Mrs. Henry Wood

Bessy Rane

Mrs. Henry Wood

Bessy Rane

ISBN/EAN: 9783337042936

Printed in Europe, USA, Canada, Australia, Japan

Cover: Foto ©Andreas Hilbeck / pixelio.de

More available books at **www.hansebooks.com**

"If you will please to get off my pony-carriage, Mr. Richard, I'll drive on."

A Novel.

BY

MRS. HENRY WOOD,

AUTHOR OF "EAST LYNNE."

LONDON:

RICHARD BENTLEY & SON, New Burlington Street.

Publishers in Ordinary to Her Majesty.

1877.

LONDON :

PRINTED BY J. OGDEN AND CO.,

172, ST. JOHN STREET, E.C.

CONTENTS.

Part the First.

Part the Second.

Part the Third.

BESSY RANE.

CHAPTER I.

THE ANONYMOUS LETTER.

IT was an intensely dark night. What with the mist that
hung around from below, and the unusual gloom above, Dr.
Rane began to think he might have done well to bring a lantern
with him, as a guide to his steps up Ham Lane, when he
should turn into it. He would not be able to spare time to
pick his way there. A gentleman—so news had been brought
to him—was lying in sudden extremity, and his services as a
medical man were being waited for.

Straight along, on the road before him, at only half a mile's
distance, lay the village of Dallory; so called after the Dallory
family, who had been of importance in the neighbourhood in
the years gone by. This little off-shoot of it was styled Dallory
Ham. The latter name gave rise to disputes amidst anti-
quarians. Some of them maintained that the word Ham was
but a contraction of hamlet, and that the correct name of the
place would be Dallory Hamlet: others asserted that the
appellation arose from the circumstance that the public green,
or common, was in the shape of a ham. As both sides brought
logic and proof irresistible to bear on their respective opinions,
contention never flagged. At no remote period the Ham had
been a wild grassy waste, given over to stray donkeys, geese,
and gipsies. They were done away with now that houses
encircled it; pretty villas of moderate dimensions, some cot-
tages and a few shops: the high road ran, as it always had
done, straight through the middle of it. Dallory Ham had
grown to think itself of importance, especially since the time

B

when two doctors had established themselves in it: Dr. Rane and Mr. Alexander. Both of them lived in what might be called the neck of the Ham, which was nearest to Dallory proper.

Standing with your face towards Dallory (in the direction the doctor was now running), his house was on the right-hand side. He had but now turned out of it. Dallory Hall, to which place Dr. Rane had been summoned, stood a little beyond the entrance to the Ham, lying back on the right amidst its grounds, and completely hidden by trees. It was inhabited by Mr. North.

Oliver Rane had come forth in great haste and commotion. He could not understand the message, except the one broad fact that Edmund North, Mr. North's eldest son, was supposed to be dying. The servant, who brought it, did not seem to understand it either. He spoke of an anonymous letter that had been received by Mr. North, of disturbance and commotion thereupon, of a subsequent encounter (a sharp, brief quarrel) between Edmund North and Mr. Alexander, the surgeon; and of a sort of fit in which Edmund North was now lying senseless.

Dr. Rane was a gentlemanly man of middle height and slender frame, his age about thirty. The face in its small regular features might have been held to possess a dash of effeminacy, but for the resolute character of the firm mouth and the pointed chin. His eyes—rather too close together—whiskers and hair, were of reddish brown, the latter worn brushed aside from the forehead; his teeth were white and even: altogether a good looking man; but one of rather too silent manners, of too inscrutable a countenance to be very pleasing.

"An anonymous letter!" Dr. Rane had repeated to himself, with a kind of groan, as he flew from his house like one greatly startled, and pursued his course down the Ham. Glancing across at Mr. Alexander's house opposite, he felt a momentary temptation to go over and learn the particulars—if, haply, the surgeon should be at home. The messenger had said that Mr. Alexander flung out of Dallory Hall in a passion, right in the midst of the quarrel; hence the summons for Dr. Rane. For Mr. Alexander, not Dr. Rane, was the Hall's medical attendant: this was the first time the latter had been called upon to act as such.

They had come to Dallory within a day of each other, these

two doctors, in consequence of the sudden death of its old practitioner; each hoping to secure the practice for himself. It was Mr. Alexander who chiefly gained it. Both were clever men; and it might have been at least an even race between them, but for the fact that Mrs. North, of Dallory Hall, set her face resolutely against Dr. Rane. The reason was inexplicable, since he had been led to believe that he should have the countenance of Mr. and Mrs. North. She did her best in a covert way to prevent his obtaining practice, pushing his rival—whom she really despised, and did not care a tittle for—into favour. Her object might not be to drive Oliver Rane from the spot, but it certainly seemed to look like it. So Mr. Alexander had obtained the lion's share of the practice in the best families, Dr. Rane but little; as to the poor, they were divided between them pretty equally. Both acted as general practitioners, and Mr. Alexander dispensed his own medicines. The rivals were outwardly cordial with each other; but Dr. Rane, no doubt, felt an inward smart.

The temptation to dash over to Mr. Alexander's passed with the thought; there was no time for it. Dr. Rane pursued his course until he came to an opening on the right, Ham Lane, into which he turned, for it was a near way to the Hall. A narrow lane, green and lovely in early summer, with wild flowers nestling on its banks, dog-roses and honeysuckles clustering in its hedges. Here was the need of the lantern. But Dr. Rane sped on without regard to inadvertent sideward steps, that might land him in the ditch. Some excitement appeared to be upon him, far beyond any that might arise from the simple fact of being called out to a gentleman in a fit; yet he was by temperament entirely self-possessed, one of the calmest-mannered men living. A stile in the hedge on the left, which he found as if by instinct, took him at once into the grounds of Dallory Hall; whence there came wafting to him the scent of hyacinths, daffodils, and other spring flowers in delicious sweetness, spite of the density of the night air. Not that Dr. Rane derived much advantage from the benefit; nothing could seem delicious to him just then.

It was more open here, as compared with the lane, and not so intensely dark. Three minutes of the same heedless pace in and out amidst the winding walks, when he turned a point at right angles, and the old stone mansion was before him. A long, grey, sensible-looking house, of only two stories high, imparting the notion of spacious rooms within. Lights shone

from some of the windows and through the fan-light over the
entrance door. One of the gardeners crossed Dr. Rane's path.

"Is that you, Williams ? Do you know how young Mr.
North is ? "

"I've not been told, sir. There's something wrong with
him, we hear."

"Is this blight ? " called back the doctor, alluding to the
curiously dark mist.

"Not it, sir. It's nothing but the vapour arising from the
day's heat. It *have* been hot for the first day o' May."

The door yielded to Dr. Rane's hand, and he went into the
hall : it was of middling size, and paved with stone. On the
left were the drawing-rooms, on the right the dining-room,
and also a room that was called Mr. North's parlour; a handsome staircase of stone wound up at the back. All the doors
were closed ; and as Dr. Rane stood for a moment in hesitation, a young lady in grey silk came swiftly and silently down
the stairs. Her figure was small and slight, her face fair, pale,
gentle, with the meekest look in her dove-like grey eyes. Her
smooth, fine hair, of an exceedingly light brown, was worn in
curls all round the head, after the manner of girls in a bygone
time. It made her look very young, but she was in reality
thirty years of age ; three months younger than Dr. Rane.
Miss North was very simple in tastes and habits, and adhered
to many customs of her girlhood. Moreover, since an illness
seven years ago, the hair had never grown very long or thick.
She saw Dr. Rane, and came swiftly to him. Their hands
met in silence.

"What is this trouble, Bessy ? "

"Oh, I am so glad you are here ! " she exclaimed, in the
soft, subdued tone characteristic of dangerous sickness in a
house. "He is lying as though he were dead. Papa is with
him. Will you come ? "

"One moment," he whispered. "Tell me, in a word, what
it all is ? The cause, I mean, not the illness."

"It was caused by an anonymous letter to papa. Edmund ——"

" But how could any anonymous letter to your papa have
caused illness to Edmund ? " he interrupted. And the tone of
his voice was so sharp, and the dropping of her hand, clasped
until then, so sudden, that Miss North, in her self-deprecation,
thought he was angry with her, and glanced upwards through
her tears.

" I beg your pardon, Bessy. My dear, I feel so grieved and confounded at this, that I am scarcely myself. It is to me utterly incomprehensible. What were the contents of the letter ?" he continued, as they hastened upstairs to the sick chamber. And Bessy North told him in a whisper as much as she knew.

The facts of the case were these. By the six o'clock post that same evening, Mr. North received an anonymous letter, reflecting on his son Edmund.—His first wife, dead now just eight-and-twenty years, had left him three children, Edmund, Richard, and Bessy.—When the letter arrived, the family had sat down to dinner, and Mr. North did not open it until afterwards. He showed it to his son Edmund, as soon as they were left alone. The charges it contained were true, and Edmund North jumped to the conclusion that only one man in the whole world could have written it, and that was Alexander, the surgeon. He went into a frightful passion ; he was given to do so on occasions ; and he had, besides, taken rather more wine at dinner than was good for him—which also he was somewhat addicted to. As ill fate had it, Mr. Alexander called just at the moment, and Mr. North, a timid man in nervous health, grew frightened at the commencing torrent of angry words, and left them together in the dining-room. There was a short, sharp storm. Mr. Alexander came out almost immediately, saying, " You are mad ; you are mad. I will talk to you when you are calmer." " I would rather be mad than bad," shouted Edmund North, coming after him. But the surgeon had already let himself out at the hall-door ; and Edmund North went back to the dining-room, and shut himself in. Two of the servants, attracted by the sounds of dispute, had been lingering in the hall, and they saw and heard this. In a few minutes Mr. North went in, and found his son lying on the ground, senseless. He was carried to his chamber, and medical men were sent for : Dr. Rane (as being the nearest), and two physicians from the more distant market town, Whitborough.

Edmund North was not dead. Dr. Rane, bending over him, saw that. He had not been well of late, and was under the care of Mr. Alexander. Only a week ago (as was to transpire later) he had gone to consult a physician in Whitborough, one of those now summoned to him. This gentleman suspected he had heart-disease, and warned him against excitement. But the family knew nothing as yet of this ; neither did Oliver

Rane. Another circumstance Edmund North had not disclosed.
When sojourning in London the previous winter, he had been
attacked by a sort of fit. It had looked like apoplexy more
than heart; and the doctors gave him sundry injunctions to
be careful. This one also, Dr. Rane thought, knowing nothing
of the former, looked like apoplexy. Edmund North was a
very handsome man, but a great deal too stout.

"Is he dead, Oliver?" asked the grieving father; who,
when alone with the doctor, and unshackled by the presence
of his wife, often called him by his Christian name.

"No; he is not dead."

And, indeed, a spasm just at that same moment passed over
the prostrate face. All the means that Oliver Rane could
think of, and use, he tried with the best heart and efforts—
hoping to recall the fast-fleeting life.

But when the two doctors arrived from Whitborough, Oliver
Rane found he was not wanted. They were professionals of
long standing, men of note in their local arena; and showed
themselves blandly cool, condescendingly patronizing to the
young practitioner. Dr. Rane had rather a strong objection
to be patronized: he withdrew, and went to Mr. North's
parlour. It was a dingy room; the shaded lamp on the table
not sufficing to light it up. Red moreen curtains were drawn
before the large French window that opened to the side
flower-garden.

Mr. North was standing before the fire. He was a little
shrivelled man with stooping shoulders, his scanty hair smoothed
across a low, broad forehead, his lips thin and querulous; his
eyes, worn and weary now, had once been mild and loving as
his daughter Bessy's. Time and care and (as some people
said) his second wife, had changed him. Oliver Rane thought
he had never seen him look so shrunken, nervous, and timid
as to-night.

"What a grievous pity it was that you should have mentioned the letter to him, Mr. North!" began the doctor,
speaking at once of what lay uppermost in his thoughts.

"Mentioned the letter to him!—why, it concerned him,"
was the surprised answer. "But I never cast a thought to its
having this kind of effect upon him."

"What was in the letter, sir?" was the doctor's next
question, put with considerable gloom, and after a long
silence.

"You can read it, Oliver."

Opening the document, he handed it to Dr. Rane. It looked like any ordinary letter. The doctor took it to the lamp.

" Mr. North,—Pardon a friend who ventures to give you a caution. Your eldest son is in some kind of embarrassment, and is drawing bills in conjunction with Alexander, the surgeon. Perhaps a word from you would arrest this : it is too frequently the first step of a man's downward career—and the writer would not like to see Edmund North enter on such."

Thus, abruptly and signatureless, ended the fatal letter. Dr. Rane slowly folded it, and left it on the table.

" Who could have written it ? " he murmured.

" Ah, there it is ! " rejoined Mr. North. " Edmund said no one could have done it but Alexander."

Standing over the fire, to which he had turned, Dr. Rane warmed his hands. The intensely hot day had given place to a cold night. His red-brown eyes took a dreamy gaze, as he revolved facts and suppositions. In his private opinion, judging only from the contents of the letter, Mr. Alexander was about the last man who would have been likely to write it.

" It is not like Alexander's writing," observed Mr. North.

" Not in the least."

" But of course this is in a thoroughly disguised hand."

" Most anonymous letters are so, I expect. Is it true that he and your son have been drawing bills together ?"

" I gather that they have drawn one ; perhaps two. Edmund's passion was so fierce that I could not question him. What I don't like is, Alexander's going off in the manner he did, without seeing me : it makes me think that perhaps he did write the letter. An innocent man would have remained to defend himself. It might have been written from a good motive, after all, Oliver ! My poor son !—if he had but taken it peaceably ! "

Mr. North wrung his hands. His tones were feeble, meekly complaining ; his manner and bearing were altogether those of a man who has been perpetually put down and no longer attempts to struggle against the cares and crosses of the world, or the will of those about him.

" I must be going," said Oliver Rane, arousing himself from a reverie. " I have to see a poor man at Dallory."

" Is it Ketler ? "

"Yes, sir. Good-night. I trust you will have cause to be in better spirits in the morning."

"Good night, Oliver."

But the doctor could not get off at once. He was waylaid by a servant, who said Madam wished to see him. Crossing the hall, the man threw open the doors of the drawing-room, a magnificent apartment. Gilded and gleaming mirrors; light blue satin curtains and furniture ; a carpet softer and thicker than moss : and all kinds of bright and resplendent things were there.

"Dr. Rane, madam."

Mrs. North sat on a couch by the fire. In the house she was called Madam—out of the house, too, for the matter of that. A severely handsome woman, with a cold, pale, imperious face, the glittering jewels in her black hair, looking as hard as she did. A *cruel* face, as some might have deemed it. When Mr. North married her, she was the widow of Major Bohun, and had one son. Underneath the chandelier, reading by its light, sat her daughter, a young lady whose face bore a strong resemblance to hers. This daughter and a son had been born since her second marriage.

"You wished to see me, Mrs. North ? "

Dr. Rane so spoke because they took no manner of notice of him. Mrs. North turned then, with her dark, inscrutable eyes; eyes that Oliver Rane hated, as he hated the cruelty glittering in their depths. He believed her to be a woman unscrupulously selfish. She did not rise ; merely motioned him to a seat opposite with a haughty wave of her white arm : and the bracelets shone on it, and her ruby velvet dress gleamed with amazing richness. He sat down with entire self-possession, every whit as independent as herself.

"You have seen this infamous letter, I presume, Dr. Rane ? "

"I have."

"Who sent it ? "

"I cannot tell you, Mrs. North."

"Have you no idea at all ? "

"Certainly not. How should I have ? "

"Could you detect no resemblance in the writing to any one's you know ? "

He shook his head.

"Not to — for instance — Alexander's ? " she resumed, making the pauses as put, and looking at him steadfastly. But

Dr. Rane saw with a sure instinct that Alexander's was not the name she had meant to speak.

"I feel sure that Mr. Alexander no more wrote the letter than—than you did, Mrs. North."

"Does it bear any resemblance to Richard North's?" she continued, after a faint pause.

"To Richard North's!" echoed the doctor, the words taking him by surprise. "No."

"Are you familiar with Richard North's handwriting?"

Oliver Rane paused to think, and then replied with a passing laugh. "I really believe I do not know his handwriting, madam."

"Then why did you speak so confidently?"

"I spoke in the impulse of the moment. Richard North, of all men, is the least likely to do such a thing as this."

The young lady, Matilda North, turned round from her book. An opera cloak of scarlet gauze was on her shoulders, as if she were cold; she pulled it closer with an impatient hand.

"Mamma, why do you harp upon Richard? He *couldn't* do it; papa told you so. If Dick saw cause to find fault with anybody, or tell tales, he would do it openly."

One angry gleam from Madam's eyes as her daughter settled to her book again, and then she proceeded to close the interview.

"As you profess yourself unable to give me information or detect any clue, I will not detain you longer, Dr. Rane."

He stood for a second, expecting, perhaps, she might offer her hand. She did nothing of the sort, only bowed coldly. Matilda North took no notice of him whatever: she was content to follow her mother's teachings when they did not clash with her own inclination. Dr. Rane had ceased to marvel why he was held in disfavour by Mrs. North: to try to guess at it seemed a hopeless task. Neither could he imagine why she opposed his marriage with Bessy; for to Bessy and her interests she was utterly indifferent.

As he left the drawing-room, Bessy North joined him, and they went together to the hall door. No servant had been rung for—it was one of Mrs. North's ways of showing contempt—and they stood together outside, speaking softly. Again the tears shone in Bessy's eyes: her heart was a very tender one, and she had loved her brother dearly.

"Oliver, is there any hope?"

"Do not distress yourself, Bessy—I cannot tell you, one way or the other."

"How am I to help distressing myself?" she rejoined, her hand resting quietly in both of his. "It is all very well for you to be calm; a medical man meets these sad things every day. You cannot be expected to care."

"Can I not?" he answered; and there was a touch of passionate emotion in the usually calm tone. "If any effort or sacrifice of mine would bring back his health and life, I'd make it freely. Good-night, Bessy."

As he stooped to kiss her, some quick firm footsteps were heard approaching, and Bessy went indoors. He who came up was a rather tall and very active man, with a plain, but nevertheless an attractive face. Plain in its irregular features; attractive from its open candour and strong good sense, from the earnest, truthful look in the deep-set hazel eyes. People were given to say that Richard North was the best man of business for miles round. It was so: and he was certainly, in mind, manners, and person a gentleman.

"Is it you, Rane? What is all this trouble? I have been away for a few hours, unfortunately. Mark Dawson met me just now with the news that my brother was dying."

The voice would have been pleasing to a degree if only from its tone of ready decision: but it was also musical as voices seldom are, clear and full of sincerity. From the voice alone, Richard North might have been trusted to his life's end. Dr. Rane gave a short summary of the illness and the state he was lying in.

"Dawson spoke of a letter that had excited him," said Richard.

"True; a letter to Mr. North."

"A dastardly anonymous letter. Just so."

"An anonymous letter," repeated the doctor. "But the effect on your brother seems altogether disproportioned to the cause."

"Where is the letter? I cannot look upon Edmund until I have seen the letter."

Dr. Rane told him where the letter was, and went out. Richard North passed on to the parlour. Mr. North, sitting by the fire, had his face bent down in his two hands.

"Father, what is all this?"

"Oh, Dick, I am glad you are come!" and in the tone there sounded an intense relief, as if he who came brought back strength and hope. "I can't make top or tail of this; and I think he is dying."

"Who is with him ?—Arthur ?"

"No; Arthur has been out all day. The doctors are with him still."

"Let me see the letter."

Mr. North gave it him, reciting at the same time the chief incidents of the calamity in a rambling sort of manner. Richard North read the letter twice: once hastily, to gather in the sense; then attentively, giving to every word full consideration. His father watched him.

"It was not so much the letter itself that excited him, Richard, as the notion that Alexander wrote it."

"Alexander did not write this," decisively spoke Richard.

"You think not ?"

"Why, of course he did not. It tells against himself as much as against Edmund."

"Edmund said no one knew of the matter but Alexander, and therefore no one else could have written it. Besides, Dick, where is Alexander ? Why is he staying away ?"

"We shall hear soon, I dare say. I have faith in Alexander. Keep this letter jealously, father. It may have been right to give you the information it contains: I say nothing at present about that; but an anonymous writer is generally a scoundrel, deserving no quarter."

"And none shall he get from me," spoke Mr. North, emphatically. "It was posted at Whitborough, you see, Dick."

"I see," shortly answered Richard. He threw his coat back as if he were too hot; and moved to the door on his way to his brother's chamber.

Meanwhile Oliver Rane went down the avenue to the front entrance gates, and took the road to Dallory. He had to see a patient there: a poor man who was lying in danger. He threw his coat back, in spite of the chill fog, and wiped his brow, and seemed altogether in a fume, as if the weather or his reflections were too hot for him.

"What a fool! what a fool!" murmured he, half aloud, apostrophizing, doubtless, the writer of the anonymous letter. Or, it might be, the unfortunate young man who had allowed it to excite within him so fatal an amount of passion.

The road was smooth and broad: a fine highway, well kept. For a short distance there were no houses, but they soon began. Dallory was a bustling village, poor and rich living in it. The North Works, as they were familiarly called, from the fact of Mr. North's being their chief proprietor, lay a little further on, and Dallory church beyond still. It was a straggling parish, make the best of it.

Amidst the first good houses that Dr. Rane came to was one superior to the rest. A large, square, handsome dwelling, with a pillared portico nearly abutting on the village pathway, and a fine garden behind.

"I wonder how Mother Gass is to-night?" thought the doctor, arresting his steps. "I may as well ask."

His knock at the door was answered by the lady herself, whom he had styled so unceremoniously "Mother Gass." A stout, comfortable-looking dame, richly dressed, with a face as red as it was good-natured, and a curiously fine lace cap, standing on end with yellow ribbon. Mrs. Gass had neither birth nor breeding; she had made an advantageous match, as you will hear further on: she possessed many good qualities, and was popularly supposed to be rich enough to buy up the whole of Dallory Ham. Her late husband had been the uncle of Oliver Rane, but neither she nor Oliver presumed upon the relationship in their intercourse with each other. In fact they had never met until two years ago.

"I knew your knock, Dr. Rane, and came to the door myself. Step into the parlour. I want to speak to you."

The doctor did not want to go in by any means, and felt caught. He said he had no time to stay; had merely called, in passing, to ask how she was.

"Well, I'm better this evening: the swimming in the head's less. You just come in, now. I say yes. I won't keep you two minutes. Shut the door, girl, after Dr. Rane."

This was to a smart housemaid, who had followed her mistress down the wide and handsome passage. Dr. Rane perforce stepped in, very unwillingly. He felt instinctively convinced that Mrs. Gass had heard of the calamity at the Hall and wished to question him. To avoid this he would have gone a mile any other way.

"I want to get at the truth about Edmund North, doctor. One of the maids from the Hall called in just now and said he had been frightened into a fit through some letter; and that you were fetched to him."

"Well, that is the truth," said the doctor, accepting the situation.

" My patience ! " ejaculated Mrs. Gass. " What was writ in the letter ? She said it was one of them enonymous things."

" So it was."

" Was it writ to himself ? "

" No. To Mr. North."

" Well, now,"—dropping her voice,—" was it about that young woman he got acquainted with ? You know."

" No, no; nothing of that kind." And Dr. Rane, as the shortest way of ending the matter, gave her the details.

" There was not much in the letter," he said, in a confidential tone. " No harm would have come of it but for Edmund North's frightful access of passion. If he dies, mind,"—the doctor added this in a dreamy tone, gazing out afar as if looking into the future—" if he dies, it will not be the letter that has killed him, but his own want of self-control."

" Don't you talk of dying, doctor. It is to be hoped it won't come to that."

" It is, indeed."

" And Mr. Richard was not at home, the girl said ! "

" Neither he nor Captain Bohun. Richard has just got in now."

Mrs. Gass would fain have kept him longer, but he told her the sick man Ketler was waiting for him. This man was one of the North workmen, who had been terribly injured in the arm ; Dr. Rane hoped to save both the arm and the life.

" That receipt for the rhubarb jam Mrs. Cumberland promised : is it ever coming ? " asked Mrs. Gass as Dr. Rane was quitting the room.

Turning back, he put his hat on the table and took out his pocket-book. Mrs. Cumberland had sent it at last. He selected the paper from amongst several others and handed it to her.

" I forgot to leave it when I was here this morning, Mrs. Gass. My mother gave it me yesterday."

Between them they dropped the receipt. Both stooped for it, and their heads came together. There was a slight laugh ; in the midst of which the pocket-book fell on the carpet. Some papers fluttered out of it, which the doctor picked up and replaced.

" Have you got 'em all, doctor ? How is the young lady's cold ? "

" What young lady's ? " he questioned.

" Miss Adair's."

"I did not know she had one."

"Ah, them lovely girls with their bright faces never show their ailments; and she is lovely, if ever there was one lovely in this terrestial world. Good-night to you, doctor; you're in a mortal hurry."

He strode to the street-door and shut it after him with a bang. Mrs. Gass looked out of her parlour and saw the same smart maid hastening along the passage: a little too late.

"Drat it, wench! is that the way you let gentlefolks show themselves out—scuttering to the door when they've got clean away from it. D'ye call that manners?"

CHAPTER II.

ELLEN ADAIR.

THE day promised to be as warm as the preceding one. The night and morning mist were gone; the sun shone hot and bright. Summer seemed to have come in before its time.

Two white gothic villas stood side by side just within the neck of Dallory Ham, a few yards of garden and some clustering shrubs lying between them. They were built alike. The side windows, facing each other over this strip of ground, were large projecting bay-windows, and belonged to the dining-rooms. These houses were originally erected for two maiden sisters; hence their relationship (if such a term may be applied to dwellings) one with the other. A large and beautiful garden lay at the back, surrounding the two villas, only a slender wire fence, that a child might have stepped over, dividing it. Entering the Ham from the direction of Dallory, these houses stood on the left; in the first of them lived Mrs. Cumberland, the mother of Oliver Rane. She had been married twice, hence the difference in name. The second house was occupied by Dr. Rane. They lay back with a strip of grass before them, the entrance doors being level with the ground; no steps.

Let us go into the doctor's: turning the handle of the door without ceremony, as Dr. Rane's more familiar patients do. The hall is small, narrowing off at the upper end to a passage, and lighted with stained glass. On the left of the entrance door is the consulting-room, not much bigger than a closet; beyond it is the dining-room, a good spacious apartment, with its bay-window, already spoken of, looking to the other house.

Opposite the dining-room across the passage, narrow here, is the white-flagged kitchen; and the drawing-room lies in front, on the right of the entrance. Not being furnished it is mostly kept shut up. A back-door opens to the garden.

Oliver Rane sat in his consulting-room; the "Whitborough Journal," damp from the press in his hand. It was just twelve o'clock and he had to go out, but the newspaper was attracting him. By seven o'clock that morning he had been at the Hall, and learnt that there was no material change in the patient lying there: he had then gone on, early though it was, to see the man, Ketler. The journal gave the details of Mr. North's seizure with tolerable accuracy, and concluded its account in these words: "We have reason to know that a clue has been obtained to the anonymous writer."

"A clue to the writer!" repeated Dr. Rane, his eyes seeming to be glued to the words. "I wonder if it's true? No, no; it is not likely," came the quiet, contemptuous decision. "How should any clue——"

He stopped suddenly; rose from the chair, and stood erect and motionless, as if some thought had struck him. A fine man; almost as good-looking at a casual glance as another who was stepping in upon him. The front door had opened, and this one was slightly tapped at. Dr. Rane paused before he answered it, and a fierce look of inquiry, as if he did not care to be interrupted, shot out from his eyes.

"Come in."

A tall, slender, and very handsome man, younger than Dr. Rane, opened the door by slow degrees. There was a peculiar cast of proud refinement on his fair features; a dreamy look in his dark blue eyes. An attractive face at all times and seasons, whose owner it was impossible to mistake for any but an upright well-bred gentleman. It was Arthur Bohun; Captain Bohun, as he was very generally called. He was the only son of Mrs. North by her former marriage with Major Bohun, and of course the step-son of Mr. North.

"Any admittance, doctor?"

"Always admittance to you," answered the doctor, who could be affable or not, as suited his mood. "Why don't you come in?"

He came in with his pleasant smile; a smile that hid the natural pride of the face. Oliver Rane put down the newspaper.

"Well, is there any change in Edmund North?"

"The very slightest in the world, the doctors think; and for the better," replied Captain Bohun. "Dick told me. I have not been in myself since early morning. I cannot bear to look on extreme suffering."

A ghost of a smile flitted across Dr. Rane's features at the avowal. He could understand a woman disliking to look on suffering, but not a man. And the one before him had been a soldier!

Captain Bohun sat down on an uncomfortable wooden stool as he spoke, gently pushing back the front of his light summer overcoat. He imparted the idea of never being put out over any earthly thing. The movement displayed his cool white waistcoat, across which fell a dainty gold chain with its hanging seal, transparent sapphire, of rare and costly beauty.

"You have begun summer early!" remarked the doctor, glancing at Captain Bohun's attire.

The clothes were of a delicate shade of grey; looking remarkably cool and nice in conjunction with the white waistcoat. Captain Bohun was always dressed well; it seemed a part and parcel of himself. To wear the rude and rough attire that some men affect now-a-days, would have been against his instincts.

"Don't sit on that stool of penitence; take the patient's chair," said the doctor, pointing to an elbow chair opposite the window."

"But I am not a patient."

"No. Or you'd be at the opposition shop over the way."

Arthur Bohun laughed. "It was of the opposition shop I came to speak to you—if I came for anything in particular. Where's Alexander? Is he keeping out of the way; or is he really gone to London as people say?"

"I know nothing of him," returned Dr. Rane. "Look here—I was reading the account they give in the newspaper. Is this last hint true?"—holding out the journal—"that a clue has been obtained to the writer of the letter?"

Arthur Bohun ran his eyes over the sentence to which the doctor's finger pointed.

"No, this has no foundation," he promptly answered. "At least so far as the Hall is concerned. As yet we have not found any clue whatever."

"I thought so. These newsmongers put forth lies by the

bushel. Just as we might, if we had to cater for an insatiably curious public. But I fear I must be going out."

Arthur Bohun brought down the fore-legs of the stool, which he had kept on the tilt, rose, and said a word of apology for having detained him from his patients. His was essentially a courteous nature, sensitively regardful of other people's feelings, as men of great innate refinement are sure to be.

They went into the dining-room, Dr. Rane having left his hat there, and passed out together by the large bay-window. The doctor crossed at once to a door in the wall that bound the premises at the back, and made his exit to the lane beyond, leaving Arthur Bohun in the garden.

A garden that on a summer's day seemed as a very paradise. With its clustering shrubs, its overhanging trees, its leafy glades, its shrubberies, its miniature rocks, its sweet repose, its sweeter flowers. Seated in a remote part of that which belonged to Mrs. Cumberland, was one of the loveliest girls that eye had ever looked upon. She wore a morning dress of light-coloured muslin, with an edging of lace on her neck and wrists. Slight, gentle, charming, with a peculiar look of grace and refinement, a stranger would have been almost startled at her beauty. It was a delightful face; the features clearly cut; the complexion soft, pure, and delicate, paling and flushing with every emotion. In the dark brown eyes there was a singularly sweet expression; the dark brown hair took a lustrously bright tinge in the sunlight.

A natural arbour of trees and branches had been formed overhead: she sat on a garden bench, behind a rustic table. Before her, at a short distance, a falling cascade trickled down the artificial rocks, and thence wound away, a tiny stream, amidst ferns, violets, primroses, and other wild plants. A plot of green grass, smooth and soft as the moss of the rocks, lay immediately at foot, and glimpses of statelier flowers were caught through the trees. Their rich perfume came wafted in a sudden breeze to the girl's senses, and she looked up gratefully from the work she was busy over; some small matter of silken embroidery.

And now you could see the exceeding refinement and delicacy of the face, the pleasant expression of the soft bright eyes. A bird lodged itself on a branch close by, and began a song. Her lips parted with a smile of greeting. By way of rewarding it, off he flew, dipped his beak into the running stream, and soared away out of her sight. As is the case sometimes in life.

c

On the table lay a handful of violets, picked short off at the blossoms. Almost unconsciously, as it seemed, her thoughts far away, she began toying with them, and fell insensibly into the French schoolgirls' play, telling off the flowers. "Est-ce qu'il m'aime?" was the first momentous question; and then began the pastime, a blossom being told off with every answer. "Oui. Non. Un peu. Beaucoup. Pas du tout. Passionnément." And so the round went on, and on again, until the last violet was reached. It came, as chance had it, with the last word, and she, in an access of rapture, her soft cheeks glowing, her sweet lips parting, caught up the flower and put it into her bosom.

"Il m'aime passionnément!"

Ah, foolish girl! The oracle seemed as true as if it had come direct from heaven. But can we not remember the ecstasy such necromancy once brought to us!

With her blushes deepening as she woke, startling, into reality; with a smile at her own folly; with a shrinking sense of maiden shame for indulging in the pastime, she pushed the violets into a heap, threaded a needleful of green floss silk, and went on with her work soberly. A few minutes, and then either eye or ear was attracted by something ever so far off, and she sat quite still. Quite still outwardly; but oh! the sudden emotion that rose like a lightning flash within! and she knew the footsteps. Every vein was tingling; every pulse was throbbing; the pink on her cheeks deepened to a very sea of crimson; the life blood of her heart rushed wildly on, and she lay her hand upon her bosom to still it.

He was passing straight on from Dr. Rane's to the other house, when he caught a glimpse of her dress through the trees, and turned aside. Nothing could have been quieter or more undemonstrative than the meeting; and yet a shrewd observer, skilled in secrets, had not failed to read the history —that both alike loved. Captain Bohun went up, calm as befitted a well-bred man: shaking hands after the fashion of society, and apparently with as little interest: but on his face the flush also shone with all its tell-tale brightness; the hand that touched hers thrilled almost to pain. She had risen to receive him: she was just as calm outwardly as he, but her senses were in one maze of wild confusion.

She began to go on with her work again in a sort of hurried, trembling fashion when he sat down. The day, for her, had turned to Eden; the flowers were brighter, the song of the birds was sweeter, the trees were of a golden green, like unto emeralds; all things seemed to discourse a sweet music.

True love—idealistic, passionate, pure love—is not fluent of speech whatever the world may say, or poets teach. Dr. Kane and Miss North thought they loved each other: and so they did, after a sensible, sober, plain manner: they could have conversed with mutual fluency for ever and a day; but their love was not *this* love. It is the custom of modern writers to ignore it: the prevailing fashion is to be matter-of-fact; realistic; people don't talk of love now and of course don't feel it: the capability of it has died out; modes have changed. Ah me! what a false age it is; as if we could put off human nature as we do a garment.

Captain Bohun was the first to break the silence. *She* had been content to live in it by his side for ever: it was more eloquent, too, than his words were.

"What a fine day it is, Ellen!"

"Yes. I think summer has come: we shall scarcely have it warmer than this in July. And oh, how lovely everything is!"

"It was hot yesterday. I had a ride of ten miles between green hedges on which the May is beginning to blossom. Envious darkness had shut out the world before I got home."

"And I sat out here all the afternoon," she answered—and perhaps she unconsciously spoke more in pursuance of the thought, that she had sat out waiting and hoping for him, than to give the information. "Where did you go, Arthur?"

"To Bretchley. Some of my old brother officers are quartered there: and I spent the day with them. What's that for?"

He alluded to the piece of work. She smiled as she held it out in her right hand, on the third finger of which was a plain gold ring. A small piece of white canvas with a pink rose and part of a green leaf already worked upon it in bright floss silk.

"Guess."

"Nay, how can I? For a doll's cushion?"

"Oh Arthur!" came the laughing exclamation. "If I tell you, you must keep counsel, mind that, for it is a secret, and I am working at it under difficulties, out of Mrs. Cumberland's sight. Don't you think I have done a great deal? I only began it yesterday."

"Well, what's it for?" he asked, putting his hand under

neath it as an excuse, perhaps, for touching the fingers it was in. "A firescreen for pretty faces?"

The young lady shook her head. "It's for a kettle-holder."

"A kettle-holder! What a prosy ending!"

"It's for Mrs. Cumberland's invalid kettle that she keeps in her bedroom. The handle got hot a day or two ago, and she burnt her hand. I shall put it on some morning to surprise her."

There ensued a pause of silence. Half their intercourse was made up of pauses: the eloquent language of true love. Captain Bohun, thinking how kindly natured was the girl by his side, played abstractedly with the heap of sweet blossoms lying on the table.

"What have you been doing with all these violets, Ellen?"

"Nothing," she replied; and down fell the scissors. But that she stooped at once, Captain Bohun might have seen the sudden flush on the delicate face, and wondered at it: a flush of remembrance. *Il m'aime passionnément.* Well, so he did.

"Please don't entangle my silk, Captain Bohun."

He laughed as he put down the skein, one of a bright gold colour. "Shall I help you to wind it, Ellen?"

"Thank you, but we don't wind floss silk. It would deaden its beauty. Arthur! do you know that the swallows have come?"

"The swallows! Then this summer weather will stay with us, for those birds have a sure instinct. It is early for them to be here."

"I saw one this morning. It may be only an avant-courier, come to report on the weather to the rest."

She laughed lightly at her own words, and there ensued another pause. Captain Bohun broke it.

"What a shocking thing this is about Edmund North!"

"What is a shocking thing?" she asked, with indifference, going on with her work as she spoke. Arthur Bohun, who was busy again with the pale blue violets, scarcely as blue as his own eyes, lifted his face and looked at her.

"I mean altogether. The illness; the letter; the grief at home. It is all shocking."

"Is Edmund North ill? I did not know it."

"Ellen!"

Living in the very atmosphere of the illness, amidst its sea of bustle, distress, and attendant facts, to Arthur Bohun it seemed almost an impossibility that she should be in ignorance of it.

"Why, what has Rane been about, not to tell you?"

"I don't know. What is the matter with Edmund North?"

Captain Bohun explained the illness and its cause. Her work dropped on her knee as she listened; her face grew pale with interest. She never once interrupted him; every sympathetic feeling within her was aroused to warm indignation.

"An anonymous letter!" she at length exclaimed. "That's worse than a stab."

"A fellow, writing one of malice, puts himself beyond the pale of decent society: shooting would be too good for him," quietly remarked Captain Bohun. "Here comes a summons for you, I expect, Helen."

Even so. One of the maids approached, saying Mrs. Cumberland was downstairs; and so the interview was broken up. Captain Bohun would perforce have taken his departure, but Miss Adair invited him in—to tell the sad story to Mrs. Cumberland. Only too glad was he of any plea that kept him by Ellen's side.

Putting her work away in her pocket, she took the arm that was held out, and they went wandering through the garden; lingering by the cascade, dreaming in the dark cypress walk, standing over the beds of beautiful flowers. A seductive time; life's gala summer; but a time that never stays, for the biting frosts of winter and reality succeed it surely and swiftly.

Nothing had been said between them, but each was conscious of what the other felt. Neither had whispered in so many words, "I love you." Ellen did not hint that she had watched for him the whole of the past live-long day with love's sick longing; he did not confess how lost the day had been to him, how worse than weary, because it did not give him a sight of her. These avowals might come in time, but they would not be needed.

Stepping in through the middle doors of the bay window, as Arthur Bohun had made his exit from the opposite one, they looked round for Mrs. Cumberland, and did not see her. She was in the drawing-room on the other side the small hall, sitting near the Gothic windows that faced the road. A pale, reticent, lady-like woman, always suffering, but making more of her sufferings than she need have done—as her son, Dr. Rane, not over-dutifully thought. Her eyes were light and cold; her flaxen hair, banded smoothly under a cap, was turning grey. But that Mrs. Cumberland was entirely occupied with self, and but little with her ward, Ellen Adair, she might have noticed before now the suggestive intimacy between that young lady and Arthur Bohun.

" Captain Bohun is here, Mrs. Cumberland," said Helen, when they entered. " He has some very sad news to tell you."

" And the extraordinary part of the business is that you should not have heard it before," added Arthur, as he shook hands with Mrs. Cumberland.

Mrs. Cumberland's rich black silk gown rustled a very little as she responded to the greeting ; but there was no smile on her grey face, her cold eyes wore no brighter light. In her way she was glad to see him : that is, she had no objection to see him ; but gladness and Mrs. Cumberland seemed to have parted company. The suffering that arises from chronic pain makes a selfish nature doubly selfish.

" What is the news that Ellen speaks of, Captain Bohun ? "

He stood leaning against the mantel-piece as he told the tale : told it systematically ; the first advent of the anonymous letter to Mr. North ; the angry, passionate spirit in which Edmund North had taken it up ; his stormy interview with the surgeon, Alexander ; the subsequent attack, and the hopelessness in which he was lying. For once Mrs. Cumberland was aroused to feel sympathy in another's sufferings : she listened with painful interest.

" And it was *Oliver* who was called in first to Edmund North ! " she presently exclaimed, with inquiring emphasis, as if unable to credit the fact.

" Yes."

" But how was it he did not step in here afterwards to tell me the news ? " added she, resentfully.

Captain Bohun could not answer that so readily. Ellen Adair, ever ready to find a charitable excuse for the world, turned to Mrs. Cumberland.

" Dr. Rane may have had to see patients. Perhaps he did not get home until too late to come here."

" Yes, he did ; I saw his lamp burning before ten o'clock," was Mrs. Cumberland's answer. " Ah ! this is another proof that I am being forgotten," she went on, bitterly. " When a woman has seen fifty years of life, she is old in the sight of her children, and they go then their own way in the world, leaving her to neglect."

"But, dear Mrs. Cumberland, Dr. Rane does not neglect you," said Ellen, struck with the injustice of the complaint. "He is ever the first to come in and amuse you with what news he knows."

"And in this instance he may have kept silence from a good motive—the wish to spare you pain," added Captain Bohun.

"True, true," murmured Mrs. Cumberland, her mind taking a more reasonable track. "Oliver has always been dutiful."

On departure, Captain Bohun crossed the road to Mr. Alexander's; a slight limp being visible in his gait. The mystery that appeared to be surrounding the surgeon's movements at present, puzzled him not a little; his prolonged absence seemed unaccountable. The surgery, through which he entered, was empty, and he opened the door leading from it to the house. A maid-servant met him.

"Is Mr. Alexander at home?"

"No, sir."

"Papa's gone to London," called out a young gentleman of ten, who came running along the passage, cracking a whip. "He went last night. They sent for him."

"Who sent for him?" asked Captain Bohun.

"The people. Mamma's gone too. They are coming home to-day; and mamma's going to bring me a Chinese puzzle and a box of chocolate if she had time to buy them."

Not much information, this. As Captain Bohun turned out again, he stood at the door, wishing he had a decent plea to take him over to Mrs. Cumberland's again. He was an idle man; living only in the sweet pastime of making that silent love.

But Mrs. North never suspected that he was making it, or knew that he was intimate at Mrs. Cumberland's. Still less did she suspect that Mrs. Cumberland had a young lady inmate named Ellen Adair. It would have startled her to terror

CHAPTER III.

IN MRS. GASS'S PARLOUR.

EARLY on the following morning the ringing out of the death-bell from the church at Dallory proclaimed to those who heard it that Edmund North had passed to his rest. He had never recovered consciousness, and died some thirty-six hours after the attack.

Amidst those who did not hear it was Oliver Rane. The doctor had been called out at daybreak to a country patient in an opposite direction, getting back between eight and nine o'clock.

He sat at his breakfast in the dining-room, unconscious of the morning's calamity. Hot coffee, broiled ham, two eggs. The table stood in front of the large bay-window.

" She has done it too much—stupid thing ! " exclaimed Dr. Rane, cutting the slice of ham in two and apostrophising his unconscious servant. " Yesterday it was hardly warmed through. Just like them !—make a complaint, and they rush to the other extreme. I wonder how things are going on there this morning ? "

He glanced up towards the distant quarter where the Hall was situated, for his query had reference to Edmund North ; and this gave him the opportunity of seeing something else : a woman stepping out of Mrs. Cumberland's dining-room. She was getting on for forty, tall enough for a May-pole, with inquisitive green eyes, sallow cheeks, remarkably thin, as if she had lost her back teeth, and a bunch of black ringlets on either side of her face. She wore the white apron and cap of a servant, but looked one of a superior class. Emerging from the opposite window, she stepped across the wire fence and approached Dr. Rane.

" What does Jelly want now ? " he mentally asked.

Jelly ! A curious name, no doubt, but it was hers. Fanny Jelly. When Mrs. Cumberland had engaged her as upper maid, she decided to call her by the latter name, Fanny being her own.

Jelly entered without ceremony—she was not given to observe much at the best of times. She had come to say that he need not provide anything for his dinner ; her mistress meant to send him in a fowl—if he would accept it.

" With pleasure, tell her," said Dr. Rane. " How is my mother this morning, Jelly ? "

" She has had a good night, and is pretty tolerable this morning," replied Jelly, giving a backward fling to her flying cap-strings—for she did not follow the new fashion of a round bit of net on the back hair and call it a cap. " The foreign letters have come in ; two for her, one for Miss •Adair."

Dr. Rane, not particularly interested in the said foreign letters, went on eating his breakfast. Jelly, with characteristic composure, stood at ease just inside the window watching the process.

"That ham is dried up to fiddle-strings," she suddenly said.

"Yes. Phillis has done it too much."

"And I should like to have the doing of her!" spoke Jelly in a wrathful tone. "It is a sin to spoil good food."

"So it is," said Dr. Rane.

"So that poor young man's gone!" she resumed, as he cracked an egg.

The doctor lifted his head quickly. "What young man?"

"Edmund North. He died at half-past seven this morning."

"Who says it?" cried Dr. Rane, a startled look crossing his face and eyes.

"The milkman told me: he heard the passing-bell toll out. You needn't be surprised, sir: there has been no hope from the first."

"But there has been hope," disputed the doctor. "There was hope yesterday at midday, there was hope last night. I don't believe he is dead."

"Well, sir, then you must disbelieve it," equably answered Jelly; but she glanced keenly out at him from her green eyes, "Edmund North is as certainly dead as that I stand here."

He seemed strangely moved at the tidings: a quiver stirred his lips, the colour in his face faded to whiteness. Jelly, having looked as much as she chose, turned to depart.

"Then we are to send in the fowl, sir?"

"Yes, yes."

"Tell Phillis, please, that it will be all ready for the spit."

He watched her dreamily as she crossed the low fence and disappeared within her proper domains; he pushed the ham, not eaten, from him, he turned sick at the underdone egg, whose shell had just been broken. What, though he preferred eggs underdone in calm times? calm times were not these. The news did indeed trouble him in no measured degree: it was so sad for a man in the prime of early life to be cut off thus: Edmund North was but a year or two older than himself: two days ago he had been as full of health and life, deep in the plans and projects of this world, thinking little of the next. Sad? it was horrible. And Dr. Rane's breakfast was spoiled for that day.

He got up to walk the room restlessly: he looked at himself in the chimney glass; possibly to see how the news might have affected his features; in all he did there was a hurried, confused kind of motion, betraying that the mind must be in a state of perturbation. By-and-by he snatched up his hat, and went forth, taking the direction of the Hall.

"I ought to call. It will look well for me to call. It is a civility I owe to them," he kept repeating at intervals, as he strode along. Just as though he thought in his inmost heart he ought *not* to call, and were seeking arguments to excuse to himself his doing so.

How eager he was to be there and see and hear all that was transpiring, he alone knew. No power could have stopped him, whether to go were suitable or unsuitable; for he had a strong will. He did not take the lane this time, but went straight alone the high road, turning in at the iron gates, and up the chestnut avenue. The young green of the trees was beautiful: birds sang on their branches; the blue sky flickered through the waving leaves. Winding on, Dr. Rane met Thomas Hepburn, the undertaker and carpenter: a sickly looking but very intelligent and respectable man.

"Is it you, Hepburn?"

"Yes, sir; I've been in to take the orders. What an awful thing it is!" he continued in a low tone, glancing round at the closed windows, as if fearful they might detect what he was saying. "The scoundrel who wrote that letter ought to be tried for murder when they discover him. And they are safe to do that, sooner or later."

"The writer could have done no great harm but for Edmund North's allowing himself to go into that fatal passion."

"An anonymous writer is—an anonymous writer," re-joined Hepburn with scorn. "They say there'll not be an inquest."

"An inquest!" repeated the doctor, to whom the idea of one had never occurred. "There's no necessity for an inquest."

"Well, doctor, I suppose the law would in strictness exact it. But Mr. North is against it, and it's thought his wishes will be respected."

"Any of the medical men can furnish a certificate of the cause of death. I could do it myself."

"Yes, of course. But I've got no time to stay talking," added the undertaker. "Good-day to you, sir."

The next to come forth from the house was Alexander, the surgeon. Dr. Rane rubbed his eyes, almost thinking they deceived him. The brother practitioners shook hands; and

Mr. Alexander—a little man with dark hair—explained what had seemed unexplainable.

It seemed that the very same evening delivery which brought Mr. North the anonymous letter, had brought one to Mr. Alexander. His was from London, informing him that he had been appointed to a post connected with one of the hospitals, and requesting him to go up *at once* for a few hours. Mr. Alexander made ready, got a fly, and started with his wife for the station, bidding the driver halt at Mr. North's iron gates. As he was in attendance at that time on Edmund North, he wished to give notice of his temporary absence. To be attacked furiously by Edmund North the moment he got inside the doors, and as it seemed to him, without rhyme or reason, put Mr. Alexander into a bit of a passion also. There was no time for elucidation, neither was a single word he said listened to, and the surgeon hastened out to his waiting fly. He had returned by the first train this morning—London was not much more than an hour's journey by rail—and found that Edmund North had died of that self-same passion. Half paralysed with grief and horror, Mr. Alexander hastened to the Hall; and was now coming from it, having fully exculpated himself in all ways in the sight of its master. Nearly as fully he spoke now to Dr. Rane; in his grief, in his straightforward candour, nothing selfish or sinister could hide itself.

The transaction in regard to drawing the bill had been wholly Edmund North's. Some months ago he had sought Mr. Alexander, saying he was in want of a sum of money,— a hundred pounds; he did not know how to put his hands just then upon it, not wishing to apply to his own family; would he, the surgeon, like a good fellow, lend it? At first, Mr. Alexander had excused himself; for one thing he had not the money—fancy a poor country surgeon with a hundred pounds loose cash, he said; but eventually he fell in with Edmund North's pleadings. A bill was drawn, both of them being liable, and was discounted by Dale, the lawyer of Whitborough. When the bill had become due (about a week ago) neither of them could meet it; and the matter was arranged with Dale by a second bill.

" What I cannot understand is, how Edmund North, poor fellow, could have pitched upon me as the writer of that letter," observed the surgeon to Dr. Rane, when he had finished his recital. He must have gone clean daft to think

it. I had no cause to disclose it; I did not fear but he would
eventually meet the bill."

"I told them you could not have written it," quietly rejoined the doctor.

Mr. Alexander brought down his hand on a tree-branch
with angry emphasis. "Rane, I'd give a thousand pounds out
of my pocket—if I were a rich man and had it—to know
who wrote the letter and worked the mischief. I never disclosed the transaction to a living soul; I don't believe Edmund North did; besides us, it was known only to the dis-
counter. Dale is a safe man; so it seems a regular mystery.
And mark you, Rane—that letter was written to damage me
at the Hall, not Edmund North."

Dr. Rane gazed at the other in great surprise. "To damage
you?"

"It is the view I take of it. And so, on reflection, does
Richard North."

"Nonsense, Alexander!"

"If ever the hidden particulars see daylight, you will find
that it is not nonsense, but truth," was the surgeon's answer.
"I must have some enemies in the neighbourhood, I suppose; most professional men have; and they no doubt hoped
to do for me with Mr. North. The Norths in a degree sway
other people here, and so I should have lost my practice, and
been driven away."

Oliver Rane had raised his cane, and was lightly flicking the
shrub by which he stood, his air that of one in deep thought.

"I confess I do not follow you, Alexander. Your ill-doing
and well-doing is nothing to Mr. North; his son's of course
was. If you lived by drawing bills, it could be no concern of
his."

"The drawing of bills on my own score would certainly be
of no moment to Mr. North; but the drawing them in *conjunction with his son* would be. Upon which of us would he naturally lay the blame? Upon a young, heedless man, as
Edmund North was; or upon me, a middle-aged, established
member of society, with a home and a family? The case
speaks for itself."

Oliver Rane did not appear quite to admit this. He thought
the probability lay against Mr. Alexander's theory, rather than
with it. "Of course," he slowly said, "looking at it in that
light, the letter would tell either way. But I think you must
be wrong."

" No, I am not. Whoever wrote that missive did it to injure me. I seemed to see it, as by an instinct, the minute Mr. North gave me the letter to read. If the motive was to drive me from Dallory, it might have been spared, and Edmund North saved for I am going to quit it of my own accord."

" To quit Dallory ? "

" In a month's time from this I and mine will have left it for London. The situation now given to me I have been try-ing for, under the rose, these six months past."

" But why do you wish to quit Dallory ? "

" To better myself, as the servants say," replied Mr. Alex-ander, " and the move will do that considerably. Another reason is that my wife dislikes Dallory. Madam turned her nose up at us socially when we first settled here ; and that, in a degree, kept the best society closed to Mrs. Alexander. She is well-born, has been reared a lady ; and of course it was enough to set her against the place. Besides, all our friends are in London ; and so, you see, if my exit into the wilderness was what that anonymous individual was driving at, he might have gained his ends without crime, had he waited but a short while."

" I hate Mrs. North," dreamily spoke Dr. Rane ; " and I am sure she hates me, though the wherefore is to me incom-prehensible."

" Look there," spoke the surgeon, dropping his voice.

Both had, simultaneously, caught sight of Mrs. North. She was passing the shrubbery close by, and looked out at them. They raised their hats. Mr. Alexander made a movement to approach her ; she saw it, and turned from him back to the dark wall with her usual sweeping step. So he remained where he was.

" She asked to see me on Tuesday night when I was leaving ; wanting to know if I could tell her who wrote the letter," said Dr. Rane.

" She suspected me, I suppose."

" She appeared to suspect—*not* you, but somebody else ; and that was Richard North."

" Richard North ! " ironically repeated Mr. Alexander. " She knows quite well that he is above suspicion ; perhaps she was only trying to divert attention from some other : she is made up of craft. Who knows but she wrote the letter herself ? "

" Mrs. North ! "

"Upon my word and honour the thought is in my mind, Rane. If the motive of the letter were as you think—to do Edmund North damage with his father,—I know of only one person who would attempt it, and that is Mrs. North."

Their eyes met: a strange light shone momentarily in Oliver Rane's. In saying that he hated Mrs. North, he spoke truth; but there was every excuse for the feeling, for it was quite certain that Mrs. North had long been working him what ill she could. His marriage with Bessy was being delayed, and delayed entirely through her covert opposition.

"That she is an entirely unscrupulous woman, and would stand at nothing, I feel sure," spoke Dr. Rane, drawing a deep breath. "But, as to the letter——?"

"Well,—as to the letter?" cried the surgeon, in the pause come to. "I don't say she foresaw that it would kill him."

"This would disprove your theory of its being written to damage you, Alexander."

"Not altogether. The damaging another, more or less, would be of no moment at all to Mrs. North; she'd crush anybody without scruple."

"I'm sure she'd crush me," spoke Dr. Rane. "Heaven knows why; I don't."

"Well, if she did write the letter, I think her conscience must smite her as she looks at the poor dead man lying there. Good day, Rane: I have not been home to see my little ones yet. Mrs. Alexander is remaining in town for a day or two."

In talking, they had walked slowly to the end of the avenue; Mr. Alexander passed through the gates, and took the road towards the Ham.

"I may as well go on at once, and see Ketler," thought Dr. Rane. "Time enough to call at the Hall as I return."

So he went on towards Dallory. Two gentlemen passed him on horseback, county magistrates, who were probably going to the Hall. The sight of them turned his thoughts to the subject of an inquest: he began speculating why Mr. North wished to evade it, and whether he would succeed. For his own part, he did not see that the case, speaking in point of law, called for one. Hepburn said it did; and he was supposed, as undertaker-in-chief to Dallory, to understand these things.

Deep in reflection, the doctor strode on; when, in passing Mrs. Gass's house, a sharp tapping at the window saluted his ear. It came from that lady herself, and she flung up the sash.

"Just come in, will you, Dr. Rane? I want you for something very particular."

He felt sure she only wanted to question him about the death, and would a great deal rather have gone on : but with her red and smiling face inviting him in peremptorily, he did not see his way clear to refuse.

"And so he is *gone*—that poor young man!" she began, meeting him in her smart dress and pink cap. "When I heard the death-bell strike out this morning, it sounded to me a'most like my own knell."

"Yes, he is gone—unhappily," murmured Dr. Rane.

"Well, now, doctor, the next thing is—what became of you yesterday?"

The transition of subject appeared peculiar.

"Became of me?" repeated Dr. Rane. "How do you mean?"

"All the mortal day I was stuck at this here parlour window, waiting to see you go by," proceeded Mrs. Gass. "You never passed once."

"Yes, I did. I passed by in the morning."

"My eyes must have gone a-maying then, for they never saw you," was Mrs Gass's answer.

"It was before my usual hour. I was called out early to a sick man in Dallory, and I took the opportunity to see Ketler at the same time."

"Then that accounts for the milk in the cocoa-nuts; and I wasted my time for nothing," was her good-tempered rejoinder.

"Why did you want to see me pass?"

Mrs. Gass paused for a moment before replying. She glanced round to see that the door was closed, and dropped her voice nearly to a whisper.

"Dr. Rane, who wrote that fatal letter?"

"I cannot tell."

"Did *you?*"

Oliver Rane stared at her, a sudden flush of anger dyeing his brow. No wonder : the question, put with emphatic earnestness, seemed an assertion, almost like that startling reproach of Nathan to David.

"Mrs. Gass, I do not know what you mean."

"I see you don't relish it, doctor. But I am a plain body, as you know; and when in doubt about a thing, pleasant or unpleasant, I like to ask an explanation straight out."

"But why should you be in doubt about this?" he inquired wonderingly. "What can induce you to connect me with the letter?"

Mrs. Gass took her portly person across the room to a desk; unlocked it, and brought forth a folded piece of paper. She handed it to Dr. Rane.

It was not a letter; it could not be the copy of one: but it did appear to be the rough sketch of the anonymous missive that had reached Mr. North. Some of the sentences were written two or three times over; in a close hand, in a scrawling hand, in a reversed hand, as if the writer were practising different styles; in others the construction was altered, words were erased, different ones substituted. Oliver Rane gazed upon it like one in complete bewilderment.

"What *is* this, Mrs. Gass?"

"Is it not the skeleton of the letter?"

"No, certainly not. And yet——" Dr. Rane broke off and ran his eye over the lines again and again. "There is a similarity in some of the phrases," he suddenly said.

"Some of the phrases is identical," returned Mrs. Gass. "When Mr. Richard North was here yesterday, I got him to repeat over to me the words of the letter; word for word, so far as he remembered 'em, and I know 'em for *these* words. Whoever writ that letter to Mr. North, doctor, first of all tried his sentences and his hand on this paper, practising how he could best do it."

"How did you come by this?"

"You left it here the night before last."

"*I* left it here!" repeated Dr. Rane, looking as if he mentally questioned whether Mrs. Gass was in her right senses.

"Yes. You."

"But you must be dreaming, Mrs. Gass."

"I never do dream—that sort of dreaming," replied Mrs. Gass. "Look here"—putting her stout hand, covered with valuable rings, on his coat sleeve—"didn't you upset your pocket-book here that night? Well, this piece of paper fell out of it."

"It could not have done anything of the sort," he repeated, getting flushed and angry again. "All the papers that fell out of my pocket-book I picked up and returned to it."

"You didn't pick up this; it must have fluttered away unseen. Just after you were gone I dropped my spectacle-case, and in stooping for it, I saw this piece of paper lying in the shade of the table's claw."

"But it could not have come out of my pocket-book. Just tell me if you please, Mrs. Gass, what should bring such a document in my possession ?"

"That's just what I can't tell. The paper was not there before candle-light; I'll answer for that much; so where else could it have come from ?"

The last words were not spoken as an assertion of her view, but as a question. Dr. Rane looked at her, she at him; both seeming equally puzzled.

"Had you any visitor last evening besides myself ?" he asked.

"Not a soul. The only person that came into the parlour, barring my own servants, was Molly Green, under-housemaid at the Hall. She lived with me once, and calls in sometimes in passing to ask how I am. They sent her into Dallory for something wanted at the chemist's, and she looked in to tell me. The thing had just happened."

Dr. Rane's brow lost its perplexity: an easy smile, as if the mystery were solved, crossed his face. The hint recently given him by Mr. Alexander was in his mind.

"I'm glad you've told me this, Mrs. Gass. The paper was more likely to have been left by Molly Green than by me. It may have dropped from her petticoats."

"Goodness bless the man! From her petticoats! Why she had run all the way from the Hall. And how was she likely to pick it up in *that* house—even though her gown-hem had been finished off with pot-hooks ?"

"What cause have I given you to suspect *me* of this ?" retorted Dr. Rane in a harsh tone.

"Only this—that I don't see where the paper could have come from but out of your own pocket-book," replied Mrs. Gass frankly. "I have no other cause to suspect you ; I'd as soon suspect myself. It is just a mystery, and nothing else."

"Whatever the mystery may be, it is not connected with my pocket-book, Mrs. Gass," he emphatically said. "Did you mention this to Richard North ?"

"No. Nor to anybody else. It was not a pleasant thing to speak of, you see."

"Not a pleasant thing for me, certainly, to be suspected of having dropped that paper. The culprit, an innocent one, no doubt, must have been Molly Green."

"I never was so brought up in all my life," cried the puzzled woman. As to Molly Green—it must be just a fancy of yours, doctor, for it never can be fact."

Oliver Rane drew his chair a little nearer to Mrs. Gass, and whispered a word of the doubt touching Mrs. North. He only spoke of it *as* a doubt; a hint at most; but Mrs. Gass was not slow to take it.

"Heaven help the woman!—if it's her work."

"But this must not be breathed aloud," he said, taking alarm. "It may be a false suspicion."

"Don't fear me: it's a thing too grave for me to mix myself up in," was the reply: and to give Mrs. Gass her due, she did look scared in no slight degree. "Dr. Rane, I am sorry for saying what I did to you. It was the impossibility, as I took it, of anything's having left it here but that flutter of papers from your pocket-book. Whoever would have gave a thought to Molly Green?"

Dr. Rane made no answer.

"She put her basket down by the door there, and came up the room to look at my geraniums; I held the candle for her. I remember she caught her crinoline on the corner of the iron fender, and it gave her a twist round. The idiots that girls make of themselves with them big crinolines! Perhaps it dropped from her then."

"Well, let us bury it in silence, Mrs. Gass; it is but a doubt at best," said the prudent but less eloquent physician. "You will allow me to take this," he added, alluding to the paper. "I should like to examine it at leisure."

"Take it, and welcome," she answered; "I'm glad to be rid of it. As to burying it in silence, we had better, I expect, both do that."

"Even to Richard North," he enjoined rather anxiously.

"Even to Richard North. I have kept secrets in my day, doctor, and can keep e'm again."

Dr. Rane put the paper in his pocket-book, deposited that in the breast pocket of his coat, and took his departure. But now, being a shrewd man, a suspicion that he would not have given utterance to for the whole world, lay on Dr. Rane— that it was more in accordance with probability that the paper had dropped out of his pocket-book than from Molly Green's petticoats, seeing they were *not* finished off with fish-hooks.

A heavy weight lying there on his breast! And he went along with a loitering step, asking himself how the paper could have originally come there.

CHAPTER IV.

ALONE WITH THE NAKED TRUTH.

OLIVER RANE was in his bed-chamber; a front apartment facing the road. It will be as well to give a word of description to this first floor, for it may prove needful as the tale goes on. There was a very large landing-place, the boards white and bare, with a spacious window looking full to the side of the other house, as the dining-room beneath it did. Wide, low, and curtainless was this landing-window; imparting in conjunction with the bare floors and walls, a staring, bleak appearance to the place. Mrs. Cumberland's opposite landing, (could you have seen it) presented quite a different aspect, with its rich carpet of many colours, its statues, vases, bookcases, and its tasty window-drapery. Dr. Rane could not afford luxuries yet; or, indeed, superfluous furniture. The stairs led down nearly close to this window, so that in coming from any of the bed-rooms, or the upper floor, to descend below, you had to face it.

To get into Dr. Rane's chamber—the best in the house—an ante-room had to be passed through, whose door was opposite to the large window. Two chambers opened from the back of the landing: they faced the back lane that ran along beyond the garden wall. Above, in the roof, were two other rooms, both three-cornered. Phillis, the old serving-woman, slept on that floor in one of them, Dr. Rane on this: the house had no other inmates.

The ante-room had no furniture: unless some curious-looking articles lying on the floor could be called such. They seemed to consist chiefly of glass: jars covered in dust, a cylindrical glass-pump, and other things pertaining to chemistry, of which science the doctor was fond. Certainly the architect had not made the most of this floor, or he would never have expended so much space on the landing. But if this ante-room was not furnished, Dr. Rane's chamber was; and well, too. The entrance door was in the middle of the beautifully papered wall of white and gold, the dressing-table and glass stood opposite before the window. The fire-place was on the left; a handsome white Arabian bedstead picked out with gold, on the right, its hangings, of green damask, matching the window drapery and in colour the soft carpet.

Other furniture stood about, all very good of its kind, and the whole in harmony.

Seated at the round table in the middle. of the room, his hand raised to support his head, was Dr. Rane. He had but just come in, and it was now one o'clock—his ordinary dinner hour. Is was that same morning told of in the last chapter, when he had quitted Mrs. Gass's house with that dangerous piece of paper weighing down his pocket and his heart. He had been detained out. As he was entering the door of the sick man, Ketler, whom he had proceeded at once to see, a bustle in the street, and much wild running of women, warned him that something must have happened. Two men had fallen into the river at the back of the North Works; and excited people were shouting that they were drowned. Not quite : as Dr. Rane saw when he reached the spot : not beyond hope of restoration. Patiently the doctor persevered in his endeavours. He got life into them at length; and stayed afterwards caring for them. After that, he had Ketler and other patients to see, and it was nearly one when he bent his steps towards home. In the morning he had said to himself that he would call at the Hall on his return ; but he passed its gates ; perhaps because it was his dinner hour, for one o'clock was striking.

Hanging up his hat in the small hall, leaving his cane in the corner—a pretty little thing with a gold stag for its head—he was making straight for the stairs, when the servant, Phillis, came out of the kitchen. A little woman of some five-and-fifty years, with high shoulders, and her head poking forward. Her chin and nose were sharp now, but the once good-looking face was meek and mild, the sweet dark eyes were subdued, and the hair, peeping from beneath the close white cap, was grey. She wore a dark cotton gown and check apron, and her arms were bare to the elbows. A tidy-looking, respectable woman, in spite of her unfashionable appearance.

"Is that you, master ? Them folks have been over from the brick-kilns, saying the woman's not so well to-day, if you'd please to go to her."

Dr. Rane nodded his head. He went on up the stairs and into his own room, the door of which he locked. Why ? Phillis was not in the habit of intruding upon him, and there was no one else in the house. The first thing he did was to take the paper received from Mrs. Gass out of his pocket-book, and read it attentively twice over. Then he struck a match, set fire to it, and watched it consume away in the empty grate. A dangerous memento, whosesoever hand had penned it; and the physician did well, in the interests of humanity, to put it out of sight for ever. The task over, he leaned against the window-frame, in the shade of the flowing damask window-curtain, and lapsed into thought. He was dwelling upon the death at Dallory Hall, and what it might bring forth.

Hepburn, the undertaker, was right. There was to be no inquest. So much Dr. Rane had learned from Richard North: who had hastened to the works on hearing of the accident to his men. The two Whitborough doctors had given the certificate of death—apoplexy, to which there had been a previous tendency, though immediately brought on by excitement—and nothing more was required by law. From a word spoken by Richard, Dr. Rane gathered that it was Madam (as Mrs. North was very generally called) who had set her veto against an inquest. And quite right too; there was no necessity whatever for one, had been the answering comment made by Oliver Rane to Richard. But now—now when he was alone with himself and the naked truth: when there was no man at hand whose opinion it might be well to humour or deceive: no eye upon him save God's, he could not help acknowledging that had he been Mr. North, had it been his son who was thus cut off from life, he should have called for an inquest to be held. Ay, ten inquests, and the law would have allowed them; if by that means he might have traced the letter home to its writer.

Quitting his place by the window, he sat down at the table and bent his forehead upon his hand. Never in his whole life had anything so affected him as this death: and it was perhaps natural that he should set himself to see whether, or not, any kind of excuse might be found for the anonymous writer.

He began by putting himself in idea into the writer's place and argued the point for him: for and against. Chiefly *for* it was on that side his bias leaned. It is very easy, as the world knows, to find a plea for those in whom we are interested or on whom misfortune falls; it is so natural to indulge for their sakes in a little sophistry. Such sophistry came now to the help of the physician.

"What cause had Edmund North to fly into a dangerous passion?" ran the self-argument. "Only a madman would have been expected to do so. There was nothing in the letter that need have excited him, absolutely nothing. It was (probably) written with a very harmless view; certainly the writer never could have dreamt that it might have the effect of destroying a life."

Destroying a man's life! A flush passed into Oliver Rane's face at the thought, dyeing neck and brow crimson. And, with it, came back the words of Hepburn—that the writer was a murderer and might come to be tried for it. A murderer! a slayer of one's inoffensive fellow-man! There is no other self-reproach under heaven that can bring home so much anguish to the conscience. But—could a man be justly called a murderer if he had never had thought or intention to do anything of the kind?

"Wait here," said Dr. Rane, beginning to speak aloud, as if he were a special pleader arguing in a law court. "Can a man be called a murderer who has never had the smallest intention to murder—who would have flown in horror from the bare idea? Let us suppose it was—Mrs. North—who wrote the letter? Alexander suspects her, at any rate. Put it that she had some motive for writing it. It might have been a good motive—that of stopping Edmund North in his downward career, as the letter intimated—and she fancied this might be best accomplished by letting his father hear of what he, in conjunction with Alexander, was doing. According to Alexander, she does not interfere openly between the young men and their father; it's not her policy: and she may have considered the means she took were legitimate under the circumstances. Well, could she for a moment imagine that any terrible consequences would ensue? A rating from Mr. North to his son, and the matter would be over. Just so: she was innocent of any other thought. Then how can she be deemed guilty?"

Dr. Rane paused. A book lay on the table: he turned its leaves backwards and forwards in abstraction, his mind never quitting the subject. Presently he resumed.

"Or—take Alexander's view of the letter—that it was written to damage him with Mr. North and the neighbourhood generally. Madam—say again—had conceived a dislike to Alexander, wished him dismissed from the house, but had no plea for doing it, and so took *that* means—the sending of a letter to her husband. Could she suspect that the result would be fatal to Edmund North? Would she not have shrunk with genuine abhorrence from penning the letter, had she foreseen it? Certainly; certainly. Then, under these circumstances, how can a man—I mean a woman—be responsible, legally or

morally, for the death ? It would be utterly unjust to charge
her with it. Edmund North is alone to blame. Clearly so.
The case is little better than a case of unintentional suicide."

Having arrived at this view of the subject—so comforting
for the unknown writer—Dr. Rane rose briskly, and began to
wash his hands and smooth his hair. He took a note-case
from his pocket, in which he was in the habit of dotting down
his daily engagements, to see at what hour he could most conveniently go to the brick-fields, in compliance with the message
just received. The sick woman was in no danger, as he knew,
and he might choose his own time. In passing through the
ante-room—which room, by the way, was generally distinguished as the Drab Room, from the unusual colour of the
walls, drab and hideous—he took up one of the glass jars, requiring it for some purpose downstairs. And then he noticed
something that displeased him.

"Phillis!" he called, putting his head out on the landing;
"Phillis!" And the woman, a very active little body, came
running up.

"You have been sweeping the Drab Room ? "

"It was so dirty, master."

"Now look you here," he cried, angrily. "If you sweep out
a room again, when I tell you it is not to be swept, I'll keep
every place in the house locked up. Some of the glass here is
valuable, and I'll not run the risk of having it broken with
brooms and brushes."

Down went Phillis, taking the reproof in silence. As Dr.
Rane crossed the landing to follow her, his eyes naturally fell
on his mother's house through the large window. The
answering window opposite, Mrs. Cumberland's, was being
cleaned by one of the servants: at the window of the dining-
room underneath, his mother was sitting. It put Dr. Rane in
mind that he had not been in to see her for nearly two days;
not since Edmund North——·

All in a moment, induced perhaps by the name, a sense of
the delusive nature of the sophistry he had been indulging,
flashed into his brain, and the truth shone out distinct and
bare. Edmund North was dead; killed by the anonymous
letter. But for that fatal letter he had been alive and well
now. A sickening sensation, as of some great oppression,
crowded over Oliver Rane, and his nerveless fingers dropped
the jar.

Out ran Phillis, lifting her hands at the crash of glittering mites lying in the passage. "He has broke one himself now," thought she, referring to the reproof about the glasses.

"Just sweep the pieces carefully into a dust-pan, and throw them away," said her master as he passed on. "The jar slipped out of my fingers."

Phillis stared a minute, getting rid of her surprise, and then turned to fetch the dust-pan. The doctor went on to the front door, instead of into the dining-room, as Phillis expected.

"Master," she called out, running after him, "your dinner's waiting. The fowl's on the table, and I was just coming in with the potatoes."

But Dr. Rane passed on as though he had not heard her, and shut the door with a bang.

He turned into his mother's house. Not by the familiar mode of the open window; he did not gain the premises by stepping over the slight fence; but he knocked at the front door, and was admitted as an ordinary visitor. Whether it was from having lived apart for so many years of their lives, or that a something was wanting of social cordiality in the disposition of each, certain it was that Dr. Rane and his mother observed more ceremony with each other, and were less familiar, than what usually obtains between mother and son.

Mrs. Cumberland sat at the open dining-room window just as he had seen her from his staircase landing; a newspaper lay behind her on a small table, put out of hand when read. Ellen Adair, as might be heard, was at the piano in the drawing-room, playing, perhaps from unconscious association, and low and softly as it was her delight to play, the "Dead March in Saul." The dirge grated on the ears of Dr. Rane.

"What a melancholy drawl!" he involuntarily exclaimed; and Mrs. Cumberland looked up, there was so much irritation in the tone.

He shook hands with his mother, but did not kiss her, which he was not accustomed to do, and stood back against the broad window, his face turned to it.

"You are a stranger, Oliver," she said. "What has kept you away?"

"I have been busy. To-day especially. They had an accident at the works—two men nearly drowned—and I have been with them all the morning."

"I heard of it. Jelly brought me in the news; she seems to hear everything. How fortunate that you were at hand!"

He proceeded rather volubly to give the particulars of the accident and of the process he adopted to recover the men; voluble for him. Mrs. Cumberland looked and listened with silent, warm affection; but that she was a particularly undemonstrative woman, she would have shown it in her manner. In her partial eyes, there was not so fine and handsome and estimable a man in all Dallory as this her only son.

"Oliver, what a dreadful thing this is about Edmund North! I have not seen you since. Why did you not come in and tell me the same night?"

He turned his eyes on her for a moment to express surprise, and paused.

"I am not in the habit of coming in to tell you when called out to patients, mother. How was I to know you wished it?"

"Nonsense, Oliver! This is not an ordinary thing: the Norths were something to me once. I have had Edmund on my knee when he was a baby; and I should have liked you to pay me the attention of bringing in the news. Only to put it on the score of gossip, it would have been welcome," she added, with a half smile at the words. "It appears to be altogether a more romantic event than one meets with every day, and such things, you know, are of interest to lonely women."

Dr. Rane made no rejoinder, possibly not having any sufficient excuse to offer for his carelessness. He stood looking dreamily from a corner of the window. Phillis (as might be seen from thence) was carrying away the fowl and a tureen of sauce. Mrs. Cumberland probably thought he was watching with critical curiosity the movements of his handmaid. She resumed:

"They say, Oliver, there has been no hope of him from the first."

"There was very little. Of course, as it turns out, there could have been none."

"And who wrote the letter? With what motive was it written?" proceeded Mrs. Cumberland, her pale grey face leaning slightly forward, as she waited for an answer.

"It is of no use to ask me, mother. Some people hold one opinion, some another; mine would go for little."

"They are beginning now to think that it was not written at all to injure Edmund, but Mr. Alexander."

"Who told you that?" he asked, a sharper accent discernible in his tone.

"Captain Bohun. He came in this morning to apprise me of the death. Considering that I have no claim upon him, that a year ago I had never spoken to him, I must say that Arthur Bohun is very kind and attentive to me. He's one in a thousand."

Perhaps the temptation to say, "It's not for your sake he is attentive," momentarily assailed Oliver Rane. But he was good-natured in the main, and he knew when to hold his tongue, and when to speak : no man better. Besides, it was no business of his.

"I entertain a different opinion," he observed, referring to the point in discussion. "Of course it is all guess work what the writer's motive was, or what it was not: there's no profit in discussing it, mother; and I must be going, for my dinner's waiting. Thank you for sending me the fowl."

"A moment yet, Oliver," she interposed, touching his arm as he was passing her to move away. "Have you heard that Alexander is going to leave ? "

"Yes: he was talking with me about it this morning."

If ever a glow of hope, of light, had been seen lately on Mrs. Cumberland's marble face, it was seen then. The tightly-drawn skin on the features had lost its grey tinge.

"Oliver, I could go down on my knees and thank Heaven for it. You don't know how grieved I have felt all through these past two years, to see you put into the shade by that man, and to know that it was I who had brought you here ! It will be all right now. New houses are to be built, they say, at the other end of the Ham, and the practice will be worth a great deal. I shall sleep well to-night."

He smiled as he shook hands with her; partly in affection, partly at her unusual vehemence. In passing the drawing-room, Ellen Adair happened to be coming out of it, but he went on. She supposed he had not observed her, and spoke.

"Ah ! how do you do, Miss Adair ? " he said, turning back, and offering his hand. "Forgive my haste; I am busy to-day."

And before she had time to say an answering syllable, he was gone; leaving an impression on her mind, she could not well have told why or wherefore, that he was ill at ease; that he had hastened away, not from pressure of business, but because he did not care to stay to talk.

If that feeling was pervading Dr. Rane, and had reference to the world in general, and not to the young lady in particular, it might not have been agreeable to him to encounter an acquaintance as he turned out of his mother's house. Mr. Alexander was swiftly passing on his way towards home from the lower part of the Ham, and stopped.

" I wish I'd never said a syllable about my going away till I was off," cried he in his free, off-hand manner—a pleasanter manner and more sociable than Dr. Rane's. " The news has been noised abroad, and I've got the whole place upon me; asking this—questioning that. One man comes and wants to know if I'll sell my furniture; another thinks he'd like the house as it stands. My patients are up in arms;—say I'm doing it to kill them. I shall have some of them in a fever before the day's over."

" Perhaps you'll not go after all," observed Dr. Rane.

" Not go! How can I help going? I'm elected to the post. Why, it's what I've been looking out for ever so long —almost ever since I've been here. No, no, Rane: a short while, and Dallory Ham will have seen the last of me."

He hastened across the road to his house, on the run, like a man who has the world's work on his busy shoulders. Dr. Rane's thoughts, as he glanced after him, reverted to the mental argument he had held in his chamber, and he unconsciously resumed it, putting himself in the place of the unknown, miserable writer, as before.

" It's almost keener than the death itself—if the motive *was* to do Alexander injury in his profession, or drive him from the place—to know that he, or she—Mrs. North—might have spared her pains! Heavens! what remorse it must be !— to commit a crime, and then find there was no necessity for it ! "

Dr. Rane wiped his brow with his white handkerchief— the day was very warm—and turned into his house. Phillis once more put the dinner on the table, and he sat down to it.

But not a mouthful could he swallow; his throat was like so much dried chip, and the food would not go down. Phillis, who was coming in for something or other, saw him leave his plate and rise from table.

" Ain't it tender, sir ? "

" Tender ? " he responded, as though he did not catch the sense of the question, and paused. " Oh, it's tender enough : but I must go to see a patient. Get your own dinner."

" Surely you'll come back to yours, sir ? "

"I've had mine—as much as I want. Take the things away."

"I wonder what's come to him?" mused the woman as his quick steps receded from the house, and she was left alone with the rejected dishes. A consciousness came dimly penetrating to her hazy brain that there was some change upon him. What it was, or where it lay, she did not define. It was unusual for his strong firm fingers to drop a glass; it was still more unusual for him to explain cause and effect. "The jar slipped from my fingers." "I've had as much as I want. I must go to see a patient." It was quite out of the common order of routine for Dr. Rane to be explanatory to his servant on any subject whatever; and perhaps it was his having been so in these two instances that took hold of Phillis.

"How quick he must have eaten his dinner!"

Phillis nearly dropped the dish of fowl. The words were spoken close behind her, and she had believed herself alone in the house. Turning round, she saw Jelly, standing half in, half out at the window.

"Well, I'm sure!" cried Phillis, wrathfully. "You needn't come startling a body in that way, Mrs. Jelly. How did you know but the doctor might be at table?"

"I've just seen him go down the lane," returned Jelly, who had plenty of time for gossiping with her neighbours, the duties at home not being onerous, and had come strolling over the garden fence now with no other object. "Has he had his dinner? It's but the other minute he was in at our house."

"He has had as much as he means to have," answered Phillis, her anger evaporating, for she liked a social gossip too. "I'm sure it's not worth the trouble of serving meals, if they are to be left in this fashion. It was the same thing at breakfast."

Jelly recollected the scene at breakfast; the startled pallor on Dr. Rane's face, when told that Edmund North was dead: she supposed that had stopped his appetite. Her inquisitive eyes turned unceremoniously to the fowl, and she saw that the merest bit of a wing was alone eaten.

"Perhaps he is not well to-day," said Jelly.

"I don't know about his being well; he's odder than I ever saw him," answered Phillis. "I shouldn't wonder but he has had his stomach turned over them two half-drowned men."

Putting the doors open, she carried the dinner-things across to the kitchen. Jelly, who assisted at the ceremony, so far as watching and talking went, was standing in the passage, when her quick eyes caught sight of two small bits of glass. She stooped to pick them up.

"Look here, Phillis! You have been breaking something. It's uncommonly careless to leave the pieces about."

"Is it!" retorted Phillis. "You've got your eyes in everything. I thought I took 'em all up," she added, looking on the ground.

"What did you break?"

"Nothing. The doctor did. He dropped one of them dusty glass jars down the stairs. It did give me a start. You should have heard the smash."

"What made him drop it?" asked Jelly.

"Goodness knows," returned the older woman. "He's not a bit like himself to-day; it's just as if something had come to him."

She began to eat her dinner as she spoke, standing, her usual mode of taking it. The whole of the fowl was put by into the larder, including the cut wing on the doctor's plate, and she contented herself with a piece of bacon and the gravy remaining in the dish. Phillis was of too economical a turn to waste dainty fowl upon herself, though quite at liberty to do so. Dr. Rane sometimes asked her what she lived upon: Phillis would answer that she lived as well as she ever had lived, and as well as she cared to live. Bread and butter and tea were her chief luxuries.

Jelly, following her customary free-and-easy habits, stood against the door-post, apparently interested in the progress of the meal. They presented a contrast, these two women, the one a thin giantess bolt upright, the other a dwarf stooping forward. Jelly, a lady's maid, held herself of course altogether above Phillis, an ignorant (as Jelly would have described her) servant-of-all-work, though condescending to drop in for the sake of gossip.

"Did you happen to hear how the doctor found Ketler?"

"As if I should be likely to hear!" was Phillis's retort. "He'd not tell me, and I couldn't ask. My master's not one of them you can put questions to, Jelly."

A silence ensued. The gossip apparently flagged to-day. Phillis had it chiefly to herself, for Jelly vouchsafed but a brief answering remark now and again. She was engaged in mental process of wondering what *had* come to Dr. Rane.

CHAPTER V.

RETROSPECT.

THERE must be some retrospect to make things intelligible; and it may as well be given at once.

Mr. North, now of Dallory Hall, had got on entirely by his own persevering industry. Of obscure, though in a certain way very respectable parentage, he had been placed as working apprentice to a firm in Whitborough. It was a firm in extensive work, not confining itself to one branch. They took contracts for public buildings, small and large: they did mechanical engineering; they had planned one of the early railways. John North—plain Jack North he was known as, then—remained with the firm when he was out of his time, and got on in it. Thrifty, steady, and plodding, he rose from one step to another; and at length, in conjunction with one who had been in the same firm, he set up for himself. This other was Thomas Gass. Gass had not risen from the ranks as North had : he was of good connections and had received a superior education; but his friends were poor. North and Gass, as the new firm called itself, began business near to Dallory; quietly at first—as all people, who truly look to get on, generally do begin. They rose rapidly. The confined premises grew into great ones; the small contracts into larger. People said luck was with them—and in truth it seemed so. The Dallory works became of note in the county, employing quite a colony of people : the masters were respected and sought after. Both of them lived at Whitborough; Mr. North with his wife and family; Mr. Gass a bachelor.

Thomas Gass had one brother; a clergyman. Their only sister, Fanny, a pretty young girl, had her home with him in his rectory, but she came often to Whitborough on a visit to Thomas. Suddenly it was announced to the world that she had engaged herself to be married to a Captain Rane, entirely against the wish of her two brothers. She was under twenty. Captain Rane, a poor naval man on half-pay, was nearly old enough to be her grandfather. Their objection lay not so much to this, as to him. For some cause or other, neither liked him. The Reverend William Gass forbid his sister to think of him; Mr. Thomas Gass (a fiery man) swore he would never afterwards look upon her as a sister, if she persisted in thus throwing herself away.

Miss Gass did persist. She possessed the obstinate spirit of her brother Thomas, though without his fire. She chose to take her own way, and married Captain Rane. They sailed at once for Madras; Captain Rane having obtained some post there, connected with the Government ships.

Whether Miss Gass repented of her ill-assorted marriage, her brothers had no means of learning: for she, cherishing anger, never wrote to them during her husband's life. It was a very short one. Barely a twelvemonth had elapsed after the knot was tied, when there came a pitiful letter from her. Captain Rane had died, just as her little son Oliver (named after a friend, she said) was born. Thomas Gass, to whom the letter had been specially written, gathered that she was left badly off; though she did not absolutely say it. He went into one of his fumes, and tossed the epistle across the desk to his partner. "You must do something for her, Gass," said John North when he had read it. "I never will," hotly affirmed Mr. Gass. "Fanny knows what I promised if she married Rane—that I would never help her during my life or after it. She knows another thing—that I am not one to go from my word. William may help her if he likes; he has not got much to give away, but he can have her back to live with him." " Help the child, then," suggested Mr. North, knowing further remonstrance to be useless. "I won't help the child," returned obstinate Thomas Gass; "I'll stick to the spirit of my promise as well as the letter." And Mr. North bent his head down again—he was going over some estimates—feeling that the affair was none of his. "I don't mind putting the boy in the tontine, North," presently spoke the junior partner. " The tontine!" echoed John North in surprise, "what tontine?" "What tontine!" returned the hard man—though in truth he was not hard in general, " why, the one that you and others are getting up; the one you have just put your baby, Bessy, in; I know of no other tontine." "But that will not benefit the boy," urged Mr. North : "certainly not now; and the chances are nine to one against its ever benefitting him." "Never mind; I'll put him in it," said Mr. Gass, whose obstinacy always came out well when spurred by opposition. "You are wanting a tenth child to close the list, and I'll put him in it." So into the tontine Oliver Rane, unconscious infant, was put.

But Mrs. Rane did not further trouble either of her brothers; or, as things turned out, require assistance from them. She remained in India; and at a year's end married a Government chaplain there, the Reverend George Cumberland, who had some private property. Little, if any, communication took place afterwards between her and her brothers; she cherished resentment for old grievances, and would not write. And so the sister and the brothers seemed to fade away from each other henceforth. We all know how relatives, parted by time and distance, become estranged, disappearing almost from memory.

While the firm, North and Gass, was rising higher and higher in wealth and importance, the wife of its senior partner died. She left three children, Edmund, Richard, and Bessy. Subsequently, during a visit to London, chance drew Mr. North into a meeting with a handsome young woman, the widow of Major Bohun. She was not long from India, where she had buried her husband. A flashing, designing, attractive syren, who began forthwith to exercise her dangerous fascinations on plain, unsuspicious Mr. North. She had but a poor pittance; what money there was belonged to her only child, Arthur; a little lad: sent out of sight already to a preparatory school. Report had magnified Mr. North's wealth into something fabulous; and Mrs. Bohun did not cease her scheming until she had caught him in her toils and he had made her Mrs. North.

Men do things sometimes in a hurry, only to repent. That Mr. North had been in a hurry in this case was indisputable—it was just as though Mrs. Bohun had thrown a spell over him; whether he repented when he woke up and found himself with a wife, a stepmother for his little ones at home, was not so sure. He was a sufficiently wise man in those days to conceal what he did not want known.

Whom he had married, beyond the fact that she was the widow of Major Bohun, he did not know from Adam. For all she disclosed about her own family, in regard to whom she maintained an entire reticence, she might have dropped from the moon, or " growed " like Topsy ; but, from the airs and graces she put on, Mr. North might have concluded they were dukes and duchesses at least. Her late husband's family were irreproachable, both in character and position. The head of it was Sir Nash Bohun, representative of an ancient baronetcy, and elder brother of the late Major. Before the wedding tour was over, poor Mr. North found that his wife was a cold, imperious, extravagant woman, not to be questioned by any means if she chose not to be. When her fascinations were in full play (while she was only the widow Bohun) Mr. North had been ready to think her quite an angel. Where had all the amiability flown ?—he rubbed his mental eyes as he asked it. People do change after marriage somehow. At least, there have been instances known of it.

A little circumstance occurred one day that—to put it mildly —had surprised Mr. North. He had been given to understand by his wife that Major Bohun died suddenly of sun-stroke; she had certainly told him so. In talking at a dinner-party at Sir Nash Bohun's with some gentlemen not long from India, he and Mr. North being side by side at table after the ladies had retired, the subject of sun-strokes came up. "My wife's former husband, Major Bohun, died of one," innocently observed Mr. North. "Died of *what ?*" cried the other, putting down his claret-glass, which he was about to convey to his mouth. "Of sun-stroke," repeated Mr. North. "Bohun did not die of sun-stroke," came the impulsive answer; "who told you he died of that?" "She did—my wife," was Mr. North's answer. "Oh!" said his friend; and drank the claret. "Why, what did he die of, if it was not sun-stroke?" asked Mr. North, with curiosity. "Well,—I—I don't know; I'd rather say no more about it," was the conclusive reply: "of course Mrs. North must know better than I." And no other words would he speak, save—as Mr. North saw—evasive ones.

They were staying at this time at Sir Nash Bohun's. In passing through London after the Continental wedding trip on their way to Whitborough, Sir Nash had invited them to make his house their resting-place. Not until the day following his conversation at the dinner-table had Mr. North an opportunity of questioning his wife; but, that some false representation, intentionally or otherwise, had been made to him on the subject of her late husband's death, he felt certain. They were alone in her dressing-room. Mrs. North, who had a mass of beautiful purple-black hair, was standing before the glass, doing something to a portion of it, when her husband suddenly accosted her. He called her by her Christian name in those first married days. It was a very fine one.

"Amanda, you told me, I think, that Major Bohun died of sun-stroke."

"Well ?" she returned carelessly, occupied with her hair.

D

"But he did not die of sun-stroke. He died of—of something else."

Mr. North had watched women's faces turn to pallor, but never in his whole life had he seen so livid a look of terror as overspread his wife's. The band of black hair dropped from her hands; even their very fingers became of a ghastly whiteness.

"Why, what is the matter?" he exclaimed.

She murmured something about a spasm of the heart, a spasm to which she was subject: an excuse, as he saw. Another moment, and she had recovered her composure, and was busy with her hair again.

"You were asking me something, were you not, Mr. North?"

"About Major Bohun: what was it he died of,—if it was not sun-stroke?"

"But it was of sun-stroke," she said, in a sharp, ringing accent, that would have required but a little more to be a scream. "What else was there that he should die suddenly of in India's burning climate? He went out in the blaze of the mid-day sun, and was brought home dead!"

And nothing more, then or afterwards, did Mr. North learn. Her manner rendered it impossible that he could press the subject. He might have applied to Sir Nash for information, but an instinct prevented his doing so. After all, it did not signify to him what Major Bohun had died of, Mr. North said to himself, and determined to forget the matter. But that some mystery must have attended Major Bohun's death, some painful circumstances which could blanch his wife's face with sickly terror, remained on Mr. North's mind as a fact not to be controverted.

Mrs. North effected changes. Almost the very day she was taken home to Whitborough, she let it be known that she should rule with an imperious will. Her husband became a very reed in her hands; yielding passively to her sway, as if all the spirit he ever owned had gone out of him. Mrs. North professed to hate the very name of trade: that one with whom she was so nearly connected should be in business, brought to her a sense of degradation and a great deal of talk of it. The quiet, modest, comfortable home at Whitborough was at once given up for the more pretentious Manor Hall at Dallory Ham, which happened to be in the market. And they set up there in a style that might have more properly pertained to the lord-lieutenant of the county. Perhaps it was her assumption of grandeur out of doors and in, combined with the haughty, imperious manner, the like of which had never before been seen in the simple neighbourhood, that caused people to call her "Madam." Or, it might have been to distinguish her in speech from the first Mrs. North.

In proportion as Mrs. North made herself hated and feared by her husband, his children, and the household, so did she become popular with society. It sometimes happens that the more fascination a woman displays to the world, the more unbearable is she in her own house. It was the case here. Madam put on all her attractions when out of doors; she visited and dressed and dined and spent; and gave fêtes again at Dallory Hall utterly regardless of expense. Little wonder, was there, that she swayed the neighbourhood.

Not the immediate neighbourhood. With the exception of the Dallory family (and they did not live there always), there was not a single person she would have visited. Some gentlepeople resided at Dallory Ham; Mrs. North did not condescend to know any of them. Report ran that when they left cards on her on her first coming to the Hall, she had returned them in blank envelopes. People living at a greater distance she made friends with, but not those around her; and with as many of the county families as would make friends with her. The pleasantest times were those when she would betake herself off on long visits, to London, or elsewhere: they grew to be looked for.

But the most decided onset made by Mrs. North was on her husband's business connections. Had Thomas Gass been a chimney-sweep, she could not have treated him with more intense contempt. It was said that if by ill-fortune she met him in the street, she would pick up her skirts with a jerk as she passed him by. Thomas Gass had his share of sense, and pitied his partner far more than he would had that gentleman gone in for hanging instead of second marriage. Mr. Gass was a very wealthy man now; and had built himself a handsome and comfortable residence in Dallory.

But, as the years went on, he was doomed to furnish food himself to all the gossips within miles. Dallory rose from its couch one fine morning, to hear that Thomas Gass, the confirmed old bachelor, had married his housekeeper. Not one of your "lady housekeepers," but a useful, good, hard-working damsel, who had passed the first bloom of youth, and had not much of beauty to recommend her. It was a nine days' wonder, nearly a rebellion. Of course, however much the neighbours might solace their feelings by ridiculing him and abusing her, they could not undo the marriage. All that remained to them was, to make the best of it; and by degrees they wisely did so. The new Mrs. Gass, who had glided so easily into her honours, shook as easily down in them. She made an excellent wife to her ailing husband—for Thomas Gass had begun to ail before his marriage—she put on no airs of being superior to what she was; she turned out to be a thoroughly capable woman of business, giving much judicious advice: she was very good to the sick and suffering, caring for the poor, ready to give a helping hand wheresover and whensoever it might be needed. In spite of her fine clothes, which sat ludicrously upon her, and of her mode of speech, which she did not attempt to get out of; above all, in spite of their own prejudices, Dallory grew to like and respect Mrs. Gass, and its small gentle-people to admit her to their houses on an equality.

And so time and years went on, Mr. North withdrawing himself more and more from personal attendance on the business, which seemed to have grown utterly distasteful to him. His sons had become young men. Edmund was a civil engineer: by profession at least, not much by practice. Never of strong health, given to expensive and idle habits, Edmund North was in general either in trouble abroad, or leading a lazy life at home, his time being much divided between going into causeless passions and writing poetry. Richard was at the works, the mainspring and prop of the business. Mr. Gass had become a confirmed invalid, and could not personally attend; Mr. North did not. There was only Richard—Dick, as they all called him; but he was a host in himself. Of far better powers to bring to bear on it than Mr. North had ever possessed, highly educated, of cultivated mind, he was a thorough man of business, and at the same time a finished gentleman. Energetic, persevering, decisive in control, but of courteous and considerate manners to the very lowest, Richard North was loved and respected. He walked through life doing his duty by his fellow-men: striving to do it to God. He had been tried at home in many ways since his father's second marriage, and borne all with patient endurance: how he was tried out of home, he alone knew.

For a long while past there had been trouble in the firm, ill-feeling between the two old partners; chiefly because Mr.

North put no limit to the sums he drew out for his private
account. Poor Mr. North at length confessed that he could
not help it: the money was wanted by his wife: though how
on earth she contrived to get rid of so much, even with all her
extravagance, he could not conceive. Mr. Gass insisted on a
separation: John North must withdraw from the firm; Richard
might take his place. Poor Mr. North yielded, meek as any
lamb. "Don't let it go abroad," he only stipulated, speaking
as if he were half heart-broken, which was nothing new; "I
should not like it to be known that I was superseded." They
respected his wishes, and the change was made privately: very
few having cognizance that the senior partnership in the firm
had passed into the hands of a young man. Thenceforth Mr.
North ceased to have control over the business; in fact, to
have any actual connection with it. Dallory suspected it not:
Mrs. North had not the faintest idea of it. Richard North
signed the cheques as he had done before, "North and Gass:"
and perhaps the bank at Whitborough alone knew that he
signed them now as principal.

Richard was the scape-goat now. Mr. North's need of
money, or rather his wife's, did not cease: the sum arranged
to be paid to him as a retiring pension—a very liberal sum,
and Mr. Gass grumbled at it—seemed to be as nothing; it
melted in Madam's hands like so much water. Richard was
constantly appealed to by his father; and responded generously,
though it crippled him.

The next change came in the shape of Mr. Gass's death.
The bulk of his property was left to his wife; a small portion,
comparatively speaking, to charities and servants; two
thousand pounds to Richard North. He also bequeathed to
his wife his interest in the business, which by the terms of the
deed of partnership he had power to do. So that his share of
the capital was not drawn out, and the firm remained, actually
as well as virtually, North and Gass. People generally supposed that the "North" was Mr. North; and Madam went
into a cold sea of indignation at her husband's name being put
in conjunction with "that woman's." In the years gone by,
Mr. North used to have a nice time of it, finding it a difficult
matter to steer his course between his partner and Madam, so
as to give offence to neither. Madam had never condescended
to notice Thomas Gass's wife in the smallest degree: she took
to abuse her now, asking her husband how he could *suffer* himself to be associated with her. Mr. North, when goaded almost

beyond bearing, had much ado to keep his tongue from retort-
ing that it was not himself that was associated with her, but
Richard.

Mrs. Gass showed her good sense in regard to the partnership, as she did in most things. She declined to interfere
actively in the business. Richard North went to her house
twice or thrice a week to keep her cognisant of what was
going on ; he consulted her opinion on great matters, just as
he had used to consult her husband's. She knew she could
trust to him. Ever and anon she would volunteer some
advice to himself personally : which was invariably good. It
could not be concealed from her that large sums (exclusively
Richard's) were ever finding their way to the Hall, and for
this she took him to task. " Stop it, Mr. Richard," she said
—always as respectful to him as she used to be in her housekeeping days : " stop it, sir. Their wants be like a bottomless
sack, the more grain you pour into it the more you may. It's
doing them no good ; *no good*, mind. An end must come to
it some time, or you'll be in the workhouse. The longer it
goes on, the more difficult it will be to put an end to, and the
harder for them." But Richard, sorely tried between prudence
and filial duty, could not bring himself to stop it so easily ;
and the thing went on.

We must now go back to Mrs. Cumberland. It was somewhat singular that, the very week Thomas Gass lay dead, she
should make her unexpected appearance at Dallory. But so it
was. Again a widow, she had come home to settle near her
brother Thomas. She arrived just in time to see him put into
his coffin. The other brother, William, had been dead for
years. Mrs. Gass, who knew all about the estrangement,
received her with marked kindness, and heartily offered her a
home for the future.

But that was declined. Mrs. Cumberland preferred to have
a home of her own, possessing ample means to set up one in a
moderate way. She gave a sketch of her past life to Mrs.
Gass. After her marriage with the Reverend George Cumberland, they had remained for some time at his chaplaincy in
the Madras presidency ; but his health began to fail, and he
exchanged to Australia. Subsequent to that, years later, he
obtained a duty in Madeira. Upon his death, which occurred
recently, she came to England. Her only son, Oliver Rane,
had been sent home at the age of seven, and was placed with
a preceptor in London. When the time came for him to

choose a profession he fixed on the medical, and qualified himself for it, studying in London, Paris, and Vienna. He passed all the examinations with great credit, including that in the College of Physicians. He next paid a visit to Madeira, remaining three months there with his mother and step-father, and then came home and established himself in London, with money furnished by his mother. But practice does not always come quickly to young beginners, and Oliver Rane found his means dwindling. He had a horror of debt, and wisely decided to keep out of it : taking a situation as assistant, and giving up the expensive house he had entered on. This had just been effected when Mrs. Cumberland returned. For the present she let her son remain as he was : Oliver had all a young man's pride and ambition, and she thought the discipline might do him good.

Mrs. Cumberland took on lease one of the two handsome gothic villas at the neck of the Ham, and established herself in it; with Jelly for a waiting maid, and two other servants for the work. This necessitated the spending the whole of her income, which was a very fair one. A portion of it would die with her, the rest was willed to her son Oliver.

In the old days when she was Fanny Gass, and Mr. North, plain John North—Jack with his friends—they were intimate as elder brother and young sister. If Mrs. Cumberland expected this agreeable state of affairs to be resumed, she was destined to find herself mistaken. Madam set her scornful face utterly against Mrs. Cumberland : just as she had against others. It did not matter. Mrs. Cumberland simply pitied the underbred woman : her health was very delicate, and she did not intend to visit anyone. The gentle-people of the neighbourhood called upon her ; she returned the call, and there the friendship ended. When invitations first came in, she wrote a refusal, explaining clearly and courteously why she was obliged to do so—that her health did not allow her to visit. If she and Mr. North met each other, as by chance happened, they would linger in conversation, and be happy in the reminiscences of the past days.

Mrs. Cumberland had thus lived on in quiet retirement for some time, when the medical man who had the practice of Dallory Ham, and some of that of Dallory, died suddenly. She saw what an excellent opportunity it would be for her son to establish himself, if he would but take up general practice, and she sent a summons for him. When Oliver arrived in answer to it, he entered into the prospect warmly; left his mother to make arrangements, and returned to London, to compass his removal. Mrs. Cumberland went to Mr. North, and obtained his ready promise to do what he could to push Oliver. It was equivalent to an assurance of success—for Dallory Hall swayed its neighbours—and Mrs. Cumberland did not hesitate to secure the other gothic villa adjoining her own (which happened to be vacant), believing the future practice would justify it. In a week's time Oliver Rane came down and took possession.

But fate was against him. Dr. Rane said treachery. A young fellow whom he knew in London had told a medical friend—a Mr. Alexander—of this good practice that had fallen in at Dallory, and that Rane was thinking to secure it for himself. What was Dr. Rane's mortification when, upon arriving at the week's end at Dallory Ham to take possession, he found another there before him. Mr. Alexander had come the previous day, was already established in an opposite house, and had called on everybody. Dr. Rane went over and reproached him with treachery—they had not previously been personally acquainted. Mr. Alexander received the charge with surprise; he declared the field was as open for him as for Dr. Rane—that if he had not thought so, nothing would have induced him to enter for it. He spoke his true sentiments, for he was a straightforward man. An agent in Whitborough had also written up to tell him of this opening; he came to look at it, and decided to try it. The priority, the right to monopolise it, was no more Dr. Rane's, he urged, than it was his. Dr. Rane took a different view, and said so : but contention would not help the matter now, and he could only yield to circumstances. So each held to his right in apparent amicability, and Dallory got two doctors instead of one ; secret rivals from henceforth.

Not for a moment did Oliver Rane think Mr. Alexander could long hold out against him, as he had secured, through his mother, the favour of Dallory Hall. Alas, a very short while showed him that this was a mistake; Dallory Hall turned round upon him, and was doing what it could to push his rival. Mrs. Cumberland went to Mr. North, seeking an explanation. He could only avow the truth—that his wife, who was both master and mistress, had set her face against Oliver, and was recommending Alexander. "John, you promised me," urged Mrs. Cumberland. "I know I did and I'd keep to it if I could," was Mr. North's dismal answer; "but nobody can hold out against her." "Why should she have taken this dislike to Oliver?" rejoined Mrs. Cumberland. "Heaven knows; a caprice, I suppose. She sets herself against people without reason : she has never taken to either Richard or Bessy; and only a little to Edmund. If I can do anything for Oliver under the rose, I'll do it: my will's good to help him, Fanny, in remembrance of our friendship of the old days."

Mrs. Cumberland took home news of her non-success to Oliver. As to Madam, she simply ignored him, throwing her patronage into the scale of his rival. How bitterly the slight sat upon his heart, none save himself could tell. Mrs. Cumberland resented it; but ah, not as he did. A sense of wrong was ever weighing his spirit down, and he thought Fate was against him. One puzzle remained on his mind unsolved—what he could have done to offend Mrs. North.

Mr. Alexander obtained a fair practice : Dr. Rane barely enough to keep himself. His wants and those of the old servant Phillis were not many. Perhaps the entire fault did not lie with Madam. Alexander had the more open manner and address, and they go a long way with people; he was also an older man, and a married man, and was supposed to carry better experience. A bitter sense of injury rankled ever in Oliver Rane's heart; of injury inflicted by Alexander. Meanwhile he became engaged to Bessy Rane. During an absence from home of Madam's, the doctor grew intimate at the Hall, and an attachment sprang up between him and Bessy. When Madam came back, his visits had to cease, but he saw Bessy at Mrs. Gass's and elsewhere.

I think that is all of retrospect—and a pretty long one it has been. It brings us down to the present time, to the period of the anonymous letter and Edmund North's death. Exactly two years ago this same month, May, the rival doctors had appeared in Dallory Ham ; and now one of them was going to leave it.

Just an incident must be told, bearing on something that has been related, and then the chapter shall close.

The summer of the past year has been a very hot one. A labouring man, working on Mr. North's grounds, suddenly fell ; and died on the spot. Mr. Alexander, summoned hastily, thought it must have been sun-stroke. "That is what my father died of," remarked Captain Bohun, who stood with the rest. Mr. North turned to him: "Do you say your father died of sun-stroke, Arthur?" "Yes, sir, that is what he died of, did you not know it?" was the ready reply. "You are sure of that?" continued Mr. North. "Quite sure, sir," repeated Arthur, turning his dreamy blue eyes full upon his step-father, in all their proud truthfulness.

Mr. North knew that he spoke in the sincerity of belief. Arthur Bohun possessed in an eminent degree the pride of his father's race. That innate, self-conscious sense of superiority that is a sort of safeguard to those who possess it : the *noblesse oblige* feeling that keeps them from wrong-doing. It is true, Arthur Bohun held an exalted view of his birth and family : in so far as that his pride in it equalled that of any man living or dead. He was truthful, generous, honourable, ; the very opposite in all respects to his mother. Her pride was an assumed pride ; a despicable, false, contemptible pride, offensive to those with whom she came in contact. Arthur's was one that you admired in spite of yourself. Of a tarnish to his honour, he could almost have died ; to bring disgrace on his own name or on his family, would have caused him to bury his head for ever. Sensitively regardful of other people's feelings, of courteous manner to all, he yet unmistakably held his own in the world. His father had been just the same ; and in his day was called "Proud Bohun."

To have asserted that Major Bohun died of sun-stroke, had any doubt of the fact lain on his mind, would have been simply impossible to Arthur Bohun. Therefore, Mr. North saw that, whatever the mystery might be, in regard to the real cause of Major Bohun's death, Arthur was not cognisant of it.

CHAPTER VI.

LOOKING AT THE FUNERAL.

In the comfortable dining-room of Mrs. Gass, securely ensconced behind the closed blinds, drawn to-day, sat that lady and a visitor. It was the day of the funeral of Edmund North ; and Mrs. Gass had put on mourning out of respect to the family : a black silk gown and white net cap : it need not be said that the change from finery improved her appearance greatly : she looked, as she herself would have phrased it, genteel to-day. This was her favourite sitting-room ; she rarely used any other : for one thing it gave her the opportunity of seeing the movements of her neighbours. The drawing-room faced the garden at the back : a spacious, beautiful apartment, opening to the smooth green lawn.

The visitor was Mrs. Cumberland. For once in her life Mrs. Cumberland emerged from her shell of cold indifference and condescended to evince somewhat of the curiosity of ordinary people. She had come to Mrs. Gass's to see the funeral pass : and that lady made much of her, for their meetings were rare. Mrs. Cumberland was in black silk too : but she rarely wore anything else. The two women sat together, talking in a subdued voice of far-back times : not that they had known each other then ; but each had interest in the past. Mrs. Gass was full of respect, never presuming on her elevation ; though they were sisters-in-law, she did not forget that she had once been but a servant in Mrs. Cumberland's family. They had not much in common, though, and the topics of conversation exhausted themselves. Mrs. Cumberland was of a silent nature, not at all given to gossip in general. She began to think the waiting long. For the convenience of two mourners, who were coming from a distance, the funeral had been put off until four o'clock.

" Holidays don't improve the working class—unless they've got the sense to use 'em as they ought," observed Mrs. Gass. " Just look at them three, ma'am. They've been at the tap— and more shame to 'em ! They'd better let Mr. Richard catch his eye upon 'em. Putting theirselves into that state, when he is a-following his brother to the grave."

She alluded to some men belonging to the Dallory Works, closed to-day. They had taken more than was seemly, and were lounging against the opposite shutters, quarrelling together. Mrs. Gass could bear it no longer ; in defiance of appearances she drew up the blind and dashed open the window.

" Be you three men not ashamed of yourselves ? I thought it was you, Dawson ! When there's any ill-doing going on, you be safe to be in it. As to you, Thomas, you'll not like to show your face to-morrow. Don't you come to me again, Smith, to beg grace for you of Mr. Richard North."

The men slunk away and disappeared down an entry. Mrs. Gass, in one sense of the word, was their mistress; at any rate, their master's partner. She shut the window and drew down the blind.

" Are the men paid for to-day, or do they lose it ? " asked Mrs. Cumberland.

" They're paid, ma'am, of course. It would be very unjust to dock them when the holiday's none of their making. Neither Mr. Richard nor me would like to be unjust."

" And he—Richard—seems to act entirely for his father."

" Mrs. Gass coughed. " Mr. North is took up with his garden, and that; he don't care to bother his head about business. It's better in younger hands."

Another pause of silence. Mrs. Cumberland felt weary.

" Is this funeral ever coming ? " she exclaimed. " There seems to be some delay."

" 'Twas a late hour to fix it for, ma'am. Old Sir what's-his-name wrote word he couldn't be here afore the afternoon ; so they put it off to four o'clock for his convenience."

Mrs. Cumberland looked up enquiringly. She did not understand.

" I mean young Bohun's relatives, ma'am. Madam's brother-in-law by her first husband."

" Sir Nash Bohun ! Is he coming ? "

" Sir Nash ; that's the name," remarked Mrs. Gass. " I know when Mr. Richard said it, it put me in mind of grinding the teeth."

" What could have induced them to ask him ? " wondered Mrs. Cumberland. " He is no relative."

" It sounds grand to have him, ma'am—and that's all *she* thinks of," returned Mrs. Gass, with slighting allusion to Madam. " Or maybe, as it was an uncommon death, they want to make it an uncommon funeral. *I* look upon it as no better than a murder."

" It is very strange about that piece of paper," observed Mrs. Cumberland.

She lowered her voice as she spoke as if the subject would not bear the broad light of day. Any surprise, greater than what appeared in Mrs. Gass's face at hearing it could not well be imagined.

" Ma'am ! Did he tell you of *that ?* "

" Did who tell me ? "

" Your son."

They looked questioningly at each other; both unconscious that they were alluding to two totally different circumstances. Cross-purposes are sometimes productive of more ill than straight ones.

It appeared that a night or two subsequent to Edmund North's death, Captain Bohun found in his own desk a sheet of folded note-paper in an envelope. It contained a few words in Edmund's handwriting, not apparently addressed to anybody in particular, but to the world in general. No date was

appended, but the ink looked fresh, as if it had been recently
written.

" *When the end comes, make no fuss with me, but bury me
quietly out of sight.—E.·N."*

Captain Bohun, not having the faintest idea of who put it
in his desk, or how it came there, carried it to Richard North.
Richard showed it to his father. From thence it spread to the
house, and to one or two others. Opinions were divided.
Mr. North thought his ill-fated son had intended to allude to
his own death : that he must have felt some foreshadowing of
it on his spirit. On the contrary, Arthur Bohun and Richard
both thought that it was nothing more than one of his scraps
of poetry : and this last idea was at length adopted. Arthur
Bohun had related the circumstance to Mrs. Cumberland, and
it was *this* she meant to speak of to Mrs. Gass. Mrs. Gass,
who knew nothing of it, thought, and quite naturally, that she
spoke of the piece of paper found on her carpet.

"Of course it *might* have been nothing more than some
ideas he had dotted down, poor fellow, connected with his
nonsensical poetry," slightingly observed Mrs. Cumberland,
who was the first to resume speech : "Richard North and
Captain Bohun fully hold to that opinion. I don't. It may be
that I am inclined to look always on the sombre side of life ;
but I can only think he was alluding to his own death."

" 'Twere odd sort of poetry," cried Mrs. Gass, after a pause
and a stare.

" The only curious part about it to my mind is, that it should
have been found in Arthur Bohun's desk," pursued Mrs.
Cumberland, the two being delightfully unconscious still that
they were at the cross-purposes. " He says he has not left
his desk unlocked at all, that he is aware of—but of course he
might have done so. Why Edmund North should have chosen
to put it in there, is a mystery."

"What has Captain Bohun's desk got to do with it ?"
enquired Mrs. Gass, beginning to feel a little at sea.

" The paper was found in Captain Bohun's desk. Though
why Edmund North should have hidden it there, remains a
mystery."

" Ma'am, whoever told you that, must have been just trying
to deceive you. It was found on this carpet."

" Found on this carpet !"

" On this very blessed carpet that we've each got our feet

on, ma'am. Right back again' the claw of that there centre
dining-table."

Again they gazed at each other. Mrs. Cumberland thought
her friend must be dreaming.

"But you are quite mistaken, Mrs. Gass. The paper—note,
or whatever it was—could not have been on this carpet at all:
not in your house, in fact. Captain Bohun discovered it in
his desk three days ago, and he has not the slightest notion of
how it came there. Mr. North took possession of it, and has
never let it go out of his hands since."

"My dear lady, they have been a-mystifying of you," cried
Mrs. Gass. "Seeing's believing. The paper was first found
by me. By me, ma'am, on this here carpet, and it was the
same night that Edmund North was first took ; not an hour
after the fit."

Mrs. Cumberland made no reply. She was drifting into the
conclusion that she had not yet had all the circumstances
related to her.

"I picked the paper up myself," continued Mrs. Gass,
anxious for the truth, as straightforward people are apt to be.
"I kept it safe here for a day and a night, ma'am, waiting to
give it back to your son : what I thought was that he had
dropped it out of his pocket-book. I never spoke of it to a
single soul, and as soon as I had the opportunity I gave it up
to him. If it was found in Captain Bohun's desk afterwards,
why—Dr. Rane, or somebody else must have put it there.
Ma'am, if, as I conclude, you've heard about the paper from
your son, I wonder he did not tell you this."

"What paper was this?" enquired Mrs. Cumberland, a dim
notion arising that they could not be talking of the same thing.

"It were the copy of that anonymous letter."

"The copy of the anonymous letter!"

"Leastways, its skeleton."

Rapidly enough came the elucidation now. Without in the
least intending to break faith with Dr. Rane, or with her own
resolution to hold the matter secret, Mrs. Gass told all she
knew, with one exception. Led on by the miserable, but very
natural misapprehension—that Mrs. Cumberland was a de-
pository of the secret as well as herself—she spoke, and had
not the least idea that she was betraying trust. That exception
was the hinted suspicion that Madam might have been the
writer. Mrs. Cumberland sat listening, still as a statue.

"And you thought that—this rough copy of the letter—it

was Oliver who dropped it ? " she exclaimed at length, moved
out of her usual apathetic calmness.

"What else could I think ? " debated Mrs. Gass. "Dr.
Rane had let fall some papers from his pocket-book five minutes before, and I picked this up as soon as he had gone. I'm
sure I never so much as gave a thought to Molly Green—
though she had come straight from the Hall. Dr. Rane said
it might have dropped from her petticoats : but it was a puzzle
to me how ; and it's a puzzle still."

A keen, enquiring sort of glance shot from the speaker's
eyes with the last words. It was but momentary and not intentional ; nevertheless, something in it caused Mrs. Cumberland's heart to quail. A cold hue spread over her grey face ;
a cold shade of recollection deadened her heart. Captain
Bohun had told her of Mr. Alexander's theory—that the letter
was written to damage *him.*

"I am sorry I spoke of this, ma'am," struck in Mrs. Gass.
"More particular that it should have been you : you'll
naturally tell Dr. Rane, and he *will* say I know how to keep
secrets—just about as the jackdaws keep theirs. It was your
telling of the other paper that misled me."

"I am quite safe," answered Mrs. Cumberland, with a
sickly smile. "The matter's nothing to me, that I should get
speaking of it again."

"Of course it's not, ma'am. After all—Halloa ! here it
comes ! "

This sudden break was caused by an interrupting sound,
the roll of a muffled drum, first advent of the advancing
funeral procession. Edmund North had belonged to a local
military corps, and was to be attended to the grave with honours. Mrs. Gass drew up the white blind an inch above the
short venetian one, which enabled them to look out unseen.
The road suddenly became lined with spectators ; men, women
and children collecting one hardly knew from whence.

The band came first—their instruments in rest ; then the
muffled drum, on which its bearer struck a note now and again.
The hearse and three mourning coaches followed, some private
carriages, and the soldiers on foot. And that was all : except
a straggling tail of spectators in the rear, with Hepburn the
undertaker and his men on either side the black coaches. The
hearse was exactly opposite Mrs. Cumberland when the band
struck up the Dead March in Saul. Suddenly to her memory
flashed a recollection of the morning, but a very few days ago,

when Ellen Adair had been playing the same dirge, and it had seemed to grate on Oliver's ear. Her eyes fixed themselves on the hearse as it passed, and she saw in mental vision the cold corpse lying within. In another moment, the music, her son, the dead, and the fatal letter, all seemed to be jumbling together in confusion in her brain : and Mrs. Cumberland sat down white and faint, and three parts senseless. The lady of the house, her eyes glued to the strip of open window, made her comments and suspected nothing of the indisposition.

"Mr. North in the first coach with his white hankecher held to his nose. And well he may hold it, poor berefted gentleman ! There's Mr. Richard sitting by the side of him. Captain Bohun's on the opposite seat :—and—who's the other ? Why ! it's the young one, Sidney North. Then they've sent for him from college, or wherever it is he stays at : Madam's doings, I'll lay. What a little whipper-snapper of a fellow it is !—like nobody but himself. He'll never be half the man his step-brothers be."

Mrs. Gass's tongue ceased with the passing of the coach. In her plentitude of curiosity she did not observe that she had no response. The second coach came in sight, and she began again.

"An old gent, upright as a dart, with snow-white hair and them features called aquiline ! It's a handsome face, if ever I saw one ; his eyes be as blue and as fine as Captain Bohun's. There's a likeness between 'em. It must be his uncle, Sir Nash. A young man sits next him with a white unhealthy face ; and the other two—why, if I don't believe it's the young Dallorys ! "

There was no answering comment. Mrs. Gass turned round to see the reason. Her visitor was sitting back in a chair, an awfully grey shade upon her face and lips.

"My patience ! Don't you feel well, ma'am ? "

"I am a little tired, thank you," replied Mrs. Cumberland, smiling languidly as she roused herself. "Looking out at passing things always fatigues me."

"Now don't you stir, ma'am ; I'll tell it off to you," came the rejoinder, spoken with warm sympathy. "There's only one coach more. And that have got but two inside of it— which is the doctors from Whitborough," added Mrs. Gass ; who in moments of unwonted excitement, whether of pleasure or pain, was apt to be signally oblivious of the courtesies of life, as conveyed in correct syntax. "I wonder they didn't in

rite Mr. Oliver—the first called in to the poor young man—
and Alexander. Not thought good enough by Madam, perhaps, to be mixed with all these here dons."

She looked after the swiftly passing pageantry with lingering
admiration. Mrs. Cumberland sat still in the chair and closed
her eyes, as if all interest in the funeral—and in life too, for
the matter of that—had passed away.

The procession wound along : through the long straggling
village street, past the Dallory Works (a mass of buildings
that lay on the left), and so to the church. It was the only
church in the parish, inconveniently far for some of the
inhabitants. Dallory Ham spoke about building one for itself ;
but that honour had not been attained to yet. In a corner of
the large churchyard lay Mrs. North, Mr. North's first wife
and Edmund's mother. The new grave was dug by her
side.

Amidst the spectators, numbers of whom had collected in
the burial ground, stood Jelly. Very much no doubt to the
astonishment of her mistress, had she seen her. To peep surreptitiously from behind blinds, was one thing ; but to stand
openly staring in the churchyard, was another ; and Mrs.
Cumberland would assuredly have ordered her away. Jelly
had come to it with a cousin of hers, Susan Ketler, the wife of
the sick man who was being attended by Dr. Rane. Jelly
had curiosity enough for ten ordinary women—which is saying
a great deal—and would not have missed the sight for the
world.

It was soon over : our burial service is not a long one : and
the coaches and mourners moved away again, leaving the field
in possession of the mob. There ensued a rush to get a view
of the coffin, as yet scarcely sprinkled with earth. Jelly and
her friend got close, and the former read the inscription.

"Edmund, son of John North and of Mary, his first wife.
Died May 3rd, 18—, aged 33."

"I should not have put 'died,' but 'murdered,' if it was
me had the writing of it," spoke Mrs. Ketler.

"And so should I, Susan," significantly replied Jelly.
"Here! let's get out of this throng."

Jelly, in her loftiness of stature and opinion, was above the
throng literally and figuratively ; but it was dense and trouble-
some. Neither death nor funeral had been of an ordinary
description ; and others besides the great unwashed were
crowding there. The two women elbowed their way out, and

passed back along the broad highway to Ketler's house in
Dallory. He was one of the best of the North workmen,
earning good wages; and the family lived in comfort.

Ketler was in the parlour, sitting up for the first time.
Under Dr. Rane's skilful treatment he was getting better
rapidly. A little one sat on his knee, held by his able arm;
the rest were around. The children had wanted (as a matter
of course) to go out and see the funeral. "No," said their
father; "they might get playing, and that would be unseemly."
He was a short, dark, honest-looking man; a good husband
and father. Jelly sat talking for a short while, and then rose
to leave.

But she was not allowed to go. To let her depart at that
hour of the afternoon without first partaking of tea, would
have been a breach in the obligations of hospitality that the
well-to-do workpeople of Dallory never wished to hear of.
Jelly, all too easily persuaded where sociability was concerned,
took off her bonnet to be comfortable, and the tray was
brought in, with plates of bread-and-butter.

Cups of beer induce men to a long sitting; cups of tea
women. Jelly (who drank four) sat on, oblivious of the
lapse of time. The chief topic of conversation was the anonymous letter. Jelly found to her surprise and anger, that
the prevailing belief here was, that it had been written by a
clerk named Wilks, who was in the office of Dale the lawyer,
and might have become cognisant of the transaction between
his master, Mr. Alexander, and Edmund North.

"Who told you that, Ketler?" sharply demanded Jelly,
after a pause, fixing her indignant eyes on the man.

"I can't rightly say who told me," replied Ketler; "it's
the talk of the place. Wilks, he denies it out and out;
but when he's in his evening cups—and that's not seldom
—he does things that next morning he has no recollection of.
Doctor Rane laughed at me, though, for saying so: a lawyer
knows better than to let private matters get out to his clerks,
says the doctor. But he don't know that Tim Wilks as some
of us do."

"Well, I would not say too much about it's being Tim
Wilks if I were you, Ketler," cried Jelly, in suppressed
wrath, brushing the crumbs off her black gown. "You
might find yourself in hot water."

And then Ketler suddenly remembered that Wilks was her
particular friend, so he turned the subject.

Jelly tore herself away at last, very unwillingly : gossip and tea-drinking formed her idea of an earthly paradise. Night was setting in ; a light, beautiful night, the moon sailing majestically in the sky.

Just past the gates of Dallory Hall, in a bend of the road where the overhanging trees on either side gave it a lonely appearance at night (and by day too, for that matter), no dwelling of any sort being within view or hail, stood a bench on the side path. It was a welcome resting-place to tired wayfarers ; it was no less welcome to wandering lovers in their evening rambles. As Jelly went hastening on, a faint sound of voices broke upon her ear from this spot, and she stilled her steps instinctively. The chance of pouncing unexpectedly upon a pair exchanging soft vows, was perfectly delightful to Jelly ; especially if it should happen to be a pair who had no business to exchange them.

Stealing softly along on the side grass, went she, until she came to the turn, and then she looked cautiously round. The bushes projected there and favoured her. To do Jelly justice, it must be affirmed that she had neither malice nor ill-will in her nature ; rather the contrary ; but a little innocent prying into her neighbours' affairs presented an irresistible temptation. What, then, was her astonishment to see—not a dying swain and his mistress, side by side : but her own mistress, Mrs. Cumberland, seated on the bench in an agony of grief, and Dr. Rane standing with folded arms before her.

Jelly, great at divining probabilities, comprehended the situation easily. Her mistress must have stayed to take tea with Mrs. Gass, and encountered her son in walking home.

To come down upon lovers with a startling reprimand was one thing ; to burst upon her mistress and Dr. Rane would be quite another. Jelly wished she had not gone stealing up like a mouse, and felt inclined to steal back again.

But the attitude and appearance of Mrs. Cumberland riveted her to the spot. Her face, never so grey as now, as seen in the moonlight, dim here, was raised to her son's, its expression one yearning agony ; her hands were lifted as if imploring some boon, or warding off some fear. Jelly's eyes opened to their utmost width, and in her plentitude of astonishment she failed to catch the purport of the first low-spoken words.

"I tell you, you are mistaken, mother," said Dr. Rane in answer, *his* voice ringing out clear enough in the still night :

though it nevertheless had a hushed tone. "Is it probable? Is it likely? *I* drop the copy of the letter out of my pocket-book! What next will you suppose me capable of?"

"But—Oliver,"—and the voice was raised a little—"how else could it have come upon her carpet?"

"I have my theory about that," he rejoined with decision. "Mother, come to your home: I'll tell you more then. Is this a fitting time or place to have thus attacked me?"

Air, voice, action, were alike sharp with authority, as he bent and took her hand. Mrs. Cumberland, saying some words of "having been surprised into speaking," rose from the bench. Jelly watched them along the road; and then sat down on the bench herself to recover her amazement.

"What on earth does it mean?"

Ah! what did it mean? Jelly was pretty sharp, but she was afraid to give her thoughts their full range. Other steps grew on her ear. They turned out to be those of Mr. Alexander.

"Is it you, Jelly! Waiting for your sweetheart?"

Jelly rose. "Standing about to look at funerals, and such things, tires one worse than a ten-mile run."

"Then why do you do it?"

"One fool makes many," returned Jelly with composure. "Sir, I'd like to know who wrote that letter."

"It strikes me the letter was written by a woman."

"A woman!" echoed Jelly, with a shriek of genuine surprise. "Good gracious, Mr. Alexander!"

"They are so sharp upon us at times, are women," he continued, smiling. "Men don't attack one another."

"And what woman do you suspect, sir?" cried Jelly, in her insatiable curiosity.

"Ah! there's the rub. I have been speaking of women in general, you see. Perhaps it was you?"

"*Me!*" exclaimed Jelly.

Mr. Alexander laughed. "I was only joking, Jelly. Good night."

But Jelly, sharp Jelly, rather thought he had not been joking, and that the suspicion had slipped out inadvertently.

She went straight home. And when she got there, Mrs. Cumberland was seated by the drawing-room fire, her face calm and still as usual, listening to the low sweet singing of Ellen Adair.

And Oliver Rane had passed in to his own house with his weight of many cares. Half wishing that he could exchange places with Edmund North in Dallory churchyard.

CHAPTER VII.

AFTER THE FUNERAL.

THE two guests, Sir Nash Bohun and his son, were departing from Dallory Hall. They had arrived the previous afternoon in time to attend the funeral, had dined and slept, and were now going again. Their coming had originated with Sir Nash. In his sympathy with the calamity—the particulars of which had been written to him by his nephew, Arthur Bohun—Sir Nash had proposed to show his concern and respect for the North family by coming with his son to attend the funeral. The offer was accepted; albeit Mrs. North was not best pleased to receive them. For some cause or other, Madam had never been solicitous to court intimacy with her first husband's brother: when thrown into his society, there was something in her manner that almost seemed to say she did not feel at ease with him.

Neither at the dinner last night nor at the breakfast this morning had the master of the house been present: the entertaining of the guests had fallen on Richard North as his father's representative. Captain Bohun was of course with them; also the rest of the family, including Madam. Madam played her part gracefully in a full suit of mourning: black crape elaborately set off with jet. For once in her life she was honest and did not affect to feel the grief for Edmund that she would have felt for a son.

Sitting disconsolately before the open window of his parlour was Mr. North. His new black clothes looked too large for him, his slippers were down at heel, his whole air was that of one who seems to have lost interest in the world. It is astonishing how aged, as compared with other moments, men will look in their seasons of abandonment. While we battle with our cares, they spare in a degree the face: but in the abandonment of despair, when all around seems dreary, and we are sick and faint because to fight longer seems impossible, look at the poor sunken face then!

The room was dingy; it has already been said; rather long but narrow; and it seemed uncared for. The door opened at the end, the window faced it. The fire-place was in the middle, on the left; opposite to it an old open secretaire, filled with seeds and papers pertaining to gardening, stood side by side with a closet door. This closet—which was, however, more of a small shut-in passage than a closet—had an opposite door opening to the dining-room. But, if the parlour was in itself dingy, the capacious window and the prospect on which it looked, brightened it. Stretching out before it, broad and large, was the gay parterre of many-coloured flowers, Mr. North's only delight for years past. In the cultivation of these flowers, he had found a refuge, a sort of shelter from the consciousness of disappointment that was ever upon him, from life's daily vexations and petty cares. Heaven is all-merciful, and some counter-balancing interest to grievous and long-continued sorrow is often supplied. " She wants me to give up my garden; but I should die; I should die, Dick," Mr. North said one day imploringly to his son Richard after a dispute with Madam. Such disputes were frequent. And yet—could it be properly called a dispute when the railing and reproach were all on one side ? Madam wanted money perpetually ; money and money, nothing but money ; and when her husband avowed—with far more deprecation than he could have used to any other woman on earth—that he was unable to furnish it, she abused him. " Give up your expensive garden," was often the burthen of her cry ; and in very fear, as it seemed, lest he should have to give it up, he had yielded so far as gradually to reduce his staff of gardeners to two. " On my word, I think it is the garden and its cares that keeps life in him," Richard North had exclaimed in a confidential moment to Mrs. Gass. "Then, Mr. Richard, sir," was the answer, " let him always have it; you and me can take care of so much as that." Richard nodded. There were times when circumstances compelled him to entrust home secrets to Mrs. Gass—and he might have had a worse depositary.

Mr. North sat looking at his flowers. He had been sitting there just as he was for the past hour, buried in reflections that were not pleasant, and the morning was getting on. He thought of his embarrassments—those applications for money from Madam, that he strove to hide from his well-beloved son Richard, and that made the terror of his life. They were apt to come upon him at the most unexpected times, in season and out of season ; it seemed to him that he was never free from them ; that he could never be sure at any minute she would not come down upon him the next. For the past few days the house had been, so to say, sacred from these carping concerns; even she had respected the sorrow in it; but with this morning, the return to every-day life, business and the world resumed its sway. Mr. North was looked upon as a man perfectly at his ease in money matters ; " rolling in wealth," people would say, as they talked of the handsome portion his two daughters might expect on their wedding-day. Local debts, the liabilities of ordinary passing life, were kept punctually paid ; Richard saw to that ; and perhaps no one in the whole outer world, save Mrs. Gass, suspected the truth and the embarrassment. Mr. North thought of his other son, he who had gone from his view for ever ; but the edge of the grief was wearing off, though he was as eager as ever to find out the writer of the anonymous letter.

But there is a limit to all things—I don't know what would become of some of us if there were not—and the mind cannot dwell for ever upon its own bitterness. Unhappy topics, as if in very fatigue, gradually drifted away from Mr. North's mind and were replaced by loving thoughts of his flowers. How could it be otherwise, when their scent came floating to him through the broad open window in a delicious sea of perfume. The assorted colours charmed the eye, the sweet aroma took captive the senses. Spring flowers, all; and simple ones. It was like a many-hued plain ; and further on, beyond the trees that bounded the grounds, a fine view was obtained of the open country over Dallory Ham. Hills and dales, woods and sunny plains, with here and there a gleam of glistening water, lay underneath the distant horizon. Mr. North looked not at the landscape, which was a familiar book to him, but at his flowers. The spring had been continuously cold and wet, retarding the appearance of these early flowers to a very remarkably late period. For the past week or two the weather had been lovely, hot with a summer brightness, and the flowers seemed to have sprung up all at once. Hyacinths, blue, pink, white, purple ; gilly-flowers in all their rich shades ; white daffodils ; primroses, double and single cowslips and polyanthuses, and so on. Just as he chose the most simple flowers to cultivate, so he called them all by their more simple and familiar names. Madam turned up her nose at both in contemptuous derision; sometimes speaking in society of Mr. North's " vulgar cottage garden." A little later the tulip beds would be in bloom. A rare collection that; a show for the world to flock to. Great people came boldly inside; small ones would peep through the shrubs and over the railings, sniffing the sweet scent, and saying the ground was like a many-hued carpet of gorgeous colours. Later on still, the roses would be out, and many thought they were the best show of all. And so the year went on, the flowers replacing each other in their loveliness.

Sadness sat on them to-day : for we see things, you know, in accordance with our own mood, not with their actual brightness. Mr. North rose with a sigh and stood at the open window. Only that very day week, about this time in the morning, his eldest son had stood there with him side by side. For this was the eighth of May. "Poor fellow!" sighed the father, as he thought of this.

Some one went sauntering down the path that led round from the front of the house, and disappeared beyond the trees; a short, slight young man. Mr. North recognized him for Sidney : Madam's son as well as his own, and he heaved a sigh almost as profound as the one he gave to the dead Edmund. Sidney North was dreadfully dissipated, and had caused already a great deal of trouble. It was suspected— and with truth—that some of Madam's superfluous money went to this son. She had brought him up badly, fostering his vanity, and indulging him in everything. By the very way in which he walked now—his head hanging moodily down, his gait slouching, his hands thrust into his pockets, Mr. North judged him to be in some dilemma. He had not wished him to be called home for the funeral ; no, though the dead had stood to him as half brother ; but Madam took her own way and wrote for him. "He'll be a thorn in her side if he lives," thought the father, his reflections unconsciously going out to that future time when he himself should be no more.

The door opened, and Richard came in. Mr. North stepped back from the window at which he had been standing.

"Sir Nash and his son are going, sir. You will see them first, will you not?"

"Going! going already! Why—I declare it is past eleven! Bless me! I hope I have not been rude, Dick? Where are my boots?"

The boots stood at hand, ready for him. He put them on in haste, and hid his slippers out of sight in the closet

What with his present grief, and what with his disinclination for society, or, as he called it, company, that had been for some time growing upon him, Mr. North had held aloof from his guests. But he was one of the last men to show incivility, and it suddenly struck him that perhaps he had been guilty of it.

"Dick, I suppose I ought to have been at the breakfast-table?"

"Not at all, my dear father; not at all. Your remaining in privacy is perfectly natural, and I am sure Sir Nash feels it to be so. Don't disturb yourself: they will come to you here."

Almost as he spoke they came in, Captain Bohun with them. Sir Nash was a very fine man with a proud face, that put you in mind at once of Arthur Bohun's, and of the calmest, pleasantest, most courteous manners possible. His son was not in the least like him; a studious, sickly man, his health delicate, his dark hair scanty. James Bohun's time was divided between close classical reading and philanthropic pursuits. He strove to have what he called a mission in life: and to make it one that might do him some service in the next world.

"I am so very sorry! I had no idea you would be going so soon: I ought to have been with you before this," began Mr. North in a flutter.

But the baronet laid his hands upon him kindly, and calmed the storm. "My good friend, you have done everything that is right and hospitable. I would have stayed a few hours longer with you, but James has to be in London this afternoon to keep an engagement."

"It is an engagement that I cannot well put off," interposed James Bohun in his small voice that always sounded too weak for a man. "I would not have made it, had I known what was to intervene."

"He has to preside at a public missionary meeting," explained Sir Nash. "It seems to me that he has something or other of the kind on hand every day in the year. I tell him that he is wearing himself out."

"Not every day in the year," spoke the son, as if taking the words literally. "This is the month for such meetings, you know, Sir Nash."

"You do not look strong," observed Mr. North, studying James Bohun.

"Not strong in appearance perhaps, but I'm wiry, Mr. North: and we wiry fellows last the longest. What sweet flowers those are," added Mr. Bohun, stepping to the threshold of the window. "I could not dress myself this morning for looking at them. I longed to put the window open."

"And why did you not?" sensibly asked Mr. North.

"I can't do with the early morning air, sir. I don't accustom myself to it."

"A bit of a valetudinarian," remarked Sir Nash.

"Not at all, father," answered the son. "It is well to be cautious."

"I sleep with my window open, James, summer and winter. Well, well, we all have our different tastes and fancies. And now, my good friend," added the baronet, taking the hands of Mr. North, "when will you come and see me? A change may do you good."

"Thank you; not just yet. Thank you all the same, Sir Nash, but later—perhaps," was Mr. North's answer. He knew that the kindness was meant, the invitation sincere; and of late he had grown to feel grateful for any shown to him. Nevertheless he thought he should never accept this.

"I will not receive you in that hot, bustling London: it is getting to be a penance to myself to stay there. You shall come to my place in Kent, and be as quiet as you please. You've never seen Peveril: it cannot boast the charming flowers that you show, but it is worth seeing. Promise to come."

"If I can. Later. Thank you, Sir Nash; and I beg you and Mr. Bohun to pardon me for all my seeming discourtesy. It has not been meant as such."

"No, no."

They walked through the hall to the door, where Mr. North's carriage waited. The large shut-up carriage. Some dim idea was pervading those concerned that to drive to the station in an open dog-cart would be hardly the right thing for these mourners after the recent funeral.

Sir Nash and his son stepped in, followed by Captain Bohun and Richard North, who would accompany them to the station. As Mr. North turned in-doors again after watching the carriage away, he ran against his daughter Matilda, resplendent in glittering black silk and jet, with endless chains of jet on her head, and neck, and arms, and skirts.

"They have invited you to visit them, have they not, papa?"

"They have invited me—yes. But I shall be none the nearer going, Matilda."

"Then I wish you would, for I want to go," she returned, speaking imperiously. "My Uncle Nash asked me. He asked mamma, and said would I accompany her : and I should like to go. Do you hear, papa ? I should like to go."

It was all very well for Miss Matilda North to say "My Uncle Nash." Sir Nash was no relation to her whatever : but that he was a baronet, she might have remembered it.

"You and your mamma can go," said Mr. North with animation, as the seductive vision of the house, relieved of Madam's presence for an indefinite period, arose mentally before him.

"But mamma says she shall not go."

"Oh does she ?" he cried, his spirits and the vision sinking together. "She'll change her mind perhaps, Matilda. I can't do anything in it, you know."

As if to avoid further colloquy, he passed on to his parlour and shut the door sharply. Matilda North turned into the dining-room, her handsome black silk train following her, her discontented look preceding her. Just then Mrs. North came down stairs, a coquettish, fascinating sort of black lace hood on her head, one she was in the habit of wearing in the grounds. Matilda North heard the rustle of the robes, and looked out again.

"Are you going to walk, mamma ?"

"I am. Have you anything to say against it ?"

"It would be all the same if I had," was the pert answer. Not very often did Matilda North gratuitously beard her mother; but she was in an ill humour : the guests had gone away much sooner than she had expected or wished, and Madam had vexed her.

"That lace hood is not mourning," resumed Miss Matilda North, defiantly viewing Madam from top to toe.

Madam turned the hood and the haughty face it encircled on her presuming daughter. The look was enough in itself; and what she might have said was interrupted by the approach of Bessy.

"Have you any particular orders to give this morning, Madam ?" Bessy asked of her step-mother—whom she as often called Madam as Mamma, the latter fond word never meeting with fond response from Mrs. North to *her*.

"If I have I'll give them later," imperiously replied Madam, sweeping out at the hall door.

"What has angered her now?" thought Bessy. "I hope and trust it is nothing connected with papa. He has enough trouble without having to bear ill-temper."

Bessy North was housekeeper. And a fine time she had of it! Between Madam's capricious orders, issued at all sorts of inconvenient hours, and the natural resentment of the servants, a less meek and patient spirit would have been worried beyond bearing. Bessy made herself the scape-goat; labouring, both by substantial help and by soothing words, to keep peace in the household. None knew how much Bessy did, or the care that was upon her. Miss Matilda North had never soiled her fingers in her life, never done more than ring the bell with a dash, and issue her imperious orders after the fashion of Madam, her mother. The two half-sisters were a perfect contrast. Certainly they presented such outwardly, as witness this morning: the one not unlike a peacock, her ornamented head thrown up, her extended train trailing, and her odds and ends of gleaming jet; the other a meek little woman in a black gown of some soft material with a bit of quiet crape upon it, and her smooth hair banded back—for she had put it plain to-day.

On her way to the kitchens, Bessy halted at her father's sitting-room, and opened the door quietly. Mr. North was standing against the window-frame, half inside the room half out of it.

"Can I do anything for you, papa?"

"There's nothing to do for me, child. What time do we dine to-day, Bessy?" he asked, after a pause.

"I suppose at six. Mrs. North has not given contrary orders."

"Very well. I'll have my bit of luncheon in here, child."

"To be sure. Dear papa, you are not looking well," she added, advancing to him.

"No? Looks don't matter much, Bessy, when folks get to be as old as I am. A thought comes over me at odd moments —that it is good to grow ugly, and yellow, and wrinkled. It makes us wish to become young and fair and pleasant to the sight again: and we can only do that through immortality. Through immortality, child."

Mr. North lifted his hand, the fingers of which had always now a trembling sort of movement in them, to his shrivelled face, as he repeated the concluding words, passing it twice over the weak, scanty brown hair that time and care had left him. Bessy kissed him fondly, and quitted the room with a sigh, one sad thought running through her mind.

" How sadly papa is breaking ! "

Mrs. North swept down the broad gravel walk leading from the entrance door, until she came to a path on the left, which led to the covered portion of the grounds. Not covered by any roof ; but the trees in places here grew so thick that shade might be had at midday. This part of the grounds was near the dark portion of the Dallory highway already mentioned (where Jelly had surprised her mistress and Oliver Rane in the moonlight the past night), only the boundary hedges being between them. Thickets of shrubs were there ; hedges of laurel, privet, sweet-briar ; clustering trees, their branches meeting over-head. Dark grottos nestled at ends of walks, covert benches were hidden in corners. It was a sweet spot, affording retirement from the world and shelter from the fierce rays of the burning sun. Madam was fond of frequenting this spot: and all the more so because sundry loop-holes gave her the opportunity of peering out beyond. She could see all who passed to and from the Hall, without being herself seen. One high enclosed walk was especially liked by her ; ensconced within its shade, quietly resting on one of its rustic seats, she could hear as well as see. Before she had quite gained this walk, however, her son Sidney crossed her path. A young man of twenty now, undersized, insufferably vain, fast, and conceited. His face might be called a pretty face: his auburn curls were arranged after the models in a hairdresser's window ; his very blue unmeaning eyes had no true look in them. Sidney North was like neither father nor mother: like nobody but his own contemptible self. Madam looked upon him as next door to an angel ; he was her well-beloved. There can be no blindness equal to that of a doting mother.

" My dear, I thought you had gone with them to the station," she said.

"Didn't ask me to go ; Dick and Arthur made room for themselves, not for me," responded Sidney, taking his pipe from his mouth to speak, and his voice was as consequential as his mother's.

A frown crossed Madam's face. Dick and Arthur were rather in the habit of putting Sydney in the shade, and she hated them for it. Arthur was her own son, but she had never regarded him with any sort of affection.

" I'm going back this afternoon, mamma."

"This afternoon! No, my boy; I can't part with you to-day."

"Must," laconically responded Sidney, puffing at his pipe. And Madam had got to learn that it was of no use saying he was to stay if he wanted to go. "How much tin can you let me have?"

"How much do you want?"

"As much as you can give me."

His demands for money seemed to be as insatiable as Madam knew her husband found hers. The fact was beginning to give her some concern. Only two weeks ago she had despatched him all she could afford: and now here he was, asking again. A slight frown crossed her brow.

"Sidney, you spend too much."

"Must do as others do," responded Sidney.

"But, my sweet boy, I can't let you have it. You don't know the trouble it causes."

"Trouble!—with those rich North Works to draw upon!" cried Sidney. "The governor must be putting by mines of wealth."

"I don't think he is, Sidney. He pleads poverty always; says we drain him. I suppose it's true."

"Flam! All old paters cry that. Look at Dick—the loads of gold he must be netting. He gets his equal share, they say; goes thirds with the other two."

"Who says it?"

"A fellow told me so yesterday. It's an awful shame that Dick should be a millionaire, and I obliged to beg for every paltry coin I want! There's not so many years between us."

"Dick has got his footing in at the works, you see," observed Madam. "Let him! I'd not have *you* degrade yourself to it for the world. He's fit for nothing but work; been brought up to it; and we can spend."

"Just so," complacently returned the young man. "And you must shell out liberally for me this afternoon, mamma."

With no further ceremony of adieu or apology, Mr. Sidney North sauntered away. Madam proceeded to her favourite shaded walk, where she kept her eyes looking out on all sides for intruders, friends or enemies. On this occasion she had the satisfaction of being gratified.

Her arms folded over the black lace shawl she wore, its hood gathered on her head, altogether very much after the fashion of a Spanish mantilla, and the gown train with its crape and jet falling in stately folds behind her, Madam had been pacing this retreat for the best part of an hour, when she caught sight, through the interstices of the leaves, of two ladies slowly approaching. The one she recognized at once as Mrs. Cumberland; the other she did not recognize at all. "What a lovely face!" was her involuntary thought.

A young, fair, lovely face. The face of Ellen Adair.

CHAPTER VIII.

MADAM'S LISTENING CLOSET.

MANY years before, when the Reverend George Cumberland held his chaplaincy in Madras, there were two friends also there with whom he was intimate—Major Bohun and Mr. Adair. The latter held a civil appointment under Government. At that time, Mr. Adair was not married. Later, this gentleman went to Australia: Mr. and Mrs. Cumberland also went there. Mr. Adair had married in the course of time. His wife died, leaving one little child, a daughter: who was despatched to England for her education. Upon its completion, William Adair wrote and begged Mrs. Cumberland to receive her: he thought it probable that he should be returning home; and if so, it would not be worth while for Ellen to go out to him. Mrs. Cumberland consented, and the young lady became an inmate of her house at Dallory Ham. Very liberal terms were offered by Mr. Adair: but this was a matter entirely between himself and Mrs. Cumberland.

Holding herself, as she did, so entirely aloof from her neighbours, there was little wonder in Madam's having remained unconscious of the fact that some months ago, nearly twelve now, a young lady had come to reside with Mrs. Cumberland. Part of the time Mrs. Cumberland had been away. Madam had also been away: and when at home her communication with Dallory and Dallory Ham consisted solely in being whirled through its roads in a carriage: no one in-doors spoke unnecessarily in her hearing of any gossip connected with those despised places; and to church she rarely went, for she did not get up in time. And so the sweet girl, who had for some time now been making Arthur Bohun's heart's existence, had never yet been seen or heard of by his mother.

For Mrs. Cumberland to be seen abroad so early was something marvellous; indeed she was rarely seen abroad at all. On this morning she came out of her room between eleven and twelve o'clock, dressed for a walk; and bade Ellen Adair make ready to accompany her. Ellen obeyed, silently wondering. The truth was, Mrs. Cumberland had picked up a very unpleasant doubt the previous day, and would give the whole world to lay it to rest. It was connected with her son. His assurances had partly pacified her, but not quite: and she determined to get a private word with Mr. North. Ellen, walking by her side along the road, supposed they were going into Dallory. Mrs. Cumberland kept close to the hedge for the sake of the shade: as she brushed the bench in passing, where she had sat the past night, a slight shudder took her frame. Ellen did not observe it; she was revelling in the beauty of the sweet spring day. The gates of Dallory Hall gained, Mrs. Cumberland turned in. Ellen Adair wondered more and more; but Mrs. Cumberland was not one to be questioned at will on any subject.

On they came, Madam watching with all her eyes. Mrs. Cumberland was in her usual black silk attire, and walked with the slow step of an invalid. Ellen wore a morning dress of lilac muslin. It needed not the lilac parasol she carried to reflect an additional lovely hue on that most lovely face. A stately, refined girl, as Madam saw, with charming manners, the reverse of pretentious.

But as Madam, fascinated for once in her life, gazed outwards, a certain familiarity in the face dawned upon her senses. That she had seen it before, or one very like it, became a conviction. "Who on earth is she?" murmured the lady to herself—for Madam was by no means stilted in her phrases at leisure moments.

"Are you going to call at the Hall, Mrs. Cumberland?" enquired Ellen, venturing to ask the question at length in her increasing surprise. And every word could be heard distinctly by Madam, for they were nearly close.

"I think so," was the answer, given in a hesitating tone. "I—I should like to tell Mr. North that I feel for his loss."

"But is it not early to do so—both in the hour of the day, and after the death?" rejoined Ellen, with deprecation.

"For a stranger it would be; for me, no. I and John North were as brother and sister once. Besides, I have something else to say to him."

Had Miss Adair asked what the something else was—which she would not have presumed to do—Mrs. Cumberland might have replied that she wished again to enlist the Hall's influence on behalf of her son, now that Mr. Alexander was about to leave. A sure indication that it was *not* the real motive that was drawing her to the Hall, for she was one of those reticent women who rarely, if ever, observe open candour even to friends. Suddenly she halted.

"I prefer to go on alone, Ellen. You can sit down and wait for me. There are benches about in the covered walks."

Mrs. Cumberland went forward. Ellen turned back and began to walk towards the entrance gates with the slow lingering step of one who waits. Mrs. Cumberland had got well on, when she turned and called.

"Ellen."

But Ellen did not hear. She had her face turned the other way.

"Ellen! Ellen Adair!"

A loud call, this, echoing on the warm summer air, echoing on the curious ears covered by the lace mantilla. Mrs. North gave a quick, sharp start. It looked very like a start of terror.

"Ellen Adair!" she repeated to herself, her hungry eyes, hungry in their fear, flashing out on the beautiful face, to see whether she could track home the resemblance *now*. "Ellen Adair? Good heavens!"

Ellen had turned at once. "Yes, Mrs. Cumberland."

"Do not go within view of the road, my dear. I don't care that all the world should know I am making a call at Dallory Hall. Find a bench and sit down, as I bade you."

Obedient as it was in her nature to be, the young lady turned promptly into one of the side paths, which brought her within nearer range of Madam's view. She, Madam, with a face from which every atom of colour had faded, leaving it white as ashes, stood still as a statue, like one confounded.

"I see the likeness: it is to *him*," she muttered. "Can he have come home?"

Ellen Adair passed out of sight and hearing. Madam, shaking herself from her fear, turned with stealthy steps to seek the house, keeping in the private paths as long as might be, which was a more circuitous way. Madam intended, unseen, to make a third at the interview between her husband and Mrs. Cumberland. The sight of that girl's face had frightened her. There might be treason in the air.

G

Mrs. Cumberland was already in Mr. North's parlour. Strolling out amidst his flowers, he had encountered her in the garden, and taken her in through the open window. Madam arriving a little later, passed through the hall to the dining room. Rather inopportunely, there sat Bessy, busy with her housekeeping account books.

"Take them elsewhere," said Madam, with an imperious sweep of the hand.

She was not in the habit of giving a reason for any command whatever : let it be reasonable or unreasonable, all to be done was to hear and obey. Bessy gathered her books up in her black apron, and went away, Madam shooting the bolt of the door after her.

Then she stole across the soft Turkey carpet and slipped into the closet already spoken of, that formed a communication (never used as such) between the dining-room and Mr. North's parlour. The door opening to the parlour was unlatched and had been ever since he put his slippers inside it an hour before. When her eyes became accustomed to the closet's darkness, Madam saw them lying there; she also saw one or two of his old brown gardening coats hanging on the pegs. Against the wall was a narrow table with an unlocked desk upon it, belonging to herself. It was clever of Madam to keep it there. Opening the lid silently, she pulled up a few of its valueless papers, and let them stick out. Of course, if the closet were suddenly entered from the parlour —a most unlikely thing to happen, but Madam was cautious— she was only getting something from her desk. In this manner she had occasionally made an unsuspected third at Richard North's interviews with his father. Letting the lace hood slip off, Madam bent her ear to the crevice of the unlatched door, and stood there listening. She was under the influence of terror still : her lips were drawn back, her face wore the hue of death.

Apparently the ostensible motive of the interview—Mrs. Cumberland's wish to express her sympathy for the blow that had fallen on the Hall—was over ; she had probably also been asking for Mr. North's influence to push her son. The first connected words Madam caught were these :

"I will do what I can, Mrs. Cumberland. I wished to do it before, as you know. But Mrs. North took a dislike—I mean took a fancy to Alexander."

"You mean took a dislike to Oliver," corrected Mrs. Cumberland. "In the old days, when you were John North without thought of future grandeur, and I was Fanny Gass, we spoke out freely to each other."

"True," said poor Mr. North. "I've not had such good days since. Ah, what a long while it seems to look back to! I have grown into an old man, Fanny, older in feeling than in years; and you—you wasted the best days of your life in a hot and pestilential climate."

"Pestilential in places and at seasons," corrected Mrs. Cumberland. "My husband was stationed in the beautiful climate of the Blue Mountains, as we familiarly call the region of the Neilgherry Hills. It is pleasant there."

"Ay, I've heard so. Get the cool breezes and all that."

"People used to come up there from the hot plains to regain their wasted health," continued Mrs. Cumberland, whose thoughts were apt to wander back to the earlier years of her exile. "Ootacamund is resorted to there, just as the colder sea-side places are, here. But I and Mr. Cumberland were stationary."

"Ootacamund?" repeated Mr. North, struck with the name. "Ootacamund was where my wife's first husband died; Major Bohun."

"No, he did not die there," quietly rejoined Mrs. Cumberland.

"Was it not there? Ah! well, it does not matter. One is apt to confuse these foreign names and places together in the memory."

Mrs. Cumberland made no rejoinder, and there ensued a momentary silence. Madam, who with the mention of the place, Ootacamund, bit her lip almost to bleeding, bent forward, and looked through the opening of the door. She could just see the smallest portion of the cold, calm, grey face, and waited in sickening apprehension of what the next words might be. They came from Mrs. Cumberland and proved an intense relief, for the subject was changed for another.

"I am about to make a request to you, John: I hope you will grant it for our old friendship's sake. Let me see the anonymous letter that proved so fatal to Edmund—little Neddums, as I and your wife used fondly to call him in his babyhood. Every incident connected with this calamity is to me so full of painful interest!" she continued, as if seeking to apologise for her request. "As I lay awake last night,

unable to sleep, it came into my mind that I would ask
you to let me see the letter."

"You may see it, and welcome," was Mr. North's ready
reply, as he unlocked a drawer in the old secretaire—bureau,
he always called it—and handed the paper to her. "I only
wish I could show it to some purpose—to somebody who
would recognise the handwriting. You won't do that."

Mrs. Cumberland answered by a sickly smile. Her hands
trembled as she took the letter, and Mr. North noticed how
white her lips had become—as if with some inward suspense
or emotion. She studied the letter well, reading it three
times over; looking at it critically in all lights. Madam in
the closet could have hit her for her inquisitive curiosity.

"You are right, John," she said, with an unmistakable
sigh of relief as she gave the missive back; "I certainly do
not recognise that handwriting. It is like no one's that I
ever saw."

"It is a disguised hand, you see," he answered. "No
question about that: and accomplished in the cleverest
manner."

"Is it true that poor Edmund had been drawing bills in
conjunction with Alexander?"

"Only one. He had drawn a good many I'm afraid during
his short lifetime in conjunction with other people, but only
one with Alexander—which they got renewed. No blame
attaches to Alexander; not a scrap of it."

"Oliver told me that."

"Ay. I have a notion that poor Edmund did not get into
this trouble for his own sake, but to help that young scamp,
his brother."

"Which brother?"

"Which brother!" echoed Mr. North, rather in mockery.
"As if you need ask that. There's only one of them who
could deserve the epithet, and that's Sidney. An awful scamp
he is. He is but twenty years of age, and he is as deep in the
ways of a bad world as though he were forty."

"I am very sorry to hear you say it. Whispers go abroad
about him, as I dare say you know, but I would rather not
have heard them confirmed by you."

"People can't say much too bad of him. We have got
Mrs. North to thank for it: it is all owing to the way she has
brought him up. When I would have corrected his faults, she
stepped between us. Oftentimes have I thought of the enemy

that sowed the tares amid the wheat in his neighbour's field."

"The old saying comes home to many of us," observed Mrs. Cumberland with a suppressed sigh, as she rose to leave. "When our children are young they tread upon our toes, but when they get older they tread upon our hearts."

"Ay, ay! Don't go yet," added Mr. North. "It is pleasant in times of sorrow to see an old friend. I have no friends now."

"I must go, John. Ellen Adair is waiting for me; she will find the time long. And I expect it would not be very agreeable to your wife to see me here. Not that I know for why, or what I can have done to her."

"She encourages nobody; nobody of the good old days," was the confidential rejoinder. "There's no fear of her; I saw her going off towards the shrubberies—after Master Sidney, I suppose. She takes what she calls her constitutional walks there. They last a couple of hours sometimes."

As Mr. North turned to put the letter into the drawer again, he saw a scrap of poetry that had been found in Arthur Bohun's desk. This he also showed his visitor. He would have kept nothing from her; she was the only link left to him of the days when he and the world (to him) were alike young. Had Mrs. Cumberland stayed there till night, he would then have thought it too soon for her to go away.

"I will do all I can for your son, Fanny," said Mr. North, as they stood for a moment at the glass doors. "I like Oliver. He is a steady, persevering fellow, and I'll help him on if I can. If I do not, the fault will not lie with me. You understand?" he added, looking at her.

Mrs. Cumberland understood perfectly—that the fault would lie with Madam. She nodded in answer.

"Mr. Alexander is going, John—as you know. Should Oliver succeed in getting the whole of the practice—and there's nothing to prevent it—he will soon be making a large income. In that case, I suppose he will be asking you to give him something else."

"You mean Bessy. I wish to goodness he had her!" continued Mr. North impulsively; "I do heartily wish it sometimes. She has not a very happy life of it here. Well, well; I hope Oliver will get on with all my heart; tell him so from me, Fanny. He shall have her when he does."

"*Shall* he!" ejaculated Madam from her closet, and in her

most scornfully defiant tone—for the conversation had not pleased her.

They went strolling away amid the parterres of flowers, Madam peering after them with angry eyes. She heard her husband tell Mrs. Cumberland to come again; to come in often; whenever she would. Mr. North went on with her down the broad path, after they had lingered some minutes with the sweet flowers. In strolling back alone, who should pounce upon Mr. North from a side path but Madam!

" Was not that woman I saw you with the Cumberland, Mr. North ? "

" It was Mrs. Cumberland : my early friend. She came in to express her sympathy at my loss. I took it as very kind of her, Madam."

" I take it as very insolent," retorted Madam. " She had some girl with her when she came in. Who was it ? "

" Some girl! " repeated Mr. North, whose memory was anything but retentive. " Ah yes, I remember : she said her ward was waiting for her."

" Who is her ward ? "

" The daughter of a friend whom they knew in India, Madam. In India or Australia; I forget which : George Cumberland was stationed in both places. A charming young lady with a romantic name : Ellen Adair."

Madam toyed with the black lace that shielded her face. " You seem to know her, Mr. North."

" I have seen her in the road; and in coming out of church. The first time I met them was in Dallory, one day last summer, and Mrs. Cumberland told me who she was. That is all I know of her, Madam—as you seem to be curious."

"Is she living at Mrs. Cumberland's ? "

" Just now she is. I—I think they said she was going to be sent out to join her father," added Mr. North, whose impressions were always hazy in matters that did not immediately concern him. " Yes, I'm nearly sure, Madam : to Australia."

"Her father—whoever he may be—is not in Europe then," slightingly spoke Madam, stooping to root up mercilessly a handful of blue-bells.

" Her father lives over yonder. That's why the young lady has to go out."

Madam tossed away the rifled flowers and raised her head to its customary haughty height. The danger had passed.

"Over yonder" meant, as she knew, some far-off antipodes. She flung aside the girl and the interlude from her recollections, just as ruthlessly as she had flung the blue-bells.

"I want some money, Mr. North."

Mr. North went into a flutter at once. "I—I have none by me, Madam."

"Then give me a cheque."

"Nor cheque either. I don't happen to have a signed cheque in the house, and Richard is gone for the day."

"What have I repeatedly told you—that you must *keep* money by you; and cheques too," was her stern answer. "Why does Richard sign the cheques always?—Why can't you sign them?"

She had asked the same thing fifty times, and he had never been goaded to give the true answer.

"I have not signed a cheque since Thomas Gass died, except on my own private account, Madam; no, nor for long before it. My account is over-drawn. I shan't have a stiver in the bank until next quarter-day."

"You told me that last week," she said contemptuously. "Draw then upon the firm account."

He shook his head. "The bank would not cash it."

"Why?"

"Because only Richard can sign. Oh dear, this is going over and over the old ground again. You'll wear me out, Madam. When Richard took first acting place at the works, it was judged advisable that he should alone sign the business cheques—for convenience' sake, Madam; for convenience' sake. Gass's hands were crippled with gout; I was here with my flowers."

"I don't care who signs the cheques so that I get the money," she retorted in a rude, rough tone. "You must give me some to-day."

"It is for Sidney; I know it is for Sidney," spoke Mr. North tremulously. "Madam, you are ruining that lad. For his own sake some check must be put upon him: and therefore I am thankful that to-day I have no money to give."

He took some short hurried steps over the corners of paths and flower-beds, with the last words, and got into his own room. Madam calmly followed. Very sure might he be that she would not allow him to escape her.

Ellen Adair, waiting for Mrs. Cumberland, had *not* felt the time long. Very shortly after she was left alone, the carriage came back from the station, bringing Arthur Bohun : Richard had been left at Whitborough. Captain Bohun got out at the gates, intending to walk up to the house. Ellen saw him come limping along—the halt in his gait was always more visible when he had been sitting for any length of time—and he at the same time caught sight of the bright hues of the lilac dress gleaming through the trees.

Some years back, the detachment commanded by Arthur Bohun was quartered in Ireland. One ill-starred night it was called out to suppress some local disturbances, and he got desperately wounded : shot, as was supposed, unto death. That he would never be fit for service again ; that his death, though it might be a lingering one, was inevitable ; surgeons and friends alike thought. For nearly two years he was looked upon as a dying man : that is, as a man who could not possibly recover. But Time, the great healer, healed him ; and he came out of his long sickness and danger with only a slight limp, more or less perceptible. When walking slowly, or when he took any one's arms, it was not seen at all. Mrs. North (who was proud of her handsome and distinguished son, although she had no love for him,) was wont to tell friends confidentially that he had a bullet in his hip yet—at which Arthur laughed.

The sight of the lilac dress caused him to turn aside. Ellen rose and stood waiting ; her whole being was thrilling with the rapture the meeting brought. He took her hand in his, his face lighting.

"Is it indeed you, Ellen ! I should as soon have expected to see a fairy here."

"Mrs. Cumberland has gone to call on Mr. North. She told me to wait for her."

"I have been with Dick to take my uncle and James to the station," spoke Captain Bohun, pitching upon it as something to say, for his tongue was never too fluent when alone with her. "He has been asking me to go and stay with him."

"Sir Nash has ?"

"Yes. Jimmy invites nobody ; he is taken up with his missionaries, and that."

"Shall you go ?"

Their eyes met as she put the question. Go ! away from her !

"I think not," he quietly answered. "Not at present. Miss Bohun's turn must come first : she has been writing for me this long while."

" That's your aunt."

" My aunt. And a good old soul she is. Won't you walk about a little, Ellen ? "

She took the arm he held out, and they paced the covered walks, almost in silence. The May birds were singing, the budding leaves were dancing. Eloquence enough for them : and each might have detected the beating of the other's heart. Madam had her ear glued to that closet door, and so missed the sight. A sight that would have made her hair stand on end.

Minutes, for lovers, fly on swift wings. When Mrs. Cumberland appeared, it seemed that she had been away no time. Ellen went forward to meet her : and Captain Bohun said he had just come home from the station. Mrs. Cumberland, absorbed in her own cares, complaining of fatigue, took little or no notice of him : he strolled by their side up the Ham. Standing at Mrs. Cumberland's gate for a moment in parting, Oliver Rane came so hastily out of his house that he ran against them.

" Don't push me over, Rane," spoke Arthur Bohun in his lazy but very pleasing manner.

" I beg your pardon. When I am in a hurry I believe I am apt to drive on in a blindfold fashion."

" Is any one ill, Oliver ? " questioned his mother.

" Yes. At Mrs. Gass's. I fear it is herself. The man who brought the message did not know."

" You ought to keep a horse," spoke Captain Bohun, as the doctor recommenced his course. " So much running about must wear out a man's legs."

" Ought !—oughts go for a great deal, don't they ? " replied the doctor, looking back. " I ought to be rich enough to keep one, but I'm not."

Captain Bohun wished them good day, and they went indoors. Ellen wondered to hear that Mrs. Cumberland was going out again. Feeling uneasy—as she said—on the score of the sudden illness, she took her way to the house of Mrs. Gass, in spite of the fatigue she had been complaining of. A long walk for her at any time. Arrived there she found that lady in perfect health ; it was one of her servants to whom Oliver had been summoned. The young woman had scalded badly her hand and arm.

" I was at the Hall this morning, and Mr. North showed me the anonymous letter," Mrs. Cumberland took occasion to say. "It evidently comes from a stranger; a stranger to us. The handwriting is entirely strange."

"So much the better, ma'am," heartily spoke Mrs. Gass. "'Twould be too bad to think it was writ by a friend."

"Oliver thinks it was Madam," pursued Mrs. Cumberland, dropping her voice. "At least—he has not gone so far as to say *he* thinks it, but that Mr. Alexander does."

"That's just the word he gave to me, ma'am. Alexander thought it, he said, but that he hisself didn't know what to think, one way or the other. As well, perhaps for us not to talk of it: least said is soonest mended."

"Of course. But I cannot help recalling a remark once innocently made by Arthur Bohun in my hearing: that he did not know anybody who could imitate different hand-writings so well as his mother. Did you "—Mrs. Cumberland looked cautiously round—"observe the girl, Molly Green, take her handkerchief from her pocket while she stood here?"

"I didn't see her with any handkercher," was the answer, given after a pause of reflection. "Shouldn't think the girl's got one. She put her basket on the sideboard there, to come forward to my geraniums, and she stood stock still, while she looked at 'em. I don't say she didn't touch her pocket; but I never saw her at it."

"It might have been. These little actions often pass un-noticed. And it is so easy for any other article to slip up un-seen when a handkerchief is drawn out of a pocket," concluded Mrs. Cumberland in a suppressed tone of almost trembling eagerness. Which Mrs. Gass noticed, and did not quite like.

But there's a little something yet to tell of Dallory Hall. When Madam followed her husband through the glass doors into his parlour, an unusually unpleasant scene ensued. For once Mr. North held out resolutely. He had no other resource, for he had not the money to give her, and did not know where to get it. That it was for Sidney, he well believed; and for that reason only would have denied it to the utmost of his poor feeble strength. Madam flounced out in one of her worst moods. Mrs. Cumberland's visit and the startling sight of Ellen Adair had brought to her unexampled annoyance. As ill-luck had it, she encountered Bessy in the hall, and upon her vented her dreadful temper. The short scene was a violent one. When it was over, the poor girl went shivering and trembling into her father's parlour. He had been standing with the door ajar, shrinking almost as much as Bessy, and utterly powerless to interfere.

"Oh, child! if I could but save you from this!" he murmured, as they stood together before the window, and he fondly stroked the soft hair that lay on his breast. "It's one of the troubles that are wearing me out, Bessy: wearing me out before my time."

He burst into tears; perhaps her own sobs set him on; and they cried in concert. Bessy North was patient, meek, enduring; but meekness and patience can both be tried beyond their strength.

"Oliver Rane wants you: you know that, Bessie. If he could see his way clear to keep you, you should go to him to-morrow. Ay! though your poor brother has just been put into his grave."

Bessy lifted her head. In these moments of dire emotion, the heart speaks out without reticence.

"Papa, I would go to Oliver as he is now, and risk it," she said through her blinding tears. "I should not be afraid of our getting on: we'd make shift together, until better luck came. He spoke a word of this to me not long ago, but his lips were tied, he said, and he could not press it."

"He thought he had not enough for you?"

"He thought you would not consider it so. I should, papa. And I think those who bravely set out to struggle on together, have as much happiness in their shifts and economy as others who begin with a fortune."

"We'll see; we'll see, Bessy. I'd like you to try it, if you are not afraid. I'll talk to Dick. But—mind!—not a word here," he added, glancing round at the door to indicate the precincts of Mrs. North. "We shall have to keep it to ourselves if we'd not get it frustrated. I wonder how much Oliver makes a year."

"Not much; but he is advancing slowly. He has talked to me about it. What keeps one will keep two, papa."

"He'll come into about two hundred a year when his mother dies. And I fear she won't live long, by what she tells me. Poor Fanny! Not that I'd counsel anybody to reckon on dead men's shoes, child. Life's uncertain: he might die before her."

"He would not reckon on anything but his own exertions, papa. He told me a secret—that he is engaged on a medical work, writing it all his spare time. It is quite certain to take, he says, to be popular, and bring him good returns. Oh! papa, there will be no doubt of our getting on. Let us risk it!"

What a bright, hopeful tone she spoke in—"let us risk it!"—her mild eyes shining, the tears dried on her cheeks. Mr. North caught the glad spirit, and resolved—Dick being willing: sensible Dick—that they should risk it.

CHAPTER IX.

IN LAWYER DALE'S OFFICE.

WHITBOROUGH was a good sized, bustling town, sending two members to parliament. In the heart of it lived Mr. Dale, the lawyer, who did a little in money lending as well. He was a short stout man, with a red pimply face and no whiskers, nearly bald on the top of his round head; and he usually attired himself in the attractive costume of a brown tail coat and white neckcloth.

On this same morning which had witnessed the departure of Sir Nash Bohun and his son from Dallory Hall, Mr. Dale, known commonly amid his townsfolks as Lawyer Dale—was seated in his office at Whitborough. It was a small room, containing a kind of double desk, at which two people might face each other. The lawyer's place at it was against the wall, his face to the room; a clerk sometimes sat, or stood on the other side when business was pressing. Adjoining this office was one for the clerks, three of whom were kept; and clients had to come through their room to reach the lawyer's.

Mr. Dale was writing busily. The clock was on the stroke of twelve, and a great deal of the morning's work had to be done yet, when one of the clerks came in : a tall, thin cadaverous youth with black hair, parted into a flat curl on his forehead.

"Are you at home, sir?"

"Who is it?" asked Mr. Dale, growling at the interruption.

"Mr. Richard North."

"Send him in."

Richard came in; a fine looking man in his deep black clothes—the lawyer could not help thinking so. After shaking hands—a ceremony Mr. Dale liked to observe with all his clients, they being agreeable—he came from behind his desk to seat himself in his dwarf elbow-chair of red patent leather, and gave Richard a seat opposite. The room was small, the

desk and other furniture large, and they sat nearly nose to
nose. Richard held his hat on his knee.

"You guess no doubt what has brought me here, Mr. Dale.
Now that my ill-fated brother is put out of our sight in his
last resting-place, I have leisure and inclination to look into
the miserable event that sent him to it. I shall spare neither
cost nor energy in discovering—if so may be—the traitor."

"You allude to the anonymous letter."

"Yes. And I have come here to ask you to give me all the
information you can about it."

"But, my good sir, I have no information to give. I don't
possess any."

"I ought to have said information of the attendant circumstances. Let me hear your history of the transaction from beginning to end : and if you can impart to me any hint of the
possible writer—that is, if you have formed any private notion
of him—I trust you will do so."

Mr. Dale could be a little tricky on occasion ; he was sometimes engaged in transactions that would not have borne the
light, and that most certainly he would never have talked of.
On the other hand, he could be honest and truthful where
there existed no reason for being the contrary : and this
anonymous letter business came under the latter category.

"The transaction was as open and straightforward as could
be," spoke the lawyer—and Richard, a judge of character and
countenances, saw he was speaking the truth. "Mr. Edmund
North came to me one day some short time ago, wanting me to
let him have a hundred pounds on his own security. I didn't
care to do that—I knew about his bill transactions, you see—
and I proposed that somebody should join him. Eventually
he came with Alexander the surgeon, and the matter was
arranged."

"Do you know for what purpose he wanted the money ? "

"For his young brother, Sidney North. A fast young man,
that, Mr. Richard," added the lawyer in a significant tone.

"Yes. Unfortunately."

"Well, he had got into some secret trouble, and came
praying to Mr. Edmund to get him out of it. Whatever
foolish ways Edmund North had wasted money in, there's this
consolation remaining to his friends—that the transaction
which eventually sent him to his grave was one of pure kindness," added the lawyer warmly.

"'My Father has enough trouble, Dale,' he said to me, 'with

one thing and another, his life's about worried out of him;
and I don't care that he should get to hear of what Master
Sidney's been doing, if it can be kept from him?' Yes; the
motive was a good one."

"How was it he did not apply to me?" asked Richard.

"Well—had you not, just about that time, assisted your
brother Edmund in some scrape of his own?"

Richard North nodded.

"Just so. He said he had not the face to apply to you so
soon again; should be ashamed of himself. Well, to go on,
Mr. Richard North. I gave him the money on the bill; and
when it became due, neither he nor Alexander could meet it:
so I agreed to renew. Only one day after that, the anonymous letter found its way to Dallory Hall."

"You are sure of that?"

"Certain. The bill was renewed on the 30th of April; here.
in this very room. Mr. North got the letter on the 1st of
May."

"It was so. By the evening post."

"So that, if the transaction got wind through that renewing,
the writer did not lose much time."

"Well now, Mr. Dale, in what way could that transaction
have got wind, and who heard of it?"

"I never spoke of it to a human being," impetuously cried
the lawyer, giving his knee a thump with his closed hand.
And Richard North felt sure that he had not.

"The transaction, from the beginning, was known only to
us three men: Edmund North, the surgeon, and myself. I
don't believe either of them mentioned it at all. I know I did
not. It's just possible Edmund North might have told his
step-brother Sidney the way he got the money—the young
scamp. I beg your pardon, Mr. Richard; I forgot he was
your brother also."

"It would be to Sidney's interest to keep it quiet," casually
remarked Richard. "Our men at the works have got a report
running amidst them—I know not whence picked up, and I
don't think they know—that the writer of the letter was your
clerk, Wilks."

"Flam!" contemptuously rejoined the lawyer. "I've
heard of that. Why should Wilks trouble his head to write
about it? Don't you believe anything so foolish."

"I don't believe it," returned Richard North. "Wilks
could have no motive whatever for it, as far as I can see.

But I think this—that he may have become cognisant of the affair, and talked of it abroad."

"Not one of my clerks know anything about it," protested Mr. Dale. "I've got three of 'em: Wilks and two others. You don't suppose, sir, I take them into my confidence in all things."

"But, is it quite impossible that any one of them—say Wilks—could have got to know of it surreptitiously?" urged Richard.

"Wilks has nothing surreptitious about him," said the lawyer. "He is too shallowed-pated. A thoroughly useful clerk here, but a man without guile."

"I did not mean to apply the word surreptitious to him personally. I'll change it if you like. Could Wilks, or either of the other two have accidentally learnt this, without your knowledge? Was there a possibility of it? Come, Mr. Dale; be open with me. Even if it were so, no blame attaches to you."

"It is just this," answered Mr Dale, accepting the solicitation to be open—"that I don't see how it was possible for any one of them to have learnt it; while at the same time, I see no other way in which it could have transpired. That's the candid truth."

"But—is it quite impossible they could have learnt it?" urged Richard North, repeating his words.

"It seems impossible to me; but it is just one of those things that one could not take a Bible oath to. I lay awake one night for half-an-hour, turning the puzzle about in my mind. Alexander says he never opened his lips upon it; I know I did not; and poor Edmund North went into his fatal passion thinking Alexander wrote the letter, because he said Alexander alone knew of it; which is a pretty sure proof he had not talked himself."

"Which brings us back to your clerks," remarked Richard North. "They might have overheard a few chance words when the bill was renewed."

"I'm sure the door was shut," debated Mr. Dale, in a tone as if he were *not* sure, but rather sought to tell himself he was sure. "Only Wilks was in, that morning; the other two had gone out."

"Rely upon it that's how it happened. The door could not have been quite closed."

"W⁻¹ I don't know. I generally shut it myself, with a

bang too, when important clients are in here. I confess,"
honestly added Mr. Dale, "that it's the only loophole I can see
If the door was unlatched, Wilks might have heard. I had
him in last night, and taxed him with it. He denies it out
and out: says that, even if the affair had reached his knowledge, he knows his duty better than to have talked of
it."

"I don't doubt that he does, when in his sober senses. But
he is not always in them."

"Oh, come, Mr. Richard North, it is not so bad as that."

Richard was silent. If Mr. Dale was satisfied with his
clerk and his clerk's discretion, he had no wish to render him
otherwise.

"He takes too much now and then, you know, Mr. Dale;
and he may have dropped a word in some enemy's hearing:
who perhaps caught it up and then wrote the letter. Would
you mind my questioning him?"

"He is not here to be questioned, or you might do it and
welcome," replied Mr. Dale. "Wilks is lying up to-day. He
has not been well for more than a week past; could hardly do
his work yesterday."

"I'll take an opportunity of seeing him then," said Richard.
"My father won't rest until the writer of this letter shall be
traced; neither, in truth, shall I."

The lawyer said good morning to his visitor, and returned
to his desk. But ere he recommenced work, he thought over
the chief subject of their conversation. Had the traitor been
Wilks, he asked himself. What Richard North had said was
perfectly true—that the young man sometimes took too much
after work was over. But Mr. Dale had hitherto found no
cause to complain of his discretion; and, difficult as any other
loophole of suspicion seemed, he finally concluded that he had
no cause now.

Meanwhile Richard North walked back to Dallory—it was
nearly two miles from Whitborough. Passing his works, he
continued his way a little further, to a turning called North
Inlet; in which were some houses, large and small, tenanted
chiefly by his workpeople. In one of these, a pretty cottage
standing back, lodged Timothy Wilks. The landlady was a
relative of Wilks's, and as he got his two rooms cheap, he did
not mind the walk once a day to and from Whitborough.

"Good morning, Mrs. Green. Is Timothy Wilks in?"

Mrs. Green, an ancient matron in a mob-cap, was on her

hands and knees, whitening the door-step. She got up at the
salutation, saw it was Richard North, and curtseyed.

"Tim have just crawled out to get a bit o' sunshine, sir.
He's very bad to-day. Would you please to walk in, Mr.
Richard?"

Here, amidst this colony of his work-people, he was chiefly
known as "Mr. Richard." Mrs. Green's husband was time-
keeper at the North works.

"What's the matter with him?" asked Richard, as he
stepped over the threshold and the bucket to the little parlour.

"Well, sir, I only hope it's not a low-fever; but it looks to
me uncommon like it."

"Since when has he been ill?"

"He have been ailing this fortnight past. The fact is, sir,
he *won't* keep steady," she added in a deploring tone. "Once
a week he's safe to come home the worse for drink, and that's
pay night; and sometimes its oftener than that. Then for
two days afterwards he can't eat; and so it goes on, and he
gets as weak as a rat. It's not that he takes much drink; it
is that a little upsets him. Some men could take half-a-dozen
glasses a'most to his one."

"What a pity it is!" exclaimed Richard.

"He had a regular bout of it a week or so ago," resumed
Mrs. Green; who when she was set off on the score of Timothy's misdoings, never knew when to stop. It was so well
known to North Inlet, this failing of the young man's, that
she might have talked of it in the market-place and not betrayed confidence. "He had been ailing before, as I said,
Mr. Richard; off his food, and that; but one night he caught
it smartly, and he's been getting ill ever since."

"Caught what smartly?" asked Richard, not understanding North Inlet idioms.

"Why the drink, sir. He came home reeling, and give his
head such a bang again the door-post that it knocked him
back'ards. I got him up somehow—Green was out—and on
to his bed, and there he went off in a dead faint. I'd no
vinegar in the house: if you want a thing in a hurry you're
sure to be out of it: so I burnt a feather up his nose and that
brought him to. He began to talk all sorts of nonsense then,
about doing 'bills' whatever that might mean, and old Dale's
money-boxes, running words into one another like mad, so
that you couldn't make top nor tail o' the sense. I'd never
seen him as bad as this, and got a'most frightened."

H

She paused to take breath, always short with Mrs. Green. The words "doing bills" struck Richard North. He immediately perceived that hence might have arisen the report (for she had no doubt talked of this publicly) that Timothy Wilks was the traitor. Other listeners could put two and two together as well as he.

"I thought I'd get in the vinegar, in case he went off again," resumed Mrs. Green, having laid in a fresh stock of breath. "And when I was running round to the shop for it—leastways walking, for I can't run now—who should I meet, turning out of Ketler's but Dr. Rane. I stopped to tell him, and he said he'd look in and see Tim. He's a kind man in sickness, Mr. Richard."

"Did Dr. Rane come?" asked Richard.

"Right off, sir, there and then. When I got back he had put cloths of cold water on Tim's head. And wasn't Tim talking! You might have thought him a show-man at the fair. The doctor wrote something on paper with his pencil and sent me off again to Stevens's the druggist's, and Stevens he gave me a little bottle of white stuff to bring back. The doctor gave Tim some of it in a tea-cup of cold water, and it sent him into a good sleep. But he has never been well, sir, since then: and now I misdoubt me but it will end in low fever."

"Do you remember what night this was?" asked Richard.

"Ay, that I do, sir. For the foolish girls was standing out by twos and threes, making bargains with their sweethearts to go a-maying at morning dawn. I told 'em they'd a deal better stop in-doors to mend their stockings. 'Twas the night afore the First of May, Mr. Richard."

"The evening of the day the bill was renewed," thought Richard. He possessed the right clue now. If he had entertained any doubt of Wilks before, this set it at rest.

"Did any of the neighbours hear Tim talking?" he asked.

"Not a soul but me and Dr. Rane here, sir. But I b'lieve he had been holding forth to a room full at the Wheatsheaf. They say he was in part gone when he got there. Oh, it does make me so vexed, the ranting way he goes on when the drink's in him. If his poor father and mother could look up from their graves, they'd be fit to shake him in very shame. Drink is the worse curse that's going, Mr. Richard—and poor Tim's weak head won't stand hardly a drop of it."

She had told all she knew. Richard North stepped over the

bucket again, remarking that he might meet Tim. Sure enough
he did. In taking a cross-cut to the works, he came upon him,
leaning against the wooden rails that bordered a piece of waste
land. He looked very ill: Richard saw that: a small, slight
young man with a mild pleasant countenance and inoffensive
manners. His mother had been a cousin of Mrs. Green's, but
superior to the Greens in station. Timothy would have held
his head considerably above North Inlet, but for being brought
down both in consequence and pocket by these oft-recurring
bouts.

Kindly and courteously, but with a tone of resolution not to
be mistaken, Richard North entered on his questioning. He
did not suspect Wilks of having written the anonymous letter;
he told him this candidly; but he suspected, nay, knew, that
it must have been penned by some one who had gathered
certain details from Wilks's tongue. Wilks, weak and ill,
acknowledged that the circumstance of the drawing of the
bill (or rather the renewing of one) had penetrated to his
hearing in Mr. Dale's office; but he declared that he had not,
so far as he knew, repeated it again.

"I'd no more talk of our office business, sir, than I'd writ
an anonymous letter," said he, much aggrieved. "Mr. Dale
never had a more faithful clerk about him than I am."

"I daresay you would not, knowingly," was Richard's
rejoinder. "Answer me one question, Wilks. Have you any
recollection of haranguing the public at the Wheatsheaf?"

Mr. Wilks's answer to this was, that he had not harangued
the public at the Wheatsheaf. He remembered being at the
house quite well, and there had been a good deal of argument
in the parlour; chiefly, he thought, touching the question of
whether masters in general ought not to give holiday on the
first of May. There had been no particular haranguing on
his part, he declared; and he could take his oath that he never
opened his lips there about what had come to his knowledge.
One thing he did confess, on being pressed by Richard—that
he had no remembrance of quitting the Wheatsheaf, or of how
he got home. He retained a faint notion of having seen Dr.
Rane's face bending over him later, but could not say whether
it was a dream or reality.

Nothing more could be got out of Timothy Wilks. That
the man was guiltless of intentional treachery there was as
little doubt of as that the treachery had occurred through his
tongue. Richard North bent his steps to the Wheatsheaf, to

hold conference with Packerton, the landlord of that much-frequented hostelric.

And any information that Packerton could give, he was willing to give; but it amounted to little. Richard wanted to get at the names of all who went into the parlour on the night of the 30th of April, during the time that Wilks was there. The landlord told over as many as he could remember; but said that others might have gone in and out. One man (who looked like a gentleman and sat by Wilks) was a stranger, he said; he had never seen him before or since. This man got quite friendly with Wilks, and went out with him, propping up his steps. Packerton's son, a smart young fellow of thirteen, going out on an errand, had overtaken them on their way across the waste ground. (In the very path where Richard had but now encountered Wilks.) Wilks was holding on by the railings, the boy said, talking with the other as fast as he could talk, and the other was laughing. Richard North wished he could find out who this man was, and where he might be seen; for, of all the rest mentioned by the landlord, there was not one at all likely to have taken up the cause and written the anonymous letter. Packerton's opinion was that Wilks had not spoken of the matter there; he was then hardly "far enough gone" to have committed the imprudence.

"But I suppose he was when he left you," said Richard.

"Yes, sir, I'm afraid he might have been. He could talk; but every bit of reason had gone out of him. I never saw anybody but Wilks just like this when they've taken too much."

Again Richard North sought Wilks, and questioned him who this stranger, man or gentleman, was. He might as well have questioned the moon. Wilks had a hazy impression of having been with a tall, thin, strange man: but where, or when, or how, he knew not.

"I'll ask Rane what sort of a condition Wilks was in when he saw him," thought Richard.

But Richard could not carry out his intentions until night. Business claimed him for the rest of the day, and then he went home to dinner.

Dr. Rane was in his dining-room that night, the white blind drawn before the window, and writing by the light of a shaded candle. Bessy North had said to her father that Oliver was busy with a medical work that he expected good

returns from when published. It was so. He spared no
labour; over that, or anything else: often writing far into the
little hours. He was a patient, persevering man: once give
him a fair chance of success, a good start on life's road, and
he would be sure to go on to fortune. He said this to himself
continually; and he was not mistaken. But the good chance
had not come yet.

The clock was striking eight, when the doctor heard a ring
at his door bell, and Phillis appeared, showing in Richard
North. A thrill passed through Oliver Rane; perhaps he
could not have told why or wherefore.

Richard sat down and began to talk about Wilks, asking
what he had to ask, entering into the question generally. Dr.
Rane listened in silence.

"I beg your pardon," he suddenly said, remembering his
one shaded candle. "I ought to have got more light."

"It's quite light enough for me," replied Richard. "Don't
trouble. I'd as soon talk by this light as by a better. To go
back to Wilks: Did he say anything about the bill in your
hearing, Rane?"

"Not a word; not a syllable. Or, if he did, I failed to
catch it."

"Old Mother Green says he talked of 'bills,'" said Richard.
"That was before you saw him."

"Does she?" carelessly remarked the doctor. "I heard
nothing of the kind. There was no coherence whatever in his
words, so far as I noticed: one does not pay much attention
to the babblings of a drunken man."

"Was he quite beside himself?—quite unconscious of what
he said, Rane?"

"Well, I am told that it is the peculiar idiosyncrasy of
Wilks to be able to talk and yet to *be* unconscious: unconscious
for all practical purposes, and for recollection afterwards.
Otherwise I should not have considered him quite so far gone
as that. He talked certainly; a little; seemed to answer me
in a mechanical kind of way when I asked him a question,
slipping one word into another. If I had tried to understand
him, I don't suppose I could. He did not say much; and I
was away from him a good deal about the house, looking for
water and rags to put on his head."

"Then *you* heard nothing of it, Rane?"

"Absolutely nothing."

The doctor sat so that the green shade of the candle happened to fall on his face, making it look very pale. Richard North, absorbed in thoughts about Wilks, could not have told whether the face was in the dark or the light. He spoke next about the stranger who had joined Wilks, saying he wished he could find out who it was.

"A tall thin man, bearing the appearance of a gentleman?" returned Dr. Rane. "Then I think I saw him, and spoke to him."

"Where?" asked Richard with animation.

"Close by your works. He was looking in through the iron gates. After quitting Green's cottage, I crossed the waste ground, and saw him standing at the gates, underneath the centre gas-lamp. I had to visit a patient down by the church, and took the near way over the waste ground."

"You did not recognize him?"

"Not at all. He was a stranger to me. As I was passing, he turned round and asked me whether he was going right for Whitborough. I pointed to the high road and told him to keep straight along it. Depend upon it, this was the same man."

"What could he have been looking in at my gates for?" muttered Richard. "And what—for this is of more consequence—had he been getting out of Wilks?"

"It seems rather curious altogether," remarked Dr. Rane.

"I'll find this man," said Richard, as he got up to say good night; "I must find him. Thank you, Rane."

But after his departure Oliver Rane did not settle to his work as before. A man, once interrupted, cannot always do so. All he did was to pace the room restlessly with bowed head, like a man in some uneasy dream. The candle burnt lower, the flame got above the shade, throwing its light on his face, showing up its hues and lines and angles. But it was not a bit brighter than when the green shade had cast over it its cadaverous hue.

"Edmund North! Edmund North!"

Did the words in all their piteous, hopeless appeal come from him? Or was it some supernatural cry in the air?

CHAPTER X.

PUT TO HIS CONSCIENCE.

A FINE morning in June. Lovely June; with its bright blue skies and its summer flowers. Walking about amidst his rose-trees with their clustering blossoms, was Mr. North, a rake in his hand. He fancied he was gardening; he knew he was trifling. What did it matter?—his face looked almost happy. The glad sunshine was over head, and he felt as free as a bird in it.

The anonymous letter, that had caused so much mischief, was passing into a thing of the past. In spite of Richard North's efforts to trace him out, the writer remained undiscovered. Timothy Wilks was the chief sufferer, and bitterly resentful thereupon. To have been openly accused of having sent it by at least six persons out of every dozen acquaintances he met, cankered the mind and curdled the temper of ill-starred Timothy Wilks. As to the general public, they were beginning to forget the trouble—as it is in the nature of a faithless public to do. Only in the hearts of a few individuals did the sad facts remain in all their rugged sternness; and of those, one was Jelly.

Poor Mr. North could afford to be happy to-day, and for many days to come. Bessy also. Madam had relieved them of her presence yesterday, and gone careering off to Paris with her daughter. They hoped she might be away for weeks. In the seductive freedom of the home, Richard North had stayed late that morning. Mr. North was just beginning to talk with him, when some one called on business, and Richard shut himself up with the stranger. The morning had gone on; the interview was prolonged; but Richard was coming out now. Mr. North put down the rake.

"Has Wilson gone, Richard?"

"Yes, sir."

"What did he want? He has stayed long enough."

"Only a little business with me, father," was Richard's answer in his dutiful care. It had not been agreeable business, and Richard wished to spare his father.

"And now for Bessy, sir?" he resumed, as they paced side by side amidst the sweet-scented roses. "You were beginning to speak about her.

"Yes, I want to talk to you. Bessy would be happier with Rane than she is here, Dick."

Richard looked serious. He had no sort of objection to his sister's marrying Oliver Rane : in fact, he regarded it as an event certain to take place, sooner or later, but he did not quite see that the way was clear for it yet.

"I make no doubt of that, father."

"And I think, Dick, she had better go to him now, while we are at liberty to do as we please at home."

"Now!" exclaimed Richard.

"Yes; now. That is before Madam comes back. Poor Edmund is but just put under the sod ; but—considering the circumstances—I think the memory of the dead must give place to the welfare of the living."

"But how about ways and means, sir ?"

"Ay, that's it : how about ways and means. Nothing can be spared from the works at present, I suppose, Dick."

"Nothing to speak of, sir."

Mr. North had felt ashamed even to ask the question. In fact, it was more a remark than a question, for he knew as well as Richard did that there was no superfluous money.

"Of course not, Dick. Rane gets just enough to live upon now, and no more. Yesterday, after Madam and Matilda had driven off, I was at the front gates when Rane passed. So he and I got talking about it—about Bessy. He said his income was small now, but that of course it would very considerably augment itself as soon as Alexander should have left. As he and Bessy are willing to try it, I don't see why they should not, Dick."

Richard gave no immediate reply. He had a rose in his hand and was looking at it absently, deep in thought. His father continued :

"It's not as if Rane had no expectations whatever. Two hundred a-year must come to him at his mother's death. And —Dick—have you any notion how Mrs. Gass's will is left ? "

"Not the least, sir."

"Oliver Rane is the nearest living relative to her late husband, Mrs. Cumberland excepted. He is Thomas Gass's own nephew—and all the money was his. It seems to me, Dick, that Mrs. Gass is sure to remember him : perhaps largely."

"She may."

"Yes; and I think will. Bessy shall go to him; and be emancipated from her thraldom here."

"Oliver Rane has got no furniture in his house."

"He has got some. The dining-room and his bed-room are as handsomely furnished as need be. We can put in a bit more. There are some things at the Hall that were Bessy's own mother's, and she shall have them. They have not been taken much account of here, Dick, amid the grand things that Madam has filled the house with."

"She'll make a fuss, though, at their being removed," remarked Dick.

"Let her," retorted Mr. North, who could be brave as the best when two or three hundred miles lay between him and Madam. "Those things were your own dear mother's, Dick; she bought them with her own money before she married me, and I have always regarded them as heir-looms for Bessy. It's just a few plain solid mahogany things, as good as ever they were. It was our drawing-room furniture in the early days, and it will do for their drawing-room now. When Rane shall be making his six or seven hundred a year, they can buy finer if they choose. We thought great things of it; I know that."

Richard smiled. "I remember once when I was a very little fellow, my mother came in and caught me drawing a horse on the centre-table with pen-and-ink. The trouble she had to get the horse out!—and the whipping I got!"

"Poor Dick! She did not whip often."

"It did me good, sir. I have been scrupulously careful of furniture of all kinds ever since."

"Ah, nothing like the lessons of early childhood for making an impression," spoke Mr. North. "'Spare the rod and spoil the child!' There was never a truer saying than that."

"Then you really intend them to marry at once," spoke Richard, returning to the question.

"I do," said Mr. North in a more decisive tone than he usually spoke. "They both wish it: and why should I hold out against them? Bessy's thirty this year, you know, Dick: if girls are not wives at that age, they begin to think it hard. It's better to marry tolerably young: a man and woman don't shake down into each other's ways if they come together late in life. You are silent, Dick."

"I was thinking, sir, whether I could not manage a couple of hundred pounds for them from myself."

"You are ever generous, Dick. I don't know what we should all do without you."

"The question is—shall I give it over to them in money, or spend it for them in furniture ?"

"In money; in money, Dick," advised Mr. North. "The furniture can be managed; and cash is cash. Spend it in chairs and tables and it seems as if there were nothing tangible to show for it."

Richard smiled. "It strikes me that the argument lies the other way, sir. The chairs and tables are tangible; whereas cash sometimes melts. However, I think it will be better to do as you advise. Bessy shall have two hundred pounds handed to her after her marriage, and they can do what they consider best with it."

"To be sure; to be sure, Dick. Let 'em be married; we'll put no impediment on it. Bessy has a miserable life of it here; and she'll be thirty on the twenty-ninth of this month. Oliver Rane was thirty the latter end of March."

"Only thirty!" cried Richard. "I think he must be more than that, sir."

"But he's not more," returned Mr. North. "I ought to know; and so ought you, Dick. Don't you remember they are both in the tontine? All the children put into that tontine were born in the same year."

"Oh, was it so ? I had forgotten," returned Richard carelessly, for the tontine had never much troubled him. He could just recollect that when they were children he and his brother were wont to tease little Bessy, saying if she lived to be a hundred years old she'd come into a fortune.

"That was an unlucky tontine, Dick," said Mr. North, shaking his head. "Of ten children who were entered for it, only three remain. The other seven are all dead. Four of them died in the first or second year."

"How came Oliver Rane to be put in the tontine ?" asked Richard. "I thought he came to life in India—and lived there for the first few years of his life. The tontine children were all Whitborough children."

"Thomas Gass did that, Richard. When he got news that his sister had this baby—Oliver—he insisted upon putting him into the tontine. It was a sort of salve to Tom Gass's conscience; that's what I thought: what his sister and the poor baby wanted then was money—not to be put into a useless tontine. Ah, well, Rane has got on without anybody's assistance, and I daresay will flourish in the end."

Richard glanced at his watch; twelve o'clock; and increased his pace; a hundred and one things were wanting him at the works. Mr. North was walking with him to the gate.

"Yes, it's all for the best, Dick; they shall come together. And we'll get the wedding comfortably over while Madam's away."

"What has been her motive, sir, for opposing Bessy's engagement to Rane?"

"Motive!" returned Mr. North. "Do you see that white butterfly, Dick, fluttering senselessly about, now up, now down?—as good ask me what *his* motive is, as ask me Madam's. I don't suppose she has any motive—except that she is given to oppose us all."

Richard concluded it was so. Something might lie also in Bessy's patient excellence as a housekeeper; Madam, ever selfish, did not perhaps like to lose her.

As they reached the iron gates, Mrs. Cumberland passed, walking slowly. She looked very ill. Mr. North arrested her, and began to speak of the projected marriage of Oliver and Bessy. Mrs. Cumberland changed colour and looked three parts scared. Unobservant Mr. North saw nothing. Richard did.

"Has Oliver not told you what's afoot?" said the former. "Young men are often shyer on these matters than women."

"It's a very small income for them to begin upon," she observed presently, when Mr. North had said what he had to say—and Richard thought he detected that she had some private objection to the union. "So very small for Bessy— who has been used to Dallory Hall."

"It won't always remain small," said Mr. North. "His practice will increase when Alexander goes; and he'll have other money, may be, later. Oh, they'll get along, Fanny. Young couples like to be sufficiently poor to make struggling upward a pleasure. I dare say you married upon less."

"Of course, if you are satisfied,—it must be all right," murmured Mrs. Cumberland. "You and Bessy."

She pulled her veil over her grey face, said good morning, and moved away. Not in the direction of Dallory—as she was previously walking—but back to the Ham. Mr.

North turned into his grounds again; Richard went after Mrs. Cumberland.

"I beg your pardon," he said—he was not as familiar with her as his father was—"will you allow me a word. You do not like this proposed marriage. Have you ought to urge against it?"

"Only for Bessy's sake. I was thinking of her."

"*Why* for Bessy's sake?"

There was some slight hesitation in Mrs. Cumberland's answer. She appeared to be pulling her veil straight.

"Their income will be so small. *I* know what a small income is, and therefore I feel for her."

"Is that all your doubt, Mrs. Cumberland?—the smallness of the income?"

"All."

"Then I think, as my father says, you may safely leave the decision with themselves. But—*was* this all?" added Richard: for an idea to the contrary had taken hold of him. "You have no personal objection to Bessy?"

"Certainly it was all," was Mrs. Cumberland's reply. "As to any personal objection to Bessy, that I could never have. When Oliver first told me they were engaged, I thought how lucky he was to get Bessy North; I wished them success with all my heart."

"Forgive me, Mrs. Cumberland. Thank you. Good morning."

Reassured, Richard North turned, and strode hastily away in the direction of Dallory. He fancied she had heard Bessy would have no fortune, and was feeling disappointed on her son's account. It struck him that he might as well confirm this; and he wheeled round.

Mrs. Cumberland had gone on and was already seated on the bench before spoken of, in the shady part of the road. Richard, in a few concise words, entering into no details of any sort, said to her that his sister would have no marriage portion.

"*That* I have long taken as a matter of course; knowing what the expenses at the Hall must be," she answered with a friendly smile. "Bessy is a fortune in herself; she would make a good wife to any man. Provided they have sufficient for comfort—and I hope Oliver will soon be making that—they can be as happy without wealth as with it, if your sister can only think so. Have you—pardon me for recalling to you what must be an unpleasant topic, Richard—have you yet gained any clue to the writer of that anonymous letter ? "

" Not any. It presents mystery on all sides."

" Mystery ? "

" As it seems to me. Going over the various attendant circumstances, as I do on occasion when I get a minute to myself, I try to fit one probability into another, and I cannot compass it. We must trust to time, Mrs. Cumberland. Good morning."

Richard raised his hat, and left her. She sat on with her pain. With her pain. Mrs. Cumberland was as strictly rigid a woman in tenets as in temperament; her code of morality was a severe one. Over and over again had she asked herself whether (it is of no use to mince the matter any longer) Oliver had or had not written that anonymous letter which had killed Edmund North : and she could not answer. But, if he had done it, why then surely he ought not to wed the sister. It would be little less than sin.

Since this secret trouble had been upon her, more than a month now, her face had seemed to have assumed a greyer tinge. How grey it looked now, as she sat on the bench, passers-by saw, and almost started at. One of them was Mr. Alexander. Arresting his quick steps—he always walked as though running a race—he enquired after her health.

" Not any better and not much worse," she answered. " Complaints, such as mine, are always tediously prolonged."

" They are less severe to bear, however, than sharper ones," said the doctor, willing to administer a grain of comfort if he could. " What a lovely day it is! And Madam's off for a couple of months I hear."

" Have the two any connection, Mr. Alexander ? "

" I don't know," he said laughing. " Her presence makes winter at the Hall, and her absence its sunshine. If I had such a wife, I'm not sure that I should think it any sin to give her an over-dose of laudanum some day, out of regard to the general peace. Did you hear of her putting Miss Bessy's wrist out ? "

" No."

" She did do it, then. Something sent her into a passion with Miss Bessy; she caught her hand and flung it away so violently that the wrist began to swell. I was sent for to bind it up. Why such women are allowed to live, I can't imagine."

"I suppose because they are not fit to die," said Mrs. Cumberland. "When are you leaving?"

"Sometime in July, I think, or during August. I enter on my new post the first of September, so there's no hurry."

Mrs. Cumberland rose and continued her slow way homewards. Passing her own house, she entered that of her son. Dr. Rane was engaged with a patient, so she went on to the dining-room and waited.

He came in shortly, perhaps thinking it might be another patient, his face bright. It fell a little when he saw his mother. Her visits to him were so exceedingly rare that some instinct whispered him nothing pleasant had brought her there. She rose and faced him.

"Oliver, is it true what I hear—that you are shortly to be married?"

"I suppose it is, mother," was his answer.

"But—is there no impediment that should bar it?" she asked in a whisper.

"Well—as to waiting, I may wait to the end, and not find the skies rain gold. If Bessy's friends see no risk in it, it is not for me to see it. At any rate, this will be a more peaceful home for her than the Hall."

"I am not talking of waiting,—or of gold,—or of risk, Oliver," she continued solemnly, placing both her hands on his arm, "is there nothing on your mind that ought to bar this marriage? is your conscience at rest? If—wait and let me speak, my son; I understand what you would say; what you have already told me—that you were innocent—and I know that I ought to believe you. But a doubt flashes up in my mind continually, Oliver; it is not my fault; truth knows my will is good to bury it up for ever. Bear with me a moment; I must speak. If the death of Edmund North lies at your door, however indirectly it was caused, to make his sister your wife will be a thing altogether wrong; little less than a sin in the sight of Heaven. I do not accuse you, Oliver; I suggest this as a possible case; and now I leave it with you for your own reflection. Oh, my son, believe me—for it seems to me as though I spoke with a prophet's inspiration this day! If your conscience tells you that you were not innocent, to bring Bessy North home to this roof will be wrong, and I think no blessing will rest upon it."

She was gone. Before Oliver Rane in his surprise could

answer a word, Mrs. Cumberland was gone. Passing swiftly out at the open window, she stepped across the garden and the dwarf wire-fence, and so entered her own home.

CHAPTER XI.

WHERE'S THE RING?

APPARENTLY Dr. Rane found nothing in his conscience that could present an impediment, and the preparations for the wedding went quietly on. Secretly might almost be the better word. In their dread lest the news should reach Madam in her retreat over the water, and bring her back to stop it, those concerned deemed it well to say nothing; and no suspicion of what was afloat transpired to the world in general.

Bessy—upon whom, from her isolated position, having no lady about her, the arrangements fell—was desired to fix a day. She named the twenty-ninth of June, her birthday. After July should come in, there was no certainty about Madam's movements; she might come home, or she might not, and it was necessary that all should be over by that time, if it was to be gone through in peace. The details of the ceremony were to be of the simplest nature: Edmund North's recent death and the other peculiar attendant circumstances forbidding the usual gaiety. The bridal party would go to church with as little ceremony as they went to service on Sundays, Bessy in a plain silk dress and a plain bonnet. Mr. North would give his daughter away, if he were well enough; if not, Richard. Ellen Adair was to be bridesmaid; Arthur Bohun had offered himself to Dr. Rane as best man. It might be very undutiful, but Arthur enjoyed the stealing a march on Madam as much as the best of them.

Mrs. Cumberland was no doubt satisfied on the score of the scruples she had raised, since she intended to countenance the wedding, and be at church. Dr. Rane and his bride would drive away from the church door to the railway station at Whitborough. The bridal tour was to last one week only: the doctor did not care to be away longer from his patients, and Bessy confessed that she would rather be at home, setting her house in order, than prolonging her stay at small roadside inns in Wales. But for the disconcerting fact of Madam's being in Paris, Dr. Rane would have liked to take Bessy across the Channel and give her her first glimpse of the French capital.

Under Madam's unjust rule, poor Bessy had never gone any-where: Matilda North had been taken half over the world.

The new household arrangements at Dr. Rane's were to be achieved during their week's absence: the articles of furniture (that Mr. North chose to consider belonged to Bessy) to be taken there from the Hall; the new carpet, Mrs. Cumberland's present, to be laid down in the drawing-room; Molly Green to enter as helpmate to Phillis. Surely Madam would not grumble at *that ?* Molly Green, going into a temper one day at some oppression of Madam's, had given warning on the spot. Bessy liked the girl, and there could be no harm in engaging her for her own housemaid.

One of those taken into the secret had been Mrs. Gass. Richard, who respected her greatly in spite of her queer grammar, and liked her too, unfolded the news. She received it in silence: a very rare thing for Mrs. Gass to do. Just as it had struck Richard in regard to Mrs. Cumberland, so it struck him now—that Mrs. Gass did not quite like the tidings.

"Well, I hope they'll be happy," she said at length, break-ing the silence, "and I hope he deserves to be. I hope it with all my heart. Do you think he does, Mr. Richard ?"

"Rane? Deserves to be happy? For all I see, he does. Why should he not ?"

"*I* don't know," answered Mrs. Gass, searching Richard's face. "Oliver Rane is my late husband's nephew, but he's three parts a stranger to me, except as a doctor; for it's him attends here, you know, sir,—as is natural—and not Alex-ander. Is he truthful, Mr. Richard ? Is he trustworthy ?"

"He is, for anything I know to the contrary," replied Richard North, a little wondering at the turn the conversation was taking. "If I thought he were not, I should be very sorry to give Bessy to him."

"And let us hope that he is, Mr. Richard, and wish 'em joy with all our hearts."

That a doubt was lying on Mrs. Gass's mind, in regard to the scrap of paper found in her room, was certain. Being a sensible woman, it could not be but that—when surrounding mists had cleared away—she should see that the only likely place for it to have dropped from, was Dr. Rane's pocket-book. Molly Green had been subjected to a cross-examination, very cleverly conducted, as Mrs. Gass thought, which left the matter exactly as it was before. But the girl's surprise was

so genuine, at supposing any receipt for making plum-pudding
(for that's how Mrs. Gass put it) could have been dropped by
her, that Mrs. Gass's mind could but revert to the pocket-
book. How far Oliver Rane was guilty, whether guilty at
all, or not, she was quite unable to decide. A small haze of
doubt remained on her mind, though she was glad enough to
put it from her. One thing struck her as curious, if not suspicious—that from the hour she handed him over the paper
to this, Dr. Rane had never once spoken of the subject. It
almost seemed to Mrs. Gass that an innocent man would,
though it had only been to say, I have found no clue to the
writer of that paper.

And if a modicum of the same hazy doubt rose to Richard
North during his interview with Mrs. Gass, it was due to her
manner. But he was upright himself, unsuspicious as the
day. The impression faded again; and he came away believing that Mrs. Gass, zealous for the Norths' honours, rather
disapproved of the marriage for Bessy, on account of the
doctor's poverty.

And so, there was no one to say a word of warning where
it might have been effectual, and the day fixed for the wedding
drew on. After all, the programme was not strictly carried
out, for Mr. North had one of his nervous attacks, and could
not go to church.

At five minutes past nine o'clock, in the warm bright June
morning, the Dallory Hall carriage drove up to Dallory church.
Richard North, his sister, and Arthur Bohun were within it.
The forms and etiquette usually observed at weddings were
slighted here, else how came Arthur Bohun, the bridegroom's
best man, to come to church with the bride? What did it
matter? So closely in its wake that the horses nearly clashed
with Mr. North's horses, came up the other carriage—which
ought to have been the first. In after days, when a strange
ending had come to the marriage life of Oliver Rane and his
wife, and Oliver was regarded with dread, assailed with
reproach, people said the marriage had been the Norths'
doings more than his. Any way, Bessy was first at church
and both were a little late.

But Mr. North was not the only one who failed them; the
other was Mrs. Cumberland. She assigned no reason for
absenting herself from the ceremony, excepting a plea that
she did not feel equal to it—which her son believed or not,
as he pleased. Her new bright dress and bonnet were spread

I

out on the bed; but she never as much as looked at them: and Ellen Adair found that she and Dr. Rane had to drive to the church alone, in the hired carriage, arriving there almost simultaneously with the other party.

Richard North took his sister up the aisle, the bridegroom following close on their steps. Ellen Adair and Captain Bohun, left behind, walked side by side. Bessy wore a pretty grey silk and plain white bonnet: she had a small bouquet in her hand that the gardener, Williams, had done up for her. Ellen Adair was in a similar dress, and looked altogether lovely. Mr. Lea, the clergyman, stood ready, book in hand. The spectators in the church—for the event had got wind at the last moment, as these events almost always do, and many came—rose up with expectation.

Of all the party, the bridegroom alone seemed to suffer from nervousness. His answering voice was low, his words were jerky. It was the more remarkable, because he was in general so self-contained and calm a man. Bessy, timid and yielding always, spoke with gentle firmness; not a shade of doubt or agitation seemed to cross her. But there occurred a frightful controtemps.

"The ring, if you please," whispered the officiating clergyman to the bridegroom when the part of the service came that the ring was needed.

The ring! Oliver Rane felt in his waistcoat pocket, and went into a spasm of consternation. The ring was not there. He must have left it on his dressing-table. The little golden symbol had been wrapped in a bit of white tissue paper, and he certainly remembered putting it into his waistcoat pocket. It was as certainly not there now: and he supposed he must have put it out again.

"I have not got the ring!" he exclaimed hurriedly.

To keep a marriage ceremony waiting in the middle, while a messenger ran a mile off to get the ring and then ran a mile back again, was a thing that had never been heard of by the clergyman or any other of the scared individuals around him. What was to be done? It was suggested that perhaps somebody present could furnish a ring that might suffice. Ellen Adair, standing in her beauty behind the bride, gently laid down the glove and bouquet she was holding, took off her own glove, and gave Oliver Rane a plain gold ring from her finger: one she always wore there. Arthur Bohun alone knew the ring's history; the rest had never taken sufficient interest in *her* to enquire it; perhaps had never noticed that she wore one.

The service proceeded to its end. Had Oliver Rane gone a pilgrimage to all the jewellers' marts in Whitborough, he could not have chosen a more perfectly-fitting wedding-ring than this. When they went into the vestry, Bessy, agitated by the mishap and the emotional position altogether, burst into tears, asking Ellen how *she* came by a wedding-ring.

The history was very simple. It arose—that is the possession of the ring—through the foolish romance of two young girls. Ellen and one of her schoolfellows named Maria Warne had formed a sincere and lasting attachment to each other. At the time of parting, when Ellen was leaving school for Mrs. Cumberland's, each had bought a plain gold ring to give the other, over which eternal friendship had been vowed, together with an undertaking to wear the ring always. Alas, for time and change! in less than six months afterwards, Ellen Adair received notice of the death of Maria Warne. The ring had in consequence become really precious to Ellen; but on this emergency she had not scrupled to part with it.

As they came out of the vestry, Ellen found herself face to face with Jelly. The clerk, and the two women pew-openers, and the sexton, considering themselves privileged people, pressed up where they chose: Jelly, who of course—living with Mrs. Cumberland—could not be at all confounded with the common spectators, chose to press with them. Her face was as long as one and a half, as she caught hold of Miss Adair.

"How *could* you, Miss Ellen?" she whispered. "Don't you know that nothing is more unlucky than for a bride to be married with anybody else's wedding-ring?"

"But it was not a wedding-ring, Jelly. Only a plain gold one."

"Anyway it was unlucky for *you*. We have a superstition in these parts, Miss Ellen, that if a maid takes off a ring from her own finger to serve at a pinch for a bride, she'll never be a wife herself. I'd not have risked it, Miss."

Ellen laughed gaily, Jelly's dismay was so real and her face so long. But there was no time for more. Richard held out his arm to her; and Oliver Rane was already taking out his bride. Close up against the door stood Mr. North's carriage, into which stepped the bride and bridegroom.

"My shawl! where's the shawl?" asked Bessy, looking round.

She had sat down upon it; and laughed gaily when Oliver drew it out. This shawl—a thin cashmere of quiet colours—was intended to be thrown on ere they reached the station. Her silk dress covered with that, and a black lace veil substituted for the white one on her bonnet, the most susceptible maid or matron who might happen to be travelling, would never take her for a bride.

Arthur Bohun deliberately flung an old white satin slipper after the carriage—it struck the old coachman's head, and the crowding spectators shouted cheerily. Richard was going to the works. He placed Ellen in the carriage that had brought her.

"Will you pardon me, that I depute Captain Bohun to see you safely home instead of myself, Miss Adair? It is a very busy day at the works, and I must go there. Arthur, will you take charge of this young lady?"

What Ellen answered, she scarcely knew. Captain Bohun got into the carriage. The situation was wholly unexpected: and if their hearts beat a little faster in the tumult of the moment's happiness, Richard at least was unconscious of it.

"It is the first wedding I ever was at," began Ellen gaily, feeling that she must talk to cover the embarrassment of the position. Both were feeling it: and got as far apart from each other as if they had quarrelled: she in one corner, he in the further one opposite. "Of course it had been arranged that I should go home with Mrs. Cumberland."

"Is she ill?"

"Dr. Rane thinks it is only nervousness: he said so as we came along. I had to come with him alone. I am sure the people we passed on the road, who had not heard about Bessy, thought it was I who was going to be married to him, they stared into the carriage so."

Ellen laughed as she said it. Arthur Bohun, drinking in draughts of her wondrous beauty, glanced at her meaningly, his blue eyes involuntarily betraying his earnest love.

"It may be your turn next, Ellen."

She blushed vividly, and looked from the window as though she saw something passing. He felt tempted there and then to speak of his love. But he had a large sense of the fitness of the time and place; and she had been placed for these few minutes under his protection: it seemed like putting him on his honour, as schoolboys say. Besides, he had fully made up his mind not to speak until he saw his way clear to marry.

Ellen Adair brought her beaming face round again. "Jelly

is in a terrible way about the ring, foretelling all kinds of ill-luck to everybody concerned, and thankful it did not happen to *her*. Will Bessy keep my ring always, do you think? Perhaps she'd not be legally married if she gave it me back and took to her own—when it is found ? "

Arthur Bohun's eyes danced a little. "Perhaps not," he replied in the gravest of tones. "I cannot tell what they would have done without it, Ellen."

"I did not tell Bessy one thing, when she asked me about it in the vestry. I will never tell her if I can help it—that Maria Warne is dead. How was it Mr. North did not come ? "

"Nervousness too, in my opinion. He said he was ill."

"Why should he be nervous ? "

"Lest it should come to his wife's ears—that he had so far countenanced the marriage as to be present at it."

"Can you tell why Mrs. North should set her face against it ? "

"No. Unless it is because other people have wished it. I should only say as much to you, though, Ellen : she is my mother."

The implied confidence sounded very precious in her ears. She turned to the window again.

"I hope they will be happy. I think there is no doubt of it. Bessy is very sweet-tempered and gentle."

"He is good-tempered too."

"Yes I think so. I have seen but little of him. There's Mrs. Gass ! "

They were passing that lady's house. She sat at the open window ; a grand amber gown on, white satin ribbons in her cap. Leaning out, she shook her handkerchief at them in violent greeting, just as though they had been the bride and bridegroom. As Ellen drew back in her corner after bowing, her foot touched something on the carpet at the bottom of the carriage.

"Why ! what is this ? "

They both stopped at once. It was the wedding-ring enclosed in its bit of tissue paper. Captain Bohun unfolded the paper.

"Dr. Rane must have lost it out of his pocket as we went along," cried Ellen. "He said, you know, that he felt so sure he had put it in. What is to be done with it ? "

"Wear it instead of your own until they come back," said Arthur. "Bessy can then take her choice of the two."

Accepting the suggestion without thought of dissent, Ellen took off her right glove and held out the other hand for the ring. He did not give it. Bending forward, he took her right hand and put it on for her.

"It fits as well as my own did."

Their eyes met. He had her hand still, as if trying the fit. Her sweet face was like a damask rose.

"I trust I may put one on to better purpose some day, Ellen," came the murmuring, whispered, tremulous words. "Meanwhile—if Bessy does not claim this, remember that I have placed it on your finger."

Not another syllable, not another look from either. Captain Bohun sat down in his corner; Ellen in hers, her hot face bent over the glove she was putting on, and fully believing that the carriage had changed into Paradise.

CHAPTER XII.

PUTTING DOWN THE CARPET.

THE days went on, and Dr. Rane's house was being made ready for the reception of the bride. No time could be lost, as the wedding tour was intended to be so short a one. As Jelly said, They'd be at home before folks could look round. Mrs. Cumberland presented the new carpet for the drawing-room; the furniture that had been the first Mrs. North's, arrived from Dallory Hall. Molly Green arrived with it, equally to take up her abode in the house of Dr. Rane. The arranging of these things, with the rest of the preparations, was carried on with a considerable deal of bustle and gossip, Jelly being in at the doctor's house continually, and constituting herself chief mistress of the ceremonies. Phillis and Molly Green, with native humility, deferred to her in all things.

It was said in a previous chapter that Jelly was one of those who retained an interest in the anonymous letter. She had a special cause for it. Jelly in her propensity to look into her neighbours' affairs, was given to take up any mysterious cause, and make it hers. Her love of the marvellous was great, her curiosity insatiable. But Jelly's interest in this matter really was a personal one and concerned herself. It was connected with Timothy Wilks.

Amidst Jelly's other qualities and endowments, might be ranked one that took almost the pre-eminence—love of admiration. Jelly could not remember to have been without an "acquaintance" for above a month at a time since the days when she left off pinafores. No sooner did she quarrel with one young man and dismiss him, than she took on another. Dallory wondered that of all her numerous acquaintances she had not got married: but, as Jelly coolly said, to have a suitor at your beck and call was one thing, and to be tied to a husband quite another. So Jelly was Jelly still; and perhaps it might be conceded that the fault was her own. She liked her independence.

The reigning "acquaintance" at this present period happened to be Timothy Wilks. Jelly patronized *him; he* was devoted to her. There was a trifling difference in their ages—some ten years probably, and all on Jelly's side—but that disparity had often happened before. Jelly had distinguished Tim by the honour of taking him to be her young man; and when the damaging whisper fell upon him, that he had probably written the anonymous letter resulting in the death of Edmund North, Jelly resented the aspersion far more than Timothy did. "I'll find out who did do it if it costs me a year's wages and six months' patience," avowed Jelly to herself in the first burst of indignation.

But Jelly found she could not arrive at that satisfactory result any quicker than other people. It's true, she possessed a slight clue that they did not, in the few memorable words she had overheard pass that moonlight night between her mistress and Dr. Rane, but they did not serve her. The copy of the letter was said to have dropped out of Dr. Rane's pocket-book on somebody's carpet, and he denied that it had so dropped. Neither more nor less could Jelly make of the matter than this: and she laboured under the disadvantage of not being able to speak of the overheard words, unless she confessed that she had been a listener. Considering who had been the speakers, Jelly did not choose to do that. From that time until this, a good two months, had the matter rankled in Jelly's mind; she had kept her ears wide open and put cautious questions whenever she thought they might avail, and all to no purpose. But in this, the first week of July, Jelly got a slight light thrown on the clue from Molly Green. The very day that damsel arrived at Dr. Rane's as helpmate to Phillis, and Jelly had gone in with her domineering orders,

the conversation happened to turn on plum-pudding—Phillis
having made a currant-dumpling for dinner, and let the water
get into it—and Molly Green dropped a few words which
Jelly's pricking ears caught up. They were only to the effect
that Mrs. Gass had asked her whether she did not let fall on
her carpet a receipt for making plum-pudding, the night of
Edmund North's attack; which receipt Mrs. Gass had said,
might have belonged to Madam, and been brought from the
Hall by Molly Green's petticoats. Jelly put a wary question
or two to the girl, and then let the topic pass without comment. That same evening she betook herself to Mrs. Gass,
acting craftily. "Where's that paper that was found on
your carpet the night Edmund North was taken?" asked
Jelly with bold tongue. Upon which Mrs. Gass was seized
with astonishment so entire that in the moment's confusion
she made one or two inconvenient admissions, just stopping
short of the half-suspicion she had entertained of Dr. Rane.

In the days gone by, when Mrs. Gass was a servant herself,
Jelly's relatives—really respectable people—had patronized
her. Mrs. Gass got promoted to what she was; but she
assumed no fine airs in consequence, as the reader has heard,
and she and Jelly had remained very good friends. Vexed with
herself for having incautiously admitted that the paper found
was the copy of the anonymous letter, Mrs. Gass turned round
on Jelly and gave her a good sharp reprimand for taking her
unawares, and for trying to pry into what did not concern her.
Jelly came away, not very much wiser than she went, but with
a spirit of unrest that altogether refused to be soothed. She
dared not pursue the enquiry openly, out of respect to her
mistress and Dr. Rane, but she resolved to pump Molly Green.
This same Molly was niece to the people with whom Timothy
Wilks lodged, and rather more friendly with the latter gentleman than Jelly liked.

On the following morning when Jelly had swallowed her
breakfast, she went into the next house with her usual lack of
ceremony. Phillis and Molly Green were on their knees
laying down the new carpet in the drawing-room, tugging and
hammering to the best of their ability, their gowns pinned
round their waists, their sleeves stripped to the elbows; Phillis
little and old, and weak-looking; Molly a comely girl of
twenty, with red cheeks.

"Well, you must be two fools!" was Jelly's greeting, after
taking in appearances. "As if you could expect to put down

a heavy Brussels yourselves! Why didn't you get Turtle's men here? They served the carpet, and they ought to come to put it down."

"They promised to be here at seven o'clock this morning, and now it's nine," mildly responded Phillis, her nice dark eyes raised to Jelly's. "We thought we'd try and do it ourselves, so as to be able to get the table, and chairs in, and the room finished. Perhaps Turtles have forgot it."

"I'd forget them, I know, if it was me, when I wanted to buy another carpet," said Jelly, tartly.

But, even as she spoke, a vehicle was heard to stop at the gate. Inquisitive Jelly looked from the window, and recognized it for Turtle's. It seemed to contain one or two pieces of new furniture. Phillis did not know that any had been coming and went out. Molly Green rose from her knees, and stood regarding the carpet. This was Jelly's opportunity.

"Now, then!" she sharply cried, confronting the girl with imperious gesture. "Did you drop that, or did you not, Molly Green?"

Molly Green seemed all abroad at the address—as well she might be. "Drop what?" she asked.

"That plum-pudding receipt on Mrs. Gass's parlour carpet."

"Well, I never!" returned Molly after a pause of surprise. "What is it to you, Jelly, if I did?"

Now the girl only so spoke by way of retort; in a sort of banter. Jelly, hardly believing her ears, took it to be an admission that she did drop it. And so the two went floundering on, quite at cross-purposes.

"Don't stare at me like that, Molly Green. I want a straight-for'ard answer. Did it drop from your skirts?"

"It didn't drop from my hands. As to staring, it's you that's doing that, Jelly, not me."

"Where had you picked up the receipt from?—Out of Mr. Edmund North's room?"

"Out of Mr. Edmund North's room!" echoed Molly in wonder. "Whatever should have brought me a-doing that?"

"It was the night he was taken ill."

"And if it was! I didn't go a-nigh him."

A frightful thought now came over Jelly, turning her quite faint. What if the girl had gone to her Aunt Green's that night and picked the paper up there? In that case it could not fail to be traced home to Timothy Wilks.

"Did you call in at your aunt's that same evening, Molly Green?"

"Suppose I did?" retorted Molly.

"And how *dare* you call in there, and bring—bring—receipts away with you surreptitious?" shrieked Jelly in her temper.

Molly Green stooped to pick up the hammer, lying at her feet, speaking quietly as she did so. Some noise was beginning to be heard outside, caused by Turtle's men getting a piano into the house, and Phillis talking to them.

"I can't think what you are a-driving at, Jelly. As to calling in at aunt's, I have a right to do it when I'm out, if time allows. Which it had not that night, at any rate, for I never went nowhere but to the druggist's and Mrs. Gass's. I scuttered all the way to Dallory, and scuttered back again; and I don't think I stopped to speak to a single soul, but Timothy Wilks."

Jelly's spirits, which had been rising, fell again to wrath at the name. "You'd better say you got it from *him*, Molly Green. Don't spare him, poor fellow; whiten yourself."

Molly was beginning to feel just a little wrathful in her turn. Though Jelly was a lady's-maid and superior to herself with her red arms and rough hands, that could not be a reason for attacking her in this way.

"And what if I did get it from him, pray? Come! A plum-pudding prescription's no crime."

"But a copy of an anonymous letter *is*," retorted Jelly, the moment's anger causing her to lose sight of caution. "Don't you try to brazen it out to me, girl."

"WHAT?" cried Molly, staring with all her eyes.

But in the intervening moment Jelly's senses had come back to her. She set herself coolly to remedy the mischief.

"To think that my mind should have run off from the pudding receipt to that letter of poor Mr. Edmund's! It's your fault, Molly Green, bothering my wits out of me! Where *did* you pick up the paper? There. Answer that; and let's end it."

Molly thought it might be as well to end it; she was getting tired of the play: besides, here were Turtle's men coming into the room to finish the carpet.

"I never had the receipt at all, Jelly, and it's not possible it could have dropped from me: that's the blessed truth. After talking to me, just as you've done, and turning me inside out, as one may say, Mrs. Gass as good as confessed that it might have fell out of her own bundle of receipts that she keeps in the sideboard drawer."

Slowly, Jelly arrived at a conviction that Molly Green, in regard to her own non-participation in dropping the paper, must be telling the truth. It did not tend to lessen her wrath.

"Then why on earth have you been keeping up this farce with me? I'll teach you manners, with your betters, girl."

"Well, why did you set upon me?" was the good-humoured answer. "There's no such great treason in dropping a plum-pudding-paper, even if I had done it—which I didn't. 'Taint a love-letter. I don't like to be brow-beat for nothing : and it's not your place to do it, Jelly."

Jelly said no more. Little did she suspect that Mr. Richard North, leaning against the door-post of the half-open drawing-room door, while he watched the movements of the men; had heard every syllable of the colloquy. Coming round to see what progress was being made in the house, before he went to the works for the day, it chanced that he arrived at the same time as Turtle's cart. The new piano was a present from himself to Bessy.

Turtle's men leaving the piano in the hall, went into the room to finish the carpet, and Jelly came out of it. She found her arm touched by Mr. Richard North. He motioned her into the dining-parlor : followed, and closed the door.

"Will you tell me the meaning of what you have just been saying to Molly Green?"

The sudden question—as Jelly acknowledged to herself afterwards—made her creep all over. For once in her life she was dumb.

"I heard all you said, Jelly, happening to be standing accidentally at the door. What was it that was dropped on Mrs. Gass's carpet the night of my brother's illness?"

"It—was—a receipt for making plum-pudding, sir," stammered Jelly, turning a little white.

"I think not, Jelly," replied Richard North, gazing into her eyes with quiet firmness. "You spoke of a copy of an anonymous letter; and I am sure, by your tone, you were then speaking truth. As I have overheard this much, you must give me an explanation."

"I'd have spent a pound out of my pocket, rather than this should have happened," cried Jelly, with much ardour.

"You need not fear to tell *me*. I am no tattler, as you know.

Had there been only the ghost of a chance to stand out

against the command Jelly would have caught at it. But
there was not. She disclosed what she knew: more than she
need have done. Warming with her subject, when the narra-
tive had fairly set in—as it was in Jelly's gossiping nature to
warm—she told also of the interview she had been a partial
witness to between Mrs. Cumberland and the doctor, and the
words she had heard them say.

Richard North looked grave—startled. He said very
little: only cautioned Jelly never to speak of the subject again
to other people.

"I suppose you will be asking Mrs. Gass about it, sir,"
cried Jelly, as he was turning to leave.

"I shall. And should be thankful to hear from her that it
really was nothing more than a receipt for plum-pudding,
Jelly."

Jelly's head gave an incredulous toss. "I hope you'll not
let her think that I up and told you spontaneous, Mr. Richard.
After saying to her that I should never open my lips about it
to living mortal, she'd think I can't keep my word, sir."

"Be at ease, Jelly; she shall not suppose I learnt it by
aught but accident."

"And I am glad he knows it, after all!" decided Jelly to
herself, as she watched him away up the Ham. "Perhaps
he'll now be able to get at the rights and the wrongs."

Richard North walked along, full of tumultuous trouble.
It could not be but that he should have caught up a suspicion
of Oliver Rane—now his brother-in-law—that he might have
been the author of the anonymous letter. How, else, could
its copy have dropped from his pocket-book—if, indeed, it had
so dropped? Jelly had not thrown so much as a shadow of
hint upon the doctor; either she failed to see the obvious in-
ference, or controlled her tongue to caution: but Richard
North could put two-and-two together. He went straight to
Mrs. Gass's, and found that lady at breakfast in her dining-
parlour, with window thrown up to the warm summer air.

"What's it you, Mr. Richard?" she cried, rising to shake
hands. "I am a'most ashamed to be found a-breakfasting
at this hour; but the truth is, I overslept myself: and that
idiot of a girl never came to tell me the time. The first part
of the night I got no sleep at all: 'twere three o'clock afore
I closed my eyes."

"Were you not well?" asked Richard.

"I'd got a touch of my stomach-pain; nothing more.

Which is indigestion, Dr. Rane says: and he's about right. Is it a compliment to ask you to take some breakfast, Mr. Richard, sir? Them eggs are fresh, and here's some downright good tea."

Richard answered that it would be only a compliment; he had breakfasted with his father and Arthur Bohun before leaving home. His eyes ran dreamily over the white damask cloth, as if he were admiring what stood on it; the pretty china, the well-kept silver, the glass with a bunch of fresh roses in it. Mrs. Gass liked to have things nice about her, although people called her vulgar. In reality Richard saw nothing. His mind was absorbed with what he had to ask, and with how he should ask it.

In a pause, made by Mrs. Gass's draining her cup of tea and pushing her plate from her, Richard North bent forward and opened the communication, speaking in a low and confidential tone.

"I have come to you thus early for a little information, Mrs. Gass. Will you kindly tell me what were the contents of the paper that was found here on your carpet, the night of Edmund's seizure?"

From the look that Mrs. Gass's countenance assumed at the question, it might have been thought that she was about to have a seizure herself. Her eyes grew round, her cheek and nose red. For a full minute she made no answer.

"What on earth cause have you to ask me that, Mr. Richard? *You* can't know nothing about it."

"Yes, I can; and do. I know that such a paper was found; I fear it was a copy of the anonymous letter. But I have come to you to learn particulars."

"My patience!" ejaculated Mrs. Gass. "To think you should have got hold of it at last. Who in the world told you, sir?"

"Jelly. But——"

"Drat that girl!" warmly interposed Mrs. Gass. "Her tongue is as long as from here to yonder."

"But not intentionally, I was about to add. I overheard her say a chance word, and I insisted upon her disclosing to me what she knew. There is no blame due to Jelly, Mrs. Gass."

"I say Yes there is, Mr. Richard. What right has she got to blab out chance words about other folk's business? Let her stick to her own. That tongue of hers is worse than a steam-engine: once set it going, it won't be stopped."

"Well, we will leave Jelly. It may be for the better that I should know this. Tell me all about it, my dear old friend."

Thus adjured, Mrs. Gass spoke; telling the tale from the beginning. Richard listened in silence.

"He denied that it came out of his pocket-book?" was the first remark he made.

"Denied it out and out. And then my thoughts turned naturally to Molly Green; for no other stranger had been in the room but them two. He said perhaps she had brought it in her petticoats from the Hall: but I don't think it could have been. I'm afraid—I'm *afraid*, Mr. Richard—that it must have dropped from his pocket-book."

Their eyes met: each hesitating to speak out the conviction lying at heart. Notwithstanding there had been confidential secrets between them before to-day. Richard was thinking that he ought not to have married Bessy—at least, until it was cleared up.

"Why did you not tell me, Mrs. Gass?"

"It was in my mind to do so—I said a word or two—but then, you see, I *couldn't* think it was him that writ it," was her answer. "Mrs. Cumberland told me she saw the anonymous letter itself, Mr. North showed it her, and that it was not a bit like any handwriting she ever met. Suppose he is innocent—would it have been right for me to come out with a tale, even to you, Mr. Richard, that he might have been guilty?"

On this point Richard said no more. All the talking in the world now could not undo the marriage, and he was never one to reproach uselessly. Mrs. Gass resumed.

"If I had spoke ever so, I don't suppose it would have altered things, Mr. Richard. There was no proof; and, failing that, you'd not have liked to say anything at all to Miss Bessy. Any way they are man and wife now."

"I hope—I *hope* he did not write it!" said Richard fervently.

Mrs. Gass gave a sweep with her arm to all the china together, as she bent her earnest, red face nearer Richard's.

"Let's remember this much to our comfort, Mr. Richard: if it *was* him, he never thought to harm a hair of your brother's head. He must have writ it to damage Alexander. Oliver Rane has looked upon Alexander as his mortal enemy,—as a

man who ought to be kicked,—as a man who did him a right
down bad turn and spoilt his prospects,—as a man upon whom
it was a'most a duty to be revenged."

"Do you think this?" cried Richard, rather at sea.

"No; but I say he thinks it. He never meant worse nor
better by the letter than to drive Alexander away from the
place where, as Rane fancies, he only got a footing by treachery.
That is, *if* he writ it: sometimes I think he did, and sometimes
I think he didn't."

"What is to be done?"

"Nothing. You can do nothing. You and me must just
bury it between us, Mr. Richard, sir, for Miss Bessy's sake.
It would be a nasty thing for her if a whisper of this should
go abroad, let him be as innocent as the babe unborn. They
are fond of one another, and it would just be a cruelty to have
stopped the marriage with *this*. He is a good-intentioned
man, and I don't see but what they'll be happy together. Let
us hope that he has made his peace with the Lord, and that it
won't be visited upon him."

"Amen!" was the mental response of Richard North.

CHAPTER XIII.

COMING HOME.

DASHING up to Dallory Hall in a fiery foam, just a week and a
day after the wedding, came Mrs. North. Madam had learnt
the news. While she was reposing in all security in Paris,
amid a knot of friends who had chosen to be there at that
season, Matilda North happened to take up a *Times* newspaper
of some two or three days old, and saw the account of the
marriage: "Oliver Rane, M.D., of Dallory Ham, to Bessy,
daughter of John North, of Dallory Hall, and of Elizabeth, his
first wife." Madam rose up, her face in a flame, and clutched
the journal to look: she verily believed Miss Matilda was
playing a farce. No: the announcement was there in plain
black and white. Making her hasty arrangements to quit
the French Capital, she came thundering home: and arrived
the very day that Dr. and Mrs. Rane returned.

A letter had preceded her. A letter of denouncing wrath,
that had made her husband shake in his shoes. Poor Mr.
North looked tremblingly out for the arrival, caught a glimpse
of the carriage and of Madam's face, and slipped out at the

back door to the fields. Where he remained wandering about for hours.

So Madam found nobody to receive her. Richard was at the works, Captain Bohun had been out all the afternoon.

Nothing increases wrath like the having no object to expend it on; and Madam foiled, might have sat for a picture of fury. The passion that had been bubbling up higher and higher all the way from Paris, found no escape at its boiling point.

One of the servants happened to come in her way; the first housemaid, who had been head over Molly Green. Madam stopped her; bit her lips for calmness, and then enquired particulars of the wedding with a smooth face.

" Was it a run-away match, Lake ? "

"Goodness, no, Madam !" was Lake's answer, who was apt to be free with her tongue, even to her imperious mistress. "Things were being got ready for a month beforehand; and my master would have gone to church to give Miss Bessy away himself, but for not being well. All us servants went to see it."

Little by little, Madam heard the details. Captain Bohun was best man; Mr. Richard took out Miss Adair, who was bridesmaid, and looked lovely to behold. The bride and bridegroom drove right away from the church door. Captain Bohun went back in the carriage with Miss Adair; Mr. Richard went off on foot to the works. Miss Bessy—leastways Mrs. Oliver Rane now—had had some furniture sent to her new home from the Hall, and Molly Green was there as housemaid. That Lake should be glowing with intense gratification at being enabled to tell all this, was only in accordance with frail human nature: she knew what a pill it was for Madam ; and Madam was disliked in the household worse than poison. But Lake was hardly prepared for the ashy tint that spread over Madam's features, when she came to the part that told of the homeward drive together of her son and Ellen Adair.

The girl was in the midst of her descriptions when Arthur Bohun came in. Madam saw him sauntering lazily up the gravel drive, and swept down in her fine Parisian costume of white-and-black brocaded silk, lappets of lace floating from her hair. They met in the Hall.

" Why! is it you, mother ? " cried Arthur in surprise—for he had no idea the invasion might be expected so soon. " Have you come home ? "

He advanced to kiss her. Striving to be as dutiful as she

would let him be, he was willing to observe all ordinary relations between mother and son : but of affection there existed none. Mrs. North drew back from the offered embrace, and haughtily motioned him to the drawing-room. Matilda sat there, sullen and listless : she was angry at being dragged summarily from Paris.

"Why did I assist at Bessy's wedding?" replied Arthur, parrying the attack with light good humour, as he invariably strove to do on these wrathful occasions. "Because I liked it. It was great fun. Especially to see Rane hunting in every pocket for the ring, and turning as red as a salamander."

"What business had you to do such a thing?" retorted Madam, her face dark with the passion she was suppressing. "How dared you do it?"

"Do what, Madam?"

Madam stamped a little. "You know without asking, sir; countenance personally the wedding."

"Was there any reason why I should not? Bessy stands to me as a sister : and I like her. I am glad she is married, and I hope sincerely they'll have the best of luck always."

"I had forbidden the union with Oliver Rane," stamped Madam. "Do you hear?—*forbidden it.* You knew that as well as she did."

"But then, don't you see, mother mine, you had no particular right to forbid it. If Matilda there took it into her head to marry some knight or other, you would have a voice in the matter, for or against; but Bessy was responsible to her father only."

"Don't bring my name into your nonsense, Arthur," struck in Matilda, with a frown.

Madam, looking from one to the other, was biting her lips.

"They had the wedding while you were away that it might be got over quietly," resumed Arthur, in his laughing way. determined not to give in an inch, even though he had to tell a home truth or two. "For my part, mother, I have never understood what possible objection you could have to Rane."

"That is my business," spoke Mrs. North. "I wish he and those Cumberland people were all at the bottom of the sea. How dared you disgrace yourself, Arthur Bohun?"

"Disgrace myself?"

"You did. You, a Bohun, to descend to a companionship with *them!* Fie upon you! And you have been said to inherit your father's pride."

"As I hope I do, in all proper things. I am unable to understand your distinctions, Madam," he added, laughingly. "Rane is as good as Bessy, for all I see. As good as we are."

Madam caught up a hand screen, as if she would have liked to fling it at him. Her hand trembled, with emotion or temper.

"There's some girl living with them. They tell me you went home with her in the carriage!"

Arthur Bohun suddenly turned his back upon them, as if to see who might be coming, for distant footsteps were heard advancing. But for that, Madam might have seen a hot flush illumine his face.

"Well? What else, mother? Of course I took her home —Miss Adair."

"In the face and eyes of Dallory!"

"Certainly. And we had faces and eyes out that morning, I can tell you. It is not every day a Miss North gets married."

"How came *you* to take her?"

"Dick asked me. There was nobody else to ask, you see. Mrs. Gass clapped us going by, as if we had been an election. She had a stiff shining yellow gown on and white bows in her cap."

His suavity was so great, his determination not to be ruffled so evident, that Mrs. North felt three parts foiled. It was not often she attacked Arthur; he always met it in this way, and no satisfaction came of it. She could have struck him as he stood.

"What *is* the true tale about the ring, Arthur?" asked Matilda, in the silence come to by Mrs. North. "Lake says Oliver Rane really lost it."

"Really and truly, Matty."

"Were they married without a ring?"

"Somebody present produced one," he replied carelessly, in his invincible dislike to mention Ellen Adair before his mother and sister: a dislike that had ever clung to him. Did it arise from the shy reticence that invariably attends love, this feeling?—or could it have been some foreshadowing, dread instinct of what the future was to bring forth?

"How came Dr. Rane to lose the ring?"

"Carelessness, I suppose. We found it in the carriage, going home. He must have dropped it accidentally."

"Peace Matilda!—Keep your foolish questions for a fitting

time," stormed Madam. "How dare you turn your back upon me, Arthur? What money has gone out with the girl?"

Arthur turned round to answer. In spite of his careless manner, he was biting his lips with shame and vexation. It was so often he had to blush for his mother.

"I'm sure I don't know, if you mean with Bessy; it is not my business that I should presume to ask. Here comes Dick: I thought it was his step. You can inquire of him, Madam."

Richard North looked into the drawing-room, all unconscious of the storm awaiting him. Matilda sat back in an easy chair tapping her foot discontentedly; Arthur Bohun toyed with a rose at the window; Madam, standing upright by the beautiful inlaid table, her train sweeping the rich carpet, confronted him.

But there was something about Richard North that instinctively subdued Madam; she had never domineered over him as she did over her husband, and Bessy, and Arthur; and at him she did not rave and rant. Calm always, sufficiently courteous to her, and yet holding his own in self-respect, Richard and Madam seldom came to an issue. But she attacked him now: demanding why this iniquity—the wedding—had been allowed to be enacted.

"Pardon me, Mrs. North, if I meet your question by another," calmly spoke Richard. "You complain of my sister's marriage as though it were a grievous wrong against yourself. What is the reason?"

"I said it should not take place."

"Will you tell me why you oppose it?"

"No. It is sufficient that, to my mind, it did not present itself as suitable. I have resolutely set my face against Dr. Rane and his statue of a mother, who presumes to call the Master of Dallory Hall John! And I forbade Bessy to think of him."

"But—pardon me, Mrs. North—Bessy was not bound to obey you. Her father and I saw no cause for objecting to Dr. Rane."

"Was it right, was it honourable, that you should seize upon my absence to marry her in this indecent manner?— before Edmund was cold in his grave?"

"Circumstances guide cases," said Richard. "As for marrying her while you were away, it was done in the interests of peace. Your opposition, had you been at home, would not have prevented the marriage; it was therefore as well to get it over in quietness."

A bold avowal. Richard stood before Madam when he made it, upright as herself. She saw it was useless to contend: and all the abuse in the world would not undo it now.

"What money has gone out with her?"

It was a question that she had no right to put. Richard answered it, however.

"At present, not any. To-morrow I shall give Rane a cheque for two hundred pounds. Time was, Madam, when I thought my sister would have gone from us with twenty thousand."

"We are not speaking of what was, but of what is," said Madam, an unpleasant sneer on her face. "Mr. North—to hear him speak—cannot spare the two hundred."

"Quite true; Mr. North has it not to spare," said Richard. "It is I who give it to my sister. Drained though we are for money perpetually, I could not, for very shame, suffer Bessy to go to her husband wholly penniless."

"She has not gone penniless," retorted Madam, brazening the thing out. "I hear the Hall has been dismantled for her."

"Oh, mother!" interposed Arthur in a burst of pain.

"Hold your tongue; it is no affair of *yours*," spoke Mrs. North. "A cart-load of furniture has gone out of the Hall."

"Bessy's own," said Richard. "It was her mother's; and we have always considered it Bessy's. A few poor mahogany things, Madam, that you have never condescended to take notice of, and that never, in point of fact, have belonged to you. They have gone with Bessy, poor girl; and I trust Rane will make her a happier home than she has had here."

"I trust they will both be miserable," flashed Madam.

Equable in temper though Richard North was, there are limits to endurance; he found his anger rising, and quitted the room abruptly. Arthur Bohun went limping after him: in any season of emotion, he was undeniably lame.

"I'd beg your pardon for her, Dick, in all entreaty," he whispered, putting his arm within Richard's, "but that my tongue is tied with shame and humiliation. It was an awful misfortune for you all when your father married her."

"We can but make the best of it, Arthur," was the kindly answer. "It was neither your fault nor mine."

"Where is the good old pater?"

"Hiding somewhere. Not a doubt of it."

"Let us go and find him, Dick. He may be the better for having us with him to-day. If she was not my mother—and upon my word and honour, Richard, I sometimes think she is not—I'd strap on my armour and do brave battle for him."

The bride and bridegroom were settling down in their house. Bessy, arranging her furniture in her new home, was busy and happy as the summer day was long. Some of the mahogany things were sadly old-fashioned, but the fact never occurred to Bessy. The carpet was bright; the piano, Richard's present, and a great surprise, was beautiful. It was so kind of him to give her one—she who was but a poor player at best, and had thought of asking Madam to be allowed to have the unused old thing in the old school-room at Dallory Hall. She clung to Richard with tears in her eyes as she kissed and thanked him. He kissed her again, and gave his good wishes for her happiness, but Bessy thought him somewhat out of spirits. Richard North handed over two hundred pounds to them: a most acceptable offering to Dr. Rane.

"Thank you, Richard," he heartily said, grasping his brother-in-law's hand. "I shall be getting on so well shortly as to need no help for my wife's sake or for mine." And Richard knew that he was anticipating the period when the other doctor should have gone, and the whole practice be in his own hands.

It was on the third or fourth morning after their return, that Dr. Rane, coming home from seeing his patients, met his fellow-surgeon, arm-in-arm with a stranger. Mr. Alexander stopped to introduce him.

"Mr. Seeley, Rane," he said. "My friend and successor."

Had a shot been fired at Dr. Rane, he could scarcely have felt more. In the moment's confused blow, he almost stammered.

"Your successor? Here?"

"My successor in the practice. I have sold him the good-will, and he has come down to be introduced."

Dr. Rane bowed. The new doctor put out his hand. That same day Dr. Rane went over to Mr. Alexander's and reproached him.

"You might at least have given me the refusal had you wanted to sell it."

"My good fellow, I promised it to Seeley ages ago," was

the answer. "He knew I had a prospect of the London appointment : in fact, helped me to get it."

What was to be said ? Nothing. But Oliver Rane felt as though a bitter blow had again fallen upon him, blighting the fair vista of the future.

"Don't be down-hearted, Oliver," whispered Bessy, hopefully, as she clung around him when he went in and spoke of the disappointment. "We shall be just as happy with a small practice as a large one. It will all come right—with God's blessing on us."

But Oliver Rane, looking back on a certain deed of the past, felt by no means sure in his heart of hearts that the blessing would be upon them.

CHAPTER XIV.

OF WHAT WAS, AND OF WHAT MIGHT BE.

BESSY RANE sat at the large window of her dining-room in the coming twilight. Some twelve months had elapsed since her marriage, and summer was round again. Her work had dropped on her lap: it was that of stitching some wristbands for her husband: and she sat inhaling the fresh sweet scent of the garden flowers, and watching Jelly's movements in the dining-room facing her—Mrs. Cumberland's. Jelly had a candle in her hand, apparently searching for something, for she was throwing its light and her own eyes into every hole and corner. Bessy stooped forward to pluck a sprig of sweet verbena, and sat on tranquilly.

At the table behind her sat Dr. Rane, writing as fast as the decreasing light would allow. Some unusual and peculiar symptoms had manifested themselves in a patient he had been recently attending, and he was making them and the case into a paper for a medical publication, in the hope that it would bring him back a remunerating guinea or two.

"Oliver, I am sure you can't see," said Bessy presently, looking round.

"It is almost blindman's holiday, dear. Will you ring for the lamp?"

Mrs. Rane rose. But, instead of ringing for the lamp, she went up to him, and put her hand on his shoulder persuasively.

"Take a quarter of an hour's rest, Oliver. You will find all the benefit of it; and it is not quite time to light the lamp. Let us take a stroll in the garden."

"You are obstructing what little light is left, Bessy; standing between me and the window."

"Of course I am. I'm doing it on purpose. Come! You ought to know a great deal better than I do that it is bad to try the eyes, sir. *Please*, Oliver."

Yielding to her entreaties, he pushed the paper from him with a sigh of weariness, and they stepped from the window into the garden. Bessy passed her hand within his arm; and, turning towards the more covert paths, they began to converse with one another in a semi-whisper.

Many a twilight half-hour had they thus paced together of late, talking together of what was and of what might be. The first year of their marriage had not been one of success in a pecuniary point of view; for Dr. Rane's practice improved not. He earned barely enough for their moderate wants. Bessy, the cash-keeper, had a difficulty in making both ends meet. But the fact was not known; never a syllable of it transpired from either of them. Dr. Rane was seen out and about a great deal, going to and fro among his patients; and the world did not suspect his returns were so poor.

The new surgeon, Seeley, had stepped into all Mr. Alexander's practice, and was flourishing. Dr. Rane's, as before, was chiefly confined to the lower classes, especially those belonging to the North Works; and from certain circumstances, these men were not so full of funds as they had been, and consequently not so well able to pay him. That Dr. Rane was bitterly mortified at not getting on better, for his wife's sake as well as his own, could not be mistaken. Bessy preached of hope cheerfully; of a bright future in store yet; but he had lost faith in it.

It seemed to Dr. Rane that everything was a failure. The medical book he had been engaged upon in persevering industry at the time of his marriage, from which he had anticipated great things both in fame and fortune, had not met with success. He had succeeded in getting it published; but as yet there were no returns. He had sacrificed a sum of money towards its publication; not a very large sum, it's true, but larger than they could afford, and nobody but themselves knew how it had crippled them. Bessy said it would come back some day with plenty of interest; they had only to keep up a good heart and live frugally.

Poor Bessy herself had one grief that she never spoke of even to him—the lack of offspring. There had been no prospect of it whatever; and she so loved children! As week after week, month after month went by without bringing sign, her disappointment was very keen. She was beginning to get a little reconciled to it now; and grew only the more devoted to her husband.

Mrs. Rane was an excellent manager in the household, spending the smallest fraction that she could, consistent with comfort. It had not yet come to the lack of *that.* At the turn of the previous winter old Phillis became ill and had to leave; and Bessy had since kept only Molly Green. By a fortunate chance Molly understood cooking; she had grown to be a really excellent servant. At the small rate of expense they lived at now, Dr. Rane might perhaps have managed to continue to meet it while he waited patiently for better luck; but he did not intend to do anything of the kind. His only anxiety was to remove to another place, as far away as might be from Dallory Ham.

Whether this thirst for migration would have arisen had his practice been successful, cannot be told. We can only relate things as they were. With the disappointment—and other matters—lying upon him, the getting away from Dallory had grown into a wild, burning desire, that never quitted him by night or by day. That one fatal mistake of his life seemed to hang over him like a curse. It's true that when he penned the letter so disastrous in its result, he had no more intention in his heart of slaying or killing than had the paper he wrote on; he had only thought of putting Alexander into disfavour at Dallory Hall; but it had turned out as it had turned out, and Dr. Rane felt that he had a life to answer for. He might have borne this; and at any rate his running away from Dallory would neither lessen the heart's burden nor add to it; but what he could not bear was the prospect of detection. Not a day passed but he saw somebody or other whose face tacitly reminded him that such discovery might take place. He felt sure that Mrs. Gass suspected him still of having written the letter; he knew that his mother doubted it; he picked up a half suspicion of Jelly; he had more than half a one of Richard North; and how many others there might be he knew not. Ever since the time when he returned from his marriage trip, he thought there had been an involuntary constraint in Richard's manner to him; it could not be his fancy. As to Jelly, the way he sometimes caught her green eyes observing him, was enough to give the shivers to a nervous man, which Dr. Rane was not. How he could have committed the fatal mistake of putting that copy—or semi-copy—of the miserable letter into his pocket-book, he never knew. He had tried his writing and his words on two or three pieces of paper, but he surely thought he had torn all up and burnt the pieces.

Over and over again, looking back upon his carelessness, he
said to himself that it was Fate. Not carelessness, in one
sense of the word. Carelessness if you will, but a carelessness
that he could not go from in the arbitrary dominion of Fate.
Fate had been controlling him with her iron hand, to bring his
crime home to him; and he could not escape it. Whatever it
might have been, however—Fate, or want of caution—it had
led to his being a suspected man by some few around him; and
continue to live amidst them he would not. Dr. Rane was a
proud-natured man, liking in an especial degree to stand well
in the estimation of his fellow-creatures; to have such a degradation as this brought publicly home to him would go well
nigh to kill him with shame. Rather than face it he would
have run away to the remotest quarter of the habitable globe.

And he had quite imbued Bessy with the wish for change.
She but thought as he thought. Never suspecting the true
cause of his wish to get away and establish himself elsewhere,
she only saw how real it was. Of this they talked, night after
night, pacing the garden paths. "There seems to have been
a spell of ill-luck attending me ever since I settled in this
place," he would say to her; "and I know it won't be lifted
off while I stop." He was saying it on this very night.

"I hate the place, Bessy," he observed, looking up at the
bright evening star that began to show itself in the clear blue
sky. "But for my mother and you I should never have stayed
in it. I wish I had the money to buy a practice elsewhere.
As it is, I must establish one."

"Yes," acquiesced Bessy. "But where? The great thing
is—what other place to fix upon."

Of course that was the chief thing. Dr. Rane looked down
and kept silence, pondering various matters in his mind. He
thought it had better be London. A friend of his, one Dr.
Jones, who had been a fellow-student in their student days,
was doing a large practice as a medical man in the neighbourhood of New York: he wanted assistance, and had proposed
to Dr. Rane to go over and join him. Nothing in the world
would Dr. Rane have liked better; and Bessy was willing to
go where he went, even to quit her native land for good; but
Dr. Jones did not offer this without an equivalent, and the
terms he named to be paid down, £500, were entirely beyond
the reach of Oliver Rane. So he supposed it must be London.
With the two hundred pounds that he hoped to get for the
good-will of his own practice in Dallory Ham—at this very

moment he was trying to negociate with a gentleman for it in private—he should set up in London, or else purchase a small share in an established practice. Anything, anywhere, to get away, and to leave the nightmare of daily-dreaded discovery behind him!

"Once we are away from this place, Bessy, we shall get on. I feel sure of it. You won't long have to live like a hermit, from dread of the cost of entertaining company, or to look at every sixpence before you lay it out."

"I don't mind it, Oliver. You know how sorry I should be if you thought of giving up our home here for my sake."

"But I don't; it's for my own as well," he hastily added. "You can't realize what it is, Bessy, for a clever medical man —and I am that—to be beaten back ever into obscurity; to find no field for his talents; to watch others of his generation rise into note and usefulness. I have not got on here! Madam has schemed to prevent it. Why she should have pushed on Alexander; why she should push Seeley; not for their sakes, but to oppose me, I have never been able to imagine. Unless it was that my mother, when Fanny Gass, and Mr. North were intimate as brother and sister in early life."

"And Madam despises the Gass family, and ours equally. It was a black-letter day for us all when papa married her."

"It is no reason why she should have set her face against *me*. It has been a fatal blight on me : worse than you and the world think for, Bessy."

"I am sure you must have felt it so," murmured Bessy. "And she would have stopped our marriage if she could."

"Whoever succeeds me here will speedily make a good practice of it. You'll see. She has kept me from doing it. There's one blessed thing—her evil influence cannot follow us elsewhere."

"I should like to become rich and have a large house, and get poor papa to live with us," said Bessy hopefully. "Madam is worrying him into his grave with her cruel temper. Oh, Oliver, I should like him to come !"

"I'm sure I'd not object," replied Dr. Rane good-naturedly.

"How they will keep up the expenses at Dallory Hall if this strike be prolonged, I cannot think. Serve Madam right!"

"Do you hear much of the trouble, Oliver ?"

"Much of it! Why, I hear nothing else. The men are fools. They'll cut their own throats as sure as a gun. Your brother Richard sees it coming."

" Sees what ?" asked Bessy, not exactly understanding.

" Ruin," emphatically replied Dr. Rane. " The men will play at bo-peep with reason until the trade has left them. Fools! Fools!"

" It's not the poor men, Oliver. I have lived amongst them, some of them at any rate, since I was a child, and I don't like to hear them blamed. It is that they are misled. Misled by the trades' unions."

" Nonsense!" replied Dr. Rane. " A man who has his living to earn ought not to allow himself to be misled. There's his work to hand; let him do it. A body of would-be autocrats might come down on me and say, ' Oliver Rane, we want you to join our society: which forbids doctors to visit patients except under its own rules and regulations.' Suppose I listened to them ?—and stayed at home, and let Seeley, or anybody else who would, snap up my practice, and awoke presently to find my means of living irrevocably gone ?—nothing left for me but the workhouse ? Should I deserve pity ? Certainly not."

Bessy laughed a little. They were going in, and she—still keeping her hand within his arm—coaxed him yet for another minute's recreation into the drawing-room. Sitting down to the piano in the fading light—the piano that Richard had given her—she began a song that her husband was fond of, " O Bay of Dublin." That sweet song set to the air of " Groves of Blarney," by the late Lady Dufferin. Bessy's voice was weak and of no compass, but true and rather sweet; and she had that, by no means common, gift of rendering every word as distinctly heard as though it were spoken : so that her singing was pleasant to listen to. Her husband liked it. He leaned against the window-frame, now as she sang, in a deep reverie, gazing out on Dallory Ham, and at the man lighting the road-side lamps. Dr. Rane never heard this song but he wished he was the emigrant singing it, with some wide ocean flowing between him and home.

" What's this, I wonder ?"

Some woman, whom he did not recognize, had turned in at his gate and was ringing the door-bell. Dr. Rane found he was called out to a patient: one of the profitless people as usual.

" Piersons want me, Bessy," he looked into the room to say. " The man's worse. I shall not be long."

And Bessy rose when she heard the street-door closed.

Taking a clean duster from the drawer, she carefully passed it over the keys before closing her piano for the night. Very much did Bessy cherish her drawing-room and its furniture. They did not use it much : not from fear of spoiling it, but because the other room with its large bay window seemed the most cheery ; and people feel more at ease in the room they commonly sit in. Bessy took pride in her house as though it had been one of the grandest in all Dallory : happy as a queen in it, felt she. Stepping lightly over the drawing-room carpet —fresh as the day when it came out of Turtle's warehouse— touching, with a gentle finger, some pretty thing or other on the tables as she passed, she opened the door and called to the servant.

" Molly, it is time these shutters were shut."

Molly Green, in a bit of a cap tilted on her hair behind, and a white muslin apron, came out of the kitchen hard by. Molly liked to be as smart as the best of them, although she had the whole work to do. Which whole was not very much when aided by her mistress's help and good-management.

" You had better light the hall-lamp," added Mrs. Rane, as she went up stairs.

It was tolerably light yet. Bessy often did what she was about to do—namely, draw down the window-blinds ; it saved Molly the trouble. The wide landing was less bare than it used to be ; at the time of Dr. Rane's marriage he had covered it with some green drugget, and put a chair and a book-shelf there. It still looked too large, still presented a contrast with the luxuriously furnished landing of Mrs. Cumberland's opposite, especially when the two wide windows happened to be open ; but Bessy thought her own good enough. Of the two back rooms, one had been furnished as a spare bed-chamber ; the other had not much in it beside Bessy's boxes that had come from the Hall. Richard had spoken kindly to her about this last chamber. " Should any contingency arise ; sickness, or else ; that you should require its use, Bessy," he said, " and Rane not find it quite convenient to spare money for furniture, let me know, and I'll do it for you." She had thanked him gratefully : but the contingency had not come yet.

Into this back room first went Bessy, passed by her boxes, closed the window, and drew the white blind down. From thence into the chamber by its side—a pretty room with chintz curtains to the window and the Arabian bed. Dr. Rane was very particular about having plenty of air in his house, and would have every window open all day long. Next, Bessy crossed the landing back again to her own chamber. She had to pass through the drab room (as may be remembered) to get to it. The drab room was just in the same state that it used to be; its floor bare, Dr. Rane's glass jars and other articles used in chemistry lying on one side it. Formerly they were strewed about anywhere : under Bessy's neat rule they were gathered together into a small space. Sometimes Bessy thought she should like to make this her own sitting and work-room : its window looked to the fields beyond Dallory Ham. Often, when she first came to the house, she would softly say to her secret heart, " What a nice day-nursery it would make ! " She had left off saying it now.

Taking some work from a drawer in her own room, which was what she went up for—for she knew that Oliver would tell her to leave off if she attempted to stitch the wristbands by candle-light—she stood for a minute at the window and saw some gentleman, whom she did not recognise, turn out of Mr. Seeley's, and go towards Dallory.

" A fresh patient," she thought to herself, with a sigh very like envy. " He gets them all. I wish a few would come to Oliver."

As she watched the stranger up the road, something in his height and make put her in sudden mind of her dead brother, Edmund. All her thoughts went back to the unhappy time of his death, and to the letter that had led to it.

" It's very good of Oliver to comfort me, saying he could not in any case have lived long—and I suppose it was so," murmured Bessy ; " but that does not make it any the less shocking. He was killed. Cut off without warning by that anonymous, wicked letter. And I don't believe the writer will be ever traced now : even Richard seems to have cooled in the pursuit, since he discovered it was not the man he had suspected."

Close upon the return of Dr. and Mrs. Rane after their marriage, the tall, thin stranger who had been seen with Timothy Wilks the night before the anonymous letter was sent, and whom Richard North and others fully believed to have been the writer, was discovered. It proved to be a poor artist, travelling the country to take sketches—who was sometimes rather too fond of being a boon companion with whatever company he might happen to fall into. Hovering hero some days, hovering there, all in pursuit of his calling, he at length made his head-quarters at Whitborough. Hearing he was suspected, he came voluntarily forward, and convinced Richard North that he at least had had nothing to do with the letter. Richard's answer was that he fully believed him. And perhaps it was Richard North's manner at this time, coupled with a remark he made to the effect that "it might be better to allow all speculation on the point to rest," that first gave Dr. Rane the idea of Richard's suspicion of himself. Things had been left at rest since : and even Bessy, as we see, thought her brother was growing cold.

Turning from the window with a sigh, given to the memory of her dead brother, she passed through the ante-room to the landing on her way downstairs. Mrs. Cumberland's landing opposite gave forth a brilliant light as usual—for that lady liked to burn plenty of lamps in her hall and staircases—and Ann, the housemaid, was drawing down the window blind. Mrs. Rane's window had never had a blind.

Molly Green was taking the supper-tray into the dining-room when she got down. Bessy hovered about it, seeing that things were as her husband liked them. She put his slippers ready, she drew his arm-chair forward ; ever solicitous for his comfort. To wait on him and make things pleasant for him was the great happiness of her life. After that she sat down and worked by lamp-light, awaiting his return.

While Dr. Rane, walking forth to see his patient and walking home again, was buried in an unpleasant reverie, like a man in a dream. That one dreadful mistake lay always with heavier weight upon him at the solitary evening hour. Now and again he would almost fancy he should see Edmund North looking out at him from the road-side hedges or behind trees. At any sacrifice he must get away from the place, and then perhaps a chance of peace might come : at least from this ever-haunting dread of discovery. He would willingly give the half of his remaining life to undo that past dark night's work.

CHAPTER XV.

MRS. GASS AMID THE WORKMEN.

THERE was trouble amidst the Dallory workpeople. It had been looming for some time before it came. No works throughout the kingdom had been more successfully carried on than the North Works. The men were well paid; peace and satisfaction had always reigned between them and their employers. But when some delegates, or emissaries, or whatever they may please to call themselves, arrived stealthily at Dallory from the Trades' Unions, and took up their stealthy abode in the place, and whispered their stealthy whispers into the ears of the men, the peace was over.

It matters not to trace the working of these insidious whispers, or how the poison spread. Others have done it far more effectively and to the purpose than I could. Sufficient to say that the Dallory workpeople caught the infection prevailing amidst other bodies of men—which the public, to its cost, has of late years known too much of—and they joined the ranks of the disaffected. First there had been doubt, and misgiving, and wavering; then agitation; then dissatisfaction; then parleying with their master, Richard North; then *demands* to be paid more and do less work. In vain Richard, with his strong good sense, argued and reasoned: showing them, in all kindness, not in anger, how mistaken was the course they were entering on, and what must come of it. They listened to him with respect, for he was liked and esteemed; but they would not give in a jot. It had been told privately to Richard that much argument and holding-out had been carried on with the Trades' Union emissaries, some of whom were ever hovering over Dallory like birds of prey: the workmen wanting to insist on the sound sense of Richard North's views of things, the others speciously disproving. But it came to nothing. The workmen yielded to their despotic lords and rulers just as submissively as others have done, and Richard's words were set at nought. They were like so many tame sheep following blindly their leader. The agitation, beginning about the time of Bessy North's marriage, continued for many months; it then came to an issue; and for several weeks now the works had been shut up.

For the men had struck. North and Gass had valuable contracts on hand, and they could not be completed. Unless matters took a turn speedily, masters and men would alike be ruined. The ruin of the first involved that of the last.

Mrs. Gass took things more equably than Richard North. In one sense she had less cause to take them otherwise. Her prosperity did not depend on the works. A large sum of hers was certainly invested in them; but a larger one was in other securities safe and sure. If the works and their capital went to nought, the only difference it would make to Mrs. Gass was, that she would have so much the less money to leave behind her when she died. In this sense therefore Mrs. Gass could take things calmly: but in regard to the men's conduct she was far more outspoken and severe than Richard.

Dallory presented a curious scene. In former days, during work time not an idle man was to be met: the village street, the various outlets, had looked almost deserted, save for the playing children. Now the narrow thoroughfares were blocked up with groups of men; talking seriously, or chaffing with each other, as might be; most of them smoking and spitting, and all looking utterly sick of the wearily-passing hours. Work does not tire a man—or woman either—half as much as idleness.

At first the holiday was agreeable from its novelty; the six days were each a Sunday, as well as the seventh; and the men and women lived in clover. Not one family in twenty had been sufficiently provident to put by money for a rainy day, good though their wages had been; but the trades' unions took care of their new protégés, and supplied them with funds. But as the weeks went on, and Richard North gave no sign of relenting—that is, of acceding to his men's demands by taking them on again at their terms—the funds did not come in so liberally. Husbands, not accustomed to be stinted; wives, not knowing how to make sixpence suffice for a shilling, might be excused if they felt a little put out; and they began to take things to the pawnbroker's. Mr. Ducket, the respectable functionary who presided over the interests of the three gilt balls at Dallory, rubbed his hands complacently as he took the articles in. Being gifted with a long sharp nose, his scent was keen, and he smelt the good time coming.

One day, in passing the shop, Mrs. Gass saw three women in it. She walked in herself; and, with scant ceremony, demanded what they were pledging. The women slunk away, hiding their property under their aprons, and leaving their errand to be completed another time. That Mrs. Gass or their master, Richard North, should see them at this work, brought humiliation to their minds and shame to their cheeks. Richard North and Mrs. Gass had both told them (to their intense disbelief) that it would come to this: and to be detected in the actual fact of pledging, seemed very like a tacit defeat.

"So you've began, have you, Ducket?" commenced Mrs. Gass.

"Began what, ma'am?" asked Ducket; a little, middle-aged man with watery eyes and weak hair; always deferent in manner to the wealthy and fine Mrs. Gass.

"Began what! Why, the spouting. I told 'em all they'd come to the pawn-shop."

"It's them that have begun the spouting, ma'am; not me."

"Where do you suppose it will end, Ducket?"

Ducket shook his head meekly, intimating that he couldn't suppose. He was naturally meek in disposition, and the brow-beating he habitually underwent in the course of business from his customers of the fairer sex had tended to subdue his spirit and make him mild as honey.

"It'll just end in their pawning every earthly thing their home has got inside of 'em, leaving them to the four naked walls," said Mrs. Gass. "And the next move 'll be into the work'us."

In the presence of Mrs. Gass, Ducket did not choose to show any sense of latent profit this wholesale pledging might bring to him. On the contrary, he affected to see nothing but gloom.

"A nice prospect for us rate-payers, ma'am, that 'nd be! Taxes be heavy enough, as it is, in Dallory parish, without having all these workmen and their families throw'd on us to eat us up."

"If the taxes was of my mind, Ducket, they'd let the men starve, rather than help 'em. When strong, able-bodied artizans have got plenty of work to do, and won't do it, it's time for them to be taught a lesson. As sure as you be standing on that side your counter, and me on this, them misbeguided men will come to want a mouldy crust."

"Well, I'd not wish 'em as bad as that," said Ducket, who,

apart from the hardness induced by his trade, was rather soft-hearted. "Perhaps Mr. Richard North 'll give in."

"Mr. Richard North give in!" echoed Mrs. Gass. "Don't you upset your brains with perhapsing that, Ducket. Who ought to give in—looking at the rights and wrongs of the question—North and Gass, or the men? Tell me that."

"Well, I think the men are wrong," acknowledged the pawnbroker, smoothing down his coarse white linen apron. "And foolish too."

Mrs. Gass nodded several times, a significant look on her pleasant-natured face. She wore a top-knot of white feathers, and they bowed majestically with the movement.

"Maybe they'll live to see it, too. They will, unless their senses come back to 'em pretty quick. Look here, Ducket: what I was about to say is this—don't be too free to take their traps in."

Ducket's face assumed a rueful cast, but Mrs. Gass was looking at him evidently waiting for an answer.

"I don't see my way clear for refusing of things when they be brought to me, Mrs. Gass, ma'am. The women 'ud only go off to Whitborough and pledge 'em there."

"Then they should go—for me."

"Yes, ma'am," rejoined the man, not knowing what else to say.

"I'm not particular squeamish, Ducket; trade's trade; and a pawnbroker must live as well as other people. I don't say but what the money he lends does sometimes a world of good to them that's got no other help to turn to—and, maybe, through no fault of their own, poor things. But when it comes to the dismantling of homes by the dozen and the score, and the leaving of families as naked and destitute as ever they were when they came into this blessed world, that's different. And I'd not like to have it on my conscience, Ducket, though I was ten pawnbrokers."

Mrs. Gass quitted the shop with the last words, leaving Ducket to digest them. In passing North Inlet, she saw a group of the disaffected collected together, and turned out of her way to speak to them. Mrs. Gass was entirely at home, so to say, with every one of the men at the works; more so, perhaps, than a lady of better birth and breeding could ever have been. She found fault with them, and commented on their failings as familiarly as though she had been one of themselves. Of the whole body of workpeople, not more than three or four had consistently raised their voices against the strike. These few would willingly have gone to work again, and thought it a terrible hardship that they could not: but of course the refusal of the many to return practically closed the gates on all. Richard North could not keep his business going with only half-a-dozen pairs of hands in it.

"Well," began Mrs. Gass, "what's the time o' day with you men?"

The men parted at the address, and touched their caps. The "time o' day" meant, as they knew, anything but the literal question.

"How much longer do you intend to lead the lives of gentlefolk?"

"It's what we was a talking on, ma'am—how much longer Mr. Richard North 'll keep the gates closed again us," returned one whose name was Webb, speaking boldly but respectfully.

"Don't you put the saddle on the wrong horse, Webb; I told you that, the other day. Mr. Richard North didn't close the gates again you: you closed 'em again yourselves by walking out. He'd open them to you to-morrow, and be glad to do it."

"Yes, ma'am, but on the old terms," debated the man, looking obstinately at Mrs. Gass.

"What have you to say again the old terms?" demanded that lady of the men collectively. "Haven't they kept you and your families in comfort for years and years? Where was your grumblings then?—I heard of none."

"But things is changed," said Webb.

"Not a bit of it," retorted Mrs. Gass. "It's you men that have changed; not the things. I'll put a question to you, Webb—to all of you—and it won't do you no harm to answer it. If these trade union men had never come among you with their persuasions and their doctrines, should you, or should you not, have been at your work now in content and peace? Come, Webb, be honest, and say."

"I suppose so," confessed Webb.

"You know so," corrected Mrs. Gass. "It is as Mr. Richard said the other day to me—the men are led away by a chimera, which means a false fancy, Webb; a sham. There's the place"—pointing in the direction of the works—"and there's your work, waiting for you to do it. Mr. Richard will give you the same wages that he has always gave; you say you won't go to work unless he gives more: which he can't afford

to do. And there it rests; you, and him, and the business, all
at a standstill."

"And likely to be at a standstill, ma'am," returned Webb,
but always respectfully.

"Very well; let's take it at that," said Mrs. Gass, with
equanimity. "Let's take it that it *lasts*, this state of things.
What's to come of it?"

Webb, an intelligent man and superior workman, looked out
straight before him thoughtfully, as if seeking a solution to the
question. Mrs. Gass, finding he did not answer, resumed:

"If the Trades' Unions can find you permanent in food
and drink, and clothes and firing, well and good. Let 'em do
it: there'd be no more to say. But if they can't?"

"They undertake to keep us as long as the masters hold
out."

"And the money—where's it had from?"

"Subscribed. All the working bodies throughout the
United Kingdom subscribe to support the Trades' Unions,
ma'am."

"I heard," said Mrs. Gass, "that you were not getting
quite as liberal a keep from the Trades' Unions as they gave
you to begin upon."

"That's true," interrupted one named Foster, who very
much resented the shortening of supplies.

Mrs. Gass gave a toss to her lace parasol. "I heard, too—
I've seen, for the matter of that—that your wives had begun
to spout their spare crockery," said she. "What'll you do
when the allowance gets less and less till it comes to nothing,
and *all* your things is at the pawnshop?"

One or two of them laughed slightly. Not at her figures
of speech—the homely language was their own—but at the
improbability of the picture she called up. It was a state of
affairs not possible to arise, they answered, while they had
the Trades' Unions at their backs.

"*Isn't* it," said Mrs. Gass. "Them that live longest 'll
see most. There's strikes agate all over the country. You
know that, my men."

Of course the men knew it. But for the nearly universal
example set by others, they might never have struck themselves.

"Very good," said Mrs. Gass. "Now look you here.
You can see out before you just as well as I can, you men;
you've got your senses as sharp as I've got mine. When the

whole country, pretty nigh, gets on the strike, where are the subscriptions to come from for the Trades' Unions? Don't it stand to common reason that there'll be nobody to pay 'em? Who'll keep you then?"

It was the very thing wanted—that all the country should be on strike; for then the masters must give in, was the reply given. And then the men stood their ground and looked at her.

Mrs. Gass shook her head; the feathers waved. She supposed it must be as Richard North had said—that the men in their prejudice really could not foresee what might be looming in the future.

"It seems no good my talking," she resumed; "I've said it before. If you don't come to repent, my name's not Mary Gass. I'm far from wishing it; goodness knows that; and I shall be heart-sick sorry for your wives and children when the misery comes upon 'em. Not for *you;* because you are bringing it on deliberate."

"Ma'am, we don't doubt your good wishes for us and our families generally," spoke Webb. "But, if you'll please excuse my saying of it, you stand in the shoes of a master, and naturally look on with the masters' sight. Your interests lie that way, ours this, and they be dead opposed to each other."

"Well, now, I'll just say something," cried Mrs. Gass. "As far as my own interest goes, I don't care a jot whether the works go on again, or whether they stand still for ever. I've got as much money as will last me my time; if every pound that's locked up in the works is lost, it'll make no sort of difference to me, or my home, or my comforts—and you ought to know this of yourselves. I shall have as much to leave behind me, too, as I care to leave. But, if you come to talk of interests, I tell you whose I do think of, more than I do of mine—and that's yours and Mr. Richard North's. I am as easy on the matter, on my own score, as a body can be; but I'm not on yours or his."

It was spoken with single-minded earnestness. In fact Mrs. Gass was incapable of attempting deceit or sophistry— and the men knew it. But they thought that, in spite of her honesty, she could but be prejudiced for the opposition cause; and consequently her words held no more weight with them than the idle wind.

"Well, I'm off," said Mrs. Gass. "I hope with all my

heart that your senses will come to you. And I say it for your sakes."

"They've not left us—that we knows on," grumbled a man in a suppressed and half-insolent tone, as if he were dissatisfied with things in general.

"I hear you, Jack Allen. If you men think you know your own business best, you must follow it," concluded Mrs. Gass. ."The old saying runs, A wilful man must have his way. One thing I'd like you to understand : that when your wives and children shall be left without a potater to their mouths or a rag to their backs, you needn't come whining to me to help 'em. Don't you forget to bear that in mind, my men."

Waiting for her at her own home, Mrs. Gass found Richard North. That this was a very anxious time for him, might be detected by the ever-thoughtful look his face wore habitually. It was all very well for Mrs. Gass, so amply provided for, to take the reigning troubles easily ; Richard was less philosophical. And with cause. His own ruin—and the final closing of the works would be nothing less—might be got over. He had his profession, his early manhood, his energies ; his capability and character alike stood high : he could have no fear of making a living for himself, even though it had to be done in the service of some more fortunate firm, and not in his own. But there was his father. If the works came to a permanent close, the income Mr. North enjoyed from them could no longer be paid. All Mr. North's resources, whether hitherto derived from them or from Richard's generosity, would vanish like the mists of a summer's morning.

"What's it you, Mr. Richard ? " cried Mrs. Gass when she entered, and saw him standing near the window of her dining-room. "I'd not have stopped out if I'd known you were here. Some of them men have been hearing a bit of my mind," she added, sitting down behind the plants and untying her bonnet-strings. "It's come to pawning of the women's best gowns now."

"Has it ? " replied Richard North, rather abstractedly, as if he were buried in thought. "Of course it must come to that, sooner or later."

"Sooner or later it 'ud come to the pawning of their skins —an' they were able to strip 'em off," spoke Mrs. Gass. "If this state of things is to last, they'll have nothing else left to of 'em to strip."

Richard wheeled round, took a chair in front of Mrs. Gass, and sat down in it. He had come to make a proposition to her; one he did not quite cordially approve of himself; and from that cause his manner was perhaps a trifle less ready than usual. Richard North had received from Mrs. Gass, at the time of her late husband's death, full power to act on his own responsibility, just as he had held it from Mr. Gass; but in all weighty matters he had made a point of consulting them: Mr. Gass while he lived, Mrs. Gass since.

"It is a question that I have been asking myself a little too often for my peace—how long this state of things will last, and what will be its end," said Richard in answer to her last words, his low tone almost painfully earnest. "The longer it goes on, the worse it will be; for the men and for us."

"That's precisely what I tell 'em," acquiesced Mrs. Gass, tilting back her bonnet and fanning her face with her handkerchief. "But I might just as well speak to so many postesses."

"Yes; talking will not avail. *I* have talked to them; and find it to be only waste of words. If they listen to my arguments and feel inclined to be impressed with them, the influences of the Trades' Union undo it all again. I think we must try something else."

"And what's that, Mr. Richard?"

"Give way a little."

"Give way!" repeated Mrs. Gass, pushing her chair some inches back in her surprise. "What! give 'em what they want?"

"Certainly not. That is what we could not do. I said give way a *little*."

"Mr. Richard, I never would."

"What I thought of proposing is this: To divide the additional wages they are standing out for. That is, offer them half. If they would not return to work on those terms, on that concession, I should have no hope of them."

"And my opinion is, they'd *not*. Mr. Richard, sir, it's them Trade Union people that upholds 'em in their obstinacy. They'll make 'em hold out, them misleading Unionists, for the whole demands or none. What do the leaders of the Union care? It don't touch their pockets, or their comforts. So long as their own nests be feathered, the working man's may get as bare as boards. Don't you fancy the rulers 'll let our men give way half. It's only by keeping up agitation that agitators live."

"I should like to put it to the test. I have come here to ask you to agree to my doing it."

"And what about the shortening of the time that they want?" questioned Mrs. Gass.

"I should not give way there. It is not practicable. They must return on the usual time: but of the additional wages demanded I would offer half. Will you assent to this?"

"It will be with an uncommon bad grace," was Mrs. Gass's answer.

"I see nothing else that can be done," said Richard North. "If only as a matter of conscience I should wish to propose it. When it ends in a comprehensive ruin—which seems only too certain, for we cannot shut our eyes to what is being enacted all over the country in almost all trades—and the women and children come to lie under our very eyes here, famished and naked, I shall have the consolation of knowing that it is the men's own fault, not mine. Perhaps they will accept this offer. I hope so, though it will leave us but little profit. If we can only make both ends meet, just to keep us going during these unsettled times, we must be satisfied. I am sure I shall be doing right, Mrs. Gass, to make this proposal."

"Mr. Richard, sir, you know that I've trusted to your judgment always, and shall trust it to the end: anything you thought well to do, I should never dissuade from. You shall make this offer if you please: but I know you'll be opening for the men a loophole. Give 'em an inch, and they'll want to take an ell."

"If they come back it will be a great thing," argued Richard. "The sight of the works standing still; the knowledge that all else involved is standing still, almost paralyses me."

"Don't you go and take it to heart at the beginning now," affectionately advised Mrs. Gass. "There's not much damage done yet."

Richard bent forward, a painful earnestness on his face. "It is of my father that I think. What will become of him if all our means are stopped?"

"I'll take care of him till better times come round," said Mrs. Gass, heartily. "And of you, too, Mr. Richard; if you won't be too proud to let me, sir."

Richard laughed; a slight, genial laugh; partly in amusement, partly in gratitude. "I hope the better times will come at once," he said, preparing to leave. "At least, sufficiently good ones to allow of business going on as usual. If the men refuse this offer of mine, they are made of more ungrateful stuff than I should give them credit for."

"They *will* refuse it," said Mrs. Gass, emphatically. "As is my belief. Not them, Mr. Richard, sir, but the Trades' Unions for 'em. Once get under the thumb of that despotic body, and a workman daredn't say his soul is his own."

And Mrs. Gass's opinion proved to be the correct one. Richard North called his men together, and laid the concession before them; pressing them to accept it in their mutual interests. The men requested a day for consideration, and then gave their answer: rejection. Unless the whole of their demands were complied with, they unequivocally refused to return to work.

"It will be worse for them than for me in the long run," said Richard North.

And many a thoughtful mind believed that he spoke in a spirit of prophecy.

CHAPTER XVI.

MORNING VISITORS.

IN the dining-parlour at Mrs. Cumberland's, with its large window open to the garden and the sweet flowers, stood Ellen Adair. It was the favourite morning-room. Mrs. Cumberland, up in good time to-day, for it was barely eleven o'clock, had stepped forth into the garden, and had disappeared amid its remoter parts.

Ellen Adair, wearing a dress of cool pink muslin, almost as thin as gauze, stood in a reverie. A pleasant one, to judge by the soft blush on her face and the sweet smile that parted her lips. She was twirling the plain gold ring round and round her finger, thinking no doubt of the hour when it was put on, and the words spoken with it. Bessy Rane had wholly refused to give back the ring she was married with, and Ellen retained the other.

The intimacy with Arthur Bohun, the silent love-making, had been going on always. Even now, she was listening lest haply his footsteps might be heard; listening with hushed

breath and beating heart. Never a day passed but he contrived to call, on some plea or other, at Mrs. Cumberland's,
morning, afternoon, or evening: and this morning he might
be coming, for aught she knew. At the close of the past
summer, Mrs. Cumberland had gone to the Isle of Wight for
change of air, taking Ellen and her maid Jelly. She hired a
secluded cottage in the neighbourhood of Niton. Singular to
say, Captain Bohun remembered that he had friends at Niton
—an old invalid brother officer, who was living there in great
economy. On and off, on and off, during the whole time of
Mrs. Cumberland's stay—and that lasted five months, for she
had gone the beginning of September, and did not come home
until the end of February—was Arthur Bohun paying visits
to this old friend. Now for a day or two; now for a week or
two; once for three weeks together. And still Mrs. Cumberland suspected nothing! It was as if her eyes were held.
Perhaps they were: there is a destiny in all things, and it
must be worked out. It is true that she did not see or
suspect half the intimacy. A gentle walk once a day by
the sea was all she took. At other times Ellen rambled at
will; sometimes attended by Jelly, alone when Jelly could not
be spared. Captain Bohun took every care of her, guarding
her more jealously than he would have guarded a sister: and
this did a little surprise Mrs. Cumberland.

"We ought to feel obliged to Captain Bohun, Ellen," she
said on one occasion. "It's not many a young man would
sacrifice his time to us. Your father, and his, and my husband the chaplain, were warm friends for a little time in
India: it must be the knowledge of that that induces him to
be so attentive. Very civil of him!"

Ellen coloured vividly. Eminently truthful, of a nature
antagonistic to deceit, she yet did not dare to say that perhaps that was *not* Captain Bohun's reason for being attentive.
How could she hint at Captain Bohun's love, plain though it
was to her own heart, when he had never spoken a syllable
to her about it? It was not impossible. So things went on
in the same routine: he and she wandering together on the
sea-shore: both of them living in a dream of Elysium. In
February, when they returned home, the scene was changed,
but not the companionship. It was an early spring that year,
warm and genial. Many and many an hour were they together in that seductive garden of Mrs. Cumberland's, with
its miniature rocks, its mossy grass soft as velvet; the birds

would be singing and their own hearts dancing. But Mrs. Cumberland's eyes were not to be always closed.

It was scarcely to be expected that so good-looking a girl as Ellen Adair should remain long without a declared suitor. Especially when there was a rumour that she would have a fortune—though how the latter arose, or whence its grounds, people would have been puzzled to tell. A gentleman of good position in the vicinity; no other than Mr. Graves, son of one of the county members; took to make rather pointed visits at Mrs. Cumberland's. That his object was Ellen Adair, and that he would most likely be asking her to become his wife, Mrs. Cumberland saw. She wrote to Mr. Adair in Australia, telling him she thought Ellen was about to receive an offer of marriage, eligible in every way. The young man was of high character, good family, and large means, she said: should she, if the proposal came, accept it for Ellen. By a singular omission, which perhaps Mrs. Cumberland was not conscious of, she did not mention Mr. Graves's name. But the proposal came sooner than Mrs. Cumberland had bargained for: barely was this letter despatched—about which in her characteristic reticence, she said not a word to anybody—when Mr. Graves spoke to Ellen and was refused. It was this that opened Mrs. Cumberland's eyes to the nature of the friendship between Ellen and Captain Bohun. She then wrote a second letter to Mr. Adair, saying Ellen had refused Mr. Graves in consequence, as she strongly suspected, of an attachment to Arthur Bohun—the son of Major Bohun, whom Mr. Adair once knew so well. That Arthur Bohun would be wishing to make Ellen his wife, there could be, Mrs. Cumberland thought from observation, no doubt: might he be accepted? In a worldly point of view, Captain Bohun was not so desirable as Mr. Graves, she added—unless indeed he should succeed to his uncle's baronetcy, which was not very improbable, the present heir being sickly—but he would have enough to live upon as a gentleman, and he was liked by every one. This second letter was also despatched to Australia by the mail following the one that took the first. Having thus done her duty, Mrs. Cumberland sat down to wait placidly for Mr. Adair's answer, tacitly allowing the intimacy to continue, inasmuch as she did not stop the visits of Arthur Bohun. Neither he nor Ellen suspected what she had done.

And with the summer weather there had come in another suitor to Ellen Adair. At least another was displaying signs

that he would like to become one. It was Mr. Seeley, the
doctor who had replaced Mr. Alexander. Soon after Mrs.
Cumberland's return from Niton in February, she had been
for a week or two alarmingly ill, and Mr. Seeley was called
in as well as her son. He had continued to be on terms of
friendship at her house; and it became rather palpable that
he very much admired Miss Adair.

Things were in this state on this summer's morning, and
Ellen Adair stood near the window twirling round and round
the plain gold ring on her finger. Presently she came out of
her reverie, unlocked a small letter-case, and began to write
in her diary.

"Tuesday.—Mrs. Cumberland talks of going away again.
She seems to me to get thinner and weaker. Arthur says the
same. He ——"

A knock at the front door, and Mr. Seeley was shown in.
He paid a professional visit to Mrs. Cumberland at least every
other morning. Not as a professional man, he told her; but
as a friend, that he might see how she went on.

Miss Adair shook hands with him, her clasp and her manner alike cold. He saw it not; and his fingers parted linger-
ingly from hers.

"Mrs. Cumberland is in the garden, if you will go to her,
Mr. Seeley," said Ellen, affecting to be quite occupied with
her letter-case. "I think she wants to see you; she is not at
all well. You will find her in the grotto, or somewhere about."

To this semi-command Mr. Seeley answered nothing, except
that he was in no hurry, and would look after Mrs Cumberland by-and-by. He was a dark man of about two-and-
thirty, with a plain, honest face; straightforward in disposition and manner, timid only when with Ellen Adair. He took
a step or two nearer Ellen, and began to address her in a low
tone, pulling one of his gloves about nervously.

"I have been wishing for an opportunity of speaking to you,
Miss Adair. There is a question that I—that I—should like
to put. One I have very much at heart."

It was coming. In spite of Ellen Adair's studious coldness to him, by which she had meant him to take a lesson and
learn that he must *not* speak, she saw that it was coming. In
the pause he made, as if he would wait for her permission to
go on, she felt miserably uncomfortable. Her nature was
essentially generous and sensitive; to have to refuse Mr.
Seeley, or any one else, made her feel as humiliated as though

she had committed a crime. And she could have esteemed the man apart from this.

They were thus standing: Mr. Seeley looking awkward and nervous, tearing at his glove as no sane man would do; Ellen turning red and white and hot and cold: when Arthur Bohun walked in. Mr. Seeley, effectually interrupted for the time, muttered a good morning to Captain Bohun and shot into the garden.

"What was Seeley saying, Ellen?"

"Nothing," she rather faintly answered.

"*Nothing!*"

Ellen glanced up at him. His face wore the haughty Bohun look; his mouth betrayed scorn enough for ten of the proud Bohuns put together. She did not answer.

"If he were saying 'nothing,' why should you be looking as you did?—with a great blush on your face, and your eyes cast down?"

"He had really said as good as nothing, Arthur. What he might have been going to say, I—I don't know. It was only that minute he had come in."

"As you please," coldly returned Arthur, walking into the garden in his turn. "If you do not think me worthy of your confidence, I have no more to say.

The Bohun blood was bubbling up in a fierce turmoil. Not in doubt of Ellen; not in resentment against her—at least only so in the moment's passion: but in angry indignation that Seeley, a common village practitioner, should dare to lift his profane eyes to Ellen Adair. Captain Bohun had suspected the man's hopes for some short time; there's an instinct in these things; and felt outrageous over it. Tom Graves's venture had filled him with resentment; but he at least was a gentleman of position.

Ellen, wonderfully disturbed, gently sat down to write again; all she did was gentle. And the diary got some sentences added to it.

"That senseless William Seeley! And after showing him as plainly as I could show, that it is useless—that I should consider it an impertinence in him to attempt to speak to me. I don't know whether it was for the worst or the best that Arthur should have come in just at that moment. For the best because it stopped Mr. Seeley's nonsense; for the worst because Arthur has now seen and is vexed. The vexation will not last, for he knows better. Here they are."

Once more Ellen closed her diary. The "Here they are," applied to the doctor and Mrs. Cumberland. They were walking slowly towards the window, conversing calmly on her ailments, and came in. Mrs. Cumberland sat down with her newspaper. As Mr. Seeley took his departure to visit other patients, Arthur Bohun returned. Close upon that, Richard North was shown in. It seemed that Mrs. Cumberland was to be rich in visitors that morning.

That Richard North should find his time hang somewhat on hand, was only natural; he, the hitherto actively-employed man, who had often wished the day's hours to be doubled, for the business he had to do in it. Richard could afford to make morning calls on his friends now, and he had come strolling to Mrs. Cumberland's.

They sat down. Arthur in the remotest chair he could find from Ellen Adair: she had taken up a bit of light work, and her fairy fingers were plying its threads deftly. Richard sat near Ellen, facing Mrs. Cumberland. He could not help thinking how lovely Ellen Adair was: the fact had never struck him more forcibly than to-day.

"How is the strike getting on, Richard?"

Mrs. Cumberland laid down her newspaper to ask the question. No other theme bore so much present interest in Dallory. From the time that North and Gass first established the works, things had gone on with one continuous smoothness, peace and plenty reigning on all sides. No wonder this startling innovation seemed like a revolution.

"It is *going* on," replied Richard. "How the men are getting on, I don't like to think. The wrong way, of course."

"Your proposition, to meet them half-way, was rejected, I hear."

"It was."

"What do they expect to come to?"

"To fortune, I should fancy," returned Richard. "To abjure work and *not* expect a fortune, must be rather a mistake. A poor look-out at the best."

"But, according to the newspapers, Richard, one half of the working classes that the country contains are out on strike. Do you believe it?"

"A vast number are out. And more are going out daily."

"And what is to become of them all?"

"I cannot tell. The question, serious though it is, appears never to occur to the men or their rulers."

" The journals say—living so much alone as I do, I have time to read many, and I make it my chief recreation—that the work is leaving the country," pursued Mrs. Cumberland.

"And so it is. It cannot be otherwise. Take a case of my own as an example. A contract was offered me some days ago, and I could not take it. Literally *could not*, Mrs. Cumberland. My men are out on strike, and likely to be out; I had no means of performing it, and therefore could only reject it. That contract, as I happen to know, has been taken by a firm in Belgium. They have undertaken it at a cheaper rate than I could possibly have done at the best of times: for labour there is cheaper. It is true. The work that circumstances compelled me to refuse, is gone over there to be executed, and I and my men are playing in idleness."

" But what will be the end of it ?" asked Mrs. Cumberland.

" The end of it ? If you speak of the country, neither you nor I can foresee."

"I spoke of the men. Not your men in particular, Mr. Richard North, but all those that we include under the name of British workmen : the vast bodies of artizans scattered in the various localities of the kingdom. What is to become of these men if the work fails ? "

"I see but one of three courses for them," said Richard, lifting his hand in some agitation, for he spoke from the depth of his heart, believing the subject to be of more awful gravity than any that had stirred the community for some hundreds of years. "They must eventually emigrate—provided that the means to do so can be found; or they must become burdens upon the public charity; or they must lie down in the streets and starve. As I live, I can foresee no better fate for them."

" And what of the country, if it comes to this?—if the work and the workmen leave it ? "

Richard North shrugged his shoulders. It was altogether a question too difficult for him. He would have liked to get it answered from somebody else very much indeed: just as others would.

" Lively conversation !" interposed Captain Bohun, in a half-satirical, half-joking manner, as he rose. It was the first time he had spoken. "I think I must be going," he added, approaching Mrs. Cumberland.

Richard made it the signal for his own departure. As they

stood, saying adieu, Bessy Rane was seen for a moment at her own window. Mrs. Cumberland nodded.

"There's Bessy," exclaimed Richard. "I think I'll go and speak to her. Will you pardon me, Mrs. Cumberland, if I make my exit from your house this way?"

Mrs. Cumberland stepped outside herself, and Richard crossed the low wire fence that divided the two gardens. Arthur Bohun went to the door, never having said a word of farewell to Ellen Adair. He stood with it in his hand looking at her, smiled, and was returning, when Mrs. Cumberland came in again.

"Won't you come and say adieu to me here, Ellen?"

The invitation was given in so low a tone that she gathered it by the form of his lips rather than by the ear; perhaps by instinct also. She went out, and they walked side by side in silence to the open hall door. Dallory Ham, in its primitive ways and manners, left its house-doors open with perfect safety by day to admit the summer air. Outside, between the house and the gate, was a strip of a bed planted with flowers. Arrived at the door, Captain Bohun could find nothing better to talk of than these, as he stood with her on the crimson mat.

"I think those lilies are finer than Mr. North's."

"Mrs. Cumberland takes so much pains with her flowers," was Ellen's answer. "And she is very fond of lilies."

They stepped out, bending over these self-same lilies. Ellen picked one. He quietly took it from her.

"Forgive me, Ellen," he murmured. "I am not a bear in general. Good-bye."

As they stood, her hand in his for the parting greeting, her flushed face downcast, shrinking in maiden modesty from the gaze of love that was bent upon her, Mrs. North's open carriage rolled past. The head of Madam was suddenly pushed as far towards them as safety permitted: her eyes glared: a stony horror sat on her countenance.

"Shameful! Disgraceful!" hissed Madam. And Miss Matilda North, by her side, started up to see what the shame might be.

Arthur Bohun had caught the words and the hiss—not Ellen—and bit his lips in a complication of feeling.

But all he did was to raise his hat—first to his mother, then to Ellen—as he went out at the gate. Madam flung herself back on her seat, and the carriage pursued its course up the Ham.

CHAPTER XVII.

THREE LETTERS FOR DR. RANE.

" You are keeping quality hours, Bessy—as our nurse used to
say when we were children," was Richard North's salutation
to his sister as he went in and saw the table laid for breakfast.

Mrs. Rane laughed. She was busy at work, sewing some
buttons on a white waistcoat of her husband's.

" Oliver was called out at seven this morning, and has not
come back yet," she explained.

" And you are waiting breakfast for him ! You must be
starving."

" I took a piece of bread-and-butter and some coffee when
Molly had hers. How is papa, Richard ? "

" Anything but well. Very much worried, for one thing."

" Madam and Matilda are back, I hear ? " continued Bessy.

" Three days ago. They have brought Miss Field with
them."

" And Madam has brought her usual temper, I suppose,"
added Bessy. " No wonder papa is suffering."

" That of course ; it will never be otherwise. But he is
troubling himself also very much about the works being
stopped. I tell him to leave all such trouble to me, but it is
of no use."

" When will the strike end, Richard ? "

Richard shook his head. It was an unprofitable theme,
and he did not wish to pursue it with Bessy. She had
enough cares of her own, as he suspected, without their being
added to. Three letters lay on the table, close by where
Richard was sitting ; they were addressed to Dr. Rane. His
fingers began turning them about mechanically, quite in
abstraction."

" I know the handwriting of two of them," remarked
Bessy, possibly fancying he was curious on the point ; " not
of the third."

" The one is from America," observed Richard, looking at
the letters for the first time.

" Yes ; it's from Dr. Jones. He would like Oliver to join
him in America."

" To join him for what ? " asked Richard.

Bessy looked at him. She saw no reason why her brother should not be told. Dr. Rane wished it kept secret from the world; but this, she thought, could not apply to her good and trustworthy brother Richard. She opened her heart and told him all; not what they were going certainly to do, for ways and means lay in doubt yet, but what they hoped to be able to do. Richard, excessively surprised, listened in silence.

They made up their minds to quit Dallory. Dr. Rane had taken a dislike to the place; and no wonder, Bessy added in a parenthesis, when he was not getting on at all. He intended to leave it as soon as ever the practice was disposed of.

"I expect this letter will decide it," concluded Bessy, touching one that bore the London post-mark. "It is from a Mr. Lynch, who is wishing to get a practice in the country on account of his health. London smoke does not do for him, he tells Oliver. They have had a good deal of correspondence together, and I know his handwriting quite well. Oliver said he expected to get his decision to-day or to-morrow. He is to pay £200 and take to the furniture at a valuation."

"And then—do I understand you aright, Bessy?—you and Rane are going to America?" questioned Richard.

"Oh, *no*," said Bessy with emphasis. "I must have explained badly, Richard. What I said was, that Dr. Jones, who has more practice in America than he knows what to do with, had offered a share of it to Oliver if he would go and join him. Oliver declined it. He would have liked to go, for he thinks it must be an exceedingly good thing; but Dr. Jones wants a large premium: so it's out of the question."

"But surely you would not have liked to emigrate, Bessy?"

She glanced into Richard's face with her meek, loving eyes, blushing a very little.

"I would go anywhere that he goes," she answered simply. "It would cost me pain to leave you and papa, Richard; especially papa, because he is old, and because he would feel it; but Oliver is my husband."

Richard drummed for a minute or two on the table-cloth. Bessy sewed on her last button.

"Then where does Rane think of pitching his tent, Bessy?"

"Somewhere in London. He says there is no place like it for getting on. Should this letter be to say that Mr. Lynch takes the practice, we shall be away in less than a month."

"And you have never told us!"

"We decided to say nothing until it was a settled thing

and then only to you, and Mrs. Cumberland, and papa. Oliver does not want the world to know it sooner than need be."

"But do you mean to say that Rane has not told his mother?" responded Richard to this in some surprise.

"Not yet," said Bessy, shaking out the completed waist-coat. "It will be sure to vex her, and perhaps needlessly; for, suppose, after all, we do not go? That entirely depends upon the disposal of the practice here."

Bessy was picking up the threads in her neat way, and putting the remaining buttons in the little closed box, when Dr. Rane was heard to enter and go into his consulting room. Away flew Bessy to the kitchen, bringing in the things with her own loving hands—and, for the matter of that, Molly Green was at her up-stairs work—buttered toast, broiled ham, a dainty dish of stewed mushrooms. There was nothing she liked so much as to wait on her husband. Her step was light and soft, her eye bright. Richard, looking on, saw how much she cared for him.

Dr. Rane came in, wiping his brow: the day was hot, and he tired. He had walked from a farm-house a mile beyond the Ham. A strangely-weary look sat on his face.

"Don't trouble, Bessy; I have had my breakfast. Ah, Richard, how d'ye do?"

"You have had your breakfast!" repeated Bessy. "At the farm?"

"Yes; they gave me some."

"Oh, dear! won't you eat a bit of the ham, or of the mushrooms, Oliver? They are so good: And I waited."

"I am sorry you should wait. No, I can't eat two break-fasts. You must eat for me and yourself, Bessy."

Dr. Rane sat down in his own chair at the table, turning it towards Richard, and took up the letters. Selecting the one from Mr. Lynch, he was about to open it when Bessy, who was now beginning her breakfast, spoke.

"Oliver, I have told Richard about it—what we think of doing?"

Dr. Rane's glance went out for a moment to his brother-in-law's, and met it. He made the best of the situation, smiled gaily, and put down the letter unopened.

"Are you surprised, Richard?" he asked.

"Very much, indeed. Had a stranger told me I was going to leave Dallory myself—and, indeed, that may well come to

be, with this strike in the air—I'd as soon have believed it.
Shall you be doing well to go, do you think, Rane ? "

"Am I doing well here ? " was the doctor's rejoinder.

"Not very, I fear."

"And, with this strike on, it gets all the worse. The
wives and children get ill, as usual, and I am called in ; but
the men have no money wherewith to pay me. I don't
intend to bring Bessy to a crust, and I think it would come
to that if we stayed here —— "

"No, no; not quite to that, Oliver," she interposed. But
he took no notice.

"Therefore I shall try my fortune elsewhere," continued
Dr. Rane. "And if you would return thanks to the quarter
whence the blow has originally come, you must pay them to
your stepmother, Richard. It is she who has driven me
away."

Richard was silent. Dr. Rane broke the seal of Mr.
Lynch's letter, and read it to the end. Then, laying it down,
he took up the one from America, and read that. Bessy,
looking across, tried to gather some information from his
countenance; but Dr. Rane's face was one which, in an ordinary way, it was no easier to read than a stone.

"Is it favourable news, Oliver ? " she asked, as he finished
the long letter, and folded it.

"It's nothing particular. Jones runs on upon politics. He
generally gives me a good dose of *them.*"

"Oh, I meant from Mr. Lynch," replied Bessy. "Is he
coming ? "

"Mr. Lynch declines."

"Declines, Oliver ! "

"Declines the negotiation. And he is not much better
than a sneak for giving me all the trouble that he has, and
then crying off at the eleventh hour," added Dr. Rane.

"It *is* bad behaviour," said Bessy, warmly. "What excuse
does he make ? "

"You can see what he says," said Dr. Rane, pushing the
letter towards her. Bessy opened it, and read it aloud for
the benefit of Richard.

Mr. Lynch took up all one side with apologies. The sub-
stance of the letter was, that a practice had unexpectedly
been offered to him at the sea-side, which he had accepted, as
the air and locality would suit his state of health so much
better than Dallory. If he could be of service in negotiating

with any one else, he added, Dr. Rane was to make use of him.

It was as courteous and explanatory a letter as could be written. But still it was a refusal : and the negotiation was at an end. Bessy Rane drew a deep breath : whether of relief or disappointment it might have puzzled herself to decide. Perhaps there lay in it a mixture of both.

" Then, after all, Oliver, we shall not be leaving ! "

" Not at present, it seems," was Dr. Rane's answer. And he put the two letters into his pocket.

" Perhaps you will be thinking again, Oliver, of America, now ? " said his wife.

" Oh no I shall not."

" Does Dr. Jones still urge you to come ? "

" Not particularly. He took my refusal for final."

She went on, slowly eating some of the mushrooms. Richard said nothing : this projected removal seemed to have impressed him to silence. Dr. Rane took up the remaining letter and turned it about, looking at the outside.

" Do you know the writing, Oliver ? " his wife asked.

" Not at all. The post-mark's Whitborough."

Opening the letter, which appeared to contain only a few lines, Dr. Rane looked up with an exclamation.

" How strange ! How very strange ! Bessy, you and I are the only two left in the tontine."

" What ! " she cried, scarcely understanding him. Richard North turned his head.

" That tontine that we were both put in when infants. There was only one life left in it besides ours—old Massey's son, of Whitborough. He is dead."

" What !—George Massey ? Dead ! " cried Richard North.

Dr. Rane handed him the note. Yes : it was even so. The other life had dropped, and Oliver Rane's and his wife's alone remained.

" My father has called that an unlucky tontine," remarked Richard. " I have heard it said that if you want a child to live, you should put it in a tontine, for the tontine lives are sure to arrive at a green old age, to the mutual general mortification. This has been an exception to the rule. I am sorry about George Massey. I wonder what he has died of ? "

" Last long, in general, do you say ? " returned Dr. Rane, musingly. " I don't know much about tontines my-self.

" Neither do I," said Richard. "I remember hearing talk of one tontine when I was a boy: five or six individuals were left in it, all over eighty then, and in flourishing health. Perhaps that was why my father and Mr. Gass took up with one. At any rate, it seems that you and Bessy are the only two remaining in this."

" I wonder if a similar condition of things ever existed before as for a man and his wife to be the two last in a tontine ? " cried Dr. Rane, slightly laughing. "Bessy, practically it can be of no use to us conjointly ; for before the money can be paid, one of us must die. What senseless things tontines are ! "

" Senseless indeed," answered Bessy. "I'd say something to it if we could have the money now. How much is it ? "

" Ay, by the way, how much is it ? What was it that each member put in at first, Richard ? I forget.—Fifty pounds, was it ? And then there's the compound interest, which has been going on for thirty years. How much would it amount to now ? "

" More than two thousand pounds," answered Richard North, making a mental calculation.

Dr. Rane's face flushed with a quick hot flush : a light shone in his eye : his lips parted, as with some deep emotions. "More than two thousand pounds ! " he echoed under his breath. "Two thousand pounds ! Bessy, it would be like a gold mine."

She laughed slightly. "But we can't get it, you see, Oliver. And I am sure neither of us wishes the other dead."

" No—no ; certainly not," said Dr. Rane.

Richard North said, "Good day," and left. Just before turning in at the gates of Dallory Hall, he met a gig containing Lawyer Dale of Whitborough, who was driving somewhere with his clerk ; no other than Timothy Wilks. Mr. Dale pulled up, to speak.

" Can it be true that George Massey is dead ? " questioned Richard as they were parting.

" It's true enough, poor fellow. He died yesterday : been ill but two days."

" I've just heard it at Dr. Rane's. He got a letter this morning to tell him."

" Dr. Rane did ? I was not aware they knew each other."

" No more did they. But they were both in that tontine. Now that George Massey's gone, Dr. Rane and his wife are the only two remaining in it. Rather singular that it should be so."

For a minute Mr. Dale could not recollect whether he had ever heard of this particular tontine; although, being a lawyer, he made it his business to know everything; and he and Richard talked of it together. Excessively singular, Lawyer Dale agreed, that a tontine should be practically useless to a man and his wife—unless one of them died.

"Very mortifying, I must say, Mr. Richard North; especially where the money would be welcome. Two thousand pounds! Dr. Rane must wish the senseless thing at Hanover. I should, I know, if it were my case. Good morning."

And quiet Timothy Wilks, across whom they talked, heard all that was said, and unconsciously treasured it up in his memory.

Richard carried home the news to his father. Mr. North was seated at the table in his parlour, some papers before him. He lifted his hands in dismay.

"Dead! George Massey dead! Dick, as sure as we are here, there must be something wrong about that tontine! They'd never drop off like this, else; one after another."

"It's not much more than a week ago, sir, that I met George Massey in Whitborough, and was talking with him. To all appearance he was as healthy and likely to live as I am."

"What took him off?"

"Dale says it was nothing more than a neglected cold." ·

"I don't like it; Dick, I don't like it," reiterated Mr. North. "Bessy may be the next to go; or Rane."

"I hope not, father."

"Well—I've had it in my head for ever so long that that tontine is an unlucky one; I think it is going to be so to the end. We shall see. Look here, Dick."

He pointed to some of the papers before him; used cheques apparently; pushing them towards his son.

"They sent me word at the bank that my account was overdrawn. I knew it could not be, and asked for my cheques. Dick, here are four or five that I never drew."

Richard took them in his fingers. The filling up was in Madam's handwriting: the signature apparently in Mr. North's.

"Do you give Mrs. North blank cheques ready signed, sir?"

"No, never, Dick. I was cured of that, years ago. When she wants money, I sometimes let her fill in the cheque, but I never sign it beforehand."

" And you think you have not signed these ? "

" Think ! I know I have not. She has imitated my signature, and got the money."

Richard's face grew dark with shame ; shame for his stepmother. But that Mr. North was her husband, it would have been downright forgery: perhaps the law, if called upon, might have accounted it such now. He took time for consideration.

" Father, I think—pardon me for the suggestion—I think you had better let your private account be passed over to me. Allow it to lie in my name ; and make my signature alone available—just as it is with our business account. I see no other way of safety."

" With all my heart ; I'd be glad to do it," acquiesced Mr. North, " but there's no account to pass. There's no account to pass, Dick ; it's overdrawn."

CHAPTER XVIII.

MADAM'S ADVICE.

A DINNER-PARTY at Dallory Hall. Arthur Bohun was in his chamber, lazily dressing for it. Not a large dinner, this : half a dozen or so, besides themselves ; and the hour six o'clock. Two gentlemen, bidden to it, would have to go away by train afterwards : on such occasions the dinner of necessity must be tolerably early.

Mr. North and Richard did not approve of Madam's dinners at the most favourable times : now, with all the care of the strike upon them and the great trouble looming in the distance if that strike lasted, the breaking up of their business, the decay of their means, they looked on these fast-recurring banquets as most reprehensible. They were without power to stop them ; remonstrance availed not with Madam. Sometimes the dinners were impromptu, or nearly so, Madam inviting afternoon callers at the Hall to stay, or bringing home a carriage-full of guests with her. As was partially the case on this day.

Captain Arthur Bohun, who liked to take most things easily, dressing included, stood hair-brush in hand. He had drawn aside from the glass, and was looking from the open window. His thoughts were busy. They ran on that little episode of the morning, when Madam, passing in her carriage, had seen him with Ellen Adair, and had chosen to make display of her

sentiments on the subject in the manner described. That it
would not end there, Arthur felt sure; Madam would inevitably
treat him to a little more of her mind. It was rather a singular
thing—as if Fate had been intervening with its usual cross
purposes—for circumstances so to have ordered it that Madam
should still be in ignorance of their intimacy. Nearly always
when Mrs. Cumberland was at home, it chanced that Madam
was away; and, when Madam was at the Hall, Mrs. Cumberland was elsewhere. Thus, during Mrs. Cumberland's prolonged stay at Niton, Madam's presence blessed her household;
the very week that that lady returned to Dallory Ham,
Madam took her departure, and had but recently returned.
She had spent the interval in Germany. Sidney North, her
well-beloved son, giving trouble as usual to all who were connected with him, had found England rather warm in early
spring, and had betaken himself to Germany. His chief point
of sojourn was Homburg, and Madam, with her daughter
Matilda, had been making it hers since the spring. Mr. North,
in the glad relief her absence brought him, had used every
exertion to supply her with the money she so rapaciously sent
home for. It would appear that the accommodation had not
been sufficient, for—as was soon to be discovered by Richard
—the cheques shown to him by his father had been drawn by
her at Homburg. And so, as Fate or Fortune had willed it,
Mrs. North had been out of the way of watching the progress
of the intimacy between her son and Ellen Adair.

A quick knock at the chamber-door, and Madam swept in,
waiting for no response, a large crimson rose, just brought
from the greenhouse, adorning her jet-black hair, her white
silk gown rustling and trailing after her. As well as though
she had already spoken, Arthur knew what she had come for.
He thought to himself that she was losing no time and must
have hurried over her toilette purposely. The carriage had
not long got home, for she and Matilda had been driving to a
distance, and remained out to luncheon. Arthur, not moving
from where he was, began brushing at his hair hap-hazard.

" I suppose I am late, Madam ? "

" Was it *you* that I passed this afternoon in Dallory Ham,
talking to some girl at a house-door ? " began Madam, taking
no notice of his remark.

" It was me, safe enough; I had been calling on Mrs.
Cumberland," replied Arthur, carelessly. " Dick also. By
the way you stared, Madam, I fancied you scarcely knew me."

A little bit of banter. Madam might take it seriously, or not, as she chose. She went round to the other side of the dressing-table, and stood opposite him at the window.

"What girl were you talking with?"

"Girl! I was with Miss Adair."

"Who *is* she, Arthur?"

"She is Mrs. Cumberland's ward."

"What do you know of her?"

"I know her as being at Mrs. Cumberland's. I see her when I go there."

Was he really indifferent? Standing there brushing away at his hair lazily, now the right way, now the wrong, speaking in the most supine manner, his apparently supreme indifference could not be exceeded. Madam scanned his face in momentary silence; *he* was closely intent upon two sparrows, fighting over a reddening cherry on the branch of the proximate tree.

"Fight away, young gentlemen; battle it out; you'll get all the better appetite for your supper."

"Will you attend to me for a short while, Captain Bohun?" spoke Madam, irritably.

"Certainly; I am attending," was the Captain's ready answer.

Just for an instant Madam paused. This was not one of the daily petty grievances that she made people miserable over, but a trouble to her of awful meaning, almost as of life or death. In this, her own grave interests, she could control her temper, and she thought it might be the best policy to do so while she dealt with it.

"Arthur, you know that you are becoming more valuable to me," she said, with soft calmness; and Arthur Bohun opened his surprised ears at the words and tone. "Since Sidney took up his abode away from England, and cannot come back to it, poor fellow, for the present you are all I have here. If I speak, it is for your welfare."

"Very good of you, I'm sure," returned Arthur, seeing she waited for him to say something, and feeling how two-faced the words were, mother of his though she was. "What is it you wish to say?"

"It's about that girl, Miss—what do you call her?—Adair. Young men will be young men; soldiers especially; I know that; but wrong is wrong, and it cannot by the most ingenious sophistry be converted into right. It is quite wrong to play with these village girls, as you seem to be doing with Miss Adair."

Arthur threw back his head as though his pride were hurt. Madam had seen just the same movement in his father.

"I have no intention of *playing* with Miss Adair."

A gleam shot from her eyes—half fear, half defiance. She bit her lip, and went on in a still softer tone.

"You cannot mean anything *worse*, Arthur."

"I do not understand you, Madam. Worse? Worse than what?"

"Anything serious. To play with village girls is reprehensible; but —— "

"I beg your pardon, mother; this is quite unnecessary. The playing with village girls—whatever that may mean— is not a habit of mine, and never has been. The caution might be more appropriate if applied to your men-servants than it is to me."

"Allow me to finish, Arthur. To play with village girls is reprehensible; but to intend anything serious with one would be far more so in your case. Will you profit by the caution?"

"If you wish me to comprehend the word 'serious,' you must speak out. What does it mean?"

"It means *marriage*," she answered, with a burst of temper—so far as tone might convey it. "I allude to this absurd intimacy of yours with Miss Adair. You must be intimate with the girl; your look and attitude, as I passed to-day, proved it."

"And if I did mean marriage, what then?"

He asked the question jokingly, laughing a little; but he was not prepared for the effect it had on his mother. Her eyes flashed fire, her lips trembled, her face turned whiter than death.

"Marriage! With *her?* You must be dreaming, Arthur Bohun."

"Not dreaming; joking," he said, lightly. "You may be at ease, Madam; I have no intention of marrying any one at present."

"You must never marry Miss Adair."

"No?"

"Arthur Bohun, you are treating all this with mockery," she exclaimed, beginning in truth to believe that he really was; and the relief was great, though the tacit disrespect angered her. "How dare you imply that you could think seriously of these village girls ?—only to annoy and frighten me."

"You must be easily frightened to-day, Madam. I don't think I did imply it. As to Miss Adair ——"

"Yes, as to Miss Adair," fiercely interrupted Madam. "Go on."

"I was about to say that, in speaking of Miss Adair, we might as well recognise her true position. It is not quite respectful to be alluding to her as a 'village girl.' She is a lady, born and bred."

"Perhaps you will next say that she is equal to the Bohuns ?"

"I do not wish to say it. Don't you think this conversation may as well cease, Madam ?" added Arthur, after a short pause. "Why should it have been raised ? One might suppose I had asked your consent to my marriage, whereas you know perfectly well that I am a poor man, with not the slightest chance of taking a wife."

"Poor men get engaged sometimes, Arthur, thinking they'll wait—and wait. Seeing you with that girl—the world calls her good-looking, I believe—I grew into an awful fright for your sake. It would be most disastrous for you to marry beneath your rank—a Bohun never holds up his head afterwards if he does that ; and I thought I ought to speak a word of warning to you. You must take a suitable wife when you do marry—one fit to mate with the future Sir Arthur Bohun."

"To mate with plain Arthur Bohun. To call me the future Sir Arthur is stretching possibility out very wide indeed, Madam," he added, laughing.

"Not at all. You will as surely succeed as that I am telling it you. Look at that puny James Bohun ! A few years at most, will see the last of him."

"I hope not, for his father's sake. Any way, he may live long enough to marry and leave children behind him. Is your lecture at an end, Madam ?" he jestingly concluded. "If so, perhaps you may as well leave me to get my coat on, or I shall have to keep the dinner waiting."

"I have another word," said Madam ; "your coat can keep. Miss Dallory dines here."

"Miss Dallory ! I thought she was in Switzerland. Did she come over in a balloon to dine with us ?"

"She is staying with her brother Frank. I and Matilda called at Ham Court just now and brought her with us."

"Did you bring him?"

"I did not see him; they said he was not in the way. But now why do I mention this?"

"As a bit of gossip for me, I suppose. It's very good of you. My coat and the dinner can certainly wait."

"I have brought Miss Dallory here for your sake, Arthur Bohun," was the rejoinder, spoken with emphatic meaning. "*She* is the young lady you will do well to think of as your future wife."

Madam went out of the room with much stately rustle, and swept down stairs. Another minute, and the door opened again to admit Richard North. Captain Bohun had not progressed further in dressing, or stirred from his place, but was leaning against the window-frame in abstraction, whistling softly.

"Madam's in a way, is she not?" began Richard in a low tone. "My window was open, Arthur, and I was obliged to catch a word here and there. I made all kinds of noises, but you did not take the hint."

"*She* didn't; and I would as soon you heard as not," was Captain Bohun's answer. "You are ready, I see, Dick."

"The course of true love never did run smooth, you know," said Richard, laughing.

"And never will. Whenever I read of the old patriarchal days, in which a man had only to fix on a wife and bring her home to his tent; and look on all that has to be considered in these—money, and suitability of family, and settlements—I wonder whether it can be the same world. Madam need not fear that I have any chance of marrying."

"Or you'd not be long a bachelor?"

"I don't know about that."

"You don't know! Why you do know, and so do I. I've seen how it is for some weeks now, Arthur."

"Seen what?"

Richard smiled.

"Seen what?"

"How it is between you and Ellen Adair."

"You think you have?"

"Think! You love her, don't you?"

Arthur Bohun put down the hair-brush gently, which he had held all the while, and moved to get his coat.

"Dick, old fellow, whether it will come to anything between us or not I cannot tell,' he said, his voice strangely deep, his brow flushing with emotion, "but I shall never care for any one else as I care for her."

"Then secure her," answered Dick.

"I might be tempted to do it, in spite of my mother, had I the wherewithal to set up a home; but I've not."

"You have more than double what Rane and Bessy have."

"Rane and Bessy! But Bessy is one in a thousand. I couldn't ask a wife to come home to me on that."

"Just as you think fit, of course. Take care, though, you don't get her snapped up. I should fear it if it were my case. Ellen Adair is the loveliest girl I ever saw, and I think her the sweetest. I could but look at her as we sat in Mrs. Cumberland's room this morning. Other men will be finding it out, Arthur, if they have not already done so."

Arthur never answered. He had gone back to his former post, and was leaning against the window-frame, looking out dreamily.

"Madam objects, I presume?"

"I presume she would if I put it to her," assented Arthur, as if the proposition admitted of no dispute.

"I don't see why she should, or you, either."

"I'm afraid, Dick, we Bohuns have our full share of family pride."

"But Mr. Adair is, no doubt, a gentleman?"

"Oh, yes. That is, not in trade," added Arthur carelessly.

"Well, a gentleman is a gentleman," said Richard.

"Of course. But I take it for granted that he holds no position in the world. And we Bohuns, you know ——"

Arthur stopped. Richard North laughed. "You Bohuns would like to mate only *with* position. A daughter, for example, of the Lord Lieutenant of the county."

"Exactly," assented Arthur, echoing the laugh, but very much in earnest for all that. "Madam has been recommending Miss Dallory to my notice."

"Who?" cried Richard, rather sharply.

"Mary Dallory."

"You might do worse," observed Richard, after a pause.

"No doubt of that, friend. She is down stairs."

"Who is down stairs?"

"She. So Madam has just informed me."

"There's the gong."

"And be hanged to it!" returned Arthur, getting into his coat. "I wish to goodness Madam did not give us the trouble

of putting on dinner dress every other day ! Neither are
entertainments seemly in your house during these troubled
times."

" What's more, I don't see how they will get paid for, if the
trouble continues," candidly spoke Richard.   " Madam must
be uncommonly sanguine to expect they can be."

" Or careless," returned Arthur Bohun in a low tone.
" Dick, my friend, it's a bad sign when a man has no good
word to give his mother."

That every grain of filial affection had long gone out of his
breast and been replaced by a feeling near akin to shame and
contempt, Arthur Bohun was only too conscious of. He strove
to be dutiful ! but it was at times a hard task. Living under
the same roof as his mother, her sins against good manners and
good feeling were brought under his notice perpetually ; he
was more sensitively alive to them than even others could be.

Since Arthur Bohun had quitted the army and recovered
from the long sickness that followed on his wound, Dallory
Hall had been his ostensible home. Latterly he had made it
really such ; for Dallory Ham, contained an attraction from
which he could not tear himself. Ellen Adair had his heart's
best love : and, far from her he could not wander. A pure,
ardent love, honourable as every true passion must be in an
honourable man, but swaying his every action with its power.
Sir Nash Bohun invited him in vain. His aunt, Miss Bohun,
with whom he was a great favourite, could not think why he
went so rarely to see her ; or, when he did go, made his visit
a flying one. Arthur Bohun possessed a few hundreds a
year : about four : just enough to keep him as a gentleman ;
and he had none of the bad habits that run away with young
men's money. Miss Bohun would leave him fairly off when
she died : so he was at ease on the score of the future.
One day, after he had been at Dallory Hall for a few
months, he put a hundred-pound bank-note into Richard
North's hands.

" What is this for ? " questioned Richard.

Arthur told him. The embarrassments in the Hall's finan-
cial department (caused by Madam) were lightly touched on :
this was Arthur's contribution towards his own share of the
cost. In the surprise of the moment Richard North's spirit
rose, and fought at it. Arthur quietly persisted.

" As long as I pitch myself among you in the home tent
here, I shall hand over this sum every six months. To you

Dick: there's nobody else to be trusted with it. If I gave it to Bessy, she would be safe to speak of it, and it might be wiled out of her."

"I never heard of such nonsense in my life," cried Richard. "You will not get me to take it. I'd not countenance anything of the kind."

"Yes you will, Dick. You'd not like me to take up my abode at the 'Dallory Arms.' I declare on my honour I shall do so, if I am forced to be as a guest at the Hall."

"But, Arthur ——"

"Dick, my friend, there's no need of argument. I mean what I say. Don't drive me away. The 'Dallory Arms' would not be very comfortable as a home; and I should drift away, goodness knows where."

"As if one inmate, more or less, made any difference in our home expenses."

"As if it did not. I have no right or claim whatever to be living on your father. Don't make me small in my own eyes, frère Richard. You know that you'd feel the same in my place, and do the same. No one need know of this but our two selves, Dick."

Richard gave in: he saw that Arthur was resolute: and after all, it was just. So he took the bank-note to account, and told his father; and Arthur Bohun stayed on, his conscience at peace. Once, in one of Madam's furious onslaughts of temper, when she spared nobody, she had abused her son for staying at the Hall, and living upon her. Upon *her!* Arthur parried the attack with a careless kind of good humour, merely saying he was Dick's guest. When Dick turned him out of the Hall he should go.

CHAPTER XIX.

MARY DALLORY.

The assembled guests waited in the drawing-room. Madam, with a face of gracious suavity, was bestowing her smiles on all, after her manner in society, her white silk dress gleaming in its richness. A slight frown crossed her brow, however, at the tardy entrance of her son and Richard North.

"We have waited for you," she rather sharply said. "Dinner has been announced."

Richard found his father did not intend to be present, and

N

that he must act as host, which was nothing new. Glancing round the room, he was advancing to Miss Dallory—there was no married lady present save Madam—when Madam's voice rang out cold and clear.

"Take Eliza Field, Richard North. Arthur, you will conduct Miss Dallory."

Now that was all wrong according to the rules of etiquette. Miss Dallory, the great heiress, whose family was of some note in the county, should have fallen to Richard : Eliza Field, a middle-aged lady, had only been Matilda North's governess. But Madam had a way of enforcing her own mandates : or, rather, of letting people know they might not be disputed. There was a moment's awkwardness : Richard and Arthur both stood with arrested footsteps ; and then each advanced to the appointed lady. But Miss Dallory nearly upset it all : she turned away from Captain Bohun to Richard, her hand outstretched.

" How do you do, Mr. Richard North ? "

He clasped it for a moment in his. Madam, who had a shrewd way of making guesses, and of seeing things that nobody else saw, had picked up a notion long ago, that had Richard North's fortunes been in the ascendant, he might have forgotten the wide gulf lying between him and Mary Dallory—she patrician-born, he plebeian—and asked her to step over it.

"I did not know you had returned, Miss Dallory, until a few minutes ago," said Richard.

" No ! I have been home two days."

They separated. Madam was sweeping on to the dining-room on the arm of a Colonel Carter, whose acquaintance she had made at Homburg, and the rest had to follow. Richard brought up the rear with Eliza Field.

Miss Dallory, a rather tall and graceful girl of two-and-twenty, sat between Arthur Bohun and Richard North. She was not particularly handsome, but very pleasing. A fair-complexioned face with plenty of good sense in it, grey eyes set rather deep in the head, and soft, dark-brown hair. Her manners were remarkably open and ready : her speech candidly independent. It was this perhaps—the pleasantness of the speech and manners—that made her a favourite with everybody.

The Dallory family were very wealthy. There were three of them : Miss Dallory and her two brothers, John and

Frank, both older than herself. They had been left orphans
at an early age: their father's will having bequeathed his
property nearly equally among the three; the portion of it
entailed on his elder son lay in another county. To the surprise of many people it was found that he had left Dallory
Hall to his daughter; so that, in point of fact, this Miss
Dallory, sitting at Mr. North's dinner-table, was the owner of
the house. It had been the residence of the Dallory family
during Mr. Dallory's lifetime: after his death, the trustees
let it on lease to Mr. North. Which lease was *purchased:* so
that Mr. North had no rent to pay for it. The lease, however, had now all but terminated. Madam hoped to be able
to get it renewed: perhaps that might be one of the reasons
why she was now setting out to pay court to Mary Dallory.
That young lady came into her property when she was one-
and-twenty; and all power lay in her own hands. Nearly
two years ago Miss Dallory had gone on the Continent with
her aunt, Mrs. Leasom. Illness had prolonged Mrs. Leasom's
stay there, and they had but just returned. Mrs. Leasom
remained at her home in London; Miss Dallory came down
at once to her younger brother's house—an exceedingly
pretty place just beyond the Ham. And that's enough of
explanation.

The dinner progressed. Miss Dallory talked chiefly with
Richard: next to whom she sat; Arthur Bohun, on the other
side, was rather silent and glum. She was telling of her
travels: and jestingly complaining of finding what she called
a grand dinner, when she had thought Mrs. North was only
bringing her to dine en famille—as her dress proved.
Which was nothing but a coloured muslin.

"Don't laugh at me, Mr. Richard North. If you had been
living in a remote village of Switzerland for months, dining
off bouilli and a thin chicken in your aunt's chamber, you
would think this grand yourself."

"I did not laugh," answered Richard. "It is a vast deal
grander than I like."

"Do you get it every day?"

"Nearly."

"Where's Mr. North?" she asked, slightly dropping her voice.

Richard shook his head. "The grandeur has tired him,
Miss Dallory. He dines nearly always in his parlour: I join
him as often as I can."

"I hear he is breaking," she continued, her deep grey eyes

looking straight at Richard, pity and concern in their depths.
"Frank says so."

"He is breaking sadly. The prolonged strain is too much
for him."

Madam glanced down the table, and spoke in a tart tone.

"Are you attending to Miss Field, Richard?"

Miss Field was on his left hand: Miss Dallory on his right.

"Yes, Madam. She heard," added he to Miss Dallory,
scarcely moving his lips.

"And it was high treason, I suppose," rejoined that young
lady, confidentially. "There have been changes in your home,
Mr. Richard, since I was last here. Mr. North's first children
were all in it, then."

"And now two of them have gone out of it. Bessy to
another home: Edmund to—his last one."

"Ah, I heard all. How sad it must have been for you
and Mr. North! John and Frank wrote me word that they
followed him to the grave."

"Very sad for him as well as us," assented Richard.
"But he is better off."

"Who sent that wicked letter?"

Richard North dropped his glance on his plate as he
answered, apparently intent on what was there. Miss
Dallory's keen eyes had been on his: and she used to read a
great deal that lay within them.

"There has been no discovery at all."

"It was thought to be Mr. Tim Wilks, I believe."

"It was certainly not he," said Richard, rather hastily.

"No! He had at least something to do with the mischief,
if he did not write the letter."

"Yes. But without intending evil. The next to leave the
home here may be myself," he added.

"You!"

"Of course you have heard that our works are at a standstill? The men have struck."

"That's old news: I heard it in Switzerland."

"If we are not able to re-open them—and I begin to think
we shall not be—I must go out in the world and seek employment elsewhere."

"Nonsense, Richard North!"

"If you reflect for a moment, you will see that it is all sober
earnest, Miss Dallory. When a man does not possess the
means of living, he must work to earn one."

She said no more then. And when she spoke again the subject was changed.

"Is Bessy's marriage a happy one?"

"Very—as it seems to me. The worst is, Rane gets on as badly as ever in his profession."

"But why does he?"

"I know not. Except that Madam undoubtedly works—always works—to keep him back."

"What a shame! He shall come and attend me. I'll get up some headaches on purpose."

Richard laughed.

"We have had changes also, since you and I met," resumed Miss Dallory. "But not sad ones. I have become my own mistress in the world; am independent of everybody. And Frank has taken up his abode at Ham Court, for a permanency."

"I hope you intend to make a good use of your independence," said Richard with gravity.

"Don't I. And I shall *be* independent; you may rely on that."

"We heard it rumoured some time ago that you were likely to lose your independence, Miss Dallory."

"I! In what way?"

"By getting married."

Their eyes met for a moment, and then dropped. Miss Dallory laughed lightly.

"Did the news penetrate as far as this? Well, it never was 'likely,' Mr. Richard North. A—gentleman asked me; but I caught up an idea that he wanted my money more than he did myself, and—so nothing came of it."

"Who was he?"

"It would not be fair to him to tell."

"Right. Thank you for correcting me," spoke Richard in his earnest way. "I ought to feel shame for asking. I beg your pardon; and his."

Happening to glance at the young lady, he saw that her face had turned crimson with blushes. A rare thing for Miss Dallory. She was too self-possessed to display emotion on light occasions.

"Have you seen Ham Court lately?" she resumed, looking up; and the blushes made her look very pretty.

"Not since your brother came to it. He has not been here long, you know. I called one day, but they said Mr. Dallory was out."

"The place is so nice now. He has made alterations, and done it up beautifully. You must come again."

"With pleasure," answered Richard. "How long shall you remain with him?"

"As long as he will have me. I am not going away yet. I shall make it my home. Frank has quiet tastes and so have I: and we intend to live together like a brother-and-sister Darby and Joan, and grow into an old maid and an old bachelor."

Richard smiled. "How is it Francis did not come with you to dinner?"

"He was not in the way to get an invitation. May I dare to tell you why?" she added below her breath. "When we saw Madam's carriage driving up, Frank disappeared. 'Say I am out, Polly,' was his order to me. He and Madam never got on well: as a little boy he was terribly afraid of her, and I think the feeling lasts. When I went to put my bonnet on, I found him shut up in his room with the blinds down. He wished me joy of my visit, and promised to come and walk home with me in the evening."

"Take care of Madam's ears," breathed Richard.

"She cannot hear me. Your neighbour even cannot. Arthur may,"—looking round at Captain Bohun· questioningly—"but I don't mind him."

"Talk away," said Arthur. "Dick and I often wish we had a remote room, with locked door and drawn blinds, to use as a refuge in home storms. Heaven knows it is the pain of my life to be able to say this."

How suggestive it was!—of the estimation in which Mrs. North was publicly held. For her son to confess this, for Miss Dallory with her refined mind and feeling to have called it forth, spoke badly for Madam.

She—Madam—rose from table early. Something in the arrangements seemed not to suit her. It was a warm and lovely evening, and they went out on the lawn. Miss Dallory slipped round the corner of the house to the window of Mr. North's parlour.

It stood open and he sat just within it. Sat with his hands on his knees, and his head drooping. Miss Dallory started back: not so much because his face was thin and worn, but at its expression of hopeless despair. In her two years' absence, he seemed to have aged ten.

She stepped over the threshold, and gently laid her hands on his. He looked up like a man bewildered.

" Why—it—it—it cannot be Mary Dallory."

" It is Mary Dallory; come home at last. You'll kiss me, won't you, dear Mr. North."

He kissed her very fondly. In the old days when John North was supposed to be the most rising man, in a commercial point of view, in the county, Mr. Dallory had thought it worth while to court his friendship, and Mr. North had been asked to stand to his little girl. Mary—after she lost her own parents—was wont to say she belonged to the Hall, and she used to be often there. Her aunt, Mrs. Leasom, who had been a Miss Dallory once, was left personal guardian to the children, with Ham Court as her residence until the younger son should be of age, to whom it would then lapse. But Mrs. Leasom spent a large portion of her time in London, and sometimes the children had not seen their native place, Dallory, for years together.

" When did you come home, my dear ? "

" To England a week ago. To Ham Court only yesterday. Do you know that you are much changed ? "

" Ay. There's nothing but change in this life, my dear. The nearer we approach the end of our days, the faster our sorrows seem to come upon us : I have had more than my share of them; and they have changed me. Turning round, to this quarter, to that quarter, I see only one source of comfort left to me in the wide world."

" And that ? " she asked, half kneeling at his feet.

" My dear son Richard. Nobody knows the good son he has been to me ; the sacrifices he has made. Nobody, save God."

Miss Dallory gave no answer to this. He was stroking her soft hair in deep abstraction, thinking no doubt of his many troubles—for he always was thinking of them—when the person in question entered ; Richard North. Miss Dallory rose and sat down on a chair decorously.

She remained but a minute or two now, and spent the time talking and laughing. Richard gave her his arm to take her back to the company. Miss Dallory apparently was in no hurry to go, for she lingered over some of the near flowerbeds.

" Is the strike a serious matter ? " she questioned, her voice taking a confidential tone.

" As serious as it is possible for any matter of the kind to be," replied Richard.

" You and your men were always on the best of terms :
why did they become dissatisfied with you ? "

" They never became dissatisfied with me. The Trades
Unions' agents stepped in and persuaded them they would
be better off if they could work less time and be paid more
wages. The men listened : it was only natural : and presented themselves to me with these new demands. I did
not grant them, and they struck. That's the whole truth in
a nutshell, Miss Dallory."

" I suppose you would not grant them ? "

" Right. I would not grant them upon principle ; I could not,
because my profits did not afford it. I am quite certain of
one thing : that if I had acceded, in a short while the men
would have demanded more. The Trades' Unions will never
allow them to be satisfied, until ——"

" Until what ? " she asked, for Richard had stopped.

" Until the country is ruined. Until its trade has left it."

" It is a serious thing," she said—and she was very grave
now. " I suppose you would take the men on again at the
old terms ? "

" And be glad to do it."

" And they will not be taken ? "

" No. I have offered, in regard to their demand for increased wages, to meet them half-way. It is of no use."

" Then I think those men deserve to learn what want of
employment means," she returned warmly. " I thought your
men were intelligent; I used to know many of them. When
I go amongst them—and that may be to-morrow—I shall
ask if they have taken leave of their senses. What does
Mrs. Gass say to it all ? "

Richard smiled a little. Mrs. Gass said more than he did,
he answered, but it was equally useless.

" And I suppose it is the strike that is troubling Mr.
North ? I do think him so changed."

" It troubles him, of course—and there are other things."

" Does it trouble *you ?* " asked Miss Dallory, in a pointed
tone, as she looked straight at him.

" Trouble me ! " he rejoined, in surprise at the superfluous
question. " Why, see you not what it involves—unless we
can go on again ? Simply ruin. Ruin for me, and for my
father with me. There's your brother."

They had reached the lawn at length, and saw Francis,
Dallory, who had come to walk home with his sister. He was

a short, fair young man with an open countenance. Madam had already seized upon him.

"Where's Arthur?" demanded Madam imperiously, as Miss Dallory came into view on Richard's arm. "I thought he was with you."

Miss Dallory answered that she had not seen Arthur Bohun since she quitted the dinner-table. Nobody had seen him—that Madam could discover. She suspected he must have gone off somewhere to smoke; and would have liked to put his pipe behind the fire.

But the pipe was not in fault. Arthur Bohun, possibly thinking there were enough without him, had surreptitiously made his escape, and gone for a stroll towards the Ham. It took him so near to Mrs. Cumberland's that he said to himself he might as well call in and ask after her headache—that she had been suffering from in the morning.

Sophistry! Nothing but sophistry. Captain Arthur Bohun did not really care whether the headache was worse or better; until a minute ago he had not even remembered that she had complained of one. The naked truth was, that he could not bear to rest for even one evening without a sight of Ellen Adair. No mother ever hungered for a lost child, as he hungered for her presence.

They were at tea. Mrs. Cumberland, Ellen, and Mr. Seeley. When Jelly showed Captain Bohun in, the doctor was just taking his second cup. Ellen, who sat at the tea-tray, asked Captain Bohun if he would like some, and he rather savagely answered, No. Warfare lay in his mind. What business had that man to be sitting there on a footing of companionship with Ellen Adair.

Mrs. Cumberland's head was a little worse, if anything, she replied, thanking Captain Bohun for his solicitude in regard to it. Mr. Seeley had given her two draughts of something—ether, she believed—in the afternoon, but they had not done the head any good. Arthur pushed back his golden hair in a passion. Then the man had had the impudence to go there in the afternoon as well as morning and evening! *How* could Mrs. Cumberland so far forget the fitness of propriety as to allow him to take tea with her—to invite him, no doubt—when she knew that by so doing he must also take it with Ellen Adair?

It might have come to a question of which would have sat out the other—for Mr. Seeley detected somewhat of the feelings

of Arthur Bohun's mind, and resented them, considering himself as good a man as he, in regard of possessing the same
right to a chance of woman's favour—but for the entrance of
Dr. Rane.   Dr. Rane appeared to have no present intention of
leaving again, for he plunged into a hot discussion with his
brother practitioner, touching some difficult question in surgery,
which seemed quite likely to continue all night, and Arthur
Bohun rose.   He would have remained on willingly, but he
was ever sensitive as to intruding, and he fancied Mrs. Cumberland might wonder why he stayed.

As he went out, Francis Dallory and his sister were passing
on their walk homeward.   Captain Bohun turned with them,
and went to the end of the Ham.

The shades of evening—nay, of night—had stolen over the
earth as he went back; the light night of summer.   The north-
west was bright with its blue-green tinge of opal; a star or
two twinkled in the heavens.   Dr. Rane was pacing his
garden walks, his wife on his arm.

"Good-night, Bessy!" he called out, to her whom he had
always regarded as his step-sister.

"Good-night, Arthur!" came the hearty rejoinder—for
Bessy had recognised his voice.

Onwards for a few steps—only a few—and it brought Arthur
Bohun level with the window of Mrs. Cumberland's drawing-
room.   It was not yet lighted.   At the window, their heads
nearly close together, stood the other doctor and Ellen Adair.
In Captain Bohun's desperate anger, he stared Ellen full in the
face, and made no movement of recognition.   Turning his
head away with a contemptuous movement, quite plainly discernible in the dusk, he went striding on.

Shakespeare never read more truly the human heart than
when he said jealousy makes the food it feeds on.   Arthur
Bohun went home nearly mad; not so much with jealousy in
its narrow sense, as with indignation at the doctor's most
iniquitous presumption.   Could he have analysed his own heart
in due fairness, he would have found full trust in the good
faith of Ellen Adair.   But he was swayed by man's erring
nature, and yielded to it wilfully.

How innocent it all was! how little suggestive of fear,
could Captain Bohun but have read events correctly.   There
had been no invitation to tea at all; Mr. Seeley had gone in
just as they began to take it, and was offered a cup by Mrs.
Cumberland.   As to the being together at the window, Ellen

had been standing there to catch the fading light for her wool work, perhaps as an excuse for leaving him and Mrs. Cumberland to converse alone; and he had just come up to her to say good-night as Captain Bohun paused.

If we did but divine the real truth of these fancies when jealousy puts them before us in its false and glaring light, some phases of our lives might be all the happier. Arthur Bohun lay tossing the whole night long on his sleepless pillow, tormenting himself by wondering what Ellen Adair's answer to Seeley would be. That the fellow in his audacity was proposing to her as they stood at the window, he could have sworn before the Lord Chief Baron of England. It was a wretched night; his tumultuous thoughts were fit to kill him. Arthur had Collins's "Ode to the Passions" by heart; but it never occurred to him to recal any part of it to profit now.

> "Thy numbers, Jealousy, to nought were fixed,
>   Sad proof of thy distressful state.
> Of differing themes the veering song was mixed:
>   And now it courted Love; now, raving, called on Hate."

CHAPTER XX.

LOVE AMONG THE ROSES.

THE early sunshine is a great purifier. Fancies find but little room in the matter-of-fact bustle of every-day life. When Arthur Bohun rose, his senses had returned to him. That Ellen Adair's love was his, and that no fear existed of her accepting any other man, let him be prince or peasant, reason told him. He wanted to see her; for *that* his heart was always yearning; but on this morning when, as it seemed, he had been judging her harshly, the necessity seemed overwhelmingly great. His impatient feet would have carried him to Mrs. Cumberland's after breakfast; but his spirit was a little rebellious yet, and kept him back. He'd not show his impatience, he thought; he'd not go down until the afternoon; and he began to resort to all kinds of expedients to kill the earlier time. He walked with Richard North the best part of the way to Dallory: he came back and wrote to his aunt, Miss Bohun; he went pottering about the flower-beds with Mr. North. As the day wore on towards noon, his restless feet betook him to Ham Lane—which the reader has not visited since he saw Dr. Rane hastening through it on the dark and troubled night that opened this history. The hedges were green now, blooming with their dog-roses of delicate pink and white, redolent with the perfume of sweet-briar. Captain Bohun went along, switching at these same pleasant hedges with his cane. Avoiding the turning that would take him out into Dallory Ham, he continued his way to another lane, less luxurious; the lane that ran along the back of the houses of the Ham, and which was familiarly called by their inhabitants "the back lane." Strolling onwards, he had the satisfaction of finding himself passing by the dead wall of Mrs. Cumberland's garden, and of seeing the roof and chimneys of her house. Should he go round and call? A few steps lower down, just beyond Dr. Rane's, there was an opening that would take him, a public-house at its corner. He had told himself he would not go until the afternoon, and now it was barely twelve o'clock; should he call, or should he not?

Moving on, in his indecision, at a slow pace, he had got just opposite Dr. Rane's back garden door, when it suddenly opened, and the doctor came forth.

"Ah, how d'ye do?" said the doctor, rather surprised at seeing Arthur Bohun there. "Were you coming in this way? The door was bolted."

"Only taking a stroll," carelessly replied Captain Bohun. "How's Bessy?"

"Quite well. She is in the dining-room, if you'll come in and see her."

Nothing loth, Arthur Bohun stepped in at once, the doctor continuing on his way. Mrs. Rane was darning stockings. She and Arthur had always been the very best of friends, quite brother and sister. Meek and gentle as ever, she looked, sitting there with her smooth, curling hair, and the loving expression in her mild, soft eyes. Arthur sat down and talked with her, his glance roving ever to that other house, seeking the form of one whom he did not see.

"Do you know how Mrs. Cumberland is this morning?" he inquired of Bessy.

"I have not heard. Mr. Seeley has been there; for I saw him in the dining-room with Ellen Adair."

Arthur Bohun's pulses froze to ice. Figuratively speaking, his golden hair bristled up, stiff and straight.

"I think they are both in the garden now."

"Are they?" snapped Arthur. "His patients must get on nicely if he idles away his mornings in a garden."

Bessy looked up from her darning. "I don't mean that Seeley's there, Arthur—I mean Mrs. Cumberland and Ellen."

As Bessy spoke, Jelly was seen to come out of Mrs. Cumberland's house, penetrate amidst the trees, and return with her mistress.

"Some one has called, I suppose," remarked Bessy.

Captain Bohun thought the gods had made the opportunity for himself expressly. He went out, stepped over the small wire fence, and disappeared in the direction that Mrs. Cumberland had come from, believing it would lead him to Ellen Adair.

In the secluded and beautiful spot where we first saw her (but where we shall not often, alas! see her again) she sat. The flowers of early spring were out then; the richer summer flowers were blooming now. A natural bower of roses seemed to encompass her about; the shrubs clustered, the trees o'er-shadowed her overhead. The falling cascade was trickling softly as ever down the artificial rocks, murmuring its mono-tonous cadence; the birds sang to it and to each other from branch to branch; glimpses of the green lawn and of bril-liantly-hued flowers were caught through the trees. Ellen Adair had sometimes thought the spot beautiful as a scene of fairy-land. It was little less so.

She was not working this morning, An open book lay before her on the rustic table; her cheek was leaning on her raised hand, from which the wrist-lace fell back, a hand so suspiciously delicate as to betoken some lack of sound strength in its owner. She wore a white dress, with a bow of pink ribbon at the throat, and a pink waist-band. There were times, and this was one, when she looked extremely fragile.

A sound as of footsteps. Ellen only thought it was Mrs. Cumberland returning, and read on. But there was a different sound in *these* steps as they gained on her ear. Her heart stood still, and then bounded on again with a tumultuous rush, her pulses tingled, her sweet face turned red as the blushing rose. Sunshine had come.

"Good morning, Miss Adair."

In a cold, resentful, haughty tone was it spoken, and he did not attempt to shake hands. The sunshine seemed to go in again with a sweep. She shut her book and opened it, shut and opened it, her fingers fluttering. Captain Bohun put his hat on the seat.

" I thought Seeley might be here " said he, seeking out a pretty rose, and plucking it carefully.

" Seeley ! " she exclaimed.

" Seeley. I beg your pardon. I did not know I spoke indistinctly, SEELEY."

He stood and faced her, watching the varying colour of her face, the soft blushes going and coming. Sometimes they increased his anger.

" May I ask if you have accepted him ? "

" Ac—cepted him ! " she stammered, in wild confusion. " Accepted what ? "

" The offer that Seeley made you last night."

" It was not last night," she replied in a confused impulse.

" Oh, then it was this morning ! May I congratulate you, or not ? "

Ellen Adair turned to her book in deep vexation. She had been caught, as it were—deluded into the tacit admission that Mr. Seeley had made the offer. And she was hurt at Arthur Bohun's words and tone. Had he no better trust in her than *this ?* As she turned the leaves of the book backwards and forwards in her agitation, as if seeking for some particular page, the plain gold ring on her finger attracted his sight. He was chafing inwardly, but he strove to appear at the most careless ease, and sat down as far from her as the bench allowed, which, seeing that it would only hold two stout people, could not be very far.

" I'd be honourable if I died for it," he remarked with indifference, sniffing at the rose. " Is it quite the thing for you to listen to another man while you wear that ring upon your finger ?"

Ellen took it off and pushed it towards him along the table.

This frightened him. He turned as white as ashes. Until this, he had only been speaking in jealously, not in belief. Her own face was becoming white, her lips were compressed to hide their trembling. And thus they sat for a minute or two, like the two simpletons they were. He looked at the ring, he looked at her.

" Do you mean it, Ellen ? " he asked, in a voice that struggled with agitation, proving how very earnest he deemed the thing was becoming—whatever it might have begun in.

She made no answer.

" Do you wish to give me back this ring ? "

" What you said was, I thought, equivalent to asking for it.""

"It was not. You know better."

"Why are you quarrelling with me?"

Moving an inch nearer, he changed his tone to gentleness, bending his head forward to speak.

"Heaven knows that it is bitter enough to do so. Have I cause, Ellen?"

Her eyes were bent down: the colour stole into her face again; a half smile parted her lips.

"You know, Ellen, it is a perfectly monstrous thing that a common man like Seeley should dare to cast his aspiring thoughts to you."

"Was it my fault?" she returned. "He ought to have seen that—that—I should not like it."

"What did you tell him?"

"That it was quite impossible; that he was making a mistake altogether. When he was gone, I complained to Mrs. Cumberland."

"Insolent jackanapes! Was he rude, Ellen?"

"Rude! Mr. Seeley!" she returned in surprise. "Quite the contrary. He has always been as considerate and respectful as a man can be. You look down on his position, Arthur, but he is as complete a gentleman in mind as you are."

"I only despise his position when he would seek to unite you to it."

"It has been very wrong of you to make me confess this. I can tell you *I* am feeling anything but 'honourable,' as you put it just now. There are things that should never be talked about; this is one. Nothing can be more unfair."

Very unfair. Captain Bohun's high-class feeling had come back to him, and he could but assent to it. He began to feel a little ashamed of himself on more points than one.

"It shall never escape my lips, Ellen, while I breathe. Seeley's secret is safe for me."

Taking up the ring, he held it for a moment, as if examining the gold. Ellen rose and went outside. The interview was becoming a very conscious one. He caught her up near the cascade, took her right hand in his, and slipped the ring upon her third finger.

"How many times has it been off?" he asked.

"Never until to-day."

"Well, there it is again, Ellen. Cherish it still. I hope— I hope—that ere long ——"

He did not finish, but she understood quite well what he

meant. Their eyes met, and each read the impassioned love seated within the other; strangely pure withal, and idealistic as ever poet dreamed of. He strained the hand in his.

"Forgive my petulance, my darling."

Save for the one sweet word and the lingering pressure of the hand; save that the variegated rose was transferred from his possession to hers, the interview had been wholly uncharacterised by the fond signs and tokens that are commonly supposed to attend the intercourse of lovers. Captain Bohun had hitherto abstained from using such, and perhaps heaven alone knew what the self-denial cost. In his ultra-refined nature he may have deemed such would be unjustifiable, until he could speak out openly and say, Will you be my wife?

"What is your book, Ellen?" he asked, as she returned to take it from the table.

"Longfellow."

"Longfellow! Shall I read it to you? can you stay out?"

"I can stay until one o'clock: luncheon time."

They sat down and he began: "The Courtship of Miles Standish." The blue sky shone down upon them through the flickering leaves, the cascade trickled, the bees hummed in the warm air, the white butterflies sported with the buds and flowers: and Ellen Adair, her hands clasping that treasure they held, the variegated rose, her eyes falling on it to hide their happiness, listened in wrapt attention, for the voice was sweeter to her than any out of heaven.

The words of that other poet—not Longfellow, as we all know—most surely were applicable to this period of the existence of Captain Bohun and Ellen Adair. One of them at least would acknowledge it amidst the bitterness of after-life.

Love took up the glass of Time, and turned it in his glowing hands;
Every moment, lightly shaken, ran itself in golden sands."

It could not last—speaking now only of the hour. One o'clock came all too soon; when he had seemingly read about ten minutes; and Miles Standish had to be left in the most unsatisfactory state. Ellen rose: she must hasten in.

"It is a pity to leave it at this," said Arthur. "Shall I come and finish it in the afternoon?"

Ellen shook her head. In the afternoon she would have to drive out with Mrs. Cumberland.

Captain Bohun went home through the green lanes, and soon found himself amidst those other flowers—Mr. North's.

That gentleman came forth from his parlour to meet him, apparently in some tribulation, a letter in his hand.

"Oh, Arthur, I don't know what to say to you ; I am so sorry," he exclaimed. "Look here. When the postman came this morning, I happened to be out on the lawn, and he gave me my two letters, as I thought, and as he must have thought, going on to the hall door with the rest. I put them in my pocket and forgot them, Arthur : my spectacles were indoors. When I remembered them only just now, I found one was directed to you in Sir Nash's hand. I am so sorry," repeated poor Mr. North in his most helpless manner.

"Don't be that, sir," replied Arthur cheerily. "It's nothing ; not of the least consequence at all," he added, opening the letter. But nevertheless, as his eyes fell on the contents, a rather startled expression took his face.

"There!" cried Mr. North, looking inclined to cry. "Something's wrong, and the delay has done mischief."

"Indeed nothing's wrong—in the sense you are thinking," repeated Arthur—for he would not have added to the poor old man's troubles for the world. "My uncle says James is not so well as he could wish : he wants me to go up at once and stay with them. You can read it for yourself, sir."

Mr. North put on his glasses. "I see, Arthur. You might have gone the first thing this morning, but for my keeping the letter. It was very stupid of the postman to give it to me."

Arthur laughed. "Indeed, I should have made no such hurry. There's not the least necessity for that. I think I shall go up this afternoon, though."

"Yes, do, Arthur. And explain to Sir Nash that it was my fault. Tell him that I am growing forgetful and useless. Fit only to be cut down, Arthur ; to be cut down."

Arthur Bohun put the old man's arm affectionately within his, and took him back to his parlour. If Mr. North had grown old it was with worry, not with years : the worry dealt out to him daily by Madam ; and Arthur would have remedied it with his best blood had he known how.

"You had better go up with me, sir ; for a little change. Sir Nash would be so glad to see you."

"*I* go up with you ! I couldn't, Arthur ; I am not equal to it now. And the strike is on, you know, and my place ought to be here while it lasts. The men look upon me still as their master, though Dick—Dick acts. And there's another thing. Arthur—I couldn't leave my roses just as they have come into bloom."

Arthur Bohun smiled; the last reason was all cogent. Mr. North stayed behind, and he went up that same afternoon to London.

CHAPTER XXI.

THE TONTINE.

The tontine. If the reader only knew how important a share the tontine—with its results—holds in this little history, he would enter on it with interest.

Tontines may be of different arrangement. In fact they are so. This one was as follows. It had been instituted at Whitborough. Ten gentlemen put each an equal sum into a common fund, and invested the whole in the joint names of ten children all under a year old. This money was to be allowed to accumulate at compound interest, until only one of these children should be left alive: that one, the last survivor, would then receive the whole of the money unconditionally.

Of these ten children whose names were inscribed on the parchment deed, Oliver Rane and Bessy North alone survived. Mr. North had been wont to call it an unlucky tontine, for its members had died off rapidly one after another. For several years only three had been left; and now one of them, George Massey, had followed in the wake of those that were gone. Under ordinary circumstances, the tontine would have excited no comment whatever, but have gone on smoothly to the end: that is, until one of the two survivors had collapsed. The other one would have had the money paid him; and nothing been thought about it, except that he was a fortunate man.

But this case was exceptional. The two survivors were man and wife. For the good fortune to lapse to one of them, the other must die. It was certainly a curious position, and it excited a great deal of comment in the neighbourhood. Dallory, as prone to gossip as other places, made it into that oft-quoted thing, a nine-days' wonder. In the general stagnation caused by the strike, people took up the tontine as a source of relief.

Practically the tontine was of no further use to the two remaining members: that is, to the two combined. They were one, so to say; and so long as they continued to be such, the

money could not lapse. If Bessy died, Dr. Rane would take
it; if Dr. Rane died, she would take it. Nothing more could
be made of it than this. It had been accumulating now just
one-and-thirty years; how much longer it would be left to
accumulate none could foresee. For one-and-thirty years
to come, in all human probability; for Dr. Rane and his wife
appeared to possess, each, a sound and healthy constitution.
Nay, they might survive ten or twenty years beyond that, and
yet not be very aged. And so, there it was; and Dallory
made the matter its own, with unceremonious freedom.

But not as Dr. and Mrs. Rane did. They had need of
money, and this huge sum (huge to them) lying at the very
threshold of their door, but forbidden to enter, was more tan-
talizing than pen can tell. Richard North had not been far
wrong in his computation: and the amount, as it stood at
present, was rather considerably over two thousand pounds.
The round sum, however, was large enough to reckon by,
without counting the odds and ends. Two thousand pounds!
Two thousand pounds theirs of right, and yet they might not
touch it because one of them was not dead!

How many hours they spent discussing the matter with
each other could never be computed. As soon as the twilight
of the evening came on, wherever they might be and whatever the occupation, the theme was sure to be drifted into.
In the dining-room when it grew too dusk for Dr. Rane to
pursue his writing; in the drawing-room, into which Bessy
would wile him, and sing to him one of her simple songs;
walking together, arm within arm, in the garden paths, the
stars in the summer sky above them, the waving trees encom-
passing them round about, the subject of the tontine would be
taken up: the tontine; nothing but the tontine. It was no
wonder that they grew to form plans of what they would do
if the money were theirs: we all know how apt we are to let
imagination run away with us, and to indulge visions that
grow to seem like reality. Dr. Rane painted a bright future.
With two thousand pounds in hand, he could establish himself in a first-class metropolitan locality, set up well, both
professionally and socially; and there would be plenty of
money for him and his wife to live upon while the practice
was growing. Bessy entered into it all as eagerly as he.
Having become accustomed to the idea of quitting Dallory,
she never glanced back at the possibility of remaining. *She*
thought his eager wish, his unalterable determination to leave

it, was connected only with the interests of his profession; *he* knew that the dread of a certain possible discovery, ever haunting his conscience, made the place more intolerable to him day by day. At any cost he must get away from it: at any cost. There was a great happiness in these evening conversations, in the glowing hope presented by plans and projects. But, where was the use of indulging such, when the tontine money (the pivot on which all was to turn) could never be theirs? As often as this damping recollection brought them up with a check, Dr. Rane would fall into a gloomy silence. Gradually, by the very force of thinking, he saw a way, or thought he saw a way, by which their hopes might be accomplished. And that was to induce the trustees to advance the money at once to him and his wife jointly.

Meanwhile the strike continued in unabated force. Not a man was at work; every one refused to do a stroke unless he could be paid for it what *he* thought right, and left off his daily labour when he chose. One might have supposed, by the independence of the demands, that the men were the masters, and North and Gass the servants. Privation was beginning to reign, garments grew scanty, faces pinched. There was not so much as a sixpence for superfluities: and under that head in troubled times must be classed the attendance of a medical man. It will readily be understood, therefore, that this state of affairs did not contribute to fill the pockets of Dr. Rane.

One day, Mr. North, sitting on the short green bench in front of his choicest carnation bed, found two loving hands put round his neck from behind. He had been three parts asleep, and woke up slightly bewildered.

"Bessy, child, is it you?"

It was Mrs. Rane. Her footfall on the grass had not been heard. She wore a cool print dress and black silk mantle; and her plain straw bonnet sat well on, around the pretty falling curls. Bessy looked quiet and simple always: and always a lady.

"Did I startle you, papa?"

"No, my dear. When I felt the arms, I thought it was Mary Dallory. She comes upon me without warning sometimes. Here's room, Bessy."

Making way for her, she sat down beside him. It was a very hot morning, and Bessy untied the strings of her bonnet. There was a slight look of weariness on her face as if she

were just a little worried with home cares. In truth she felt
so : but all for Oliver's sake. If the money came not in so
freely as to make matters easy, she did not mind it for herself, but for him.

"Papa, I have come to talk to you," she began, laying one
of her hands on his knee affectionately. "It is about the
tontine money. Oliver thinks that it might be paid to us
conjointly ; that it ought to be."

"I know he does," replied Mr. North. "It can't be done,
Bessy."

Her countenance fell a little. " Do you think not, papa ? "

" I am sure not, child."

" Papa, I am here this morning to beg of you to use your
interest for us with Sir Thomas Ticknell. Oliver knows
nothing of my coming. He said last night, when we were
talking, that if you could be induced to throw your interest
into our scale, the bank might listen to you. So I thought to
myself that I would come to you in the morning and ask."

"The bank won't listen to me, or to anybody else, in this
matter, Bessy. It's against the law to pay the tontine over
while two of you are alive, and the Ticknells are too strict to
risk it. I shouldn't do it myself in their places."

" What Oliver says is this, papa. The money must, in the
due course of events, come to either him or me, whichever of
us shall survive the other. We have therefore an equal interest in it, and possess at present an equal chance of succeeding
to it. No one else in the wide world, but our two selves, has
the smallest claim to it, or ever can have. We are the only
survivors of the ten ; the rest are all dead. Why, then,
should the trustees not stretch a point and let us have the
money while it can be of use to us conjointly ? Oliver says
they ought to do it."

" I know he does," remarked Mr. North.

" Has Oliver spoken to you, papa ? "

" No," said Mr. North. " I heard about it from Dick.
Dick happened to be at the bank yesterday, and Thomas
Ticknell mentioned to him that Dr. Rane had been urging
this request upon them. Dick said Sir Thomas seemed quite
horrified at the proposition ; they had told Dr. Rane, in
answer, that if they could consent to such a thing it would be
no better than a fraud."

" So they did," replied Bessy. " When Oliver was relating
it to me after he came home, he could not help laughing—in

spite of his vexation. The money is virtually ours, so where would the fraud lie ? "

" To be virtually yours is one thing, Bessy; to be legally yours is another. You young women can't be expected to understand business questions, my dear ; but your husband understands them. Of course it would be a great boon to get the two thousand pounds while you are both together ; but it would not be a legal thing for the bankers to do, and they are right in refusing it."

" Then—do you think there is no chance for us, papa ? "

" Not a bit of it, child."

A silence ensued. Mr. North sat watching his carnations, Bessy watching, with a far-off gaze, the dark-blue summer sky, as if the difficulty might be solved there. In spite of her father's opinion, she thought the brothers, Thomas and William Ticknell, unduly hard.

The Ticknells were the chief bankers of Whitborough. Upon the institution of the tontines, the two brothers, then in their early prime, had been made trustees to it, in conjunction with a gentleman named Wilson. In the course of time, Mr. Wilson died : and Mr. Thomas and Mr. William Ticknell grew into tolerably aged men ; they wanted now not much of the allotted span, three score years and ten. The elder brother had gone up to court with some great local matter, and he came back Sir Thomas. These two gentlemen had full power over the funds of the tontine. They were straight-forward, honourable men ; of dispositions naturally cautious ; and holding very strict opinions in business. Increasing years had not tended to lessen the caution, or to soften the strict tenets : and when Dr. Rane, soliciting a private inter-view with the brothers, presented himself before them with a proposition that they should pay over the tontine funds to him and his wife conjointly, without waiting for the death of either, the few hairs remaining on the old gentlemen's white heads rose up on end.

Truly it had seemed to them, this singular application, as touching closely upon fraud. Dr. Rane argued the matter with them, putting it in the most feasible and favourable light : and it must be acknowledged that, to his mind, it appeared a thing not only that they might do, but that it would be in them perfectly right and honest to do. All in vain ; they heard him with courtesy, but were harder than adamant. Richard North happened to go in upon some business soon after the conclusion of the interview, and the brothers—they were the bankers to North and Gass—told him confidentially of the application. Richard imparted it to his father: hence Mr. North heard Bessy without surprise.

Regarded in the narrow, legal view, of course the Messrs. Ticknell might be right; but, taking it broadly and comprehensively, there could be no doubt that it seemed hard upon Oliver Rane and his wife. The chief question that had presented itself to Richard North's mind was, if the money were handed over now, would the Messrs. Ticknell be quite secure from ulterior consequences? They said *not.* Upon Richard North's suggesting that a lawyer might be consulted on the point, Sir Thomas Ticknell answered that, no matter what a lawyer might say, they should never incur the responsibility of parting with the tontine money so long as two of its members were living. "And I think they must be right," Richard remarked afterwards to his father. Turning to Bessy, sitting by him on the bench, Mr. North repeated this. Bessy listened in dutiful silence, but shook her head.

"Papa, much as I respect Richard's judgment, clever as I know him to be, I am sure he is wrong here. It is very strange that he should go against me and Oliver."

"It is because of his good judgment, my dear," replied Mr. North simply. "I'd trust it against the world, on account of his impartiality. When he has to decide between two opposite opinions, he invariably puts himself, or tries to put himself, in either place, weighs each side, and comes to a conclusion unbiassed. Look at this strike, now on: Dick has been reproached with leaning to the men's side, with holding familiar argument with them, for and against; a thing that few masters would do: but it is because he sees they really believe they have right on their side, and he would treat their opinions with respect, however mistaken he may know them to be."

"Richard cannot think the men are not to blame!" exclaimed Mrs. Rane.

"He lays the blame chiefly where, as *he* says, it is due—on the Trade Union. The men were deluded into listening to it at first; and they can't help obeying its dictates now: they have given themselves over to it, body and soul, Bessy, and can no more escape than a prisoner from a dungeon. That's Richard's view, mind; and it makes him all leniency; I'd try and bring 'em to their senses in a different way, if I had the power and the means left me."

" In what way, papa ? "

" Bessy, if I were what I once was—a wealthy man, independent of business—I'd close the works for good : break 'em up : burn 'em if need be : anything but re-open them. The trade should go where it would, and the men after it ; or stop here and starve, just as they chose. It's not I that would have my peace of life worried out of me by these strikes ; or let men that I have employed and done liberally by always, dictate to me. You've heard of the old saying—cutting off the nose to spite the face : that's just what the men will find they have done. They'll find it, Bessy, to their cost, as sure as that we two are sitting here."

Mr. North laid hold of the hoe that was resting on the elbow of the bench, and struck it lightly on the ground. Meaning no doubt to give emphasis to his words. Bessy Rane passed from the subject of the strike to that which more immediately concerned her.

" Richard is honest, papa ; he would never say what he did not think ; but he may be mistaken sometimes. I *cannot* understand how he can think the Ticknells right in refusing to let us have the money. If there were the slightest, smallest, reason for their keeping it back, it would be different : but there's none."

" Look here, Bessy. If they go by the strict letter of the law, they cannot do it. The tontine deed was drawn up as tightly as any deed, can be : it expressly says that nine of the members must be dead, and only the tenth remaining, before the money can be withdrawn from where it is invested. The Ticknells can't get over this."

" Papa—forgive me—you should not say can't, but won't," spoke Mrs. Rane. " They can do it if they please ; there's nothing to prevent it. All power, to act, lies with them ; they are responsible to none : if they paid over the money to Oliver to-morrow, not an individual in the whole world, from the queen upon her throne to the youngest clerk in their counting-house, could call them to account for it. The strictest judge on the bench might not say to them afterwards, You have paid away money that you had no right to pay."

" Stop a bit, Bessy—that's just where the weak point lies. The Ticknells say that if they parted with the money now, they might be called upon for it again at some future time."

Bessy sat in amazement. "Why! How could that be?"

Mr. North raised his straw hat and rubbed his head before he replied. It was a somewhat puzzling question.

"Dick put it somehow in this way, my dear: that is, Thomas Ticknell put it to him. If you should die, Bessy, leaving your husband a widower with children (or, for the matter of that, if he should die, leaving you with some) the children might come upon the Ticknells for the money over again. Or Rane might come upon them, if he were the one left; or you, if you were. It was in that way, I think Dick said, but my memory is not as clear as it used to be."

"As if we should be so dishonourable! Besides—there could be no possibility of claiming the money twice. Having received it once, the Ticknells would hold our receipt for it."

Mr. North shook his head. "The law is full of quips and turns, Bessy. If the trustees paid over this money to you and your husband now, against the provisions of the tontine deed, I suppose it is at least a nice question whether the survivor of you could not compel them to pay it again."

Bessy held her breath. "Do *you* think they could be compelled, papa?"

"Well, I don't know, Bessy. I fancy perhaps they might be. Dick says they are right, as prudent men, to refuse. One thing you and Oliver may rest assured of, my dear—that, under the doubt, the Ticknells will never be got to do it as long as oak and ash grow."

Bessy Rane sighed, and began to tie her bonnet. She had no idea that the paying of the money would involve the trustees in any liability, real or fancied, and hope went out of her from this moment. By nature she was as just as Richard; and she could not henceforth even wish that the bankers should incur the risk.

"Dick's indoors, my dear, if you'd like to ask him what Thomas Ticknell said; he would explain it to you better than I have. No haste now, to go off in a morning: there's no works open to go to."

"I have heard enough, papa; I quite understand it now," was Mrs. Rane's answer. "It will be a dreadful disappointment to Oliver when he hears that no chance, or hope, is left. It would have been—oh such a help to us."

"He is not getting on very well, is he, Bessy?"

"No. Especially since the strike set in. The men can't pay."

"Seeley must feel it as well as Oliver."

"Not half as much; not a quarter. His practice chiefly lies amid the richer classes. Well, we must have patience. As Oliver says, Fortune does not seem to smile upon us just now."

"If I could put a hundred-pound note, or so, into your hand, while these bad times are being tided over, I'd do it, Bessy, with all my heart. But I can't. Tell Oliver so. The strike is bringing us no end of embarrassment, and I don't know where it will end. It was bad enough before, as you remember, Bessy: but we had always Richard as a refuge."

"Richard will take care of you still, papa; don't be troubled; in some way or the other, I am sure he will. As to ourselves, we are young, and can wait for the good time coming."

Very cheerily she spoke. And perhaps felt so. Bessy's gentle nature held a great deal of sunshine.

"I wonder Oliver's mother does not help him," remarked Mr. North.

"Her will would be glad to do it, papa, but she lives up to every farthing of her income: beyond it, I fancy, sometimes. She has luxuries around her, and her travelling about costs a good deal. Mrs. Cumberland is not one to cut and contrive, or to put up with small lodgings on her different sojourns. Sometimes, as you know, she travels post: it is easier, she says; and that is very expensive."

"You'll come indoors a bit, won't you, Bessy?" said Mr. North as she rose. "Miss Field and Matilda were sitting in the hall just now, for coolness."

She hesitated for a moment, and then walked on by his side. Mrs. Rane's visits to the Hall were rare. Madam had not been cordial with her since her marriage; and she had never once condescended to enter Bessy's home.

The hall was empty. Bessy was about to enter the drawing-room in search of Matilda, when the door opened to give Madam egress. The two touched each other. Madam started haughtily, stepped back, and shut the door in Bessy's face. Next moment, a hand was extended over Bessy's shoulder, and threw it wide.

"By your leave, Madam," said Richard North calmly. "Room for my sister."

He marshalled her in as though she had been a duchess. Madam, drawing her lace shawl around her shoulders, swept

majestically out, vouchsafing neither word nor look. It was
nothing more than the contempt often dealt to Bessy: but
Richard's blood went up in a boil.

That the refusal of the trustees to part with the funds of the
tontine was irrevocable, there could be no doubt: nevertheless,
Oliver Rane declined to see it. The matter got wind, as
nearly everything else seemed to do in Dallory, and many of
the public took his part. It was a frightful shame, they
thought, that a man and his wife could not be let enjoy together the money that was their due, but must wait for one or
the other's death before they got it. Jelly's tongue made itself
particularly busy. Dr. Rane was not a favourite of hers on the
whole, but she espoused his cause warmly in this.

" It's such a temptation," remarked Jelly to a select few,
one night at Ketler's, whither she had betaken herself to blow
up the man for continuing to hold out on strike, to which
movement Jelly was a determined foe.

" A temptation?" rejoined Tim Wilks respectfully, who
made one of her audience. " In what way, Miss Jelly?"

" In what way," retorted Jelly with some scorn. " Why in
the way of *stealing* the money, if it is to be got at; or of
punching those two old bankers' heads. When a man's kept
out of his own through nothing but some naggering crotchet,
it's enough to make him feel desperate, Tim Wilks."

" So it is, miss," acquiesced meek Timothy.

"If my mistress withheld my wages from me—which it's
twenty pounds a year, and her left-off silks—I should fight
at it, I know: perhaps take 'em. And *this* is two thousand
pounds."

" Two thousand pounds!" ejaculated honest Ketler in a low
tone of reverence, as he lifted his hands. "And for the doctor
to be kept out of it because his wife's not dead ! It *is* a shame."

" I'd not say, either, but it might bring another sort of
temptation to some men, besides those mentioned by Miss
Jelly," put in Timothy Wilks with hesitation.

"And pray what would that be?" demanded Jelly in a tart
voice—for she made it a point to keep Timothy under before
company.

" The putting of his wife out of the way on purpose to get
the money, Miss Jelly," spoke Tim with deprecation. And
the words caused a sudden pause.

" You—you don't mean the murdering of her !" shrieked
Mrs. Ketler, who was a timid woman and apt to be startled.

"Yes I did," replied Timothy Wilks. "Some might be found to do it. No offence to Dr. Rane. I'm putting the supposititious case of a bad man; not of him."

CHAPTER XXII.

AT THE SEA-SIDE.

THE summer was slowly passing. At a small and obscure sea-side place on the East coast was located Mrs. Cumberland. She had engaged part of one of the few good houses there—houses that let at an enormous price in the season to visitors—and lived in it with Ellen Adair, and her maid to wait on her. Not Jelly this time, but the housemaid Ann. Mrs. Cumberland's own house at Dallory was being painted inside during her absence. She had deemed it well to leave Jelly in charge: and so brought Ann instead.

They had been in this place, Eastsea, for some weeks now; and Ellen privately believed that this sojourn was never coming to an end. Any thing more wearisome than it was to her, could not have been found. Arthur Bohun was in London at his uncle's, where he had been staying for some time. It was several weeks since he and Ellen had met: to her it seemed as many months. James Bohun was still ill, but fluctuated much; at one time appearing to be past recovery, at another as if he were all but well. He would not part with Arthur; Sir Nash said he must not think of leaving. Under the circumstances, Arthur did not see his way clear to get away.

Another person was fluctuating. And that was Mrs. Cumberland. Her complaint, connected with the heart, was just one of those that may snap life suddenly, or allow it to be prolonged for years. That she was gradually growing worse, there could not be a doubt of; but it was by almost imperceptible degrees. No change could be noted from day to day; it was only by comparing her present state with what it had been three, or six, or twelve months before, that the decay could be seen. Sometimes, for days together, she would feel very ill, be quite unable to quit her room; and again she would have an interval of ease, almost of seeming recovery, and walk and drive out daily. Dr. Rane had come over twice to see his mother: staying but a few hours. His opinion was, that she might yet, with care, live for years; and probably many. At the same time, he knew that there could be, speaking only in a medical point of view, no certainty of it.

It was during this sojourn at Eastsea that Mrs. Cumberland received news from Mr. Adair. He wrote in answer to Mrs. Cumberland's letter—the first of the two letters already told of—wherein she had spoken of the probability of Ellen's being sought in marriage by a gentleman every way desirable, but in which she had omitted, probably from inadvertence, to mention the gentleman's name. Mr. Adair's answer, now received, was to the effect that—fully relying on Mrs. Cumberland's judgment—he could not *desire* better for his daughter than that so suitable a marriage should be entered into; and accorded it his cordial consent.

But this involved a most unhappy contretemps: of which no one as yet was, or could be, conscious. That first letter of Mrs. Cumberland's had alluded to Mr. Graves: *she took this consent to apply to Arthur Bohun.* It takes time, as everybody knows, for a letter to get to Australia from England and an answer to come back again. Whether, during the lapse of weeks, Mrs. Cumberland actually forgot that her first letter had applied to Mr. Graves; or whether in her sickness, memory had grown confused between the two, and she remembered only the last letter, must ever remain a question. Certain it was, that she took this present cordial approbation of Mr. Adair's to apply to Arthur Bohun. It might be, that she had entirely forgotten having written about Mr. Graves.

With her usual reticence, she said nothing to Ellen Adair. Not a word. Time enough for that when Arthur Bohun should speak—if he ever did speak. She held the consent ready for use if necessity ever required it; and was at ease.

" Ellen, how you mope ! "

Ellen Adair looked up, faintly blushing at the abrupt charge, which came from Mrs. Cumberland.

" Mope ! " exclaimed Ellen.

" My dear, you do nothing else. I don't think you like Eastsea."

" Not very much. At least—it is rather dull."

" Well, I suppose you can but find it so ; confined in-doors half my time, as I am. At Niton you had often Captain Bohun to go out with : now you have to go alone."

Ellen turned away, a soft blush rising to her face at the remembrance of Niton. " Shall you be going home soon, do you think, Mrs. Cumberland ? " she asked.

"Oh dear no. I had a note from Jelly this morning, and she says the house is not half done. Lazy idlers, workpeople are! once you get them into a place you can't get them out. But if Jelly were ready for us I should not go. This air is doing me good on the whole. Perhaps I shall stay the winter here."

Ellen's heart fell within her. All the autumn in this place, that verily seemed to her like the fag end of the world, and all the winter! Should she *ever* again get the chance of seeing her heart's love, Arthur Bohun? And he?—perhaps he was forgetting her.

"Do you feel well enough to come out, Mrs. Cumberland?"

"No. I am sorry, Ellen, but you must go alone. Get your things on at once, child: the afternoon will be passing."

Ellen sighed. It was of no moment to her whether she went out or stayed in: she obeyed mechanically, and went forth. Quite alone. Generally speaking Ann attended her, but the servant was this afternoon wanted by her mistress.

The sunshine played in small sparkles on the clear blue sea, ever changing its hue for one different and more beautiful, as the light autumn clouds floated above it in the sky. Ellen Adair sat in a sheltered place and watched it. It was her favourite seat: one hewn out of the rocks, and apparently frequented only by herself, as she had never yet been disturbed in it. Except the small strip of beach before her, nothing was to be seen from it but the sea and the sky. Over-head, she could hear the children's voices at play: the tide below was coming in with gentle monotony. Ellen had a book with her, and she had her diary; she had read a few pages in the . one, she had written some lines in pencil in the other: and so the hours passed, and she was utterly dreary. The weary day was but the type of the other weary days that at present made the sum total.

"Will it ever come to an end?" she murmured, having watched a tiny pleasure-boat shoot past and disappear, leaving her to her silent solitude. "Shall we ever get back to Dallory Ham, and—and the friends that live there? I suppose a winter *might* be got through in this place, and one be alive at the end of it, but ——"

A gentleman in deep mourning walking by on the strip of beach, looking this way, looking that. Ellen's thoughts were cut short summarily, and she rose with a faint cry: the cry of intense joy that is so near akin in its sound to that of exquisite pain.

For it was no other than Captain Arthur Bohun. He had not heard it; but he saw her; it was for her he had been looking: and he turned to her with an outstretched hand. For a moment she felt utterly bewildered, half doubting the reality of the vision. But oh yes, it was he; it was he! The sea, and the sky, and the rocks, and the monotony—they had all changed into paradise.

"How do you do, Ellen?"

Nothing more than this commonplace greeting was spoken. They stood in silence, their hands clasped. His lips were quivering slightly, proving how ardent was the feeling that stirred him, at this, their renewed meeting; Ellen, blushing and paling by turns, was agitated almost to pain. A long look in each other's eyes: both saw what the meeting was to the other. Sitting down quietly by her side on the ledge of rock, he accounted for his unexpected appearance. On his arrival at Eastsea that afternoon, he had gone at once to call at Mrs. Cumberland's. Ann said her mistress was lying down, and that Miss Adair was on the beach.

"Did you think I was never coming to see you, Ellen? I did. I could not get away from my uncle's while James was so ill."

"Is he—dead?" hesitated Helen, looking pointedly at the black clothes.

"Oh no. It is a cousin of Sir Nash's and of my father's who is dead: a very old man who has lived for years in the south of France. James Bohun is very much better."

"I thought, by the deep mourning, it must be he."

"Is it deep? I suppose it looks so, being all black. We men cannot put on what you ladies call half mourning. Neither should I wish to in the present instance, for the good old man has been generous to me."

They fell into silence, each feeling the rapture of the other's presence, after the prolonged separation, as something more than human. So intense was it that Ellen, at least, might have been content to die in it there and then. The sea changed ever its beautiful colours, the sky seemed to smile on them, the children played over-head, a flute from some unseen boat in the distance was playing softly. No: Eden never could have been sweeter than this.

"What have you been doing, all this while by yourself at Eastsea?" he at length asked her.

"Very much what I am now, I think—sitting here to watch the sea," she answered. "There has been nothing else to do. It was always dull."

"Has Mrs. Cumberland had any visitors?"

"Dr. Rane has been here twice. He gives a poor account of things at Dallory. The strike shows no signs of coming to an end; and the men are in want."

"So Dick says. I get a letter from him sometimes."

A great amount of talking, this. They lapsed into silence again. The tide turned; a big steamer went by in the distance.

"Do you hear that, Ellen?"

A man's soft tenor voice had struck up a love song overhead: "Ellen Adair." Robin Adair, as the world more often has it. Arthur Bohun used to hear it sung as "Ellin Adair," when he was recovering from his wound in Ireland; the Irish insisted on it that that was the original song; and he had sometimes got Ellen to sing it so for him since. The children ceased their play; the verses went on, and they, these unseen two below the rocks, listened to the end, catching every word distinctly.

> "Yet her I loved so well,
>   Still in my heart shall dwell.
> Oh! I shall ne'er forget
>   Ellen Adair."

"Nor I," softly spoke Arthur, as the refrain died away.

They quitted the seat at length. As they passed through the town, the man was singing before a house: "The Minstrel Boy." His hat was in his hand; he looked as though he had seen better days and might have been a gentleman once. Captain Bohun put a shilling into the hat.

Mrs. Cumberland was up when they got in. Ann had told her of Captain Bohun's appearance and that he had gone to find Miss Adair. Mrs. Cumberland took a few minutes for consideration, and then decided on her course of conduct, and that was to speak to Captain Bohun.

It might have been all very well, while she was armed with no authority, tacitly to countenance Captain Bohun's frequent visits; but now that she had authority, she deemed it right, in justice to Ellen, to take a different standing. If Captain Bohun had serious intentions, well and good; if not, she should request him to bring the intimacy to a close. Feeling the responsibility that lay upon her as the sole guardian in Europe of Ellen Adair, she thought she should be justified in saying thus much, for, unless Arthur Bohun proposed to make the young lady his wife, it was cruel to allow her to love him.

When Mrs. Cumberland once made her mind up to any resolve, she did not usually lose time in putting it in practice, and she lost none here. Taking the opportunity this same evening, when Ellen was out of the room, sent from it by herself on some errand of excuse, she spoke to Captain Bohun.

But the most fastidious man living could not have taken exception to what she said. She spoke entirely as a lady. Captain Bohun's appearance that day at Eastsea—coupled with the remembrance of his frequent sojourns at Niton when they were staying there, and his constant visits to her house at Dallory Ham—had revived a faint idea that had sometimes presented itself to her mind, namely, that he might be growing attached to Ellen Adair. Mrs. Cumberland did not wish to enlarge on this point; it might be, or it might not be; Captain Bohun alone knew; perhaps she was wholly mistaken; all she wished to say was this—that if Captain Bohun *had* no future thoughts in regard to Miss Adair, she must request him to terminate his intimacy at once. When she got back to Dallory Ham she would be glad to see him at her house occasionally, just as any other visitor; but nothing more.

To this Arthur Bohun answered candidly enough. He did like Ellen Adair; if circumstances permitted he would be only too glad to make her his wife; but, as Mrs. Cumberland knew, he had hitherto been very poor. As he pleased, Mrs. Cumberland remarked; the matter was entirely for his own consideration; she did not attempt to press it, one way or the other; if he saw no chance of his circumstances improving, he should freely say so, and terminate his visits; she could not allow Ellen to be played with. And upon that, Arthur begged to have the night for reflection; he would see Mrs. Cumberland in the morning, and give her his decision.

It was left at that. When Ellen returned to the room—entirely unsuspicious of what had been said during her few minutes' absence from it—Captain Bohun took his departure. Arrived at the hotel where he had put up, he devoted himself to the consideration of the grave question, weighing it in all its bearings as fairly as his love for Ellen allowed him to do. Of course that biassed him.

He had enough to marry upon now. By the death of the relative for whom he was in mourning, he had come into about eight hundred a year. With his own income, that made twelve. Quite sufficient to begin upon, though he was a Bohun. But—there were deterring considerations. In some way, as he suspected, his mother, in her fear of Ellen Adair, had contrived to instil a suspicion into the mind of Sir Nash, that Arthur, unless he were closely controlled, might be making a very disgraceful mésalliance. Sir Nash had all the pride of the Bohuns, and it frightened him. He spoke to Arthur, telling him that unless he married entirely to the approbation of his family, he should never allow him to succeed to the estates. No, nor to the title if he could help it. If James died, he, Sir Nash, would marry first, and leave direct heirs.

This, it was, that now crippled the decision of Arthur. One fact was known to him—that James Bohun, since this illness set in, had joined his father in cutting off the entail, so that the threat of leaving the estates away from Arthur (even though he succeeded to the title) was easy of accomplishment. What was to be done ? Part with Ellen Adair he could not. Oh, if he might but make her his wife without the world knowing it; the world abroad, and the world at home ! *Might* this be ? Very slowly Arthur Bohun arrived at a conclusion—that the one only plan, if Mrs. Cumberland and Ellen would accede to it, was a private marriage.

Arguments are so easy when inclination lies with them. The future looks very much as we ourselves paint it. They might be married at once, here at Eastsea. If James Bohun recovered and lived, why there could be no question of the title or the estates lapsing to Arthur, and he might avow his marriage as soon as he pleased. If James died, he should not, as he fully believed, have to conceal it long, for he thought Sir Nash's life quite as precarious as James's. A few months, perhaps only weeks, and he might be able to tell the world that Ellen was his wife. He felt an inclination to whisper it beforehand to his good friend and aunt, Miss Bohun. But, he must first of all ascertain from Mrs. Cumberland what was the social standing of Mr. Adair. Unless he were a gentleman undeniable, Ellen could be no fit wife for a Bohun. Arthur, swayed by his love, had hitherto been content to take this assumed fact for granted; now he saw the necessity of ascertaining it more explicitly. It was not that he had any real doubt, only it was but right to make sure.

Mr. Adair held some post under the British Government,

formerly in India, for a long while now in Australia. His wife had died young; his only child, Ellen, had been sent to a first-class school in England for her education. Upon its completion, Mr. Adair had begged of Mrs. Cumberland to receive her; he had some floating thoughts of returning home himself, so that he did not wish Ellen to go out to him. An impression was afloat in Dallory that Ellen Adair would inherit a good fortune; also that Mrs. Cumberland received liberal remuneration for the expenses of the young lady. These generalities Arthur Bohun knew; but he knew no more.

He paid the promised visit to Mrs. Cumberland in the morning. Ellen was on the beach with the maid; there was no interruption, and their converse was long and confidential. Heaven alone knew how Arthur Bohun succeeded in getting Mrs. Cumberland to believe in the necessity for the marriage being kept private. He did succeed. But he used no subterfuge; he frankly told of the prejudice his mother had taken against Ellen Adair, and that she had gained the ear of Sir Nash. In short, the same arguments he had used to himself the previous evening, he urged now. Mrs. Cumberland—naturally biassed against Madam for the injury she strove to work Dr. Rane—thought it a frightful shame that she should strive to destroy the happiness and prospects of her own son Arthur, and she sympathised with him warmly,. It was this feeling that rendered her more easy than she would otherwise have been—in short, that made her give her consent to Arthur's plan. To counteract the would-be bitter wrong contemplated by Mrs. North, she considered would be a merit on Arthur's part, instead of a sin. And then, when things were so far settled, and the speedy marriage determined on, Mrs. Cumberland astonished Captain Bohun by putting Mr. Adair's letter into his hands, explaining how it came to be received, and what she had written to that gentleman to call it forth. "So that her father's blessing will rest on the marriage," remarked Mrs. Cumberland; "but for that fact, I could not have consented to a private one."

This gave Arthur the opportunity to ask about the position of Mr. Adair, which, in the heat of argument, he had been forgetting. Certainly he was a gentleman, Mrs. Cumberland answered, and of very good Scotch family. Major Bohun, Mr. Adair, and her own husband, George Cumberberland, had been firm friends in India at the time of Major

Bohun's death. She could not help thinking, she added in conclusion, that it was the remembrance of that early friendship which induced Mr. Adair to give so ready and cordial a consent to his daughter's union with Major Bohun's son.

And so there the matter ended, all couleur-de-rose; Arthur believing that there could be no possible objection to his marrying Ellen Adair; nay, that the way had been most markedly paved for it through this letter of Mr. Adair's; Mrs. Cumberland deeming that she was not indiscreet in permitting the marriage to be a private one. Both were unsuspicious as the day. He, that there existed any real bar; she, that Mr. Adair's consent applied to a very different man from Arthur Bohun.

Captain Bohun went out from Mrs. Cumberland's in search of Ellen, with the light of love flushing his cheeks. He found her in the same favourite sheltered spot, hedged in from the gaze of the world. Again alone. The servant had gone to the shops, ribbon buying. Their salutations hitherto had been nothing but decorum and formality, as witness that of the previous day.

"Good morning," said Ellen, rising and holding out her hand.

Instead of taking it, he took *her.* Took her in his arms with a half-cry of pent-up emotion, and laid her sweet face upon his breast, kissing it with impassioned kisses. Ellen, utterly astonished, could not get away.

"Do not shrink from me, Ellen. You are going to be my wife."

CHAPTER XXIII.

A LAST PROPOSAL.

AFFAIRS grew more unsatisfactory at Dallory as the weeks went on. The strike continued; the men utterly refusing to return to work except on their own terms, or, rather, the Trades' Union refusing to allow them. Supplies to them became more scanty. If not actual famine, something near akin to it began to reign. North Inlet, once so prosperous, looked like a half-starved place out at elbows—the same as its inhabitants. Oh, what senseless folly it was! What would it end in? Mrs. Gass had tired of going amid the men to tell them her mind and try to bring them to reason; but Miss Dallory went. Miss Dallory could make no impression whatever. The men were moody, miserable, three parts starved: they would have been glad to go back to work again almost on no pay at all, only as a relief to the present weary idleness; but they belonged to the famous Trades' Union now, and must obey its dictates. Mary Dallory got in a passion sometimes, and asked whether they were men, or cravens, that they had no pity for their poor helpless children.

One day Mrs. Gass and Miss Dallory went forth together. Not of premeditation. One of Ketler's children was ill and weakly; incipient consumption, Dr. Rane said; she was a sweet little child, mild and gentle; and Miss Dallory would sometimes carry her strengthening things. It was a frightful shame, she would tell Ketler, that he should let even this poor sick little one starve: and Ketler humbly acknowledged to his own heart that the child *was* starving; and felt it to his backbone. The man was as well meaning a man as heaven ever sent into the world; anxious to do his duty: but he had signed himself a member of the Trades' Union, and was completely helpless.

Miss Dallory wore a print gown, and was altogether a vast deal less fine than Jelly. She had a small basket in her hand, containing fresh eggs. As she passed Mrs. Gass's that lady was standing at her open parlour window, in all the glory of a gorgeous green satin robe, and white bonnet with bird-of-paradise feather. She dearly loved rich clothes, and saw no reason why she should not wear them.

"Where be you bound to, my dear?" asked the grandly-dressed lady, as Mary stopped.

"I want to take these eggs to little Cissy Ketler. Mrs. Gass, I cannot *think* what is to become of all the poor children if this state of things should last much longer."

"I'm sure I can't. It goes again the grain to see 'em want; but when we give 'em food or help, it's just so much premium offered to the father's incorrigible obstinacy and idleness, my dear."

"But the child is sick," said Mary Dallory. "And so are many other children."

"They'll be worse afore long. My dear, I was not a talking at you, in saying that. But I don't see where it's all to end. We can't set up hospitals for the children and women, even with the best will to do it. And the will, I, for one, have not. Once get their wives and children took care of, and the men 'ud lead the lives of gentlemen to the close o' the chapter.

Here; I'll walk with you, my dear; and we can talk going along."

She came forth, drawing on her lemon-coloured gloves: and they went towards Ketler's. North Inlet looked deserted to-day. Not a man was lounging in it. The few stragglers to be seen were walking along briskly in the direction of the works; as if they had business on hand, and were without their pipes. Mrs. Gass arrested one who was passing her.

"What's up, Dawson?"

"We've been called together, ma'am, to meet Mr. Richard North. He have got som'at to say to us. Happen, maybe, he's a going to give in at last."

"Is he!" retorted Mrs. Gass. "I don't think you need worrit your inside with that idea, Dawson. It's a deal more likely that he's going to warn you he'll sell the works out and out—if he can get any fool to buy 'em."

The man passed on. Mrs. Gass, as she turned to speak to Miss Dallory, gave a flourish with her small white lace parasol and a toss to the bird-of-paradise.

"Had anybody told me men could be so obstinate, in regard to thinking themselves in the right, I'd not have believed it: but seeing's believing. My dear, suppose we just step on to the works, and learn what the matter is that Mr. Richard has in hand."

The men, going in at the iron gates, branched round to their own entrance. Mrs. Gass took Miss Dallory to a private one. It led at once into what might now be called the audience chamber, for Richard North was already haranguing the men in it: a long and rather narrow room, with a counter running across it. It used to be the pay-room of the men: perhaps some of them, entering it now, recalled those prosperous days with a sigh. Richard North did not see the ladies come in. He stood with his back to them, in his usual every-day attire, a plain black frock coat and grey trousers, with fine white linen. His hands rested on the counter as he talked to the men, who faced him on the other side of it; a crowd of them, all with attentive countenances. Mrs. Gass signed to Miss Dallory to halt; not to conceal themselves from Richard, but simply lest their advance should interrupt what he was saying. And so they remained listening, Richard unconscious that he had any other audience than his workpeople.

The matter was this. A contract had just been offered to North and Gass. It was one of value, and would certainly, if

accepted, keep the men employed for some time. It was offered
at a certain price. Richard North made his calculations and
found that he could accept it, provided the men would work on
the former terms: but he could not if the rate of wages had to
be raised. Considering the present hopeless condition of the
men, imagining that they must have had pretty nearly sufficient experience of idleness and empty cupboards to bring them
to, at least, exercise reason, he determined to lay the proposal
before them—that they might accept or reject it. In a clear
and concise manner he stated this, and the men heard him
respectfully to the end. One of them then advanced a few steps
before the rest, and answered. Answered without the smallest
deliberation ; without so much as a pretence of inquiring what
the feelings of his fellows might be.

"We can't do it, sir."

Richard North raised his hand for silence, as if the man had
spoken before his time.

"Do you fully understand the case in all its bearings ?" resumed Richard : "if not, take time to reflect until you do
understand it. Look at it comprehensively ; take into consideration the future as well as the present. Listen again.
This contract has been offered me : it is a good one, as you
must know. It will set our works going again ; it will be the
means of bringing back the business that seems to be drifting
more hopelessly away from us day by day. It will provide
you with employment, with wages that you not so long ago
thought liberal; and will place you again in what may be
called prosperity—great prosperity as compared with what
exists at present. Your homes may be homes of plenty again,
your children can eat and drink. In short, both to you and
to me, this contract offers just the turn of the tide. I wish to
accept it : I see nothing but ruin before my father and myself
if I cannot : what I see before you I do not care to speak
of, if you are not wise enough to see it for yourselves. The
decision lies with you, unfortunately ; I wish it lay with
myself. Shall I take it, or shall I not ?"

"We couldn't return at them rate of wages, nohow," spoke
up a voice from the thick of the throng.

"It is the last chance that I shall offer you," proceeded
Richard. "For your sakes I would strongly advise you to
take it. Heaven is my witness that I am honest in saying
'for your sakes.' We have been associated together for many
years, and I cannot see the breaking up of old ties without

first using every effort to re-unite them. I must give my answer to-morrow, and accept this work or reject it. Little time is allowed me for decision, therefore I am unable to give much to you. Virtually the acceptation or rejection lies with you; for, without you, I could not fulfil it: but I cannot help a remark in passing, that for such a state of things to exist argues something rotten at the core in the relations between master and men. At six o'clock to-morrow morning the great bell shall be rung, calling you to work as formerly. My men, I hope you will all respond to it."

No, not at the terms offered, was the answer gathered by Richard North from the buzz that rose around.

" I cannot offer you better."

" No—and no. Not at them."

" I have said that this is the last chance," repeated Richard. " I shall never give you the option of working for me again."

The men couldn't help that. (The fact was, they only three parts believed it.) One ventured a supposition that if the works were sold, the new firm that bought might give them work on new terms.

" No," said Richard North. " I am very different from you, my men. You see work at your hand, and will not do it. You look forward to the future with (as I must suppose) easy apathy, giving neither care nor anxiety how you and your families are to live. I, on the contrary, am only anxious to work; at a reduced rate of profit, on a smaller scale if it must be; but, any way, to work. Night after night I lie awake, tormented with lively apprehensions for the future. What seemed, when you first turned out, to be a mere temporary stoppage, that reason and good sense on both our sides could not fail to rectify, has assumed gigantic proportions and a permanent aspect. After some time I gave way; offering to split the difference, as to wages, if you would return ——"

" But we wanted the whole," came an interruption. " And you didn't give way as to time."

" I could not do either," said Richard North, firmly. " I offered all I was able. That is a thing of the past: let it go. I now make you this last and final offer; and I think it only fair to tell you what my course will be if you reject it. I shall go over to Belgium and see if I cannot engage Belgian workmen to come here and take your places."

A dead silence fell on the room. Ketler broke it.

" You'd surely not do that, sir ! "

" Not do it ! Why you force it on me. I must either get a
new set of men, or else **give** up the works entirely. As I do
not feel inclined to the latter course, the former alone is open
to me."

" We'll have none o' them Belgiums here !" cried a threatening voice from the outskirts of the crowd.

" Allow me to tell you, Thoms, to tell you all, that the
Belgians will not ask your leave to come," spoke Richard,
drawing his head to its full height. " Would you act the
part of dogs-in-the-manger ? I offer *you* the work; offer
it *now;* and I heartily wish you to accept it, but if you
do not, I shall certainly endeavour to get others here who will."

" Drat them Belgicks ! Who be *they* that they should
snatch the bread out of honest Englishmen's mouths ! "

" What are the honest Englishmen about, to let them
snatch it ? " retorted Richard. " Look here, my men ;
listen," he continued, as he leaned forward and raised his
hands impressively. " If you (I speak of the country's hands
collectively) refuse to work, it can signify very little to you
practically whether the work goes to Belgium (or elsewhere)
to be done, or whether strangers come and do it here. *It
must end in one or the other.*"

" It shan't never end in them frogs o' foreiguers coming
here," spoke Thoms again, vexed that his voice should have
been recognized by Richard North. And this second interruption was hissed down by his more sensible comrades; who
sharply bade him hold his tongue, and hear the master.
Richard put up his hand.

" We will take it, for the moment's argument, at what
Thoms says—that strangers would not, or should not, come
here. In that case the other result must supervene—that the
work of the country would pass away from it. It has already
begun to pass ; you know it, my men ; and so do your rulers
the Trades' Unions. How it affects their nerves I don't
pretend to say ; but, when once this tide of desolation has set
in fairly as a settled result, there won't be much need of
their agitation. As truly as that I live, as that I now stand
here and speak to you, I believe this will come. In different
parts of the country whole places are being dismantled—the
work has left it. Do you suppose North Inlet is the only spot
where the provision shops may as well be closed because the
men have no longer money to spend in them ? Any newspaper you take up will tell you to the contrary. Read about

the ship-building in the East of London; how it has gone away, and whole colonies of men are left behind starving. Gone to Scotland; to the banks of the Tyne; gone anywhere that men can be found to work. It is the same with other trades. Whose fault is this?—Why the men's own."

Murmurs. "No. No."

"No! Why, here's a very present illustration of it. Whose fault is it that my works here are shut up, and you are living in idleness—or, we'll say, starving in idleness, if you like the word better. If I am unable to take this present contract now offered, and it goes elsewhere, whose doings will it be, but yours? Don't talk nonsense, my men. It is all very well to say that the Trades' Unions don't allow you to take the work. I have nothing to do with that: you and the Unions may divide the responsibility between you."

"The fact is, sir, that we are not our own masters," said Ketler.

"Just so. And it seems that you cannot, or will not, emancipate yourselves from your new slavery and become again your own masters. However, I did not call you together to go over this old ground, but to lay before you the option of returning to work. You have the day to consider of it. At six o'clock to-morrow the call-bell will ring —— "

"'Twon't be of no use ringing it, sir," interrupted Ketler, some sadness in his tone.

"At six o'clock to-morrow morning the call-bell here will ring," authoritatively repeated Richard North. "You respond to it and I shall heartily welcome you back. If you do not, my refusal must go in, and the job will lapse from me. If we part to-day it is our final parting, for I shall at once take measures to secure a fresh set of workpeople. Though I get but ten together at first, and the work I undertake be insignificant in proportion, *I'll get them.* It will be something like beginning life again : and you will have forced it on me."

"And of all pig-headed idiotics that mortal master ever had to deal with, sure you men be the worst!"

The undignified interruption emanated from Mrs. Gass. Richard looked round, in great surprise; perhaps all the greater when he saw also Miss Dallory. Mrs. Gass came forward; talking here, talking there; her bird-of-paradise nodding time to her words. As usual she told the men some home truths; sounding none the less forcibly because her language was as their own—homely.

"Is this true?" asked Miss Dallory in a low tone, as Richard went back to shake hands with her. "Shall you really re-open the works again with another set of men?"

"Yes—if these do not return. It will be better, however quietly I may have to begin, than going out to seek my fortune in the world. At least, I have lately been thinking so."

"*Will* the men return?"

"I am afraid to give you my true opinion. Lest it should seem like a bad omen."

"And now you have given it me. It is also mine. They are blind, to infatuation."

"Not so much blind, I think, as that they are—I have just said so to them—in a state of slavery from which they dare not emancipate themselves."

"And who would?—under the specious promises of the Trades' Unions? Don't blame them too much, Mr. Richard North. If some great strong body came down on you and me with all kinds of agitation and golden promises for the future, we might believe in them too."

Richard shook his head. "Not if the great strong body lived by the agitation: and took our hard-earned money to keep themselves and the golden promises going."

Mary Dallory laughed a little. "Shall you ring that great bell in the morning?"

"Yes. Certainly I shall."

"Ah, well—the men will only laugh at you from their beds. But I daresay you can stand that. Oh dear me! What need there is that the next world should be great and good, when this is so foolish a one!"

The meeting had broken up. Richard North and some few of the more intelligent of the men—those who had filled the more important posts at the works—remained talking yet together. Mrs. Gass, and Mary Dallory with her basket of fresh eggs, went away together.

Women stood about with anxious faces, watching for the news. They were tired of the strike: heartsick, as some of them feelingly expressed it. Nothing teaches like experience: the women were as eager for the strike at one time as ever the men could be, believing it would bring a tide of prosperity in its wake. They had not bargained for what it had brought: misery, and dismantled homes, and semi-starvation. But for being obliged to keep up as others did—as we all have to do, whatever may be the life's struggles, the heart's bitter care—

there were those amidst them who would have lain down to die in sheer hopelessness.

Mrs. Ketler stood at her door in a tattered black net cap— the once tidy woman. She was shading the sun from her eyes as she looked out for her husband. It prevented her noticing the approach of the ladies ; and when they accosted her she backed into her house in her timid fashion, rather startled, attempting some words as by way of apology. The little girl who was sick—a wan child of seven years old—was being nursed by one somewhat older. Miss Dallory looked round to see that there was a chair left capable of being sat upon, and took the invalid on her own lap. Nearly all the available things the house once contained had been parted with ; either pledged or sold. Miss Dallory gave the eggs to the mother, and a half-pint bottle of beef tea that lay at the bottom of the basket.

"How is Cissy to-day ? " she asked tenderly of the child.

"Cissy tired," was the little one's answer.

"Has Cissy finished the strawberry-jam ? "

Cissy nodded.

" Then let your big boy come to Ham Court for some more," said Miss Dallory, turning to the mother.

The "big boy" was the eldest. He had been employed at the works, but was of course condemned to be idle, like the rest.

"Bain't you pretty nigh tired of this sort o' thing," demanded Mrs. Gass, who had come to an anchor on a wooden bucket turned upside-down.

The woman knew what she meant by "this sort o' thing," and gave a groan. It was very expressive, showing *how* tired she was of it, and how hopeless were prospects of any change.

"I've heard about the master's offer, ma'am ; but the men mean to reject it," she said. "Smith stopped to tell me as he went by. The Lord above knows what is to become of us ! "

"If the men do reject it, they'll deserve to sit for the rest of their lives on a iron plough-share with all its spikes sticking into 'em," retorted Mrs. Gass—her own present uncomfortable seat probably suggesting the idea. "Any way, I hope they'll never get the pricks out o' their consciences."

"It's the Trades' Union," said the woman in a low tone, giving a scared look around. "The men can't do as they would."

"Not do as they would!" echoed Mrs. Gass. "Don't *you* pick up their folly and retail it to me again, Susan Ketler. If the men was fools enough to be drawed into joining the Union at first—and I'd not blame 'em too much for that, for the best of us gets led away at times by fair promises that turn out in the end to be smoke, or worse—they ought not to be so pig headed as to keep there. Now that they've seen what good that precious Trades' Union is doing for 'em, and what it's likely to do, they should buckle on the armour of their common sense and leave it. Mr. Richard North has this day gave them the opportunity of doing so. Every man Jack of 'em can go back to work to-morrow morning at the ringing of the bell : and take up again with good wages and comfort. If they refuse they'll be not so much fools as something worse, Susan Ketler : they'll be desperately wicked."

"They are afraid," murmured the woman. "They have tied themselves by word and bond to the Union."

"Then let 'em *untie* theirselves. Don't tell me, Susan Ketler. Afraid? What of? Could the Union kill 'em for it? Could the men be hung and drawn-and-quartered for leaving it? Who *is* the Union? Giants that were born with thunderbolts in their hands and power from the Creator to use 'em to control people's wills ?—or just simple men like themselves : workmen too once, some of 'em, if reports are true. You'd better not try to come over me with your fallacies, Susan Ketler. Facts is facts, and reason's reason. If these men *chose* to do it, they could send the Trades' Union to the right about this day, and come back, with one accord, to work and their senses to-morrow. Who's to hinder it ?"

Susan Ketler ventured to say no more. She only wished she dared say as much to her husband and the men. But, what with common sense, as Mrs. Gass called it, on the one side, and the Trades' Union sophistries pulling on the other, the steering along in North Inlet just now was perplexing in the extreme. Mrs. Gass rose from her uneasy seat, and departed with Mary Dallory.

CHAPTER XXIV.

AT NIGHT: UNDER THE CEDAR-TREE.

THERE was commotion that day in Dallory. An offer like this of Richard North's, coming as it did in the very midst of distress and prolonged privation, could not be rejected off-hand without some dissenting voices. The few men who had not joined the Union, who only wished to get back to work, pleaded for its acceptance as if they were pleading for very life. Strangers also—that is, gentlemen who had no direct interest in the question—went about amid the men, striving to impress upon them where their obligations lay, and what their course ought to be. One of these was Dr. Rane. There had been a good deal of sickness lately—when is there not where privation reigns?—and the doctor's services were in much requisition. In every house he went that day, to every workman with whom he came in contact, he spoke forcibly and kindly: urging them most strongly not to reject this opportunity of putting themselves right with the world. It was one, he said, that might never occur again, if neglected now. Dr. Rane, while blaming the men, was sorry for them; pityingly sorry for their wives and children.

He had had a very fatiguing day. When the dusk of evening came on, he went and sat in the garden, tired and weary. Bessy was gone to spend the evening at Ham Court with Mary Dallory; and the doctor had promised to fetch her home. His ruminations still ran, as ever, on the getting away from Dallory; but at present there seemed to be little chance of his doing it: unless he could dispose of his practice here, he would not have the wherewithal to establish himself in another place. Had Oliver Rane been a less healthy man than he really was, he would long ago have thought himself into a nervous fever.

It grew darker. Dr. Rane struck his repeater—for it was too dark to see—wondering whether if was time to go for his wife. No; not quite he found; he could delay another quarter of an hour yet. And he lapsed back into his musings.

The seat he had chosen was underneath the great cedar-tree at the extreme corner of the garden, close to the wire fence that divided his ground from Mrs. Cumberland's, and also close against that lady's back door. An intervening leafy foliage of clematis and woodbine would have hidden him from anyone on the other side even at daylight, and Dr. Rane felt as much in private as he would have been in an African desert. From his own troubles his thoughts went roaming off to other matters : to the long sojourn of his mother at Eastsea, to wondering when she meant to come home ; and thence on to speculate on what the workmen's answer to Richard North's call would be.

"Will they show the white feather still ? and it is nothing less, this cowardly grovelling to the dictates of the Union," soliloquised Dr. Rane ; "or will they respond to Dick like men of sense, and go back to him ? But for those agitators ——"

"I can tell you what it is, Mr. Tim Wilks—if you don't choose to keep your time and your promises, you need not trouble yourself to come worrying after me later. A good two mortal hours by the clock have I been at Green's waiting for *you*."

The above, succeeding to the sound of footsteps in the lane, and uttered in the sharpest tones of Jelly, cut short the musings of Dr. Rane. A short squabble ensued : Jelly scolding ; Tim Wilks breathlessly explaining. From what the doctor, sitting in silence, and unsuspected, could gather, it appeared that Jelly must have had some appointment with Tim (no doubt of her own imperious making) which he had failed to keep, and that he had come running after her, only catching her up at the garden door.

Jelly put the key in the lock, and stepped inside the garden : the servants sometimes chose that way of entrance in preference to the front. During the absence of Mrs. Cumberland Jelly acted as the house's mistress, entertained her friends, and went in and out at will. Mr. Wilks meekly remained where he was, not daring to cross the threshold without her permission.

"Is it too late for me to come in, Miss Jelly ?" asked he.

"Yes, it is too late," retorted Jelly ; the pair of them not having the slightest notion that any eavesdropper was near. Though the word could not justly be applied to Dr. Rane : he did not want to hear what was said ; felt rather annoyed at the noise and interruption.

"I couldn't get home before," resumed Timothy, "though I'm sure I nearly ran my legs off all the way from Whitborough. When a young man has his day's work to perform, and that in a lawyer's office, he is obliged to stop in beyond hours if required."

"Don't tell me," said Jelly, who stood with the half-closed door in her hand in the most inhospitable manner. "You could have come home if you chose."

"But I couldn't, Miss Jelly."

"You are always stopping beyond hours now. That is, *saying* that you are."

"Because we have been so busy lately," answered Tim. "Our head clerk, Repton, is away through illness, and it puts more work on us others. Dale's as cranky as he can be: he works us like horses. If you'll believe me, Miss Jelly, I didn't have time to go out and get any tea. I've not had bit or drop inside me since one o'clock to-day."

This piteous view of affairs a little mollified Jelly; and she dropped her tart tone. Dr. Rane was wishing the talkers would go away. He would have gone himself, but that he did not altogether care to betray his proximity.

"Why does that old Dale not get another clerk?" demanded Jelly. "I should tell him plainly if I were you, Tim, that going without my regular meals did not suit me."

"We should not dare to say that. Much he'd listen if we did! As to getting another clerk, I believe he is doing it. Repton's doctor says he'll never be well again, so Dale thinks it's of no good waiting for him."

"*You* were to be put up in Repton's place, if ever he went out of it," said Jelly, quickly.

"I know I was"—and Timothy Wilks's voice took so strangely rueful a tone that it might have made Dr. Rane laugh under more open circumstances. "But when Dale made that promise, Miss Jelly, you see the affair of the anonymous letter had not taken place."

"What anonymous letter?"

"The one that killed Edmund North."

"Why, you don't mean to insinuate that Dale lays the blame of that on *you?*"

"I don't suppose he thinks I sent it. Indeed I'm sure he does not. But he was anything but pleasant over it to me at the time, and he has never been quite the same to me since."

"He is an unjust owl," said Jelly.

"One does not look for much else than injustice from lawyers."

"Does Dale say that letter is the reason of his not pro-
moting you to Repton's place?"

"He doesn't say it : but I know just as well, that it is so,
as if he did."

Jelly struck the key two or three times against the door.
She was thinking.

"That's through your tongue, Timothy Wilks. You know
you did talk of the matter out of the office."

"They say so," confessed Timothy. "But if I did, I'm
sure I've been punished enough for it. It's hard that it
should stick to me always like pitch. Why don't they find
the writer of the letter, and plaster *him?* He was the
villain; not me."

"So he was," said Jelly. "Tim, what would you say if
I told you I knew who it was?"

"I? Excuse me, Miss Jelly, but I should not quite believe
it."

Jelly laughed. Not a loud laugh, was it, but rather de-
risive, and full of *power.* Its peculiar significance penetrated
through the slender thicket of green, to him who was seated
under the cedar-tree, betraying to him all too surely that
Jelly knew his dangerous secret. Even Tim Wilks, less sensitive, was struck with the sound.

"Surely, Miss Jelly, you do not mean that you know who
wrote the letter?"

"I could put my finger out from where I now stand, Tim,
and lay it on the right person," she answered in a low, im-
pressive tone, little suspecting how literally true were the
words.

Tim seemed struck aghast. He drew a deep breath.

"Then, why don't you, Miss Jelly?"

"Because—" Jelly stopped short. "Well, because there are
certain considerations that make it inconvenient to speak."

"But you ought to speak. Indeed you ought, Miss Jelly.
If Lawyer Dale got to hear of this, he'd tell you that it's
quite obligatory."

Again there broke forth a laugh from Jelly. But quite a
different laugh this time—one of light mirth. Tim decided
that she had been only laughing at *him.* He resented it in
his heart, as much as he was capable of resenting anything.

"You shouldn't make game of a young man in this manner,
Miss Jelly! I'm sure I thought you were in earnest. You'd
make a fine play-actor."

Q

" Shouldn't I ? " assented Jelly, " and take in the audience nicely, as I take in you. Well," changing her tone, " you must be soft, Tim Wilks! The idea of believing that *I* could know who wrote the letter ? "

The hint about Lawyer Dale had frightened Jelly, bringing back the prudence which her impulsive sympathy with Tim's wrongs had momentarily scared away. All she could do, then, was to strive to undo the impression raised. There existed certain considerations, and they made it, as she had aptly said, inconvenient to speak. But she felt vexed with herself, and resented it on Tim.

" Look here," cried she, " I can't stand at this gate all night, jabbering with you; so you can just betake yourself off. And the next time you make a promise to be home by a certain hour to take a late cup of tea with friends at Mrs. Green's, I'll trouble you to keep it. Mind that, Mr. Wilks."

Mr. Wilks had his nose round the post, and was beginning some deprecatory rejoinder, but Jelly slammed the door, and nearly snapped the nose off. Locking it with a click, she put the key in her pocket, and marched on to the house.

Leaving Dr. Rane alone to the night dews under the heavy cedar-tree. *Were* the dews falling ?—or was it that his own face gave out the damp moisture that lay on it ? He sat still as death.

So, then, Jelly did know of it! as he had before half-suspected ; and he had been living, *was* living, with a sword suspended over him. It mattered not to speculate upon how she acquired the terrible secret : she knew it, and that was enough. Dr. Rane had not felt very safe before ; but now it seemed to him as though he were treading on the extreme verge of a precipice, whose edge was crumbling from under him. There could be no certainty at any moment that Jelly would not declare what she knew: to-morrow—the next day —the day after : how could he tell which day or hour it might be ? Oliver Rane wiped his face, his hand anything but a steady one.

The " certain considerations that made it inconvenient to speak," to which Jelly had confessed, meant that she was in service with Mrs. Cumberland, and that he was Mrs. Cumberland's son. While Jelly retained her place, she would not perhaps be deliberately guilty of the bad faith of betraying, as it were, her mistress. Not deliberately : but there were so many chances that might lead to it. Lawyer Dale's questionings might bring it about—and who could answer for it that such might not at once set in at a word from Wilks?—or she might be quitting Mrs. Cumberland's place—or taking upon herself to right Tim with the world—or speaking, as she had evidently spoken that night, upon impulse. Yes, yes; there were a hundred and one chances now of his betrayal!

He must get away from Dallory without delay. "Out of sight, out of mind," runs the old proverb—and it certainly seemed to Dr. Rane that if *he* were out of sight the chances of betrayal would be wonderfully lessened. He could battle with it better, too, at a distance, if discovery came; perhaps wholly keep it from his wife. Never a cloud had come between him and Bessy: rather than let *this* disclosure come to her—that he had been the one who caused her brother's death —he would have run away with her to the wilds of Africa. Or, perhaps from her.

Run away! The thought brought a remembrance to his mind. That self-same morning another letter had arrived from his friend in America, Dr. Jones. Dr. Jones had again urged on Oliver Rane his acceptance of the offer—to join his practice there—that he had previously made, saying it was an opportunity he might never have again throughout his life-time. Dr. Rane fully believed it: it was, beyond doubt, a very excellent offer; but, alas! he had not the requisite money to embrace it. Five hundred pounds—besides the expenses of the voyage and the removal: Dr. Rane had not, to spare, five hundred shillings. The tontine money came flashing through his brain. Oh, if he could but get it!

The air grew really damp; but he still sat in the dark under the shade of the cedar-tree, reviewing plans and projects, ways and means. To him it was growing as a very matter of life or death.

How long he sat, he knew not: but by-and-by the faint sound of Dallory church clock was wafted to him through the clear air. He counted the strokes—ten. Ten? *Ten?* Dr. Rane started up: he ought to have gone for his wife long and long ago.

Boom! boom! boom! Six o'clock in the morning; and the great bell ringing out from the works of North and Gass! It was a bell Dallory had not heard of late, and sleepy people turned in their beds. Many had been listening for it, know-ing it was going to be rung; some got up and looked from their windows to see whether the street became alive with workmen, or whether it remained silent.

Richard North was within the works. He had come out thus early, hoping to welcome his men. Three or four entered with him. The bell rang its accustomed time, and then ceased; its sound dying away, and leaving a faint echo in the air. There was no other answer: the men had not responded to the call. Nothing more, than that faint vibration of sound remained to tell of the appeal made by Richard North.

Richard North threw up, compulsorily, the offered contract; and proceeded on a journey without loss of time. Some said he went to Scotland, some to Belgium; but the utmost known about it was that his departure had reference to business. But that he was a temperate man, and given to pity as much as to blame, he could have cursed the men's blind folly. What was to become of them? The work was there, and they drove it away from their doors, driving all chance with it of regaining prosperity. They were forcing him to their supersedure: they were bringing despair, famine, death upon a place where content and comfort had used to reign. Yes, death: as you will find later. Sure never did greater blindness than this, fall on mortal sight!

Days went on, and grew into weeks: not many: and Richard North was still absent. Prospects seemed to be looking gloomy on all sides. To make matters worse, some cases of fever began to manifest themselves at Dallory. Dr. Rane and his brother practitioner, Mr. Seeley, only wondered that something of the kind had not broken out before.

Amidst other places that wore an air of gloom was the interior of Dallory Hall. Madam's insatiable demands for money had been very partially responded to of late: not at all since the absence of Richard. Even she, with all her imperious scorn of whence supplies came, provided they did come, began to realize the fact that gold can no more be drawn from exhausted coffers than blood from a stone. It did not tend to render her temper sweeter.

She sat one morning in what she was pleased to call her boudoir—a charming apartment opening from her dressing-room. Several letters lay before her, brought up by her maid: she had carelessly tossed them aside for some hours, but was getting to them now when it was near mid-day. Not very pleasant letters, any of them, to judge by Madam's dark face. One was from Sidney at Homburg, imploring for assistance (which had not recently been sent him) in a piteous manner; two or three were rather urgent demands for the payment of private accounts of Madam's rather long delayed; one was a polite excuse from Frank Dallory and his sister for not accepting a dinner invitation. There was not a single pleasant letter amidst the lot.

"I wonder what Dick North means by staying away like this!—and leaving orders at Ticknell's that no cheques are to be cashed!" growled Madam in self-soliloquy. "He ought to be here. He ought to force those miserable men of his back to work, whether they will or not. He's away; Arthur's away; Sidney's away: and with this uncertain state of things out-doors and trouble in, the house is worse than a dungeon. People seem to be getting shy of it: even Mary Dallory stays without the gates. That girl's an artful flirt: as Matilda said yesterday. If Arthur and Dick were back she'd come fast enough: I should like to know which of the two she most cares for. It is absurd though, to speak of her in conjunction with Dick North. *Dick North!* As well suppose she would take up with one of his workmen. I think I'll go off somewhere for a while. Should it be true, this suspicion of fever, the place will not be safe. I shall want a hundred pounds or two. And Sidney must have money. He says he'll do something desperate if I don't send it—but he has said that before. Confound it all! Why does not gold grow upon trees?"

Madam's dress this morning was a striped lilac silk of amazing rustle and richness. Letting it all out behind her, she went down the stairs and through the hall, sweeping the dust along in a little cloud. Mr. North was not in his parlour; Madam went about looking for him; sweeping still.

To her surprise she found him in the drawing-room; it was not often he ventured into that exclusive place. He had a shabby long coat on down to his heels, and a straw hat. Madam's scornful head went up fifteen inches when she saw him there.

"What do you want?" she asked in a tone that plainly said he had about as much right in the room as an unwelcome stranger.

"I have come to beg a bit of cotton of Matilda to tie up these flowers," was Mr. North's answer, showing some in his hand—and indeed it was only then he was preferring the request. "Thomas Hepburn's little boy is here, and I thought I'd give the child a posy."

"A posy!" mockingly repeated Madam, despising the homely term.

"I have no cotton," said Matilda, who lay back in a chair, reading. "What should bring cotton in a drawing-room?"

"Ah well—I can bind a piece of the variegated grass round," said Mr. North with resignation. "I'm sorry to have troubled you, Matilda."

"And when you have disposed of your 'posy,' I am coming to your parlour," said Madam.

Mr. North groaned as he went out. He knew what "coming to his parlour" meant—that his peace would be destroyed for the day. There were moments when he thought heart and mind and brain must alike give way under home worries and Madam's.

"When did this come?" enquired Madam, pointing to a letter that stood upright on the mantel-piece: one addressed to Richard North, in her son Arthur's writing.

"This morning," shortly answered Matilda, not looking up from her book.

"Yes, Arthur can write often enough to Dick. This is the second letter that has come for him within a week. What did you do with the other?" Madam broke off to ask.

"Put it into Dick's room against he comes home."

"But Arthur does not trouble himself to write to us, or to let us know aught of his movements," resumed Madam. "We have not had a syllable from him since he wrote word that old Bohun was dead. Is he still in London?—or at his aunt's?—or where?"

"I'm sure I don't know where," retorted Matilda, fractious at being interrupted.

Neither did she care. Madam turned the letter over in idle curiosity: but the post-mark was illegible, not to be deciphered. Leaving it on the mantel-piece, she went to look after Mr. North. He stood on the lawn, doing something to a dwarf-tree of small and most beautiful roses. There was some wind to-day, and the skirts of his coat waved a little in the breeze.

"Did you hear what I said—that I was coming to your parlour?" demanded Madam, swooping down upon him majestically. "*Money must be had.* I want it; Sidney wants it; the house wants it. I——"

Mr. North had straightened himself.   Desperation gave him a little courage.

"I'd give it you if I had it.   I have always given it you. But what is to be done when I have it not?   You must see that it is not my fault, Madam."

"I see that when money is needed it is your place to get it," coolly returned Madam.   "Sidney cannot live upon air. He ——"

"It seems to me that he lives upon gold," Mr. North interrupted in a querulous voice.   "There's no end to it."

"Sidney must have money," equably went on Madam.   "I must have it, for I purpose going away for a time.   You will therefore ——"

"Goodness me ! here's the telegraph man."

This second interruption was also from Mr. North.   Telegraphic messages were somewhat rare at Dallory Hall ; and its master went into a fluster.   His fears flew to his well-beloved son, Dick.   The messenger was coming up the broad walk, a despatch in his hand.   Mr. North advanced to meet him ; Madam sailing behind.

"It is for Captain Bohun, sir," spoke up the man, perceiving something of Mr. North's tremor.

"For Captain Bohun ! " interposed Madam.   "Where's it from ? "

"London, Madam."

Motioning to the messenger to go to the house and get his receipt, she tore it open without the smallest ceremony, and read its contents :

" Dr. Williams to Arthur Bohun, Esq.:

" James Bohun is dying.   Sir Nash wishes you to come up without delay."

Looking here, looking there, stood Madam, her thoughts busy.   Where could Arthur be ?   Why had he left London ?

"Do *you* know ? " she asked roughly of Mr. North.

"Know what, Madam ? "

"Where Arthur Bohun is."

Mr. North stared a little.   "Why, how should I know ? " he asked.   "It's ever so long since Arthur wrote to me.   He sends me messages when he writes to Dick."

Madam swept into the drawing-room.   She took the letter from the mantel-piece, and coolly broke its black seal asunder. Even Matilda's scruples were aroused at this.

"Oh, mamma, don't!" she exclaimed, starting up and

putting her hand over the letter. "Don't open that. It would not be right."

Madam dexterously twitched the letter away, carried it to the window and read it from end to end. Matilda saw her face turn ghastly through its paint, as if with fright.

"Serves her right," thought the young lady. "Mamma, what is amiss?"

Madam crumpled the letter into a ball of creases in her agitated hand: but no answer came from her white lips. Turning abruptly up the stairs, she locked herself into her chamber.

"She is in a passion of fright—whatever the cause may be," quoth Miss Matilda, in self soliloquy.

Ere the day had closed, the household was called upon to witness Madam's sudden departure by train. She went alone : and gave not the slightest clue where she might be going, or when she would be back.

Matilda North had aptly worded the paroxysm : "a passion of fright." Madam was in both. For that rifled letter had given her the news of Arthur Bohun's present place of locality —and that he was by the side of Ellen Adair. What had become of Dick? the letter asked. He must make haste and come, or he would be too late. Madam did not understand at all. There followed a mysterious intimation to Dick; to Dick,, whom Arthur so trusted and who was true as steel; it was more obscure even than the rest ; but it seemed to hint at— yes, to hint at—marriage. Marriage? Madam felt her flesh creep all over.

"A son of mine marry *her !*" she breathed. "Heaven help me to avert the danger."

About the last woman, one would think, who ought to call for help from Heaven.

CHAPTER XXV.

A SECOND FLY AT THE DOOR.

THE tide came rippling up on the sea shore in gentle ridges of sparkling foam, with a monotonous, soothing murmur. The waves to-day showed themselves not ; the air was densely still : but in the western sky little black clouds were rising, no bigger yet than a man's hand ; and as the weather-wise old fishermen glanced to the spot, they foretold a storm.

Two people, pacing the beach side by side, regarded neither the sea nor the threatened storm. Need you be told who they were ?—Arthur Bohun and Ellen Adair. What were the winds and the waves to them in their trance of happiness ? Amidst the bitter misery that was soon to set in for both of them, the recollection of this short time spent at Eastsea, these few weeks since their love had been declared, and their marriage was approaching, would seem like an impossible dream.

The private marriage, consented to by Mrs. Cumberland, must not be confounded with a secret marriage. It was to be kept from the world in general : but not from every friend they possessed. Mrs. Cumberland intended to be present as Ellen's guardian ; and she very much urged that some friend of Arthur's should also attend. He acquiesced, and fixed on Richard North. Captain Bohun purposed to tell his aunt, Miss Bohun, his true friend in every way : but not until the wedding was over : he would trust nobody beforehand, he said, save Mrs. Cumberland and Dick. Even Dick he did not trust yet. He commanded Dick's presence at Eastsea, telling him that his coming was imperative : that there must be no refusal. Finding Dick did not respond in any way, Arthur wrote again ; but still only mysteriously. The first letter was the one put aside by Miss Matilda North, the second was the one opened by Madam.

But there were moments when, in spite of his happiness, Arthur Bohun had qualms of conscience for his precipitation : and the more especially did they press upon him immediately after the marriage was decided upon. For, after all, he really knew nothing, or as good as nothing, of Mr. Adair's position : and the proud Bohun blood bubbled up a little, as a thought crossed him that it was just possible he might find too late that, in point of family, hers was not fit to have been mated with his.

The human heart is very treacherous : given over to self-deceit, and to much sophistry. So long as a thing is coveted, when it seems next door to unattainable, we see nothing but the desirability of gaining it, the advantages and happiness it must bring. But, let this great desire be attained, and lo ! we veer round with a vengeance, and repent our haste. For instantly every reason and argument that could bear against it, true or false, rise up within us with mocking force, and we say, Oh that I had waited before doing this thing ! It is that deceitful heart of ours that is in fault, nothing else; placing upon all things its own false colouring.

At first, as they sat together under cover of the rocks, or on the more open benches on the sands, or wandered to the walks inland and the pretty rural lanes, his conversation would turn on Mr. Adair. But Ellen seemed to know as little of her father as he did.

"It is strange you don't remember more of him, Ellen!" he suddenly said on one occasion when he was alone with her at Mrs. Cumberland's.

"Strange! Do you think so?" returned Ellen, turning round from the bay window where she was standing. "I was sent to Europe at eight years old, and children of that age so soon forget. I seem to recollect a gentleman in some kind of white coat, who cried over me and kissed me, and said mamma was gone to live in heaven. His face was a pleasant one, and he had bright hair; something the colour of yours."

She thought Arthur had alluded to personal remembrance. But he had not meant that.

"I remember another thing—that papa used to say I was just like my mother, and should grow up like her," resumed Ellen. "It seems ages ago. Perhaps when I see him I shall find that my memory has been giving me an ideal father; that he is quite different from what I have pictured."

"You know none of your Scotch relatives, Ellen?"

"None."

"Or in what locality they live?"

"No."

"Why does not Mr. Adair come home?"

"I don't know. He has been thinking of it for some years; and that's why he put me with Mrs. Cumberland instead of having me sent out to him. I am sure he must respect Mrs. Cumberland very much," added Ellen after a pause. "His letters prove it. And he often mentions her late husband as his dear friend and chaplain. I'll show you some of the letters if you like. Would you? I keep all papa's letters."

Arthur Bohun's face lighted up at the proposition. "Yes," he said with animation. "Yes. As many as you please."

She crossed the room to unlock her desk, took out three or four letters indiscriminately from a bundle lying there, and brought them to him. He detained the pretty hands as well as the letters, and took some impassioned kisses from the blushing face, turned up unconsciously to his. Sweeter kisses than Arthur Bohun would ever impress upon any other face in after life. Ellen had almost learned not to shrink from them in her maiden modesty; he vowed to her that it was now his best right and privilege.

But the letters told him nothing. They were evidently a gentleman's letters; but of the writer's position or family they said not a word. Arthur returned them with a half sigh: it was of no use, he thought, to disturb himself any more about the matter. After all, his own father and Mr. Adair had been close friends in India, and that was a kind of guarantee that all must be right. This decided, he delivered himself up to his ideal happiness: and the day of the wedding was finally fixed.

This afternoon, when they were pacing the beach, unseeing the little clouds rising in the west, was the marriage eve. It is the last day they need thus walk together as mere formal acquaintances, not daring to touch each other's hands in view of the public gaze, or to walk arm within arm: for at that little church whose spire is not a stone's-throw off, they will to-morrow be made man and wife. A strange light of happiness sits on Arthur Bohun's cheek, a stranger still is ever fluttering at his heart. The day and the hour are drawing very near to its realization: and not so much as a thought has crossed his mind that any untoward fate could arise to mar it.

Ah, but might not those dark clouds have read him a lesson? Just as the black trifling circlets out there might rise into an overwhelming storm, before which both man and beast must bow their heads, so might be rising, even then, some unseen threatening wave in the drama of his life. And it was so: though he suspected it not. Even now, as they walked, the clouds were growing bigger: just as was the unseen thunder-storm that would descend upon their lives and hearts. Suddenly, in turning to face the west, Arthur saw them. They were pretty big now.

"Look at those clouds, getting up! I hope the weather's not going to change for us to-morrow, Ellen. What does that mean?" he asked of a man who was doing something to his small boat, now high and dry upon the beach.

The sailor glanced indifferently to where the finger pointed.

"It means a storm, master."

"Shall we get it here, do you think?"

"Ay. Not till to-morrow, may be. I fancy we shall, though"—turning up his nose and seeming to sniff around, as if the storm were pervading the air. "I knowed there was going to be a change."

"How did you know it ?"

"Us fishermen smells a storm afore it comes, master. My foot tells it me besides. I got him jammed once, and he have had the weather in him ever since."

"And you think it's going to be a change altogether ? "

"Ay that it be, master."

They walked on. "That will be two untoward events for us," remarked Captain Bohun ; but he spoke with a jesting smile, as if no untoward events could mar their security of happiness. "We want a third to complete it, don't we, Ellen ? "

"What are the two ? "

"This threatened bad weather for to-morrow's one ; Dick's non-coming is the other. I am vexed at that."

For, on this same morning, Mrs. Cumberland had received a letter from her son. Amidst other items of news, Dr. Rane mentioned that Richard North was absent : it was supposed in Belgium, but nobody knew for certain. This explained Richard's silence to Captain Bohun, and put out the hope that Richard would be at the wedding. Dr. Rane also said another thing—which was anything but pleasant news : that beyond all doubt fever was breaking out at Dallory, though it was not yet publicly known. The doctor added that he feared it would prove to be of a malignant type, and he felt glad his mother was away. Bessy was well, and sent her love.

"Will you rest a little before going in ? "

They were passing the favourite old seat under the rocks, as Captain Bohun asked it. Ellen acquiesced, and they sat down. The black clouds came higher and higher : but, absorbed in their own plans, in their own happiness, had the heavens become altogether overshadowed it would have been to them as nothing. In a low voice they conversed together of the future ; beginning with the morrow, ending they knew not where. Their visions were of the sweetest rose-colour ; they fully believed that bliss so great as their own had never been realized on earth. His arm was round Ellen as they sat, her hand lay in his, she could feel his warm breath on her cheek, her shoulder seemed to be resting against his heart. To all intents and purposes they seemed as entirely alone in this sheltered nook as they could have been in the wilds of the desert. The beach was shingly ; footsteps could not approach without being heard : had anybody passed, they would have been seen sitting with as decorous a space between them as though they had quarrelled : but the shore seemed deserted this afternoon.

The arrangement for the marriage was as follows :—At half-past eleven o'clock, Arthur, Ellen, and Mrs. Cumberland would enter the little church by a private door, and the ceremony would take place. Richard North was to have been deputed to give her away, but that was over now. Arthur had the licence ; he had made a friend of the clergyman, and all would be done quietly. He and Ellen were to go away for a few days: she would then return to her home with Mrs. Cumberland, and be to the world still as Miss Adair. After that, Arthur would take his own time, and be guided by circumstances for declaring the marriage: but he meant, if possible, to at once introduce Ellen to his aunt, Miss Bohun. And Ellen Adair? Not a scruple rested on her mind, not a doubt or hesitation on her heart; her father had given his cordial approbation—as expressed in the letter to Mrs. Cumberland—and she was full of the sweetest peace.

" Did you feel that, Ellen ? "

It was a faint, quivering breeze that seemed to pass over them with sharp quickness and to be dying away in a moan. Some white sails out at sea flapped a little, and the boats turned homewards.

" We had better be going, too, my love ; or we may have it upon us."

She rose as he spoke, and they walked homewards. The sky was getting darker; the shades of evening were beginning to gather. Mrs. Cumberland had been lying down and was dressing, the maid said—if Captain Bohun would wait. Ellen took off her bonnet and mantle.

" While we are alone, let me see that I have not made a mistake in the size, Ellen."

Taking from his pocket a bit of tissue paper, he unfolded it and disclosed a wedding-ring. Ellen turned the colour of fifteen peonies as he tried it on.

" I—thought," she timidly began amidst her blushes, " that you meant this to be my wedding-ring "—indicating the plain gold one she habitually wore on her right hand.

" No. Rane bought that one. This will be mine."

It was an exact fit. Captain Bohun had not allowed for the probability of those fragile fingers getting larger with years. As he held it on for a minute, their eyes met. Ellen suddenly

recalled that long-past day in Dallory church, when she had
taken Maria Warne's ring to serve for Bessy North, with the
scene in the carriage afterwards, when Arthur Bohun put the
other one on, and his sweet words: she recalled the scene in
the garden when he put it on again.   This was time the third.

"If this should ever get too small for me?" she murmured as he took it off the finger.

"Oh, but that—if ever—won't be for ages and ages."

Not for ages, and ages!   If they, in their innocent uncon-
sciousness, could but have seen the cruel Fate that was
already coiling its meshes around them!

The storm did not come that night.   But whether, in
aggravation for the delay, it chose to expend itself with
double violence, certain it was that such a one had seldom
been seen at Eastsea as raged in the morning.   The sky was
lurid, angry, and black; the sea tossed itself; the wind
howled; the rain came dashing down at intervals as if from
so many buckets: all nature seemed at warfare.

In much distress lay Mrs. Cumberland.   Exceedingly
subject of late to outer influences, whether it might be this
unusual storm that made her ill, she knew not, but she felt
unable to rise from her bed.   The hour for the marriage was
drawing on.   It had been fixed for a late one: half-past
eleven.   The clergyman had a funeral at half-past ten; and
Mrs. Cumberland had said *she* could not be up and ready
before that.   At a little after eleven Arthur Bohun came up
in the fly that was to convey them to church.   Mrs. Cumberland sent to ask him to go up stairs to her; and he found her
in tears.   A curious sight: she was so self-contained a woman.

"I cannot help it, Captain Bohun: indeed I cannot.   Had
not the marriage better be put off for a day?   I may be
better to-morrow."

"Certainly not," he answered.   "Why should it?   I am
very sorry for Ellen's sake; she would have felt more comfortable at your being in church.   But your presence is not
essential to the ceremony, Mrs. Cumberland."

"Her father and mother were my dear friends.   It seems
as though I should fail in my duty if I were to allow her to go
to church without me."

Arthur Bohun laughed.   He would not hear a word—was
it likely that he would?   In less than an hour's time all responsibility in regard to Ellen would be transferred to him, he
answered, for he should be her husband.

"The marriage will stand good, believe me, dear Mrs. Cumberland, though you do not witness it," were his last words as he went down stairs.

Ellen was ready. She wore an ordinary silk dress of light quiet colour, and a plain white bonnet: such as she might have walked out in at Eastsea. There was nothing, save her pale face and quivering lips, to denote that she was a bride. To have to go to church alone was very unpalatable, and she could with difficulty suppress her tears.

"My dearest love, I am more grieved at it for your sake than you can be," he whispered. "Take a little courage, Ellen; it will soon be over. Once you are my wife, I will strive to shelter you from all vexation."

But this illness of Mrs. Cumberland's made a hitch in the programme. For Arthur Bohun to go out with Mrs. Cumberland and Ellen in a fly, was nothing; he sometimes accompanied them in their drives: but to go out alone with Ellen, and in that storm, would have excited the curiosity of Ann and the other servants. Arthur Bohun rapidly decided to walk to church, braving the rain: Ellen must follow in the fly. There was no time to be lost. It was twenty minutes past eleven.

"Shall I put you in the carriage first, Ellen?" he stayed to ask.

"No. I think you had better not."

"My darling, you *will come?*"

Did a doubt cross him, that he should say this? But she answered that she would: he saw she spoke sincerely. He wrung her hand and went out to the door.

Had the fly multiplied itself into two flies?—and were they squabbling for precedence? Certainly two were there: and the one wet driver was abusing the other wet driver for holding his place close before the door, and not allowing him to draw up to it.

"Arthur! Good Heavens, how fortunate I am! Arthur Bohun! don't you see me?"

Every drop of blood in Arthur Bohun's veins seemed to stand still and turn to ice, as he recognized his mother's voice and his mother's face. Madam, driven hastily from the railway station, had come to bear him off in the body. That his wedding was over for that day, instinct told him: she would have gone and forbidden the banns. He stepped to her fly door.

In after-life, he never could recall clearly these next few minutes. Madam spoke of the telegram that had been received at Dallory. She said—giving to matters her own colouring—that James Bohun was in extremity; that he only waited to see Arthur to die; that he was crying out for him : not a moment was to be lost. She had hastened to London on receipt of the telegram, and had now come down this morning straight to fetch him.

"Step in, Arthur. We must catch the quarter-to-twelve train."

"I—I cannot go," he answered.

"Not go !" screamed Madam. "But I command you to go. Would you disobey the last sacred wishes of a dying man ?"

Well, no; he felt that he could not do that. "A quarter to twelve ?" he said rather dreamily. "You must wait, Madam, while I speak to Mrs. Cumberland. There's plenty of time."

He went indoors with his tale, and up to Mrs. Cumberland, like one in a dream. He was forced to go, he bewailed, but not for more than a day, when he should be back to complete the marriage. What could she answer ? In her bewilderment she scarcely understood what had happened or what had not. Leaping downstairs again, he closed the door of the sitting-room upon himself and Ellen, and clasped her to his heart.

"My darling ! But for this, you would have been on your way to become my wife. Come what may, Ellen, I shall be down again within a few hours. God bless you, my love ! Take care of these."

They were the ring and licence; he handed them to her lest he might lose them. Before Ellen could recover herself, while yet her face was glowing with his farewell kisses, he was being rattled away in the fly with Madam to the station.

Crafty Madam ! Waiting there in the fly at the door and making her observations, she had read what the signs meant almost as surely as though it had been told to her. The other fly waiting, and Ellen dressed ; going out in it on that day of storm ; Arthur out of mourning, and his nice attire covered over with a light over-coat—she guessed the truth (aided by the mysterious hint in the letter she had rifled) and believed full surely that it was nothing less than MARRIAGE she had interrupted. Not a word said she on the road to the station. The getting him away was a great victory gained : it would not do to risk the marring of it. But when they were in the train, and the whistle had sounded, and they were fairly off, then Madam spoke. They had the compartment to themselves.

"Arthur, you cannot deceive me : any attempt at it would be useless. You were about to marry Ellen Adair."

She spoke quietly, almost affectionately; when the bosom is beating with a horrible dread, calmness of manner obtains, more than passion. For a single moment there wavered in Arthur Bohun's mind a doubt of whether it should be avowal or evasion, but not for longer. As it had come to this, why he must take his standing. He raised his head proudly.

"Right, mother. I am going to wed Ellen Adair."

Madam's pulses began to beat nineteen to the dozen. Her head grew hot, her hands grew cold.

"You *were*, you mean, Arthur."

"Yes. Put it as you like. What was interrupted to-day,. will be concluded to-morrow. As soon as I have seen James,. I shall return to Eastsea."

"Arthur! Arthur Bohun! It must never be concluded. Never."

"Pardon me, mother. I am my own master."

"A Bohun may not wed shame and disgrace."

"Shame and disgrace cannot attach to *her*. Madam, I must beg you to remember that in a few hours that young lady will be my wife. Do not try my temper too sorely."

"No, not to her, but to her father," panted Madam—and Arthur felt frightened, he knew not why, at her strong emotion. "Would you wed the daughter of a—a—"

Madam paused. Arthur looked at her; his compressed lips. trembled just a little.

"Of a what, mother? Pray go on."

"Of everything that is bad. A forger. A convict."

There was a dead pause. Nothing to be heard but the whirling train. "A—what?" gasped Captain Bohun, when he could get his breath.

"A Convict," burst forth Madam in a scream; for her agitation was becoming irrepressible. "Why do you make me repeat painful things?"

"Mother! Of whom do you speak?"

"Of her father: William Adair."

He fell back in the carriage like one who is shot. As one from whom life and all that can make it sweet, had suddenly gone out for ever.

CHAPTER XXVI.

A PANIC.

THE funerals were going about in Dallory. Dr. Rane's prog-nostications had proved correct; the fever was a real fever. It spread, and a panic set in.

As yet it had been confined to the poor. To those who for some months now had been living in squalor and despair and poverty. Some called it the famine fever; some a relapsing fever; some typhus: but, whatever the name accorded to it, one thing was certain—that it was of a malignant and fatal type.

It possessed a rather singular feature: that it seemed to burst out all at once—in a single night. Before the doctors had well made themselves sure that anything of the kind was in the air, before most of the public had so much as heard of it, it came. The probability of course was that it had been for some days smouldering. On the afternoon that witnessed Madam's departure from Dallory Hall (after the receipt of the telegram and the reading of Dick's letter) there had not been one decided case: in the morning no less than seven cases had shown themselves. After that, it spread rapidly.

Madam remained away. James Bohun was dead, and she stayed with Sir Nash. Matilda North, taking French leave, went up there to join her without an invitation; she did not care to stay amidst the sickness. So the master of Dallory Hall was alone, and enjoyed his liberty as much as trouble had left him capable of.

A week or ten days had passed on now since the outbreak, and the funerals were going about Dallory. The two medical men, Dr. Rane and Mr. Seeley, were worked nearly off their legs. The panic that had set in was at its height. Dallory had been an exceptionally healthy place: people were unused to this state of things, and got frightened. Some of the better families took flight; for the sea-side, or elsewhere. The long-continued distress, resulting on the strike, had pre-disposed the poorer classes for it. It was they whom it chiefly attacked, but there were now two or three cases amid their betters. This was no time for the medical men to speculate whether they should or should not be paid; they put all such considerations aside, and gave the poor sufferers their best care. Dr. Rane in particular was tenderly assiduous with his patients. In spite of that fatal letter and the mistake—nay, the sin—it involved, he was a humane-natured man. Were he a successful practitioner, making his hundreds a year, or his thousands, as might be, he would be one of the first and readiest to give away largely of his time and skill to any who could not well afford to pay him.

The last person whom the fever had attacked was one of the brothers Hepburn of Dallory, undertakers, carpenters, and coffin-makers. Both of them were sickly men; but exceedingly steady and respectable. The younger brother, Henry, was the one seized: it was universally assumed that he caught it in the discharge of certain of the duties of his calling, and the supposition did not tend to decrease the public panic. Dr. Rane thought him a bad subject for the illness, and did all he could.

Bessy Rane stood in her kitchen, making an apple pudding. It is rather a sudden transition of subject, from sickness to puddings, but only in accordance with existing life. Whatever calamity may be decimating society abroad, the domestic routine of daily existence goes on at home in just its ordinary course. Molly Green was pudding-maker in general: but Molly was hastening over her other work that day, for she had obtained leave to go home in the evening to see her mother: a woman who had been ailing for years with chronic sickness, and lived at Whitborough. So Bessy this morning took upon herself the pudding.

Mrs. Rane stood at the table; a brown holland apron tied over her light morning gown, her sleeves turned up to the middle of her arms above her wrists. Hands and wrists and arms were alike pretty. The apples lay in a basin ready pared, and she was rolling out the crust. Ever and anon she glanced at the kitchen clock. Her husband had been called out at early morning, four o'clock, and she was getting a little anxious. Now it was close upon eleven. It cannot be said that Bessy was afraid of the fever for him: she shared in the popular belief that medical men are generally exempt from infection; but she was always glad to see him come home safe and well.

His latch-key was heard in the door while she was thinking of him. Dr. Rane went straight up-stairs to the unused top-room, changed his clothes, and washed his hands and face—a precaution he always took when he had been with fever patients. Bessy put the kitchen door open, that he might see where she was when he came down.

"Pudding-making, Bessy!" he cried, looking in. "Why don't you let Molly do that?"

"Molly's busy. She wants to go home this evening, Oliver, as soon as we can spare her, and not come back until to-morrow night. She had a letter this morning to say her mother has at last taken to her bed, and the doctor thinks her very ill. I have given her leave to go."

"But how shall you manage without her?"

"I shall have old Phillis in. Molly has been to her, and she says she'll be glad to come."

Dr. Rane said no more. It was quite the same to him whether Molly, or Phillis, did what was wanted. When men are much harassed in spirit, they cannot concern themselves with petty details.

"I was thinking, Oliver, that—if you don't mind—as we can have Phillis, I would leave it to Molly whether to come back to-morrow night, or not. If her mother is really growing worse, the girl may like to stay a day longer with her."

"My dear, do just as you like about it," was the doctor's rather impatient answer.

"Your breakfast shall be ready in a moment, Oliver."

"I have taken breakfast. It was between eight and nine before I could get away from Ketler's, and I went and begged some of Mrs. Gass. After that I went round to the patients."

Bessy was putting the crust into the basin. She lifted her hands and turned in some dismay.

"Surely, Oliver, they have not got the fever at Ketler's!"

Dr. Rane slightly laughed. "Not the fever, Bessy: something else. The baby. It was Ketler who called me up this morning."

"Oh dear," said Bessy, going on with her pudding. "I thought that poor baby was not expected for a month or two. How will they manage to keep it? It seems to me that the less food there is for them, the quicker the babies come."

"That's generally the case," observed Dr. Rane.

"Is the mother well?"

"Tolerably so."

"And—how are other things going on, Oliver?"

He knew, by the tone of her voice, that she meant the fever. Bessy never spoke of that without a kind of timidity.

" Neither worse nor better. It's very bad still."

" And fatal? "

" Yes, and fatal. Henry Hepburn is in danger."

" But he'll get over it ? " rejoined Bessy quickly.

" I don't think so. His brother will have it next if he does not mind. He is as nervous over it as he can be. I am off now, Bessy, up the Ham."

" You will be in to dinner ? "

" Before that, I hope."

Bessy settled to her pudding again, and the doctor departed. Not into danger this time, for the fever had not yet shown itself in Dallory Ham. Scarcely a minute had elapsed when the door-bell rang, and Molly went to answer it. Mrs. Rane, her hands all flour, peeped from the kitchen, and saw Mr. North.

" Oh papa! How glad I am to see you! Do you mind coming in here ? "

Mind ! Mr. North felt far more at home in Bessy's kitchen than in his wife's grand drawing-room. He had brought a small open basket of most lovely hot-house flowers for Bessy. He put it on the table, and sat down on one of the wooden chairs in peace and comfort. Richard had not returned, and he was still alone.

" Go on with your pudding, my dear. Don't mind me. I like to see it."

" It's all but done, papa. Molly will tie it up. Oh, these beautiful flowers ! " she added, bending her face down to them. " How kind of you to think of me ! "

" I'm going up to Ham Court about some seeds, child ; the walk will do me good, this nice day. I feel stronger and better, Bessy, than I did."

" I am so glad of that, papa."

" And so I thought—as I was intending to call in here— that I'd cut a few blossoms, and bring with me. How's the fever getting on, Bessy ? "

" It is not any better, I am afraid, papa."

" So I hear. They say that Henry Hepburn's dying."

Bessy felt startled. " Oh, I trust not ! Though I think—I fear—Oliver has not very much hope of him."

" Well, I've heard it. And I came here, Bessy, to ask if you would not like to come to the Hall for a week or two. It might be safer for you. Are you at all afraid of catching it, child ? "

" N—o," answered Bessy. But it was spoken dubiously, and Mr. North looked at her.

" Your husband has to be amongst it pretty well every hour of his life, and I can but think there must be some risk for you. You had better come to the Hall."

" Oliver is very particular to change his clothes when he comes in ; but still I know there must of course be some little risk," she said. " I try to be quite brave, and not think of it, papa : and I have a great piece of camphor inside here "— touching the bosom of her dress—" at which Oliver laughs."

" Which is as good as confessing that you are nervous about it, Bessy," said Mr. North.

" Not much, papa. A doctor's wife, you know, must not have fancies."

" Well, you come up to the Hall to-day, Bessy. It will be a change for you, and pleasant for me, now I'm all alone ; it'll be like some of the old days come back again, you and me together. As to Oliver, I daresay he'll be glad to have the house to himself a bit, while he is so busy."

Bessy, wiping the flour off her hands on a towel, consented. In point of fact, her husband had proposed, some days back, that she should go away : and she did feel half afraid of taking the fever through him.

" But it cannot be until to-morrow, papa," she said, as Mr. North rose to depart, and she accompanied him to the door, explaining that Molly was going home. " I should not like to leave Oliver alone in the house for the night. Phillis will be here to-morrow : she can stay and sleep, should Molly Green not return."

" Very well," said Mr. North.

It was left at this. Bessy opened the door for her father, and watched him on his way up the Ham.

Dr. Rane came back to dinner ; and found his patients allowed him an hour's peace to eat it in. Bessy informed him of the arrangement she had made : and that he was to be a bachelor from the morrow for an indefinite period. The doctor laughed, making a jest of it : but nevertheless he glanced keenly from under his eyelids at his wife.

" Bessy ! I do believe you are afraid ! "

" No, not exactly," was her answer : " I don't think 'afraid' is the right word. It is just this, Oliver : I do not get nervous over it ; but I cannot help remembering rather often that you may bring it home to me."

"Then, my dear, go—go by all means where you will be out of harm's way, so far as I am concerned."

Dinner over, Dr. Rane hastened out again, on his way to see Mrs. Ketler. He had just reached that bench in the shady part of the road at the neck of the Ham, when he saw Jelly coming along. The doctor only wished there was some convenient shelter to dart into, by which he might avoid her. Ever since the night when he had heard that agreeable conversation as he sat under the cedar-tree, Jelly's keen green eyes had been worse to him than poison. She stopped when she met him.

" So that child of Susan Ketler's is come, sir ! "

" Ay," said Dr. Rane.

" What in the world brings it here now ? "

" Well, I don't know," returned the doctor. " Children often come without giving their friends due notice. I am on my way thither."

" And not as much as a bedgown to wrap it in," resentfully went on Jelly, " and not a bit o' tea or oatmeal in the place for her ! My faith ! baby after baby coming into the world all round, and the men out on strike ! This makes seven—if they'd all been alive : she'll be contented perhaps when she's got seventeen."

" It is the way of the world, Jelly. Set up the children first, and consider what to do with them afterwards."

" What's this that's the matter with Tim Wilks, sir ? " demanded Jelly, abruptly changing the subject.

" With Tim Wilks ! I did not know that anything was the matter with him."

" Yes, there is," said Jelly. " I met old Green just now, and he said Timothy Wilks was in bed ill. They thought it might be a bilious attack, if it was not the fever."

" I'll call in and see him," said Dr. Rane. " Has he been drinking again ? "

Jelly's eyes flashed with resentment. Considering that Tim had really kept sober and steady for the past year and half, she looked on the question as a frightful aspersion. And the more especially so as proceeding from Dr. Rane.

" *I* can answer for it that he has not been drinking—and so, as I supposed, might everybody else," was her tart reply. " Timothy Wilks is worried, sir ; that's what it is. He has never been at ease since people accused him of writing that anonymous letter : and he never will be till he is publicly cleared of it. Sir, I think he ought to be."

Was it an ice-bolt that seemed to shoot through Oliver Rane's heart ?—or only a spasm ? Something took it : though he managed to keep his countenance, and to speak with calm indifference.

"Cleared ? Cleared of what ? I fancied it had been ascertained that Wilks was the man who spoke of the affair out of Dale's office. He can't clear himself from that. As to any other suspicion, no one has cast it on him."

"Well, sir—of course *you know best*," answered Jelly, recollecting herself and cooling down : but she could not help giving the words an emphasis. "If Tim should become dangerously ill, it might have to be done to set his mind at rest."

"What might have to be done ?" demanded Dr. Rane with authority.

And Jelly did not dare to answer the direct question. She could boast and talk *at* people in her gossiping way so long as she felt safe, but when it came to anything like proving her words, she was a very coward. Dr. Rane was looking at her, waiting for her to speak, his manner uncompromising, his countenance stern.

"Oh well, sir, I'm sure I don't know at all," she said, her tongue feeling as if it had dried up. "And I'm sure I hope poor Tim has not got the fever."

"I'll call and see him," repeated Dr. Rane, proceeding on his way. Jelly curtsied and went on hers.

When beyond her view, he took out his handkerchief and wiped his face, damp as with the dews of death. He must, he *must* get away from Jelly and Dallory ! But for having a wife on his hands, he might have felt tempted to make a hasty flitting to America and join Dr. Jones. Join Dr. Jones ?— But where was the wherewithal to do it ? He had it not. His thoughts turned, as they ever did on these occasions, to that money of his locked up in the Tontine. *Of his :* that was how Dr. Rane had got to regard it. That money would bring him salvation. If he could but obtain it ——

A bow from some white haired old gentleman, passing in a carriage. Dr. Rane returned it, the singular coincidence of his appearance at that moment flashing through his mind. For it was Sir Thomas Ticknell. Yes : it truly seemed to him that that Tontine money would be nothing less than salvation. He went on with a great fear and pain in his throbbing heart, wondering for how long or short a time Jelly would hold her counsel.

The next morning was Thursday. It brought news that nearly struck people dumb: Henry Hepburn, the undertaker, was dead, and Mrs. Rane had been seized with the fever. Dr. Rane's account was, that his wife had been very restless all night; he gave her a composing draught, which seemed to do good for the time: but upon attempting to get up she was attacked with nausea and faintness, and had to go back to bed. The symptoms that subsequently set in he feared were those of the fever.

It was an awkward time for Bessy to be ill, as Molly Green had gone home: but Phillis, an excellent substitute, was there. She attended on Mrs. Rane, and the doctor went abroad to his patients. Mr. North, disappointed at Bessy's non-arrival, hearing of her indisposition, came to the house; but Bessy sent down an urgent message by Phillis, begging him not to run into any danger by coming up to her chamber. And Mr. North, docile and obedient—as Madam in her imperiousness had trained him to be—left his best love, and went back home again.

In the course of the morning Dr. Rane called in at Hepburn's. It was a kind of double shop and double house; in the one were sold articles of furniture, in the other the carpenter's work was carried on. Thomas Hepburn and his family lived in the first; Henry, now dead, had occupied the last. He was a married man, but had no children. When Dr. Rane entered the second shop, he did not at first see Thomas Hepburn; the two shutters up at the window made the place dark, after coming in from the bright sunshine. Thomas Hepburn saw him, however, and came forward from the workshop behind, where he had been looking on at his men. Various articles seemed to be in the course of active construction, coffins amidst the rest.

" I am very sorry for this loss, Hepburn," began the doctor.

" Well, sir, I've not had any hope from the first," sighed Hepburn, his face looking careworn and unusally sickly in the semi-light. " I don't think poor Henry had."

" The fact is, Hepburn, he had not strength to carry him through the disorder; it did not attack him lightly. I did all I could."

" Yes, sir, I'm sure of that " returned Hepburn—and what

with his naturally weak voice, and the hammering that was
going on behind, Dr. Rane had to listen with all his ears to
catch the words. "We've been an ailing family always:
liable to take disorders, too, more than others."

Dr. Rane made no reply for the moment. He was regarding the speaker. Something in his aspect imparted the suspicion that the man was in actual present fear.

"You must keep up a good heart, you know, Hepburn."

"I'd rather go a hundred miles, sir, than do what I've got
to do just now amid the dead," said Hepburn, glancing round.
"*That's* how my brother took it."

"Let a workman go instead of you."

The undertaker shook his head. "One *has* to go with me;
and the other is just as afraid as afraid can be. No, I must
go on myself. There'll be double work for me, now Henry's
gone."

"Well, Hepburn, I begin to think the fever is on the turn,"
said the doctor cheerily, as he walked away.

The day wore on. Mrs. Rane's symptoms were decidedly
those of fever, and the doctor went all the way to Whitborough
himself (not far in actual distance, only that he could not well
spare the time) to tell Molly Green she was to keep where she
was, out of harm's way, and not return until sent for. When
he got back home his wife was worse. Phillis met him at the
door, and said her poor mistress's face was scarlet, and she
rolled her head from side to side. Phillis wanted to stay the
night, but the doctor would not have it: there was no necessity, he said, and she had better not be longer in the infection
than could be helped. So Phillis went away at ten o'clock.

Between eleven and twelve, just as Mr. Seeley was preparing for rest, Dr. Rane came in and asked him to go over to
see his wife. The surgeon went at once. Bessy was lying in
bed in her comfortable chamber, just as Phillis had described—
her face scarlet, her head turning uneasily on the pillow. A
candle stood on the table, dimly lighting the room; Mr.
Seeley took it close to inspect her face; but Bessy put up her
hand and turned her head away, as if the light hurt her.

"She seems slightly delirious," whispered Mr. Seeley apart,
and Dr. Rane nodded. After that, the two doctors talked
together a little on the stairs, and Mr. Seeley went away, saying he would come again in the morning.

In the morning, however, Dr. Rane went over to tell him
that his wife, after a most restless night, had dropped into a

quiet doze, and had better not be disturbed. He felt sure she was better. This was Friday.

Phillis arrived betimes. She found a wet sheet flapping in the grey ante-room, just outside the bed-chamber door, which Dr. Rane had saturated with disinfecting liquid. Jars of disinfectants stood on the wide landing, on the staircase, and in other parts of the house. Phillis had no fear, and went in behind the flapping sheet. She could make nothing of Mrs. Rane. Instead of the scarlet face and restless head, she now lay buried in her pillow, still, and pale, and intensely quiet. Phillis offered her some tea; Mrs Rane just opened her eyes, and feebly motioned it away with her hand, just as she had motioned away the light the previous night. "It's a sudden change," thought Phillis. "I don't like it."

Later in the morning, Dr. Rane brought up Mr. Seeley. She lay in exactly the same position, deep in the pillow. What with that, and what with the large night-cap, the surgeon could get to see very little of her face.

"Don't disturb me," she faintly said, when he would have aroused her sufficiently to get a good look. "I am easy now."

"Do you know me?" questioned Mr. Seeley, bending over her.

"Yes," she answered, opening her eyes for a moment. "Let me sleep; I shall be better to-morrow."

"How do you feel?" he asked.

"Only tired. Let me sleep."

"Bessy," said her husband, in the persuasive voice he used to the sick, "won't you just turn to Mr. Seeley?"

"To-morrow. I want to go to sleep."

And so they did not disturb her further. After all, sleep does wonders, as Dr. Rane remarked.

It might have been that Mr. Seeley went away somewhat puzzled, scarcely thinking that the fever had been on her sufficiently long to leave this kind of exhaustion.

As the day grew older, a rumour was whispered that Mrs. Rane was dying. Whence it arose none could trace, unless from a word or two dropped by Dr. Rane himself to Thomas Hepburn. They happened to meet in the street, and the undertaker stopped to enquire after Mrs. Rane. She was in a most critical state, was the doctor's answer; the night would decide it, one way or the other.

Phillis went up to her mistress several times. Dr. Rane kept the hanging sheet well saturated, and flapped it often.

Mrs. Rane never seemed to rouse herself throughout the day : seemed, in fact, to sleep through it. Phillis began to hope that it was indeed comfortable, refreshing sleep, and that she would awake better.

"You'll let me stay here to-night, master?" she said, when there was nothing more to do, as Dr. Rane—who had been out—came in, and passed by the kitchen.

"No need," he answered in his decisive manner. "Be here the first thing in the morning."

Phillis put on her shawl and bonnet, wished him good-night, and departed. It was about ten o'clock. Dr. Rane saw her out and went up to the sick chamber. In less than five minutes he came down again with a white face, opened the front door, and strode across the road to' Mr. Seeley's. The latter was in his surgery, in the act of pouring out some medicine into a small phial.

"Seeley! Seeley! My wife is gone!"

What with the suddenness of the interruption, and what with the words, the surgeon was so startled that he dropped the bottle.

"Gone!" he cried. "Do you mean *dead?*"

"I do."

"Why, when I saw you at dusk, you told me she was sleeping comfortably!" said the surgeon, staring at Dr. Rane. "Phillis also said it."

"And so she was. She was to all appearance. Heaven is my witness that I thought and believed the sleep then to be natural—that it was refreshing her. She must have died in it. I went up now, and found her—found her—getting cold. She must have been dead more than an hour."

Oliver Rane put his arm on Mr. Seeley's counter and bent his face to hide his emotion. The surgeon in the midst of his surprise, had hardly ever felt so sorry for any one as he felt in that moment for his brother practitioner.

CHAPTER XXVII.

WHAT JELLY SAW.

"It was too true; Mrs. Rane was dead," said sympathising people one to the other; for even that same night the sad tidings went partially out to Dallory. What with the death of Hepburn the undertaker, and now the doctor's wife—both

prominent people, so to say, in connection with the sickness—
something like consternation fell on such as heard it. Dr.
Rane carried the news himself to Dallory Hall, catching Mr.
North just as he was going to bed, and imparting it to him in
the most gentle and soothing manner he knew how. Fearing
that if he left it until morning, it might reach him abruptly,
the doctor thus made haste. From thence he went on to
Hepburn's. He had chanced to meet Francis Dallory in
coming out of Seeley's ; he met some one else he knew ; these
imparted the tidings to others ; so that many heard of it that
night.

But now we come to a very strange and singular thing that
happened to Jelly. Jelly in her tart way was sufficiently
good-hearted. There was sickness in Ketler's house: the
wife had her three days' old infant : the little girl, Cissy, got
worse and weaker : and Jelly chose to sacrifice an afternoon
to the nursing of them. Much as she disapproved of the man's
joining the Trades' Union and upholding the strike, often as
she had assured him that both starving and the workhouse,
whichever he might prefer, were too good for him, now that
misfortune lay upon the house, Jelly came-to a little. Susan
Ketler was her cousin ; and, after all, *she* was not to blame for
her husband's wrong doings. Accordingly, in the afternoon
of the last day of Mrs. Rane's illness, Jelly went forth to
Ketler's, armed with some beef-tea, and a few scraps for
the half-famished children, the whole enclosed in a reticule
bag.

" I shall take the latch-key," she said, in starting, to the
cook, who was commonly called Dinah, " so you can go to
bed. If Susan Ketler's very ill I'll stop late. Mind you put
a box of matches on the slab in the hall."

Susan Ketler was not very ill, Jelly found ; but the child,
Cissy, was. So ill, that Jelly hardly knew whether to leave
her at all, or not. The mother could not attend to her ;
Ketler had gone tramping off beyond Whitborough after
Union work, and had not come back. Only that she thought
Mrs. Cumberland would not be pleased if she came to hear
that Jelly, the confidential servant left in charge, had stayed
out for a night, leaving the house with only the cook in it, she,
Jelly, had certainly stayed. At past twelve poor Ketler got
home, dead beat, sick, faint, having walked several miles
without food. Jelly blew him up a little—she considered that
the man who could refuse work when his children were

starving, because he belonged to the Trades' Union, deserved
nothing but blowing-up on any score—bade him look to Cissy,
told him ungraciously that there was a loaf in the pan, and
came away. Ketler, fit to drop though he was, civilly offered
to see her home; but all the thanks he got in return, was a
recommendation to attend to his own concerns and not to
meddle with hers.

It was a fine, still night, rather too warm for the sickness
that lay on Dallory; and Jelly walked on at a swift pace, her
reticule, empty now, on her arm. Some women might have
felt timid at the midnight walk: Jelly was too strong-minded.
She certainly found it a little lonely on entering the Ham, as
if the road under the overshadowing trees, beginning now to
lose some of their leaves, had something weird about it. But
this part was soon passed; and Jelly came to the houses, and
within sight of home. Not a soul met she: it was as dreary,
as far as human companionship went, as could be. A black
cat sprang suddenly from the hedge, and tore over the road
almost across Jelly's feet; and it made her start.

She began thinking about Mrs. Rane; quite unconscious of
the death that had taken place. When Jelly left home in the
afternoon Mrs. Rane was said to be in danger: at least such
was Phillis's opinion, privately communicated: but, late in the
evening, news had been brought to Ketler's that all danger
was over; that Mrs. Rane was in a refreshing sleep, and going
on safely to recovery.

"And I'm downright glad of it, poor young lady!" said
Jelly, half aloud, as she turned in at her gate. "Doctors' wives
are naturally more exposed to the chance of catching infectious
sickness. But on the other hand they have the best advice
and care."

It was striking one. Letting herself in with the latch key,
Jelly felt for the box of matches, passing her hand cautiously
over the marble table. And passed it in vain: no matches
were there.

"Forgetful hussy!" ejaculated Jelly, apostrophizing the
unconscious Dinah. "Much good she's of!"

So Jelly crept quietly upstairs in the dark, knowing she
had matches in her own chamber: and in a minute came upon
another of the negligent Dinah's delinquencies. She had
omitted to draw down the blind of the large window on the
landing.

"She has been out at that back-door, talking to people,"

quoth Jelly in her wrath. "Just like her! Won't she get a taste of my tongue in the morning!"

Turning to draw down the blind herself, she was suddenly arrested, with the cord in her hand, by a sight in the opposite landing—Dr. Rane's. Standing there, dressed in something white, which Jelly at the time took for a nightgown or petticoat, was Mrs. Rane. The landing was faintly lighted, as if by some distant candle, invisible to Jelly; but Mrs. Rane was perfectly distinct, her features and even their expression quite clear. The first thought that crossed Jelly was, that Mrs. Rane was delirious: but she looked too still for that. She did not move; and the eyes had a fixed stare, as it seemed to Jelly. But that she herself must have been invisible from the surrounding darkness, she would have thought Mrs. Rane was staring at *her*. For a full minute this lasted: Jelly watching, Mrs. Rane never stirring.

"What in the world brings her standing there?" quoth Jelly in her amazement. "And what can she be staring at? It can't be at me."

But at that moment Jelly's bag slipped off her arm, and fell on the carpet with a bang. It caused her to shift her gaze from the opposite landing for a single second—it really did not seem longer. When she looked again, the place was in darkness: Mrs. Rane and the faint light were alike gone.

"She has no business to be out of her bed—and the doctor ought to tell her so if he's at home," thought Jelly. "Anyway, she must be a great deal better: for I don't think it's delirium."

She waited a short while, but nothing more was seen. Drawing down the blind with a jerk, Jelly picked up her bag, and passed on to her own chamber—one of the back rooms on this first floor. Where she slept undisturbed until morning.

She lay late. Being amenable to nobody while Mrs. Cumberland was away, the house's mistress in fact, as well as Dinah's, Jelly did not hurry herself. She was no laggard in general, especially on a Saturday, but felt tired after her weary afternoon at Ketler's and from having gone so late to rest. Breakfast was ready in the kitchen when she got down; Dinah—a red-faced young woman in a brown-spotted cotton gown—being busy at the fire with the coffee.

"Now then!" began Jelly—her favourite phrase when she was angry. "What have you got to say for yourself?

Whereabouts on the slab did you put those matches last night?"

Dinah, taken-to, tilted the kettle back. Until that moment she had not thought of her negligence.

"I'm afraid I never put 'em at all," she said.

"No you *didn't* put 'em," retorted Jelly with stinging emphasis. "But for having matches and a candle in my room, I must have undressed in the dark. And I'd like to know why you didn't put 'em; and what you were about not to?"

"I'm sure I'm sorry," said Dinah, who was a tractable kind of girl. "I forgot it, I suppose, in the upset about poor Mrs. Rane."

"In the upset about poor Mrs. Rane," scornfully repeated Jelly. "What upset you, pray, about her?—And you've never been out to fasten back the shutters!"

"She's dead," answered Dinah—and the ready tears came into the girl's eyes. "That's what I've got the shutters half-to for. I thought you'd most likely not have heard it."

A little confusion arose in Jelly's mind. Thought is quick. Mrs. Rane's death (as she supposed) could not possibly have occurred before morning : the neglect, as to the matches, was last night. But, in the shock of the news she passed this over. Her tart tone went away as by magic : her face changed to an amazed sadness.

"Dead? When did she die, Dinah?"

"It was about nine o'clock last night, they think. And she lay an hour after that in her bed, Jelly, getting cold, before it was found out."

On hearing this, Jelly's first impression was that Dinah must be playing with her. The girl came from the fire with the coffee, wiping her eyes.

"Now what d'ye mean, girl? Mrs. Rane didn't die last night—as I can answer for."

"Oh but she did, Jelly. Dr. Rane went up to her at ten o'clock—he had been out till then—and found her dead. I can tell you, I didn't half like to go all the way up to bed by myself to that top floor, and me alone in the house, knowing she was lying there at the very next door."

Jelly waited to take in the full sense of the words, staring at Dinah while she did it. What *was* all this?

"You must have taken leave of your senses, girl," she said, as she began to pour out the coffee.

"I'm sure I've not," said Dinah. "Why?"

"To tell me Mrs. Rane died last night. How did you pick up the tale?"

"Jelly, it's no tale. It's as true as you and me's here. I. was standing at the front gate for a breath of air, before shutting-up, when Dr. Rane came out of his house in a haste like, and went across to Mr. Seeley's. It struck me that Mrs. Rane might be worse and that he had gone to fetch the other, so I stayed a bit to see. Presently—it wasn't long—he came back across the road again. Mr. Francis Dallory happened to be passing, and he asked after Mrs. Rane. She was dead, the doctor said; and went on to tell him how he had found her. You needn't look as if you thought I was making-up stories, Jelly. They stood close by the doctor's gate, and I heard every word."

Jelly did not precisely know how she looked. If this was true, why—what could be the meaning of that which she had seen in the night?

"She can't be dead?"

"She is," said Dinah. "Why should you dispute it?"

Jelly did not say why. She gulped down her hot coffee at a draught, and went out, eating a piece of bread-and-butter. She did not believe it. Dinah evidently did: but the girl might have caught up some misapprehension: or, as Jelly mentally put it, "heard cross-wise."

The first thing that struck Jelly when she got outside, was the appearance of the doctor's house. It was closely shut up, doors and windows, and the blinds were down. As Jelly stood, looking up, she saw Mr. Seeley standing at his door without his hat. She went over and accosted him.

"Is it true, sir, that Mrs. Rane is dead?"

"Quite true," was the answer. "She died yesterday evening, poor lady. It was terribly sudden."

Jelly felt a very queer sensation take her. But she was in a fog of disbelief yet. Mr. Seeley was called to from within, and Jelly returned and knocked softly at Dr. Rane's door. Phillis opened it, her eyes swollen with crying.

"I say, Phillis, whatever is all this?" demanded Jelly, in a low tone. "When did she die?"

"Stop a bit," interposed Phillis, arresting her entrance. "You'd better not come in. I am not afraid: and, for the matter of that, somebody must be here: but it isn't well for those to run risks that needn't. The doctor says it was the quickest and most malignant case of them all."

6

"I never caught any disorder in my life, and I don't fear that I ever shall," answered Jelly, quietly making her way to the kitchen. "*When* did she die, Phillis?"

"About nine o'clock last evening, as is thought. The minute and hour won't never be known for sure: at ten, when the doctor found her, she was getting cold. And for us below to have thought her quietly sleeping!" wound up Phillis with a sob.

The queer sensation grew into tremor. Jelly had never experienced anything like it in her whole life. She stood against the dresser, staring at Phillis helplessly.

"I don't *think* she could have died last evening," whispered Jelly presently.

"And I'm sure I as little thought she was dying," returned Phillis. "The last time I went up was about half-after seven: she was asleep then; that I'm positive of; and it seemed a good healthy sleep, for the breathing was as regular as could be. Sometime after eight o'clock, master went up: he came down and said she was still sleeping, and he hoped she'd sleep till morning, and I'd better not go up again for fear of disturbing her. I didn't go up, Jelly. I knew if she woke and wanted anything she'd ring: the bell-rope was to her hand. Master went out to a patient, and I cleared up the kitchen here. He came in at ten o'clock. I was ready to go, but asked him if I should stay all night. There was no need, he answered, missis being better; and I went. I never heard nothing more till I come this morning. The milkman got to the door just as I did; and he began saying what a sad thing it was that she had died. 'Who had died,' I asked him, and he said, 'Why, my missis.' Jelly, you might have knocked me down with a breath of wind."

By Jelly's looks at this moment, it seemed as if a breath of wind might do the same for her. Her face and lips had turned of a yellow whiteness.

"The master opened the door to me: and told me all about it: about his finding her dead close upon my going out," continued Phillis. "He's frightfully cut up, poor man. Not that there's any tears, but his face is heavy and sad, like one looks who has never been in bed all night—as he hasn't been. I found a blanket on the dining-room sofa, so he must have lain down there."

"Where is he now?" asked Jelly.

"Out. He was fetched to somebody at Dallory. I must

stir up the pots," added Phillis, alluding to the earthern jars that were about with the disinfectants. "Master charged me to do it every hour. It's safer for the undertaker's men and others that have to come to the house."

Taking a piece of stick, she went into the hall, to wherever stood a jar, and gave the contents a good stir. The dining-room door was open: Dr. Rane's solitary breakfast was laid there, waiting for him. From thence, Phillis went up the staircase to the other jars. Jelly followed.

"Nasty stuff! I do hate the smell of it," muttered Phillis. "I'd not come up if I were you," she added to Jelly, in the low, hushed voice that we are all apt to use when near the dead.

Jelly disregarded the injunction. She believed herself safe: and was not prone to take advice at the best of times. "Whatever's that?" she exclaimed when she reached the landing.

The sheet that had been flapping for two days outside the bedroom door, now flapped, wet as ever, on the landing before the door of the ante-room. Dr. Rane deemed this the better place for it now. Phillis gave it some knocks with the stick to bring out its saving properties.

Compared with the gloom of the rest of the house, behind its drawn blinds, this landing, with its wide, staring, uncovered window, was strikingly bright. Jelly glanced round, it might have been thought nervously, only that she was not a nervous woman. Here, in the middle of the floor, at one o'clock in the morning, her face turned to that window, had stood Mrs. Rane. If not Mrs. Rane—who?—or what?

"Phillis," whispered Jelly, "I should like to see her."

"You can't," answered Phillis.

"Nonsense. I am not afraid."

"But you can't, Jelly. She is fastened down."

"She is!—Why what do you mean?" broke off Jelly.

Phillis took up a corner of the sheet, unlocked the door—in which the key was left—and opened it half an inch for Jelly to peep in. There, in the middle of the grey room stood a closed coffin, supported on trestles. In the shock of the surprise Jelly fell back against the wall, and began to tremble.

The idea that came over her—as she said to some one afterwards—was, that Mrs. Rane had been put into the coffin alive. What with the sight of the previous night (and Jelly did not yet admit to herself the full thought of what that sight might have been), and what with this, she felt in a kind of be-wildered horror. Recovering herself a little, she pushed past the sheet into the room, but with creeping, timid steps.

"Jelly, I'd not go in! The master charged *me* not."

But Jelly never heard. Or, if she heard, did not heed. It was a common deal shell: its lid nailed down. Jelly touched it with her fore-finger.

"*When* was she put in here, Phillis?"

"Sometime during the night."

"And fastened down at once?"

"To be sure. I found it like this when I came this morning."

"But—why need there have been such haste?"

"Because it was safest so. Safest for us that are living," as my master said. "The leaden one will be here to-day."

Well—of course it was safer. Jelly could but acknowledge it, and recovered herself somewhat. She wished she had not seen—that—in the night. It was that sight, so unaccountable, that was turning her mind upside down.

With her customary lack of ceremony, Jelly opened the bedroom door and looked in. It had not been put to rights: Phillis said her master would not let her go in to do anything to it until the two rooms should have been fumigated. Medicine bottles stood about; the bed-clothes lay over the foot of the bed, just as Hepburn's men must have flung them when they removed the dead. On the dressing-table lay a bow of blue ribbon that poor Bessy had worn in her gown the last day she had one on, a waistband with its buckle, and other trifles. Jelly began to feel oppressed, as if her breath were getting short, and came away hastily. Phillis stood on the landing beyond the sheet.

"It seems like a dream, Phillis."

"I wish we could awake and find it was one," answered Phillis, practically, as she turned the key in the lock; and they went down stairs.

Not a minute too soon. Before they had well reached the kitchen, Dr. Rane's latch-key was heard.

"There's the master," cried Phillis under her breath, as he turned into his consulting-room. "It's a good thing he didn't find us up there."

"I want to say a word to him, Phillis; I think I'll go in," said Jelly, taking a sudden resolution to acquaint Dr. Rane with what she had seen. The truth was, her mind felt so unhinged, knowing not what to believe, what to disbelieve, that she thought she must speak, or die.

"Need you bother him now?—what's it about?" asked Phillis. "I'd let him get his breakfast first."

But Jelly went on to the consulting-room door; and found herself nearly knocked over by the doctor—who was turning swiftly out of it. She asked if she could speak to him: he said Yes, if she'd be quick; but he wanted to catch Mr. Seeley before the latter went out.

"And your breakfast, master?" called out Phillis in a pitying tone.

"I'll take some presently," was the answer. "What is it that you want, Jelly?"

Jelly carefully closed the door before speaking. She then entered on her tale. At first the doctor supposed, by this show of caution, that she was going to consult him on some private ailment, St. Antony's fire in the face, for instance, or St. Vitus's dance in the legs; and thought she might have chosen a more opportune time. But he soon found it was nothing of the kind. With her hands pressing heavily the elbow of the patients' chair, Jelly told her tale. The doctor stood facing her, his arms folded, his back to the drawn-down blind. At first he did not appear to understand.

"Saw my wife upon the landing in her nightgown?" he exclaimed,—and Jelly thought he looked startled. "Surely she was not so imprudent as to get out of bed and go there!"

"But, sir, it is said that she was then dead!"

"Dead when? She did not die until nine o'clock. She could not have known what she was doing," continued Dr. Rane, passing his hand over his forehead. "Perhaps she may have caught a chill. Perhaps ―― "

"You are misunderstanding me, sir," interrupted Jelly. "It was in the night I saw this; some hours after Mrs. Rane's death."

Dr. Rane's face took a puzzled expression. He looked narrowly at Jelly, as if wondering what it was she would say.

"Not *last* night?"

"Yes, sir. Or, I'd rather say this morning; for it was one o'clock. I saw her standing there as plainly as I see you at this moment."

"Why, Jelly, you must have been dreaming?"

"I was as wide awake, sir, as I am now. I had just got home from Ketler's. I can't think what it was I did see," added Jelly, dropping her voice.

"You saw nothing," was the decisive answer—and in the doctor's tone there was some slight touch of anger. "Fancy plays tricks with the best of us: it must have played you one last night."

"I have been thinking whether it was possible that—that—she was not really dead, sir," persisted Jelly. "Whether she could have got up, and ——"

"Be silent, Jelly. I cannot listen to this folly," came the stern, checking interruption. "You have no right to let your imagination run away with you, and then talk of it as something real. I desire that you will never speak another word upon the subject to me; or to anyone."

Jelly's green eyes seem to have borrowed the doctor's look of puzzled doubt. She gazed into his face. This was a most curious business: she could not see as yet the faintest gleam of any solution to it.

"It was surely her I saw on the landing, sir, dead or alive. I could swear to it. Such things have been heard of before now as swoons being mistaken for death. When poor Mrs. Rane was left alone after her death—that is, her supposed death—if she revived; and got up; and came out upon the landing ——"

"Hold your tongue," interposed the doctor, sharply. "How dare you persist in this nonsense, woman! You must be mad or dreaming. An hour before the time you speak of, my poor wife, dead and cold, was where she is now—fastened down in her shell."

He flung out of the room with an indignant movement; leaving Jelly speechless with horror.

"Fastened down," ran her thoughts, "at twelve o'clock—dead and cold—and I saw her on the landing at one! Oh my goodness, what does it mean?"

CHAPTER XXVIII.

DESOLATION.

AT the front-parlour window at Eastsea, sat Ellen Adair—looking for one who did not come. Whatsoever troubles, trials, mysteries might be passing elsewhere, Eastsea was going

on its usual monotonous routine. How monotonous, Ellen
Adair could have answered: and yet, even here, something like
mystery seemed to be looming in the air.

"Come what may, Ellen, I shall be down again within a
few hours," had been Arthur Bohun's parting words to her.
But the hours and the days passed on, and he came not.

To have one's marriage suddenly interrupted, and the bridegroom borne off from, so to say, the very church-door, was no
more agreeable to Ellen Adair than it would be to any other
young lady. She watched him away in the fly, while his
kisses were yet warm upon her lips. All that remained, was
to make the best of the situation. She took off her bonnet
and dress, and locked up the ring and licence he had begged
her to take care of. Until the morrow she supposed; only
until the morrow. Mrs. Cumberland sent out a message to
the fly-man (*her* fly-man, not Madam's), by Ann the servant
—from whom (Ann) she hoped to avert suspicion—to the
effect that, finding herself unable to get up, she could not take
her drive, but he was to bring the fly at the same hour on the
morrow. Mrs. Cumberland also wrote a line to the clergyman.

The morrow came; and went. Ellen scarcely stirred from
the window—which commanded a view of the road from the
station—but she did not see Captain Bohun. "Sir Nash's
son must be worse, and he cannot leave," she said to herself,
striving to account naturally for the delay, while at the same
time an under-current of vague uneasiness lay within her,
which she made believe not to recognize, or listen to. "There
will be a letter to-morrow morning—or else, himself."

But on the morrow morning there was no letter. Ellen
watched the postman pass the house, and she turned sick and
white. Mrs. Cumberland—who was better and had risen betimes, expecting Captain Bohun, and that the marriage would
certainly take place that day—took the absence of letters with
philosophy.

"He might as well have written a line, of course, Ellen;
but it only shows that he is coming in by the first train. That
will be due in twenty minutes."

Ellen stood at the window, watching : her spirit faint, her
heart beating. That vague under-current of uneasiness had
grown into a great recognized fear now—but a fear she knew
not of what. She made no pretence to eat breakfast; she
could not have swallowed a morsel had it been to save her

life: Mrs. Cumberland said nothing, except that she must take some after Captain Bohun had come.

"There's the train, Ellen. I hear the whistle."

The window had a dwarf Venetian blind; Ellen sat behind it, glancing through the staves. Three or four straggling passengers were at length perceived, making their way down the street. But not one of them was Captain Bohun. The shock of disappointment was turning her heart to sickness, when a station fly came careering gaily up the street.

Ah me, how hope rose again! She might have known he would take a fly, and not *walk* up. The driver seemed making for their house. Ellen's eyes grew bright; her pale cheeks changed to rose-colour.

"Is that fly coming here, my dear?"

"I think so, Mrs. Cumberland."

"Then it's Captain Bohun. We must let the clergyman know at once, Ellen."

The fly stopped at their house, and Ellen hid her head; she would not seem to be looking for him, though he was so soon to be her husband. But—something was called out to the driver in a shrill voice from the inside; upon which he started his horse on again, and pulled up at the next door. A lady and child got out. It was *not* Captain Bohun.

I wonder whether disappointment so great ever fell on mortal woman? Great emotions, be they of joy or sorrow, are always silent. The heart alone knoweth its own bitterness, says the wise King, and a stranger may not intermeddle with its joy. Ellen laid her hands a minute or two on her bosom; but never a word spoke she.

"He'll be here by the next train," said Mrs. Cumberland. "He *must* come, you know, Ellen."

She watched throughout the livelong day. How its hours dragged themselves along she knew not. Imagination pictured all kinds of probabilities that might bring him at any minute. He might post down: he might alight by mistake at the wrong station, and walk on: he might have come by the last train, and be putting himself to rights at the hotel after travelling. Five hundred such ideas, alternating with despair, presented themselves. And thus the weary day went on. Towards night the same delusive hope of the morning again rose; the same farce, of the apparent arrival of Captain Bohun, was once more enacted.

It was dusk: almost dark: for Ellen, watching ever, had

not thought about lights; and Mrs. Cumberland, tired with her long day, was gone into the small back dining-room to lie on the sofa undisturbed. The last train for the night was steaming in: Ellen heard the whistle. If it did not bring Captain Bohun she thought she could only give him up for ever.

A short interval of suspense; and then—surely he was coming! A fly or two came rattling along the street from the station: and one of them—yes—one of them drew up at the door. Ellen, thinking she had learnt wisdom, said to herself that she would not get up any expectation in regard to this. Foolish girl! when her whole heart was throbbing and beating.

One of the house servants had gone out, and was opening the fly door. A gentleman's hand pitched out a light over-coat; a gentleman himself leaped out after it, and turned to get something from the seat. Tall and slender, Ellen took it to be Captain Bohun: the light coat was exactly like his.

And the terrible suspense was over! She should now know what the mystery had been. He had written most likely, and the letter had miscarried: how stupid she was not to have thought of that before! She heard his footsteps in the passage: he was coming in: in another instant she should be in his arms, feeling his kisses on her lips. It was a moment's delirium of happiness: neither more nor less. Ellen stood looking at the door, her breath hushed, her cheeks changing, her nervous hands clasped one within the other.

But the footsteps passed the sitting-room. There seemed to be some talking, and then the house subsided into silence. Where was he? Whither had he gone? Not into the dining-room, as Ellen knew, for Mrs. Cumberland might not be awakened. Gradually the idea came creeping in, and then bounded onwards with a flash that, after all, it might not have been Captain Bohun. A faint cry of despair escaped her, and she put her hands up as if to ward off some approaching evil.

But the suspense at least must be put an end to; it was too heavy to bear; and she rang the bell. Ann, who mostly waited on them, answered it.

"For lights, I suppose, Miss Ellen?"

"Yes. Who is it that has just come here in a fly?"

"It's the landlady's son, miss. Such a fine, handsome man!"

When Mrs. Cumberland entered, Ellen sat, pale and quiet, on the low chair. In good truth the inward burden was becoming hard to bear. Mrs. Cumberland remarked that Captain Bohun had neither come nor written, and she thought it was not good behaviour of him. And, with that, she settled to her evening newspaper.

"Why, Ellen! Here's the death of James Bohun," she presently exclaimed. "He died the day after Arthur left. This accounts for the delay, I suppose."

"Yes," murmured Ellen.

"But not for his not writing," resumed Mrs. Cumberland. "That is very strange. I hope," she added smiling, "that he is not intending to break with you because he is now heir-presumptive to a baronetcy."

Mrs. Cumberland, as she spoke, happened to look over the newspaper at Ellen, and was struck by her face. It was pale as death; the eyes had a kind of wild fear, the lips were trembling.

"My dear child, you surely did not take what I said in earnest! I spoke in jest. Captain Bohun is not a man to behave dishonourably; you may quite rely upon that. Had he come into a dukedom, you would still be made his duchess."

"I think I'll go to bed, if you don't mind my leaving you alone," said Ellen, faintly. "My head aches."

"I think you had better, then. But you have been tormenting yourself into that headache, Ellen."

To bed! It was only a figure of speech. Ellen sat up in her room, knowing that neither bed nor sleep could bring her ease—for her dreams these past two nights had been worse than reality. She watched for hours the tossing sea—that had never calmed properly down since the storm.

The morning brought a letter from Captain Bohun. To Mrs. Cumberland; not to Ellen. Or, rather a note, for it was not long enough to be called a letter. It stated that most urgent circumstances had prevented his returning to Eastsea—and he would write further shortly. He added that he was very unwell, and begged to be remembered to Miss Adair.

To Miss Adair! The very formality of the message and name—Miss Adair, and not Ellen—told a tale. Something was wrong: it was evident even to Mrs. Cumberland. The letter was short, constrained, abrupt; and she turned it about in haughty wonder.

"What can the man mean? *This* is not the way to write when things are at their present crisis. Here are the ring and licence waiting; here's the clergyman holding himself and the church in readiness from day to day; here are you fretting out your heart, Ellen, and he writes such a note as this! But for its being his own handwriting, I know what I should think."

"What?" asked Ellen, hastily.

"Why, that he is worse than he says. Delirious. Out of his senses."

"No, no; it is not that."

"I think if it's not, it ought to be," sharply retorted Mrs. Cumberland. "We must wait for his next letter, I suppose; there's nothing else to be done."

And they sat down to wait. And the weary days dragged their slow length along.

Any position more cruelly difficult than that of Captain Bohun cannot well be conceived. Madam's communication to him did not stop at the one first revelation; she added another to it. At first there had been no opportunity for more; the train stopped at a branch station just beyond Eastsea, and the carriage became filled with passengers. Arthur, in his torment, would have put further questions to his mother, praying for confirmation, for elucidation; but Madam whispered a demand to know whether he was mad, that he should speak *there*, and then turned her back upon him. The people went all the way to London, but as soon as Arthur had put his mother in a cab, on their way to Sir Nash Bohun's, he began again. The storm that raged at Eastsea had apparently extended its fury to London; the rain beat, the wind blew in gusts, the streets were as deserted as it is possible for London streets at a busy hour of the afternoon to be. Arthur shuddered a little as he glanced out on the black pools, the splashing mud; outer influences seemed just now to be nearly as black as his fate.

"Mother, things cannot rest here," he said, putting up both windows with a jerk. "You evaded my questions in the train; you must answer them now."

"Would you have had me speak before half a dozen people?—and proclaim to them what I know of that man— William Adair?"

"Certainly not: but you might have spoken for my ear

alone. Cannot you see how dreadful this suspense must bo to me? I am engaged to marry Ellen Adair: if not to-day, some other day. And now you tell me that, which—which ——"

Which ought to break it off, he was about to say: but emotion stopped him. He raised his hand and wiped the cold moisture from his forehead. Madam bent down, and kissed his hand. He did not remember to have been kissed by her since he was a child. Her voice took a soft, tender tone; something like tears stood in her eyes.

"I can see how you suffer, Arthur; I am sure you must love her, poor young lady; and I'd give anything not to have to inflict pain or disappointment on you. But what else can I do? You are my son: your interests are dear to me: and I must speak. Don't you remember how I have always warned you against Miss Adair? But I never suspected there would be cause for it so great as this?"

He did remember it. This new soft mode of Madam's became her well. In the midst of his own sea of troubles Arthur spared a moment to think he had in a degree misjudged her, and to regret it.

"I cannot understand how so frightful a charge can be brought against Mr. Adair," spoke Arthur. "What you tell me sounds like a fable. I had been given to understand that he and my father were close friends."

"As they were, once."

"And yet you say that he, Mr. Adair, was a—a ——"

"A convict," spoke Madam, supplying the words. "I cannot give you details, Arthur: only facts. He was tried, out there, and convicted. He got a ticket-of-leave—which I dare say may not have expired yet."

"And his crime?—What was it."

"I told you. Forgery."

"Did *you* ever know him?"

"Of course I did: at the time when he was intimate with your father. We never quite knew who he was, Arthur; or who his people were at home, or what had taken him out originally to India; but Major Bohun was unsuspicious as the day, unsuspicious as *you*. There arose great trouble, Arthur; gambling and wickedness, and I can't tell you what: and through it all, nearly up to the last, your father believed in Adair."

"Was he a convict *then?*"

"No, no; all that came afterwards: not the crime, perhaps, but discovery, trial, and conviction. Arthur—how sorry I am to say it, I can never express—your father's son had better go and marry that miserable drab, than a daughter of William Adair."

She pointed to a poor wretch that was passing. A skeleton of a woman, with a dab of paint on her hollow cheeks, and a tawdry gown trailing in the mud.

Arthur pressed his hands on his temples; all kinds of confused thoughts were fighting together within his breast.

"Did Mrs. Cumberland know of this?" he asked.

"I cannot say. *Her husband did.* At the time it all happened, Mrs. Cumberland was away in ill-health. I should think she would hear it from her husband afterwards."

"Then—how could she encourage me to enter into this contract of marriage with Miss Adair?" returned Arthur, in a flash of resentment.

"You must never see her again, Arthur; you must never see her again. Go abroad for a time if need be: it may be the better plan."

"What am I to say to them?" he cried in self-commune. "After all, Ellen is not responsible for her father's sins."

A spasm of fright caught Madam. Was this information not sufficient?—would he carry out the marriage yet?

"Arthur, there's worse behind," she breathed. "Why can't you be satisfied?—why do you force me to tell you all?—I'd have spared you the rest."

"What rest?" he asked, his lips turning white.

"About that man—William Adair."

"What rest?"

"He killed your father."

"Killed—my father?"

"Yes he did. He forged his name; he ruined him: and in the shock—in the shock—he ——"

Madam stopped. "What?" gasped Arthur.

"Well, the shock killed your father."

"Do you mean that he died of it?"

"He could not bear the trouble; and he—shot himself."

Madam's face was white now: white with emotion. Arthur, in *his* emotion, seized her hand, and gazed at her.

"It is true," she whispered. "He shot himself in the trouble and disgrace that Adair brought upon him. And you, his son, would have married the man's daughter!"

With a horrible fear of what he had all but done,—with a remorse that nearly turned him mad,—with a sort of tacit vow never again to see Mrs. Cumberland or Ellen Adair, Arthur Bohun dropped his mother's hand with a suppressed groan, and kept silence until they stopped before the house of Sir Nash Bohun.

Mechanically he looked up at the windows, and saw that the shutters were open. So James was not dead. Arthur gave his hand to Madam, to help her in.

But James Bohun was as ill as he could be. Sinking fast; and very palpably nearer death than when Madam had started from the house at break of dawn. In fact there had then been some hope, for he had rallied in the night. Arthur never knew that. He supposed his mother had truly come off to fetch him, in solicitude that he should be present at the final close : he suspected not that she had frantically hastened down to disturb him in his paradise.

And this was Arthur Bohun's present position. It is not possible (as was just remarked) to imagine one more cruelly difficult. Bound by every tie of honour to Ellen Adair, only not married to her through a mere chance, she waiting for him now—now, each hour as it passed—to return and complete the ceremony ; and loving her as he should never love any other in this world. And—in the very midst of these obligations— to have made the sudden and astounding discovery that Ellen Adair was the only woman living who must be barred to him ; whom, of all others, of all the many numbers that walk the earth, he must alone not make his wife. The position would have been bewildering to a man without honour ; to Arthur Bohun, with his fastidiously high standard of it, innate in him from his birth, it was simply awful. And the word is not used in its slight and careless sense, as it has become the fashion to use it of late years.

For the few hours that James Bohun lasted, Arthur did nothing. It may almost be said that he *thought* nothing, for his mind was in a chaos of confusion. On the day following his arrival James died : and he, Arthur, was then heir-presumptive. To many, it might have been looked upon that he was quite as secure of the succession as though he were heir-apparent ; for Sir Nash was old and ailing. A twelvemonth ago Sir Nash Bohun had been full of life ; upright, energetic, to all appearance strong, hearty, and likely to outlive his son. But since then he had changed rapidly ; and the once healthy man seemed to have little health in him. Medical men told him that if he would go abroad and partake for some months of certain medicinal springs, he might—and in all probability would—regain his health and strength. Sir Nash would have tried it but for the decaying health of his son. James could not leave home; Sir Nash would not leave him.

What though Arthur Bohun *was* the heir? In his present distress, it was to him worse than nothing. A Bohun could not live with tarnished honour : and his must be tarnished to the end of his days. To abandon Ellen Adair would bring the red stain of indelible shame to his cheek ; to marry her would be, of the two, the worst disgrace. What, then, was the expected rank and wealth to him?—better that he should go out to some land of exile and hide his head for ever.

He knew not what to do ; even at this present passing moment, he knew it not. What *ought* he to do ? Torn with conflicting emotions, now swayed this way, now that, he could not see which way his duty lay in this very present dilemma. Think not that, in saying this, it was the marriage he was in doubt over ; *that* had been given up in his own mind for ever. But what was he to say to Ellen ?—what to Mrs. Cumberland. Where seek for an excuse or plea for his conduct ? They were expecting him, no doubt, by every train, and he did not go. He did not mean to go. What could he write ?—what say ? On the day of James Bohun's death, he took the pen in his hand and sat down : but he never wrote a word. The true cause he could not urge. He could not say to Ellen, Your father was a convict, he has (or had) a ticket-of-leave, he caused my father's death ; and so our union must not take place. If he merely said, I have heard things against your father, Ellen would naturally ask what things—for that *she* knew nothing of the past or the disgrace attaching to her father, was clear as day. "I tell you these dreadful truths in confidence," Madam had said to Arthur, "you must not speak of them. You might be called upon for proofs—and proofs would be very difficult to obtain at this distance of time. The Reverend George Cumberland knew all, even more than I ; but he is dead : and it may be that Mrs. Cumberland knows nothing. I should almost think she does not : or she would never have sought to marry you to Adair's daughter. You can only be silent, Arthur ; you must be, for the girl's sake. By speaking merely a hint of what her father was, you would blight her life and prospects. Let her have her fair chance :

though she may not marry you, she may be chosen by some one else : don't you be the one to hinder it. If the story ever comes out through others, why—you will be thankful, I dare say, that it was not through you."

And there, listening to this, assenting to it with his whole heart, stood Arthur. He speak a word that would blight the life of Ellen Adair ? No: he was blighting it enough himself. But, see you not how this compulsory reticence held him ? He might not assign the true reason for his shameful conduct —and to him it appeared shameful in the worst degree : while he could not find or invent any other plea of excuse.

He sat with the pen in his hand, and did not write a word. There was no word in the whole English language, or collection of words, that would have served him. "My darling love, Fate has parted us, but I would a great deal rather die than have to write it, and I shall hold you in my heart for ever." Something like that he would have liked to say, had it been practicable. But it was not with romance he had to deal, but with stern reality.

He put the ink and pens up for the day, and lay back in his chair with a face almost as white as that of his dead cousin ; and felt as though he were dying himself. Man has rarely gone through a mental conflict such as this, and come out scatheless. He saw no way out of his dilemma ; no way that was, or could be, open to him.

On the third day he spoke to Sir Nash. It was not that a suspicion of his mother's veracity on this point crossed his mind: it did not: for she had shown too much agitation herself for him to doubt that the revelation was genuine. Therefore, it was not to have the tale confirmed that he spoke, but in the fulness of his bitter heart.

They were alone in the library. Sir Nash began talking of different things ; of Arthur's probable succession ; of his dead son. James, never strong, had worn himself out between philanthropy and close reading, he said. Arthur, he hoped, would take a lesson, embrace rational pursuits, and marry. He, Sir Nash, understood there was a charming young lady waiting to be asked by him ; of good family, of good fortune, everything in her favour: he alluded to Miss Dallory.

"Did you know anything of the cause of my father's death, sir ?" questioned Arthur, who had stood listening, in silence, his elbow on the mantel-piece, his hand supporting his brow.

Sir Nash replied by another question: and he glanced keenly at Arthur as he put it.

"Do *you* know?"

"I always thought that he died of sunstroke. But my mother has at length disclosed to me the truth. He—died in a different way."

"He shot himself," said Sir Nash, in a low tone. "My brother got suddenly overwhelmed with a load of trouble, and he—he was unable to bear it. Poor Tom!"

Arthur questioned of the particulars: he was hoping to hear them. But Sir Nash could not tell him a syllable more than he already knew: in fact, the baronet seemed in a fog about it altogether.

"Of course I never got hold of the details as if I had been on the spot, Arthur," he said. "Your poor father fell into the meshes of a villanous scoundrel, one Adair, who had somehow forged his way by false pretences into society—which I suppose is not difficult to do, out there. And this Adair brought some scandalous disgrace on him from which there was no escape: and—and Tom, poor fellow, could not survive it. He was simplicity itself in honour, trusting implicitly, believing all men to be as upright as he, until he found them otherwise. If he had a failing, it was on the side of pride—but I'm afraid most of us Bohuns think too much of that. A less proud man might have got over it. Tom could not. He died, rather than live with his name tarnished."

Arthur Bohun, standing there and looking more like a ghost than a living man, thought of the blow his own honour had just received—the tarnish that would rest on it for aye.

"And you don't know the details, uncle?" he resumed. "I wonder you did not stir in it at the time—and bring Adair to justice."

"On the contrary, we hushed it up. We have never spoken of it, Arthur, above our breath. Tom was gone; and it was as well to let it lie. It took place in some out-of-the-way district of India; and the real truth was not known to half a dozen people. The report there was that Major Bohun died of sunstroke; it spread to Europe, and we let it circulate uncontradicted. Better, we thought, for Tom's little son—you, Arthur —that the real facts of the death should be allowed to rest, if they would rest."

There ensued a pause. Presently Arthur lifted his face; and

T

spoke, as Sir Nash supposed, banteringly. In good truth, it was in desperation.

"It would not do, I suppose, for a gentleman to marry Adair's daughter?"

Sir Nash turned to him quickly. "Why do you ask this? I believe you know the girl."

"I will tell you, Uncle Nash. No one could have been nearer marrying another than I was marrying Ellen Adair. Of course it is at an end: I cannot do it now."

Sir Nash Bohun stared for a minute, as if unable to take in the absurdity of the words. He then drew up his fine old head with a proud dignity.

"Arthur! Arthur Bohun! a gentleman had better do as your poor father did—shoot himself—than marry Ellen Adair."

And Arthur Bohun, in his bitter misery, wondered whether he had *not* better do it, rather than live the life that must remain to him now.

CHAPTER XXIX.

IN THE CHURCHYARD.

NOTHING of late years had affected Mr. North so much as the death of Bessy Rane. The calamity of his son Edmund's death, encompassed though it was by the doubt and trouble connected with the anonymous letter, did not touch him as this did. Perhaps he had been unconscious until now how very dear Bessy was to his heart.

"Why should Bessy have died?" he asked over and over again in his deep distress, the tears rolling down his cheeks. "*She* was not starved; *she* had plenty of stamina to meet it. They had been calling it a famine fever, some of them, but why should a famine fever attack *her?* I knew she was exposed to danger, her husband coming home continually from his fever patients; but if she did take it, why should she not have got over it? Others get over it, many of them, most of them; who have not half the strength or the good constitution that Bessy had. And why, why did she die so soon?"

No one could answer him. Not even Dr. Rane. Fever was capricious; attacking badly or lightly at its will, the latter said. And death was capricious, he added in a lower tone, often seizing upon those whom we most care to save.

Dallory in general echoed Mr. North's sentiments. The

death of Mrs. Rane—or Bessy North, as many had always continued to call her—was the greatest shock that had fallen on them since the outbreak of the fever. Mrs. Gass, braving infection—but, like Jelly, she did not fear it—went down to Dr. Rane's house on the Monday morning to express her sympathy, and relieve herself of some of her surprise. She felt much grieved, she was truly shocked : Bessy had always been a favourite of hers ; it seemed impossible to realize the fact that she was dead. Her mental arguments ran very much as did Mr. North's spoken ones—Why should Bessy, well fed, well nourished, have died, when so many half starved ones recovered ? But the point that pressed most forcibly on Mrs. Gass was the quickness of the death. None had died so soon after seizure as Bessy, or anything like so soon ; it seemed unaccountable tl at she should not have battl d longer for life.

Phillis received Mrs. Gass in the darkened drawing-room ; her master was out. Dr. Rane could not stay indoors to indulge his grief and play propriety, as most men can ; danger and death were abroad, and the physician had to go forth and try to avert both from others, in accordance with his duty to Heaven and to man. That he felt his loss keenly, people saw ; there was no outward demonstration of it, neither sighs nor tears ; but he seemed like a man upon whom some heavy weight had fallen ; his manner preoccupied, his bearing almost unnaturally still and calm. Phillis and Mrs. Gass were talking, and, if truth must be told, crying together, when the doctor came in. Phillis, standing by the centre table, had been giving the particulars of the death, so far as she knew them, just as she had given them to Jelly the morning after. Mrs. Gass, seated in the green velvet chair, had untied the strings of her black bonnet—for she had not come down in satins and birds-of-paradise to-day, but in respectful black—and was wiping her eyes with her broad-hemmed handkerchief while she listened.

The old servant retired at the entrance of her master. He took a seat, and prepared to go through the interview with equanimity, though he heartily wished Mrs. Gass anywhere else. His house was desolate ; infected also ; he thought that visitors, for their own sake and his, had better keep away. They had not met since the death, and Mrs. Gass, though the least exacting woman in the world, took it a little unkindly that he had not been in, knowing he passed her house several times in the day.

In a subdued tone, in accordance with the closed blinds and perhaps with his own heart, Oliver Rane gave to Mrs. Gass a summary of Bessy's illness and death. He had done all he could to keep her in life, he said; all he could. Seeley had come over to see her once or twice, and knew that nothing more had remained in his power.

"But, doctor, I heard say that on the Friday you told people she was getting better and the danger was over," urged Mrs. Gass, with a sob.

"And I thought it was so," he answered. "What I took to be sleepiness from the exhaustion left by the fever, and what Seeley took to be sleepiness—fatigued nature taking rest to renovate itself—must have been the exhaustion of approaching death. We are deceived thus sometimes."

"But, doctor, she never had but a day's fever. Was that enough to kill her from exhaustion?"

"She had a day and a night. But consider how strong the fever was: I never before saw anything like it. We must not always estimate the duration of a fever, Mrs. Gass, in regard to the effect on the patient, so much as its power. I'm sure the shock and surprise to me—speaking only *as* shock and surprise—were worse than they could have been to any one else."

Yes, Mrs. Gass believed that, and warmly sympathized with him. She then expressed a wish to see the coffin. "Would it be well for her to go up?" he asked. "Oh dear yes," Mrs. Gass answered, "she was not afraid of anything;" and the doctor took her up without further hesitation. There was not much danger now, if any, he observed, as he pulled aside the sheet, which still hung there, saturated, for her to enter the grey room. He had fumigated the place well.

Everything was completed. Hepburn's men had been to and fro, and all was finished. The outer coffin was covered with black cloth, bearing the inscription on the lid. Mrs. Gass's eyes fairly gushed out tears as she read it.

"BESSY RANE.
AGED 31."

"But you have never put the date of the death, doctor!" cried Mrs. Gass, the omission striking her.

"No? True. That's Thomas Hepburn's fault; I left it to him. The man is half crazed just now, what with grief for his brother and fear for himself. It will be put on the grave."

From Dr. Rane's Mrs. Gass went to Dallory Hall, knowing Madam was absent. Otherwise she'd not have ventured there. And never was guest more welcome to its master. Poor Mr. North spoke out to her all his grief for Bessy, weeping bitterly.

But of all the people who felt this death, none were affected by it like Jelly. She could not rest; day and night wild thoughts tormented her. The idea at first picked up kept floating through her head, and sometimes she could not get it out for hours: that Mrs. Rane had been shut into her coffin alive; that what she saw was *herself*, and not her spirit—and this, in spite of the discrepancy, as to time and possibility. But Jelly knew that this could not be, and her imagination would go out to another wild improbability, though she did not dare to follow it—that the poor lady had not died a natural death. One night there came surging into Jelly's brain the supposititious case put by Timothy Wilks, that some men might be found who would put their wives out of the way for the sake of getting the tontine money. Jelly tossed from side to side in her uneasy bed, and stared at the candle—for she no longer cared to sleep in the dark—and tried to get rid of the wicked notion. But she never got rid of it again; and when she rose in the morning, pale, and trembling, and weary, she believed that the dread mystery had solved itself to her, and would be found in *this*.

What ought she to do? Going about that day like one in a dream, moping here, halting there, the question perpetually presented itself. Jelly was at her wits' end with indecision: one time (chiefly at night) she'd resolve to tell of the apparition, and of her suspicion of Dr. Rane; by day she would fling the ideas from her, and call herself a fool for yielding to them. Dinah could not make out what ailed her, she was so strange and dull, but privately supposed it might be the state of Mr. Timothy Wilks. For that gentleman was confined to his bed with some attack connected with the liver.

The day of the funeral drew on. Wednesday. It had been a little retarded to allow of the return for it of Richard North. News had been received of him the morning after Bessy's death. It may readily be imagined what Richard's consternation and grief must have been to hear of his sister's death; whom he so recently left well, and happy, and as likely to live as he was.

The funeral was fixed for twelve o'clock. Richard only

arrived the same morning at ten. He had been delayed twelve
hours by the state of the sea, the Ostend boat not putting out.
One cannot control wind and weather: and sometimes they
act for us—as we think—in a spirit of contrariety. Jelly, in
the feeling of superstition that lay upon her, thought the ele-
ments had been conspiring to keep Richard North back from
following one to the grave who had not been sent to it by
Heaven.

Long before twelve o'clock struck, groups had formed
about the churchyard. The men, out on strike, and their
wives, were there in force: partly because it was a break to
their monotonous idleness, partly out of respect to their
many-years master. The whole neighbourhood sincerely re-
gretted Bessy Rane; she had never made an enemy in her life.

In the church people of the better class assembled fast, all
wearing mourning. Mrs. Gass was in her pew, in an upright
bonnet and crape flowers. Seeing Jelly come in looking very
woe-begone, she hospitably opened the pew door to her. And
this was close upon the entrance of the funeral.

The first to make his appearance was Thomas Hepburn in
his official capacity; quite as woe-begone as Jelly, and more
sickly. The rest followed. The coffin, which Mrs. Gass had
seen the other day, and touched, was placed on its stand; for
the few last words of this world. Dr. Rane, as white as a
sheet; and Mr. North, leaning on his son Richard's arm, comprised the followers. No strangers were invited: Dr. Rane
thought, considering what Bessy had died of, they might not
care to attend. People wondered whether Captain Bohun
had been bidden to it. If so, he certainly had not come.

It seemed but a few minutes before they were moving out
of the church again. The grave had been dug in the churchyard corner, near to Edmund North's: and he, as may be
remembered, lay next his mother. Mrs. Gass and Jelly took
their seats on a remote bench, equally removed from the ceremony and the crowd. The latter stood at a respectful
distance, not caring, from various considerations, to go too
near. Not a word had the two women as yet spoken to each
other. The bench they sat on was low, and over-shadowed
by the trees that bordered the narrow walks. Not ten people
in the churchyard were aware that anybody sat there. Jelly
was the first to break the silence.

" How white he looks ! "

It was rather abrupt; as Mrs. Gass thought. They could

see the clergyman in his surplice through the intervening trees, and the others standing bare-headed around him.

"Do you mean the doctor, Jelly?"

"Yes," said Jelly, "I mean him."

"And enough to make him, poor bereft man, when the one nearest and dearest to him is suddenly cut off by fever," gravely rejoined Mrs. Gass. "In the midst of life we are in death."

Now, or never. Sitting there alone with Mrs. Gass, surrounded by these solemn influences, Jelly thought the hour and the opportunity had come. Bear with the secret much longer, she could not; it would wear her to a skeleton, dry up her tongue, worry her into a fever perhaps; and she had said to herself several times that Mrs. Gass, with her plain common sense, would be the best person to tell it to. Yes, she mentally repeated, now or never.

"*Was* it the fever that cut her off?" began Jelly significantly.

"Was it the fever that cut her off?" echoed Mrs. Gass. "What d'ye mean, Jelly?"

Jelly turned her face to the speaker, and plunged into her tale. Beginning, first of all, with the apparition she had certainly seen, and how it was—the staying late at Ketler's, and Dinah's having left the blind undrawn—that she had come to see it. There she paused.

"Why, what on earth d'ye mean?" sharply demanded Mrs. Gass. "Saw Mrs. Rane's ghost! Don't be an idiot, girl."

"Yes, I saw it," repeated Jelly, with quiet emphasis. "Saw it as sure as I see them standing there now to bury her. There could be no mistake. I never saw her plainer in life. It was at one o'clock in the morning, I say, Mrs. Gass; and she was screwed down at twelve: an hour before it."

"Had you took a drop too much beer?" asked Mrs. Gass after a pause, staring at Jelly to make sure the question would not apply to the present time. But the face that met hers was strangely earnest: too much so even to resent the insinuation.

"It was her ghost, poor thing: and I'm afraid it 'll walk till justice lays it. I never knew but one ghost walk in all my life, Mrs. Gass: and he had been murdered."

Mrs. Gass made no rejoinder. She was taken up with looking at Jelly. Jelly went on.

"It's said there's many that walk: the world's full of such tales; but I never knew but that one. When people are put to an untimely end, and buried away out of sight, and their secrets with 'em, it stands to reason that they can't rest quiet in their graves. *She* won't."

Mrs. Gass put her hand with a slap on the black shawl that covered Jelly's arm, and kept it there. "Tell me why you be saying this."

"It's what I want to do. If I don't tell it somewhere I shall soon be in the grave myself. Fancy! me living at the very next door, and nobody in the house just now but Dinah!"

Jelly spoke out all: that she believed Dr. Rane might have "put his wife out of the way." Mrs. Gass was horrified. Not at the charge: she didn't believe a word; but at Jelly's presuming to fancy it. She gave Jelly a serious reprimand.

"It was him that wrote that anonymous letter, you know," whispered Jelly.

"Hush! Hold your tongue, girl. I've warned you before to let that alone."

"And I'm willing."

"This is downright wicked of you, Jelly. Dr. Rane loved his wife. What motive do you suppose he could have had for killing her?"

"To get the tontine money," replied Jelly in a whisper.

The two women gazed at each other; gaze meeting gaze. And then Mrs. Gass grew on a sudden whiter than Dr. Rane, and began to shiver as though some strange chill had struck her.

CHAPTER XXX.

IN HIS SICK ROOM.

Leaning back on the pillows of an invalid's chair was Arthur Bohun, looking as yellow as gold. He had had an attack of jaundice. The day of James Bohun's funeral it had poured with rain; Arthur got wet, standing at the grave, and caught a chill. It terminated in the yellow jaundice—the distressed state of his mind no doubt doing its full part towards bringing on the malady. At first the doctors were afraid of bilious fever, but the danger of that passed. He was recovering now. Sir Nash, at whose house he lay, was everything that was kind.

Madam was kind also: at least she made a great professing show of it. Her private object in life just now was to get

her son to marry Miss Dallory. Madam cared no more for
her son Arthur or his welfare than she did for Richard North ;
but she had the shrewdness to foresee that the source, whence
her large supplies of money had hitherto come, was now dried
up : and she hoped to get some out of Arthur for the future.
The marrying an heiress, wealthy as Mary Dallory, would
vastly increase his power and means of helping her. Moreover, she wished to be effectually relieved from that horrible
nightmare that haunted her still—the possibility of his wedding
Ellen Adair.

So Madam laid her plans—as it was in her scheming nature
ever to be laying them—and contrived to get Miss Dallory (at
that time in London with her aunt) to Sir Nash Bohun's for
a few days' visit when Arthur was recovering. The young
lady was there now ; and Matilda North was there ; and they
both spent a good portion of every day with Arthur ; and Sir
Nash made much of Mary Dallory, partly because he liked her
for herself, and partly because he thought there was a probability that she would be Arthur's wife. During his illness,
Captain Bohun had had time to reflect : not only time, but
calmness, in the lassitude it cast on him mentally and bodily :
and he began to see his immediate way somewhat clearer. To
hold off and say nothing, give no explanation to the two
ladies at Eastsea, to whom he was acting (as he felt) so base
a part, was the very worst form of cowardice ; and, though
he could not explain to Ellen Adair, he was now anxious to
do so to Mrs. Cumberland. Accordingly the first use he made
of his partially-recovered health, was to cause writing materials
to be put on the bed and pen her a note in very shaky cha-
racters. He spoke of his serious illness, stated that certain
"untoward circumstances" had occurred to intercept his
plans, but that as soon as he was sufficiently well to travel he
should beg of her to appoint a time when she could allow him
a private conference.

The return post brought him a letter from Ellen. Rather
to his consternation. Ellen assumed—not unnaturally, as the
reader will find, a page or two further on—that the sole cause
of his mysterious absence was illness ; that he had been ill
from the first, and unable to travel. It ran as follows :—

"My DEAREST ARTHUR,—I cannot express to you what my
feelings are this morning ; so full of joy, yet full of pain. Oh
I cannot tell you what the past two or three weeks have

been to me; looking back, it almost seems a wonder that I *lived* through them. For I thought—I thought—I will not say here what I thought, and perhaps I could not, only that you were never coming more; and that it was to me agony worse than death. And to hear now that you could not come: that the cause of your silence and absence has been dangerous illness, brings to me a great sorrow and shame. Oh Arthur, my dearest, forgive me! Forgive also my writing to you in this free manner; but it almost seems to me as though you were already my husband. Had you been called away but half an hour later you would have been, and perhaps even might have had me with you in your illness.

"I should like to write pages and pages, but you may be too ill yet to read much, and so I will stop here. May God watch over you and bring you round again.

"Ever yours, Arthur, yours only, with the great love of my whole heart,　　　　　　　　　　　"ELLEN ADAIR."

And Captain Arthur Bohun, in spite of the cruel fate that had parted them, in spite of his best hope never to see her more, pressed the letter to his heart, and the sweet name, Ellen Adair—sweeter than any he would ever hear—to his lips, and shed tears of anguish over it in the feebleness induced by illness.

They might take Mary Dallory to his room as much as they pleased; and Matilda might exert her little wiles to subtly praise her, and Madam hers to leave them "accidentally" together; but his heart was too full of another, and of its own bitter pain, to allow room for as much as a responsive thought to Mary Dallory.

"Arthur is frightfully languid and apathetical!" spoke Miss North one day in a burst of resentment. "I'm sure he is quite rude to me and Mary: he'll let us sit there by him for an hour, and never speak."

"Consider how ill he has been—and is," was the remonstrating answer of Sir Nash.

Mrs. Cumberland's span of life was drawing into a very narrow space: and it might be that she was beginning to suspect this. For some months she had been getting inwardly weaker; but the weakness had for a week or two been visibly and rapidly increasing. The unaccountable behaviour of Captain Bohun had tried her—for Ellen's sake. She was responsible to Mr. Adair for the welfare of his daughter, and the matter was a source of daily and hourly annoyance to her mind. When this second tardy note arrived, she considered it, in one sense, a satisfactory explanation; in another, not; since, if Captain Bohun had been too ill to write himself, why did he not get some one else to write to her and say so? However, she was willing to persuade herself that all would be right; and she told Ellen, without showing her the note, that Captain Bohun had been dangerously ill, unable to come or write. Hence Miss Ellen's return letter.

But, apart from the silent progress of the illness in itself, nothing had done Mrs. Cumberland so much harm as the news of her daughter-in-law's death. It had been allowed to reach her abruptly, without the smallest warning. I suppose there is something in our common nature that urges us to impart sad tidings to others. We are all alike in it. However grievous and horrible they may be, we find pleasure in imparting them: and Dinah, Jelly's friend and underling, proved no exception. On the day after the death, she sat down and indited a letter to her fellow-servant, Ann, at Eastsea, in which she detailed the short progress of Mrs. Rane's illness, and described the death as "awful sudden." Ann, before she had well mastered the cramped lines, ran with white face and open mouth to her mistress; and Miss Adair afterwards told her that she ought to have known better. That it was too great a shock for Mrs. Cumberland in her critical state, the girl in her repentance saw. Mrs. Cumberland asked for the letter, and scarcely had it out of her hand for hours and hours. Dead! apparently from no cause; for the fever had lasted but a day, Dinah said, and was gone again. Mrs. Cumberland, in her bewilderment, began actually to think it was a fable.

Not for two or three days did she receive confirmation from Dr. Rane. Of course the doctor did not know and did not suppose that any one else would be writing to Eastsea; and he was perhaps willing to spare his mother the news as long as he could. He shortly described the illness—saying that he, himself, had entertained but little hope from the first, from the severity of the fever. But all this did not tend to soothe Mrs. Cumberland; and in the two or three weeks that afterwards went on, she faded palpably. Little wonder the impression, that she was growing worse, made its way to Dallory.

CHAPTER XXXI.

JELLY'S TROUBLES.

WITH the same rapidity, to outer appearance, that the sickness had come on, so did it subside in Dallory. Mrs. Rane's was the last serious case : the last death ; the very few attacks afterwards were of the mildest description ; and within a fortnight of the time that ill-fated lady was laid in the ground, people were fumigating their houses and throwing their rooms open to the renewed healthy air.

The inhabitants in general, rallying their depressed courage, thought the sooner they forgot the episode the better. Save perhaps by the inmates of those houses from which some one had been taken, they did soon forget it. It was surprising—now that magnifying fear was at an end and matters could be summed up dispassionately—how few the gaps were. With the exception of Henry Hepburn the undertaker and Mrs. Rane, they lay entirely amidst the poor working people out on strike, and, of those, principally amidst the children. Mrs. Gass told men to their faces that the fever had come of nothing but famine and deprivation, and that they had only themselves to thank for it. She was in the habit, as the reader knows, of dealing out to them some home truths : but she had dealt out something else during the sickness—and that was, good nourishing food. She continued to do so still to those whose frames had been weakened by it : but she gave them due warning that it was only temporary help, which they'd never have received from her but for the fever. And so the visitation grew into a thing of the past, and Dallory was itself again.

One, there was, however, who could not forget : with whom that unhappy past, or rather a calamity left by it, was present night and day. Jelly. That Dr. Rane had in some way wilfully caused the death of his wife, Jelly was as sure of as though she had seen it done. Her suspicion pointed to laudanum ; or to some preparation of the kind. Suspicion? Nay, with her it was a certainty. In that last day of Bessy Rane's life, when she was described as sleeping, sleeping, always sleeping ; when her sole cry had been—" I am easy, only let me sleep," Jelly now felt that Dr. Rane knew she had been quietly sleeping away to death. Indelibly as though it had been written

on her heart with the pen of truth, lay the conviction. About
that, there could be neither doubt nor hesitation in her mind :
the difficulty was—what ought to be her own course ?

In all Jelly's past life she had never been actually superstitious ; if told that she was so now, she would have replied
Yes, because circumstances forced it upon her. That Mrs.
Rane's spirit had appeared to her that memorable night to one
sole intent—namely, that she, Jelly, should avenge her dreadful end by disclosing it to the public, Jelly believed as implicitly as she believed in the Gospel. Not a soul in the whole
wide world but herself (save of course Dr. Rane) had the
faintest idea that the death was not a natural one. Jelly
moaned and groaned, and thought her fate unjustly hard that
she should have been signalled out by heaven (for that's how
she solemnly put it) for the revelation, when there were so
many other people in the community of Dallory. Jelly had
fits of real despondency, when she didn't quite know whether
her head was on or off, or whether her mind wouldn't "go."
Why couldn't the ghost have appeared to somebody else, she
mentally asked at these moments : to Phiilis, say ; or to
Dinah ; or to Seeley the surgeon ; just because she had been
performing an act of charity in sitting-up with Ketler's sick
child, it must show itself to *her !* And then Jelly's brain would
go off into suppositions, that it might have puzzled one, wiser
than she was, to answer. Suppose she had not been at
Ketler's that night, the staircase blind would have been drawn
down at dusk as usual, she would have gone to bed at her
customary hour, seeing nothing, and been spared all this
misery. But no. It was not to be. She went to Ketler's ;
she stayed with the sick child to a strangely late hour, because
Ketler himself was detained out : when she reached home she
found no light placed for her ; she found the blind not down,
both through Dinah's omission : and so—she saw what she did
see. And although Jelly, in her temper, might wish to throw
the blame on Ketler for staying out, and on Dinah for her
negligence, she recognized the finger of Destiny in all this, and
knew she could not have turned aside from it.

What was she to do ? Living in mortal dread of seeing again
the apparition, feeling somehow a certainty within herself that
she should see it, Jelly pondered the question every hour of the
day. Things could not rest as they were. On the one hand,
there was her natural repugnance to denounce Dr. Rane (just
as there had been in the case of the anonymous letter), not

only because she was in the service of his mother, but for his own sake; for Jelly, with all her faults, as to curiosity and the like, had not a bad heart. On the other, there was the weighty secret revealed to her by the dead woman—and the expression is not wrong, for, *but* for that apparition Jelly would have known no more than the rest of the world—and the obligation it laid upon her. Yet—*how* could she speak?—when the faintest breath of such an accusation against her son, would assuredly kill Mrs. Cumberland in her present critical state! and to Jelly she was a good and kind mistress. No, she could never do it. With all this conflict within her, no wonder Jelly lost flesh and appetite : she had been thin enough before, she was like a veritable skeleton now. As to the revelation to Mrs. Gass, Jelly might just as well have made it to the moon. For that lady, after the first shock was passed, absolutely refused to give credence to the tale : and had appeared ever since, by her manner, to ignore it as completely as though it had never been spoken.

Gradually Jelly grew disturbed by another fear—that she might be taken up as an accomplice after the fact. She was sure she had heard of such cases: and she tormented Tim Wilks nearly out of his patience—that gentleman having recovered his temporary indisposition—by asking perpetual questions of what the law might do to a person who found out that another had committed some crime, and concealed the knowledge : say stole a purse, for instance, and kept the money—for that's how Jelly generally put it.

One night, when Jelly, by some fortunate chance, had really got to sleep early—for she more often lay awake till morning light—a ring at the door-bell suddenly aroused her. Mrs. Cumberland had caused a loud night-bell to be affixed to the door : in case of fire, she said : it hung on this first landing, close, so to say, to Jelly's head, so that she awoke instantly. Dinah, sleeping above, might have heard it just as well as Jelly; but Dinah was a hard sleeper—most people are so who have plenty of work to do and nothing to worry them—and the bell, as Jelly knew, might ring for an hour before it awoke her. However, Jelly lay still, not caring to get up herself, hoping against hope, and wondering who in the world could be ringing, unless it was somebody mistaking their house for Dr. Rane's. Which had happened before.

Ring; ring. It was not a loud ring by any means; but a gentle one, as if the applicant did it in deprecation. Jelly lay on. She was not afraid that it was connected with the sight she was always in mortal dread of again seeing, since ghosts don't come ringing to announce their visits, after the manner of men and women. In fact, the surprise, and the speculating who it could be, put the fear for the time being altogether out of Jelly's head.

Ring; ring; ring. Rather a loud peal this turn, as if a little impatience mingled with the deprecation.

"Drat that girl!" cried Jelly in her wrath, finding that she must get up after all.

Flinging on a warm shawl, and putting her feet into her shoes, Jelly proceeded to the front room—Mrs. Cumberland's chamber when she was at home—threw up the window, and called out to know who was there. A little man, stepping back from the door into the bright moon-light, looked up to answer—and Jelly recognized the form and voice of Ketler.

"It's me," said he.

"You!" interrupted Jelly, not allowing the man to continue. "What on earth do you want here at this hour?"

"I came to tell you the news about Poor Cissy. She's dead."

"Couldn't it wait?" tartly returned Jelly overlooking the sad nature of the tidings in her anger at being disturbed out of her bed. "Would it have run away, that you must come and knock folks up to tell it as if you'd been the telegraph?"

"It was my wife made me come," spoke Ketler, with much humility. "She's in a peck o' grief, Jelly, and nothing 'ud do but I must come right off and tell you; she thought, mayhap, you'd not be gone to bed."

"Not gone to bed at twelve o'clock at night!" retorted Jelly. "And there it is, striking: if you've got any ears to hear. You must be a fool, Ketler."

"Well, I'm sorry to have disturbed you," said the man, with a sigh. "I'd not have done it of myself; but poor Susan was taking on so, I couldn't say her nay. We was all of us so fond of the child; and—and ——"

Ketler broke down with a great sob. The man had loved his child: and he was weak and faint with hunger. It a little appeased Jelly: not very much.

"I suppose you don't expect me to dress myself and come off to Susan at this hour?" she resentfully exclaimed, her tone, however, not quite so sharp.

"Law bless you, no," answered Ketler. "What good would that do? It couldn't bring Cissy back to life."

"Ketler, it's just this—instead of being upset with grief, you and Susan, you might be thankful that the child's taken out of the distress of this world. She won't cry for food where she's gone, and find none."

The man's sobs were renewed at the last suggestion. But Jelly had really meant it in the light of consolation.

"She was your god-child, Jelly."

"You needn't tell it me," answered Jelly. "Could I have saved her life at any trouble or cost, I'd not have grudged it. If I had a home of my own I'd have taken her to it, but I'm only in service, as you know. Ketler, it is the strike that has killed that child."

Ketler answered nothing.

"Cissy was a weakly child and required extra comforts; as long as you were in work she had them, but when that dropped off—leastways, when *you* dropped it, I should say," amended Jelly, who did not let the opportunity slip for dealing out a modicum of reproach—"of course the child suffered. And now she's gone. She is better off, Ketler."

"Yes," assented the man as if he were heart-broken. "If it wasn't for the thought of the rest, I wish it was me that was gone instead."

"Well, give my love to Susan and say I'm sorry for it altogether, and I'll come down sometime in the morning. And, look here, Ketler—what about the money for the burial? You've not got anything towards it, I expect."

Ketler caught up his breath. "Not a penny."

"Well, I know you'd not like the poor little thing to be buried by the parish, so I'll see what's to be done, tell Susan. Good night."

Jelly shut down the window with a bang. She really looked upon the strike as having led to the child's death—and in a remote degree possibly it had; so what with that, and what with the untimely disturbance from her bed, her tartness of manner was somewhat excusable.

In passing back across the landing to her own chamber, with no more superstitious thoughts in her mind just then than if she had never had cause to entertain such, the large window became suddenly illuminated. Jelly stopped. Her heart, as she would herself have expressed it, leaped into her mouth. The light came from the outside; no doubt from Dr. Rane's. Jelly stood stock still. And then—what desperate courage impelled her she never knew, but believed afterwards it must have been something akin to the fascination of the basilisk—she advanced to the window, and pulled aside the white blind.

But she did not see Bessy Rane this time, as perhaps she had expected; only her husband. Dr. Rane had a candle in his hand, and was apparently picking up something he had let fall quite close to the large opposite window. It was this candle that had lighted up Jelly's window. In another moment he lodged the candle on a chair that stood there, so as to have both hands at liberty. Jelly watched. What he had dropped appeared to be several articles of his deceased wife's clothing, some of which had come unfolded in the fall. He soon had them within his arm again, caught up the candle, and went down-stairs. Jelly saw and recognized one beautiful Indian shawl, scarlet with a gold border, which had been a present from her own mistress to Bessy.

"He is going to pack them up and sell them, the wicked man!" spoke Jelly in her strong conviction. And her ire grew very great against Dr. Rane. "I'd almost rather have seen the spirit of his poor wife again than *this*," was her bitter comment, as she finally went into her room.

Putting aside all the solemn doubts and fears that were making havoc with Jelly's mind, her curiosity was insatiable. Perhaps no woman in all Dallory had so great a propensity for prying into other people's affairs as she. Not, it must be again acknowledged, to do them harm, but simply in her world-wide inquisitiveness.

On the following morning, when Jelly attired herself to go to Ketler's after breakfast—which meal was seasoned throughout with reproaches to Dinah for not hearing the night bell— she bethought herself that she could first of all step into the next door. Ostensibly for the neighbourly object of informing Phillis of the death of the child; really, to pick up any items of information there might be to pick up. Dr. Rane, it may be here remarked, had given Molly Green a character to get herself another place, himself preferring to retain the elder servant, Phillis, who, however, only went to him by day. The doctor was alone in his house at night, and Jelly believed he dared not have even old Phillis in, knowing it was haunted. He made no secret now of his intention to quit Dallory. As soon as his practice should be disposed of, and the tontine money paid, away he would go.

Jelly coolly walked out of the window of Mrs. Cumberland's

dining-room, and through that of the doctor's. She had seen him go out some little time before. Phillis was upstairs, putting her master's chamber to rights, and Jelly sought her there. She told of the fright Ketler had given her by coming at midnight to bring the news about Cissy; and Phillis, who had a tender heart, dropped a tear or two to the child's memory. Cissy had been loved by everybody.

"Miss Dallory will be sorry to hear this when she comes back," remarked Phillis.

"I say, Phillis, what does your master mean to do with Mrs. Rane's clothes?" abruptly asked Jelly.

Phillis, dusting the looking-glass at the moment, paused in her occupation, as if considering.

"I'm sure I don't know, Jelly. He pointed out a few of the plain things to me one day, and said I might divide them between myself and Molly Green, but that he'd not like to see us wear them till he was gone away. As of course we shouldn't, being in black for her."

"She had lots of beautiful clothes. I'm sure the shawls, and scarfs, and embroidered robes, and worked petticoats, and other valuable Indian things that my mistress was always giving her, would have set up any lady's wardrobe. What will he do with *them?*"

Phillis shook her head, and pointed to a large, high chest of drawers. Her heart was full yet when she spoke of her late mistress.

"They are all in there, Jelly."

Are they, thought Jelly. But Phillis was going down now, her occupation finished. Jelly lingered behind, and thrust her black bonnet out at the window, as if looking at something up the road. When Phillis had descended the stairs, Jelly tried the drawers. All were locked except one. That one, which Jelly softly drew open, was filled with articles belonging to the late Mrs. Rane; none of them, so far as Jelly could gather by the cursory glance and touch, of much value.

"Yes," she said bitterly. "He keeps these open for show, but he is sending away the best. Those other drawers, if they could be looked into, are empty."

If ever Jelly had been startled in all her life at human footstep, it was to hear that of Dr. Rane on the stairs. How she got the draw shut, how she got her bonnet stretched out at the window again as far as ever it would stretch, she hardly knew. The doctor came in. Jelly, bringing in her head, apparently as much surprised as if a rhinoceros had walked up, apologised and explained rather lamely. She supposed Phillis must have gone down, she said, while she was watching that impudent butcher's boy; she had made bold to step up to tell Phillis about Ketler's little girl.

" Ah, she is gone," observed Dr. Rane, as Jelly was walking out. " There has been no hope of her for some time."

" No, sir, I know there hasn't," replied Jelly, somewhat recovering her equanimity.

" I told Ketler that he may thank the strike for it."

Jelly got out with this, and was whisking through the grey room, when the doctor spoke again.

" Have you heard from your mistress this morning, Jelly ? "

" No, sir."

" Well, I have. I am very much afraid that she is exceedingly ill, Jelly ? "

" Dinah got a letter from Ann a day or two ago, sir ; she said in it that her missis was looking worse, and seemed lower than she'd ever known her."

" Ay, I wish she would come home. Eastsea is far away, and I cannot be running there perpetually," added the doctor, as he shut the chamber door in Jelly's face.

CHAPTER XXXII.

COMING HOME TO DIE.

TIME went on again; nearly a fortnight. Dallory had relapsed into its old routine, and the fever was forgotten. Houses had recovered the smell of soap and scrubbing : their inhabitants were back again ; and amidst them Mrs. North and her daughter Matilda.

The chief news Madam found to interest her was, that Richard North had opened the works again. The glow of hope it raised within her was bright indeed ; for she looked upon it as an earnest that supplies would come in again for the future as they had in the past. That she would find herself mistaken was exceedingly probable ; Richard himself could have said a certainty. Madam had the grace to express some calm regret for the untimely death of Bessy, in the hearing of Mr. North and Richard ; she had put herself and Matilda into deeper mourning than they had assumed for

James Bohun.   It was all of the most fashionable and costly
kind; and the master of Dallory Hall, poor helpless man, had
the pleasure of receiving the bills for it from the London
court-milliners and dressmakers.   But Madam never enquired
into the particulars of Bessy's illness and death; in her opinion
the less fevers were talked of the better.

Yes: the North works were re-opened.   Or, to be quite
correct, they were close on the point of it.   Upon how small
a scale he must begin again, Richard, remembering the mag-
nitude of past operations, felt almost ashamed to think.   But,
as he good-humouredly remarked, half a loaf was better than
no bread.   He must get a living; he had not a fortune in the
bank, or elsewhere, to fly to; and he preferred doing this to
seeking employment under other firms, if indeed anything
worth having had been to be found; but the country's trade
was in a most depressed state, and hundreds of gentlemen,
like himself, had been thrown out.   It was the same thing as
beginning life over again; just a little venture, that might
succeed or might not; one in which he must plod on carefully
and cautiously, even to keep it going.

The whole staff of operatives would at first be under twenty
men.   The old workmen, idly airing themselves still in North
Inlet, laughed derisively when they heard this.   Twenty men,
indoor and out, including the master hisself, in that there big
block o' buildings, they shouted to one another.   What was
they a-going to make—wheelbarrers?—bridges for dogs to
trot across?—railway carriages to carry dolls?   The men
were pleasantly sarcastic over it, thinking perhaps they concealed their real bitterness of heart.   The new measure did
not find favour with them.   How should it, when they stood
in the light of excluded parties?   Some eight or ten, who had
never been willing upholders of the strike, who had been
ready to return to work all along, would be taken on again;
the rest, foreigners, Richard North was bringing over from
abroad.   And the ire of the disaffected was great.

Truly the men were like the dog in the manger—as Richard
North formerly told them.   They would not do the work themselves: had Richard now again offered it to them, they would
have declined it, as before: and yet they wished to prevent
others doing it.   Ay, and intended to prevent, luck being good
for it.   The strike and its disastrous accompaniments seemed
to have wholly changed the character of these poor mistaken
operatives.   They used, speaking of them as a whole, to be

as respectable and civil and sensible a body of men as one
could wish to find; but now they were sullen and depressed,
almost ferocious, next door to desperate. Out at pocket and
elbows; out of hope and heart; their homes were desolate,
their wives resentful, their children ragged, sickly, dying.
Neither men nor women, neither growing children nor infants,
ever knew now what it was to have a substantial meal of good
wholesome food. And of course the question lay heavily on
the minds of the most thoughtful—Where and in what way
was it to end? Richard North had told them—in starvation,
or the workhouse; and the prospect looked nearer now than
it had then. The only thing money seemed to be found
pretty readily for, was tobacco: since the men might still be
seen with their pipes. Beer also could be bought occasionally
—and perhaps they required it, in their state of long-continued incipient famine.

Mrs. Gass entered cordially into Richard's plans. She
would have put money wholesale into his new undertaking—
or, as she generally expressed it, his new venture; and in
truth it might be called new, and a venture also. But Richard
would not have it. Some portion of her capital that had been
embarked in the firm of North and Gass, remained in it of
necessity—all, in fact, of it that was not lost—but this she
reckoned as nothing, and wanted to help Richard further.
"It's o' no good crying after spilt milk, Mr. Richard," she
said to him, philosophically; "and I've still got a deal more
than I shall ever want." But Richard was firm: he would
not be helped further: it was a risk, and he preferred to
incur it alone.

Perhaps there were few people living that Richard North
liked better than Mrs. Gass. He even liked her homely mode
of speech; it was honest, genuine; far more to be respected
than if she had made a show of attempting what she could
not have kept up. Richard had grown to know her worth:
he recognized it more surely day by day. In his uncomfortable home at Dallory Hall—which had long to him been
anything but a home—he had got into the habit of almost
making a second one with Mrs. Gass. Never a day passed
but he spent an hour or two of it with her; and she would
coax him to remain for meals as often as she could.

He sat one afternoon at her well-spread tea-table. His
arrangements were pretty well organized now; and in a day
the works would open. The foreign workmen had come, and

were lodged with their families in the places appointed for them. Two policemen, paid by Richard, had also taken up their position in Dallory, purposely to protect them. Of course the object of the officers was not made known : Richard North would not be the one to provoke hostilities, or even let it be suspected he feared them ; but he was quite aware of the ill-feeling obtaining amidst his former workmen.

"Blessed idiots, they be," said Mrs. Gass, confidentially, as she handed Richard a cup of tea. "They want a lesson read to 'em, Mr. Richard ; that's what it is."

"I can't tell about that," dissented Richard. "I should have thought they could hardly find a better lesson than these last few months must have been."

"Ah, you don't know 'em, as I do, Mr. Richard. I'm almost double your age, sir ; and there's nothing gives one experience like years."

Richard laughed. "Not double my age yet, old friend."

"Any ways, I might have been your mother—if you'll excuse my saying of it," she persisted. "You be hard upon thirty-three, and I'm two years turned fifty."

It was in this plain manner that Mrs. Gass usually liked to make her propositions so undeniable. Certainly she might, so far as age went, have been Richard's mother.

"I know them men better than you do, Mr. Richard ; and I say they want a lesson read to 'em yet. And they'll get it, sir. But we'll leave the subject for a bit, if you please. I've been tired of it for some time past, and I'm sure you have. To watch men, once sensible, act like fools, and persist in acting, spite of everybody and everything, is wearying to one's patience. Is it to-morrow that you open ?"

"The day after."

"Well, now, Mr. Richard, I'd like to say another word upon a matter that you and me don't agree on—and it's not often our opinions differs, is it, sir ? It's touching your capital. I know you'll want more than you can command : it would give me a real pleasure if you'll let me find it."

Richard smiled, and shook his head decisively. "I cannot say more about it than I have said before," was his reply. "You know all I have urged."

"Look here : promise this," returned Mrs. Gass. "If ever you find yourself at a pinch as things go on, say you'll come to me. I don't ask you, should the concern turn out a losing one, a hopeless one (which I know it won't, unless them

precious Trades' Union men sets it a-fire, like the incendaries
they are, and I can call 'em nothing better), for in that case I
know cords wouldn't draw you to have help from me. But
when you are getting on, and money would be useful, and its
employment safe and sure, I shall look out for you to come to
me. Now, that's enough. I want to put a question, Mr.
Richard, that delicacy has kept me from bothering you with
before. What about their expenses at Dallory Hall? *You*
can't pretend to keep 'em up."

"Ah," said Richard, "that has been my great nightmare.
But I think I see a way through it—at least, in my own
mind. First of all, I have given notice to Miss Dallory that
we shall not require the lease renewed: it will be up, you
know, next March."

"Good," observed Mrs. Gass.

"My father knows nothing of it—it is of no use to trouble
him earlier than need be; and of course Madam does not.
She imagines that the lease will be renewed as a matter inevitable. Miss Dallory will, at my request, keep counsel—or,
rather, her brother Francis for her, for it is he who transacts
her business."

"They know then that you are the real lessee of Dallory
Hall? Lawk a mercy, what a simpleton I be!" broke off
Mrs. Gass. "Of course they must have knowed it when the
transfer was made."

Richard nodded. "As soon as Christmas turns I shall
begin to look out for a moderate house in lieu of the Hall;
one that I shall have hopes of being able to keep up. It shall
have a good garden for my father's sake. There'll be frightful rebellion on the part of Madam and Matilda, but I can't
help that. I cannot do more than my means will allow."

"Look here, Mr. Richard; don't you worry yourself about
not being able to keep up a house for Mr. North. I'll do my
part to that: all of it, if need be. He and my husband were
partners and friends, and grew rich together. Mr. North has
lost his savings, but I have kept mine; and I shall never see
him wanting in any comfort while he lives. We'll look out
for a pretty villa-cottage with a lovely garden; and he'll be
happier in it than he has ever been in that grand big Hall. If
Madam don't like to bring her pride down to it, let her be off
elsewhere—and a good riddance of bad rubbish! I say, though,
Mr. Richard, have you heard the news about Mary Dallory?"

"What news?" he asked.

"That's she's going to be married to Captain Bohun."

Richard North drank down his tea at a gulp. His face had flushed a little.

"I hear that Madam wishes it, and is working for it," he answered. "Miss Dallory was staying with them when they were at Sir Nash Bohun's."

"I know that Madam has given it out that they're going to marry one another," rejoined Mrs. Gass. "By the way, Mr. Richard, how is Captain Bohun getting on, after his fit of the jaunders?"

"He is better. Nearly well."

Mrs. Gass took a good bite of buttered toast. "I shall believe in that there marriage when it has taken place, Mr. Richard; not before. Unless I am uncommonly out, Captain Bohun cares for another young lady too well to think of Mary Dallory. Folks mayn't suspect it; and I b'lieve don't. But I have' had my eyes about me."

Richard knew that she alluded to Ellen Adair.

"They are both as sweet and good girls as ever lived, and a gentleman may think himself lucky to get either of 'em. Mr. Richard, your coat-sleeve is a-touching of the potted-ham."

Richard smiled a little as he wiped his cuff. Mourning was always bad wear, he remarked, showing every little stain. And then he said a few words about her for whom it was worn —which he had rarely done since she died.

"I cannot get reconciled to her death," he said in a low tone. "At times can scarcely believe in it. To have been carried off after only a day of fever! it seems incredible."

And Mrs. Gass felt that the words startled her to tremor. She turned away lest he should see it in her countenance.

Bad news arrived from Mrs. Cumberland. Only a morning or two later, a thundering knock at the front door disturbed Jelly and Dinah at their breakfast. Upon its being opened by the latter, Dr. Rane walked straight into the kitchen without ceremony, an open letter in his hand. Jelly rose and curtseyed. She had been markedly respectful to the doctor of late, perhaps in very fear lest he should suspect the curious things her mind was running on.

"My mother will be home to-night, Jelly."

"To-night, sir!" exclaimed Jelly in her surprise.

"She is much worse. Very ill indeed. She says she is coming home to die."

Jelly shrieked: startled out of her equanimity.

"It is only three lines—she writes herself," continued Dr. Rane, just showing the letter in his hand, as if in confirmation. "They were to go to London yesterday, stay there the night, and will come home to-day. Of course you will have all things in readiness."

"Yes, sir. And what about meeting my mistress at the station?"

"I shall go myself," said Dr. Rane.

He went away with the last words. Jelly sat still for a few minutes to digest the news, and came to the conclusion that "coming home to die" was but a figure of speech of Mrs. Cumberland's. Then she rose up to begin her preparations, and overwhelmed the bewildered Dinah with fifteen orders at once.

During the day, Jelly, in pursuance of something or other she wanted, was walking at a sharp pace towards Dallory, when in passing the Hall gates she found herself accosted by Mrs. North. Madam was taking her usual promenade in the grounds, and had extended it to the gates. Jelly stood still in sheer amazement; it was the first time within her recollection that Madam had condescended to address herself or any other inhabitant of the neighbourhood.

How was Mrs. Cumberland?—and *where* was she? Madam graciously asked. And Jelly in the moment's haste, answered that she was at Eastsea.

"To stay the winter, I believe," went on Madam. "And Miss Adair—is she with her?"

"I ought to have said *was* at Eastsea," corrected Jelly, who did not like Madam well enough to be more than barely civil. "My mistress is worse, and is coming home to-day. Miss Adair is with her of course. I must wish you good morning, Madam, I've got my work before me." And away went Jelly, leaving Madam a mental compliment:

"Nasty proud cat! she had got some sly motive for asking, I know."

And so the day went on.

The early dusk of the autumn evening was beginning to fall, together with a storm of rain, when the carriage containing Mrs. Cumberland stopped at her door. Jelly ran out; and was met by Ellen Adair; who spoke in a frightened whisper:

"Oh Jelly, she is so ill! she cannot speak."

The doctor stood helping his mother out. Ann was

gathering small articles in her arms from beside the driver. Jelly caught one glimpse of her mistress's face and fell back in alarm. Surely that blue look was for death!

"She ought not to have come," murmured Dr. Rane in Jelly's ear. "Go and ask Seeley to step over—while I get my mother upstairs."

There was some bustle and confusion for the time. Mrs. Cumberland was put in the easy chair in her room, and undressed so far as her bonnet and travelling wraps went. She refused to go to bed. In half an hour or so, when she had somewhat recovered the fatigue, she looked and seemed considerably better, and spoke a little, expressing a wish for some tea. The doctors left her to take it, enjoining strict quiet. Jelly knelt down before her mistress, to hold the cup and saucer.

"What did she die of, Jelly?" came the unexpected question.

"Who?" asked Jelly, wonderingly.

Mrs. Cumberland made a motion in the direction of her son's house: she and her voice were alike of the faintest. "Bessy Rane."

Jelly gave a start that went well-nigh to upset the tea. She felt her face growing white: but she could not move to hide it.

"Why don't you speak! What did she die of?" ·

"Ma'am, don't you know? She caught the fever."

"It troubles me, Jelly; it troubles me. I've done nothing but dream of her ever since. And what will Oliver do without her?"

The best he can, Jelly had a great mind to answer. But all she said, was, to beg her mistress to leave these questions until the morning.

"I don't think any morning will dawn for me," was Mrs. Cumberland's remark. "I sent you word I was coming home to die. I wanted to come for many reasons. I knew the journey would do me harm; I put it off too long. But I had to come home: I could not die away from it."

Every consoling thing that Jelly could think of, she said, assuring her mistress it was nothing but the journey that put her on to these low thoughts.

"I want to see Mr. North," resumed Mrs. Cumberland. "You must go and bring him to me."

"Not to-night," said Jelly.

" To-night. Now. There's no time to lose. To see him was one of the things I had to come home for."

And Mrs. Cumberland, ill though she was, was resolute to be obeyed as ever she had been in her days of health. Jelly had the sense to know that refusal would excite her worse than any result of compliance, and prepared to obey. As she passed out of the presence of Mrs. Cumberland, she saw Ellen Adair sitting on the stairs, anxiously listening for any sound from the sick room that might tell how all was going on within it.

" Oh Miss Ellen ! You should not be there."

" I cannot rest anywhere, Jelly. I want to know how she is. She is my only friend on this side of the wide world."

" Well now, Miss Ellen, look here—you may come in and stay with her, while I am away: I was going to call Ann. But mind you don't talk."

Flinging on a shawl, Jelly started on the run for Dallory Hall. It was an inclement night, pouring with rain. And Ellen Adair took up her place in obedient silence by the side of the dying woman—for she *was* dying, however ignorant they might be of the fact. Apart from Ellen's natural grief for Mrs. Cumberland, thoughts of what her own situation would be, if she lost her, could but intrude on her mind, bringing all kinds of perplexity. It seemed to her that she would have neither home nor protector.

CHAPTER XXXIII.

RICHARD NORTH'S REVELATION.

For a wonder, the dinner-table at Dallory Hall was a solitary one. Solitary, in so far as that only the family then at home sat at it. Madam headed it; Mr. North was at the foot; Richard on one side; Matilda on the other. Scarcely a word was being spoken. Madam was in one of her imperious humours—indeed, when was she out of them ?—the servants waited in silence.

Suddenly there rang out a loud crashing peal from the hall-bell. Richard, who was already beginning to be disturbed by vague fears of what his ex-workmen's hostilities might bring them to do, sat back in his chair absently, and turned his head.

" Are you expecting any one, Dick ? " asked his father.

"No, sir. Unless it be a message to call me out."

It was, however, a message to call out Mr. North; not Richard. Mrs. Cumberland wanted to see him. "On the instant," the servant added : for that was what Jelly had imperatively said.

Mr. North laid down his knife and fork and stared at the man. He did not understand.

"Mrs. Cumberland is at Eastsea," he cried.

"No, sir, she has just got home, and she wants to see you very particular. It's the lady's maid who has brought the message."

"Mr. North cannot go," broke forth Madam loudly to the servant. "Go and say so."

But Jelly, to whom the words penetrated as she stood in the hall, had no notion of her mistress's wishes being set at nought by Madam. Jelly had a great deal of calm moral and physical courage—in spite of the supernatural terrors that had recently held influence over her—some persons might have said her share of calm impudence also : and she made no ceremony of putting her black bonnet, shiny with wet, inside the room.

"My mistress is dying, sir; I don't think there can be a doubt of it," she said, advancing to Mr. North. "She wishes to say a few last words to you, if you'll please to come. There's no time to be lost, sir."

"Bless me!—poor Fanny!" cried Mr. North, rising : and his hands began to tremble a little. "I'll come at once, Jelly."

"You will *not*," spoke Madam, as if she were issuing an imperial edict.

"I must," said Mr. North. "She is dying, Madam, don't you hear?"

"I say No, you will not."

"The wishes of the dying must be respected by the living," interposed Jelly, still to Mr. North. "Otherwise there's no telling what ghosts might haunt 'em after."

The grammar was rather obscure, but the meaning of the words plain enough. Mr. North took a step or two towards the door : Madam came round and put herself before him, with her intercepting words :

"My will is law in this house and out of it you do not go."

For a minute or two the master (the master !) of Dallory Hall looked utterly helpless, as if he were going to cry like a child. Then he cast an appealing look at his son. Richard rose, laying down his table-napkin.

"Leave the room for an instant," he quietly said to the servants, including Jelly. And they filed out.

"My dear father, is it your wish to see Mrs. Cumberland?"

"Oh, Dick, you know it is," spoke the poor brow-beaten man. "There's not much left to me in life now to care for; but if I let her die without going to her there'll be less."

"Then you shall go," said Richard. Madam turned to him; passion in her eye, and on her tongue.

"How *dare* you attempt to oppose me, Richard North? I say your father shall not go forth at the beck and call of this crazy woman."

"Madam, I say he shall," calmly spoke Richard.

"Do you defy me? Has it come to that?"

"Why yes, if you force me to: it is not my fault. Pardon me if I speak plainly—if I set you right upon one point, Madam," he added. "You have just said your will is law in the house and out of it: in future it must, on some occasions, yield to mine. This is one. My father will go to Mrs. Cumberland's. Say no more, Madam: it will be useless; and I am going to admit the servants."

From sheer amazement Madam was still. Resolution—the resolution born of conscious power to will and to execute—lay in every tone and glance of Richard North. Before she could collect her energies, the door was opened to the servants, and she heard Richard's order to make ready and bring round the close carriage instantly. Instantly.

"Mr. North will be with your mistress as soon as you are, Jelly," said he. And Jelly nodded, as she took her departure.

But there ensued a scene. Madam had called Mrs. Cumberland a crazy woman: she seemed nothing less than one herself. Whatever her private objection might have been to her husband's holding an interview with Mrs. Cumberland—and there could be no question that she had one—Richard fairly thought she was going mad in her frenzied attempts to prevent it. She stamped, she raved, she threatened Mr. North, defying him to go, she violently pushed him into his chair backwards, she ordered the servants to bar the house doors against his egress, she rushed round to the stables herself and counter-manded the carriage; she was in fact as nearly mad, as a woman, short of being a caged lunatic, can be. Matilda cried: indifferent as that young lady remained in general to her mother's ordinary fits of temper, she was frightened now. The servants collected in dark nooks of the hall, and stood peeping; Mr. North stole into his parlour, and thence, by the window, to a bench in the garden, where he sat in the dark and the rain, shaking in every limb. Of his own accord he had surely never dared to go, after this: but Richard was his sheet anchor. Richard alone maintained his calm equanimity, and carried matters through. The servants obeyed his slightest word, only the lift of his finger; with sure instinct they saw who could be, and was, the Hall's real master: and the carriage at length came to the door.

But all this had caused delay. And more might have been caused—for what will an unrestrained and determined woman not do—but that just as the wheels, grating on the wet gravel struck on Madam's ear, her violence culminated in a kind of fainting fit. For the time at least she could not move, and Richard took the opportunity to put his father in the carriage. It was astonishing how confidingly the old man trusted to Richard's protection. He clung to his hand.

"Won't you come also, Dick? I hardly dare go alone. She'd be capable of coming after me, you know."

Richard's answer was to step in and sit down beside his father. It was eight o'clock when they got to Mrs. Cumberland's. Jelly, with a reproachful face, showed them into a sitting-room.

"You can't go up now, sir; you'll have to wait!" said she.

"Is she any better?" asked Richard.

"She's worse," replied Jelly; "getting weaker and weaker with every quarter of an hour. Dr. Rane thinks she'll last till morning. I don't. The clergyman's up there now."

And when the time came for Mr. North to be introduced into the room, Mrs. Cumberland was almost past speaking to him. They were alone—for she motioned others away. Mr. North never afterwards settled with himself what the especial point could have been that she had wished to say to him; unless it was the request that he should take charge of Ellen Adair.

Her words were faint and few, and apparently disjointed, at times seeming to have no connection the one with the other. Mr. North—sitting on a chair close in front of her, holding one of her hands, bending down his ear to catch what fell from her white lips—thought her mind wandered a little. She asked him to protect Ellen Adair—to take her home to the Hall until she should be claimed by her husband or her father. It might be but a few days, she added, before the former came, and he would probably wish the marriage to take place at once; if so, it had better. Then she went on to say something about Arthur Bohun, which Mr. North could not catch at all. And then she passed abruptly to the past matter of the anonymous letter.

"John, you will forgive it! You will forgive it!" she implored, feebly clasping the hand in which hers lay.

"Forgive that?" returned Mr. North, not in dissent but in surprise that she should speak on the subject.

"For my sake, John. We were dear friends and playfellows in the old days—though you were older than me. You'll forgive it won't you, John, for my sake; because I am dying, and because I ask it of you?"

"Yes, I will," said John North: "I don't think as much about it as I did," he added. "I'd like to forgive everybody and everything before I go, Fanny; and my turn mayn't be long now. I forgive it heartily; heartily," he repeated, thinking to content her. "Fanny, I never thought you'd go before me."

"God bless you! God reward you," she murmured. "There was no ill intention, you know, John."

John North did not see why he merited reward, neither could he follow what she was talking of. It might be, he supposed, one of the hallucinations of mind that sometimes attend the dying.

"I'll take every care of Ellen Adair: she shall come to the Hall and stay there," he said, for that he could understand. "I promise it faithfully to you, Fanny."

"Then that is one of the weights off my mind," murmured the dying woman. "There were so many on it. I have left a paper, John, naming you and Richard her guardians for the time being. She's of good family, and very precious to her father. There has been so short a space to act in: it was only three or four days ago that I knew the end was coming. I did not expect it would be quite so soon."

"It mostly comes when it's not expected," murmured poor John North: "there's a many of us seem to be going very near together. Edmund was the first; then Bessy; now it's you, Fanny: and the next will be me. God in His mercy grant that we may all meet in a happier world, and be together for ever!"

Richard North had remained below in the dining-room

with Ellen Adair. The heavy crimson curtains were drawn before the large garden window, a bright fire blazed in the grate. Ellen in her black dress, worn for Bessy, sat in the warmth: she felt very chilly after her journey, was nervous at the turn the illness seemed to be taking; and every now and then a tear stole silently down her sweet face. Richard walked about a little as he glanced at her. He thought her looking, apart from the present sorrow, pale and ill. Richard North was deliberating whether to say a word or two upon a matter that puzzled him. He thought he would.

"I have been across the Channel, you know, Ellen, since you left for Eastsea," he began. He had grown sufficiently intimate at Mrs. Cumberland's, after his enforced term of idleness set in, to drop the formal " Miss Adair " for her Christian name. And she had always called him " Richard: " or " Mr. Richard."

"Yes, we heard of it. You went to engage workmen did you not ? "

"Something of that. When I got back home, I found a letter or two waiting for me from Arthur Bohun, who was then at Eastsea. Madam had opened one."

Ellen looked up, and then down again immediately. Richard North saw a change pass over her face, as though she were startled.

" I could not quite understand the letters; I think Arthur intended me not to fully understand them. They spoke of some—some event that was coming off, at which he wished me to be present."

Ellen saw that he did understand: at least, that he believed he did. She rose from her seat and went close to him, speaking in agitation.

" Will you grant me a request, Richard ? I know you can be a firm friend; you are very true. Do not ever think of it again—do not speak of it to living man or woman."

" I presume it did *not* take place, Ellen."

" No. And the sooner it is altogether forgotten, the better."

He took her hand between his, and drew her to the fire. They stood before it side by side.

" I am glad you know that I am your firm and true friend, Ellen; you may trust me always. It is neither idle curiosity nor impertinence that makes me speak. Madam stopped it, I conclude."

"I suppose so. She came and fetched him away; James Bohun was dying and wanted him. Since then I—I hardly know. He never came down again. He has been very ill."

"Yes, very. Let him get his health again; it will be all right. That's all, my dear. I should like to take a little care of you as though you were my sister."

"Care!" she replied. "Oh Richard, I don't see what will become of me, or where I shall go. They say Mrs. Cumberland will not live till morning; and papa, you know, is so far away."

Jelly appeared with some coffee; and stayed for a minute or two to gossip, after the bent of her own heart. The carriage and the horses and the coachman were waiting outside in the rain. Dr. Rane was in and out, in his restlessness. It was an anxious night with him. He would, how willingly! have restored his mother for a time, had human skill alone been necessary to do it.

Before the interview with Mr. North was over—and it did not last twenty minutes—Mrs. Cumberland had changed considerably. Her son went into the room as Mr. North left it; and he saw at once how fallacious was the hope he had entertained of her lasting until morning.

Poor Mr. North, broken alike in health and heart, weak in spirit almost as a child, burst into a fit of tears as soon as he entered the dining-room. Richard spoke a few soothing words to him: Ellen Adair, who had rarely, if ever, seen a man cry, stood aghast.

"They are all going, Dicky," he sobbed; "all going one by one. We were a'most boy and girl together; I a big one, Fanny a little mite that I'd often hold on my knee. I loved the child; she was as pretty a little thing as you'd wish to see. She's younger than me by a good deal, and I never thought she'd go before me. There'll be only you left, Dicky; only you."

Ellen touched Richard's elbow: she held a cup of coffee in her hand. "If he can be brought to drink it, it may do him good," she whispered, crying for company.

Mr. North drank the coffee. Afterwards, when he had sat awhile—breaking out ever and anon with the reminiscences of the old days—he said he should like another cup. Richard, as he handed it to him, reminded him that the carriage was waiting; upon which Mr. North, who had quite forgotten the fact, tried to drink it all down at once, and had a fit of choking.

"I'd like to know how she is before I go, Dicky," he said when it was over. "Whether there's any change."

A change indeed. Even as the words left his lips, some slight commotion was heard in the house, following upon Dr. Rane's voice, who had come out of the chamber to speak. The last moment was at hand. Ellen Adair went up, and Jelly went up. Mr. North said he must wait a bit longer.

In five minutes all was over. Ellen Adair, brought down by Dr. Rane, was convulsed with grief. Mr. North said she should go back with them to the Hall, and bade Jelly find what things she might want. At first Ellen refused: it seemed strangely sudden, almost unseemly, to go out of the house thus immediately; but when she came to reflect how lonely and undesirable would be her position if she stayed in it, she grew eager to go. To tell the truth, she felt half afraid to stay: she had never been in personal contact with death, and the idea lay upon her as a dread to be shrunk from.

So a small portmanteau was hastily repacked—not an hour had elapsed since it was unpacked—and taken out to the carriage, Jelly undertaking to send the larger box in the morning. And Ellen was in the carriage driving to the Hall with Mr. North and Richard.

"I am glad to come," she said to them, catching up her breath. "It is so very kind of you to receive me in this extremity."

"Not at all, my dear," answered Mr. North. "The Hall will be your home until we get instructions from your father. Mrs. Cumberland has appointed me and Richard as your temporary guardians: I was telling Dick so when you were upstairs."

And Ellen burst into fresh tears, and said again and again how kind it was of them. Richard North felt that he loved her as dearly as any sister.

But there would be words to the bargain: they had not taken Madam into consideration. The supposition that she would object to it never occurred to Mr. North or Richard; Madam was so very fond of having company at Dallory Hall. When the coachman, tired of being in the wet, dashed up at a canter, and they descended and entered into the blaze of light, and Madam, standing a little back, saw the young lady and the luggage, her face of surprise was a picture.

" What does this intrusion mean ? " she demanded, slowly advancing.

" It means, Madam, that Mrs. Cumberland is dead, and that she has left Miss Adair in my charge and Dick's for a bit," answered Mr. North with trembling courtesy, remembering the frightful mood he had run away from. While Richard, catching the ominous words and eye of Madam, hastily took Ellen into the drawing-room, introduced her to Matilda, and shut the door on them.

" You say Mrs. Cumberland is dead ! " had been Madam's next words to Mr. North.

" Yes, she's dead. It has been frightfully sudden."

" What did she want with you ? " resumed Madam, her voice sinking almost to a whisper; and, but that Mr. North was not an observant man, he might have seen her very lips growing white with some dread suspense.

" I don't know what she wanted," he replied—" unless it was the promise from me to take care of Miss Adair. She was nearly past speaking when I got to see her; things had made me late, Madam."

" Did she—did she——. By the commotion that woman, Jelly, made, one would have supposed her mistress had some vast secret to impart," broke off Madam. "Had she ? "

" Had who ? " asked Mr. North, rather losing the thread of the dialogue.

" Mrs. Cumberland," said Madam, with a slight stamp. And, in spite of her assumed careless petulance, she watched her husband's face for the answer as if she were watching for one of life or death. " Did she impart to you any—any private matter ? "

" She had none to impart, Madam, that I am aware of. I shouldn't think she had. She rambled in her talk a bit, as the dying will do; about our old days, and about the anony- mous letter that killed Edmund. There was nothing else, except that she wanted me to take temporary charge of Miss Ellen Adair, until we can hear from her father."

Mr. North was too simply honest to deceive, and Madam believed him. Her old arrogance resumed its sway as fear died out.

" What did she tell you about *him*—the father ? "

" Nothing ; not a word, Madam : what should she ? I tell you her mind and her speech were both all but gone. She rambled on about the old days and the anonymous letter

and I couldn't follow her even in that, but she said nothing else.

All was right then. The old will and the old arrogance
were in full swing now; Madam was herself again.

"Miss Adair goes back to Mrs. Cumberland's to night,"
said she. "I do not receive her, or permit her to remain here."

"Eh ?—what ? " cried Mr. North ; and Richard, who had
been stepping up, stood still to listen. " Why not, Madam ? "

" Because I do not choose to," said Madam. " That's why."

" Madam, I'd not do it for the world. Send her back to the
house with the dead lying in it, and where she'd have no protector ! I couldn't do it. She's but a young thing. The
neighbours would cry shame upon me."

" She goes back at once," spoke Madam in her most decisive
tones. " The carriage may take her, as it rains; but back she
goes."

" It can't be, Madam, it can't, indeed. I'm her guardian,
now, and responsible. I promised that she should stay at
Dallory Hall."

And Madam went forthwith into another of her furious
rages ; she stamped and shook with passion. Not at being
thwarted : her will was law always, and she intended it to be
so now ; but at Mr. North's *attempting* to oppose it.

"You were a fool for bringing her at all, knowing as you
might that I should not allow her to stay," stamped Madam.
"The hall is mine : so long as I am mistress of it, no girl
picked up anywhere on a wet night, no brat at fault for a place
to put her head in, shall find admittance here. *She goes back
at once.*"

Mr. North seemed ready to drop. The piteous look of hopeless despair, piteous in its utter helplessness, laid hold of his
face. Richard drew nearer, and he caught sight of him. All
this had taken place in the hall under the great lamp.

"Dick, what's to be done ? " wailed Mr. North. "I should
die of the shame of turning her out again. I wish I could die ;
I've been wishing it many times to-night. It's time I was gone,
Dick, when I've no longer a roof to offer a poor young lady a
week or two's shelter under."

"But you have one, my dear father. At least I have, which
comes to the same thing," added Richard, calmly composed as
usual. "Madam "—politely, but nevertheless authoritatively
taking Madam's hand to lead her into the dining-room—" will
you pardon me if I interfere in this ? "

" It is no business of yours," said Madam.

" Excuse me, Madam, but it is. I think I had better take
it on myself exclusively, and relieve my father—for really,
what with one thing and another, he is not capable of bearing
much."

" Oh, Dick, do ; do!" interposed poor Mr. North, timorously
following them into the dining-room. " You are strong, Dick,
and I am weak. I was strong once, though."

" Madam," said Richard, " this young lady, Miss Adair,
will remain here at the Hall until we get instructions from
her father."

Madam was turning livid. Richard had never taken such
a tone until to-night. And this was the second time ! She
would have liked to strike him. Had he been some worthless
animal, her manner could not have expressed more gratuitous
contempt.

" By what right, pray, do *you* interfere ?"

" Well, Madam, Mrs. Cumberland expressed a wish that I
as well as my father, should act as Miss Adair's guardian."

" There's a paper left that says it," eagerly put in Mr. North.

" And what though you were appointed fifty times over
and fifty to that ; do you suppose it would give you the right
to bring her here—to thrust her into my home ?" shrieked
Madam.   " Don't you believe it, Richard North."

" Madam," said Richard, quietly, " the home is mine."

" On sufferance," was the scornful rejoinder.   " But I think
the sufferance has been allowed too long."

" You have known me now many years, Madam : I do not
think in all those years you have found me advance a proposition that I could not substantiate. In saying the home here
was mine I spoke what is literally true. I am the lessee of
Dallory Hall. You and my father (my dear father "—turning to him—" I know you will pardon me for the few plain
words I must speak) are here on sufferance. My guests, as
it were."

" It is, every word, Gospel truth," spoke up poor Mr. North,
glad to his heart that the moment for her enlightenment had
at length come.   " Dick holds the lease of Dallory Hall, and
he is its real master. For several years now we have all
been pensioners on his bounty. He has worked to keep us,
Madam, in this his own house ; and he has done it nobly and
generously."

It seemed to Madam that her brain went whirling about in

a maze, for the words brought conviction. Richard the true master! Richard's money that they had been living upon!

"I am grieved to have been obliged to state this, Madam," Richard resumed. "I shall wish never to allude to it further, and I will continue to do the best I can for all. But—in regard to Miss Ellen Adair, she must remain here, and she must be made welcome."

CHAPTER XXXIV.

UNDER THE SAME ROOF.

A CRAFTY and worldly-wise cunning woman, like Mrs. North, can change her tactics as readily as the wind changes its quarters. The avowal of Richard, that he was the true master of Dallory Hall, so far as holding all power to act in his hands went—had been the greatest blow to her of any she had experienced in all these later years. It struck, don't you see, the death-warrant of *her* power; for she knew that she should never be allowed to rule again with an unjust and iron hand, as it had been her cruel pleasure to do. In all essential things, where it was needful for him to interfere, she felt that Richard's will and Richard's policy would henceforth outsway her own.

Madam sat in her dressing-room that night, mentally looking into the future. Or rather striving to look. But it was very dim and misty. The sources whence she had drawn her large supplies were gone; the unlimited power was gone. Would it be worth while for her to remain at the Hall, she questioned, under the altered circumstances. Since the death of James Bohun, and her short sojourn with Sir Nash, an idea had occasionally crossed her mind that it might be desirable to take up her residence with the baronet—if she could only scheme to accomplish it. From some cause or other she had formerly not felt at ease when with Sir Nash; but that was wearing off. At any rate, a home in his well-appointed establishment would be far preferable to Dallory if its show and expense could not be kept up; and all considerations gave way before Madam's own selfish interest.

Already Madam tasted of deposed power. Ellen Adair was to remain at the Hall, and—as Richard had emphatically enjoined—to be made welcome. Madam shut her teeth and her hands fiercely as she thought of it. Ellen Adair, whom she so hated and dreaded! she lost herself in a speculation of

what Richard might have done had she persisted in her
refusal. Would he have taken up his power in the hearing
of the servants, and said I am your true master; you must
obey my decrees now, things must be according as I wish
them? Would he have said to Madam, This is my house,
and you must either fall in with my wishes or—there's the
door and you can walk out of it? She had been too wise to
provoke this: and had yielded an acquiescence, tacitly at any
rate, to the stay of Ellen Adair.

But as Madam sat there, thinking of this, thinking of that,
a doubt slowly loomed into her mind, whether it might not,
after all, be the best policy for Ellen Adair to be at the Hall.
The dread that Arthur Bohun might possibly renew his wish
to marry her, in spite of all that had been said and done, lay
occasionally on Madam. In fact it had never left her. She
could not make a child of Arthur and keep him at her apron-
string: he was free to go hither and thither at will; and no
matter in what spot of the habitable globe Ellen might be
located, there was no earthly power that could stop his going
to her if he wished to go. Why then, surely it *was* safer and
better that the girl should be under her own eye, always in
her own immediate presence. Madam laughed a little as she
rose from her musings; she could have found in her heart to
thank Richard North for bringing this about.

And so, with the morning, Madam was quite prepared to
be gracious to Ellen Adair. Madam was one of those accom-
modating people who are ready, as we are told, to hold a
candle to a certain nameless personage, if they think their
interest may be served by doing it. Matilda North, who
knew nothing whatever of Madam's special reasons for disliking Miss Adair—save that she had heard her mother once
scornfully speak of her as a low, nameless young woman, a
nobody—was coldly civil to her on Richard's introduction.
But the sweet face, the gentle voice, the superior manners,
won even on her; and when the morning came Matilda felt
rather glad that the present monotony of the Hall was relieved
by such an inmate, and asked her all about the death of Mrs.
Cumberland.

And thus Ellen Adair was located at Dallory Hall. But
Mrs. North had not bargained for a cruel perplexity that was
to fall upon her ere the day was over: no less than the return
to it of Captain Bohun.

It has been mentioned that Sir Nash was ailing. In

Madam's new scheme, undefined and incomplete though it was at present—that of possibly taking up her residence in his house—she had judged it well to inaugurate it by trying to ingratiate herself into his favour so far as she knew how. She would have liked to make herself necessary to him. Madam had heard a hint broached of his going over to certain springs in Germany, and as she knew she should never get taken with him there, though Arthur might, she just schemed a little to keep him in England. During the concluding days of her stay with him, Sir Nash had been overwhelmed with persuasions that he should come down to Dallory Hall, and get up his health there. To hear Madam talk, never had so salubrious ·a spot been discovered on the earth's surface as Dallory; its water was pure, its air a species of tonic in itself; for rural calmness, for simple delight, it possessed attractions never before realized save in Arcadia. Sir Nash, in answer to all this, had not given the least hope of trying its virtues; and Madam had finally departed believing that Dallory would never see him.

But on this morning, the one after Ellen Adair's arrival, Madam, amidst other letters, got one addressed to her in her son Arthur's handwriting. According to her frequent habit of late—though why she had fallen into it she could not herself have told—she let her letters lie, unlooked at, until very late in the morning; just before luncheon she opened them; Arthur's the last: she never cared to hear from *him.* And then Madam opened her eyes as well as the letter. She read that Sir Nash had come to a sudden resolution to accept her proffered hospitality for a short time, and that he and Arthur would be with her that day. Now at this very moment of reading, they were absolutely on their road to Dallory Hall.

Madam sat staring. Could she stop it, was her first thought. It was very undesirable that they should come. Ellen Adair was there; and besides, after this new and startling revelation of Richard's, Madam was not quite sure that she might continue to crowd the house with guests at will. But there was no help for it; ransack her fertile brain as she would, and did, there seemed no possible chance of preventing the travellers' arrival. Had she known where a message would reach them, she might have telegraphed that the Hall was burning, or that yellow fever had broken out in it.

Mrs. North was not the first who has had to make the best of an unlucky combination of circumstances. She gave orders amidst her sevants to prepare for the reception of the guests; and descended to the luncheon table with a smooth face, say-ing there not a word. Richard was out, or she might have told him: he was so busy over the re-opening of those works of his, that he was now only at home night and morning. It happened, however, that on this day he had occasion to come home for some deed of agreement that lay in his desk.

It was about four o'clock in the afternoon—a showery one —and Richard North was approaching the gates of the Hall with the long swinging step of a man of business, when he saw some one approach them more leisurely from the other side. It was Mary Dallory. He did not know she had come back; and his face had certainly a flush of surprise on it, as he lifted his hat to greet her.

"I got home yesterday evening," she said, smiling. "Forced to it. Dear old Frank wrote the most woe-begone letters imaginable, saying he could not get on without me."

"Did you come from Sir Nash Bohun's?" asked Richard.

"Sir Nash Bohun's! No. What put that in your head? I was at Sir Nash Bohun's for a few days some ages ago— weeks, at any rate, as it seems to me—but not lately. I have been with my aunt in South Audley Street."

"London must be lively at this time," remarked Richard rather sardonically; as if, like Francis Dallory, he resented her having stayed there.

"Very. It *is*, for the tourists and people have all come back to it. I suppose you'd have liked me to stay here and catch the fever. Very kind of you! I was going in to see your father."

He glanced at her with a half smile, and held out his arm after passing the gates.

"I am not sure that I shall take it. You have been very rude, Mr. Richard."

Richard dropped it at once, begging her pardon. His air was that of a man who has received a disagreeable check. But Miss Dallory had been joking only; she glanced up at him, and a hot flush of vexation overspread her face. Richard held it out once more, and they began talking as they went along. Some drops were beginning to fall, and he put up his umbrella.

He told her of Mrs. Cumberland's death. She had not heard of it, and expressed her sorrow. But she had had no acquaintance with Mrs. Cumberland, could not remember to have seen her more than once, and that was more than three years ago : and the subject passed.

"I hear you have begun business again," she said.

"Well—I might answer you as Green, my old time-keeper, answered me to-day. I happened to say to him, 'We have begun once more, Green:' 'Yes, in a sort, sir,' said he, gruffly. I have begun 'in a sort,' Miss Dallory."

"And what kind of ' sort ' is it ? "

"In just as cautious and quiet a way as it is well possible for a poor man to begin," answered Richard. "I have no capital, as you must be aware; or at least, as good as none."

"I daresay you could get enough of that if you wanted it. Some of your friends have plenty of it, Mr. Richard."

"I know that. Mrs. Gass quarrels with me every day, because I will not take hers, and run the risk of making ducks and drakes of it. No. I prefer to feel my way alone; to stand or fall by myself, Miss Dallory."

"I have heard Richard North called obstinate," remarked the young lady, looking into the damp air.

"When he believes he is right. I don't think it is a bad quality, Miss Dallory. My dear sister Bessy used to say——"

"Oh ! Richard, what about her ?—what of Bessy ? " interrupted Mary Dallory, all ceremony thrown to the winds at the mention of the name. "I never was so painfully shocked in all my life as when I opened Frank's letter telling me she was dead. What *could* have killed her ? "

"It was the fever, you know," answered Richard, sadly. "I never shall forget what *I* felt when I heard it. I was in Belgium."

"It seemed very strange that she should die so quickly."

"It seems strange to me still. I have not cared to talk about her since: she was my only sister and very dear to me. Rane says it was a most violent attack: and I suppose she succumbed to it quickly, without much struggle."

"That poor little Cissy Ketler is gone, too."

"Yes."

"Is Ketler one of the few men who have gone back to work ? "

"Oh ! dear no."

"Do you know I should like to shake those men until they come to their senses ? "

The rain had ceased : but they were walking on, uncon-

scious of it, under the umbrella. By-and-by the fact was discovered, and the umbrella put down.

" Who's this?," exclaimed Richard. " Visitors for Madam, I
suppose."

Richard alluded to the sound of carriage-wheels behind.
He and Miss Dallory had certainly not walked as though they
were winning a wager, but they were close to the house now;
and reached its door simultaneously with the carriage.
Richard stood in very amazement, when he saw its inmates
—Arthur Bohun, thin and sallow; and Sir Nash.

There was a hasty greeting, a welcome, and then they all
entered together. Madam, Matilda, and Miss Adair were in
the drawing-room. Arthur came in side by side with Miss
Dallory; he was holding her hand; they were talking together, and a slight flush illumined his thin face. Ellen, feeling
shy amidst them all, remained in the back ground: she would
not press forward: but a general change of position brought
her and Arthur close to each other; and she held out her hand
timidly, with a rosy blush.

He turned white as death. He staggered back as though
he had seen a spectre. Just for a minute he was utterly
unnerved; and then, some sort of presence of mind returning
to him, he looked another way without further notice, and
began talking again with Miss Dallory. But Miss Dallory had
no longer leisure to waste on him. *She* had caught sight of Ellen,
whom she had never seen, and was wonderfully struck. Never
in her whole life had she found a face so unutterably lovely.

" Mr. Richard "—touching his arm, as he stood by Arthur
Bohun, and the young lady had to stretch before Arthur to
get to it—" who is that young lady ? "

" Ellen Adair."

" Is *that* Ellen Adair ? Oh ! what a sweet face it is ! I
never saw one so lovely. Do take me to her, Mr. Richard."

Richard introduced them. Arthur Bohun, his bosom beating with shame and pain, turned to the window : a sick faintness was stealing over him; he was very weak yet. How he
loved her !—*how* he loved her ! More; ay, ten times more, as
it seemed to him, than of yore. And yet, he must only treat
her with coldness ; worse than if she and he were strangers.
What untoward mystery could have brought her at Dallory
Hall ? He stole away, on the plea of looking for Mr. North.
Madam, who had all her eyes about her and had been using
them, followed him out.

There was a hasty colloquy. He asked why Miss Adair was there. Madam replied by telling (for once in her life) the pure truth. She favoured him with a short history of the previous night's events that had culminated in Richard's assumption of will. The girl was there, as he saw, concluded Madam, and she could not help it.

"Did Mrs. Cumberland before she died reveal to Miss Adair what you told me about—about her father?" enquired Arthur, from between his dry and feverish and trembling lips.

"I have no means of knowing. I should think *not*, for the girl betrays no consciousness of it in her manner. Listen, Arthur," added Madam, impressively laying her hand on his arm. "It is unfortunate that you are subjected to be in the same house with her; but I cannot, you perceive, send her from it. All you have to do is to avoid her; never allow yourself to speak to her; never be for a moment alone with her. You will be safe then."

"Yes, it will be the only plan," he mechanically answered, as he quitted Madam, and went on his way.

Meanwhile Ellen Adair little thought what cruelty was in store for her. Shocked though she had been the first moment by Arthur Bohun's apparent non-recognition, it was so improbable a rudeness for *him* to be capable of, in his almost ultra-native courteousness, even to a stranger, that she soon decided he had purposely not greeted her until they should be alone, or else had really not recognized her.

In crossing the Hall an hour later, Ellen met him face to face. He was coming out of Mr. North's parlour as she was passing it. No one was about; they were quite alone.

"Arthur," she softly said, smiling at him and putting out her hand.

He went red and white, and hot and cold. He lifted his hat, which he happened to be wearing, having come straight in through the glass doors, and politely murmured some words that sounded like "I beg your pardon, Miss Adair:" but he did not attempt to touch her offered hand. And then he turned short round, and traversed the room back to the garden, putting on his hat again.

It seemed to her as though she had received her death-blow. There could no longer be any doubt or misapprehension after this, as to what the future was to be. Every drop of blood in her body seemed to rush to her heart and set it beating; the feeling was one akin to terror. Ellen Adair crept into the

drawing-room, empty then, and leaned her aching brow against
the window frame.

Presently Matilda North entered. The young lady had her
ins and outs of curiosity the same as her mother, and fancied
some great sight was to be seen. She increased her speed.

"What are you looking at, Miss Adair?"

"Nothing," answered Ellen, lifting her head. And in
truth she had not been looking out at all.

"Ah! I see," significantly spoke Miss North.

Walking slowly side by side along a distant path, went
Captain Bohun and Miss Dallory. Matilda, acting on a hint
from Madam, would not let slip the opportunity.

"Captain Bohun is losing no time, is he?"

"In what way?" enquired Ellen.

"Don't you know that they are engaged? He is to marry
Miss Dallory. We had all kinds of love passages, I asure
you, when he was ill at my uncle's, and she was there
helping me to nurse him."

It was a wicked and gratuitous lie: there had been no
"love passages," or semblance of them. But Ellen believed
it.

"Do you say they are engaged?" she murmured.

"Of course they are. It will be a love match too, for he is
very fond of her—and she of him, I think Richard was once
a little bit *gone* in that quarter; but Arthur has put him out.
Sir Nash is so pleased at Arthur's choice; and mamma is
delighted. They are both very fond of Mary Dallory."

And that all-but completed ceremony only a few weeks back
in the Church at Eastsea!—and the ring and licence she held
in store still!—and the deep, deep love they had owned to each
other, and vowed to maintain for ever—what did it all mean?
Ellen Adair, asked the question of herself in her agony. And
as her heart returned the common-sense answer—fickleness:
faithlessness—she felt as if a great sea of fire were scorching
away hope and peace and happiness. The iron had entered
into her soul.

CHAPTER XXXV.

IN THE HOUSE TOGETHER.

It was a curious position, that of some of the present inmates
of Dallory Hall. Sir Nash Bohun, who went down to
accompany Arthur more than anything else, and who had

not intended to remain above a day or two, stayed on. The quiet life after the bustle of London was grateful to him; the sweet country air really seemed to possess some of the salubrious properties Madam had ascribed to it. He liked to sit amidst Mr. North's flower beds—that is to say, where the flowers had been, for it was getting too near winter for many to be seen now. He liked to watch the falling of the leaves from the dying trees; dying until the early spring should come round and renew their vitality. Sir Nash was about to go abroad a long, long way when that genial spring-time should set in, and try the effect of some medicinal waters, that bear the reputation of renewing failing strength. Until then, he was grateful for any change, any society that served to pass the time.

Sir Nash had been as much struck with the exceeding beauty of Ellen Adair as strangers mostly were. That she was a very sweet girl, one of those who seem made to be specially loved, he could but see. In the bustle of their first arrival, he had not noticed her: there were so many besides her to be greeted; and Miss Dallory amidst them, whose appearance was entirely unexpected and consequently a surprise. Not until they were assembling for dinner, did Sir Nash observe her. His eyes suddenly rested on a most beautiful girl in a simple black silk evening dress, its low body and sleeves edged with white tulle, and a black necklace on her pretty neck. He was wondering who she was, when he heard Richard North speak of her as Ellen Adair. Sir Nash drew Arthur Bohun to the far end of the drawing-room, ostensibly to look at one of Turner's pictures.

"Arthur, who *is* she? It cannot be *his* daughter! Adair's?"

"Yes, sir, it is."

"Mercy be good to her!" cried Sir Nash in his compassionate dismay. "What an awful calamity! She looks entirely charming in herself; fit to mate with a prince of the blood-royal."

"And she is so."

"To have been born to a blighted name; an inheritance of ignominy!" continued Sir Nash. "Poor thing! poor thing! Does she know about it?"

"No, I am sure she does not," replied Arthur warmly, his tone one of intense pain. "She believes her father to be as honourable and good as you are."

For the very fact of Ellen's having put out her hand to him in the hall with that bright and confiding smile, had convinced Arthur Bohun that at present she knew nothing.

It made his own position all the worse : for, to her, his behaviour must appear simply infamous. Yet, how tell her ? —what excuse make ? Here they were, located in the same house ; and yet they could only be to each other as formal strangers. An explanation was due to Ellen Adair ; but from the very nature of the subject, he could not give it. If he had possessed the slightest notion that she was putting it down to a wrong cause—to an engagement with Miss Dallory—he would at least have set that right. But who was likely to tell him ? No one. Madam and Matilda, be you very sure, would not : still less Ellen herself. And so the complication would, and must, go on ; just as unhappy complications do sometimes go on. But there is this much to be said—that the setting straight the only point that might have been set straight, would not have made any difference to the breach between the two who had been hopelessly separated.

And Sir Nash Bohun never once brought himself to enter on any sort of intercourse with Ellen Adair. He would not have chosen, had he known it beforehand, to take up his sojourn under the same roof with one whose father had played so fatal a part with his long-ago-dead brother : it had been contrived by circumstances. In herself the young lady was so unobjectionable—nay, so deserving of respect and homage —that Sir Nash was won out of his projected coldness ; and he would smile pleasantly upon her when paying the slight, unavoidable courtesies of every-day life. But he never lingered near her, he never entered on prolonged conversation : a bow or two, and good morning and good-night, comprised their acquaintanceship. He got to pity her ; almost to love her ; and he relieved his feelings at least once a day in private by sending sundry unorthodox epithets after the man, William Adair, for blighting the name held by this fair and sweet young lady.

It was not a very sociable party, take it on the whole. Sir Nash had a sitting-room assigned him, and stayed much in it : his grief for his son was not over, and perhaps never would be. Mr. North was often shut up in his parlour, or walking with bent head amid the garden paths. Madam kept greatly aloof, nobody knew where ; Matilda was buried in her novels, French and English, or chattering somewhere above to Madam's French maid. Richard was at the works all day. Ellen Adair, feeling herself a kind of interloper, stayed in her chamber, or went to remote parts of the garden and sat there in solitude. As to Arthur Bohun, he was an invalid still, weak and ill, and would often not be seen until luncheon or dinner-time. There was a general meeting at meals, and a sociable evening after it.

Madam had not allowed matters to take their course without a prompting word from herself. On the day after Sir Nash and Arthur arrived, she came, all smiles and suavity, knocking at the door of Ellen's chamber. She found that young lady weeping bitter tears—who stammered out, as she wiped them away and strove for composure, some excuse about feeling so greatly the sudden death of Mrs. Cumberland. Madam was gracious, considerate; as she could be when she pleased: she poured some scent on her own white handkerchief, and held it to Miss Adair's nose. Ellen thanked her and gave it back again, and smoothed her hair back with her hand, and dried her tears, and rose up out of the emotion as a thing of the past.

"I am sorry it should have happened that Sir Nash chose this time to come," spoke Madam; "you might just now have preferred to be alone with us. Captain Bohun is still so very unwell that Sir Nash says he could but bring him."

"Yes," mechanically replied Ellen, really not knowing what part it was she assented to.

"And Arthur—of course he was anxious to come; he knew Mary Dallory would be back," went on Madam, with candour, like a woman without guile. "We are all delighted at the prospect of his marrying her. Before he was heir to the baronetcy it of course did not so much matter how he married, provided it were a gentlewoman of family fit to consort with the Bohuns. But now that he has come into the succession through poor James's death, things have changed. Did you know that Sir Nash has cut off the entail?" abruptly broke off Madam.

Ellen thought she did. The fact was, Arthur had told Mrs. Cumberland of it at Eastsea: but Ellen did not understand much about entails, so the matter had passed from her mind.

"The cutting off the entail has placed Arthur entirely in his uncle's hands," continued Madam. "If Arthur were to offend him, Sir Nash might not leave him a ten-shilling piece.

It is fortunate for all of us that Mary Dallory is so charming : Sir Nash is almost as fond of her as is Arthur.   And she is a great heiress, you know : she must have at the very least three or four thousand a year.   Some people say it's more ; the minority of the Dallory children was so long."

" It is a great deal," murmured Ellen.

" Yes.   But it will be very acceptable.   I'm sure, by the way affairs seem to be going on with Mr. North and Richard, it looks as though Arthur would have us all on his hands.   It has been a *great* happiness to us, his choosing Miss Dallory for his wife.   I don't believe he thought much of her before his illness.   She was staying with us in town during that time, and so—and so the love grew, and Arthur made up his mind.   He had the good sense to see the responsibility that James Bohun's death left on him, to make a suitable and proper choice."

Ellen had learnt a lesson lately in self-control, and maintained her calmness now.   She did not know Madam (except by reputation) quite as well as some people did, and was taken-in to believe she spoke in all sincerity.   One thing she could not decide—whether Madam had known of the projected marriage at Eastsea, or not.   She felt inclined to fancy that she had not, and Ellen hoped it with all her whole heart. Madam lingered on yet to say a few more words.   She drew an affecting picture of the solace, the joy, the consolation this projected union of her son with Mary Dallory brought to her, his mother ; and—as if she were addressing an imaginary audience in the ceiling—turned up her eyes and clasped her hands, and declared she must put it to the honour and good feeling of the world in general never to attempt anything by word or deed that might tend to mar this blessed state of things.   With that she kissed Ellen Adair, and said, now that she had apologised for their not being quite alone at the Hall and explained how it happened that Sir Nash came, she would leave her to dress.

As the days went on, something happened to intensify the state of affairs—or, at least, to strengthen Ellen's view of them—Mary Dallory came on a visit to the Hall.   Her brother Francis went away from home to join a shooting party, and Madam seized upon the occasion to invite his sister. She came, seemingly nothing loth ; and with her a great trunkful of paraphernalia. Matilda North had once said, when calling Mary Dallory a flirt, that she'd come fast enough to

Y

the Hall when Richard and Arthur were there. Any way, she came now. After this, Arthur Bohun would be more downstairs than he was before; and he and she would be often together in the grounds; sitting on benches under the evergreens or strolling along the walks side by side. Sometimes Arthur would take her arm with an invalid's privilege; his limp at the present time was more perceptible than it ever had been: and sometimes she would take his. They seemed to be always talking, their heads close together after the manner of those who hold confidential intercourse. Ellen Adair would watch them through this window, through that window, and press her trembling fingers on her aching heart. She saw it all: or thought she did. Arthur Bohun had found that his future prospects in life, his heirship in fact, depended upon his wedding Miss Dallory, or some one equally eligible; and so he had resolved to forget the sweet romance of the past, and embrace reality.

She thought he might have spoken to her. So much was certainly due to her; to her who had all but been made his wife. His present treatment of her was simply despicable; next door to wicked. Better that he had explained only as Madam did: what was there to hinder his telling her the truth? He might have said to her, ever so briefly: "Such and such things have arisen, and my former plans are frustrated, and I cannot help myself." But no; all he did was to avoid her: he never sought to touch her hand; his eyes never met hers if he could guard against it. It was exactly as though he had grown to despise her, and sought to show it. *Had* he? When Ellen's fears suggested the question—and it was in her mind pretty often now—she would turn sick with despair, and wish to die.

The truth was this. Arthur Bohun's fears lest he should betray his still ardent love, caused him to be more studiously cold to Ellen than he need have been. A strange yearning would come over him to clasp her to his heart and sob out his grief and tenderness: and the very fear lest he might really do this some day, lest passion and nature should become too strong for prudence and conventionality, made him shun her and seem to behave, as Ellen thought it, despicably. He knew it himself: he called himself far more despicable than Ellen could call him: a coward, a knave, a miserably-dishonoured man. And so, that's the way things went on at Dallory Hall: and were likely to go on.

One afternoon, a few days after Mrs. Cumberland was interred, Ellen went out to see her grave. Madam, Miss Dallory, Matilda, and Sir Nash had gone out driving : Arthur had been away somewhere since the morning, Mr. North was over the celery-bed with his head gardener. There was only Ellen : she was alone and lonely, and she put her black things on and walked through Dallory to the churchyard. It happened that she met three or four people she knew ; and she stayed to talk with them. Mrs. Gass was one ; the widow of Henry Hepburn was another. But she got on at last, feeling a little shy at being seen abroad alone : in walking so far as Dallory Mrs. Cumberland had always caused a servant to attend her.

The grave had been made not far from Bessy Rane's. Ellen had no difficulty in distinguishing the one from the other, though as yet there was not a stone to mark either. Mrs. Cumberland's was near that of the late Thomas Gass ; Bessy's was close to Edmund North's. A great winter tree, an evergreen, overshadowed this corner of the churchyard, and she sat down on the bench that went round its trunk. Bessy's grave was almost at her feet ; two yards, or so, away.

She leaned her face on her hand, and was still. The past, the present, the future ; Mrs. Cumberland, Bessy Rane, Edmund North ; her own bitter trouble, and other things— all seemed to be struggling together tumultuously in her brain. But, as she sat on, the tumult cleared itself a little, and she lost herself in imaginative thoughts of that heaven where pain and care shall be no more. Could they see her ? Could Mrs. Cumberland look down and see her, Ellen Adair, sitting there in her sorrow ? A fanciful idea came to her that perhaps the dead were the guardian angels appointed to watch the living : to be " in charge over them, to keep them in all their ways." If so, why then who was watching *her* ?—it must be her own mother, Mary Adair. Could these guardian angels pray for them ?—intercede with the mighty God and the Saviour that their sins here might be blotted out ? How long Ellen gave to these thoughts she never knew : but she wound up with crying softly to herself, and she wondered how long it would be before she joined them all in heaven.

Somebody, approaching from the back of the tree, came round with a slow step and sat down on the bench. It was a gentleman in black, she could see that much, though he was nearly on the other side of the tree's trunk, and so had his back to her. Ellen found she had not been observed, and prepared to leave. It had grown dusk in the twilight of the dull evening. As she stooped to pick up her handkerchief, which had fallen, the gentleman turned and saw her. Saw as well the tears on her face. It was Captain Bohun.

He got up quicker than he had sat down, intending no doubt to move away. But in his haste he dropped his stick —a great thick stick that he used for support in walking since his illness—and it fell across Ellen's feet. She stooped in some confused impulse to pick it up, and so did he.

"Thank you—I beg your pardon," he said, with an air of self-humiliation so great that it might have wrung a tender heart to see. And then he felt that he could not for very shame go off without some notice, as he had been thinking to do. Though why he stayed to speak and what he said, it might have puzzled him at the moment to tell. Instinct, more than reason, prompted the words.

"She was taken off very suddenly."

Standing close, though he was, to Bessy's grave, Ellen thought he looked across at Mrs. Cumberland's. And the latter had been latest in her thoughts.

"Yes. I feared we should not get her home. And I feel sure that the journey was fatal to her: that, if she had remained still, she would not have died quite so soon."

"It was of Bessy I spoke."

"Oh —— I thought you meant Mrs. Cumberland. Mrs. Cumberland's death has made so much difference to me, that —— that —— I suppose my mind runs on her. This is the first time I have been here."

Both of them were agitated to pain : both could fain have pressed their hearts tightly to still the frightful beating there.

"Ellen, I should like to say a word to you," he suddenly exclaimed, turning his face to her for a moment, and then turning it aside again. "I am aware that nothing can excuse the deep shame of my conduct in not having attempted any explanation. To you I cannot attempt it. I should have given it to Mrs. Cumberland if she had not died."

Ellen made no answer. Her handkerchief lay in her hand, and she looked down upon it.

"The subject was so intensely painful and—and awkward —that at first I did not think I could have mentioned it even to Mrs. Cumberland. Then came my illness. After that, while I lay day after day, left to my own reflections, things began to present themselves to me in rather a different light; and I saw that to maintain my silence would be the most wretched shame of all. I resolved to disclose everything to Mrs. Cumberland, and leave her to repeat it to you if she thought fit—at least, as much of it as would give you the clue to the cause of my strange and apparently unjustifiable conduct."

Ellen's fingers were pulling at the hem of her handkerchief, this way and that. She did not speak.

"Mrs. Cumberland's death, I say, prevented this," continued Captain Bohun, who had gathered somewhat of courage now the matter was opened, and stood fully turned to her, leaning both hands on his stick : "and I have felt since in a frightful dilemma, from which I see no escape. To you I cannot enter on an explanation : nor yet am I able to tell you why I cannot. The subject is altogether so very painful——"

Ellen lifted her head suddenly to speak. Every drop of blood had deserted her face, leaving it of an ashy whiteness. The movement caused him to pause.

"I know what it is," she managed to say from between her white and trembling lips.

"You—know it?"

"Yes. All."

Alas for the misapprehensions of this world. *He* was thinking only of the strange disclosure made to him concerning Mr. Adair; *she* only of his engagement to Miss Dallory. At her avowal all kinds of thoughts came surging through his brain. All! She knew it *all!*

"Have you known it long?" he questioned in a low tone.

"The time may be counted by days."

He jumped to the conclusion that Mrs. Cumberland had disclosed it to her on her death-bed. And Ellen's knowledge of it bettered his position just a little. But, looking at her, at her pale sweet face and downcast eyes, at the anguish pervading every line of her countenance, and which she could not hide, Arthur Bohun's heart was filled to overflowing with a strange pity, that seemed to wring it to breaking. He drew nearer to her.

"Thank God that you understand, Ellen—that at least you do not think me the shameless scoundrel I must otherwise have appeared," he whispered, his voice trembling with its deep emotion. "I cannot help myself : you must see that I cannot, as you know all. The blow nearly killed me. My

fate—our fate, if I may dare still so far to couple your name
with mine—is a very bitter one."

Ellen had begun to shiver inwardly. Something in his
words grated terribly on her ear : and pride enabled her to
keep down outward emotion.

"You left the ring and license with me," she abruptly said,
in perhaps an access of bitterness of temper. "What am I
to do with them ? "

"Burn them—destroy them," he fiercely replied. "They
are worthless to us now."

But he so spoke only in his anguish. Ellen interpreted it
differently.

"God help us both, Ellen! A cruel, wicked fate has
parted us for this world : but we may be permitted to be
together in the next. It is all my hope now."

Should she be able to keep down the emotion and the bitter
grief ? It was shaking and trying her.

"Heaven bless you and take care of you, Ellen! Our
paths in life must lie apart, but I pray always that yours may
be a happy one."

Without further word, without touching her hand, thus he
went. Limping on to the broad path, and thence down it
towards the gate of the churchyard.

There are moments into which a whole lifetime of agony
seems to be compressed. Such a one was this for Ellen Adair.
Dusk was coming on now rapidly, but she sat on, her head
bent low on her hands. They were, then, separated for ever ;
there was no further hope for her !—he himself had confirmed
it. She wondered whether the pain would kill her ; whether
she should be able to battle with it, or must die of the
humiliation it brought. The pain and the humiliation were
strong and sharp now—now as she sat. By-and-by there
stole again into her mind those thoughts which Captain
Bohun's appearance had interrupted—the heavenly place of
rest to which Bessy and Mrs. Cumberland had passed. Insensibly it soothed her : and imagination went roving away
unchecked. She seemed to see the white robes of the Redeemed ; she saw the golden harps in their hands, and the
soft sweet light around them, and the love and peace. The
thoughts served to show her how poor and worthless, as compared with the joys of that Better Land, were the trials and
pains of this world : how short a moment, even at the longest,
they had to be endured : how quickly and surely all here

must pass away! Yes, she might endure with patience for the time! And when she lifted her head, it was to break into a flood of violent and yet soothing tears, that she could not have shed before.

"Father in Heaven, Thou seest all my trouble and my agony. I have no one in the world to turn to for shelter—and the blast is strong. Vouchsafe to guide and cover me!"

But it was close upon night. With a wet handkerchief and eyes still streaming, she rose to make her way out of the churchyard. In a sheltered nook that she passed, sat a man: and Ellen started a little, and quickened her pace. It was Captain Bohun. Instead of going away, he had turned back to wait. She understood it at once: at that hour he would not leave her alone in the grave-yard. He wished to be chivalrous to her still, for all his barefaced faithlessness. In the very teeth of his avowed desertion of her, his words and manner had proved that he loved her yet. Loved *her*, and not another. It brought its own comfort to Ellen Adair. Of course it ought not, but it did: for the human heart at best is frail and faulty.

Captain Bohun followed her out of the churchyard, and kept her in sight all the way home, every fibre of feeling he possessed aching for her. He had seen the signs and traces of her fit of weeping; he knew what must be the amount of her anguish. He might have been ready to shoot himself could it have restored peace to her; he felt that he should very much like to shoot Mr. Adair, whose bad deeds had entailed this misery upon them.

At the Hall gates he was overtaken by Richard, striding home in haste to dinner. Richard, passing his arm through Arthur's, began telling him that he feared he was going to have some sharpish trouble with his ex-workmen.

And as they, the once fond lovers, sat together afterwards at table, and in the lighted drawing-room, Arthur as far from her, according to custom, as he could get, none present suspected, or could suspect, the scene that had taken place in the churchyard. Ellen Adair's eyes looked heavy; but that was nothing unusual now. It was known that she grieved for Mrs. Cumberland.

CHAPTER XXXVI.

JELLY'S TWO EVENING VISITS.

JELLY—to whom we are obliged to refer rather frequently, as she holds some important threads of the story in her hands—found times went very hard with her. A death within the house in addition to the death close without it, were almost more than Jelly could well do with in her present state of mind. The very peculiar and startling circumstances that had characterized Mrs. Rane's demise did not attend Mrs Cumberland's: but it had been very sudden at last, and Jelly was sincerely attached to her mistress.

Dr. Rane was left sole executor to his mother's will. It was a very simple one: she bequeathed him all she had. That was not much; for a portion of her income died with her. He found that he had two hundred a year—as he had known all along he should have—and her household furniture. Of ready money there was little. When he should have discharged trifling claims and paid the funeral expenses, some twenty or thirty pounds would remain over, and that was all.

Dr. Rane acted promptly. He discharged two of the servants, Ann and Dinah, retaining Jelly for the present to look after the house. He wished, if he could, to get the furniture taken-to with the house, for he knew how ruinous in general is a sale to the pocket; so he advertised it in the local papers. He had been advertising his practice—I think this has been said previously—but nothing satisfactory had come of it. Inquiries had been made, but they all dropped through. Perhaps Dr. Rane was too honest to say his practice was worth much, or to conceal the fact that Mr. Seeley had the best of it in Dallory. Neither was the tontine money as yet paid over; and, putting out of consideration all other business, the doctor must have waited for that.

Now, of all things that could have happened, Jelly most disliked and dreaded the being left to herself in the house. From having been as physically bold as a woman can be, she had latterly become one of the most timid. She started at her own shadow; she would not for the world have gone alone at night into the room where Mrs. Cumberland died. A shivering kind of fear lay on her constantly. Having seen one ghost, Jelly could not feel sure that she should not see two. Some people hold a theory that there is given to a very few persons in this world—and not to others—the faculty, or gift, or whatever you may please to call it, of discerning supernatural sights and things pertaining to the other world. Jelly had heard this: and she took up the notion that for some wise purpose she had been suddenly endowed with it. To stay in the house alone was more than her brain would bear; and she seized upon Ketler's eldest girl, a starved damsel of thirteen, called at home "Riah," to come and be with her. As it was a mouth less to feed, and they had tried to get Riah a place in vain—for the failure of trade affected all classes, and less servants seemed to be wanted everywhere—Ketler and his wife were very glad to let her go.

How do rumours get about? Can anybody tell? How did a certain rumour get about and begin to be whispered in Dallory? Certainly no one there could have told. Jelly could have been upon her Bible oath if necessary (or thought she could) that she had not sent it floating. It was a very ugly one, whoever had done it.

Late one afternoon Jelly received a call from Mrs. Gass's smart housemaid. The girl brought a letter from her mistress; Mrs. Gass wanted very particularly to see Jelly, and had sent to say that Jelly was to go there as soon as she could. Jelly made no sort of objection. She had been confined to the house much more closely of late than she approved of: partly because Dr. Rane had charged her to be in the way in case people called to look over it: partly because she had found out that Miss Riah had a tendency to walk off, herself, if she could get Jelly's back turned.

"Now, mind you sit still in the kitchen and attend to the fire, and listen to the door; and perhaps I'll bring you home a pair of strings for that bonnet of yourn," said Jelly to the girl, when she was ready to start. "The doctor will be in by-and-by, so don't you attempt to get out of the way."

With these injunctions, Jelly began her walk. She had on her best new mourning—a merino gown of fine texture and fringed shawl of the same—and was in a complaisant mood. It looked inclined to rain—the weather had been uncertain of late—but Jelly had her umbrella: a silk one that had belonged to her mistress, and that Dr. Rane had given, with many other things, to Jelly. She rather wondered what Mrs. Gass wanted with her, but supposed it was to tell her of a situation. It had been arranged that if an eligible one offered, Jelly should

be at liberty to go, and a woman be placed in the house to take
care of it. Mrs. Gass had said she would let Jelly know if she
heard of anything desirable. So away|went Jelly with a fleet
foot, little thinking what there was in store for her at her
walk's end.

Mrs. Gass, wearing mourning also, was in her usual sitting-
room, the dining-parlour. As Jelly entered, the smart maid
was carrying out the tea-tray. Mrs. Gass stirred up her fire,
and bade Jelly to a chair near it, drawing her own pretty close
to her.

"Just see whether that girl have shut the door fast afore I
begin," suggested Mrs. Gass.   "It won't do to have ears
a-listening to me."

Jelly went, saw the door was closed, came back and sat
down again. She noticed that Mrs. Gass looked keenly in her
face, as if studying it before speaking.

"Jelly, what is it that you have been a-saying about Dr
Rane?"

The question was so unexpected that Jelly did not immediately answer it.   Quite a change, this, from an offer of a
nice place.

"I've said nothing," she replied.

"Now don't you repeat that to me. You have. And it
would have been a'most as well for you that you had cut your
tongue out afore doing it."

"I said—what I did—to you, Mrs. Gass.   To nobody else."

"Look here, girl—the mischief's done, and you'd a great
deal better be looking it full in the face than denying of it.
There's reports getting up about Dr. Rane, in regard to his
wife's death, and no mortal woman or man can have set 'em
afloat but *you*. This morning I was in North Inlet, looking a
bit after them scamps of workmen that won't work, and won't
let others work if they can help it: and after I had gave a
taste of my mind to as many of 'em as was standing about, I
stepped in to Mother Green's. She has the rheumatics—and
he has got a touch of 'em. Talking with her of one thing and
another, we got on to the subject of Dr. Rane and the tontine;
and she said two or three words that frightened me; that
frightened me, Jelly; for they pointed to the suspicion that the
doctor had sacrificed his wife to get it. I pretended to understand nothing—she didn't speak out broad enough for me to
take it up and answer her—and it was the best plan *not* to
understand ——"

"For an old woman, Mother Green has got the longest tongue I know," interrupted Jelly.

"You've got a longer," retorted Mrs. Gass. "Just wait till I've finished, girl. 'Twas a tolerable fine morning, and after that I went walking on, and struck off down by the Wheatsheaf. Packerton's wife was a-standing at the door with cherry ribbons in her cap, and I stopped to talk to her. *She* brought up Dr. Rane; and lowered her voice as she did it as if it was high treason; asking me if I'd heard what was being said about his wife's not having died a natural death. I did give it the woman; and I think I frightened her. She acknowledged that she only spoke from a hint dropped by Timothy Wilks, and said she had thought at the time it couldn't have anything in it. But what *I* have got to say to you is this," continued Mrs. Gass to Jelly more emphatically, "whether it's Tim Wilks that's spreading the report, or whether it's Mother Green, they've both got it in the first place from you."

Jelly sat in discomfort. She did not like this. It is nothing to be charged with a fault when you are wholly innocent; but when conscience says you are partly guilty it is another thing. Jelly was aware that one night at Mother Green's, taking supper with that old matron and Timothy, she had so far yielded to the seductions of social gossip as to forget her usual reticence; and had said rather more than she ought. Still, at the worst, it had been but a word or two: a hint, but not a specific charge.

"I may have let fall an incautious word there," confessed Jelly. "But it was nothing anybody can take hold of."

"Don't you make sure of that," reprimanded Mrs. Gass. "We are told in the sacred writings—which it's not well to mention in ordinary talk, and I'd only do it with reverence—of a grain of mustard seed, that's the least of all seeds when it's sown, and grows into the greatest tree. You remember Who it is says that, Jelly, so it's not for me to enlarge upon it. But I may say this much, girl, that that's an apt exemplification of gossip. You drop one word, or maybe only half a one, and it goes spreading out pretty nigh over the world."

"I'm sure, what with the weight and worry this dreadful secret has been on my mind, a'most driving me mad, the wonder is that I've been able to keep as silent as I have," put in Jelly, who was getting cross. Mrs. Gass resumed.

"If the thing is what you think it to be—a dreadful secret,

and it is brought to light through you, why I don't know that you'd get blamed—though there's many a one will say you might have spared yonr mistress's son and left it for others to charge him. But suppose it turns out to be no dreadful secret; suppose poor Bessy Rane died a natural death in the fever, what then?—where would you be?"

Jelly took off her black gloves as if they had grown suddenly tight for her hands. She said nothing.

"Look here, girl. My belief is that you've just set a brand on fire! one that won't be put out until it's burnt out. My firm belief also is, *that you be altogether mistaken.* I have thought the matter over with myself hour after hour; and, except at the first moment when you whispered it to me in the churchyard, and I own I was startled, I have never been able to bring my common sense to believe in it. Oliver Rane loved his wife too well to hurt a hair of her head."

"There was that anonymous letter," cried Jelly.

"Whatever hand he might have had in that anonymous letter—and nobody knows the truth on't whether he had or whether he hadn't—I don't believe he was the man to hurt a hair of his wife's head," repeated Mrs. Gass. "And for you to be spreading it about that he murdered her!"

"The circumstances all point to it," said Jelly.

"They don't."

"Why, Mrs. Gass, they do."

"Let's go over 'em, and see," said Mrs. Gass, who had a plain way of convincing people. "Let's begin at the beginning. Hear me tell 'em."

She went over the past minutely. Jelly listened, growing more uncomfortable with every moment. There was absolutely not one fact inconsistent with natural death. It is true the demise had been speedy, but the cause assigned for it, exhaustion, might have been the real one; and the hasty fastening down of the coffin was no doubt a simple measure of precaution, taken out of regard to the welfare of the living. No; as Mrs. Gass put it in her straightforward, sensible way, there was positively not a single fact that could be urged for supposing Mrs. Rane came to an untimely end. Jelly twirled her gloves, and twisted her hands, and grew hot—not with the fire.

"There was what I saw—the ghost," she said.

But Mrs. Gass ridiculed the ghost—that is, the idea of it—beyond every earthly thing. Jelly, however, would not give way there; and they had some sparring.

" Ghost, indeed ! and you come to this age ! It was the beer, girl; the beer."

" I hadn't had a drop of beer," protested Jelly, almost crying. "How was I to get beer at Ketler's ? They've got none for themselves. I had had nothing inside my lips but tea."

" Well ; beer or no beer, ghost or no ghost, it strikes me, Jelly, that you have done a pretty thing. This bad story is as sure to get wind now as them geraniums of mine will get air when I open the window to-morrow morning. You'll be called upon to substantiate your story; and when you can't— and I'm sure that you know that you can't—the law may have you up to answer for it. I once knew a man that rose a bad charge against another ; he was tried for it, and got seven years' transportation. You may come to the same."

A very agreeable prospect ! If Jelly's bonnet had not been on, her hair might have gone up on end with horror. There could be no doubt that it was she who had started the report ; and in this moment of repentance she sat really wishing she had first cut her foolish tongue out.

"Nothing can be done now," concluded Mrs. Gass. "There's just one chance for you—that the rumour may die away. If it will, let it; and take warning to be more cautious in future. The probability is that Mother Green and Tim Wilks have mentioned it to others besides me and Packerton's wife: if so, nothing will keep it under. You have been a great fool, Jelly."

Jelly went away in mortal fright. Mrs. Gass had laid the matter before her in its true light. Suspect as she might, *she had no proof;* and if questioned by authority could not have deduced one.

" Dr. Rane have been in here three times after you," was young Riah's salutation when Jelly got home.

" Dr. Rane has ?"

" And he said the last time you oughtn't to be away from the house so long with only me in it," added the damsel, who felt aggrieved, on her own score, at being left.

" Oh, did he ! " carelessly returned Jelly.

But she began considering *what* Dr. Rane could want. For her parting charge to Riah, that Dr. Rane was coming in, had been a slight invention of her own, meant to help keep that young person to her duty. Just as she had decided that it might have reference to this same report, which he might have heard, and Jelly was growing more and more ill at ease in consequence, he came in. She went to him in the dining-room.

"Jelly," said the doctor, "I think I have let the house."

"Have you, sir?" returned Jelly, blithely, in the agreeable revulsion of feeling. "I'm sure I am glad."

"But only for a short while," continued Dr. Rane. "Two ladies of Whitborough are seeking for temporary change of air, and will take it if it suits them. They are coming to-morrow to look at it."

"Very well, sir."

"They will occupy the house for a month certain, and perhaps continue in it longer. They pay liberally, and it will give me time to let it for a permanency. If you feel inclined to take service with them, I believe there'll be room."

"Who are they?" asked Jelly.

"Mrs. and Miss Beverage. Quakers."

She knew the name. Very respectable people; plenty of money.

"You'll show them over it to-morrow when they come: I may or may not be in the way at the time," concluded Dr. Rane.

Jelly attended him to the door. It was evident he had not heard the rumour that had reached Mrs. Gass; or, at least, did not connect Jelly with it. But how was he likely to hear it? The probability was, that all Dallory would be making a ball of it before it got near *him.*

Jelly could not eat her supper. She had taken too nauseous a dose of medicine at Mrs. Gass's to leave room for appetite. Neither did she get any sleep. Tossing and turning on her bed, lay she: the past doubt and the present dread troubling her brain until morning light.

But, when Jelly had thus tormented herself and regarded the matter in all its aspects, the result was, that she still believed her own version of the tale—namely, that Mrs. Rane had not come fairly by her death. True it was, that she had no proof to offer in corroboration: but she began wondering whether such proof might not be found. At any rate, she resolved to search for it. Not openly; not to make use of; but quietly and cautiously: to hold in her hand, as it were, in case of need. She could not tell how to look for this, or where to begin. No one had seen Mrs. Rane after death—except of course the undertakers. Jelly resolved to question them: perhaps something might be gleaned.

It was afternoon before the expected ladies came. Two nice-speaking women, dressed after the sober fashion of their sect. Mrs. Beverage, a widow, was sixty; her daughter nearly forty. They liked the house, and said they should take it; and they liked Jelly, and engaged her to stay as upper maid, intending to bring two servants of their own. After their departure, Jelly had to wait for Dr. Rane: it would not do for him to find only Riah again. He came in while Jelly was at tea. She told him the ladies wished to enter as soon as convenient; and the doctor said he would at once go over to see them at Whitborough.

This left Jelly free. It was getting late when she set forth on her expedition, and she startled at the hedge shadows as she went along. The mind is swayed by its thoughts present; and Jelly's were of all kinds of uncanny and unpleasant things. Jelly's disposition was not a secretive one, rather the contrary, and she hated to have to do with what might not be discussed in the broad light of day.

The commencement of her task was at any rate not difficult: she could enter the Hepburns' house without excuse or apology, knowing them sufficiently well for it. When they were young, Thomas Hepburn, his wife, and Jelly had all gone to the same day-school, and been companions. Walking through the shop without ceremony, save a nod to young Charley, who was minding it, Jelly turned into the little parlour: a narrow room with the fire-place in the corner surmounted by an old-fashioned high wainscot of wood, painted stone-colour. Thomas Hepburn, who seemed to be always ailing with something or other, had got a patch of inflammation on his left arm, and his wife was binding bruised lily leaves round it. Jelly, drawing near to look on, at once expressed her disapprobation of the treatment, saying the leaves would only "draw."

"I can't think how it should have come, or what it is," he observed. "I don't remember to have hurt it in any way."

Jelly took the seat on the other side the fire-place, and Mrs. Hepburn, a stout healthy woman, sat down to the small round table and began working by lamplight. Thomas Hepburn, nursing his arm, which pained him, led all unconsciously to the subject Jelly had come to speak upon. Saying that if his arm was not better in the morning, he should show it to Dr. Rane, he thence went on to express his sorrow that the doctor should talk of leaving Dallory, for they liked him so much both as a gentleman and a doctor.

'But after such a loss as he has experienced in his wife,

poor lady, no wonder the place is distasteful to him," went on Hepburn. And Jelly felt silently obliged for the words that helped her.

"Ah, that was a dreadful thing," she observed. "I shall never forget the morning I heard of it, and the shock it gave me."

"I'm sure I can never forget the night he came down here, and said she was dead," rejoined the undertaker. "It was like a blow. Although I was in a degree prepared for it, for the doctor had told me in the afternoon what a dangerous state she was in—and I didn't like his manner when he spoke: it seemed to say more than his words. I came home and told Martha here that I feared it was all over with Mrs. Rane. Poor Henry was lying dead at the same time."

"And the answer I made to Thomas was, that she'd get over it," said Mrs. Hepburn, looking up from her sewing at Jelly. "I thought she would: Bessy North was always hearty and healthy. You might have taken a lease of her life."

"We had shut up the shops for the night, though the men were at work still next door, when the doctor came," resumed Thomas Hepburn, as if he found some satisfaction in recalling the circumstances for Jelly's benefit. "It was past eleven o'clock: but we had to work late during that sad time; and Henry's illness and death seemed to make a difference of nearly as much as two hands to us. I was in the yard with the men when there came a knocking at the shop door: I went to open it, and there stood the doctor. 'Hepburn,' said he, 'my poor wife is gone.' Well, I did feel it."

Jelly gave a groan by way of expressing her sympathy. She was inwardly deliberating how she could best lead on to what she wanted to ask. But she never was at fault long.

"I have heard you express distaste against some of the things that go to make up your trade, Thomas Hepburn, but at least they give you the opportunity of taking last looks at people—which we don't get," began Jelly. "I'd have given I don't know how much out of my pocket to have had a farewell look at Mrs. Rane."

"That doesn't always bring pleasure to the feelings—or to the sight either," was the answer of the undertaker.

"Did you go to her?" asked Jelly.

"No. I sent the two men: Clark and Dobson. They took the coffin at once: the doctor had brought the measure."

" And they screwed her down at once," retorted Jelly, with
more expressive quickness than she had meant to use.

" Ay! It was best. We did it in some other cases that
died of the same."

" Did the men notice how she looked—whether there was
much change?" resumed Jelly, in a low tone. " Some faces
are very sweet and placid after death: so much so that one
can't help thinking they are happy. Was Mrs. Rane's?"

" The men didn't see her," said Hepburn.

" Not see her!"

" No. The doctor managed that they should not. It was
very kind of him. Dobson he'd had an awful dread all along
of catching the fever; and Clark was beginning to fear it a
little: Dr. Rane knew this, and said he'd not expose them to
the risk more than could be helped. The men carried the
coffin up to the ante-room, and he said he would manage to
do all the rest."

Jelly sat with open mouth and eyes staring. The undertaker put it down to surprise.

" Medical men are used to these things, Jelly. It comes as
natural to them as to us. Dr. Rane said to Clark that he
would call over Seeley if he found he wanted help. I don't
suppose he would want it: she was small and light, poor
young lady."

Jelly found her tongue. " Then they—Clark and Dobson
—never saw her at all!"

" Not at all. She was in the far room. The door was
close shut, and well covered besides with a sheet wet with
disinfecting fluid. There was no danger, Dr. Rane assured
them, so long as they did not go into the room where she
lay. The men came away wishing other people would
take these precautions; but then, you see, doctors understand things. He gave them each a glass of brandy-and-
water too."

" And—then—*nobody* saw her!" persisted Jelly, as if she
could not get over the fact.

" I daresay not," replied Thomas Hepburn.

" He must have hammered her down himself!" nearly
shrieked Jelly.

" He could do it as well as the men could. They left the
nails and hammer."

" Well—it—it—seems dreadful work for a man to have to
do for his wife," observed Jelly after a pause, staring over

Mr. Hepburn's head into vacancy, as if she were mentally watching the hammering.

"He did violence to his own feelings out of consideration for the men," said the undertaker. "And I must say it was very good of him. But, as I've observed, doctors know what's what, and how necessary it is to keep away from danger in perilous times."

"Did he manage the one of lead as well as the first? 'twould be heavy for him, wouldn't it?" continued Jelly in a hard kind of tone, which she found it utterly impossible to suppress. "And there was the third one to come, after that."

"I went and soldered down the lead myself. The men took up the last one and made all ready."

"Yes!" thought Jelly. "As soon as her poor dear face was safely nailed in, so that it couldn't tell tales, he might let anybody, that would, do the rest."

"Were you not afraid of the risk, Thomas Hepburn?" asked Jelly, somewhat tauntingly, for she despised the man for being so simply unsuspicious. "Soldering takes up some time don't it?"

"The rooms had been well disinfected then, the doctor said. We took no harm."

That Thomas Hepburn held the most perfect faith in Dr. Rane, and never had discerned cause for the smallest suspicion of unfair play, was self-evident. Jelly, in her superior knowledge, in her wrath altogether, could have shaken him for it. In his place she felt mentally sure she should not have been so obtuse. Jelly forgot that it was only that knowledge of hers that enabled her to see what others did not: and that while matters, looked at from Hepburn's point of view, were all right; looked at from hers, with a clue in her head, they were all wrong.

"Well I must be wishing you good evening, I suppose," she said. "I've left only that Riah in the house—and she's of no mortal good to anybody, except for company. With people dying about one like this, one gets to feel dull, all alone."

"So one does," answered the undertaker. "Don't go yet."

Jelly had not risen. She sat looking at the fire, evidently in deep thought. Presently she turned her keen eyes on the man.

"Thomas Hepburn, did you ever see a ghost?"

He took the question as calmly and seriously as though she had said, Did you ever see a funeral. And shook his head slightly in dissent.

"I can't say I ever saw one myself. I've known those that have. That is, that say and believe they have. And I'm sure I've no reason to say they've not. One hears curious tales now and then."

"They are not pleasant things to see," remarked Jelly a little dreamily.

"Well, no; I daresay not."

"For my part, I don't put faith in ghosts," said hearty Mrs. Hepburn, looking up with a laugh. "None will ever come near me, I'll answer for it. I've too many children about me, and too much work to do, for pastime of that sort. Ghosts come from nothing but nervous fancies."

Jelly could not contradict this in the positive manner she would have liked, so it was best to say nothing. She finally got up to go—that Riah would be falling asleep with her hair in the candle.

And in spite of the prospective attractions of a supper of toasted cheese and ale, which she was pressed to stay and partake of, Jelly departed. Things had become as sure and clear to her as daylight.

"I don't so much care now if it does come out," she said to herself as she hastened along. "What Thomas Hepburn can tell as good as proves the doctor's guilt. I knew it was so. And I wish that old Dame Gass had been smothered before she sent me in to that doubt and fright last night!"

But the road seemed frightfully lonely now; and Jelly literally sprang aside from every shadow.

CHAPTER XXXVII.

MISCHIEF BREWING IN NORTH INLET.

MORNING, noon, and night, whenever the small body of new workmen had to pass to and from the works, they were accompanied by the two policemen specially engaged for their protection, while others hovered within call. North Inlet, the ill-feeling of its old inhabitants increasing day by day, had become a dangerous place to walk in. It was not that all the men would have done violence. Ketler, for instance, and others, like him, well-disposed men by nature, sensible and quiet, would not have lifted a hand against those who had, in one sense of the word, displaced them. But they did this: they stood tamely by to look on, knowing quite well that some of their comrades only waited for their opportunity to kill, or disable—as might be—Richard North's new followers. North Inlet was not quite so full as it used to be: for some of the old inhabitants, weary and out of patience with hope deferred (hope they hardly knew of what, unless for the good time of plenty and equalization promised by the Trades' Union), had gone away on the tramp, with their wives and little ones, seeking for a corner of the earth where work might be found, enough to bring in a crust to eat and a roof to shelter them. Others had decamped without their wives and children: and were in consequence being hunted for by the parish. North Inlet, take it on the whole, was in a sore plight. The men and women, reduced (most of them) by want and despair to apply to the parish for relief, found none accorded them in answer. They had brought themselves to this pass; they had refused to work when work in plenty was to be had; and to come and ask to be supported in idleness by the parish was a procedure not to be tolerated; as one resolute guardian, sitting at the head of a table, fiercely told them. Not as much as a loaf of bread would they get, added another, taking up the song. If it came to the pass that they were in danger of dying of hunger (as the applicants urged), why they must come into the house with their wives and families— and a humilating shame that would be for able-bodied men, the guardian added—but they would receive no relief out of doors. So North Inlet, not choosing to go into that unpopular refuge for the destitute, stayed out of it. And a fine plight its natives were in!

There was absolutely nothing left to pledge. Except children. And the pawnbroker, Ducket, could not be persuaded to take in them. Ducket had scarcely done so well by the strike as he had privately anticipated. He had not quite bargained for homes being offered to him wholesale; for a glut of goods; and the goods were mostly of that insignificant, if useful character, that does not make a noise in the market. When nearly all the community are seeking to sell, it is clear that few can be wanting to buy.

An ignominious picture Ducket's interior premises presented. He was so over-laden that the collection had to hang in sight as well as out of it. A motly crowd. Strangers might have taken it for no better than a rag-and-bone shop, or a travelling tinker's caravan come to a standstill. Gowns (out at gathers and slit at cuffs), petticoats, hats, bonnets, shoes, boots, coats, waistcoats, beds, books, saucepans, gridirons, tables, chairs, frying-pans, birdcages, sheets, blankets, Italian and flat irons, Dutch ovens, tea-kettles, brooms, umbrellas, candlesticks, mops, and a model of a ship under a glass-case. That's only a few items of the list that would meet the eye on paying a visit to Mr. Ducket's: it was too comprehensive and varied for any recollection to record. The ship had belonged to Ketler, one made and given him by his brother, who was mate of a vessel trading to Ceylon.

Now, with all these articles, once beloved household gods, staring them in the face whenever they passed Ducket's; with ragged backs and empty stomachs, with the past life of plenty to look back upon (and thirst perpetually for, after the manner of the fabled Tantalus), and no prospect whatever to look forward to, there was little wonder that this misguided body of men grew to find out that something of the old Satan was in them yet. A great deal of it, too. Perhaps remorse held its full share. They had intended it to have been so entirely for the better when they threw up work; and it had turned out so surprisingly for the worse. They had meant to return to work on their own terms; earning more and toiling less: they had been led to believe that this result lay in their proper hands, and was as sure and safe as that the sun is overhead at noonday. Instead of that—here they were, in as deplorable a condition as human beings can well be. Time had been, not very long ago either, that the false step might have been redeemed; Richard North had offered them their places again and on the old terms. Ay, and he had once conceded a portion of their demands—as they remembered well. But that time and that offer had gone by for ever. Fresh men (few though they were) worked in their places, and they themselves were starving.

The feeling against these new men was bitter enough; it was far more bitter against the small number of old workmen who had gone back again. We are told that the heart of man is deceitful and desperately wicked: our own experience shows us that it is desperately selfish. They saw the employed men doing the work which was once theirs; they saw them with good strong coats on, and food to eat. They themselves had neither coats nor food: and the work they had rejected. It

wonld not have seemed so hard had the work lain altogether
in abeyance, or taken itself off from the place entirely: but to
see these others doing it and living in comfort was more than
mortal temper conld brook.   Only to watch the workmen
going home regularly to their meals while they had no meals
to go to, was dreadful.

This was not all.   The men, seeing some things in the
external world with a jaundice eye—yellow as ever was poor
Arthur Bohun's when he had the actual disease—held to it
that the fact of these others having taken work again, was the
cause that kept themselves out of it.   Richard North 'ud ha'
come-to they said, but for these curs what had went sneaking
back again to lick his hand.   They called them worse names
than that, but there's no need of repetition.   If all on us had
held out, Dick North must ha' give in.   And this they repeated so constantly, in their ire, one to another, that at last
they got actually to believe it.   It was quite wrong, and they
were wholly mistaken: for had Richard North not begun
again in the cautious way he did, and at the old rate of wages
and time, he would not have recommenced at all: but the
men refused to see this, and held to their notion, making it
into a worse grievance than the lack of food.   It is so convenient to have something substantial on which to vent blame:
and unlimited power and permission to punch the obnoxious
heads would have afforded intense gratification.   Oh, it was
very hard to bear.   To see this small knot of men re-estab-
lished in work, and to know that it was their own work once,
and might have been theirs still!   Peeping through hedges,
hiding within door-ways, standing sulkily or derisively in the
open ground, they would watch the employed men going to
and fro, the two policemen tramping by their side.   Many a
bitter word, many a crushed oath, many a silent threat was
levelled at the small band.   Murder had been done from a
state of mind not half as bad as they cherished.

"What be you a-looking at, with them evil signs on your
faces?"

A gronp of malcontents, gazing out from a corner of North
Inlet at the daily procession, fonnd this question suddenly
sounding on their ears.   Mrs. Gass had stepped out of a
dwelling close by, and put it.   Their eyes were following the
escorted line of men coming home to their twelve o'clock
dinner, so that she had not been observed.

They turned to her, and their faces dropped the threaten-

ing expression. A man named Poole, not too well respected
at the most prosperous of times, and one of the worst
malcontents since, took upon himself to answer. Boldly
too.

"We was a-taking the measure o' that small lot o' convics.
A-wishing we could brand 'em."

"Ah," said Mrs. Gass. "It strikes me some of you have
been wishing it before to-day. I'd like to give you a bit of
advice, my men; and you, especially, Poole. Take care you
don't become convicts yourselves."

"For two pins, I'd do what 'ud make me one; I'd do it
to-day if others 'ud back me up," was the rejoinder of Poole,
who was in a more defiant mood than even he usually dared
to show. He was a big, thick-set man, with shaggy light
hair and a complexion of brick-dust. His clothes, originally
fustian, had been worn and torn and jagged and patched and
darned, until now they hardly held together : his clumsy shoes
let in the water and the toes peeped out.

"You are a nice jail-bird, Poole! I don't think you ever
were much better than one," added Mrs. Gass. To which
candid avowal Poole only replied with a growl.

"These hard times be enough to make jail-birds of all of
us," interposed another—Foster ; but speaking with civility.
"Why don't the Government come down and interfere, and
prevent our work being took out of our hands by these
branded rascals ?"

"You put the work out of your own hands," said Mrs.
Gass. "As to interference, I should have thought you'd had
about enough of that, by this time. If you had not suffered
them blessed Trades' Unionists to interfere with you, my men,
you'd have been in full work now, happy and contented as
the day's long."

"What we did, we did for the best."

"What you did, you did in defiance of common sense, and
of the best counsels of your best friends," she said. "How
many times did your master show you what the upshot would
be if you persisted in throwing away your work ?—how much
breath did I waste over you, as I'm a-doing now, asking you
all to avoid a strike—and after the strike had come, day after
day begging of you to end it ?—could any picture be truer
than mine was when I said what you'd bring yourselves to ?
—rags, and famine, and desolate homes. Could any plight be
worse than this pickle that you've dropped to now ?"

" No, it couldn't," answered Foster. " It's so bad that I say Government ought to interfere for us."

' If I was Government, I should interfere on one point—and that's with them agitating Unionists," bravely spoke Mrs. Gass. " I should put *them* down a bit."

" This is a free country, ma'am," struck in Ketler, who made one of the group.

" Well, I'd used to think it was, Ketler," she said; " but old ways seem to be turned upside down. What sort of freedom do you enjoy just now ?— how much have you had of it since you bound yourselves sworn members of the Trades' Unions ? You have wanted to work and they've not let you : you'd like to be clothed and fed as you used to be and to clothe and feed your folks at home, and they deny your exercising the means by which you may do it. What freedom or liberty is there in that ?—Come, now, Ketler, tell me as a reasonable man."

" If the Trades' Unions could do as they wish, there'd be work and comfort for all of us."

" I doubt that, Ketler."

" But they can't do it," added Ketler. " The masters be obstinate and won't let 'em."

" That's just it," said Mrs. Gass. " If the Trades' Unions held the world in their hands, and there was no such things as masters and capital, why then they might secure their own way. But the masters have their own interests to look after, their businesses and what's embarked in 'em to defend : and the two sides are totally opposed one to another, and all that comes of it, or that will come of it is squabbling. You lose your work, the masters lose their trade, the Unionists fight it out fiercer than ever—and, between it all, the commerce of the country is coming to an end. Now, my men, that is the bare truth ; and you can't deny it if you try till midnight."

" 'Twouldn't be no longer much of a free country, if the Government put down the Trades' Unions," spoke a man satirically ; one Cattleton.

" But it ought to put down this arbitrary way they've got of preventing others working that want to work," maintained Mrs. Gass. " The Unionists be your worst enemies. I'm speaking, as you know I have been all along, of the head among 'em that make laws for the rest ; not of poor sheep like you that have joined the society in innocence. If them heads like to live without work themselves, and can point out a way by which others can live without it, well and good; there's no law against that, nor oughtn't to be: but what I say Government ought to put down is this—their forcing you men to reject work when it's offered you. It's a sin and a shame that, through them, the country should be brought to imbecility, and you, its once free and brave workmen, to beggary."

"The thought has come over me at times that under the new state of things we are no better than slaves," confessed Ketler, his eyes wearing an excited look.

Mrs. Gass nearly executed a triumphant dance. " Now you've just said it, Ketler. Slaves. That's exactly what you are ; and I wish to my heart all the workmen in England could open their eyes to it. You took a vow to obey the dictates of the Trades' Union; it has bound you hand and foot, body and soul. If a job of work lay to your hand, you dare not take it up, the Union masters saying you shall not; no, not though you saw your little ones dying with famine before your eyes. It's the worse kind of slavery that ever fell on the land. Press-gangs used to be bad enough, but this beats 'em hollow."

There was no reply from any one of the men. Mrs. Gass had been a good friend to their families even recently ; and the old habits of respect to her, their mistress, had sway still. Perhaps some of them, too, silently assented to her reasoning.

" It's that much, the coercive interference, that I'd have put down," she resumed. " Let every workman be free to act on his own judgment, to take work or to leave it. Not but what it's too late to say it : as far as I believe, the mischief has gone too far to be remedied."

" It be mighty fine for the masters to cry out and say the Trades' Unions is our enemies ! Suppose we choose to call 'em our friends ? "

The words came from Poole. He had been lounging against the wall in sulky defiance, smoking and spitting by turns, and sending the puffs of smoke into Mrs. Gass's bonnet : at any rate, taking no care that they did not get there. She did not mind smoke, however ; and she wore only her old black chip to-day, with its crape flowers.

" Put it at that, Poole, if you like," said she equably. " The society's your good friend, let's say. How has it showed its friendship ? what has it done for you ? "

Mr. Poole did not condescend to say.

"It's not so hard to answer, Poole. The proofs lie on the surface—there's not one of the lot of you but may read 'em off-hand. It threw you all out of your good place of work that you had held for years under a good master, that you might have held, the chances were, up to the last day of your lives. It dismantled your homes and sent your things to the pawn-shop—you may go and look at 'em now, ornamenting the walls and hooks at Ducket's. It has reduced you to a mouldy crust, where you'd used to have good joints of fat beef; it has took your warm shoes and coats away, and sends you abroad half-naked. Your children are starving, some of them dead; your wives are worn out with trouble and discontent. And this not for a temporary time but for good: for, there's no prospect for you. No prospect, that I can see, as I am a living woman. That's what your friends, as you call 'em, have done for you; and for thousands and thousands beside you. I don't care what they meant: let it be that they meant well by you, and that you meant well—as I'm sure you did—in listening to 'em: the result is what I've said. And you are standing here this day, ruined men."

Mr. Poole puffed fiercely.

"What is to become of you, and of the others ruined like you, the Lord in Heaven only knows. It's a solemn question. When the best trade of the country's driven from it, there's no longer a place for workmen. Emigration, suggests some of the newspapers. Others say emigration's over-done for the present. We don't know what to believe. Any way, it's a hard thing that a good workman should find no employment in his native land, but must be packed off from it, something like as if he was transported, to be a exile for ever."

Poole, not liking the picture, broke into a furious oath or two. The other men looked sad enough.

"You have been drinking, Poole," said Mrs. Gass with dignity. "Keep a civil tongue in your mouth before me if you please."

"I've not had no more nor half a pint," growled Poole.

"And that was half a pint too much," said Mrs. Gass. "When people's insides are reduced by famine, half a pint is enough to upset their brains in a morning."

"What business have Richard North to go and engage them frogs o' Frenchmen?" demanded Poole—who had in truth taken too much for his good. "What business have them other ratted fellows, as ought to have stuck by us, to

go back to him? It's Richard North as wants to bo
transported."

"Richard North was a good master to you. Tho world
never saw a better."

"He's a rank bad man now."

"No, no—drat th' tongue!" put in Ketler to Poole. "No
good to abuse *him*."

"If you men had had a spark of gratitude, you'd have
listened to Mr. Richard North, when he prayed you to go
back to him," said Mrs. Gass. "No, you wouldn't; and
what has it done for him? Why just ruined him, my men:
a'most as bare as you be ruined. It have took his hopes from
him; it have wasted his money, what little he had; it have
played the very dickens with his prospects. The business
he had before never will and never can come back. If once
you split a mirror to pieces, you can't put it together again.
Mr. Richard has got a life of work to look forward to; he
may get a living, but he won't do much more. You men
have at least the satisfaction of knowing that while you did
for your own prosperity, you did also for his."

They had talked so long—for there has been no space to
record all that passed—that it was hard upon one o'clock, and
the small band of workmen and the two policemen were
coming past again, back towards the works. The malignant
look rose on Poole's face: a savage growl stuck in his
throat.

"There'll be mischief yet," thought Mrs. Gass, as she
turned away.

Sounds of a woman's sobbing were proceeding from an
open door as she went down North Inlet, and Mrs. Gass
stepped in to see what might be the matter. They came from
Dawson's wife. Dawson had been beating her. The unhappy
state to which they were reduced tried the tempers of the
men—of the women also, for that m tter—rendering some of
them little better than ferocious beasts. In the old days,
when Dawson could keep himself and family in plenty, never
a cross word had been heard from him: but all that was
changed: and under the new order of things, it often came to
blows. The wife had now been struck in the eye. Smarting
under that, under ills of body and ills of mind, the woman
enlarged on her wrongs to Mrs. Gass, and showed the mark;
all of which at another time she would certainly have concealed. The home was miserably bare; the children, was

and thin, were in tatters like their mother; it was a comprehensive picture of wretchedness.

"And all through them idiots having throwed up their
work at the dictates of the Trades' Union!" was the wrathful
comment of Mrs. Gass, as she departed. "They've done for
themselves in this world : and, to judge by the unchristian
lives they be living, seem to be going on for the chance of
doing for theirselves in the next."

As she reached her own house, the smart housemaid was
showing Miss Dallory out of it. That young lady, making a
call on Mrs. Gass, had waited for her a short while, and was
going away. They now went in together. Mrs. Gass,
throwing open the door of her handsome drawing-room, began
recounting at full the events of the morning; what she had
heard, what seen.

"There'll be mischief done as sure as a gun," she concluded.
"My belief is, that some of 'em would kill Mr. Richard if they
got the chance."

Mary Dallory looked startled. "Kill *him!*" she cried.
"Why, he has been their good friend always. He would have
been so still, had they only let him."

"He's a better friend to 'em still than they know of," said
Mrs. Gass, nodding her head. "Miss Mary, if ever there was
a Christian man on earth, it is Richard North. His whole
life has been one long thought for others. Who has kept up
Dallory Hall but him? Who would have worked and slaved
on, and on, not for benefit to himself, but to maintain his
father's home, finding money cheerfully for Madam's wicked
extravagance, to save his poor father pain, knowing that the
old man had already more than he could bear. At Mr.
Richard's age he ought, before this, to have been making a
home for himself and marrying: it's what he would have done
under happier circumstances : but he has not been able ; he
has sacrificed himself for others. He has done more for the
men than they think of ; ay, even at the time that they were
bringing ruin upon him—as they have done—and since.
Richard North is worth his weight in gold. Heaven, that sees
all, knows he is; and he will sometime surely be rewarded for
it. It may not be in this world, my dear ; for a great many
of God's own best people go down to their very graves in
nothing but disappointment and sorrow : but he'll find it in
the next."

Never a word answered Mary Dallory. It might almost

have been thought from her silence she did not subscribe to
the sentiments. All she said was, that she must go. And
Mrs. Gass went with her to the front door, talking. They had
nearly reached it, when Miss Dallory stopped to put a question,
lowering her voice as she did so.

"Have you heard any rumour about Dr. Rane?"

Mrs. Gass knew what must be meant as certainly as though
it had been spoken. She turned cold, and hot, and cold
again. For once her ready tongue failed her.

"It is something very dreadful," continued Miss Dallory.
"I do not like to speak it out. It—it has frightened me."

"Lawk, my dear, don't you pay no attention to such rubbish
as rumours," returned Mrs. Gass heartily. "*I* don't. Folks
says all sorts of things of me, I make little doubt; just as they
be ready to do of other people. Let 'em! We sha'n't sleep
none the worse for it. Good-bye. I wish you'd have stayed
to take a mouthful of my dinner. It's as lovely a turkey-
poult as ever you saw, and a jam dumpling."

CHAPTER XXXVIII.

DAYS OF PAIN.

PACING the shrubbery walk at Dallory Hall, a warm grey
woollen shawl wrapped closely round her, clipping the narrow
crape tucks of her flowing black silk dress; and her pale, sweet,
sad face turned up to the lowering sky, was Ellen Adair. The
weather, cold and dull, gave tokens of coming winter. The
last scattered leaves left on the nearly bare trees fell fluttering
to the earth; the wind, sighing through the branches, had a
melancholy sound. All things seemed to speak of decay.

This ungenial cold had brought some complication with it.
Just as Sir Nash Bohun was about to quit Dallory Hall,
taking Arthur with him, the bleak wind struck him in an
unguarded moment, and laid him up with inflammation of the
chest. Sir Nash took to his bed. One of the results was,
that Arthur Bohun must remain at the Hall, and knew not
how long he might have to be a fixture there. Sir Nash
would not part with him. He had taken to regard him quite
as his son.

Ellen Adair thought Fate was very cruel to her, taking one
thing with another. And so it was. While they were together,
she could not begin to forget him: and, to see him so con-

tinually with Mary Dallory, brought to her the keenest pain. She was but human : jealousy swayed her just as it does other people.

Another thing was beginning to trouble her—she did not hear from Mr. Adair. It was very strange. Never a letter had come from him since that one containing the permission to wed Arthur Bohun (as Mrs. Cumberland had read it), received at Eastsea. Ellen could not understand the silence. Her father used to write so regularly.

"He ought not to remain here," she murmured passionately as she walked, alluding to Arthur Bohun. "*I* cannot help myself; I have nowhere else to go : but he ought to go in spite of Sir Nash."

A greyer tinge seemed to float over and settle in the sky. The shrubbery seemed to grow darker. It was but the first advent of dusk, coming on early that melancholy evening.

"Will there ever be any brightness in my life again ?" she continued, clasping her hands in pain. "Is this misery to last for ever ? Did anyone, I wonder, ever go through such a trial and live ? Scarcely. I am afraid I am not very strong to bear things. But oh—who could bear it ? Last night I dreamt that Arthur came smiling to me, and said, 'I have only been playing with you, Ellen: how could you think it was anything else ?'—and in the strange tumult of joy that rushed over me, I awoke. For a few minutes after when remembrance rushed over me, I thought I should have died with the pain. If I could but have remained in the dream for ever ! "

She sat down on one of the benches, and bent her aching brow on her hands. What with the gloom around, and her dark dress, some one who had turned into the walk, came sauntering on without observing her. Arthur Bohun. He started when she raised her head : his face was every whit as pale and sad as hers; but he could not help seeing how ill and woe-begone she looked.

"I fear you are not well," he stopped to say.

"Oh—thank you—not very," was the confused answer.

"This is a trying time. Heaven knows I would save you from it if I could. I would have died to spare you. I would die still if by that means things for you could be righted. But it may not be. Time alone must be the healer."

He had said this in rather a hard tone, as if he were angry with somebody or other ; perhaps Fate ; and went on his way with a quicker step, leaving never a touch of the hand, never a loving word, never a tender look behind him; just as it had been that day in Dallory Churchyard. Poor girl! her heart felt as though it were breaking there and then.

When the echo of his footsteps had died away, she drew her shawl closer round her slender throat and passed out of the shrubbery. Hovering in a cross walk, unseen and unsuspected, was Madam. Not often did Madam allow herself to be off the watch. She had scanned the exit of Captain Bohun; she now saw Ellen's; and Madam's evil spirit rose up within her, and she advanced with an awful frown.

"Have you been walking with Captain Bohun, Miss Adair?"

"No, Madam."

"I—*thought*—I heard him talking with you."

"He came through the shrubbery when I was sitting there, and spoke to me in passing."

"Ah," said Madam. "It is well to be cautious. Captain Bohun is to marry Miss Dallory, remember: the less any other young woman has to say to him, the better."

To this speech—rather remarkable as coming from one who professed to be a gentlewoman—Ellen made no reply, save a bow as she passed onwards, with an erect head and self-possessed step, leaving Madam to her devices.

They seemed to be at her on all sides. There was no comfort anywhere, no solace. Ellen could have envied Bessy Rane in her grave.

And the farce that had to be kept up before the world! That very evening, as fate had it, Captain Bohun took Miss Adair in to dinner and sat next her, through some well intentioned blundering of Richard's. It had pleased Madam to invite a party; some seven or eight; it did not please Mr. North to come in to dinner as he had been expected to do. Richard had to be host, and to take in a stout lady in green velvet, who was to have fallen to his father. There was a minute's confusion; Madam had gone on; Richard jumbled the wrong people together as if he were shaking up beans in a bag; and finally said aloud, "Arthur, will you take in Miss Adair?" And so they sat, side by side, and nobody observed that they did not converse (for that consisted of perhaps three monosyllables throughout the meal) or that anything was wrong. It is curious the length of time that two people may have lived estranged from each other in a household, and the rest suspect it not. Have you ever noticed this?—or tried it? It is remarkable, but very true.

After dinner came the drawing-room; and the evening was a more social one than had been known of late. Music, cards, talking. Young Mr. Ticknell (a relative of the old banker's at Whitborough) was there: he had one of the sweetest voices ever accorded to man, and delighted them with his unaffected singing. One song, that he chose after a few jesting words with Ellen, in allusion to her name, two of them at least had not bargained for. "Ellen Adair." Neither had heard it since that evening at Eastsea; so long past now, in the events that had followed, that it seemed to be removed from them by ages.

They had to listen. They could not do else. Ellen sat at the corner of the sofa in her pretty black net dress with its one white flower, that Mr. North had given her, in the middle of the corsage, and nothing at all, as usual, in her smooth brown hair; *he* was leaning against the wall, at right angles with her, his arms folded. And the verses went on to the last one.

> " But now thou art cold to me,
> 　　　　　Ellen Adair:
> But now thou art cold to me,
> 　　　　　Ellen my dear
> Yet her I loved so well,
> Still in my heart shall dwell,
> Oh! I shall ne'er forget
> 　　　　　Ellen Adair."

She could not help it. Had it been to save her life, she could not have helped lifting her face and glancing at him as the refrain died away. His eyes were fixed on her, a wistful, yearning expression in their depths; an expression so sad that in itself it was all that can be conceived of pain. Ellen dropped her face again; her agitation at that moment seeming greater than she knew how to suppress. Lifting her hand to shade her eyes, the plain gold ring, still worn on it, was conspicuously visible.

"You look as though you had all the cares of the nation on your shoulders, Arthur."

He started at the address: which came from Miss Dallory. She had gone close up to him. Rallying his senses, he smiled and answered carelessly. The next minute Ellen saw them walking across the room together, her hand within his arm.

The morning following this, Jelly made her appearance at the Hall, bringing up two letters. They were from Australia, from Mr. Adair. One was addressed to Mrs. Cumberland, the other to Ellen. Dr. Rane had bade Jelly bring them both : he considered that Miss Adair was now the only proper person to open Mrs. Cumberland's. Ellen carried it to Mr. North, asking if she ought to open it—if it would be right. Certainly, Mr. North answered, and confirmed the view Dr. Rane had taken, as conveyed in the message brought by Jelly.

Ellen carried the two letters to a remote and solitary spot in the garden, one that she was fond of frequenting, and in which she had never yet been intruded upon. She opened her own first : and there read what astonished her.

It appeared that after the despatch of Mr. Adair's last letter to Mrs. Cumberland (the one already alluded to, that she had read with so much satisfaction to Arthur Bohun at Eastsea), he had been called from his station on business, and had remained absent some two or three months. Upon his return he found other letters awaiting him from Mrs. Cumberland, and learnt, to his astonishment, that the gentleman proposing marriage to Ellen was Arthur Bohun, son of the Major Bohun with whom Mr. Adair had once been intimate. (The reader has not forgotten how Mrs. Cumberland confused matters together in her mind, or that in her first letter she omitted to mention any name.) Dashing off some peremptory lines to Ellen—these that she was now reading—Mr. Adair retracted his former consent. He absolutely forbade her to marry, or ever think again of, Arthur Bohun : a marriage between them would be nothing less than a calamity for both, he wrote, and also for himself. He added that in consequence of some unexpected death in his family, he had become its head, and was making preparations to return to Europe.

Wondering, trembling, Ellen dropped the letter, and opened Mrs. Cumberland's. An enclosure fell from it : a draft for a large sum of money; which, as it appeared, Mrs. Cumberland was in the habit of receiving half-yearly for her charge of Ellen. Mr. Adair wrote in still more explicit terms on the subject of the proposed marriage to Mrs. Cumberland—almost in angry ones. *She*, of all people, he said, ought to know that a marriage between his daughter and the late Major Bohun's son would be unsuitable, improper, and most distasteful to himself. He did not understand how Mrs. Cumberland could have laid any such proposal before him,

A A

or allowed herself to think of it for a moment : unless indeed she had never been made acquainted with certain facts of the past, connected with himself and Major Bohun and Major Bohun's wife, which Cumberland had known well. He concluded by saying, as he had to Ellen, that he hoped shortly to be in England. Both the letters had evidently been written in great haste and much perturbation : all minor matters being accounted as nothing, compared with the distinct and stern embargo laid on the marriage.

"So it has happened for the best," murmured Ellen to her breaking heart, as she folded up the letters and hid them away.

She took the draft to Mr. North's parlour. He put on his spectacles, and mastered its meaning by the help of some questions to Ellen.

"A hundred and fifty pounds for six months ! " exclaimed he. "But surely, my dear, Mrs. Cumberland did not have three hundred a year with you ! It's a vast sum—just for one young lady."

"She had two hundred, I think," said Ellen. "I did not know what the exact sum was until to-day : Mrs. Cumberland never used to talk to me about these matters. Papa allows me for myself fifty pounds every half-year. Mrs. Cumberland always gave me that."

"Ah," said Mr. North. "That's a good deal, too."

"Will you please to take the draft, sir ; and let me have the fifty pounds from it at your convenience ? "

Mr. North looked up as one who does not understand.

"The money is not for me, child."

"But I am staying here," she said, deprecatingly.

He shook his head as he pushed back the slip of paper.

"Give it to Richard, my dear. He will know what to do about it, and what's right to be done. And so your father is coming home ! We shall be sorry to lose you, Ellen. I am getting to love you, child. It seems that you have come in the place of my poor lost Bessy."

But Ellen was not sorry. The arrival of Mr. Adair would at least remove her from her present position, where every hour, as it passed, could but bring fresh pain.

CHAPTER XXXIX.

MRS. GASS IN THE SUNSHINE.

A FINE and genial day in Dallory. As if the winter were minded to give place to a few hours' brightness before it finally set in, or to make scant amends for the late season of cold and wet and boisterous winds, there intervened a day of almost summer weather. Mrs. Gass threw open her window and sat behind the geraniums enjoying the sun, exchanging salutations and gossip with as many of her acquaintance amidst the passers-by whose time would allow them to stop for it.

"How d'ye do, doctor? Isn't this a lovely day?"

It was Dr. Rane, hurrying past. He turned for an instant to the window, his brow clearing. For some time now a curious look of care and perplexity had sat upon it.

"Indeed it is," he answered. "I hope it will last. Are you pretty well, Mrs. Gass?"

"I'm first-rate," said that lady. "A fine day, with the wind in the healthy north, always sets me up. I say, doctor, have you got the tontine money paid yet?"

"No," said Dr. Rane, his voice changing to a somewhat sullen tone. "There are all kinds of forms to be gone through, seemingly; and the Brothers Ticknell do not make themselves ill with haste. The two old men are past business, in my opinion. They were always slow and tiresome; it is something more than that now."

"Do you stir 'em well up?" questioned Mrs. Gass.

"When I get the chance of doing it; but that's very rare. Go when I will I can scarcely ever see anybody but the confidential clerk, old Latham; and he is as slow and methodical as his masters. 'We are not quite ready for you, sir; these matters must take their due course,' he says to me. I suppose the money will come, but I am tired of waiting for it."

"And what about your plans when you get it, doctor? Be they all cut and dried?"

"Time enough when I get the money to decide on them," said the doctor, shortly.

"But you still intend to leave Dallory Ham?"

"Oh, yes, I shall do that."

"You won't be going to that America place?"

"I think I shall. It is more than likely."

"Well, I'd not banish myself from my native country for the best medical practice that ever shoes dropped into. You might be getting Red Indians for patients."

Dr. Rane laughed a little; and there shone a kind of eager light in his eyes that seemed to speak of glad anticipation, of hope. Only himself knew how thankful he would be to get to another country and be clear of this.

"I wonder," soliloquised Mrs. Gass to herself, as he walked on his way, "whether it is all straight-for'ard about that tontine? Have the Ticknells heard any of these ugly rumours that's flying about; and be they keeping it back in consequence? If not, why it ought to have been paid over to him before this. The delay is odd—say the best of it. How d'ye do, sir? A nice day."

A gentleman, passing, had raised his hat to Mrs. Gass. She resumed her thread of thought.

"The rumours be spreading wider and getting nastier. They'll go up with a bang presently, like a bomb-shell. I'm hearty sorry for him; for I don't believe—no, I *don't*—that he'd do such a frightful thing. If it should turn out he did—why, then I shall blame myself ever after for having procrastinated of my intentions."

Mrs. Gass paused in thought, and began to tell over those intentions, with a view, possibly, to see whether she was very much to blame.

"Finding Oliver and his wife couldn't get the tontine paid 'em—and a hard case it was!—I had it in my mind to say to 'em, 'I'll advance it to you. You'll both be the better for something in my will when I'm gone—the doctor being my late husband's own nephew, and the nearest relation left of him—and if two thousand pound of it will be of real good to you now, you shall have it.' But I didn't say it at once—who was to suppose there was such mortal need for hurry—and then she died. If the man's innocent—and I believe he is—that Jelly ought to have the end of her tongue burnt off with caustic. She——halloa! Why, there you are! Talk of the dickens and he'll appear."

"Were you talking of me?" asked Jelly: for Mrs. Gass had raised her voice with the surprise and brought it within Jelly's hearing. She had a small basket on her arm, under her black shawl, and turned to the window with the question.

" I was a-thinking of you," responded Mrs. Gass. " Be you come out marketing ? "

" I'm taking a few scraps to Ketler's," replied Jelly, just showing the basket. " My mistress has given me general leave to give them any trifles not likely to be wanted at home. The cook's good-natured too. *This* is a jar of mutton-dripping, and some bones and scraps of bread."

" And how do you like the Beverages, Jelly ? "

" Oh, very well. They are good ladies ; but so serious and particular."

Mrs. Gass rose from her seat, pushed aside a corner of the stand of geraniums, and leaned her arms upon the window-sill, so as to bring her hearty red face nearly within Jelly's bonnet.

" I'll tell you what I was a-thinking of, girl : it was about these awful whispers that's flying round. Go where you will you may hear 'em. Let it be within a dwelling-house or at the corner of a street, people's tongues be a cackling secretly of Dr. Rane's wife, and asking what she died of. I knew it would be so, Jelly."

Jelly turned a trifle paler. " They'll die away again perhaps," she said.

" Perhaps," repeated Mrs. Gass, sarcastically. " It's to be hoped they will for your sake. Jelly, I'd not stand in your shoes to be made a queen to-morrow."

" I'd not stand in somebody else's," returned Jelly, aggravated to the avowal. " I shall have some pretty good proof at hand if I'm forced to bring it out."

" What proof ? "

" Well, I'd rather not say. You'd only ridicule it, Mrs. Gass, and blow me up into the bargain. I must be going."

" I guess it's moonshine, Jelly—like the ghost. Good-morning."

Jelly went away with a hard and anything but a happy look, and Mrs. Gass took her seat again. Very shortly there came creeping by, following the same direction as Jelly, a poor shivering woman, with a ragged shawl on her thin shoulders, and a white, pinched, hopeless face.

" Is that you, Susan Ketler ? "

Susan Ketler turned and dropped a curtsey. Some of the women of North Inlet were even worse off than she was. She did have help now and then from Jelly.

" Yes, ma'am, it's me."

"I say, how long do you think yon North Inlet people will be able to keep going—as things be at present?" demanded Mrs. Gass.

"The Lord above only knows," said the woman, looking upwards with a piteous shiver. "Here's the winter a-coming on."

"What does Ketler think of affairs now?"

Ketler's wife shook her head. The men were not fond of disclosing what they might think, unless it was to one another. Ketler never told her what *he* did.

"Is he still in love with the Trades' Unions, and what they've done for him? My opinion is this, Susan Ketler," continued Mrs. Gass, after a pause: "that in every place where distress reigns, as it does here, and where it can be proved that the men have lost their work through the dictates of the society, the parish ought to go upon the society and make it feed the men and their families. If a law was passed to that effect, we should hear less of the doings of the Trades' Union people than we do. They'd draw in a bit, Susan; they'd not give the gaping public quite so many of their procession-shows, and their flags, and their speeches. It would be a downright good law to make, mind you. A just one, too. If the society forbids men to work, and so takes the bread necessary for life out of their mouths, it is but fair they should find 'em bread to replace it."

A kind of hopeful look came into the woman's eyes. "Ma'am, I said as good as this to Ketler only yesterday. Seeing that it was the society that had took the bread from us, and that the consequences had been bad instead of good, for we were starving, the society ought to put us into work again. It might bestir itself to do that : or else support us while we got into something."

Mrs. Gass smiled pityingly. "You must be credulous, Susan Ketler, to fancy the society can put 'em into work again. Where's the work to come from? Well, it's not your fault, my poor woman, and there's more people than me sorry for you all. I say," Mrs. Gass lowered her voice, "be any of the men talking treason still? You know what I mean."

Susan Ketler glanced over both her shoulders to see that nobody was within hearing, before she gave the answering whisper.

"They be always a-talking it. I can see it in their faces as they stand together. Not Ketler, ma'am, he'd stop it if he could : he don't wish harm to none."

"Ah. I wish to goodness they'd all betake themselves off from the place. Though it's hard to say it, for there's no other open to 'em that I see. Well, you go on home, Susan. Fanny Jelly's just gone there with a basket of scraps. Stay a minute, though."

Mrs. Gass quitted the room, calling to one of her servants. When she came back she had a half-pint physic bottle corked up.

"It's a drop of beer," she said. "For yourself, mind, not for Ketler. You want it, I know. Put it under your shawl. It'll wash down Jelly's scraps."

The woman went along with a grateful sob. And Mrs. Gass sat on and enjoyed the sunshine. Just then Mary Dallory came by in her little low pony-carriage. She often drove about in it alone. Seeing Mrs. Gass, she pulled up. That lady, making no ceremony, went out in her cap and stood talking.

"I hear you have left the Hall, my dear," she said, when the gossip was coming to an end.

"Ages ago," replied Miss Dallory. "Frank is home again, and he wanted me."

"How did you enjoy your visit on the whole ? "

"Pretty well. It was not very lively, especially after Sir Nash was taken ill."

"He is better, Mr. Richard tells me," said the elder lady.

"Yes; he can sit up now. I went to see him yesterday."

"Captain Bohun looks but poorly still.

"His illness was a bad one. Fancy his getting jaundice ! I had thought it was only old people who got that."

"Them jaunders attacks young and old. Once the liver gets out of order, there's no telling. Captain Bohun was born in India; and they be more liable to liver complaint, it's said, than others. You are driving alone to-day as usual," continued Mrs. Gass.

"I like to be independent. Frank won't put himself into this little chaise; he says it is no higher than a respectable wheelbarrow; and I'm sure I am not going to have a groom stuck at my side."

"If all tales told are true, you'll soon run a chance of losing your independence," rejoined Mrs. Gass. "People say a certain young lady, not a hundred miles at this moment away from my elbow, is likely to give away her heart."

Instead of replying, Mary Dallory blushed violently. Observant Mrs. Gass saw and noticed it.

"Then it is true!" she exclaimed.

"What's true?" asked Mary.

"That you are likely to be married."

"No, it is not."

"My dear, you may as well tell me. You know me well - that I'll keep counsel."

"But I have nothing to tell you. How can I imagine what you mean?"

"'Twasn't more than a hint of it I had: that Captain Bohun —Sir Arthur as he will be—was making up his mind to Miss Dallory, and she to him. Miss Mary, is it so?"

"Did Madam tell you that?"

"Madam wouldn't be likely to tell me—all of us in Dallory are just as so much dust under her feet; quite beneath being spoken to. No: 'twas her maid, Parrit, dropped it to me. She had heard it through Madam though."

Mary Dallory laughed a little and flicked the ear of the rough Welsh pony. "I fancy Madam would like it," she said.

"Who wouldn't?" rejoined Mrs. Gass. "I put the question to Richard North—Whether there was anything in it? He answered that there might be; he knew that it was wished for."

"Richard North said that, did he—that it might be? Of course, so it might—and may—for aught he can tell."

"But my dear Miss Mary, is it?"

"Well—to tell you the truth, the offer's not made yet. When it comes, why then—I daresay it will be all right."

"Meaning that you'll take him."

"Meaning that—oh but it is not right to tell tales beforehand, even to you, Mrs. Gass," she broke off, with a sunny laugh. "Let the offer come. I wish it would."

"You would like it to come, child?"

"Yes, I think I should."

"Then be sure it will. And God bless you, my dear, and bring you happiness whatever turns out. Though it is not just the marriage I had carved out in my own mind for one of the two of you."

She meant for Arthur Bohun. Mary Dallory thought she meant herself; and laughed again as the pony trotted away.

The next friend that passed the window after Mrs. Gass resumed her seat, was Richard North. He did not stop at the window, but went in. Some matter of business connected with the winding up of the old firm of North and Gass, had arisen, rendering it necessary that he should see Mrs. Gass.

"Do as you think best, Mr. Richard," she said, after they had talked together for a few minutes. "Please yourself, sir, and you'll please me. We'll leave it at that: I know it's all safe in your hands."

"Then I will do as I propose," said Richard.

"I've had Miss Dallory here—that is, in her pony-chay afore the door," observed Mrs. Gass. "I taxed her with what I'd heard about her and Captain Bohun. She didn't say it was, and she didn't say it wasn't: but Mr. Richard, I think there's truth in it. She as good as said she'd like him to make her an offer: and she did say Madam wished it. So I suppose we shall have wedding cards afore a year's gone over our heads. In their case—him next step to a baronite, and she rolling in money—there's nothing to wait for."

"Nothing," mechanically answered Richard North.

"But I did think, as to him, that it would have been Ellen Adair. Talking of that, Mr. Richard, what is it that's amiss with her?"

"With her?—with whom?" cried Richard, starting out of a reverie.

"With that sweet young lady, Ellen Adair?"

"There's nothing amiss with her that I know of."

"Isn't there! There *is*, Mr. Richard, if my judgment and eyes is to be trusted. Each time I see her, she strikes me as looking worse and worse. You notice her, sir. Perhaps now the clue has been given you'll see it too. I once knew a little girl, Mr. Richard, that was dying quietly under her friends' very eyes, and they never saw it. Never saw it at all, till a aunt came over from another county; she started back when she saw the child and says, 'Why, what have you been doing with her? she's dying.' They was took aback at that, and called in the first doctor: but it was too late. I don't say Ellen Adair is dying, Mr. Richard; 'taint likely; but I'm sure she is not all right. Whether it's on the mind, or whether it's on the body, or whether it's on the nerves, I'm not prepared to say; but its somewhere."

"I will take notice," said Richard.

"Anything fresh up about the men, Mr. Richard?"

"Nothing. Except that my workmen are getting afraid to stir out at night, and the disaffection increases amidst the others. I cannot see what is to be the end of it," he continued. "I do not mean of this rivalry, but of the sad state to which the men and their families are reduced. I often wish I did not think of it so much: it is like a chain binding me that I cannot get loose from. I wish I could help them to get work elsewhere."

"Ah!" said Mrs. Gass, "work elsewhere is very nice to look at in dreamland; but I'm afraid it'll never be seen for 'em in reality. It's not as if work was going a-begging: it have been broke up everywhere, Mr. Richard; and shoals and shoals of men, destitute as our own, be tramping about at this minute, like so many old ravens with their mouths open, ready to pick up any that may fall."

Richard North went home, his mind full of what Mrs. Gass had said about Ellen Adair. *Was* she looking so ill? He found her sitting in the open seat near what would be in spring the tulip bed; Mr. North having just gone in and left her. Yes: Richard saw that she did look ill; the face was wan, the eyes were sad and weary. She was coughing as he went up to her: it was a short, hacking cough, not a violent one. Some time ago she had caught a cold, and it seemed to hang about her still.

"Are you well, Ellen?" he asked, as he sat down beside her.

"Yes, I believe so," was her reply. "Why?"

"Because I don't think you look well."

A soft colour, like the pink on a sea-shell, stole over her cheeks as Richard said this. But she kept silence.

"You know, Ellen, we agreed to be as brother and sister. I wish to take care of you as such: to shield you from all ill so far as I can. Are you happy here?"

A moment's pause, and then Ellen took courage to say that she was not happy.

"I would like to go elsewhere," she said. "Oh Richard, if it could but be managed!"

"But it cannot," he answered.

"I have plenty of money, Richard."

"My dear, it is not that. Of course you have plenty. I fancy, by sundry signs, that you will be a very rich young lady," he added, slightly laughing. "But you have no near friends in England, and we could not entrust you to strangers.

" If I could board somewhere?—in some clergyman's family, or something of that."

" Ellen ! "

She raised her hand from underneath the grey shawl—her favourite out-door covering, for the shawl was warm—and passed it across her brow. In every movement there was a languor that spoke of weariness of body or weariness of spirit.

" When Mr. Adair comes home, if he found you had been placed out somewhere 'to board,' what would he think and say of us? Put the question to yourself, Ellen."

" I would tell him I went of my own accord."

" But, my dear, you cannot be allowed to do things of your own accord if they are not expedient. I and my father are appointed to take charge of you, and see that you do not. You must remain with us, Ellen, until Mr. Adair shall come."

It was even so. Ellen's better judgment acknowledged it, in the midst of her great wish to get away. A wish : and not a wish. To be where Arthur Bohun was, brought her still the most intense happiness; and this, in spite of the pain surrounding it, she would not willingly have relinquished : but the cruelty of his conduct—of their estrangement—was more than she knew how to bear. It was making her ill, and she felt that it was. There was, however, no help for it. As Richard said, she had no friends to whom they could entrust her. The lady in whose house she was educated had recently died, and the establishment was being broken up.

Ten times a day she longed to say to Arthur Bohun, " You are ungenerous to stay here. I cannot help myself, but you might." But pride tied her tongue.

" It may be months yet before papa comes, Richard."

" And if it should be ! We must try to make you happier with us."

" I think I must go in," she said, after a pause of silence. " The day has been very fine, but it is getting cold now."

Folding the grey shawl closer to her throat, as if she felt the chill there, and coughing a little as she walked, Ellen crossed round to the hall door and entered. Richard, occupied in watching her and busy with his own thoughts, did not perceive the almost silent approach of Arthur Bohun, who came slowly up from behind.

" Well, Dick, old fellow ! "

" Why, where did you spring from ? " asked Richard, as Arthur flung himself down in the place vacated by Ellen.

"I have been under that tree yonder, smoking a cigar. It has a good broad trunk to lean against."

"I thought the doctors had forbidden you to smoke."

"So they have. Until I should get stronger. One can't obey orders quite strictly always. I don't suppose it matters much one way or the other. You have been enjoying a confidential chat, Dick."

"Yes," replied Richard. He had not felt very friendly in his heart towards Arthur for some time past. What was the meaning of his changed behaviour to Ellen Adair?—what of the new friendship with Mary Dallory? Richard North could not forgive dishonour; and he believed Arthur Bohun was steeping himself in it to the backbone.

"Were you making love, Dick?"

Richard turned his eyes in silence on the questioner.

"She and I have had to part, Dick. I always thought you admired and esteemed her almost more, perhaps quite more, than you do any other woman. So if you are thinking of her ——"

"Be silent," sternly interrupted Richard, rising in anger. "Are you a man?—are you a gentleman? Or are you what I have been thinking you lately—a false-hearted, despicable knave?"

Whatever Arthur Bohun might be, he was just then in desperate agitation. Rising, too, he seized Richard's hands.

"Don't you see that it was but sorry jesting, Richard? Pretending to a bit of pleasantry with myself, to wile away for a moment my awful weight of torment. I am all that you say of me; and I cannot help myself."

"Not help yourself?"

"As heaven is my witness, no! If I could take you into confidence—and perhaps I may one of these days, for I long to do it—you would see that I tell you truth."

"Why have you parted with Ellen Adair?—she and you *have* parted? You have just said so."

"We have parted for life. For ever."

"You were on the point of marriage with her but a short time back?"

"No two people can be much nearer marriage than she and I were. It was within half an hour of it, Dick; and yet we have parted."

"By your doings, or hers?"

"By mine."

" I thought so."

" Dick, I have been *compelled* to it. When you shall know all, you will acknowledge that I could not do otherwise. And yet, in spite of this—this compelling power—I feel that to her I have been but a false-hearted knave, as you aptly style me : a despicable, dishonourable man. My father fell into dishonour—or rather had it forced upon him by another—and he could not survive it ; he shot himself. Did you know it, Dick ?"

" Shot himself ! " repeated Richard in his surprise. " No, I never knew that. I thought he died of sunstroke."

" My father shot himself," wailed Arthur. " He could not live dishonoured. Dick, old fellow, there are moments when I feel tempted to do as he did."

" What—because you have parted with Ellen ? "

" No. That's bitter enough to bear ; but I can battle with it. It is the other thing, the dishonour. That is always present with me, always haunting me night and day ; I know not how to live under it."

" I do not understand at all," said Richard. "You are master of your own actions."

" In this case I have not been : my line of conduct was forced upon me. I cannot explain, Don't judge me too harshly, my friend. I am bad enough, heaven knows, but not quite as bad, perhaps, as you have been deeming me."

And, wringing the hands he held in a grasp of pain, Arthur Bohun went limping away, leaving Richard lost in wonder.

He limped away to indulge his pain where no mortal eye could be upon him. Parted from Ellen Adair, the whole world was to him as nothing. The sense of dishonour lay ever upon him, the shame of his conduct to her was present to him night and day. With all his heart he wished James Bohun had not died, that there might have been no question of his succession. He would then have gone somewhere away with her, change his name, be happy in obscurity. But there was no place unfrequented by man and tourists ; he could not hide his wife's face ; and she might be recognized as the daughter of Adair the convict. Besides, would it not be an offence against heaven if he wedded the daughter of the man who had caused the death of his father ? No ; happiness might not be his. Look where he would, there was nothing around him but a sea of pain.

CHAPTER XL.

ONCE AGAIN.

JELLY lived, so to stay, with her feet on a volcano. She felt that, figuratively speaking, there was not an hour of the day or night but she might be blown up. The rumours as to the death of Mrs. Rane were becoming more frightful; they stole up and down Dallory like an insinuating tongue of flame, and Jelly had the satisfaction of knowing that it was she who had first set the flame alight. It was all very well for her to say that she had made herself safe by securing the evidence Thomas Hepburn could give: but in her secret conscience she knew that she was *not* secure; and that, even in spite of that evidence, Dr. Rane might chance to be innocent. If so, why a pretty box she would find herself in. There was no help for it; she could do nothing. The flaming tongue went twisting itself in and out, and she could not still it.

One night Jelly was lying awake, according to custom now, buried deep in some horrid visions that had lately begun to haunt her: now of being chained to some other woman and working in a gang; now of stepping incessantly up a revolving treadmill; and now of picking oakum with her nails and teeth. Twisting round in the bed, to escape, if possible, these imaginary pictures, she suddenly heard her door knocked at. A loud hasty knock; and now a louder. Jelly went into a hot fume, and then turned cold as ice. Had the officers of the law come to arrest her?

"Who's there?—what is it?" she asked faintly, not daring to sit up in bed.

"Art thee awake, Jelly?" came the gentle response, as her door was opened a few inches. "I am very sorry to have to ask thee to get up, but my mother is worse. Make haste, please."

Had Miss Beverage's voice been that of an angel, it could not have seemed sweeter to Jelly just then. The relief was great.

"I'll get up instantly, ma'am," was the ready answer—and Miss Beverage wondered that it should have in it a tone of joyous gratitude. "I'll be with you at once."

Mrs. Beverage was subject to violent but rare attacks of dangerous spasms. She had felt ill before she went to bed, but hoped it would be nothing. Jelly and her own two servants were soon at her bedside. She was very ill. Some of them ran to get hot water ready; Jelly thought it would be well to call in Dr. Rane.

"I should like the doctor to see her; at the same time I grieve to arouse him from his sleep," said Miss Beverage.

"Law, ma'am, that's nothing to doctors; they are used to it," cried Jelly.

"Mother, would thee like Oliver Rane fetched?" asked Miss Beverage, bending over the suffering lady.

"Yes—yes," was the feeble answer. "I am very ill, Sarah."

"Thee go, then, Jelly."

Away went Jelly. Unbarring their own front door, she passed out of it, and approached Dr. Rane's. The doctor's professional lamp burnt clearly, and, to her great surprise, Jelly saw that the door was not closed.

"He cannot have gone to bed to-night," she thought, as she walked in without ringing. It was past three.

But the house seemed to be in stillness and darkness. Jelly left the front door open, and the light shone a little way into the passage. She tried the surgery door; it was locked outside; she tried the dining-room; the key of that was also turned; the kitchen door stood open, but it was all in darkness.

"He has gone to bed and forgot to shut up," was the conclusion Jelly now arrived at. "I'll go up and call him."

Groping her way upstairs, she had nearly reached the top, when a pale white light suddenly illumined the landing—just the same kind of faint semi-light that Jelly saw once before, and that she remembered all too well. Raising her head hastily to look, for it had been bent downwards, there stood —what?

Not quite at the moment did Jelly know what. Not in the first startled access of terror did she recognize clearly the features of Bessy Rane. It was she, all too surely: that is, the likeness of what she had been. She seemed to stand almost face to face with Jelly: Jelly nearly at the top of the staircase, she facing it before her. The light was even more faint in front of the figure than behind: but there was no mistaking it. What it was dressed in or whence it came, Jelly never knew: there it was—the form and the face of Bessy Rane. With an awful cry of agony, that echoed to the ends of the empty house in the night's silence, Jelly turned and flew down again.

She never looked behind. Out at the front door went she, banging it, in her terror, to keep in what might be following her; and she nearly gave vent to another scream when she found herself touched by someone coming in at the gate, and saw that it was Dr. Rane.

"I am called out to a country patient," he quietly said. "While I was putting the horse to the gig, an impression came over me that I had left my house door open, so I thought I had better come back and see. What are you doing here at this hour, Jelly? Anybody ill?"

Jelly was in frightful distress and confusion of mind. Clutching hold of his arm as if it gave her protection, she sobbed for an instant or two in hysterical nervousness. Dr. Rane stared at her, not knowing what to make of it. He began to think she must require his services herself.

"Sir—do you know—do you know who is in the house?"

"Nobody's there: unless they've got in these last few minutes through the door—which I suppose I did leave open," was Dr. Rane's rejoinder, and his calm composure contrasted strongly with Jelly's emotion. "When I go out of my house at night, I carry my household with me, Jelly."

"Your wife's there," she whispered with a bursting sob. "Sir, it is as true as that I am alive to tell it."

"What do you say?"

Jelly's answer was to relate what she had seen. When Dr. Rane had gathered in her full meaning, he turned very angry.

"Why you must be mad, woman," he cried in a low voice of concentrated passion. "This is the second time. How dare you invent such folly?"

"I swear that her ghost walks, and that it is in there now," exclaimed Jelly, nearly beside herself. "It is on the landing, exactly where I saw it before. Why should she come again? —why should she haunt that one particular spot? Sir, don't look at me like that. You know I would not invent such a thing."

"Your fancy invents it, and then you speak of it as if it were fact. How dare you?"

But he could not appease Jelly: he could not talk her out of the belief of her eyesight. And the doctor saw it was useless to try.

" Why, why should her poor ghost walk?" bewailed Jelly, wringing her hands in distress.

" I'm sure I don't know why it should walk," returned the doctor, as if he would humour Jelly and at the same time make a mockery of her words. " It never walks when I am in the house." But the ridicule was lost on Jelly.

" She can't lie quiet in her grave. What cause is there?— oh, what dreadful mystery is it?"

Dr. Rane looked as though he would have liked to knock Jelly down. "I begin to think that you are either a fool or a knave," he cried. " What brought you in my house at three o'clock in the morning?"

The question, together with his almost irrepressible rage, served to recal Jelly's scattered senses. She told about the illness of Mrs. Beverage, and asked if he would come in.

" No, I cannot come," said Dr. Rane quite savagely, for it seemed that he could not get over his anger. " I am called out to a case of sudden emergency, and have no time to waste over Mrs. Beverage. If she wants a doctor, get Seeley."

He opened his door with his latch-key, and shut it fiercely after him. However, it seemed that he got over his ill humour, for when Jelly was slowly walking across the road towards Mr. Seeley's, Dr. Rane came out again, called her back, and said he would spare a minute or two.

With a sharp caution to Jelly not to make the same foolish exhibition of herself to others that she had to him, he went up to Mrs. Beverage—who was then easier, and had dozed off to sleep. Giving a few general directions in case the paroxysm should return, Dr. Rane departed. About ten minutes afterwards, Jelly was in her room, which looked towards the lane at the back, when she heard his gig come driving down it and stop at his garden door. After waiting there a short while— he had probably come in for some case of instruments—it went away quickly across country.

The horse and gig that the doctor used belonged to the public-house hard by. Dr. Rane had a key of the stables, so that if he wanted to go out during the night, he could harness the horse to the gig without disturbing any one. When medical men are not able to keep horses and grooms of their own, they put up contentedly with many shifts that richer practitioners would not.

" If he had not said beforehand that he was putting the horse to, I should have thought he'd gone out because he

B B

daredn't stay in the house," muttered Jelly, as she flattened
her face against the window pane, to look after the doctor and
the gig. She could see neither; the night was very dark.

Jelly's mind was in a chaos. What she had witnessed
caused her still to shake and tremble as though she had the
ague; and she did fully believe that she was in danger of
becoming what the doctor had told her she was already—
mad.

Suddenly, there arose a cry in the house. Mrs. Beverage
was worse. The paroxysm had returned so violently that it
seemed to the frightened beholders as though she would die in
it. Dr. Rane was not attainable, and Miss Beverage sent one
of the under servants running for Mr. Seeley. Who came
promptly.

In about an hour the danger had passed; the house was
quiet again, and Mr. Seeley was at liberty to return to his
rest. He had crossed the road to his own door when he heard
a step following him. Turning round he saw Jelly.

"Surely she is not ill again!" he hastily exclaimed.

"No, sir, she is all right I think now. Mr. Seeley," added
Jelly in agitation so marked that he could not help noticing
it, "I want to speak to you: I want to tell you something. I
must tell somebody, or I shall never live till morning light."

"Are *you* ill?" questioned Mr. Seeley.

"When I was holding the flannels just now, and otherwise
helping you, sir, you might have seen that I hadn't all my
wits about me. Miss Beverage looked at me once or twice,
as much as to ask what had become of 'em. Mr. Seeley, I
have got the weight of a most awful secret upon me, and I
can't any longer bear with it."

"A secret!" repeated Mr. Seeley.

Jelly drew so near to him that her arm touched his. She
pointed to the house of Dr. Rane, and lowered her voice to
speak in a whisper.

"Mrs. Rane's there."

He looked across at the house—so apparently still and
peaceful behind its white blinds; he turned and looked at
Jelly. Not a syllable did he understand of her meaning.

"Mrs. Rane comes again, sir. She haunts the house. I
have seen her twice with my own eyes. Once, the night of
her death, just after she had been put in her coffin; and again
this blessed night."

"Why, what on earth do you mean?" questioned Mr. Seeley

in amazement. "Mrs. Rane haunts the house?—I don't comprehend."

"Her ghost does, sir. It is in it now."

The surgeon put his back against his door-post, and seemed as though he should never leave off staring at Jelly. He fully thought her mind was wandering. A minute or two passed in utter silence.

"My good woman, you need a composing draught as badly as Friend Beverage did just now. What is the matter with you, Jelly."

In reply, Jelly told her story,—in regard to the appearance of Mrs. Rane—told it from the beginning. But she cautiously avoided all mention of suspicion as to unfair play: in fact she did not mention Dr. Rane's name. Mr. Seeley listened quietly, as though he were hearing a fairy tale.

"Have you spoken of this to Dr. Rane?" was his first question.

"Yes, sir: both times. To-night I met him as I was rushing out of the house in my terror."

"What does he say to it?"

"He ridicules it. He says it's my fancy, and is in a towering rage with me. Mrs. Gass asked whether I had been drinking beer. People are hard of belief as to such things."

"You told Mrs. Gass, then?"

"I told her the first time. I was in great distress and perplexity, and I mentioned it to her as we sat together in the churchyard looking at Mrs. Rane's funeral."

"What did Mrs. Gass say?"

"She cautioned me never to speak of it again to living soul. Neither of that, nor of—of anything. But this blessed night, sir, I have seen it again: and if it is to go on like this, I shall soon be in a lunatic asylum."

Mr. Seeley had no faith in ghosts. At the same time he saw how implicit was Jelly's belief in what she fancied she had seen, and the distressed state of mind it had induced. What to answer for the best, he did not know. If he threw ridicule on the story, it would make no sort of impression: if he pretended to receive it as truth, it could not bring her ease.

"Jelly," said he on impulse, "I should not believe in a ghost if I saw one."

"I didn't believe in them once," answered Jelly. "But seeing brings belief."

"I'm sure I don't know what to say to you," was his candid avowal. "You are evidently so imbued with your own view of the matter, that any contrary argument would be useless."

"What troubles me is this," resumed Jelly, as if she had not heard him. "*Why* is it that she is unable to rest, poor thing? What's the reason?"

"I should say there was no reason," observed Mr. Seeley.

"Should you, sir?"

Jelly spoke significantly, and he looked at her keenly. There was a professional lamp over the door, as there was over Dr. Rane's; and their faces were distinct to each other. The tone had been a slip in the heat of argument, and Jelly grew cautious again.

"What am I to do, sir?"

"Indeed I cannot tell you, Jelly. There is only one thing to do, I should say—get out of the fancy again as quickly as you can."

"You think I did not see it!"

"I think all ghost-stories proceed purely from an excited imagination," said the surgeon.

"You have not lived here very long, sir, but you have been here quite long enough to know that I've not got much imagination. I don't remember that, before this happened, I ever felt excited in my whole life. My nature's not that way. The first time I saw her, I had come in, as I say, from Ketler's; and all I was thinking of was Dinah's negligence in not putting out the matches for me. I declare that when I saw her, poor thing, that night, with her fixed eyes staring at me, I was as cool as any cucumber. She stood there some time, looking at me with a stoney stare, as it seemed, and I stood in the dark, looking at her. I thought it was herself, Mr. Seeley, and felt glad that she was able to be out of bed. In the morning, when I heard she was dead, and shut up in her coffin, I thought she must have been shut in it alive. You were the first I asked whether it was true that she was dead," added Jelly, warming with the sudden recollection. "I saw you standing here at the door after Dinah told me, and I stepped over."

The surgeon nodded. He remembered it.

"To-night when I went for Dr. Rane, there was not a thought or particle of superstition in my mind. I was troubled about Mrs. Beverage, and wondering what carelessness brought the doctor's front door open. And there she

stood !—facing me as I went up the stairs—just in the same
identical spot that she had stood the time before. Ugh ! "
broke off Jelly, with a shudder. "But don't say again, sir,
please, that it was my excited imagination."

"I could tell you stories of the imagination that would surprise you, Jelly."

"If it was not Mrs. Rane—that is, her apparition—that
appeared to me to-night, sir, and that appeared to me the
other night, I wish these eyes may never behold anything
again," spoke Jelly solemnly. And Mr. Seeley saw how worse
than futile it would be to contend farther.

" Jelly, why have you told me this ? I do not see how I
can help you."

"I've told it you because the weight of keeping it to myself
was greater than I could bear," she replied. "It's an awful
thing, and a cruel thing, that it should be just *me* that's
signalled out for it. I think I know why : and I am nearly
torn to pieces with the responsibility. As to helping me, sir,
I don't think that you or anybody else can do that. Did you
see Mrs. Rane after she died ?"

The question was put abruptly, but in a tone that Jelly
meant to be indifferent. Mr. Seeley replied in a very matter-
of-fact manner.

" No."

" Well, I'll wish you good-night, sir. Keeping you talking
here will do no good."

" Good-morning, I should say," returned the surgeon.

Jelly had reached her own gate, when she paused for
a moment and then turned back across the road. The surgeon
had not moved. He still had his back against his door-post,
and was apparently gazing at Dr. Rane's. Jelly said what
she had come back to say.

" You will please not speak of this again to any one, Mr.
Seeley. There are reasons why."

" Not I, Jelly," was the hearty rejoinder. "I don't want to
be laughed at in Dallory as the retailer of a ghost-story."

" Thank you, sir."

With that, the surgeon passed into his dwelling, and Jelly
went over to hers. And the winter's night wore on to its close.

In the favourable reaction that had fallen on Mrs. Beverage,
Jelly might have gone to rest again had she so chosen. But
she did not. There could be neither rest nor sleep for her.
She sat by the kitchen fire, and drank sundry cups of tea : and

rather thought, what with one perplexity and another, that it was not sinful to wish herself dead.

In the morning about seven o'clock, when she was upstairs in her chamber, she heard the noise of a gig in the lane, and looked out. It was Dr. Rane, returning from his visit to his sick patient. His face was white. An ordinary passer-by would have said the doctor was cold: Jelly drew a different conclusion.

"It's his conscience," she mentally whispered. "It's the thought of having to dwell in his house now that he knows what's in it. He might have set it down to my fancy the first time: he can't this. Who knows, either, but what she appears to *him?*—who knows? but it strikes me his nerves are made of iron. He must have been driving like mad, too, by the way the gig's splashed!" added Jelly, catching a glimpse of the state of the vehicle as it whirled round the corner towards the public-house. "Good heavens! what is to be done? —what is to be done about this dreadful secret? Why should it have fallen on ME?"

CHAPTER XLI.

COMING VERY NEAR.

It is not all at once, when rumours of this grave character arise, that they come to a climax. Time must be allowed them to grow and settle. It came at length, however, here. The doubts ripened to convictions: the semi-suppressed breathings widened into broad assertions: Oliver Rane had certainly murdered his wife for the sake of getting the tontine money. People affirmed it one to another as they met in the street— that is (throwing the onus off themselves), said that others affirmed it. Old Phillis heard it one day, and nearly fell down in a fit. She did not altogether believe it: but nevertheless from that time she could not speak to her master without visibly shaking. The doctor thought she must be suffering from incipient palsy. At length it penetrated to Dallory Hall, to the ears of Madam; and upon Madam it produced an extraordinary effect.

It has been stated throughout that Mrs. North had conceived a violent dislike to Dr. Rane; or at least, that she persistently acted against him in a manner that gave the impression that she had. As if she had only waited for this rumour to accuse him of something tangible, Madam took it up and made the cause her own. She never appeared to question the truth of the report, or to enquire what its grounds might be; she drove about, almost like a mad woman, here, there, and everywhere, unequivocally asserting that Bessy Rane had been poisoned, and that her husband, Oliver Rane, had done the deed.

In good truth Mrs. North had been, if not mad, in a state of inward ferment for some short while past, ever since she had become cognizant of the expected return to England of Mr. Adair. Why she should dread this, and why it should excite her—and she did dread it and it did excite her in no measured degree—she alone knew. Nobody around her had the least idea that the coming home of Mr. Adair would be more to her than the arrival of any stranger might be. Restless, nervous, anxious, with an evil and crafty look in her eyes, with ears that were ever open, with hands that could not be still, waited Madam. The household saw nothing—only that her tyranny became more unbearable day by day.

It almost seemed as though she seized upon the whispered accusation of Dr. Rane as a vent for some of her uneasiness on this other score to exercise itself upon. He must be brought to the bar of justice to answer for his crime, avowed Madam. She drove to the houses of the different county magistrates, urging this view upon them; she besieged the county coroner in his office, and bade him get the necessary authority and issue his orders for the exhumation of the body.

The coroner was Mr. Dale. There had recently been a sharp contest for the coronership (which had become vacant) between a doctor and a lawyer: the latter was Dale, of Whitborough, and he had gained the day. To say that Madam, swooping down upon him with this command, startled him considerably, would be saying little, as describing his state of astonishment. Occupied very much just now with the proceedings attaching to his new honour, and the accounts it personally involved him in (which he made many a wry face over), Lawyer Dale had found less time for gossiping about his neighbours' affairs than usual; and not a syllable of the flying rumour had reached him. So little did he at first believe it, and so badly did he think of Madam for the part she was playing, that, had she been a man, he would have given her the lie direct. But she was persistent, repeating over and over to him the charge in the most obnoxious and least delicate manner possible : Oliver Rane had poisoned his wife during her attack of fever, and he had done it to get the tontine money. She went over the grounds for suspicion, dwelling on them one by one ; and perhaps the lawyer's belief in Dr. Rane's innocence was just a trifle shaken—which he did not acknowledge. After some sparring between them— Mr. Dale holding back from interference, she pressing it on— the coroner was obliged to admit that if a demand for an inquest were formally made to him he should have no resource but to call one. Finally he undertook to institute some private enquiries into the matter, and see whether there were grounds to justify so extreme a course. Madam sharply replied that if there were the smallest disposition shown on his part to stifle the enquiry, she should at once cause the Secretary of State to be communicated with. And with that she swept down to her carriage.

"Perhaps, of all classes of men, lawyers are most brought into contact with the crimes and follies committed by the human race. Mr. Dale had not been at all scrupulous as to what he undertook ; and many kinds of curious matters had come under his experience. Leaning back in his chair after Madam's visit, revolving this point of the story, revolving that, his opinion changed, and he came to the conclusion that, on the face of things, it did look very much as though Dr. Rane had been guilty. Lawyer Dale had no cause to wish the doctor harm ; especially the awful harm a public investigation might entail : had the choice lain with him, he would have remained quiescent, and consigned the doctor to his conscience. But he saw clearly that Mrs. North would not suffer this to be, and that it was more than probable he would have to act.

The first move he made, in his undertaking to institute some private enquiry, was to seek an interview with Mr. Seeley. He went to it himself ; the matter was of too delicate a nature to be confided to a clerk. In his questions he was reticent, after the cautious custom of a man of law, giving no clue, and intending to give none, as to why he put them ; but Mr. Seeley had heard of the rumoured accusation, and spoke out freely.

"I confess that I could not quite understand the death," he avowed : "but I do not suspect that Dr. Rane, or any one else had any hand in it. She died naturally, as I believe. Mr. Dale, this is a horrible thing for you to bring against him."

" *I* bring it ! " cried Mr. Dale. " I don't bring it; I'd rather
let the doubt lie and die out. It is forced upon me."

" Who by ? These confounded scandalmongers ? "

" By Mrs. North."

" Mrs. North ! " echoed the surgeon in surprise. " You
don't mean to say the North family are taking it up."

" I don't know about the family. Madam is, and with a
vengeance. She won't let it sleep. There is an evident
animus in her mind against Dr. Rane, and she means to
pursue the charge to its last extremity."

Mr. Seeley felt vexed to hear it. When these rare and
grave charges are brought against one of the medical body,
the rest, as a rule, would rather resent it than entertain it.
And, besides, the surgeon liked Dr. Rane.

" Come; you may as well tell me the truth," cried the
lawyer, breaking the silence. " You'll have to do it publicly,
I fancy."

" Mr. Dale," was the answer, " I have told you the truth
according to my belief. Never a suspicion of foul play crossed
my mind in regard to Mrs. Rane's death. I saw nothing to
give rise to one."

" You did not see her after she died: nor for some hours
before it ? "

" No."

" You think she went off naturally."

" Most certainly I think she did."

" But, look here—we lawyers have to probe opinions, you
know, so excuse me. If you were to find it proved that she
went off in—in a different way, you'd not be surprised; eh,
Seeley ? "

" I should be very much surprised."

" Hang it, man, don't you know what I mean? You would
not be able, from your recollection of the facts attending the
case, to confute it, or to bring forward a single confronting
proof to say she did not ? "

" Well, no ; I should not be able."

" There's the difficulty, you see," resumed the lawyer;
" there's where it will lie. You believe Rane was innocent, I
may believe him innocent; but nobody possesses positive
proofs of it, to bring forward, that might serve to stop the
enquiry. It will have to go on as sure as fate."

" Cannot *you* stop it, Mr. Dale ? "

" I promise you this : that I'll put as many impediments in

the way of it as I can. But once I am called upon publicly
to act, my own power to delay will be over."

That was the end of the interview. It had a little
strengthened the lawyer's doubts, if anything. Mr. Seeley
had not seen her after death. What he was going to do next
Mr. Dale did not say.

By the day following this, perhaps the only two people
accustomed to walk up and down the streets of Dallory who
still remained in blissful ignorance of the trouble afloat, were
Dr. Rane himself, and Richard North. Nobody had dared to
mention it to *them*. Richard, however, was soon to be en-
lightened.

Business took him to his bankers' in Whitborough. It
was of a private nature, requiring to be transacted between
himself and one of the old brothers at the head of the firm.
After it was over they began talking about general things,
and Richard asked incidentally whether much further delay
would take place in paying the tontine money to Dr. Rane.

"I am not sure that we shall be able to pay it him at all,"
replied Sir Thomas Ticknell.

"Why not?" asked Richard in surprise.

For answer, the old gentleman looked significantly at
Richard for a short space of time, and then demanded whether he was still in ignorance of what had become the chief
public topic.

Bit by bit, it all came out. The brothers Ticknell, it appeared, had heard the report quite at the first: there are
never wanting kind friends to do a fellow-man an injury when
they can; and somebody had hastened to the bankers with
the news. Richard North sat aghast as he listened. His
sister was supposed to have come by her death unfairly! For
once in his life he changed to the hue of a sick man, and his
strong frame trembled. Sir Thomas made him drink a glass
of old wine.

"We hear the new coroner, Dale, has got it in hand now,"
remarked Sir Thomas. "I suppose there'll be a fine public
scandal."

Recovering in some degree the shock, Richard North
took his departure, and went over to Dale's, whose offices
were nearly opposite. The lawyer was there, and made no
scruple of disclosing what he knew to Richard.

"It's a pity that I've got to take the matter up," said Dale.
"Considering the uncertainty at present attending it—that

.he doctor may be innocent—considering also that it cannot bring the dead to life, and that it will be a most painful thing for old Mr. North—and for you too, Mr. Richard—I think it would be as well to let it alone."

"But who is stirring in it ?" asked Richard.

"Madam."

"Madam ! Do you mean Mrs. North ?"

"To be sure I do. I don't say but what public commotion and officious people would soon have brought it to the same issue; but any way, Mrs. North has forestalled them." And he told Richard of Madam's visit to him.

"You say you have been making some private enquiries," observed Richard.

Mr. Dale nodded.

"And what is your candid opinion ? Tell it me, Dale."

But the lawyer hesitated to say to him, I think Dr. Rane may have been guilty. Hesitated not only because it was an unpleasant assertion to make to Dr. Rane's brother-in-law, but also because he really had doubts whether it was so or not.

"I hold no decided opinion as yet," he said. "I may not be able to form one until the post-mortem examination has taken place ——"

"You do not mean to say that they will—that they will disturb my sister !" interrupted Richard North, his eyes full of horror.

"Why that's the first thing they will do—if the investigation goes on at all," cried the lawyer. "That's always the preliminary step. You are forgetting."

"I suppose I am," groaned Richard. "This has been a great shock to me. Dale, you cannot believe him guilty !"

"Well, I can't tell; and that's the fact," candidly avowed the lawyer. "There are certainly some suspicious circumstances attending the case : but at the same time, they are only such that Dr. Rane may be able to explain satisfactorily away."

"How have the doubts arisen ?" questioned Richard. "There were none—I suppose—at the time."

"So far as I can at present ascertain, they have sprung from some words incautiously dropped by Fanny Jelly, the late Mrs. Cumberland's maid. Whether Jelly saw anything at the time of Mrs. Rane's illness to give rise to suspicion I don't know. I have not yet got to see her. It is necessary to go about this business cautiously, Mr. Richard North; and Jelly, I expect, will be no willing witness."

"Did Madam tell you this arose from Jelly?"

"Oh dear no. Madam does not concern herself as to whence the suspicions came; she says to me: 'There they are, and you must deal with them.' I got the information from my clerk, Timothy Wilks. In striving to trace the rumours back to their source, I traced them to him. Carpeting him here before me in this room, I insisted upon his telling me whence he obtained them. He answered me readily enough, 'From Jelly.' It seems Jelly was spending an evening at his aunt's, or cousin's, or grandmother's—whatever it is. I mean the wife of your time-keeper, Mr. Richard North. Wilks was present: only those three; the conversation turned upon Mrs. Rane's death, and Jelly said a few words that startled them. I quite believe that was the commencing link of the scandal."

"What can Jelly know?" exclaimed Richard dreamily.

"I can't tell. The report is, that Mrs. Rane had something wrong given to her by her husband the last day of her life: and that his object was to get the tontine money, which he could not touch while she lived. A curious thing that the husband and wife should be the two last left in that tontine!" added the lawyer: "I've said so often."

"But even"—Richard stopped from pain—"if this had been so, how could Jelly have learnt it?"

"Well, things come out in strange ways sometimes; especially if they are things that ought not to see the light. I've noticed it. Jelly's mistress was away, and she may have gone in to help nurse Mrs. Rane in her illness: we don't yet know how it was."

Richard North rose to depart. "At any rate, I do not see that it was Madam's place to take it up and urge on an inquiry," he remarked. "She should have left that to the discretion of my father and myself."

"She was in a regular fever over it," cried Mr. Dale. "She talked of sending an application to the Secretary of State. I shouldn't wonder but what it is already gone up."

From the lawyer's house, Richard went direct to that of the late Mrs. Cumberland. The dusk of evening was then drawing on. As he reached the door, Miss Beverage, in her Quaker's bonnet of dove-coloured silk, approached it from an opposite direction. Raising his hat, he asked whether he could be allowed a five minutes' interview with Jelly. Miss Beverage, who knew Richard by sight, was very chatty and pleasant : she took him into the drawing-room and sent Jelly to him. And Jelly felt half inclined to faint as she shut the door, for she well knew what must be coming.

But, after some fencing with Richard's questions, Jelly gave in. He was resolute in requiring to hear all she could tell, and at length she made a clean breast of it. She related what she knew, and what she suspected, from beginning to end ; and before she had finished, a strangely soothing relief, that Richard should know it, grew up within her.

"For I shall consider that the responsibility is now taken off my shoulders, sir," she said. "And perhaps it has been nothing, but this, that the ill-fated lady has wanted me to do, in coming again."

In all the tale, the part that most struck Richard North, was Jelly's positive and clear assertion that she had since twice seen Mrs. Rane. He was simply astounded. And, to tell the truth, he did not seek to cast ridicule or disbelief on it. Richard North was an educated and practical man of plain common sense, with no more tendency to believe in supernatural appearances than are such men in general ; but his mind had been so unhinged since the interview with Sir Thomas Ticknell, that he almost felt inclined to admit the possibility of his sister's not resting in her grave.

He sat with his head leaning on his hand. Collecting in some degree his half scattered senses, he strove to go over dispassionately the grounds of suspicion. But he could make nothing more of them than Dale had said. Grounds for it there certainly were, but none but what Dr. Rane might be able to explain away. Jelly drew her own deductions, and called them proofs : but Richard saw that of proofs as yet there were none.

"I've lived in mortal horror, ever since that first night, of seeing it again," said Jelly, interrupting his reverie. "Nobody can imagine, sir, what a dreadful time it has been. And when I was least thinking of it, it came the second time."

"To whom have you repeated this story of having seen her ?" asked Richard.

"The first time I told Dr. Rane and Mrs. Gass. This last time I told the doctor and Mr. Seeley."

"Jelly," said Richard quietly, "there is no proof that any-thing was wrong, except in your fancy."

" And the hasty manner that she was hid out of the way,
sir—no woman called in to do anything for her; no soul
allowed to see her !" urged Jelly. " If it wanted proof positive before, it can't be thought to want it since what Thomas
Hepburn related to me."

" All that may have been done out of regard to the welfare
of the living," said Richard.

Jelly gave a disbelieving sniff. To her mind it was clearer
than daylight.

But at this juncture, a servant came in to know if she
should bring lights. Richard took the opportunity to depart.
Of what use to prolong his stay? As he went out he saw
Mr. Seeley standing at his door. Richard crossed over and
asked to speak with him : he knew of Dale's interview with
the surgeon.

" Can Rane have been guilty of this thing, or not ?" questioned Richard, when they were closeted together.

But, no. Not even here could Richard get at any decided
opinion. It might have been so, or it might not, Seeley
replied. For himself, he was inclined to think it was *not;*
that Mrs. Rane's death was natural.

Leaving again, Richard paced up and down the dark road.
His mind was in a tumult. He, with Seeley, could not think
Dr. Rane was guilty. And, even though he were, he began
to question whether it would not be better for his father's
sake, for all their sakes, to let the matter lie. Richard, pursuing his natural bias, put the two aspects together, and compared them. On the one side there would be the merited
punishment of Oliver Rane and vengeance on Bessy's wrongs ;
the other would bring a terrible amount of pain, of exposure,
almost of disgrace. And Richard truly feared for the effect
it might have on Mr. North. Before his walk was over, he
decided that it would be infinitely best to hush the scandal up,
should that be still possible.

But, for his own satisfaction, he wished to get at the truth.
It seemed to him that he could hardly live in the uncertainty.
Taking a rapid resolution, he approached Dr. Rane's ; knocked
at the door, and asked old Phillis if he could see her
master.

She at once showed him into the dining-room. Dr. Rane,
weary perhaps with the cares of the day, had fallen back in
his chair asleep. He sprung up at the interruption ; a startled,
almost frightened expression appeared in his face. Richard

North could but notice it, and his heart failed him, for it seemed to speak of guilt. Phillis shut them in together.

How Richard opened the interview, he scarcely knew, and could never afterwards recal. He soon found that Dr. Rane remained as yet in total ignorance of the stir that was abroad; and this rendered his task all the more difficult. Richard entered on the communication in the most delicate manner that the subject admitted of. Dr. Rane did not receive it kindly. He first swore a great oath, and then—his fury checked suddenly in its midst as if by some latent thought or fear—he sank back in his chair and bent his head on his breast, like a man struck dumb with tribulation.

"I think *you* need not have given credit to this report against me, Richard North," he presently spoke in a reproachful accent. "But I believe you lost confidence in me a year and a half ago."

He so evidently alluded to the anonymous letter that Richard did not affect to misunderstand him. It might be better to speak openly.

"I believe you wrote that, Rane."

"True. I did. But not to injure your brother. I thought Alexander must be a bad man—that he must be leading Edmund North into money difficulties to serve himself. I had no cause to spare him, but the contrary, for he had injured me, was injuring me daily; and I wrote what I did to Mr. North, hoping it might expose Alexander and damage him. There: you have it. I would rather have had my hand cut off"—flinging it out with emotion—"than have hurt your brother. I wished afterwards that it had been cut off first. But it was too late then."

And because of that anonymous letter Dr. Rane knew, and Richard felt, that the accusation, now made, gathered weight. When a man has been guilty of one thing, we think it a reason why he may be guilty of another.

A silence ensued. They sat, the table between them. The room was rather dark. The lamp had a shade on it, the fire had burned low; before the large window were stretched the sombre curtains. Richard North would have given some years of his life for this most distressing business never to have come into it.

He went on with what he had to say. Dr. Rane, motionless now, kept his hand over his face while he listened. Richard told of the public commotion; of the unparalleled

shock it had been to himself, of the worse shock he feared it
might bring his father. Again there was an interruption:
but Dr. Rane in speaking did not raise his face.

"Is my personal liberty in danger?"

"Not yet—in one sense. I believe you are under the sur-
veillance of the police."

"Watched by them?"

"Yes. But only to see that you do not get away."

"That is—they track me out and home, I am to understand? I am watched in and out of my patients' houses. If
I have occasion to pay country visits, these stealthy blood-
hounds are at my heels, night or day?"

"I conclude it is so," answered Richard.

"Since when has this been?"

"Since—I think since the day-before-yesterday. There is
a probability, as I hear, that the Secretary of State will be
applied to. If——"

"For what purpose?"

"For his authority to disturb the grave," said Richard in a
low tone.

Dr. Rane started up, a frenzy of fear apparent in his face.

"They—they—surely they are not talking of doing *that?*"
he cried, turning white as death.

"Yes they are. To have her disturbed will be to us the
most painful of all."

"Stop it, for the Lord's sake!" came the imploring cry.
"Stop it, Richard North! Stop it!"

But at that moment there burst upon their ears a frightful
clatter outside the door. Richard opened it. Dr. Rane, who
had sunk on his seat again, never stirred. Old Phillis, coming
in from the scullery after a cleaning bout, had accidentally let
fall nearly a small cart-loadful of pots and pans.

CHAPTER XLII.

"EST-CE QU'IL M'AIME?"

WINTRY weather set in again. The past few days had been
intensely cold and bleak. Ellen Adair sat in one of her
favourite out-door seats. Well sheltered from the wind by
artificial rocks and clustering evergreens, and well wrapped-
up besides, she did not seem to feel the frost.

Her later days had been one long great trial. Compelled

to meet Arthur Bohun perpetually, yet shunned by him as far
as it was possible for him to shun her without attracting too
much the observation of others, there were times when she
felt as though her position at the Hall were killing her.
Something, in fact, *was* killing her. Her state of mind was a
mixture of despair, shame, and self-reproach. Captain Bohun's
conduct brought to her the bitterest humiliation. Looking
back on the past, she thought he despised her for her ready
acquiescence in that wish of his for a private marriage : and
the self-repentance, the humiliation it entailed on her was of
all things the hardest to bear. She almost felt that she could
die of the memory—just as other poor creatures, whose sin
has been different, have died of their shame. To her mistaken
vision, it seemed as though the wrong deed she had consented
to—the secret marriage—were quite as much of a shame if not
of a sin. The view presented perpetually to her mind was,
that Captain Bohun so regarded it ; and had nothing for her
but scorn. This was the thought that tried her, that em-
bittered her peace by night and by day : it was doing her .
more harm than all the rest. Her cheeks would redden, her
fingers tingle with shame as she recalled that fond letter she
had written to him from Eastsea, when even then, though she
did not know it, he had given her up. To one so sensitively
organised as Ellen Adair, reared in all the graces of reticent
and refined feeling, this compelled sojourn at Dallory Hall
could indeed be nothing less than a fiery ordeal, from which
there might be no escape to former health and strength.

Very still she sat to-day, nursing her pain. Her face was
wan, her breathing short : that past cold she had caught
seemed to hang by her strangely. No further news had been
received from Mr. Adair, and Ellen supposed he was on his
way home. After to-day her position would not be quite so
trying, for Arthur Bohun was quitting Dallory. Sir Nash
had decided that he was strong enough now to travel, and
they were to depart together at two o'clock. It was past
twelve now. And so—the sunshine of Ellen Adair's life had
gone out. Never, as she believed, would a gleam come into
it again.

In spite of the commotion beyond the walls of the Hall
now increasing daily and hourly to a climax, in spite of
Madam's never resting personal exertions to urge it on, and
to crush Oliver Rane, no word of the dreadful accusation had
as yet transpired within to its chief inmates. Mr. North, his

daughter Matilda, Ellen Adair, Sir Nash Bohun, and Arthur; all were alike in ignorance. The servants of course knew of it, going out to Dallory, as they often did : but Madam had issued her sharp orders to them to hold their tongues; and Richard had begged them not to speak of it for their master's sake. As to Sir Nash and Arthur Bohun, Richard was only too glad that they should depart without hearing the scandal.

He himself was doing all he could to stop proceedings and allay excitement. Since the night of his interviews with Jelly, Mr. Seeley, and Dr. Rane, Richard had devoted his best energies to the work of suppression. He did not venture to see any official person, the coroner excepted, or impress his views on the magistrates; but he went about amid the populace, and poured oil on the troubled waters. "For my father's sake, do not press this on," he said to them; "let my sister's grave rest."

"Just like Dick North," quoth they, one to another. "He was always for peace."

In effect he said the same to the coroner; begging of him, if possible, to stop it; and he implied to all, though not absolutely asserting it, that Dr. Rane could not be guilty. So that Ellen Adair, sitting there, had not this knowledge to give her additional trouble.

A little blue leaf—as it looked—suddenly caught her eye, peeping up from a mossy and tangled green nook, at the foot of the rocks. She rose, and stooped to see. It was a winter violet. Plucking it, she sat down again, and fell into thought.

For it had brought vividly before her memory, that long-past day, when she had played out her play of violets in the garden at Mrs. Cumberland's. "*Est-ce qu'il m'aime ? Oui. Non. Un peu. Beaucoup. Pas du tout. Passionnément. Il m'aime passionnément.*" False augurs, those flowers had been! Deceitful blossoms which had combined to mock and sting her. The contrast between that time and this brought to Ellen Adair a whole flood-tide of intense misery. And those foolish violets were hidden away still! Should she carry this in-doors and add it to them?

By-and-by she began to walk towards the house. Turning a corner presently she was brought suddenly to the midst of three excited people : Captain Bohun, Miss Dallory, and Matilda North. The two former had met accidentally in the walk. Miss Dallory's morning errand at the Hall was to say good-bye to Sir Nash; and before she and Captain Bohun had

well exchanged greetings, Matilda bore down upon them in a
state of agitation, calling wildly to Arthur to stay and hear
the tidings *she* had just heard.

The tidings were those that had been so marvellously long
kept from her and from others at the Hall—the accusation of
Dr. Rane. Matilda North had just learnt them in an accidental
manner : in her horror and surprise she had run after her half-
brother, Arthur, to repeat the story. Ellen Adair found her
talking in wild excitement. Arthur, rather yellow still, was
turning to a pale straw colour as he listened ; Mary Dallory,
to whom it was no news, had covered up her face.

But Arthur Bohun and Matilda North were strong enough
to bear it without any very palpable effect. Ellen Adair was
not. As she drank in the meaning of the dreadful words—that
Bessy had been murdered—a deadly sickness seized upon her
heart ; and she had only time to sit down on a garden bench
before she fainted away.

" You should not have told it so abruptly, Matilda," cried
Arthur almost passionately. " It has made even me feel ill.
Get some water : you'll go quicker than I should."

Alarmed at Ellen's state, and eager to be of service, both
Matilda and Miss Dallory ran in search of the water. Arthur
Bohun sat down on the bench to support her. His path in life
was to lie that way, and hers this, the further apart the better ;
but he could not in humanity—no, nor in love either—walk
away now and leave her to recover alone as she best could.

Her head lay on his breast, as he placed it. She was entirely
without consciousness : he saw that. His arm encircled her
waist ; he took one of her lifeless hands between his, to rub it.
Thus he sat, gazing down at the pale thin face so near to his ;
the face which he—he—had helped to rob of its bloom.

Oh, but he loved her still ! loved her better than he did all
the rest of the world put together ! Holding her there to his
beating heart, he knew it. He knew that he only loved her
the more truly for their bitter estrangement. His frame was
trembling, his pulses were thrilling with the rapture this
momentary contact brought him. If he might but embrace
her, as of old ! Should he ? Why not ? No human soul,
save himself, would ever know it. A strangely irrepressible
yearning, to touch her lips with his, came into his eyes and
heart. Glancing keenly around first, lest any prying eyes
should be in ambush, he slightly lifted the pale sweet face, and
bent down his own.

" Oh, my darling ! My lost darling !"

Lips, cheeks, brow were kissed again and again, with a soft impassioned tenderness, with a kind of hungry rapture. It was so long since he had touched them ! Was he ever going to leave off ? A sigh—more than one—escaped him ; a little sound of irrepressible emotion : and he knew not whether it contained most of bliss or of agony.

This treatment was quite effective ; more so than the water could have been. Ellen drew a deep breath, and stirred uneasily. As soon as she began really to revive, he managed to get his coat off and fold it across the head and arm of the bench. When Ellen awoke to conciousness, she had her head leaning on it ; and Captain Bohun stood at a very respectful distance, gingerly chafing one of her hands. Never a suspicion crossed her mind of what he had been doing.

" You are better," he said, " I am so glad !"

The words, in *his* voice, aroused her fully. She lifted her head and opened her eyes, and gazed around her in bewilderment, at first remembering nothing. But what Matilda had said came back with a rush.

" Is it true ?" she exclaimed, looking piteously at him. " It never can be true !"

" I don't know," he answered. " If false, it is almost as dreadful to us who hear it. Poor Bessy ! I loved her as my very dear sister."

Ellen, exhausted by the fainting fit, her nerves unstrung by the news, burst into a flood of distressing tears. Matilda and Miss Dallory running up with water, wine, and smelling-salts, found her sobbing aloud.

" It is the reaction after the faintness," said Captain Bohun to them in a whisper.

But she soon recovered her equanimity, so far as outward calmness went, without the aid of any of the remedies—which she declined. Rising from the bench, she turned towards the house. Her steps tottered a little.

" Do give your arm to support Miss Adair, Captain Bohun," spoke Mary Dallory in a sharp quick tone, surprised perhaps that he did not. And upon that, Captain Bohun went to Ellen's side, and held it out.

" Thank you," she answered, and refused it with a slight movement of the head.

They walked on at first all in a group, as it were. But Matilda and Miss Dallory got far ahead, the former talking in

a most excited state about Bessy Rane and the miserable accusation in regard to her. Ellen's steps were slower; which she
could not help; and Captain Bohun kept by her side.

"May I wish you good-bye here, Ellen?" he suddenly
asked, stopping towards the end of the shrubbery, through
which they had been passing.

"Good-bye," she faintly answered.

He took her hand. That is, he held out his own, and Ellen
almost mechanically put hers into it. To have made a to-do,
by refusing, would have hurt her pride worse than all. He
kept it within his, clasping his other hand upon it. For a
moment his eyes met hers.

"It may be, that we shall never again cross each other's
path in life, Ellen. God bless you, my love, and keep you
always! I wish to heaven, for both our sakes, that we had
never met!"

"Good-bye," she coldly repeated as he dropped her hand.
And they walked on in silence and gained the lawn, where the
two in advance had turned to wait for them.

But this was destined to be an eventful day: to others, at
least, if not to them. At the appointed time, Sir Nash Bohun
and Arthur took their departure; Richard North, who had
paid the baronet the attention of coming home to luncheon—
for there was no concealment now as to who was the true host
at Dallory hall—seeing them into their carriage.

"You have promised to come and stay with me, Richard,"
said the baronet, at the last hand-shake.

"Conditionally. When my work shall allow me leisure,"
answered Richard, laughing.

"Can't you go with us to the station, Dick?" put in Arthur.

"Not to-day, I fear. I must hold an immediate interview
with Madam—something important. If you waited for me
you might lose the train."

Arthur bent his face—one of pain now—close to Dick's, and
whispered.

"Is it money-trouble again, Richard?"

"No; not this time."

"If she brings *that* on you in future, turn her over to me.
Yes, Richard: I must deal with it now."

Farewells were exchanged, and the carriage drove away.
Richard, stepping backwards, trod on Miss Dallory.

"I beg your pardon!" he exclaimed. "Have I hurt you?
I did not know you were there."

" Of course you have not hurt me : and I had no business
to be there. I stood to wave my handkerchief to them.
Good afternoon, Mr. Richard."

" Are you going ? " he asked.

" I am engaged to spend the afternoon and take tea with
Mrs. Gass. That luncheon was my dinner. I saw you looking
at me as if you thought I eat a great deal."

" Miss Dallory ! "

She laughed slightly.

" To confess the truth, I don't think I noticed whether you
eat anything or nothing," said Richard. " I have a great deal
of trouble on my mind just now—of more kinds than one.
Good afternoon."

He would be returning to Dallory himself in perhaps a few
minutes, but he never said to her " Stay, and I will walk
with you." Miss Dallory thought of it as she went away. It
had indeed crossed Richard's mind to say so : but he arrested
the words as they were about to leave his lips. If she was to
be Arthur Bohun's wife, the less Richard saw of her the
better.

Enquiring for Madam when he went indoors, he found she
was ensconsed in her boudoir. Richard went up, knocked at
the door, and opened it. Madam appeared not to approve of
the procedure ; she bore down on him with a swoop, and
would have shut him out.

" What do you want here, Richard North ? I am not at
liberty. I cannot admit you."

" Pardon me, Madam, I must speak with you for five
minutes," he answered, passing quietly in.

By something he had heard that morning from Dale, Richard
had reason to suppose that Mrs. North was still actively pursuing the charge against Dr. Rane ; that is, was urging in high
quarters the imperative necessity for an investigation.
Richard had come to ask her whether this was the case, and
to beg her, once for all, to be still. He sat down uninvited
while he put the question.

But Madam acknowledged nothing. In fact, she led him
to believe that it was entirely untrue ; that she had not
stirred in it at all since the caution Richard had given her,
not to, some days ago. It was simply impossible for him to
know whether what she said might be depended on—for she
told more falsehood than truth habitually. Richard could
only hope.

"It would be a terrible exposure for us," he urged. "Madam, I beg you; I beg you for all our sakes, be *still*. You know not what you would do."

She nodded an ungracious acquiescence: and Richard departed for his works, casually mentioning to Mr. North, as he passed him in the garden, that he should not be home until night. Like Miss Dallory, he had intended the mid-day meal to serve for his dinner.

"Dick," cried Mr. North, arresting him, "what's the matter with Matilda? She seems to be in a fine commotion over something or other."

Richard knew not what to answer. If his father had to be told, why better that he himself should be the teller. There was still a chance that it might be kept from him.

"Something or other gone wrong, I suppose, sir. Never mind. How well those new borders look!"

"Don't they, Dick! I'm glad I had them put."

And Richard went on to his works.

CHAPTER XLIII.

A FINE NIGHT'S WORK.

NIGHT had fallen. And it was not a bright or pleasant one.

Some few skulkers had gathered behind the dwarf hedge, that skirted the piece of waste land near the North Works. An ill-looking lot of men, seen as at present: for they had knelt down so as to bring themselves nearly on a level with the top of the hedge. Their eyes just cleared it, and the view beyond was not interrupted. Poole was in the middle; his face sternly savage, and a pistol in his right hand.

Of all the men who had returned to work, the most obnoxious to the ex-hands was one named Ralley. It was not so much because he had been a turn-coat—that is, after holding out to the eleventh moment, had finally gone back at the twelfth—that the men hated him, as because they believed him to be treacherous. Ralley had been red-hot for the strike; had done more by his agitation than any one man to bring it about. He had resolutely refused all the overtures made by Richard North: and yet—he had gone back when the works were finally re-opened. For this the men heartily despised him—far more than they did those who had been ready to go

back all along. In addition to this, they had been suspecting
—and lately had felt sure—that he was a snake in the grass.
That he had laid himself out to pick up, fairly or stealthily, as
might be, bits of information about them, their doings and
sayings, their miserable condition, and threats of revenge, and
carried them to the works and to Richard North. And so—
the contents of this pistol, that Poole held in his hand, were
meant for Ralley.

For a long time the malcontents of North Inlet had been
burning to take vengeance on somebody : some new treachery
on Ralley's part, or suspected treachery, had come to light,
and they determined to shoot *him.* Oh, poor, misguided,
foolish men ! As if it would make things better for them !
Suppose they killed Ralley, how would it ease their condition ?
Ralley had not suffered half what they suffered. He was
an unmarried man ; and, during the strike, he had been helped
by his relatives, who were pretty well off, so that he had
known neither starvation nor rags, as they had : and this
made his returning to work look all the worse in their eyes.
Ralley was about the age of Richard North, and not unlike
him in height and figure : so much like him, indeed, that since
their evil act had been determined on, one of the others had
bade Poole take care he did not mistake the master for him.
Poole's sullen rejoinder was, that 'twould not much matter if
he did.

The night was dark ; a drizzling rain had come on, and that
part was not too well lighted. The small band, about to issue
from the gates of the works, would come down by this waste
land and pass within some fifteen yards of them. Poole had
been a famous marksman in his day, and felt sure of his aim.
John Allen knelt at his right hand, one Denton at the other ;
another beyond on either side : five in all.

Five o'clock struck. Almost simultaneously with it was
heard the bell at the works, giving token that it was time for
the men to go to tea. Three or four sharp, quick strokes :
nothing more.

"That's Green, I'll swear," cried Denton, alluding to the
ringer. "I didn't know he was back again : his rheumatics
must be better."

"Hush—sh—sh !" was all Denton got. And there ensued
a death-like silence. Not for long. Poole broke it.

"Where the devil are they ?—why don't they come ?"

Ay, why did they not come ? Simply because there had

been scarcely sufficient time for it. But every moment, to these would-be murderers, kneeling there, seemed like a long drawn-out period.

" Here they be," whispered Denton.

It was so. The men were coming out at the gate, about twenty of them; two and two; the policemen to-night heading the string. At times the officers were behind it, at other times on either side. Poole rose cautiously and prepared to take aim. They were coming across from the gates at a kind of right angle, and presently would pass the hedge, side-ways. This was the second night the men had thus lain in ambush. The previous one they had alike awaited; but Ralley happened to be then on the other side his companion in the march, and so for the time was saved.

Allen stretched his head up. His sight was as keen as a sailor's.

" Which side's he on, Jack?" whispered Poole. " I don't see him yet."

For answer John Allen put his hand quickly on Poole's arm to lower the pistol. " No good again, mates," said he. " Ralley ain't there."

" Not there!" retorted Poole with a vile oath.

" I'm as nigh sure as I can be of it," said Allen. " Wait till they come nearer."

It proved to be so. Ralley for some cause or other was not with the men.

" Rat him!" cried Denton, furiously.

Tramp, tramp, tramp; their tread sounded regular in the stillness of the night as they passed, the policemen throwing their eyes on all sides. Poole had crouched down again. He and his companions in evil kept very still: it would not do to let either movement be seen, or noise be heard.

The steps died away in the distance, and the conspirators ventured to raise their heads. Allen happened to look in the direction of the gates.

" By Jorkins here he is!" burst forth Allen almost with a scream. " Something kept him back. Now's our time, mates. Here's Ralley."

" That ain't his hat, Jack Allen," dissented one.

" Hat be smothered! it's *him*," said John Allen.

Ralley was coming on very quickly, a dark, low-crowned hat drawn down on his brows. A minute's silence, during which you might have heard their hearts beat, and then——

Poole fired. Ralley gave a cry; staggered, and walked on. He was struck, no doubt, but not killed.

"Your boasted aim has failed, Poole," cried Denton with a savage oath.

Not more savage than Poole's, though, as he burst through, or over, the low hedge. What the bullet had not done, the pistol itself should. Suddenly, with a shriek and a cry, Allen burst after him, shouting to him to stay his hand.

"It's the master, Poole; it's not Ralley. Stop, you fool! —it's the master."

Too late. It was, indeed, Richard North. And Mr. Poole had felled him by a wicked blow on the temple.

Mrs. Gass and Mary Dallory were seated at tea in a subdued mood—for the conversation had turned on those dreadful rumours that, in spite of Richard North, could not be hushed, but on the contrary were growing worse hourly Stoutly was Mrs. Gass asserting that she had more faith in Dr. Rane than to believe them, when some commotion dawned on their ears from the street. Mrs. Gass stopped in the midst of a sentence.

"What's that?" she cried.

Fleet steps seemed to be running hither and thither; voices were raised in excitement. They distinctly heard the words, "Mr. Richard," "Richard North." Mrs. Gass drew aside her crimson curtains, and opened the window.

"Here—is it you, Smith?" she said, arresting a man who was running in the wake of others. "What is it? What's up?"

"I don't rightly know, ma'am," he answered. "They are saying that Mr. Richard North has been shot dead."

"Lord help us!" cried Mrs. Gass. She shut down the window and brought her face round to the light again. Every bit of colour had gone out of it. Mary Dallory stood rigidly upright, her hands clasped, still as one who had been turned into stone.

"Did you hear what he said, child?"

"I heard," was the scarcely spoken answer that the lips formed.

Mrs. Gass caught up a bonnet, which happened to lie on a chair, tilted it on her head, and went into the street. At the entrance to North Inlet a crowd was gathered, men and women. As in all such cases, reports varied. Some said it had taken place in the high road to Whitborough, some said at the works, some said near Dallory Hall. So the mob was puzzled which way to go and not miss the sight. Thoms was talking at the top of his voice as Mrs. Gass got up; anxious, perhaps, to disclaim complicity on his own score.

"They've had it in their heads to do it, some o' them bad uns have. I could name names, but I won't. If the master had knowed all, he'd ha' went about in fear of his life this long while past."

This was enough for Mrs. Gass. Gathering her black silk skirts in her hands that they should not trail in the mud, her bonnet lodged sideways, and her face paler than the assemblage had ever seen it, she stood, unmindful of the rain, and told them what she thought.

"If you've shot Richard North, you have shot the best and bravest man you'll ever know in this life. You'll never find such a friend again. Oh, he was brave. Brave to do good in the midst o' difficulties, brave to forbear. Don't *you* boast, Thoms, with your glib tongue. None of you men round me now may be the one that's shot him, but you've been all rowing in the same boat. Yes, you have. You mayn't have planned out murder yourselves—I'd not answer for it that you've not—but, any way, you knowed that others was a-planning it, and you winked at it and held your tongues. Who has been the friend to you that Richard North has? Since you've been part starving, and your wives and children's been part starving, where has all the help come from, d'ye suppose, that has kept you from starving quite? Why, from him. The most of it has come from him. The money I gave was his, the things I bought was mostly paid for by him. A little of it came from me, not much; I was too angry with your folly; but he couldn't see you quite clam, and he took care you shouldn't. Look at how you were all helped through the fever; and meat, and bread, and beer gave to you to get up your strength a bit, after it! Who did all that? Why Richard North. You thought it was me; but it was him; only he wouldn't have it known. That was his return for all the black ingratitude you'd showed, in refusing to work for him and bringing him to ruin. Pray God he may not be dead! but if he is, there's a good man gone to his reward. Is that you, Ketler?"

"Yes, it's me," answered Ketler, who was standing in the shadow, a worse gloom on his face than the night cast.

" When that child of yourn died, Cissy—and many a little help did she get in life from him—who took care that she shouldn't be buried by the parish but Richard North ? He met Fanny Jelly, and he put some money into her hand, and charged her to let it be thought it was *hers.* ' They are in great distress, I know, Jelly,' he said ; ' let this be used in any way that's best for them.' Go and ask Jelly, if you don't believe me : I had it from her. And that's the master you've been conspirating together to help to kill, Ketler !"

Ketler swallowed down a rising sob. " I'd never have raised a hand again the master ; no, nor countenanced it. If anybody has said I would, it's a lie."

" There's not one of you but knew what mischief was in the wind, or might have knew it ; and you've countenanced it by keeping silence," retorted Mrs. Gass. " You are a pack of cowards. First of all you ruin him by throwing up his work, and when you find yourselves all a-clamming together, or nigh upon it, you turn round on him and kill him. May the Lord forgive you ! I never will."

Some disturbance. A tramping of feet, and a shouting of running boys. Mrs. Gass was pushed aside with others to make way for the cause of interruption passing. Poole, Denton, John Allen, and one more were marching by in handcuffs, marshalled by some policemen. A telling hiss greeted them.

" 'Twas a mistake," said Jack Allen, in answer to the hiss, reckless under his untoward fate. " 'Twas meant for Ralley, not for the master."

" Is he dead ? " called out Mrs. Gass.

But amidst the confusion she got no answer. And at that moment she became aware of a pale countenance near her, peeping out from a muffling of wool.

" Good gracious, Mary, child ! You shouldn't be out here."

" I have been with you all the while."

" Then, my dear, you just betake yourself home again. I'll come in as soon as I can learn the truth, and where he is."

Mrs. Gass had not long to wait. Almost as she spoke, Richard North appeared : and thereupon ensued more excitement than ever. Blood was trickling from his temple, but he appeared quite sensible, and was walking slowly, helped by two men.

" Thank God !" said Mrs. Gass aloud : and the words were heartily echoed. " To my house, men. Mr. Richard, sir, it is but a few steps more, and we'll soon get the doctor. A fine

night's work, this is ! " she concluded, not speaking in reference to the weather, but to the "work."

Little Barrington, the druggist, came out of his shop, and
helped to put Richard on Mrs. Gass's sofa. They got his
coat off. The left arm was injured, as well as the temple.
Barrington staunched the blood, trickling from the latter ; but
the arm he preferred not to meddle with. "He had better
be kept quite quiet, until the surgeon comes," said the
druggist to Mrs. Gass.

Mrs. Gass cleared the room. About fifty excited messen-
gers had run to the Ham for Mr. Seeley or Dr. Rane, or both
if they should be found at home. She stood at the front
door, looking out and waiting.

Richard North, three parts in a faint, lay with his eyes
closed. Opening them in the still room, he saw Mary
Dallory kneeling by the sofa, pale and sad. He smiled
faintly, and her tears began to drop.

"Don't be alarmed," he whispered. "It might have been
worse."

"I would have given my life to save yours, Richard," she
impetuously exclaimed in the delirium of the moment. And,
leaning forward, the tears fell now on his face.

His right hand went out a little and hers met it.

"Richard, I wish I might stay and nurse you. You have
no sister," she added, as an after-thought. "Matilda is useless in a sick-room."

Richard North nervously pressed her fingers. "Don't try
me too much, Mary. I am caring for you already more than
is good for my peace. Don't tempt me."

"And if I were to tempt you ?—Though I don't quite take
the meaning," she rejoined softly and nervously. "What then ?"

"I might say what I ought not." And there he paused.

"It would make it all the harder for me," he continued.
"I am a man of the people ; a man of work. You will belong
to—to one of a different order."

She knew he alluded to Arthur Bohun, and laughed slightly.

But, though she said no more, she left her hand in his, their
fingers entwining together. Richard thought it was done
solely in compassion.

And now there was a bustle heard, and in came Mr. Seeley,
his face hot with running. The hands parted, and Mary
Dallory went round to the other side of the table, standing
there in decorum.

CHAPTER XLIV.

DISTURBING THE GRAVE.

By twos and threes, by fours and fives, by tens and by dozens, the curious and excited groups were wending their way to Dallory churchyard. For a certain work was going on there, which had never been performed in it within the memory of the oldest inhabitant.

Richard North was lying at Dallory Hall, incapacitated. When Mr. Seeley—assisted by Dr. Rane, who came in—examined int ohis injuries at Mrs. Gass's, he pronounced them not to be grave. The bullet had struck a fleshy part of the arm, and passed off from it, leaving a wound. Care and rest only would be necessary to heal it; and the same might be said with regard to the blow on the temple. Perfect quiet was essential, perfect rest, to guard against any after conse-quences. Mrs. Gass wished Richard to stay at her house and be nursed through it; but he thought of the trouble it would cause in her regular household, and said he preferred to be taken home. It was Mr Seeley who continued to attend him by Richard's own wish; not Dr. Rane. The public thought the rejection of the latter ominously significant, in spite of Richard's recent exertions to do away with the impression of his guilt.

"Understand: absolute quiet both of body and mind," enjoined Mr. Seeley, not only to Richard himself but to the family and servants. "If you have that, Mr. Richard, you will be about again in a short time: if you do not have it, I cannot undertake to answer for the result."

But Richard North, with his good common sense, was an obedient patient. He knew how necessary it was, if only for his recommenced business, that he should not long be laid by, and he kept as quiet as Mr. Seeley could wish. No stranger was allowed to disturb him; none of the household presumed to carry him the smallest particle of news, public or domestic. It was during this confinement of Richard's that Ellen Adair received her summons for departure. Her father had arrived in London, and wrote to Mrs. Cumberland—all uncon-scious of that lady's death—begging that she and Ellen would join him there. He apologized to Mrs. Cumberland for not coming to Dallory, but said that family business required his

presence in London. Mr. North at first proposed to take
Ellen up himself: but he was really not fit to do it: and it
was decided that Parrit, Madam's maid, should attend her
thither.

Ellen was allowed to go in and bid good-bye to Richard
before her departure. She burst into tears as she strove to
thank him for his kindness.

"You must come and see papa as soon as you are well
enough, Richard. When I tell him how kind you have been,
he will want to see and thank you."

"Good-bye, my dear," said Richard, releasing her hand.
"I trust you will soon get up all your good spirits again, now
your father has come."

She smiled faintly: it was not on her father—so imper-
fectly, if at all, remembered—that her spirits depended. As
Ellen was passing through the hall to enter the carriage that
would take her to the station, she found herself touched by
Madam, and drawn into the dining-room.

"You have not seemed very happy with us, Miss Adair.
But I have tried to make you so."

"Yes, Madam, I am sure you have; and I thank you very
much," returned Ellen gratefully—for Madam really did
appear to have been most kind to her of late. "I trust papa
will have an opportunity of thanking you and Mr. North
personally."

Madam coughed. "If you think I deserve thanks, I wish
you would do me a slight favour in return."

"If I can. Certainly."

"Some years ago, when we were in India," proceeded
Madam, "my late husband, Major Bohun, and your father
were acquainted with each other. Some unpleasant circumstances took place between them: a quarrel in fact. Major
Bohun considered he was injured; Mr. Adair thought it was
himself who was. It was altogether very painful, and I
would not for the world have that old matter raked up again;
it would cost me too much pain. Will you, then, guard from
Mr. Adair's knowledge that I, Mrs. North, am she who was
once Mrs. Bohun."

"Yes, I will," said Ellen in the hasty impulse of the
moment, without pausing to consider whether circumstances
would allow her to do so.

"You promise me this."

"Yes, certainly. I will never speak of it to him, madam."

"Thank you, my dear." And Madam kissed her, and co.
her out arm in arm to the carriage.

Day by day Richard North never failed to question the surgeon in a whisper, whether there was anything fresh arising
in regard to the accusation against Dr. Rane. The answer
was invariably No. In point of fact, Mr. Seeley, not hearing
more of it himself, supposed there was not; and at length,
partly in good faith, partly to calm his patient, who was restless on the subject, he said it had dropped through.

Had it! During Richard's active opposition, Madam had
found her hands somewhat crippled ; for she scarcely deemed
it might be altogether to her own interest at the Hall to set
him at defiance : but the moment he was laid up, she was at
work again more actively than ever. It was nothing but a
Providence, Madam considered, that had put Richard out of
the way for a time : and could Madam have released Poole
from the consequences of his act, and sent him on his road rewarded, she had certainly done it. She gained her point.
Poor Mrs. Rane was to be taken up from her grave.

Dale, who had it in hand, went about the proceedings as
quietly and secretly as possible. He was sorry to have to do
it, for he bore no ill-will to Richard North, but the contrary,
and he knew how anxious he was that this should not be done;
while at the same time the lawyer hated Madam. But, he had
no choice : he had received his orders, as coroner, to call an
inquest, and could not evade it. He issued his instructions in
private, strictly charging the few, who must act, to keep
silence abroad. And not a syllable transpired beforehand.

The work was commenced in the dark of the winter's morning. By ten o'clock, however, the men had been seen in the
churchyard, and secrecy was no longer possible. Like wild-
fire ran the news to all parts of Dallory—Mrs. Rane was
being taken up. Never had there been excitement akin to
this. People rushed about like maniacs. They made nothing
of knocking at the doors of others who were strangers to them
and leaving the tidings : the street was in an uproar, the
windows were alive with heads : had Dallory suddenly found
itself invaded by a destroying army, the commotion could not
have been greater,

Oh, then began the exodus to the churchyard. It was as
though strings of pilgrims were flocking to a shrine. Mr.
Dale had foreseen this probability, and was prepared. A body
of police appeared in the churchyard, and the pilgrims found

they could not approach the actual spot beyond the limits of a respectful distance. Naturally resenting this, they relieved their feelings by loud talking.

Jelly was there. Never nearer losing her reason than now. Between dismay at what she had set afloat, and horror at the crime about to be revealed, Jelly was not clear whether she stood on her head or her heels. When the news was carried to her of what was going on, Jelly nearly fainted. Now that it had come to the point, she felt that she would have given the world never to have meddled with it. It was not so much of the responsibility to herself that she thought, as of the dreadful aspect of the thing altogether. She went into a fit of trembling, and ran into her chamber to hide it; when somewhat recovered, she asked leave of Mrs. Beverage to be allowed to go out for a few hours. To have been compelled to remain indoors would have driven her quite mad. The morning was getting late when Jelly arrived at the scene, and the first person she particularly noticed there was Mrs. Gass.

But Mrs. Gass had not come forth in idle curiosity as most others had done—and there were some superior people, in regard to station, amidst the mob. Mrs. Gass was inexpressibly shocked and dismayed that it should really have come to this. Oliver Rane was her late husband's nephew; she truly did not think he could have been guilty : and she had hastened to the spot to see whether any argument or persuasion might avail at this, the twelfth hour, to arrest proceedings and spare this disgrace to the North and Gass families.

But no. But no. Stepping over the barrier-line that the police had drawn, without the smallest regard to the remonstrance of a red-faced inspector, who was directing things, Mrs. Gass approached the small throng around the grave. She might have spared herself the pains. In answer to her urgent appeal she was told that nobody here had any power now; it was gone out of their hands. In getting back, crestfallen, Mrs. Gass encountered Jelly.

" Well," said she, regarding Jelly sternly, " be you satisfied with your work ? "

Jelly never answered. In her shame, her regret, her humiliation at what she had done, she could almost have wished herself labouring at some expiating treadmill.

" Any way, girl, you might have had the decency to keep away," went on Mrs. Gass.

" I couldn't," said Jelly, meekly. " I couldn't stop at home and bear it."

" Then I'd have gone a mile or two the tother way," re-ported Mrs. Gass. " You've got a face of your own—to show .t here. And a conscience too."

A frightful noise interrupted them : something between a shout and a yell. The heavy coffin was at length deposited on the ground with the tired pick-axes beside it, and the populace were expressing their mixed sentiments at the sight: some in a round of applause at this great advance in the show : others in a condemnatory groan of scorn meant for him who had caused it—Dr. Rane. Mrs. Gass, what with the yelling, and what with the coffin and pick-axes, and what with the crush, had never felt so cruelly humiliated in all her days ; and she retired behind a remote tree to hide her face of pain.

" Where is he, the murderer ? Why don't he come and look on at his poor victim ? She'll soon be open to sight. The crowner ought to ancuff him and haul him here.—Rabbit them watchful perlice ! They've got eyes behind 'em. They wants to be blowed up with a can o' powder. Look at old Jekyll there and his red face !—Ugh ! the poisoner ! What had poor Bessy North done to him, that he should put her in there ! The lead's thick enough ! it'll take time to open *that*. Bones ! Blood ! Fire !"

These sentences, amidst many others, penetrated to Mrs. Gass's ears. Just then Thomas Hepburn appeared in sight, his face very sad and pale.

" Hepburn," said Mrs. Gass, " I can't think they'll find anything wrong in there. My belief is she died natural. Unless there were better grounds to go upon than I know of, they ought not to have gone to this shameful length"

" Ma'am, I don't think it, either," assented the man. " I'm sure it has been more like a dream to me than anything else, since I heard it. Folks say it is Madam at the Hall that has forced it on."

Had Mrs. Gass been a man, she might have felt tempted to give Madam a very strong word. What right had she, in her ill-conditioned malice, to inflict this pain on others ?

" Whatever may be the upshot of this, Thomas Hepburn, it will come home to her as sure as that we two be talking here. What are you going there for ?" added Mrs. Gass, for he was preparing to make his way towards the open grave.

"I've had orders to be here, ma'am. Some of those law
officials don't understand this sort of work as well as I do."

He crossed over, the police making way for him, Inspector
Jekyll giving him a nod. Jelly was standing not far from
Mrs. Gass, leaning her forehead against a tree, as she strained
her eyes to look on. By the eagerness displayed by the crowd,
and the difficulty there was in keeping them back, it might
have been supposed they thought that they had only to get to
see the face of the dead body, lying within, to have all suspicion of Dr. Rane turned into fact.

The work went on. Now during an interval of almost
breathless silence ; now amidst a halfsuppressed roar. Suddenly, a frightful report was whispered from one to another ;
though who first spoke it, or whence it arose, none could discover—that their righteous curiosity was not to be gratified.
That as soon as the shell should be disinterred from the
leaden coffin, it was to be taken away unopened with what it
contained.

Unopened ! would they stand this ? Were they Englishmen, and should a miserable jackanapes-at-law (meant for
Dale) treat them in this way. Had not Bessy North grown
amidst them, and would they not see justice done her ? No,
no ; they had not come here to be cheated. They'd look on
her if they died for it.

The leaden covering came off amidst a tumult, and the
common deal shell alone remained now. So determined were
the mob, so threatening grew their aspect and movements—
and it was a pretty formidable mob now, as to numbers—that
a timorous old magistrate, who was present, left the grave :
and, putting up his hands for a hearing, assured them that
the shell was to be opened, and should be opened, there on
the ground.

It was at this juncture that another spectator came slowly
up—although it might have been supposed that the whole of
Dallory was already there. The mob, their excited faces
turned to the old magistrate and to Thomas Hepburn, who
was already at work, did not see his approach. Which was
perhaps as well : for it was Dr Rane.

Even from him had these proceedings been kept secret,
perhaps especially from him : and it was only now, upon
coming forth to visit a patient in Dallory, that he learnt what
was taking place in the churchyard. He came to it at once :
his countenance was stern, his face whiter than death.

Mrs. Gass saw him; Jelly saw him. Mrs. Gass silently moved to prevent his further approach, putting her portly black silk skirts in his way. Her intentions were good.

"Go back," she whispered. "Steal away before you are seen. Look at this unruly mob here. They might tear you to pieces, doctor, in the humour they are in."

"Let them—when I have stopped *that*," he recklessly answered, pointing to what Thomas Hepburn was doing.

"You are mad, doctor," cried Mrs. Gass in excitement. "Stop that! Why, look, sir, how impossible it would be, even with the best wish, to stop it now. A nail or two more knocked up, sir, and the lid's off."

It was as she said. Dr. Rane saw it. He took out his handkerchief, and passed it over his damp face.

"Richard North gave me his word that he would stop it, if it came to such a pass as this," he murmured to himself more than to Mrs. Gass.

"Richard North knows no more o' this than it seems you knew of it," she said. "He is shut up in his room at the Hall, and hears nothing. Doctor, take advice and get away," she imploringly whispered. "There's time yet."

"No," he doggedly said. "As it has gone so far, I'll stand my ground now."

Mrs. Gass groaned. The sound was lost in a rush—a fight —a hoarse roar—policemen contending against King Mob, King Mob against policemen. It turned even Mrs. Gass pale. Dr. Rane voluntarily arrested his advancing steps. Jelly lifted her face and peered out from the distant tree.

The lid had been lifted, and the open shell stood exposed. It was more than the excited numbers could witness, and be still. Inspector Jekyll and his fellows keep them back from looking into it? Never. A short, sharp struggle, and the police and their staves were nowhere. With a triumphant whoop the crowd flew forward.

But a strange hush, seemingly of consternation, had fallen on those who stood at the grave; a hush fell on these interlopers as they reached it. The coffin was empty.

Of all unexpected stoppages to proceedings, official or otherwise, a more complete one than this had never fallen. The old magistrate, the coroner—who had just come striding over the ground, to see how things were going on—Thomas Hepburn, and others generally, stared at the empty coffin in profound perplexity.

And the draggle-tail mob, when it had taken its fill of star-ing also, elbowing each other in the process, and fighting rue-fully for place and precedence, burst out into a roar. Not at all a complimentary one to Dr. Rane.

"He have sold her for dissection, he have! He never put her in at all, he didn't! He had a sham funeral! 'Twarn't enough to poison of her, but he must sell her a'ter it!"

To accuse a man of these heinous offences behind his back and beyond his hearing, is one thing, but it is not felt to be quite so convenient to do it in his presence. The sight of Dr. Rane walking calmly (not to say impudently) across the churchyard into their very midst, struck a kind of timidity on the spirits of the roarers. Silence supervened. They even parted to let him pass, backing on each other's feet without mercy. Dr. Rane threw his glance on the empty coffin, and then on those who stood around it.

"Well," said he, "why don't you take me?"

And not a soul ventured to reply.

"I have murdered my wife, have I? If I *have*, why you know I deserve no quarter. Come, Mr. Coroner, why don't you issue your edict to arrest me? You have your officers handy."

The exceeding independence with which this was spoken, the impudent freedom of Dr. Rane's demeanour, the scornful mockery of his tone, could not be surpassed. He had the best of it now; might say what he pleased, and laugh derisively at them at will : and they knew it. Even Dale, the coroner, felt small—which is saying a good deal of a lawyer.

Turning round, the doctor walked slowly back again, his umbrella swinging, his head aloft in the air. Mrs. Gass met him midway.

"Tell me the truth for the love of goodness, doctor. I have never believed it of you. You did not help her to her death?"

"Help her to her death?" he retorted. "No : my wife was too dear to me for that. I'd have killed the whole world rather than her—if it must have come to killing at all."

"And I believe you, doctor," was the hearty response. "And I have told everybody, from the first, that the charge was wicked and preposterous."

"Thank you, Mrs. Gass."

He broke from her from any further questions she might have put, and stalked away towards Dallory, coolly saying that he had a patient to see.

As to the crowd, they really did not know what to make of this : it was a shameful cheat. The small throng of officials, including the police, seemed to know as little. To be enabled to take Oliver Rane into custody for the poisoning of his wife they must first find the wife, and ascertain whether she had been poisoned. Lawyer Dale had never met with so bewildering a check in the long course of his practice ; the red-faced Inspector stroked his chin, and the old magistrate clearly had not got his proper mind back yet.

By the appearance of the shell, it appeared pretty evident that the dead body had never been in it at all. What had he done with it ?—where could he have hidden it ? A thought crossed Mr. Jekyll, experienced in crime, that the doctor might have concealed it in his house—or buried it in his garden.

" How was it you did not feel the lightness of the shell when you put it into the lead, you and your men ?" asked the Inspector, turning sharply to Thomas Hepburn.

" We did not do it," was the undertaker's answer. " Dr. Rane undertook that himself, on account of the danger of infection. We went and soldered the lead down, but it was all ready for us."

A clearer suspicion of guilt, than this fact conveyed, could not well be found : as they all murmured one to another. The old magistrate rubbed up his hair, as if by that means he could rub up his intellect.

" I don't understand," he said, still bewildered. " Why should he have kept her out of the coffin ? If he—if he did what was wrong, surely to bury her out of sight would be the safest place to hide away his crime. What do you think about it, Jekyll ?"

" Well, your worship, I can only think that—that he might have feared some such proceeding as this, and so secured himself against it," was the Inspector's answer. " I don't know, of course : it is only an idea."

" But *where* is the body, Jekyll ?" persisted the magistrate. " What could he have done with it ?"

" It must be our business to find out, your worship."

" Did he cut her up ?" demanded the mob. For which interruption they were chased backwards by the army of discomfited policemen.

" She may be about his premises still, your worship," said the Inspector, hazarding the opinion. " If so, I should say she is lying a few feet below the surface somewhere in the garden."

" Bless my heart, what a frightful thing ! " cried his worship. " And about this ?   What is going to be done ?"

He pointed to the coffins and the open grave.   Yes : what was to be done ?   Lawyer Dale searched his legal memory and could not remember any similar precedent to guide him. A short counsel was held, the outsiders groaning and hissing an accompaniment to it.

" When her bones is found, poor lady, they'll want Chris'an bur'al : as good let the grave lie open," interposed one of the grave-diggers respectfully—who no doubt wished to be spared the present labour of filling-in the earth.   To which opinion the gentlemen, consulting there, condescended to listen.

And, finally, that course was decided upon : Thomas Hepburn being requested to have the coffins removed to his place, pending inquiry.   And the gentlemen dispersed, and the mob after them.

A very dissatisfied mob it was, shuffling and trampling out of the churchyard.   They did not get much pleasure now, poor things, in their enforced idleness, their semi-starvation : and to be balked in this way was about as mortifying a termination as the day could have had.   There was only one worse to be imagined—and that was a possibility not glanced at : that it should have been discovered poor Mrs. Rane died naturally.

The last person left in the churchyard—except a man or two who stayed to guard the coffins, while means were being brought to take them away—was Jelly.   To have watched Jelly's countenance when the empty shell stood revealed, would have been as good as looking at a picture.   The mouth opened, the jaw dropped, the eyes were strained.   It was worse than even Jelly had supposed, and Dr. Rane was a greater villain.   Not content with taking his wife's life, he had also taken her body.   Whether he had disposed of it in the manner affirmed by the mob, or in that suggested by the Inspector, or in any other way, the doctor must be one of the most hardened criminals breathing—his brazen demeanour just now in the graveyard would bear out *that*.   And now the trouble was no nearer its clearance than before, and Jelly almost wished, as she had wished many a time lately, that she could die.   Hiding herself from the spectators stood she, her brow pressed against the friendly tree's trunk, her heart faint within her. When the echoes of the trampling mob died away in the distance, Jelly lifted her head to depart also, drawing her black shawl around her with a shudder.

"*That's* why she can't rest, poor lady; she's not laid in consecrated ground. A the worst, I never suspected this."

CHAPTER XLV.

A NIGHT EXPEDITION.

SEVEN o'clock was striking out on a dark winter's night, as a hired carriage with a pair of post horses drew up near to the gates of Dallory Hall. Apparently the special hour had been agreed upon for a rendezvous; for before the clock had well told its numbers, a small group of people might have been seen approaching the carriage from different ways.

There issued out from the Hall gates, Mr. North, leaning on the right arm of his son Richard. Richard had quitted his chamber to join in this expedition. His left arm was in a sling, and he looked pale; but he was fast advancing towards recovery; and Mr. Seeley, consulted confidentially, had given him leave to go. Mrs. Gass came up from the direction of Dallory; and Dr. Rane came striding from the Ham. A redfaced portly gentleman in plain clothes, who was standing by the carriage, greeted them: without his official costume and in the dark night, few would have recognised him for Inspector Jekyll, who had been directing in the churchyard the day before. Mrs. Gass, Mr. North, and Richard, got into the carriage. The Inspector was about to ascend to the box, the postillion being on the horses, but Dr. Rane said he would prefer to sit outside himself. So Mr. Jekyll got inside, and the doctor got up; and the carriage drove away down Dallory Ham.

Peering out after it, in the dark night, behind the post of the gates, was Mrs. North. Someone by her side—it was only a servant-boy—ran off, at a signal from her, towards the stables with a message, as fast as his legs would carry him. There came back in answer Madam's carriage—which must have been waiting for the signal—with a pair of fresh fleet horses.

"Catch it up, and keep it in sight at a distance," were her orders to the coachman, as she stepped in. So the post carriage was being tracked and followed: a fact none of its inmates had the slightest notion of.

In her habit of peeping and prying, of listening at this door, of putting her ear to that, of glancing surreptitiously into other people's letters, and of ferreting generally, Madam had become aware during the last twenty-four hours that some unusual stir was shaking the equanimity of Mr. North and Richard: that some journey, to be taken in secret by Mr. North, and kept secret, was being determined on. Conscience —when it is not a good one—is apt to suggest all kinds of unpleasant things, and Madam's whispered to her that this hidden expedition had reference to herself; and—perhaps—to a gentleman who had recently arrived in England—William Adair.

Madam's cheeks turned pale through powder and rouge, and she bit her lips and her nails in impotent rage. She could have found means, no doubt, to keep Mr. North indoors, though she had broken his leg to do it; she could have found means to keep Richard also, had she known he was to be of the party: but of what avail? Never a cleverer woman lived, than Madam, and she had the sense to know that a meeting with Mr. Adair (and she believed the journey had reference to nothing else) could not be prevented in this way: it must take place sooner or later.

A carriage was to be in waiting near the Hall gates after dark, at seven o'clock—Madam got hold of so much. Where was it going? In which direction? For what purpose? At least Madam could ascertain that. She gave private orders of her own: and as night approached, retired to her room with a headache, forbidding Mr. North and the household to disturb her. Mr. North, as he eat his dinner in his parlour, thought how well things were turning out. He had been haunted with a fear of Madam's pouncing upon him, in the moment of departure, with a demand to know the why and the wherefore.

Madam, attired for a journey likewise, had escaped from the Hall long before seven, and taken up her place amidst the shrubs near the entrance gates, her position conveniently commanding both the way from the house and the road outside it. On the stroke of seven, steps were heard advancing; and Madam strained her eyes.

Richard! *Richard!* Who had not yet been out of his sick room! But for his voice, as he spoke to his father, and the black sling, so clear as he passed her, Madam would have thought the night was playing tricks with her eyesight.

She could not see who else got into the carriage: but she did see Dr. Rane come striding by; and she thought it was he upon the box when the carriage passed. Dr. Rane? Madam, catching up her breath, wondered what private histories Mrs. Cumberland had confided to him, and how much of them he was now on his way to bear testimony to. Madam was altogether on the wrong scent—the result of her suggestive conscience.

In a twinkling almost, she was shut up in her own carriage, as described, her coachman alone outside it.

The man had no difficulty in obeying orders. The post-carriage was not as light as Madam's. Keeping at a safe distance, he followed in its wake, unsuspected. First of all, from the Ham down the back lane, and then through all kinds of unfrequented, cross-country by-ways. Altogether, as both drivers thought, fifteen or sixteen miles.

The post-carriage drew up at a solitary house, on the outskirts of a small hamlet. Madam's carriage halted too, further off. Getting out of it, she told her coachman to wait: and she stole cautiously along under cover of the hedge, to watch proceedings. It was then about nine o'clock.

They were all going into the house: a little crowd of them, as it seemed to Madam; and the post-carriage went slowly away, perhaps to an inn. What had they gone to that house for? Was Mr. Adair in it? Madam was determined to see. She partly lost sight of prudence in her desperation, and was at the door just as it closed after them. Half a minute and she knocked softly with her knuckles. It was opened by a young girl with a scarlet country face, and red elbows.

"Law!" said she, "I thought they was all in. Do you belong to 'em?"

"Yes," said Mrs. North.

So she went in also, and crept up the dark staircase, after them, directed by the girl. "Fust door you comes to at the top." Madam's face was growing of a ghastly whiteness: she fully expected to see William Adair.

The voices would have guided her without anything else. Several were heard talking together inside the room: her husband's she distinguished plainly: and, she thought, Madam certainly thought, he was sobbing. Madam went into a heat at that. What revelation had Mr. Adair been already making? He had lost no time.

The door was not latched. Madam cautiously pushed it an

inch or two open so as to enable her to see in. She looked very ugly just now, her lips drawn back from her teeth with emotion, something like a hyena's. Madam looked in: and saw, not Mr. Adair, but—Bessy Rane.

Bessy Rane. She was standing near the table, while Dr. Rane was talking. Standing quite still, with her placid face, her pretty curls falling, and a violet-coloured merino gown on, that Madam had seen her wear a dozen times. In short, it was just like Bessy Rane in life. On the table, by the side of the one candle, lay some white work, as if just put out of hand.

In all Madam's life she had perhaps never been so frightened as now—with present sheer fright. The truth did not occur to her. She surely thought it was an apparition, as Jelly had before thought; or that—or that—Bessy had in some mysterious manner been conveyed hither from that empty grave. In these moments of confusion the mind is apt to run away with itself. Madam's was not strong enough to endure the shock, and be silent. With a piercing shriek, she turned to fly, and fell against the whitewashed chimney that the architect of the old-fashioned house had thought fit to carry upwards through the centre of it. The next moment she was in hysterics.

Bessy was the first to run to attend her. Bessy herself, you understand, not her ghost. In a corner of the capacious old room, built when ground was cheap, was Bessy's bed; and on this they laid Mrs. North. Madam was not long in recovering her equanimity: but she continued where she was, making believe she was exhausted, and put a corner of her shawl over her face. For once in her life her face had some shame in it.

Yes: Bessy was not dead. Humanly speaking, there had never at all been any more probability of Bessy's demise than there was of Madam's at this moment. Dr. Rane is giving the explanation, and the others are standing to listen, except Mr. North, who has sat down in an elbow chair of polished wood, while Richard leans the weight of his undamaged arm on its back. Mrs. Gass has pushed back her bonnet from her beaming face; the Inspector looks impassive as befits his calling, but on the whole pleased.

"I am not ashamed of what I have done," said Dr. Rane, standing by Bessy's side; "and I only regret it for the pain my wife's supposed death caused her best friends, Mr. North and Richard. I would have given much to tell the truth to Mr.

North, but I knew it would not be safe to intrust it to him, and so I wished to let it wait until we should have left the country. For all that has occurred you must blame the tontine. That is, blame the Ticknells, who obstinately, wrongly, cruelly kept the money from us. There were reasons—my non-success in my profession for one—why I wished to quit Dallory, and start afresh in another place· I and my wife talked of it until it grew, with me, into a disease ; and I believe Bessy got to wish for it at last almost as I did."

"Yes, I did, Oliver," she put in.

"Look at the circumstances," resumed Dr. Rane, in his sternest tones, and not at all as though he were on his defence. "There was the sum of money—two thousand pounds—belonging to me and my wife jointly, and they denied our touching it until one of us should be dead ! It was monstrously unjust. I think you must acknowledge that much, Mr. Inspector."

"Well—it did seem hard," acknowledged that functionary.

"I know *I* thought it so," said Mrs. Gass.

"It was worse than hard," spoke the doctor passionately. "I used to say to my wife that if I could take it out of the old trustees' hands by force, or stratagem, I should think it no shame. Idle talk, it was! never meant to be anything else. But I'll get on. The fever broke out in Dallory, and Bessy was taken ill. She thought it was the fever, and so did I. I had fancied her a little afraid of it, and was in my heart secretly thankful to Mr. North for inviting her to the Hall. But for her putting off the going to it for a day—which she did herself through the absence of Molly Green—what happened later could never have taken place."

Dr. Rane paused, as if considering how he should go on with his story. After a moment he resumed it, looking straight at them, as he had been looking all along.

"I wish you to understand that every word I am telling you—and shall tell you—is the strict truth. The truth, upon my honour, and before Heaven. And yet, perhaps, even after this, you will scarcely give me credit when I say—that I did believe my wife's illness was the fever. All that first day (she had been taken ill during the night with sickness and shivering) I thought it was the fever. Seeley thought it. She was in a very high state of feverishness, and no doubt the fear of the fever for her served somewhat to bias our judgment. Bessy herself said it was the fever, and would not hear a word of hope to the contrary. But at night— the night of the first day, remember—she had nearly an hour of sickness; and was so relieved by it, and grew so cool and collected, that I detected the nature of the case. It was nothing but a bad bilious attack, accompanied by a very unusual degree of fever; but not *the* fever. 'You have cheated me, my darling,' I said in a jesting way as I kissed her, 'I shall not get the tontine.'—Here she stands by my side to confirm or refute it," broke off Dr. Rane, but indeed they could all see he was relating the simple truth. "'Can you not pretend that I am dead, Oliver?' she answered faintly, for she was still exceedingly ill; 'I'll go away, and you can say I died.' Now, of course Bessy spoke this jest-ingly, as I had done: but nevertheless the words did lead to what afterwards took place. *I* proposed it—do not lay the blame on Bessy—that she really should go away, and I should give out that she was dead."

A slight groan from the region of the bed, smothered at once by a pretended snore. Dr. Rane continued.

"In prospective it seemed very easy of accomplishment— very. But had I foreseen all the disagreeable proceedings, the artifice, the trouble, that must inevitably attend such an attempted deceit, I should never have entered upon it. Had I properly reflected, I of course might have foreseen it: but I did not reflect. Like a great many schemes that we enter upon in life, the mind skips the working, and is content to skip it, and looks only to the end accomplished. Nearly all that night Bessy and I conversed together: chiefly planning how she should get away and where she should stay. By morning, what with the fatigue induced by this prolonged vigil, and the exhaustion left from her illness, she was thoroughly worn out. It had been agreed between us that she should simulate weariness and a desire to sleep, the better to evade a discovery of her, so far, restoration; but there was no need to simulate; she was both sleepy and exhausted."

"I never was so sleepy before in all my life," interrupted Bessy.

"The day went on. At ten o'clock, when Phillis left, I went up to my wife's room, and told her the time for acting had come," pursued Dr. Rane. "Next I crossed over to Seeley's with the news that my wife was gone: and I strove to show the grief I should have felt had it been true. Cross-ing back to my home again, I saw Frank Dallory, and told him. 'The play is inaugurated,' I said to Bessy when I went in—and then I betook myself to Mr. North; and then on to Hepburn's. Do you remember, sir, how I tried to soothe your grief ?—speaking persistently of hope—though of course you could not see that any hope remained," asked Dr. Rane, turning to Mr. North. "I dared not speak more plainly, though I longed to do it."

"Ay, I do remember," answered Mr. North.

"The worst part of all the business was the next; the bringing in of the shell," continued the doctor. "Worse, because I had a horror of my wife seeing it. I contrived that she did not. Hepburn's men brought it up to the ante-room: Bessy was in bed still in the front room, and she heard them: I could not help that. When they left, I put it down by the side of the wall with the trestles, threw some of my coats carelessly upon it, and so hid it. It was time then for Bessy to get up. While she was dressing, I went round to the stables, where the gig and horse I use are kept, to make sure that the ostler had gone to bed—for he had a habit sometimes of sitting up late. It was during this absence of mine that Bessy, dressed all but her gown, went to the landing to listen whether or not I had come in. The chamber door was open, so that the light shone on the landing; it happened to be at that moment that Jelly was at the opposite window, and she— later—took it to be Mrs. Rane's ghost that she saw."

The sight of Mrs. Gass's amused face was something good. She nodded in triumph.

"I thought it might be beer," said she. "I told Jelly what an uncommon idiot she was. Ghost, indeed !"

"Bessy made herself ready, took some refreshment, and I brought the gig to the back door in the garden, and drove my wife away. The only place open at that time of night—or rather morning—would be some insignificant open railway station. We fixed on Hewley. I drove her there; and left her sitting under cover in solitary state—for I had to get back with the horse and gig before people were astir. As soon as the morning was pretty well on, so as not to be remarked by strangers, Bessy walked to Churchend, about five miles' distance, and took a lodging in this house—this same room. Where she has been ever since—and it is a vast deal longer time than we calculated on. Poison my wife !" added Dr. Rane, with some emotion, as he drew her to him involuntarily, with a gesture of genuine love. "She is rather

too precious to me for that. *You* know; don't you, my
darling."

The happy tears stood in her eyes as she met his. He
stooped and kissed her, very fondly.

"If my wife were taken from me, the Ticknells might keep
the tontine money, and welcome; I should not care for it without Bessy. It was chiefly for her sake that my great desire
to possess it arose," he added, emphatically. "I could not
bear that she should be reduced to so poor a home after
Dallory Hall. Bessy constantly said that she did not mind
it, but *I* did; minded it for her."

"Couldn't you have managed all this without the funeral?"
asked Richard North, speaking for the first time.

"*How* could I?" returned Dr. Rane. "There were no
means of avoiding it. When my wife was given out as dead,
she had to be buried, or Mr. Inspector Jekyll, there, might
have been coming in to ask the reason why. Had I properly
thought of all that must be done, I should, as I say, never have
attempted it. It was hateful to me; and I declare that I don't
know how I could, or did, carry it through. Once or twice I
thought I must stick fast, and confess, to my shame, that
Bessy was alive—but I felt that might be worse, of the two,
than going on with it to the end. I hope the Ticknells will
suffer for what they have cost me."

"Jelly says she saw the ghost twice," observed Mrs. Gass,
her eyes twinkling still.

"Ah! that was Bessy's fault," said Dr. Rane, shaking his
head at his wife, in mock reproval, as we do at a beloved
child when it is naughty. "She was so imprudent as to
come home for a few hours—walking across country by easy
stages and getting in after nightfall. It was about her clothes.
I have been over here twice at night—or three times, is it not,
Bessy?—and brought her things each time. But I brought
the most valuable of them: Bessy said she must have the
others; and at last, as I tell you, she came herself, to look after
them. I think the clothes were only an excuse—eh, Bessy?"

"Partly," acknowledged Bessy. "For, oh! I longed for a
sight of home. Just one more sight as a farewell. I had quitted
it in so bewildered a hurry. It again led to Jelly's seeing me. I
was at my large chest-of-drawers, papa," she continued, as if
speaking for Mr. North alone. "Oliver had gone round to get
the gig to bring me back; I thought I heard him come in
again, and went to the landing to listen. It was not he, but

Jelly; and we met face to face. I assure you she frightened *me*—for consequences—quite as much as I did her."

"And Bessy, my dear, what have the people here thought about it all the time?" inquired Mr. North. "Do they know who you are?"

"Why of course not, papa. They think I am a lady in poor health; staying here for the sake of country air—and I did feel and look very ill when I came. It is an old widow lady who has the house, and the girl you saw is her servant. They are not curious. They know us only as Mr. and Mrs. Oliver, and think we live at Bletchley. I want to know who it was that pushed matters to extremity in regard to these proceedings against my husband," added Mrs. Rane, after a pause. "It was not you, papa: and Richard was doing his best to hush it all up. Richard had known the truth since an interview he held with Oliver. Who was it, papa?"

Madam tumbled off the bed, moaning a little, as if she were very weak. Bessy had not the slightest idea that Madam had been the culprit.

"Who was it, Mr. Jekyll?" continued Bessy.

The Inspector looked up to the ceiling and down to the floor; and then thought the candle wanted snuffing. Which it certainly did. Madam said in a shrieking voice as he was putting down the snuffers, that she should depart. If the others chose to stay and countenance all this unparalleled iniquity, *she* could not.

She stood, upright as ever, tossing back her head, all her native impudence returning to her. Dr. Rane quietly put himself in her path as she was gaining the door.

"Mrs. North, pardon me if I request you to give me a little information ere you depart, as it is probably the last time we shall meet. What has been the cause of the long-continued and persistent animosity you have borne towards me?"

"Animosity to *you!*" returned Madam, flippantly. "I have borne none."

The exceeding coolness of the avowal, in the teeth of facts, struck them as almost ludicrous. Mr. North raised his head and gazed at her in surprise.

"You have pursued me with the most bitter animosity since the first moment that I came to Dallory, Madam," said Dr. Rane, quietly and steadily. "You have kept practice from me; you have done what you can to crush me. It is you who urged on this recent charge against me—a very present proof of what I assert. But for you it might never have been made."

Madam was slightly at bay: she seemed just a little flurried. Rallying her powers, she confronted Dr. Rane and told him that she did not think him skilful and did not personally like him; if she had been biassed against him, the feeling must have taken its rise in that—there was nothing else.

Another of her shuffling untruths—and they all knew it for one. But they would get nothing better from her.

The fact was this. Madam had feared that Mrs. Cumberland could, and perhaps would, throw some light on a certain episode of the past years: which contingency Madam had dreaded above any earthly thing: for this she had wished and hoped to drive Mrs. Cumberland from the place, and had deemed that if she could drive away Oliver Rane, his mother might follow. That was the real truth: but no living person, save Madam, suspected it.

She quitted the room with the last denial, conscious that she did not just now appear to advantage—the sneaking act of tracking them this night, Madam, with all her sophistry, could not plead an excuse for. They let her go. Even the Inspector did not pay her the courtesy of opening the door for her exit, or of lighting her down the crooked old wooden stairs. It was Bessy who ran to do it.

"When you found things were going to be pushed against you, sir, why did you not declare the truth?" asked the Inspector of Dr. Rane.

"I knew that the moment I declared the truth, all hope of the tontine money would be at an end; that I should have done what I had done for nothing," answered Dr. Rane. "Richard North undertook to give me notice in time if things should be pushed to an extremity; but he got disabled, you know, and could not. Until they were in the act of disturbing the grave, I had no warning of it."

A pause of silence followed the answer. Dr. Rane resumed.

"Ill-luck seems to have attended it from the first. Perhaps nothing better was to be expected. Jelly's having seen my wife was a great misfortune. And then look at the delay as to the tontine money! Had the trustees paid it at once, Bessy and I should have been safe away long ago."

"Where to?" asked Mrs. Gass.

"America. It is where we shall now go, in any case. As

E E

I have not the money to join Dr. Jones as partner, I daresay he'll be glad of me as an assistant."

"Look here," said Mrs. Gass. "I don't say that what you've done is anything but a very wrong thing, doctor; but it might have been worse: and, compared to what a lot o' fools were saying, it seems but a trifle. I was once about to make you an offer of some money. Finding you couldn't get the tontine paid to you and your wife; which, as I've told you, I thought was a shame, all circumstances considered; I resolved to advance it to you myself. Mrs. Rane's death stopped me: leastways, her reported death. You won't get it now, doctor, for certain, from the Ticknells—for I suppose they'll have to be told the truth: and so you shall have it from me. Two thousand pounds is ready for you, at your command."

A red spot of emotion flushed Dr. Rane's pale face. He gazed at Mrs. Gass eagerly, as if asking whether it could be true.

"It's all right, doctor. You are my late husband's nephew, you know, and all the money was his. You'll find yourself and your wife substantially remembered in my will; and as two thousand pounds of it may do you good now, it shall be advanced to you."

Bessy stole round to Mrs. Gass, and burst into tears on her bosom. Happy, grateful tears. The doctor, the scarlet flush deepening on his face, took Mrs. Gass's hand and clasped it.

"And I wish to my very heart I had made no delay in the offer at first," cried Mrs. Gass. "It'll always be a warning to me not to put off till to-morrow what should be done to-day. And so, doctor, there's the money ready; and Bessy, my dear, I don't see why you and he need banish of yourselves to America. You might get a good practice, doctor, and not go further nor London."

"I must go to America; I must go," said the doctor, hastily. "Neither I nor Bessy would like now to stay in England."

"Well, perhaps you may be right," acquiesced Mrs. Gass.

"But it's a long way," said Mr. North.

"It may not be for ever, sir," observed Dr. Rane, cheerfully. "I know I shall do well there; and when I have made a fortune perhaps we may come back and live in London. Never again in Dallory. Or, if not to live, to visit. The old and the new world are brought very near each other now, sir."

Is it of any use pursuing the interview to its close ? When they went out again, after it was over, Madam's carriage was only then driving off. Madam's coachman had put up his horses somewhere ; and neither he nor they could be readily found. There was apparently no house open in the primitive village, and Madam had the pleasure of undergoing an hour or two's soaking in a good, sound, down-pouring of rain.

"I shall have to make things right with the authorities ; and I suppose Hepburn may keep the coffins for his pains," quaintly remarked Mr. Inspector Jekyll.

But the carriage took back one less than it had brought. For Dr. Rane did not return again to Dallory.

Part the Third.

CHAPTER XLVI.

ARTHUR BOHUN'S SHAME.

A well-spread dessert table of glass and china and plate, glittering under the rays of the handsome chandelier in the dining-room of Sir Nash Bohun's town house. Sir Nash and his nephew Arthur are seated at it, one guest between them. It is General Strachan; an old officer, Scotch by birth, who had just come home, after passing the best part of his life in India.

The winter was departing. Arthur Bohun looked better, Sir Nash pretty well. In a month or two both intended to depart for the German springs, that were to renovate Sir Nash's life.

General Strachan had been very intimate with Sir Nash Bohun in early life, before he went out at all to India. After he went out he had been equally intimate with Major Bohun: but he was only Captain Strachan then.

"And so you think Arthur like his father," observed Sir Nash, as he passed the claret.

"The very image of him," replied the general. "I'm sure I should have known him for Tom Bohun's son had I met him accidentally in the street. Adair saw the likeness, too."

"What Adair's that?" carelessly asked Sir Nash.

"William Adair. You saw me with him at the club door this morning. We were going in at the moment when you came up."

Perhaps Sir Nash was a little struck with the name. He called to mind a good-looking, slender, gentlemanly man, who had been arm-in-arm with the general at the time mentioned.

"But what Adair is it, Strachan?"

"What Adair? Why, the one who was in India when—when poor Tom died. He was Tom's greatest friend. Perhaps you have never heard of him?"

"Yes I have, to my sorrow," said Sir Nash. "It was he who caused poor Tom's death."

General Strachan apparently did not understand. "Who caused poor Tom's death?"

"Adair."

"Why bless me, where could you have picked up that?" cried the general in surprise. "If Adair could have saved Tom's life at any sacrifice to himself he'd have done it. They were close, firm friends to the last."

Sir Nash seemed to be listening as though he heard not. "Of course we did not get at the particulars of my brother's death, over here, as we should have got at them had we been on the spot," he remarked. "We were glad, rather, to hush it up for the sake of Arthur. Poor Tom got into some trouble, some disgrace, and Adair led him into it. That's what we have always heard."

"Then you heard wrong, Bohun," said the general somewhat bluntly. "Tom got into debt, and I don't know what all, but it was not Adair that led him into it. Who could have told you it was?"

"Mrs. Bohun, Tom's widow."

"Oh, she," returned the general, in an accent of contempt that spoke volumes. "Why she—but never mind now," he broke off, suddenly glancing at Arthur as he remembered that she was his mother. "Let bygones be bygones, Bohun," he added, sipping his claret; "no good to recal them. Only don't continue to believe aught against William Adair. He is one of the best men living, and always has been."

Arthur Bohun, who had sat still as a stone, leaned his pale face a little towards the general, and spoke.

"Did not this Mr. Adair, after my father's death, get into disgrace, and—and undergo its punishment?"

"Never. Adair got into no disgrace."

"Has he been a convict?" continued Arthur in a low, clear tone.

"A WHAT?" cried the general, putting down his glass and staring at Arthur in amazement. "My good young fellow, you cannot know of whom you are speaking. William Adair has been a respected man all his life: he is just as honourable as your father was—and the world knew pretty well what poor

Tom's fastidious notions on the point of honour were. Adair is a gentleman amidst gentlemen; I can't say better of him than that, though I talked for an hour. He is come into all the family honours and fortune; which he never expected to do. A good old Scotch family it is, too; better than mine. There, we'll drop the subject now; no good to reap up things that are past and done with."

Sir Nash asked no more: neither did Arthur. Some instinct lay within both of them that, for their own sakes, it might be better not.

But when the General left—which he did very soon, having an evening engagement—Arthur went out with him. Arthur Bohun knew, as well as though he had been told, that his wicked mother—he could but think of her so in that moment —had dealt treacherously with him; to answer some end of her own, she had calumniated Mr. Adair. Cost him what pain and shame it might, he would clear it up now.

"Will you give me the particulars—that which you would not give my uncle," began Arthur in agitation, the moment they were out of the house, as he placed his hand on the General's arm. "No matter what they are, I must know them."

"I'd give them to your uncle, and welcome," said the plain old soldier. "It was to you I would not give them."

"But I must learn them."

"Not from me."

"If you will not tell them, I shall apply to William Adair."

"William Adair can give them you if he pleases. I shall not. Take advice, my dear young friend, and don't enquire."

"I will tell you what I suspect—that if anyone had a hand in driving my father to—to do what he did do, it was his wife; my mother. You may tell me now."

"No. Because she is your mother."

"But I have the most urgent reason for wishing to know the particulars."

"Well, Arthur Bohun, I'd rather not tell you, and that's the truth. If poor Tom could hear me in his grave, I don't think he'd like it, you see. No, I can't. Ask Adair, first of all, whether he'd advise it, or not."

"Where is he staying?"

"Grosvenor Place. He and his daughter are in a furnished house there. She is very delicate."

"And—you say—I beg your pardon, General," added

Arthur in agitation, detaining him as he was going away—
"You say that he is an untainted gentleman."

"Who? Adair? As untainted as you or I, my young
friend. Good night."

In his mind's miserable tumult, any delay seemed dreadful,
and Arthur Bohun turned at once to the house in Grosvenor
Place. He asked if he could see Mr. Adair.

The servant hesitated. "There is no Mr. Adair here, sir,"
he said.

Arthur looked up at the number. "Are you sure?" he
asked of the man. "I was informed by General Strachan that
Mr. Adair had taken this house, and was living here."

"The General must have said Sir William, sir. Sir William
Adair lives here."

"Oh—Sir William," spoke Arthur, "I—I was not aware
Mr. Adair had been knighted."

"Knighted, sir! My master has not been knighted, sir,"
cried the man, as if he were indignant at the charge. "Sir
William has succeeded to the baronetcy through the death of
his uncle, Sir Archibald."

What with one thing and another, Arthur's head seemed to
be in a whirl. Sir Archibald Adair had been well known to
him by reputation: a proud old Scotch baronet, of a proud
old lineage. And so this was Ellen's family! And he had
been deeming her not fit to mate with him, a Bohun!

"Can I see Sir William? Is he at home?"

"He is at home, sir. I think you can see him."

In the dining-room of the house sat Sir William Adair
when Arthur was shown in—his after-dinner coffee on a stand
by his side, a newspaper in his hand. He was a slight man
of rather more than middle height, with an attractive countenance. The features were good, their expression was noble
and pleasing. It was impossible to associate such a face and
bearing with anything like dishonour.

"I believe my name is not altogether strange to you, sir,"
said Arthur as the servant closed the door. "I hope you will
pardon my intrusion—and especially that it should be at this
late hour."

Sir William had risen to receive him. He could but mark
the agitation with which the words were spoken. A moment's
vacillation, and then he took Arthur's hand and clasped it
within his own.

"If I wished to be cold to you I could not," he said warmly.

" For, to me, you seem to be your father come to life again. He and I were friends."

" And did you wish to be cold to me ?" asked Arthur.

" I have felt cold to you this many a year. Worse than that."

" But why, Sir William ?"

" Ah—why. I cannot tell you. For one thing, I have pictured you as resembling another, more than him."

" You mean my mother."

Sir William looked at Captain Bohun before he replied. " Yes, I do. Will you take a seat : and some coffee ?"

Arthur sat down, but it may be questioned whether he as much as heard that coffee was mentioned. Sir William rang the bell and ordered a cup of it to be brought in. Arthur leaned forward to speak ; his blue eyes solemnly earnest, his hand a little outstretched. Sir William almost started.

" How strangely like him you are !" he exclaimed. " The look, the gesture, the voice, all are your father's over again. I could fancy that you were Thomas Bohun—as I *last* saw him in life."

" You knew him well,—and my mother ? You knew all about them ?"

" Quite well. I knew you too when you were a little child."

" Tell me one thing, then," said Arthur, his emotion increasing. " *Was* she my mother ?"

The question surprised Sir William Adair. " She was certainly your mother, and your father's wife. Why do you ask it ?"

" Because—she has so acted—that I—that I—have many a time wished she was not. I have almost hoped it. I wish I could hope it now."

" Ah," said Sir William. It was all he said.

" Did you care much for my father, Sir William ?"

" More than I ever cared for any other man. I have never cared for one since as I cared for him. We were young fellows then, he and I ; not much older than you are now ; but ours was a true friendship."

" Then I conjure you, by that friendship, to disclose to me the whole history of the past : the circumstances attending my father's shocking death, and its cause. Speak of things as though my mother were no blood relative of mine. I wish to heaven she never had been !"

" I think you must know somewhat of the circumstances," spoke Sir William. " Else why should you say this ?"

" It is because I know part that I must know the whole. My mother has—has—*lied* to me," he concluded, bringing out the word with a painful effort. " She has thrust a false story upon me, and—I cannot rest."

" Arthur Bohun, although you conjure me by your late father, and for his sake I would do a great deal, I fear that I ought not to do this."

" General Strachan bade me come to you. I begged of him to tell me, but he said no. Does he know all ?" broke off Arthur.

" Every tittle. I think he and I and your mother are nearly the only three left who do know it. There were but some half-dozen of us altogether."

" And do you not think that I, Major Bohun's only son, should at least be made acquainted with as much as others know ? Tell it me, Sir William : for my lost father's sake."

" The only difficulty is—that you must hear ill of your mother."

" I cannot hear worse of her than I know," impetuously returned Arthur. " Perhaps it was not as bad as I am imagining that it may have been."

But Sir William held back. The coffee came in and Arthur drank it at a gulp, scalding hot, and sent the cup away again. He seemed on the brink of a fever in his impatience. And, whether it was that, or to clear the memory of Major Bohun, or that he deemed it a righteous thing to satisfy Major Bohun's son, or that he yielded to over-persuasion, Sir William Adair spoke.

They sat nearly together, the small coffee table between them. Whether the room was light, or whether the room was dark, neither remembered. It was a miserable tale they were absorbed in ; one that need not be very much elaborated here.

William Adair, when a young man, quarrelled with his family, or they with him, and an utter estrangement took place. His father and mother were dead, but his uncle, Sir Archibald, and other relatives, were left. He, the young man, went to the Madras Presidency, appointed to some post there in the civil service. His family made a boast of discarding him ; he, in return, was so bitterly incensed and resentful against them, that had it been well practicable, he would have abandoned the very name—Adair. Never a word did he breathe to anyone of who or what his family was; his Scotch accent betrayed his country, but people knew no more. That he was a gentleman, and in a gentleman's position, was apparent, and that was all-sufficient.

A strong friendship ensued between him and Major Bohun. During one hot season it happened that they both went up in search of health to the Blue Mountains, as Indians call the beautiful region of the Neilgherry Hills. Mrs. Bohun accompanied her husband; Mr. Adair was not married. There they made the acquaintance of the Reverend George Cumberland, who was stationed at Ootacamund with his wife. Ootacamund was at that time filled, and a great deal of gaiety (a great deal considering what the place was) was going on; Mrs. Bohun was noted for it. There was some gambling nightly: and no votary joined in it more persistently than she. Major Bohun removed with her to a little place at a short distance, and a few others went also; the chaplain, George Cumberland, was one.

There came a frightful day for Major Bohun. Certain claims suddenly swooped down upon him; debts; promissory notes, bearing his signature in conjunction with William Adair's. Neither understood what it could mean, for they had given nothing of the kind. A momentary thought arose to Major Bohun—that his wife was implicated; but only so far as that she might have joined in this high play; nothing worse. He had become aware that she had a passion for gambling, and the discovery had frightened him: in fact, it was to wean her from undesirable associates and pursuits that he had come away on this holiday; the ostensible plea, health, was not the true one. But this was not known even to his best friend, William Adair. "Let me investigate this, let me deal with it," said the major to Mr. Adair. But Mr. Adair, not choosing to let a man forge his name with impunity—and he had no suspicion it was a woman—did not heed the injunction, but addressed himself to the investigation. And a nice nest of iniquity he found. He traced the affair home to one Rabbetson—but that was in all probability an assumed name—a man bad in every way; who was no better than a blackleg; who had wormed himself into society to prey upon it, and upon men and women's failings. This man Mr. Adair confronted with Major Bohun; and then—and then—the fellow, brought to bay, braved it out by disclosing who his helpmate was—Mrs. Bohun.

It was even so. Mr. Adair sat aghast at the revelation. Had he suspected this, he would have kept it to himself. How far she had connected herself with this man, it was best not to enquire: and they never did enquire, and never knew One thing was certain—the man could afford to take a high ground. He went out from the interview bidding them do their worst—which with him would not be much, he affirmed; for it was not he who had issued the false bills, but the major's wife. And they saw he spoke the truth.

Arthur Bohun listened to this now, sitting still as a statue.

"I never saw any man so overcome as Bohun," continued Sir William Adair. "He took it to heart; to heart. 'And she is the mother of my child!' he said to me; and then he gave way, and held my hands in his, and sobbed upon my shoulder. 'We will hush it up; we will take up the bills and the other obligations,' I said to him: though in truth I did not see how I should do my part in it, for I was a poor man: he was poor also; his expenses and his wife kept him so. 'It cannot be hushed up, Adair,' he answered; 'it has gone too far.' Those were the last words he ever said to me; it was the last time I saw him alive."

"Go on," said Arthur, without lifting his head.

"Mrs. Bohun came into the room, and I quitted it. I saw by her face that she knew what had happened; it was full of evil as she turned it on me. Rabbetson had met her when he was going out, and whispered some words in her ear. What passed between her and Major Bohun I never knew. Before I had been five minutes in my rooms she stood before me; she had followed me down. Of all the vituperation that a woman's tongue can utter, hers lavished about the worst on me. It was I who had brought on the crisis, she said; it was I who had taken Rabbetson to her husband. I quietly told her that when I took Rabbetson to Major Bohun, I had not the remotest idea that she was mixed up with the affair in any way! and that if I had known it, known what Rabbetson could say, I never should have taken him, but have striven to deal with it myself, and keep it dark for my friend Bohun's sake. She would hear nothing; she was like a mad woman; she cursed me; she swore that not a word of it was true; that Rabbetson did not say it, could not have said it, but that I and Major Bohun had concocted the tale between us. In short, I think she was, for the time being, mad."

"Stay a moment, Sir William," interrupted Arthur.

"Who was she? I have never known. I don't think my father's family ever did know."

"Neither did I ever know—to a certainty. A cousin, or sister, or some relative of hers, had married a doctor in practice at Madras, and she was out there on a visit to them. Captain Bohun—as he was then—caught by her face and figure, both fine in those days, fell in love with her and married her. He found afterwards that her father kept an hotel somewhere in England."

So! This was the high-born lady who had set up for being above all Dallory. But for the utmost self-control Arthur Bohun would have groaned outright.

"Go on, please," was all he said. "Get it finished."

"There is not much more," returned Sir William. "I went looking about for Bohun everywhere that afternoon; and could not find him. Just before sun-down he was found—found as —as I daresay you have heard. The spot was retired and shady, and his pistol lay beside him. He had not suffered: death must have been instantaneous."

"The report here was that he died of sun-stroke," said Arthur, breaking a long pause.

"No doubt. Mrs. Bohun caused it to be so reported. The real facts transpired but to few: Cumberland, Captain Strachan, myself, and two or three others."

"Did Mrs. Cumberland know of them?" suddenly asked Arthur, a thought striking him.

"I daresay not. I don't suppose her husband would disclose to her the shameful tale. She was not on the spot at the time; had gone to nurse some friend who was sick. I respected both the Cumberlands highly. We made a kind of compact among ourselves, we men, not to speak of this story ever, unless it should be to defend Bohun, or for some other good purpose. We wished to give Mrs. Bohun a chance to redeem her acts and doings in her own land, for which she at once sailed. Arthur, if I have had to say this to *you*, it is to vindicate your dead father. I believe that your mother has dreaded me ever since."

Dreaded him! Ay! and foully aspersed him in her insane dread. Arthur thought of the wicked invention she had raised, and passed his hands upon his face as if he could shut out the remembrance.

"What became of Rabbetson?" he asked, in a low tone.

"He disappeared. I think, else, I should surely have shot

him in his turn, or kicked him to death. I saw him afterwards in Australia dying in the most abject misery."

"And the claims?—the bills?"

"I took them upon myself; and contrived to pay—with
time."

"You left India for Australia?" continued Arthur, after a
pause.

"My health failed, and I petitioned our government to
remove me to a different climate. They complied, and sent
me to Australia. I stayed there, trying to accumulate a com-
petency that should enable me to live at home with Ellen as
befitted my family: little supposing that I was destined to
become its head. My two cousins, Sir Archibald's sons, have
died one after the other."

Arthur Bohun had heard all he wished, perhaps all there
was to tell. If—if he could make his peace with Ellen, the
old relations between them might yet be renewed. But while
his heart bounded with the hope, the red shame crimsoned his
brow as he thought of the past. Glancing at the time-piece
on the mantle-shelf, he saw it was only half-past nine; not
too late.

"May I see your daughter, sir?" he asked in a low tone.
"We used to be good friends."

"So I suppose," replied Sir William. "You made love to
her, Mr. Arthur Bohun. You would have married her, I
believe, but that I stopped it."

"You—stopped it!" exclaimed Arthur, quite at sea: for
he had not known of the letter received by Ellen.

"I wrote to Ellen, telling her I must forbid her to marry
you. I feared at the time of writing that the interdict might
not arrive in time. But it seems it did."

"Yes," abstractedly returned Arthur, letting pass what he
did not understand.

"You see, I had been thinking of you always as belonging to her—your mother—more than to him. That mistake is over. I shall value you now as *his* son; more I dare
say than I shall ever value any other young man in this
world."

Arthur's breath came fast and thick. "Then—you—you
will give her to me, sir!"

Sir William shook his head in sadness. Arthur misunder-
stood the meaning.

"The probability is, sir, that I shall be Sir Arthur Bohun;

that I shall succeed my uncle in the baronetcy. Would it not satisfy you ? "

"You can see her if you will," was Sir William's answer, but there was the same sad kind of denial in his manner. "I would not say No now for your father's sake. She is in the drawing-room. Upstairs, front room. I will join you as soon as I have written a note."

Arthur found his way to it by instinct. Ellen was lying back in an easy chair; the brilliant light of the chandelier shining on her face. Opening the door softly, it—that face—was the first object that struck his sight. And he started back from it in a kind of amazed terror.

Was it *death* that he saw written there ? All too surely the conviction came home to him.

Oh ! but it was a more momentous interview than the one just over. Explaining he knew not how, explaining he knew not what, save that his love had never left her, Arthur Bohun knelt at her feet, and they mingled their sobs together. For some minutes neither could understand the other : but elucidation came at last. Arthur told her that the wicked tale, the frightful treachery which had parted them was but a concocted fable on his mother's part, and then he found that Ellen had never known anything about the tale.

"What then did you think was the matter with me ?" he asked.

And she told him. She told him without reserve, now that she found how untrue it was : she thought he had given her up for another. Madam had informed her he was about to marry Miss Dallory.

He took in the full sense of what the words implied : of the very abject light in which his conduct must have appeared to her. Going to marry Mary Dallory ! a groan burst from him : he covered his face to hide its shame and trouble.

"Ellen ! Ellen ! You *could* not have thought it of me."

"It was what I did think. How was I to think anything else ? Your mother said it."

"Lord forgive her her sins ! " he wailed, in his despair. Ellen hid her face.

"It was enough to kill you, Ellen. No wonder you look like this."

She was panting a little. Her breath seemed very short.

"Pray heaven I may be enabled to make it up to you when you are my wife. I will try hard, my darling."

" I shall not live for it, Arthur."

A spasm took his heart. The words struck him as being so very real.

" Arthur, I have known it for some time now. You must not grieve for me. I think even that death is rather near."

" What has killed you ? I ? "

A flush passed over her wan face. Yes, he had killed her. That is, his conduct had : the sensitive crimson betrayed it.

" I suppose the fact is, I should not in any case have lived long," she said, aloud. " I believe they feared something of the kind for me years ago. Arthur, don't! Don't weep; I cannot bear it."

Sir William Adair had just told him how his father had wept in *his* misery. And before Arthur could well collect himself, Sir William entered.

" You see," he whispered aside to Arthur, " why it may not be. There will be no marriage for her in this life. I am not surprised. I seem to have expected it always : my wife, her mother, died of decline."

Arthur Bohun quitted the house, overwhelmed with shame and sorrow. What regret is there like unto that for past mistaken conduct which can never be repaired, never remedied in this world ?

CHAPTER XLVII.

NO HOPE.

Once more, and for good, does the scene change to Dallory.

Seated on the lawn-bench at Dallory Hall in the sweet spring sunshine—for the time has again gone on—was Ellen Adair. Sir William Adair and Arthur Bohun were pacing amidst the flower-beds that used to be Mr. North's. Arthur stooped and plucked a magnificent pink hyacinth.

" It is not treason, sir, is it ? " he asked, smiling.

" What is not treason ? " returned the elder man.

" To pick this."

" Pick as many as you like," said Sir William.

" Mr. North never liked us to pluck his flowers. Now and then Madam would make a ruthless swoop upon them for her entertainments. It grieved his heart bitterly : and I think that was whence we got an idea that he did not like us to pluck them."

" No wonder," said Sir William.

The restoration to the old happiness, the clearing-up of the
dreadful cloud that had so fatally told upon her, seemed to
infuse new vigour into Ellen's shortening span of life.   With
the exception of her father, everybody thought she was recovering : the doctors admitted, rather dubiously, that
it "might be." She got wonderfully well through the winter,
went out and about almost as of old ; and when more genial
weather set in, it was suggested by friends that she should be
taken to a warmer climate.   Ellen opposed it; it would be of
no avail she knew, perhaps only hasten on the end ; and after
a private interview Sir William had with the doctors, *he*
did not second it.   Her great wish was to go to Dallory :
and arrangements for their removal thither were made.

Dallory Hall was empty, and Sir William found that he
could occupy it for the present if he pleased.   Mr. North
had removed to the house that had been Mrs. Cumberland's,
leaving his own furniture (in point of fact it was Richard's)
at the Hall, hoping the next tenant, whoever that might
prove to be, would take to it.   Miss Dallory seemed quite
undecided what to do with the Hall, whether to let it for
a term again, or not.   But she was quite willing that Sir
William Adair should have it for a month or two.

And so he came down with Ellen, bringing his servants.
This was only the third day after their arrival, and Mr. Arthur
Bohun had arrived.   Sir William had told him he might come
when he would.

The change seemed to have done Ellen good, and she had had
her visitors.   Mrs. Gass had been there; Mr. North had
come ; and Richard ran in for a few minutes daily.   Sir
William welcomed them all heartily ; Mrs. Gass warmly ; for
she was the sister-in-law of Mrs. Cumberland, and Ellen had
told him of Mrs. Gass's goodness of heart.   She had untied
her bonnet, tilting it to the back of her head without ceremony, and stayed luncheon with them.

Mr. North was alone in his new home, and was likely to be ;
for his wife had relieved him of her society.   Violently indignant
at the prospect of removal from such a habitation as the Hall
to that small home of the late Mrs. Cumberland's, Madam
went off to London with Matilda, and took Sir Nash Bohun's
house by storm.   Not an hour, however, had she been in it,
when Madam found all her golden and aspiring dreams must
be scattered to the four winds.   Never again would Sir Nash
receive her as a guest or tolerate her presence.   The long

hidden truth, as connected with his unfortunate brother's death, had been made clear to him: first of all by General Strachan, next by Sir William Adair, with whom he became intimate.

What boots it to tell of the interview between Arthur and his mother? It was of a painful character. There was no out-spoken reproach, there was no loud voice raised. In a subdued manner, striving all the while for calmness, Arthur told her she had wilfully destroyed both himself and Ellen Adair; her life, for she was dying; his happiness. He recapitulated all that had been disclosed to him relating to his father's death; and Madam, brought to bay, never denied its accuracy.

"But that I dare not presume deliberately to fly in the face of one of Heaven's express Commandments, I would now cast you off for ever," he concluded in his bitter pain. "Look upon you again as my mother, I cannot. I will help you when you need help; so far will I act the part of a son to you; but all respect for you has been forced out of me; and I would prefer that we should not meet very often."

Madam went off the same day to Germany, Matilda and Parrit, the maid, in her wake. Letters came from her to say she should never go back to Dallory; never; probably never set her foot on British soil again; and therefore she desired that a suitable income might be secured to her abroad.

And so Mr. North had his new residence all to himself— save for Richard. Jelly had taken up her post as his housekeeper, general manager, and upper servant; with a boy and a maid under her; and there was one outdoor gardener. All of whom she domineered over to her heart's content. Jelly was regaining some of her lost flesh, and more than her lost spirits. Set at rest in a confidential interview with Mr. Richard, as to the very tangible nature of the apparition she had seen, Jelly was herself again. Mr. North thought his garden lovely, more compact even than the extensive one at the Hall; he was out in it all day, working a bit between whiles, and felt at peace. Mrs. Gass came to see him often; Mary Dallory nearly daily: he had his good son Richard to bear him company in the evening: and altogether Mr. North was in much comfort. It had been Richard's intention to take a lodging for himself; but the departure of Madam

changed his plans, and he went into the new house with his
father. Dr. Rane's house remained empty: old Phillis, to
whom also had been disclosed the truth, being there to take
care of it. The doctor's personal effects had been sent to him
by Richard.

And that's all that need be said of the changes just yet.

"Ellen looks much better, sir," remarked Arthur Bohun,
as he twirled the pink hyacinth he had plucked.

"A little fresher, perhaps, from the country air," answered
Sir William.

"I have not lost hope: she may be mine yet," he
murmured.

Sir William did not answer. He would give her to Arthur
now with his whole will and heart, had her health permitted
it. Arthur himself looked ill; in the last few months he
seemed to have aged years. An awful amount of remorse
was ever upon him; his life, in its unavailing regret, seemed
to be one long agony.

They turned across to where she was sitting. "Would you
not like to walk a little, Ellen?" asked her father.

She rose at once. Arthur held out his arm, and she took it
Sir William was quite content that it should be so: Arthur,
and not himself. The three paced the lawn. Ellen wore a
lilac silk gown and warm white burnouse cloak. An elegant
girl yet, though worn nearly to a shadow, with the same sweet
face as of yore.

But she was soon tired, and sat down again, Arthur by her
side. One of the gardeners came up for some orders, and Sir
William went away with him.

"I have not been so happy for many a day, Ellen, as I am
this one," began Captain Bohun. "You are looking quite
yourself again. I think—in a little while—that you may be
mine."

A blush, beautiful as the rose-flush of old, sat for a moment
on her cheeks. She knew how fallacious was the hope.

"I am nearly sure that Sir William thinks so, and will soon
give you to me," he added.

"Arthur," she said, putting her wan and wasted hand on
his, "don't lay the hope to heart. The—the disappointment,
when it came, would be all the harder to bear."

"But, my darling, you are surely better!"

"Yes, I seem so, just for a little time. But I fear that I
shall never be well enough to be your wife."

"It was so very near once, you know," was all he whispered.

There was no one within view, and they sat, her hand clasped in his. The old expressive silence that used to lie between them of old, ensued now. They could not tell to each other more than they had told. In the most unexpected reconciliation that had come, in the bliss it brought, all had been disclosed. Arthur had heard all about her self-humiliation and anguish; he knew of the treasured violets, and their supposed treachery: she had listened to his recital of the weeks of despair; she had seen the letter, written to him from Eastsea, worn with his kisses, his tears, and kept in his bosom still. No: of the past there was nothing more to tell each other; so far, they were at rest.

Arthur Bohun was still unconsciously twirling that pink hyacinth about in his fingers. Becoming aware of the fact, he offered it to her, putting it in her lap. A wan smile parted her lips.

"You should not have given it to me, Arthur."

"Why?"

Ellen took it up and smelt it. The perfume was very strong.

"Why should I not have given it to you?"

"Don't you know what the hyacinth is an emblem of?"

"No."

"Death."

One quick, pained glance at her. She was smiling yet, and looking rather fondly at the flower. Captain Bohun took both the flower and hand into his.

"I always thought you liked hyacinths, Ellen."

"I have always liked them very much indeed. And I like the perfume—although it has something in it faint and sickly."

He quietly flung the flower on the grass, and put his boot on it to stamp out its beauty. A nearer emblem of death, now, than it was before; but he did not think of that.

"I'll find you a sweeter flower presently, Ellen. And you know ——"

A visitor was crossing the lawn to approach them. It was Mary Dallory. She had not yet been to see Ellen. Something said by Mrs. Gass had sent her now. Happening to call on Mrs. Gass that morning, Mary heard for the first time of the love that had so long existed between Captain Bohun and Miss Adair, and that the course of the love had been forcibly interrupted by Madam, who had put forth the plea to Ellen that her son was engaged to Miss Dallory.

Mary sat before Mrs. Gass in mute surprise, recalling facts and fancies. "I know that Madam would have liked her son to marry me; the hints she gave me on the point were too broad for me to mistake that," she observed to Mrs. Gass. "Neither I nor Captain Bohun had any such thought or intention; we understood each other too well."

"Any way, you once took in me," said Mrs. Gass.

Mary laughed. "It was only in sport: I did not think you were serious."

"They believed in it at the Hall."

"Oh, did they? So much the better."

"My dear, I am afraid it was not for the better," dissented Mrs. Gass rather solemnly. "They say that it has killed Miss Ellen Adair."

"What?" exclaimed Mary.

"Ever since that time when she first went to the Hall on Mrs. Cumberland's death, she has been wasting and wasting away. Her father, Sir William, has now brought her to Dallory, not to try if the change might restore her, for nothing but a miracle would do that, but because she took a whim to come. Did you hear that she was very ill?"

"Yes, I heard that."

"Well, then, I believe it is nothing else but this business that has made her ill—Captain Bohun's deserting of her for you. She was led to believe it was so—and until then, they were wrapt up in each other."

Mary Dallory felt her face grow hot and cold. She had been entirely innocent of ill intention; but the words struck a strange chill of repentance to her heart.

"I—don't understand," she said in a frightened tone. "Captain Bohun knew there was nothing between us; that there was not the shadow of a pretence of it: why did he not tell her better?"

"Because he and she had parted on another score; they had been parted through a lie of Madam's, who wanted him to marry you. I don't rightly know what the lie was; something frightfully grave; something he could not repeat again to Miss Adair; and Ellen Adair never heard it, and thought it was as Madam said—that he had turned his love over to you."

Mary sat as one struck dumb, thinking of the past. There was a long pause.

"How did you get to know this?" she breathed.

"Ah, well—partly through Mr. Richard. And I sat an

hour talking with poor Miss Ellen yesterday, and caught a hint or two then."

"I will set it straight," said Mary; feeling, though without much cause, bitterly repentant.

"My dear, it has been all set straight between 'em since the winter. Nevertheless, Miss Mary, 'twas too late. Madam did her crafty work well."

"Madam deserves to be drawn through the place at the cart's tail," was the impulsive rejoinder of Miss Dallory.

She betook herself to the Hall there and then. And this explains her approach. Things had become pretty clear to her as she walked along. She had never been able to account for the manner in which Ellen seemed to have shunned her, to have avoided all approach to intimacy or friendship. That Mary Dallory had favoured the impression that was abroad of Arthur Bohun's possible engagement to her, she was now all too conscious; or, at any rate, had not attempted to refute it. But she had never thought she was doing harm to any one.

Just as Arthur Bohun had started back when he first saw Ellen in the winter, so did Miss Dallory start now. Wan and wasted! ay, indeed. Mary felt half sick, to think what share she had held in it.

She said nothing at first. Room was made for her on the bench, and they talked of indifferent matters. Sir William came up, and was introduced. Presently he and Arthur strolled to a distance.

Mary spoke then. Just a word or two, she said of the misapprehension that had existed; and burst forth into her exculpation.

"Ellen, I would have died rather than have caused you pain. Oh if I had but known! Arthur and I were familiar with each other as brother and sister: never a thought of aught else was in our minds. If I let people think there was, why— it was done in a kind of coquetry. I had somebody else in my head, you see, all the while; and that's the truth. And I am afraid I enjoyed the disappointment that would ensue for Madam."

Ellen smiled faintly. "It seems to have been a complication altogether. A kind of ill-fate that I suppose there was no avoiding."

"You must get well, and be his wife."

"Ay. I wish I could."

But none could be wishing that as Arthur was. Hope deceived him ; he confidently thought that a month or two would see her his. Just for a few days the deceitful improvement in her continued.

One afternoon they drove to Dallory churchyard. Ellen and her father ; Arthur sitting opposite them in the carriage. A fancy had taken her that she would once more look on Mrs. Cumberland's grave ; and Sir William said he should like to see it.

The marble stone was up now, with its inscription, "Fanny, widow of the Reverend George Cumberland, Government Chaplain, and daughter of the late William Gass, Esq., of Whitborough." There was no mention of her marriage to Captain Rane. Perhaps Dr. Rane fancied the name was not in very good odour just now, and so omitted it. The place where the ground had been disturbed, to take up those other coffins, had been filled in again with earth.

Ellen drew Sir William's attention to a green spot near, overshadowed by the drooping branches of a tree that waved its leaves in the breeze, and flickered the grass beneath with ever-changing light and shade.

"It is the prettiest spot in all the churchyard," she said, touching his arm. "And yet no one has ever chosen it."

"It is very pretty, Ellen; but solitary."

"Will you let it be here, papa ?"

He understood the soft whisper, and slightly nodded, compressing his lips. Sir William was not deceived. Years had elapsed, but, to him, it seemed to be his wife's case over again. There had been no hope for her ; there was none for Ellen.

CHAPTER XLVIII.

BROUGHT FORCIBLY HOME TO HIM.

BACK in an easy chair she lay, in the little room that was once Mr. North's parlour. The window was flung open to the sweet flowers, to the balmy air ; and Ellen Adair drank in alike their beauty and their perfume.

She took to this room as her own sitting-room the day she came back. She liked it. Sir William, seeing that, had caused the shabby old carpet and chairs and tables to be put out, and fresh and bright furniture brought in. How willingly, had it been possible, would he have kept her in life !

Just for a few days had hope lasted—no more. The change in her had come on suddenly, and was unmistakable. She wore a white gown, tied round the waist with a pink girdle, and a little bow of pink ribbon—her favourite colour—at the neck. She sought to look well yet ; her toilet was attended to, her bright hair was arranged carefully as ever. But the maid did all that. The wan face was very sweet still, the soft brown eyes had all their old lustre. Very listless was the worn white hand lying on her lap ; loosely sat the plain gold ring on it—the ring that, through all the toil and trouble, had never been taken off. Ellen was alone. Sir William had gone by appointment to see over Richard North's works.

A sound as of steps on the gravel. Her father *could* not have come back yet ! A moment's listening, and then the red hectic flushed her face ; for she knew the step too well. Captain Bohun had returned, then !

Captain Bohun had gone to London to see Sir Nash off on his projected Continental journey to those springs that were to make him young again. Sir Nash had looked for Arthur to accompany him, but he now acknowledged that Ellen's claims were paramount to his. Ellen had thought he might have been back yesterday.

He came in at the glass doors, knowing he should probably find her in the room. But his joyous smile died away when he saw her face. His step halted ; his already held-out hand dropped at his side.

"*Ellen !*"

In a timid, frightened, wailing tone was the word spoken. Only three days' absence, and she had faded like this ! Was it a relapse ?—or what had she been doing to cause the change ?

For a few minutes, perhaps neither of them was sufficiently collected to know what passed. In his shock of abandonment, he knelt by the chair, holding her hands, his eyes dropping tears. The remorse ever gnawing at his heart was very cruel just then. Ellen bent towards him, and whispered that he must be calm—must bear like a man : things were but drawing a little nearer.

"I should have been down yesterday, but that I waited in town to make sundry purchases and preparations," he said. "Ellen, I thought that—perhaps—next month—your father would have given you over to me."

"Did you ? " she faintly answered.

"You must be mine," he continued, in too deep emotion to weigh his words. "If you were to die first, I—I think it would kill me."

"Look at me," was all she answered. "See whether it is possible."

"There's no knowing. It might restore you. The fresh scenes, the warm pure climate that I would take you to—we'd find one somewhere—might do wonders. I pointed this out to Sir William in the winter."

"But I have not been well enough for it, Arthur."

"Ellen, it must be! Why, you know; you know that you were almost my wife. Half an hour later, and you would have been."

She released one of her hands, and hid her face upon it. Captain Bohun grew more earnest in his pleading; he was really thinking this thing might be.

"I shall declare the truth to Sir William Adair—and I know that I ought to have done so before, Ellen. When he shall know how very near we were to being man and wife, he will make no further objection to giving you to me now. My care and love will restore you if any thing can."

She had put down her hand again, and was looking at him, a little startled and her cheeks hectic.

"Arthur, hush. Papa must never know this while I live. Do as you will afterwards."

"I shall tell him before the day's out," persisted Captain Bohun. And she began to tremble with agitation.

"No, no. I say no. I should die with the shame."

"What shame?" he rejoined.

"The shame that—that—fell upon me. The shame of—after having consented to a secret marriage, you should have left me as you did, and not fulfilled it, and never told me why. It lies upon me still, and I cannot help it. I think it is that that has helped to kill me more than all the rest. Oh, Arthur, forgive me for saying this! Do not you renew the shame now."

Never had his past conduct been brought so forcibly home to him. Never had his heart so ached with its repentant pain. He stood up and laid her face upon his breast, and the scalding tears fell from his eyes upon it.

"The fear, lest the secret should be discovered, lay upon me always," she whispered. "While I was staying here that time it seemed to me one long mental torment, a pain of prolonged crucifixion. Had the humiliation come, I could never have borne it. Spare me still, Arthur."

Every word she spoke was like a dagger thrusting its sharp

point into his heart. *She* was going—going rapidly—where neither pain nor humiliation could reach her. But he had, in all probability, a long life before him, and must live out his bitter repentance.

"Oh, my love, my love! I wish I could die for you!"

"Don't grieve, Arthur; I shall be better off. You and papa must comfort one another."

He was unconsciously turning round the plain gold ring on her wasted hand, a sob now and again breaking from him. How real the past was seeming to him; even the hour when he had put that ring on, and the words he spoke with it, were very present. What remained of it all? Nothing, save that she was dying.

"I should like to give you this key now, while I am well enough to remember," she suddenly said, detaching a small key from her watch-chain. "It belongs to my treasure-box, as I used to call it at school. They will give it you when I am dead."

"Oh, Ellen!"

"The other ring is in it, and the licence—for I did not burn it, as you bade me that day in the churchyard; and the two or three letters you ever wrote me; and my journal, and some withered flowers, and other foolish trifles. You can do what you like with them, Arthur; they will be yours then. And oh, Arthur! if you grieve any more now, like this, you will hurt me, for I cannot bear that you should suffer pain. God bless you, my darling, my almost husband! We should have been very happy with one another."

Lower and lower bent he his aching brow, striving to suppress the anguish, that went well-nigh to unman him. Her own tears were falling.

"Be comforted," she whispered; "Arthur, be comforted! It won't be for so many years, even at the most; and then we shall be together again, in Heaven!"

*　　　*　　　*　　　*　　　*

And so she died. A week or two more of lingering pain and suffering, and then she was at rest. And that was the ending of one of the sweetest girls this world has ever known —Ellen Adair.

CHAPTER XLIX.

CONCLUSION.

THE genial spring gave place to a fiery summer; and summer, in its turn, was giving place to autumn. There is nothing of much note to record of the interval; just a passing word of gossip here and there.

Dallory, as regards North Inlet, was no longer a crowded place. The poor workmen, with their wives and families, had mostly drifted away from it; some few were emigrating, some had brought their minds (or, as they expressed it, their stomachs) to accept that last and hated refuge, the work-house; and they seemed likely, so far as present prospects looked, to be permanent recipients of its hospitality. The greater portion, however, had wandered away to different parts of the country, seeking for that employment they could no longer get in their native place. Poole and the other conspirators had been tried at the March assizes. Richard North pleaded earnestly for a lenient sentence on them : and he was listened to. Poole got a term of penal servitude, shorter than it would otherwise have been, and the others hard labour. One and all, including Mr. Poole, declared that they would not willingly have injured Richard North.

So, what with one thing and another, North Inlet had too much room in it, and was now at peace. There was no longer any need of special policemen. As to Richard, he was going on steadily and quietly; progressing a little, not much. Some five or six men had been added to his small number, of whom Ketler was one; Ketler having, as Jelly said, come to his senses. But the works would never be what they had been. For one thing, Richard had not capital; and if he had, perhaps he might not now have cared to embark it. Provided he could gain a sufficient income for expenses, and employ his time and energies, it was all he asked.

Madam lived abroad permanently. Mr. North (Richard really) allowed her two hundred a year; her son Arthur two; Sir Nash two. Six hundred a year; but it was pretty plainly intimated to Madam that this income was only guaranteed so long as she kept herself aloof from them. Madam retorted that she liked the Continent too well to leave it for snuffy old England.

Matilda North had married a French count, whom they had

met at Baden-Baden. She, herself, made the announcement to her step-brother Arthur in a self-possessed letter, telling him that as the Count's fortune was not equal to his merits, she should depend upon him (Arthur) to assist them yearly. Sidney North had also married. Tired, possibly, with his most uncertain existence, finding supplies from home were now the exception rather than the rule, and not daring to show his face on English soil to entreat for more, Mr. Sidney North entered into the bonds of matrimony with a wealthy American dame who was a few years older than himself; the widow of a great man who had made his fortune by the oil springs. It was to be hoped he would keep himself straight now.

And Mr. North, feeling that he was securely freed from Madam, was happy as a prince, and confidentially told people that he thought he was growing young again. Bessy wrote to him weekly; pleasant, happy letters. She liked her new home in the new world very much indeed; and she said Oliver seemed not to have a single care. The new firm, Jones and Rane, had more patients than they could well attend to, and all things were well with them. In short, Dr. and Mrs. Rane were evidently both prosperous and happy. No one was more pleased to know this than Mrs. Gass. *She* flourished; and her beaming face was more beaming than ever when seen abroad, setting the wives of Richard North's workmen to rights, or looking out from behind her geraniums.

Dallory Hall was empty again. William Adair had quitted it, his mission there over. Richard North was thinking about removing the furniture; but in truth he did not know what to do with it. There was no hurry, for Miss Dallory said she did not intend to let it again at present.

Perhaps the only one not just now in a state of bliss was Jelly. Jelly had made a frightful discovery of iniquity—Tim Wilks was faithless. For several months now (as it came out) Mr. Wilks had transferred his allegiance from herself to Molly Green, whom he was courting at Whitborough in secrecy. At least, keeping it from Jelly. The truth was, poor Tim did not dare to tell her. Jelly heard of it in a manner that astounded her. Spending a Sunday at Whitborough with Mrs. Beverage's servants, Jelly went to morning service at one of the churches. "Fate" took her to a particular church, she said. And there she heard the banns of marriage read out for the first time of asking, between Timothy Wilks, bachelor, and Mary Green, spinster. Jelly nearly shrieked aloud in her indignation. Had the culprits been present, she might have felt obliged to box their ears afterwards in coming out. It proved to be all true. Tim and Molly were going to be married, and Tim was furnishing a pretty cottage at Whitborough.

And that is how matters were at present in Dallory.

One autumn day, when the woods were glowing with their many colours, and the guns might be heard making war on the partridges, Richard North overtook one of his Flemish workmen at the base of a hill about half a mile from his works. The man was wheeling a wheelbarrow that contained sand, but not in the handy, ready manner that an Englishman would, and Richard took it himself.

" Can't you learn, Snaude ?" he said, addressing the man by name. "Look here; you should stoop: you must not get the barrow nearly upright. See how you've spilt the sand."

Wheeling it along and paying attention to nothing else, Richard took no notice of a basket-carriage that was clattering down the opposite hill. It pulled up when it reached him. Looking up, Richard saw Miss Dallory. Giving the wheelbarrow over to the man, Richard took the hand she held out.

" Yes," he said laughing, " you stop to shake hands with me now, but you won't do it soon."

"No? Why not?" she questioned.

"You saw me wheeling the barrow along?"

"Yes. It did not look very heavy."

"I have to put my hands to all sorts of things now, you perceive, Miss Dallory."

" Just so. I hope you like doing it."

" Well, I do."

"But I want to know what you mean by saying I shall soon not stop to speak to you."

"When you become a great lady. Report says you are about to marry."

"Does it? Do you still think, sir, I am going to take a Bohun ?"

" There has been some lord down at your brother's place, once or twice. The gossips in Dallory say that he comes for you."

" Then you can tell the gossips that they are a great deal wiser than I am. Stand still, Gyp"—to the shaggy pony.

"I would not have him; and I'm sure he has not the remotest idea of having me. Why, he is hardly out of his teens! I daresay he thinks me old enough to be his godmother."

Miss Dallory played with the reins, and then glanced at Richard. He was looking at her earnestly, as he leaned on the side of the low carriage.

"That young man has come down for the shooting, Mr. Richard. Frank takes him out to it every day. As for me, I do not intend to marry at all. Never."

"What shall you do then?"

"Live at Dallory Hall. Frank *is* going to be married, to the lord's sister. Now there's some information for you, but you need not proclaim it. It is true. I shall remove myself and my bundles to the Hall, and live in it till I die."

"It will be very lonely for you."

"Yes, I know that," she answered in a sad tone. "Most old maids are lonely. There will be Frank's children, perhaps, to come and stay with me sometimes."

Their eyes met. Each understood the other as exactly as though a host of words had been spoken. She would have *one* man for a husband—if he would have her.

Richard went nearer. His lips were pale, his tones hoarse with emotion.

"Mary, it would not be suitable. Think of your money; your birth. I told you once before not to tempt me. Why you know—you *know* that I have loved you, all along, too well for my own peace. In the old days when those works of ours"—pointing to the distant chimneys—"were of note, and we wealthy, I allowed myself to cherish dreams that I should be ashamed to confess to: but that's all over and done with. It would not be suitable now."

She blushed, and smiled; and turned her head away from him to study the opposite hedge while she spoke.

"For my part, I think there was never anything so suitable since the world was made."

"Mary, I cannot."

"If you will please get off my basket-chaise, sir, I'll drive on."

But he did not stir. Miss Dallory played with the reins again.

"Mary, *how* can I? If you had nothing, it would be different. I cannot live at Dallory Hall."

"No one else ever shall." But Richard had to bend to catch the whisper.

"The community would cry shame upon me. Upon the poor man of work, Richard North."

"How dare you call yourself names, Mr. Richard? You are a gentleman."

"What would John and Francis say?"

"What they pleased. Francis likes you better than anybody in the world; better than—well, yes, sir—better than I do."

He had one of her hands now. She knew, she had known a long while, how it was with him—that he loved her passionately, but would never, under his altered circumstances, tell her so. And, moreover, she knew that he was aware she knew it.

"But Mary, since—since before you returned from Switzerland up to this hour, I have not dared to think the old hopes could be carried out, even in my own heart."

"You think it better that I should grow into an old maid, and you into an old bachelor. Very well. Thank you. Perhaps we shall both be happier for it Let me drive on, Mr. Richard."

He drew her nearer; he made her turn to him. The great love of his heart shone in his face and eyes. A face of emotion then. She dropped the reins, regardless of what the rough pony might please to do, and put her other hand upon his.

"Oh, Richard, don't let us carry on the farce any longer! We have been playing it all these months and years. Let us at least be honest with each other: and then, if you decide for separation, why—it must be so."

But, as it seemed, Richard did not mean to decide for it. He glanced round to make sure that nobody was in the lonely road: and, drawing her face to his, left some strangely ardent kisses on it.

"I could not give up my works, Mary."

"Nobody asked you to, sir."

"It is just as though I had left the furniture in the Hall for the purpose."

"Perhaps you did."

"Mary!"

"There's the pony going. Stand still, Gyp. I won't give up Gyp, mind Richard. I know he is frightfully ragged and ugly, and that you despise him more than tongue can tell;

bnt I won't give him up. He can be the set-off bargain against your works, sir."

"Agreed," answered Richard, laughing. And he chose to seal the bargain.

Mary said again that she must drive on; and did not. How long they would really have stayed it was impossible to say, but for the man's coming back from the works with the empty wheelbarrow for more sand.

* * * * *

And there's no more to say. When the next spring came round, Richard North and his wife were established at Dallory Hall. Somewhere about the time of the marriage, there occurred a little warfare. Mary, who owned a great nest of accumulated money, wanted Richard to take it for his business. Richard steadily refused. A small portion would be useful to him; that he would take; but no more.

"Richard," she said to him one day, before they had been married a week, "I do think you are more obstinate upon this point than any other. You should hear what Mrs. Gass says about it."

"She says it to me," returned Richard, laughing. "There's not my equal for obstinacy in the world, she tells me."

"And you know there's not, sir."

But the next minute he put aside lightness and grew strangely serious. "I cannot give up business, Mary; I have already said so ——"

"I should despise you if you did, Richard," she interrupted. "I have money and gentility—I beg you'll not laugh, sir; you have work, and brains to work with; so we are equally matched. But I wish you'd take the money."

"No," said Richard. "I will never again enter on gigantic operations, and be at the beck and call of the Trades' Unions. There's another reason against it—that it would require larger supervision on my part. And as I have now divided duties to attend to, I shall not increase them. I should not choose to neglect my works; I should not choose to neglect my wife."

"A wilful man must have his way," quoth Mary.

"And a wilful woman shall have hers in all things, save when I see that it would not be for her good," rejoined Richard, holding his wife before him by the waist.

"I daresay I shall!" she saucily answered. "Is that a bargain, Richard?"

"To be sure." And Richard sealed it as he had the other one some months before.

And so we leave Dallory and its people at peace. Even Jelly was in feather. Jelly, ruling Mr. North indoors, and giving her opinion, unasked, in a free and easy manner whenever she chose, as to the interests of the garden (which opinion poor Mr. North enjoyed instead of reproved, and grew to look for)—Jelly had taken on another "young man," in the person of Mr. Francis Dallory's head gardener. He was a staid young Scotchman; very respectful to Jelly, and quite attentive. Mr. Seeley had moved into Dr. Rane's old house, and old Phillis was his housekeeper; so that Jelly's neighbourly relations with the next door were continued as usual.

On Arthur Bohun there remained the greatest traces of the past. Sir Nash was restored to health; and Arthur, in his never-ceasing remorse, would sometimes hope that he would marry again: he should almost hate to succeed to the rank and wealth to which he had, in a degree, sacrificed one who had been far dearer to him than life. Arthur's ostensible home was with Sir Nash; but he was fond of coming to Dallory. He had stayed twice with Mr. North; and Richard's home, the Hall, would be always open to him. The most bitter moments of Arthur Bohun's life were those that he spent with Sir William Adair: never could he get rid of the consciousness of having wronged him, of having helped to make him childless. Sir William had grown to love him as a son— which was but an additional stab for Arthur's aching heart.

And whenever Arthur Bohun came to Dallory, he would pay a visit to a certain white tomb in the churchyard. Choosing a solitary evening for it, after dusk had fallen, and staying by it for hours, there he indulged his dreadful grief. Who can tell how he called upon her?—who can tell how he poured out all the misery of his repentant heart, praying to be forgiven? Neither she nor Heaven could answer him in this world. She was gone; gone; all his regret was unavailing to recal her: there remained nothing but the marble stone, and the simple name on it:

"ELLEN ADAIR."

J. OGDEN AND CO., PRINTERS, 172, ST. JOHN STREET, E.C.